Cakes and Ale

AND TWELVE SHORT STORIES

BOOKS BY W. SOMERSET MAUGHAM

NOVELS

The Magician	
Catalina	Ashenden
Then and Now	The Razor's Edge
The Moon and Sixpence	Up at the Villa
Mrs. Craddock	Christmas Holiday
Cakes and Ale	Theatre
The Painted Veil	The Narrow Corner
Of Human Bondage	Liza of Lambeth

SHORT STORIES

Encore	Trio
Quartet	Creatures of Circumstance
The Trembling of a Leaf	The Mixture as Before
Ah King	Cosmopolitans
The Casuarina Tree	First Person Singular
East and West	The World Over

The Complete Short Stories of
W. Somerset Maugham
Volume I. East and West
Volume II. The World Over
Cakes and Ale and Twelve Short Stories

ESSAYS

The Art of Fiction	The Vagrant Mood
France at War	Strictly Personal
The Summing Up	Books and You
A Writer's Notebook	The Maugham Reader
Points of View	

TRAVEL

On a Chinese Screen	Don Fernando
The Gentleman in the Parlour	The Land of the Blessed Virgin

PLAYS

For Services Rendered	A Man of Honour
The Breadwinner	Penelope
The Sacred Flame	Jack Straw
Sheppey	Lady Frederick
The Constant Wife	The Tenth Man
The Circle	Landed Gentry
The Explorer	The Unknown
Mrs. Dot	Smith
Our Betters	The Land of Promise
Six Comedies	

OTHER

Purely for My Pleasure
Selected Prefaces and Introductions
of W. Somerset Maugham

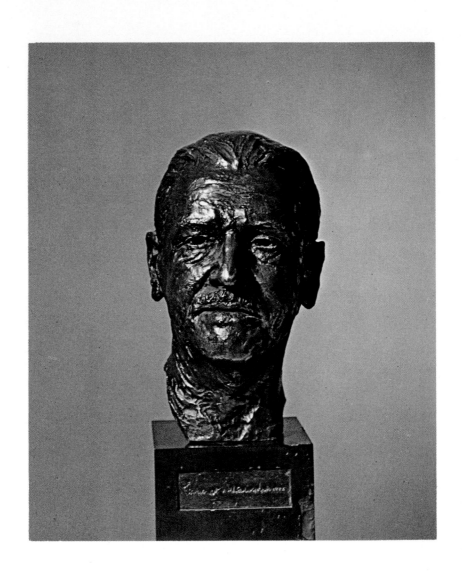

W. SOMERSET MAUGHAM

Cakes and Ale

AND TWELVE SHORT STORIES

Selected and with an Introduction

by Angus Wilson

DOUBLEDAY & COMPANY, INC., GARDEN CITY, NEW YORK

1967

All of the characters in this book are fictitious, and
any resemblance to actual persons, living or dead,
is purely coincidental.

CONTENTS

CONTENTS

INTRODUCTION
by Angus Wilson

Somerset Maugham wrote at one time or another more than one hundred short stories. Some are masterly; none is less than highly competent. To select a dozen of these is inevitably to mix critical judgement with personal taste. All the stories in this book are first class, but another editor might have replaced half of them with other stories of Maugham and yet not have lowered the standard of the whole book.

I make no defence for this personal choice except in one particular. Half the stories in this book are set in Malaysia or relate to that part of the world; two more are set in the South Seas. Some of Maugham's admirers may think that this choice gives a disproportionately narrow picture of the master's wide interests and knowledge of the world. What of his ironic vision of the Anglo-Saxons in the Mediterannean world? I have, in fact, included two stories of this area—one pure comedy, *The Three Fat Women of Antibes;* the other, *The Lotus Eater,* one of the most moving and forbidding of the author's works in his occasional moods of stern morality. What of the comedy of the London and Home Counties scene in the years from 1914 to 1930? It is here that I plead guilty to omission. Such glimpses of England as the reader will get from this selection are oblique: London seen as the unfamiliar, scaring "home" of the English men and women on occasional leaves from Malaysia—in, for example, *Before the Party* and *Virtue.* I believe this is to give a more exact and a more just picture of Maugham's essential and remarkable contribution to the literature of the human comedy. Only in one of his later works, I think, does Maugham turn his satirical eye on to the English literary scene with the same steadiness exactitude and humanity that he always shows for his fellow English expatriates. This, of course, is in the brilliant short novel included in this volume, *Cakes and Ale.* And here his satirical success is complete because it is set off by his creation of his most lovable, warm character Rosie, and by some of the best and most affectionate reconstructions of the Kentish scenes of his boyhood.

From *Of Human Bondage* onwards, Maugham was essentially a lonely writer, an observer of life with a keen eye and a sharp ear, and, above all, an extraordinary sense of the hidden loneliness in others. This isolation is the source both of his exceptional powers and his limitations. It makes him a master of irony and compassion, but it cuts him off from the more fundamental sources of love and passion; it tempers his admiration for courage with an equal belief in prudence as we may see in *The Lotus Eater;* it makes him compassionate with the rebel but it tempers that compassion with distrust of the heart as a guide to life as we can see in *Virtue;* but equally as we may see in *Footprints in the Jungle* he has little belief that the conventions and laws of society are an adequate measure of human worth. A sort of gregarious solitude as of a man always the silent fourth at bridge, the observer at the edge of a cocktail party, or the careful withdrawn host at dinner marks him, and gives his work a wonderful poise and accuracy and loving care, but marring it at times with those pretences and defences with which lonely men in society always surround themselves. He can be ungraciously malicious where he feels unsure of himself; he is charged often with a superficial cynicism, but perhaps it is more important that this cynicism, as so often with lonely people, topples on the edge of sentimentality as we may see in his treatment of the surely odious Walker in *Mackintosh.* This basic insecurity makes him, I think, at his most superficial when confronted with the clever, sophisticated world of London from which he was so often a self-imposed exile; in compensation it makes him the peculiar confidant and loving confessor of all those ordinary, tongue-tied, convention bound exiles who once ruled and traded in the British Empire in Asia. At home as he was in the whole world of European smart society it seems absurd to class him with the young District Officer in *Virtue,* Morton from Malay, who is lost amid Piccadilly's bright lights when home on leave, or with that most loveable of Maugham characters, Mrs. Hamlyn in *P. & O.* who needs the mystery of death to awaken her heart as she returns from Japan in frozen loneliness to a London that means nothing to her; yet basically it is, I believe, with these exiles that his place lay and about whom he wrote most feelingly.

For this reason I have preferred to omit the well known witty stories of London social or literary life like *Jane* or *The Creative Impulse;* their wit, I think, too shallowly covers the resentment of the outsider. Exile on the other hand awakens his love as in *P. & O.,* his compassion as in *Footprints in the Jungle,* and, best of all, his tragic acceptance as in *The Force of Circumstance.*

No author, I suppose, has more cleverly converted his defects into assets, not only by his assumption of the classic and stoic framework of life through which the lost romantic is only occasionally allowed yearningly to peer, but far more by the perfection of his craft, imposing upon his carefully limited material and even more rigorous form, and then becoming so completely master of this highly artificial technique that his stories appear to flow with the ease and simplicity of ordinary, everyday muddled life. The discipline is so beautiful that he has rightly become the model in English of the "classic" form of short story, so that however those of us who practise this craft may try to diverge into greater impressionism, more immediacy or whatever else we may feel "truer to life," we have always to measure our achievements against the rigorous perfection of form he has handed down to us. The appearance of simplicity, of course, is his masterly deception. His sentences, his prose have simplicity, the simplicity of rigorous pruning; but the form of his narratives is extraordinarily complex and any simplicity they appear to offer is a careful result of art. The narrator—frequently an "I" figure, any resemblance of which to himself Maugham always artfully denied—is in control, but within his narrative how dexterously and nimbly the story moves from mouth to mouth, from viewpoint to viewpoint, and backwards and forwards in time. It is by these alternations that Maugham achieves all his affects of irony, of pathos and of knowledge of life the more apparently certain because it is handed out to us, the readers, so casually. Consider for a moment the narration of *Before the Party:* we are in full middle class suburbia whose narrowness and hypocrisy the author wishes to expose. Mrs. Skinner is wearing the ospreys sent to her by her late son-in-law from Malaya. The family assembles in the hall ready to leave for a garden party where they will meet the bishop. But now it seems that Kathleen, the youngest daughter, when playing golf, has heard a less happy story of her brother-in-law's death than the one her widowed sister Millicent had brought back from Malaya. Suicide? Really, says Mr. Skinner, the most orthodox of solicitors, I should have been told the truth. And then Millicent begins to tell the truth. Her story moves back and forth in time, with interjections from the family. Is it true, asks Kathleen, that he drank? Like a fish, his widow abruptly replies. The ospreys begin to make Mrs. Skinner distressed. And then the bereaved widow goes flatly on with her macabre story of D.T.s at a remote Malay station. And at last we know that it was neither a natural death nor drink nor suicide, for she tells how she murdered her husband. And then they must all go off, sharing her secret, to meet the bishop. They'll get used to it in time, she tells them. But Mr. Skinner in the car must point out that really as a respectable solicitor he should never have been told the truth.

It all seems so easy, and so do the other eleven in the book but they are the end result of the most complex and economic narration, which is totally successful in giving the appearance of reality and ease to what is in fact a complete subjection of life to the discipline of art. This artistic discipline and skill with words will surely earn the admiration of new and younger readers for whom the setting of Imperial exile will now have the additional fascination of historical curiosity.

ANGUS WILSON

Cakes and Ale

AND TWELVE SHORT STORIES

The Three Fat Women
of Antibes

One was called Mrs. Richman and she was a widow. The second was called Mrs. Sutcliffe; she was American and she had divorced two husbands. The third was called Miss Hickson and she was a spinster. They were all in the comfortable forties and they were all well off. Mrs. Sutcliffe had the odd first name of Arrow. When she was young and slender she had liked it well enough. It suited her and the jests it occasioned though too often repeated were very flattering; she was not disinclined to believe that it suited her character too: it suggested directness, speed and purpose. She liked it less now that her delicate features had grown muzzy with fat, that her arms and shoulders were so substantial and her hips so massive. It was increasingly difficult to find dresses to make her look as she liked to look. The jests her name gave rise to now were made behind her back and she very well knew that they were far from obliging. But she was by no means resigned to middle age. She still wore blue to bring out the colour of her eyes and, with the help of art, her fair hair had kept its lustre. What she liked about Beatrice Richman and Frances Hickson was that they were both so much fatter than she, it made her look quite slim; they were both of them older and much inclined to treat her as a little young thing. It was not disagreeable. They were good-natured women and they chaffed her pleasantly about her beaux; they had both given up the thought of that kind of non-sense, indeed Miss Hickson had never given it a moment's con-sideration, but they were sympathetic to her flirtations. It was understood that one of these days Arrow would make a third man happy.

"Only you mustn't get any heavier, darling," said Mrs. Richman.

"And for goodness' sake make certain of his bridge," said Miss Hickson.

They saw for her a man of about fifty, but well-preserved and of distinguished carriage, an admiral on the retired list and a good golfer, or a widower without encumbrances, but in any case with a substantial income. Arrow listened to them amiably, and kept to herself that fact that this was not at all her idea. It was true that she would have liked to marry again, but her fancy turned to a dark slim Italian with flashing eyes and a sonorous title or to a Spanish don of noble lineage; and not a day more than thirty. There were times when, looking at herself in her mirror, she was certain she did not look any more than that herself.

They were great friends, Miss Hickson, Mrs. Richman and Arrow Sutcliffe. It was their fat that had brought them together and bridge that had cemented their alliance. They had met first at Carlsbad, where they were staying at the same hotel and were treated by the same doctor who used them with the same ruthlessness. Beatrice Richman was enormous. She was a handsome woman, with fine eyes, rouged cheeks and painted lips. She was very well content to be a widow with a handsome fortune. She adored her food. She liked bread and butter, cream, potatoes and suet puddings, and for eleven months of the year ate pretty well everything she had a mind to, and for one month went to Carlsbad to reduce. But every year she grew fatter. She upbraided the doctor, but got no sympathy from him. He pointed out to her various plain and simple facts.

"But if I'm never to eat a thing I like, life isn't worth living," she expostulated.

He shrugged his disapproving shoulders. Afterwards she told Miss Hickson that she was beginning to suspect he wasn't so clever as she had thought. Miss Hickson gave a great guffaw. She was that sort of woman. She had a deep bass voice, a large flat sallow face from which twinkled little bright eyes; she walked with a slouch, her hands in her pockets, and when she could do so without exciting attention smoked a long cigar. She dressed as like a man as she could.

"What the deuce should I look like in frills and furbelows?" she said. "When you're as fat as I am you may just as well be comfortable."

She wore tweeds and heavy boots and whenever she could went about bareheaded. But she was as strong as an ox and boasted that few men could drive a longer ball than she. She was plain of speech, and she could swear more variously than a stevedore.

Though her name was Frances she preferred to be called Frank. Masterful, but with tact, it was her jovial strength of character that held the three together. They drank their waters together, had their baths at the same hour, they took their strenuous walks together, pounded about the tennis court with a professional to make them run, and ate at the same table their sparse and regulated meals. Nothing impaired their good humour but the scales, and when one or other of them weighed as much on one day as she had the day before neither Frank's coarse jokes, the *bonhomie* of Beatrice nor Arrow's pretty kittenish ways sufficed to dispel the gloom. Then drastic measures were resorted to, the culprit went to bed for twenty-four hours and nothing passed her lips but the doctor's famous vegetable soup which tasted like hot water in which a cabbage had been well rinsed.

Never were three women greater friends. They would have been independent of anyone else if they had not needed a fourth at bridge. They were fierce, enthusiastic players and the moment the day's cure was over they sat down at the bridge table. Arrow, feminine as she was, played the best game of the three, a hard, brilliant game, in which she showed no mercy and never conceded a point or failed to take advantage of a mistake. Beatrice was solid and reliable. Frank was dashing; she was a great theorist, and had all the authorities at the tip of her tongue. They had long arguments over the rival systems. They bombarded one another with Culbertson and Sims. It was obvious that not one of them ever played a card without fifteen good reasons, but it was also obvious from the subsequent conversation that there were fifteen equally good reasons why she should not have played it. Life would have been perfect, even with the prospect of twenty-four hours of that filthy soup when the doctor's rotten (Beatrice) bloody (Frank) lousy (Arrow) scales pretended one hadn't lost an ounce in two days, if only there had not been this constant difficulty of finding someone to play with them who was in their class.

It was for this reason that on the occasion with which this narrative deals Frank invited Lena Finch to come and stay with them at Antibes. They were spending some weeks there on Frank's suggestion. It seemed absurd to her, with her common sense, that immediately the cure was over Beatrice who always lost twenty pounds should by giving way to her ungovernable appetite put it all on again. Beatrice was weak. She needed a person of strong will to watch her diet. She proposed then that on leaving Carlsbad they should take a house at Antibes, where they could get plenty of exercise—everyone knew that nothing slimmed you like swimming—and as far as possible could go on with the cure. With a cook of their own they could at least avoid things that were obviously fattening. There was no reason why they should not all lose several pounds more. It seemed a very good idea. Beatrice knew what was good for her, and she could resist temptation well enough if temptation was not put right under her nose. Besides, she liked gambling, and a flutter at the Casino two or three times a week would pass the time very pleasantly. Arrow adored Antibes, and she would be looking her best after a month at Carlsbad. She could just pick and choose among the young Italians, the passionate Spaniards, the gallant Frenchmen, and the long-limbed English who sauntered about all day in bathing trunks and gay-coloured dressing-gowns. The plan worked very well. They had a grand time. Two days a week they ate nothing but hard-boiled eggs and raw tomatoes and they mounted the scales every morning with light hearts. Arrow got down to eleven stone and felt just like a girl; Beatrice and Frank by standing in a certain way just avoided the thirteen. The machine they had bought registered kilogrammes, and they got extraordinarily clever at translating these in the twinkling of an eye to pounds and ounces.

But the fourth at bridge continued to be the difficulty. This person played like a foot, the other was so slow that it drove you frantic, one was quarrelsome, another was a bad loser, a third was next door to a crook. It was strange how hard it was to find exactly the player you wanted.

One morning when they were sitting in pyjamas on the terrace overlooking the sea, drinking their tea (without milk or sugar) and eating a rusk prepared by Dr. Hudebert and guaranteed not to be fattening, Frank looked up from her letters.

"Lena Finch is coming down to the Riviera," she said.

"Who's she?" asked Arrow.

"She married a cousin of mine. He died a couple of months ago and she's just recovering from a nervous breakdown. What about asking her to come here for a fortnight?"

"Does she play bridge?" asked Beatrice.

"You bet your life she does," boomed Frank in her deep voice.

"And a damned good game too. We should be absolutely independent of outsiders."

"How old is she?" asked Arrow.

"Same age as I am."

"That sounds all right."

It was settled. Frank, with her usual decisiveness, stalked out as soon as she had finished her breakfast to send a wire, and three days later Lena Finch arrived. Frank met her at the station. She was in deep but not obtrusive mourning for the recent death of her husband. Frank had not seen her for two years. She kissed her warmly and took a good look at her.

"You're very thin, darling," she said.

Lena smiled bravely.

"I've been through a good deal lately. I've lost a lot of weight."

Frank sighed, but whether from sympathy with her cousin's sad loss, or from envy, was not obvious.

Lena was not, however, unduly depressed, and after a quick bath was quite ready to accompany Frank to Eden Roc. Frank introduced the stranger to her two friends and they sat down in what was known as the Monkey House. It was an enclosure covered with glass overlooking the sea, with a bar at the back, and it was crowded with chattering people in bathing costumes, pyjamas or dressing-gowns, who were seated at the tables having drinks. Beatrice's soft heart went out to the lorn widow, and Arrow, seeing that she was pale, quite ordinary to look at and probably forty-eight, was prepared to like her very much. A waiter approached them.

"What will you have, Lena dear?" Frank asked.

"Oh, I don't know, what you all have, a dry Martini or a White Lady."

Arrow and Beatrice gave her a quick look. Everyone knows how fattening cocktails are.

"I daresay you're tired after your journey," said Frank kindly.

She ordered a dry Martini for Lena and a mixed lemon and orange juice for herself and her two friends.

"We find alcohol isn't very good in all this heat," she explained.

"Oh, it never affects me at all," Lena answered airily. "I like cocktails."

Arrow went very slightly pale under her rouge (neither she nor Beatrice ever wet their faces when they bathed and they thought it absurd of Frank, a woman of her size, to pretend she liked diving) but she said nothing. The conversation was gay and easy, they all said the obvious things with gusto, and presently they strolled back to the villa for luncheon.

In each napkin were two little antifat rusks. Lena gave a bright smile as she put them by the side of her plate.

"May I have some bread?" she asked.

The grossest indecency would not have fallen on the ears of those three women with such a shock. Not one of them had eaten bread for ten years. Even Beatrice, greedy as she was, drew the line there. Frank, the good hostess, recovered herself first.

"Of course, darling," she said and turning to the butler asked him to bring some.

"And some butter," said Lena in that pleasant easy way of hers.

There was a moment's embarrassed silence.

"I don't know if there's any in the house," said Frank, "but I'll enquire. There may be some in the kitchen."

"I adore bread and butter, don't you?" said Lena, turning to Beatrice.

Beatrice gave a sickly smile and an evasive reply. The butler brought a long crisp roll of French bread. Lena slit it in two and plastered it with the butter which was miraculously produced. A grilled sole was served.

"We eat very simply here," said Frank. "I hope you won't mind."

"Oh, no, I like my food very plain," said Lena as she took some butter and spread it over her fish. "As long as I can have bread and butter and potatoes and cream I'm quite happy."

The three friends exchanged a glance. Frank's great sallow face sagged a little and she looked with distaste at the dry, insipid sole on her plate. Beatrice came to the rescue.

"It's such a bore, we can't get cream here," she said. "It's one of the things one has to do without on the Riviera."

"What a pity," said Lena.

The rest of the luncheon consisted of lamb cutlets, with the fat carefully removed so that Beatrice should not be led astray, and spinach boiled in water, with stewed pears to end up with. Lena tasted her pears and gave the butler of a look of enquiry. That resourceful man understood her at once and though pow dered sugar had never been served at that table before handed her without a moment's hesitation a bowl of it. She helped herself liberally. The other three pretended not to notice. Coffee was served and Lena took three lumps of sugar in hers.

"You have a very sweet tooth," said Arrow in a tone which she struggled to keep friendly.

"We think saccharine so much more sweetening," said Frank, as she put a tiny tablet of it into her coffee.

"Disgusting stuff," said Lena.

Beatrice's mouth drooped at the corners, and she gave the lump sugar a yearning look.

"Beatrice," boomed Frank sternly.

Beatrice stifled a sigh, and reached for the saccharine.

Frank was relieved when they could sit down to the bridge table. It was plain to her that Arrow and Beatrice were upset. She wanted them to like Lena and she was anxious that Lena should enjoy her fortnight with them. For the first rubber Arrow cut with the newcomer.

"Do you play Vanderbilt or Culbertson?" she asked her.

"I have no conventions," Lena answered in a happy-go-lucky way, "I play by the light of nature."

"I play strict Culbertson," said Arrow acidly.

The three fat women braced themselves to the fray. No conventions indeed! They'd learn her. When it came to bridge even Frank's family feeling was forgotten and she settled down with the same determination as the others to trim the stranger in their midst. But the light of nature served Lena very well. She had a natural gift for the game and great experience. She played with imagination, quickly, boldly, and with assurance. The other players were in too high a class not to realise very soon that Lena knew what she was about, and since they were all thoroughly good-natured, generous women, they were gradually mollified. This was real bridge. They all enjoyed themselves. Arrow and Beatrice began to feel more kindly towards Lena, and Frank, noticing this, heaved a fat sigh of relief. It was going to be a success.

After a couple of hours they parted, Frank and Beatrice to have a round of golf, and Arrow to take a brisk walk with a young Prince Roccamare whose acquaintance she had lately made. He was very sweet and young and good-looking. Lena said she would rest.

They met again just before dinner.

"I hope you've been all right, Lena dear," said Frank. "I was rather conscience-striken at leaving you with nothing to do all this time."

"Oh, don't apologise. I had a lovely sleep and then I went down to Juan and had a cocktail. And d'you know what I discovered? You'll be so pleased. I found a dear little tea-shop where they've got the most beautiful thick fresh cream. I've ordered half a pint to be sent every day. I thought it would be my little contribution to the household."

Her eyes were shining. She was evidently expecting them to be delighted.

"How very kind of you," said Frank, with a look that sought to quell the indignation that she saw on the faces of her two friends. "But we never eat cream. In this climate it makes one so bilious."

"I shall have to eat it all myself then," said Lena cheerfully.

"Don't you ever think of your figure?" Arrow asked with icy deliberation.

"The doctor said I must eat."

"Did he say you must eat bread and butter and potatoes and cream?"

"Yes. That's what I thought you meant when you said you had simple food."

"You'll get simply enormous," said Beatrice.

Lena laughed gaily.

"No, I shan't. You see, nothing ever makes me fat. I've always eaten everything I wanted to and it's never had the slightest effect on me."

The stony silence that followed this speech was only broken by the entrance of the butler.

"*Mademoiselle est servie*," he announced.

They talked the matter over late that night, after Lena had gone to bed, in Frank's room. During the evening they had been furiously cheerful, and they had chaffed one another with a friendliness that would have taken in the keenest observer. But now they dropped the mask. Beatrice was sullen, Arrow was spiteful and Frank was unmanned.

"It's not very nice for me to sit there and see her eat all the things I particularly like," said Beatrice plaintively.

"It's not very nice for any of us," Frank snapped back.

"You should never have asked her here," said Arrow.

"How was I to know?" cried Frank.

"I can't help thinking that if she really cared for her husband she would hardly eat so much," said Beatrice. "He's only been buried two months. I mean, I think you ought to show some respect for the dead."

"Why can't she eat the same as we do?" asked Arrow viciously.

"She's a guest."

"Well, you heard what she said. The doctor told her she must eat."

"Then she ought to go to a sanatorium."

"It's more than flesh and blood can stand, Frank," moaned Beatrice.

"If I can stand it you can stand it."

"She's your cousin, she's not our cousin," said Arrow. "I'm not going to sit there for fourteen days and watch that woman make a hog of herself."

"It's so vulgar to attach all this importance to food," Frank boomed, and her voice was deeper than ever. "After all the only thing that counts really is spirit."

"Are you calling *me* vulgar, Frank?" asked Arrow with flashing eyes.

"No, of course she isn't," interrupted Beatrice.

"I wouldn't put it past you to go down in the kitchen when we're all in bed and have a good square meal on the sly."

Frank sprang to her feet.

"How dare you say that, Arrow! I'd never ask anybody to do what I'm not prepared to do myself. Have you known me all these years and do you think me capable of such a mean thing?"

"How is it you never take off any weight then?"

Frank gave a gasp and burst into a flood of tears.

"What a cruel thing to say! I've lost pounds and pounds."

She wept like a child. Her vast body shook and great tears splashed on her mountainous bosom.

"Darling, I didn't mean it," cried Arrow.

She threw herself on her knees and enveloped what she could of Frank in her own plump arms. She wept and the mascara ran down her cheeks.

"D'you mean to say I don't look thinner?" Frank sobbed. "After all I've gone through."

"Yes, dear, of course you do," cried Arrow through her tears. "Everybody's noticed it."

Beatrice, though naturally of a placid disposition, began to cry gently. It was very pathetic. Indeed, it would have been a hard heart that failed to be moved by the sight of Frank, that lion-hearted woman, crying her eyes out. Presently, however, they dried their tears and had a little brandy and water, which every doctor had told them was the least fattening thing they could drink, and then they felt much better. They decided that Lena should have the nourishing food that had been ordered her and they made a solemn resolution not to let it disturb their equanimity. She was certainly a first-rate bridge player and after all it was only for a fortnight. They would do whatever they could to make her stay enjoyable. They kissed one another warmly and separated for the night feeling strangely uplifted. Nothing should interfere with the wonderful friendship that had brought so much happiness into their three lives.

But human nature is weak. You must not ask too much of it. They ate grilled fish while Lena ate macaroni sizzling with cheese and butter; they ate grilled cutlets and boiled spinach while Lena ate *pâté de foie gras;* twice a week they ate hard-boiled eggs and raw tomatoes, while Lena ate peas swimming in cream and potatoes cooked in all sorts of delicious ways. The chef was a good chef and he leapt at the opportunity afforded him to send up one dish more rich, tasty and succulent than the other.

"Poor Jim," sighed Lena, thinking of her husband, "he loved French cooking."

The butler disclosed the fact that he could make half a dozen kinds of cocktails and Lena informed them that the doctor had recommended her to drink burgundy at luncheon and champagne at dinner. The three fat women persevered. They were gay, chatty and even hilarious (such is the natural gift that women have for deception) but Beatrice grew limp and forlorn, and Arrow's tender blue eyes acquired a steely glint. Frank's deep voice grew more raucous. It was when they played bridge that the strain showed itself. They had always been fond of talking over their hands, but their discussions had been friendly. Now a distinct bitterness crept in and sometimes one pointed out a mistake to another with quite unnecessary frankness. Discussion turned to argument and argument to altercation. Sometimes the session ended in angry silence.

Once Frank accused Arrow of deliberately letting her down. Two or three times Beatrice, the softest of the three, was reduced to tears. On another occasion Arrow flung down her cards and swept out of the room in a pet. Their tempers were getting frayed. Lena was the peacemaker.

"I think it's such a pity to quarrel over bridge," she said. "After all, it's only a game."

It was all very well for her. She had had a square meal and half a bottle of champagne. Besides, she had phenomenal luck. She was winning all their money. The score was put down in a book after each session, and hers mounted up day after day with unfailing regularity. Was there no justice in the world? They began to hate one another. And though they hated her too they could not resist confiding in her. Each of them went to her separately and told her how detestable the others were. Arrow said she was sure it was bad for her to see so much of women so much older than herself. She had a good mind to sacrifice her share of the lease and go to Venice for the rest of the summer. Frank told Lena that with her masculine mind it was too much to expect that she could be satisfied with anyone so frivolous as Arrow and so frankly stupid as Beatrice.

"I must have intellectual conversation," she boomed. "When you have a brain like mine you've got to consort with your intellectual equals."

Beatrice only wanted peace and quiet.

"Really I hate women," she said. "They're so unreliable; they're so malicious."

By the time Lena's fortnight drew to its close the three fat women were barely on speaking terms. They kept up appearances before Lena, but when she was not there made no pretences. They had got past quarrelling. They ignored one another, and when this was not possible treated each other with icy politeness.

Lena was going to stay with friends on the Italian Riviera and Frank saw her off by the same train as that by which she had arrived. She was taking away with her a lot of their money.

"I don't know how to thank you," she said, as she got into the carriage. "I've had a wonderful visit."

If there was one thing that Frank Hickson prided herself on more than on being a match for any man it was that she was a gentlewoman, and her reply was perfect in its combination of majesty and graciousness.

"We've all enjoyed having you here, Lena," she said. "It's been a real treat."

But when she turned away from the departing train she heaved such a vast sigh of relief that the platform shook beneath her. She flung back her massive shoulders and strode home to the villa.

"Ouf!" she roared at intervals. "Ouf!"

She changed into her one-piece bathing-suit, put on her espadrilles and a man's dressing-gown (no nonsense about it) and went to Eden Roc. There was still time for a bathe before luncheon. She passed through the Monkey House, looking about her to say good morning to anyone she knew, for she felt on a sudden at peace with mankind, and then stopped dead still. She could not believe her eyes. Beatrice was sitting at one of the tables, by herself; she wore the pyjamas she had bought at Molyneux's a day or two before, she had a string of pearls round her neck, and Frank's quick eyes saw that she had just had her hair waved; her cheeks, her eyes, her lips were made up. Fat, nay vast, as she was, none could deny that she was an extremely handsome woman. But what was she doing? With the slouching gait of the Neanderthal man which was Frank's characteristic walk she went up to Beatrice. In her black bathing-dress Frank looked like the huge cetacean which the Japanese catch in the Torres Straits and which the vulgar call a sea-cow.

"Beatrice, what are you doing?" she cried in her deep voice. It was like the roll of thunder in the distant mountains. Beatrice looked at her coolly.

"Eating," she answered.

"Damn it, I can see you're eating."

In front of Beatrice was a plate of *croissants* and a plate of butter, a pot of strawberry jam, coffee and a jug of cream. Beatrice was spreading butter thick on the delicious hot bread, covering this with jam, and then pouring the thick cream over all.

"You'll kill yourself," said Frank.

"I don't care," mumbled Beatrice with her mouth full.

"You'll put on pounds and pounds."

"Go to hell!"

She actually laughed in Frank's face. My God, how good those *croissants* smelt!

"I'm disappointed in you, Beatrice. I thought you had more character."

"It's your fault. That blasted woman. You would have her down. For a fortnight I've watched her gorge like a hog. It's more than flesh and blood can stand. I'm going to have one square meal if I bust."

The tears welled up to Frank's eyes. Suddenly she felt very weak and womanly. She would have liked a strong man to take her on his knee and pet her and cuddle her and call her little baby names. Speechless she sank down on a chair by Beatrice's side. A waiter came up. With a pathetic gesture she waved towards the coffee and *croissants*.

"I'll have the same," she sighed.

She listlessly reached out her hand to take a roll, but Beatrice snatched away the plate.

"No, you don't," she said. "You wait till you get your own."

Frank called her a name which ladies seldom apply to one another in affection. In a moment the waiter brought her *croissants*, butter, jam and coffee.

"Where's the cream, you fool?" she roared like a lioness at bay.

She began to eat. She ate gluttonously. The place was beginning to fill up with bathers coming to enjoy a cocktail or two after having done their duty by the sun and the sea. Presently Arrow strolled along with Prince Roccamare. She had on a beautiful silk wrap which she held tightly round her with one hand in order to look as slim as possible and she bore her head high so that he should not see her double chin. She was laughing gaily. She felt like a girl. He had just told her (in Italian) that her eyes made the blue of the Mediterranean look like pea-soup. He left her to go into the men's room to brush his sleek black hair and they arranged to meet in five minutes for a drink. Arrow walked on to the women's room to put a little more rouge on her cheeks and a little more red on her lips. On her way she caught sight of Frank and Beatrice. She stopped. She could hardly believe her eyes.

"My God!" she cried. "You beasts. You hogs." She seized a chair. "Waiter."

Her appointment went clean out of her head. In the twinkling of an eye the waiter was at her side.

"Bring me what these ladies are having," she ordered.

Frank lifted her great heavy head from her plate.

"Bring me some *pâté de foie gras*," she boomed.

"Frank!" cried Beatrice.

"Shut up."

"All right. I'll have some too."

The coffee was brought and the hot rolls and cream and the *pâté de foie gras* and they set to. They spread the cream on the *pâté* and they ate it. They devoured great spoonfuls of jam. They crunched the delicious crisp bread voluptuously. What was love to Arrow then? Let the Prince keep his palace in Rome and his castle in the Apennines. They did not speak. What they were about was much too serious. They ate with solemn, ecstatic fervour.

"I haven't eaten potatoes for twenty-five years," said Frank in a far-off brooding tone.

"Waiter," cried Beatrice, "bring fried potatoes for three."

"*Très bien, Madame.*"

The potatoes were brought. Not all the perfumes of Arabia smelt so sweet. They ate them with their fingers.

"Bring me a dry Martini," said Arrow.

"You can't have a dry Martini in the middle of a meal, Arrow," said Frank.

"Can't I? You wait and see."

"All right then. Bring me a double dry Martini," said Frank.

"Bring three double dry Martinis," said Beatrice.

They were brought and drunk at a gulp. The women looked at one another and sighed. The misunderstandings of the last fortnight dissolved and the sincere affection each had for the other welled up again in their hearts. They could hardly believe that they had ever contemplated the possibility of severing a friendship that had brought them so much solid satisfaction. They finished the potatoes.

"I wonder if they've got any chocolate éclairs," said Beatrice.

"Of course they have."

And of course they had. Frank thrust one whole into her huge mouth, swallowed it and seized another, but before she ate it she looked at the other two and plunged a vindictive dagger into the heart of the monstrous Lena.

"You can say what you like, but the truth is she played a damned rotten game of bridge, really."

"Lousy," agreed Arrow.

But Beatrice suddenly thought she would like a meringue.

Mackintosh

He splashed about for a few minutes in the sea; it was too shallow to swim in and for fear of sharks he could not go out of his depth; then he got out and went into the bath-house for a shower. The coldness of the fresh water was grateful after the heavy stickiness of the salt Pacific, so warm, though it was only just after seven, that to bathe in it did not brace you but rather increased your languor; and when he had dried himself, slipping into a bath-gown, he called out to the Chinese cook that he would be ready for breakfast in five minutes. He walked barefoot across the patch of coarse grass which Walker, the administrator, proudly thought was a lawn, to his own quarters and dressed. This did not take long, for he put on nothing but a shirt and a pair of duck trousers and then went over to his chief's house on the other side of the compound. The two men had their meals together, but the Chinese cook told him that Walker had set out on horseback at five and would not be back for another hour.

Mackintosh had slept badly and he looked with distaste at the paw-paw and the eggs and bacon which were set before him. The mosquitoes had been maddening that night; they flew about the net under which he slept in such numbers that their humming, pitiless and menacing, had the effect of a note, infinitely drawn out, played on a distant organ, and whenever he dozed off he awoke with a start in the belief that one had found its way inside his curtains. It was so hot that he lay naked. He turned from side to side. And gradually the dull roar of the breakers on the reef, so unceasing and so regular that generally you did not hear it, grew distinct on his consciousness, its rhythm hammered on his tired nerves and he held himself with clenched hands in the effort to bear it. The thought that nothing could stop that sound, for it would continue to all eternity, was almost impossible to bear, and, as though his strength were a match for the ruthless forces of nature, he had an insane impulse to do some violent thing. He felt he must cling to his self-control or he would go mad. And

now, looking out of the window at the lagoon and the strip of
foam which marked the reef, he shuddered with hatred of the
brilliant scene. The cloudless sky was like an inverted bowl that
hemmed it in. He lit his pipe and turned over the pile of Auck-
land papers that had come over from Apia a few days before.
The newest of them was three weeks old. They gave an impression of incredible dullness.

Then he went into the office. It was a large, bare room with
two desks in it and a bench along one side. A number of natives
were seated on this, and a couple of women. They gossiped
while they waited for the administrator, and when Mackintosh
came in they greeted him.

"*Talofa li.*"

He returned their greeting and sat down at his desk. He began
to write, working on a report which the governor of Samoa had
been clamouring for and which Walker, with his usual dilatoriness,
had neglected to prepare. Mackintosh as he made his notes reflected vindictively that Walker was late with his report because
he was so illiterate that he had an invincible distaste for anything
to do with pens and paper; and now when it was at last ready,
concise and neatly official, he would accept his subordinate's work
without a word of appreciation, with a sneer rather or a gibe, and
send it on to his own superior as though it were his own composition. He could not have written a word of it. Mackintosh
thought with rage that if his chief pencilled in some insertion it
would be childish in expression and faulty in language. If he
remonstrated or sought to put his meaning into an intelligible
phrase, Walker would fly into a passion and cry:

"What the hell do I care about grammar? That's what I want
to say and that's how I want to say it."

At last Walker came in. The natives surrounded him as he
entered, trying to get his immediate attention, but he turned
on them roughly and told them to sit down and hold their tongues.
He threatened that if they were not quiet he would have them
all turned out and see none of them that day. He nodded to
Mackintosh.

"Hulloa, Mac; up at last? I don't know how you can waste
the best part of the day in bed. You ought to have been up before
dawn like me. Lazy beggar."

He threw himself heavily into his chair and wiped his face with a large bandana.

"By heaven, I've got a thirst."

He turned to the policeman who stood at the door, a picturesque figure in his white jacket and *lava-lava,* the loin cloth of the Samoan, and told him to bring *kava.* The *kava* bowl stood on the floor in the corner of the room, and the policeman filled a half coconut shell and brought it to Walker. He poured a few drops on the ground, murmured the customary words to the company, and drank with relish. Then he told the policeman to serve the waiting natives, and the shell was handed to each one in order of birth or importance and emptied with the same ceremonies.

Then he set about the day's work. He was a little man, considerably less than of middle height, and enormously stout; he had a large, fleshy face, clean-shaven, with the cheeks hanging on each side in great dew-laps, and three vast chins; his small features were all dissolved in fat; and, but for a crescent of white hair at the back of his head, he was completely bald. He reminded you of Mr. Pickwick. He was grotesque, a figure of fun, and yet, strangely enough, not without dignity. His blue eyes, behind large gold-rimmed spectacles, were shrewd and vivacious, and there was a great deal of determination in his face. He was sixty, but his native vitality triumphed over advancing years. Notwithstanding his corpulence his movements were quick, and he walked with a heavy, resolute tread as though he sought to impress his weight upon the earth. He spoke in a loud, gruff voice.

It was two years now since Mackintosh had been appointed Walker's assistant. Walker, who had been for a quarter of a century administrator of Talua, one of the larger islands in the Samoan group, was a man known in person or by report through the length and breadth of the South Seas; and it was with lively curiosity that Mackintosh looked forward to his first meeting with him. For one reason or another he stayed a couple of weeks at Apia before he took up his post and both at Chaplin's hotel and at the English club he heard innumerable stories about the administrator. He thought now with irony of his interest in them. Since then he had heard them a hundred times from Walker himself. Walker knew that he was a character, and, proud of his reputation, deliberately acted up to it. He was jealous of his "legend" and anxious that you should know the exact details of any of the celebrated stories that were told of him. He was ludicrously angry with anyone who had told them to the stranger incorrectly.

There was a rough cordiality about Walker which Mackintosh at first found not unattractive, and Walker, glad to have a listener to whom all he said was fresh, gave of his best. He was good-humoured, hearty, and considerate. To Mackintosh, who had lived the sheltered life of a government official in London till at the age of thirty-four an attack of pneumonia, leaving him with the threat of tuberculosis, had forced him to seek a post in the Pacific, Walker's existence seemed extraordinarily romantic. The adventure with which he started on his conquest of circumstance was typical of the man. He ran away to sea when he was fifteen and for over a year was employed in shovelling coal on a collier. He was an undersized boy and both men and mates were kind to him, but the captain for some reason conceived a savage dislike of him. He used the lad cruelly so that, beaten and kicked, he often could not sleep for the pain that racked his limbs. He loathed the captain with all his soul. Then he was given a tip for some race and managed to borrow twenty-five pounds from a friend he had picked up in Belfast. He put it on the horse, an outsider, at long odds. He had no means of repaying the money if he lost, but it never occurred to him that he could lose. He felt himself in luck. The horse won and he found himself with something over a thousand pounds in hard cash. Now his chance had come. He found out who was the best solicitor in the town —the collier lay then somewhere on the Irish coast—went to him, and, telling him that he heard the ship was for sale, asked him to arrange the purchase for him. The solicitor was amused at his small client, he was only sixteen and did not look so old, and, moved perhaps by sympathy, promised not only to arrange the matter for him but to see that he made a good bargain. After a little while Walker found himself the owner of the ship. He went back to her and had what he described as the most glorious moment of his life when he gave the skipper notice and told him that he must get off *his* ship in half an hour. He made the mate captain and sailed on the collier for another nine months, at the end of which he sold her at a profit.

He came out to the islands at the age of twenty-six as a planter.

He was one of the few white men settled in Talua at the time of the German occupation and had then already some influence with the natives. The Germans made him administrator, a position which he occupied for twenty years, and when the island was seized by the British he was confirmed in his post. He ruled the island despotically, but with complete success. The prestige of this success was another reason for the interest that Mackintosh took in him.

But the two men were not made to get on. Mackintosh was an ugly man, with ungainly gestures, a tall thin fellow, with a narrow chest and bowed shoulders. He had sallow, sunken cheeks, and his eyes were large and sombre. He was a great reader, and when his books arrived and were unpacked Walker came over to his quarters and looked at them. Then he turned to Mackintosh with a coarse laugh.

"What in Hell have you brought all this muck for?" he asked.

Mackintosh flushed darkly.

"I'm sorry you think it muck. I brought my books because I want to read them."

"When you said you'd got a lot of books coming I thought there'd be something for me to read. Haven't you got any detective stories?"

"Detective stories don't interest me."

"You're a damned fool then."

"I'm content that you should think so."

Every mail brought Walker a mass of periodical literature, papers from New Zealand and magazines from America, and it exasperated him that Mackintosh showed his contempt for these ephemeral publications. He had no patience with the books that absorbed Mackintosh's leisure and thought it only a pose that he read Gibbon's *Decline and Fall* or Burton's *Anatomy of Melancholy*. And since he had never learned to put any restraint on his tongue, he expressed his opinion of his assistant freely. Mackintosh began to see the real man, and under the boisterous good-humour he discerned a vulgar cunning which was hateful; he was vain and domineering, and it was strange that he had notwithstanding a shyness which made him dislike people who were not quite of his kidney. He judged others, naïvely, by their language, and if it was free from the oaths and the obscenity which made up the greater part of his own conversation, he looked upon them with suspicion. In the evening the two men played piquet. He played badly but vaingloriously, crowing over his opponent when he won and losing his temper when he lost. On rare occasions a couple of planters or traders would drive over to play bridge, and then Walker showed himself in what Mackintosh considered a characteristic light. He played regardless of his partner, calling up in his desire to play the hand, and argued interminably, beating down opposition by the loudness of his voice. He constantly revoked, and when he did so said with an ingratiating whine: "Oh, you wouldn't count it against an old man who can hardly see." Did he know that his opponents thought it as well to keep on the right side of him and hesitated to insist on the rigour of the game? Mackintosh watched him with an icy contempt. When the game was over, while they smoked their pipes and drank whisky, they would begin telling stories. Walker told with gusto the story of his marriage. He had got so drunk at the wedding feast that the bride had fled and he had never seen her since. He had had numberless adventures, commonplace and sordid, with the women of the island and he described them with a pride in his own prowess which was an offence to Mackintosh's fastidious ears. He was a gross, sensual old man. He thought Mackintosh a poor fellow because he would not share his promiscuous amours and remained sober when the company was drunk.

He despised him also for the orderliness with which he did his official work. Mackintosh liked to do everything just so. His desk was always tidy, his papers were always neatly docketed, he could put his hand on any document that was needed, and he had at his fingers' ends all the regulations that were required for the business of their administration.

"Fudge, fudge," said Walker. "I've run this island for twenty years without red tape, and I don't want it now."

"Does it make it any easier for you that when you want a letter you have to hunt half an hour for it?" answered Mackintosh.

"You're nothing but a damned official. But you're not a bad fellow: when you've been out here a year or two you'll be all right. What's wrong about you is that you won't drink. You wouldn't be a bad sort if you got soused once a week."

The curious thing was that Walker remained perfectly uncon scious of the dislike for him which every month increased in the breast of his subordinate. Although he laughed at him, as he grew

accustomed to him, he began almost to like him. He had a certain
tolerance for the peculiarities of others, and he accepted Mackintosh as a queer fish. Perhaps he liked him, unconsciously, because
he could chaff him. His humour consisted of coarse banter and
he wanted a butt. Mackintosh's exactness, his morality, his sobriety,
were all fruitful subjects; his Scot's name gave an opportunity for
the usual jokes about Scotland; he enjoyed himself thoroughly
when two or three men were there and he could make them all
laugh at the expense of Mackintosh. He would say ridiculous
things about him to the natives, and Mackintosh, his knowledge
of Samoan still imperfect, would see their unrestrained mirth when
Walker had made an obscene reference to him. He smiled good-
humouredly.

"I'll say this for you, Mac," Walker would say in his gruff loud
voice, "you can take a joke."

"Was it a joke?" smiled Mackintosh. "I didn't know."

"Scots wha hae!" shouted Walker, with a bellow of laughter.
"There's only one way to make a Scotchman see a joke and that's
by a surgical operation."

Walker little knew that there was nothing Mackintosh could
stand less than chaff. He would wake in the night, the breathless
night of the rainy season, and brood sullenly over the gibe that
Walker had uttered carelessly days before. It rankled. His heart
swelled with rage, and he pictured to himself ways in which he
might get even with the bully. He had tried answering him, but
Walker had a gift of repartee, coarse and obvious, which gave
him an advantage. The dullness of his intellect made him im-
pervious to a delicate shaft. His self-satisfaction made it impossible to wound him. His loud voice, his bellow of laughter, were
weapons against which Mackintosh had nothing to counter, and
he learned that the wisest thing was never to betray his irritation.
He learned to control himself. But his hatred grew till it was a
monomania. He watched Walker with an insane vigilance. He
fed his own self-esteem by every instance of meanness on Walker's
part, by every exhibition of childish vanity, of cunning and of
vulgarity. Walker ate greedily, noisily, filthily, and Mackintosh
watched him with satisfaction. He took note of the foolish things
he said and of his mistakes in grammar. He knew that Walker
held him in small esteem, and he found a bitter satisfaction in his
chief's opinion of him; it increased his own contempt for the nar-

row, complacent old man. And it gave him a singular pleasure to know that Walker was entirely unconscious of the hatred he felt for him. He was a fool who liked popularity, and he blandly fancied that everyone admired him. Once Mackintosh had overheard Walker speaking of him.

"He'll be all right when I've licked him into shape," he said. "He's a good dog and he loves his master."

Mackintosh silently, without a movement of his long, sallow face, laughed long and heartily.

But his hatred was not blind; on the contrary, it was peculiarly clear-sighted, and he judged Walker's capabilities with precision. He ruled his small kingdom with efficiency. He was just and honest. With opportunities to make money he was a poorer man than when he was first appointed to his post, and his only support for his old age was the pension which he expected when at last he retired from official life. His pride was that with an assistant and a half-caste clerk he was able to administer the island more competently than Upolu, the island of which Apia is the chief town, was administered with its army of functionaries. He had a few native policemen to sustain his authority, but he made no use of them. He governed by bluff and his Irish humour.

"They insisted on building a jail for me," he said. "What the devil do I want a jail for? I'm not going to put the natives in prison. If they do wrong I know how to deal with them."

One of his quarrels with the higher authorities at Apia was that he claimed entire jurisdiction over the natives of his island. Whatever their crimes he would not give them up to courts competent to deal with them, and several times an angry correspondence had passed between him and the Governor at Upolu. For he looked upon the natives as his children. And that was the amazing thing about this coarse, vulgar, selfish man; he loved the island on which he had lived so long with passion, and he had for the natives a strange rough tenderness which was quite wonderful.

He loved to ride about the island on his old grey mare and he was never tired of its beauty. Sauntering along the grassy roads among the coconut trees he would stop every now and then to admire the loveliness of the scene. Now and then he would come upon a native village and stop while the head man brought him a bowl of *kava*. He would look at the little group of bell-shaped huts with their high thatched roofs, like beehives, and a smile would spread over his fat face. His eyes rested happily on the spreading green of the breadfruit trees.

"By George, it's like the garden of Eden."

Sometimes his rides took him along the coast and through the trees he had a glimpse of the wide sea, empty, with never a sail to disturb the loneliness; sometimes he climbed a hill so that a great stretch of country, with little villages nestling among the tall trees, was spread out before him like the kingdom of the world, and he would sit there for an hour in an ecstasy of delight. But he had no words to express his feelings and to relieve them would utter an obscene jest; it was as though his emotion was so violent that he needed vulgarity to break the tension.

Mackintosh observed this sentiment with an icy disdain. Walker had always been a heavy drinker, he was proud of his capacity to see men half his age under the table when he spent a night in Apia, and he had the sentimentality of the toper. He could cry over the stories he read in his magazines and yet would refuse a loan to some trader in difficulties whom he had known for twenty years. He was close with his money. Once Mackintosh said to him:

"No one could accuse you of giving money away."

He took it as a compliment. His enthusiasm for nature was but the drivelling sensibility of the drunkard. Nor had Mackintosh any sympathy for his chief's feelings towards the natives. He loved them because they were in his power, as a selfish man loves his dog, and his mentality was on a level with theirs. Their humour was obscene and he was never at a loss for the lewd remark. He understood them and they understood him. He was proud of his influence over them. He looked upon them as his children and he mixed himself in all their affairs. But he was very jealous of his authority; if he ruled them with a rod of iron, brooking no contradiction, he would not suffer any of the white men on the island to take advantage of them. He watched the missionaries suspiciously and, if they did anything of which he disapproved, was able to make life so unendurable to them that if he could not get them removed they were glad to go of their own accord. His power over the natives was so great that on his word they would refuse labour and food to their pastor. On the other hand he showed the traders no favour. He took care that they should not cheat the natives; he saw that they got a fair reward for their work and their copra and that the traders made no extravagant profit on the wares they sold them. He was merciless to a bargain that he thought unfair. Sometimes the traders would complain at Apia that they did not get fair opportunities. They suffered for it. Walker then hesitated at no calumny, at no outrageous lie, to get even with them, and they found that if they wanted not only to live at peace, but to exist at all, they had to accept the situation on his own terms. More than once the store of a trader obnoxious to him had been burned down, and there was only the appositeness of the event to show that the administrator had instigated it. Once a Swedish half-caste, ruined by the burning, had gone to him and roundly accused him of arson. Walker laughed in his face.

"You dirty dog. Your mother was a native and you try to cheat the natives. If your rotten old store is burned down it's a judgment of Providence; that's what it is, a judgment of Providence. Get out."

And as the man was hustled out by two native policemen the administrator laughed fatly.

"A judgment of Providence."

And now Mackintosh watched him enter upon the day's work. He began with the sick, for Walker added doctoring to his other activities, and he had a small room behind the office full of drugs. An elderly man came forward, a man with a crop of curly grey hair, in a blue *lava-lava*, elaborately tatooed, with the skin of his body wrinkled like a wine-skin.

"What have you come for?" Walker asked him abruptly.

In a whining voice the man said that he could not eat without vomiting and that he had pains here and pains there.

"Go to the missionaries," said Walker. "You know that I only cure children."

"I have been to the missionaries and they do me no good."

"Then go home and prepare yourself to die. Have you lived so long and still want to go on living? You're a fool."

The man broke into querulous expostulation, but Walker, pointing to a woman with a sick child in her arms, told her to bring it to his desk. He asked her questions and looked at the child.

"I will give you medicine," he said. He turned to the half-caste clerk. "Go into the dispensary and bring me some calomel pills."

He made the child swallow one there and then and gave another to the mother.

"Take the child away and keep it warm. Tomorrow it will be dead or better."

He leaned back in his chair and lit his pipe.

"Wonderful stuff, calomel. I've saved more lives with it than all the hospital doctors at Apia put together."

Walker was very proud of his skill, and with the dogmatism of ignorance had no patience with the members of the medical profession.

"The sort of case I like," he said, "is the one that all the doctors have given up as hopeless. When the doctors have said they can't cure you, I say to them, 'come to me.' Did I ever tell you about the fellow who had a cancer?"

"Frequently," said Mackintosh.

"I got him right in three months."

"You've never told me about the people you haven't cured."

He finished this part of the work and went on to the rest. It was a queer medley. There was a woman who could not get on with her husband and a man who complained that his wife had run away from him.

"Lucky dog," said Walker. "Most men wish their wives would too."

There was a long complicated quarrel about the ownership of a few yards of land. There was a dispute about the sharing out of a catch of fish. There was a complaint against a white trader because he had given short measure. Walker listened attentively to every case, made up his mind quickly, and gave his decision. Then he would listen to nothing more; if the complainant went on he was hustled out of the office by a policeman. Mackintosh listened to it all with sullen irritation. On the whole, perhaps, it might be admitted that rough justice was done, but it exasperated the assistant that his chief trusted his instinct rather than the evidence. He would not listen to reason. He browbeat the witnesses and when they did not see what he wished them to called them thieves and liars.

He left to the last a group of men who were sitting in the corner of the room. He had deliberately ignored them. The party consisted of an old chief, a tall, dignified man with short, white hair, in a new *lava-lava,* bearing a huge fly wisp as a badge of office, his son, and half a dozen of the important men of the village. Walker had had a feud with them and had beaten them. As was characteristic of him he meant now to rub in his victory, and because he had them down to profit by their helplessness. The facts were peculiar. Walker had a passion for building roads. When he had come to Talua there were but a few tracks here and there, but in course of time he had cut roads through the country, joining the villages together, and it was to this that a great part of the island's prosperity was due. Whereas in the old days it had been impossible to get the produce of the land, copra chiefly, down to the coast where it could be put on schooners or motor launches and so taken to Apia, now transport was easy and simple. His ambition was to make a road right round the island and a great part of it was already built.

"In two years I shall have done it, and then I can die or they can fire me, I don't care."

His roads were the joy of his heart and he made excursions constantly to see that they were kept in order. They were simple enough, wide tracks, grass covered, cut through the scrub or through the plantations; but trees had to be rooted out, rocks dug up or blasted, and here and there levelling had been necessary. He was proud that he had surmounted by his own skill such difficulties as they presented. He rejoiced in his disposition of them so that they were not only convenient, but showed off the beauties of the island which his soul loved. When he spoke of his roads he was almost a poet. They meandered through those lovely scenes, and Walker had taken care that here and there they should run in a straight line, giving you a green vista through the tall trees, and here and there should turn and curve so that the heart was rested by the diversity. It was amazing that this coarse and sensual man should exercise so subtle an ingenuity to get the effects which his fancy suggested to him. He had used in making his roads all the fantastic skill of a Japanese gardener. He received a grant from headquarters for the work but took a curious pride in using but a small part of it, and the year before had spent only a hundred pounds of the thousand assigned to him.

"What do they want money for?" he boomed. "They'll only

spend it on all kinds of muck they don't want; what the missionaries leave them, that is to say."

For no particular reason, except perhaps pride in the economy of his administration and the desire to contrast his efficiency with the wasteful methods of the authorities at Apia, he got the natives to do the work he wanted for wages that were almost nominal. It was owing to this that he had lately had difficulty with the village whose chief men now were come to see him. The chief's son had been in Upolu for a year and on coming back had told his people of the large sums that were paid at Apia for the public works. In long, idle talks he had inflamed their hearts with the desire for gain. He held out to them visions of vast wealth and they thought of the whisky they could buy—it was dear, since there was a law that it must not be sold to natives, and so it cost them double what the white man had to pay for it—they thought of the great sandal-wood boxes in which they kept their treasures, and the scented soap and potted salmon, the luxuries for which the Kanaka will sell his soul; so that when the administrator sent for them and told them he wanted a road made from their village to a certain point along the coast and offered them twenty pounds, they asked him a hundred. The chief's son was called Manuma. He was a tall, handsome fellow, copper-coloured, with his fuzzy hair dyed red with lime, a wreath of red berries round his neck, and behind his ear a flower like a scarlet flame against his brown face. The upper part of his body was naked, but to show that he was no longer a savage, since he had lived in Apia, he wore a pair of dungarees instead of a *lava-lava*. He told them that if they held together the administrator would be obliged to accept their terms. His heart was set on building the road and when he found they would not work for less he would give them what they asked. But they must not move; whatever he said they must not abate their claim; they had asked a hundred and that they must keep to. When they mentioned the figure, Walker burst into a shout of his long, deep-voiced laughter. He told them not to make fools of themselves, but to set about the work at once. Because he was in a good humour that day he promised to give them a feast when the road was finished. But when he found that no attempt was made to start work, he went to the village and asked the men what silly game they were playing. Manuma had coached them well. They were quite calm, they did not attempt to argue

—and argument is a passion with the Kanaka—they merely shrugged their shoulders: they would do it for a hundred pounds, and if he would not give them that they would do no work. He could please himself. They did not care. Then Walker flew into a passion. He was ugly then. His short fat neck swelled ominously, his red face grew purple, he foamed at the mouth. He set upon the natives with invective. He knew well how to wound and how to humiliate. He was terrifying. The older men grew pale and uneasy. They hesitated. If it had not been for Manuma, with his knowledge of the great world, and their dread of his ridicule, they would have yielded. It was Manuma who answered Walker.

"Pay us a hundred pounds and we will work."

Walker, shaking his fist at him, called him every name he could think of. He riddled him with scorn. Manuma sat still and smiled. There may have been more bravado than confidence in his smile, but he had to make a good show before the others. He repeated his words.

"Pay us a hundred pounds and we will work."

They thought that Walker would spring on him. It would not have been the first time that he had thrashed a native with his own hands; they knew his strength, and though Walker was three times the age of the young man and six inches shorter they did not doubt that he was more than a match for Manuma. No one had ever thought of resisting the savage onslaught of the administrator. But Walker said nothing. He chuckled.

"I am not going to waste my time with a pack of fools," he said. "Talk it over again. You know what I have offered. If you do not start in a week, take care."

He turned round and walked out of the chief's hut. He untied his old mare and it was typical of the relations between him and the natives that one of the elder men hung on to the off stirrup while Walker from a convenient boulder hoisted himself heavily into the saddle.

That same night when Walker according to his habit was strolling along the road that ran past his house, he heard something whizz past him and with a thud strike a tree. Something had been thrown at him. He ducked instinctively. With a shout, "Who's that"? he ran towards the place from which the missile had come and he heard the sound of a man escaping through the bush.

He knew it was hopeless to pursue in the darkness, and besides he was soon out of breath, so he stopped and made his way back to the road. He looked about for what had been thrown, but could find nothing. It was quite dark. He went quickly back to the house and called Mackintosh and the Chinese boy.

"One of those devils has thrown something at me. Come along and let's find out what it was."

He told the boy to bring a lantern and the three of them made their way back to the place. They hunted about the ground, but could not find what they sought. Suddenly the boy gave a guttural cry. They turned to look. He held up the lantern, and there, sinister in the light that cut the surrounding darkness, was a long knife sticking into the trunk of a coconut tree. It had been thrown with such force that it required quite an effort to pull it out.

"By George, if he hadn't missed me I'd have been in a nice state."

Walker handled the knife. It was one of those knives, made in imitation of the sailor knives brought to the islands a hundred years before by the first white men, used to divide the coconuts in two so that the copra might be dried. It was a murderous weapon, and the blade, twelve inches long, was very sharp. Walker chuckled softly.

"The devil, the impudent devil."

He had no doubt it was Manuma who had flung the knife. He had escaped death by three inches. He was not angry. On the contrary, he was in high spirits; the adventure exhilarated him, and when they got back to the house, calling for drinks, he rubbed his hands gleefully.

"I'll make them pay for this!"

His little eyes twinkled. He blew himself out like a turkey-cock, and for the second time within half an hour insisted on telling Mackintosh every detail of the affair. Then he asked him to play piquet, and while they played he boasted of his intentions. Mackintosh listened with tightened lips.

"But why should you grind them down like this?" he asked. "Twenty pounds is precious little for the work you want them to do."

"They ought to be precious thankful I give them anything."

"Hang it all, it's not your own money. The government allots you a reasonable sum. They won't complain if you spend it."

"They're a bunch of fools at Apia."

Mackintosh saw that Walker's motive was merely vanity. He shrugged his shoulders.

"It won't do you much good to score off the fellows at Apia at the cost of your life."

"Bless you, they wouldn't hurt me, these people. They couldn't do without me. They worship me. Manuma is a fool. He only threw that knife to frighten me."

The next day Walker rode over again to the village. It was called Matautu. He did not get off his horse. When he reached the chief's house he saw that the men were sitting round the floor in a circle, talking, and he guessed they were discussing again the question of the road. The Samoan huts are formed in this way: Trunks of slender trees are placed in a circle at intervals of perhaps five or six feet; a tall tree is set in the middle and from this downwards slopes the thatched roof. Venetian blinds of coconut leaves can be pulled down at night or when it is raining. Ordinarily the hut is open all round so that the breeze can blow through freely. Walker rode to the edge of the hut and called out to the chief.

"Oh, there, Tangatu, your son left his knife in a tree last night. I have brought it back to you."

He flung it down on the ground in the midst of the circle, and with a low burst of laughter ambled off.

On Monday he went out to see if they had started work. There was no sign of it. He rode through the village. The inhabitants were about their ordinary avocations. Some were weaving mats of the pandanus leaf, one old man was busy with a *kava* bowl, the children were playing, the women went about their household chores. Walker, a smile on his lips, came to the chief's house.

"*Talofa-li,*" said the chief.

"*Talofa,*" answered Walker.

Manuma was making a net. He sat with a cigarette between his lips and looked up at Walker with a smile of triumph.

"You have decided that you will not make the road?"

The chief answered.

"Not unless you pay us one hundred pounds."

"You will regret it." He turned to Manuma. "And you, my lad, I shouldn't wonder if your back was very sore before you're much older."

He rode away chuckling. He left the natives vaguely uneasy. They feared the fat sinful old man, and neither the missionaries' abuse of him nor the scorn which Manuma had learnt in Apia made them forget that he had a devilish cunning and that no man had ever braved him without in the long run suffering for it. They found out within twenty-four hours what scheme he had devised. It was characteristic. For next morning a great band of men, women, and children came into the village and the chief men said that they had made a bargain with Walker to build the road. He had offered them twenty pounds and they had accepted. Now the cunning lay in this, that the Polynesians have rules of hospitality which have all the force of laws; an etiquette of absolute rigidity made it necessary for the people of the village not only to give lodging to the strangers, but to provide them with food and drink as long as they wished to stay. The inhabitants of Matautu were outwitted. Every morning the workers went out in a joyous band, cut down trees, blasted rocks, levelled here and there and then in the evening tramped back again, and ate and drank, ate heartily, danced, sang hymns, and enjoyed life. For them it was a picnic. But soon their hosts began to wear long faces; the strangers had enormous appetites, and the plantains and the bread-fruit vanished before their rapacity; the alligator-pear trees, whose fruit sent to Apia might sell for good money, were stripped bare. Ruin stared them in the face. And then they found that the strangers were working very slowly. Had they received a hint from Walker that they might take their time? At this rate by the time the road was finished there would not be a scrap of food in the village. And worse than this, they were a laughing-stock; when one or other of them went to some distant hamlet on an errand he found that the story had got there before him, and he was met with derisive laughter. There is nothing the Kanaka can endure less than ridicule. It was not long before much angry talk passed among the sufferers. Manuma was no longer a hero; he had to put up with a good deal of plain speaking, and one day what Walker had suggested came to pass: a heated argument turned into a quarrel and half a dozen of the young men set upon the chief's son and gave him such a beating that for a week he lay bruised and sore on the pandanus mats. He turned from side to side and could find no ease. Every day or two the administrator rode over on his old mare and watched the progress of the road. He was not a man to resist the temptation of taunting the fallen foe, and he missed no opportunity to rub into the shamed inhabitants of Matautu the bitterness of their humiliation. He broke their spirit. And one morning, putting their pride in their pockets, a figure of speech, since pockets they had not, they all set out with the strangers and started working on the road. It was urgent to get it done quickly if they wanted to save any food at all, and the whole village joined in. But they worked silently, with rage and mortification in their hearts, and even the children toiled in silence. The women wept as they carried away bundles of brushwood. When Walker saw them he laughed so much that he almost rolled out of his saddle. The news spread quickly and tickled the people of the island to death. This was the greatest joke of all, the crowning triumph of that cunning old white man whom no Kanaka had ever been able to circumvent; and they came from distant villages, with their wives and children, to look at the foolish folk who had refused twenty pounds to make the road and now were forced to work for nothing. But the harder they worked the more easily went the guests. Why should they hurry, when they were getting good food for nothing and the longer they took about the job the better the joke became? At last the wretched villagers could stand it no longer, and they were come this morning to beg the administrator to send the strangers back to their own homes. If he would do this they promised to finish the road themselves for nothing. For him it was a victory complete and unqualified. They were humbled. A look of arrogant complacence spread over his large, naked face, and he seemed to swell in his chair like a great bullfrog. There was something sinister in his appearance, so that Mackintosh shivered with disgust. Then in his booming tones he began to speak.

"Is it for my good that I make the road? What benefit do you think I get out of it? It is for you, so that you can walk in comfort and carry your copra in comfort. I offered to pay you for your work, though it was for your own sake the work was done. I offered to pay you generously. Now *you* must pay. I will send the people of Manua back to their homes if you will finish the road and pay the twenty pounds that I have to pay them."

There was an outcry. They sought to reason with him. They told him they had not the money. But to everything they said he replied with brutal gibes. Then the clock struck.

"Dinner time," he said. "Turn them all out."

He raised himself heavily from his chair and walked out of the room. When Mackintosh followed him he found him already seated at table, a napkin tied round his neck, holding his knife and fork in readiness for the meal the Chinese cook was about to bring. He was in high spirits.

"I did 'em down fine," he said, as Mackintosh sat down. "I shan't have much trouble with the roads after this."

"I suppose you were joking," said Mackintosh icily.

"What do you mean by that?"

"You're not really going to make them pay twenty pounds?"

"You bet your life I am."

"I'm not sure you've got any right to."

"Ain't you? I guess I've got the right to do any damned thing I like on this island."

"I think you've bullied them quite enough."

Walker laughed fatly. He did not care what Mackintosh thought.

"When I want your opinion I'll ask for it."

Mackintosh grew very white. He knew by bitter experience that he could do nothing but keep silence, and the violent effort at self-control made him sick and faint. He could not eat the food that was before him and with disgust he watched Walker shovel meat into his vast mouth. He was a dirty feeder, and to sit at table with him needed a strong stomach. Mackintosh shuddered. A tremendous desire seized him to humiliate that gross and cruel man; he would give anything in the world to see him in the dust, suffering as much as he had made others suffer. He had never loathed the bully with such loathing as now.

The day wore on. Mackintosh tried to sleep after dinner, but the passion in his heart prevented him; he tried to read, but the letters swam before his eyes. The sun beat down pitilessly, and he longed for rain; but he knew that rain would bring no coolness; it would only make it hotter and more steamy. He was a native of Aberdeen and his heart yearned suddenly for the icy winds that whistled through the granite streets of that city. Here he was a prisoner, imprisoned not only by that placid sea, but by his hatred for that horrible old man. He pressed his hands to his aching head. He would like to kill him. But he pulled himself together. He must do something to distract his mind, and since he could not read he

thought he would set his private papers in order. It was a job
which he had long meant to do and which he had constantly put
off. He unlocked the drawer of his desk and took out a handful
of letters. He caught sight of his revolver. An impulse, no sooner
realized than set aside, to put a bullet through his head and so
escape from the intolerable bondage of life flashed through his
mind. He noticed that in the damp air the revolver was slightly
rusted, and he got an oil rag and began to clean it. It was while
he was thus occupied that he grew aware of someone slinking
round the door. He looked up and called:

"Who is there?"

There was a moment's pause, then Manuma showed himself.

"What do you want?"

The chief's son stood for a moment, sullen and silent, and when
he spoke it was with a strangled voice.

"We can't pay twenty pounds. We haven't the money."

"What am I to do?" said Mackintosh. "You heard what Mr.
Walker said."

Manuma began to plead, half in Samoan and half in English.
It was a sing-song whine, with the quavering intonations of a
beggar, and it filled Mackintosh with disgust. It outraged him that
the man should let himself be so crushed. He was a pitiful object.

"I can do nothing," said Mackintosh irritably. "You know that
Mr. Walker is master here."

Manuma was silent again. He still stood in the doorway.

"I am sick," he said at last. "Give me some medicine."

"What is the matter with you?"

"I do not know. I am sick. I have pains in my body."

"Don't stand there," said Mackintosh sharply. "Come in and let
me look at you."

Manuma entered the little room and stood before the desk.
"I have pains here and here."

He put his hands to his loins and his face assumed an expression
of pain. Suddenly Mackintosh grew conscious that the boy's eyes
were resting on the revolver which he had laid on the desk when
Manuma appeared in the doorway. There was a silence between
the two which to Mackintosh was endless. He seemed to read the
thoughts which were in the Kanaka's mind. His heart beat violently. And then he felt as though something possessed him so that
he acted under the compulsion of a foreign will. Himself did not

make the movements of his body, but a power that was strange to him. His throat was suddenly dry, and he put his hand to it mechanically in order to help his speech. He was impelled to avoid Manuma's eyes.

"Just wait here," he said, his voice sounding as though someone had seized him by the windpipe, "and I'll fetch you something from the dispensary."

He got up. Was it his fancy that he staggered a little? Manuma stood silently, and though he kept his eyes averted, Mackintosh knew that he was looking dully out of the door. It was this other person that possessed him, that drove him out of the room, but it was himself that took a handful of muddled papers and threw them on the revolver in order to hide it from view. He went to the dispensary. He got a pill and poured out some blue draught into a small bottle, and then came out into the compound. He did not want to go back into his own bungalow, so he called to Manuma.

"Come here."

He gave him the drugs and instructions how to take them. He did not know what it was that made it impossible for him to look at the Kanaka. While he was speaking to him he kept his eyes on his shoulder. Manuma took the medicine and slunk out of the gate.

Mackintosh went into the dining-room and turned over once more the old newspapers. But he could not read them. The house was very still. Walker was upstairs in his room asleep, the Chinese cook was busy in the kitchen, the two policemen were out fishing. The silence that seemed to brook over the house was unearthly, and there hammered in Mackintosh's head the question whether the revolver still lay where he had placed it. He could not bring himself to look. The uncertainty was horrible, but the certainty would be more horrible still. He sweated. At last he could stand the silence no longer, and he made up his mind to go down the road to the trader's, a man named Jervis, who had a store about a mile away. He was a half-caste, but even that amount of white blood made him possible to talk to. He wanted to get away from his bungalow, with the desk littered with untidy papers, and underneath them something, or nothing. He walked along the road. As he passed the fine hut of a chief a greeting was called out to him. Then he came to the store. Behind the counter sat the trader's daughter, a swarthy broad-featured girl in a pink blouse and a white drill skirt. Jervis hoped he would marry her. He had money, and he had told Mackintosh that his daughter's husband would be well-to-do. She flushed a little when she saw Mackintosh.

"Father's just unpacking some cases that have come in this morning. I'll tell him you're here."

He sat down and the girl went out behind the shop. In a moment her mother waddled in, a huge old woman, a chiefess, who owned much land in her own right; and gave him her hand. Her monstrous obesity was an offence, but she managed to convey an impression of dignity. She was cordial without obsequiousness; affable, but conscious of her station.

"You're quite a stranger, Mr. Mackintosh. Teresa was saying only this morning: 'Why, we never see Mr. Mackintosh now.'"

He shuddered a little as he thought of himself as that old native's son-in-law. It was notorious that she ruled her husband, notwithstanding his white blood, with a firm hand. Hers was the authority and hers the business head. She might be no more than Mrs. Jervis to the white people, but her father had been a chief of the blood royal, and his father and his father's father had ruled as kings. The trader came in, small beside his imposing wife, a dark man with a black beard going grey, in ducks, with handsome eyes and flashing teeth. He was very British, and his conversation was slangy, but you felt he spoke English as a foreign tongue; with his family he used the language of his native mother. He was a servile man, cringing and obsequious.

"Ah, Mr. Mackintosh, this is a joyful surprise. Get the whisky, Teresa; Mr. Mackintosh will have a gargle with us."

He gave all the latest news of Apia, watching his guest's eyes the while, so that he might know the welcome thing to say.

"And how is Walker? We've not seen him just lately. Mrs. Jervis is going to send him a sucking-pig one day this week."

"I saw him riding home this morning," said Teresa.

"Here's how," said Jervis, holding up his whisky.

Mackintosh drank. The two women sat and looked at him, Mrs. Jervis in her black Mother Hubbard, placid and haughty, and Teresa, anxious to smile whenever she caught his eye, while the trader gossiped insufferably.

"They were saying in Apia it was about time Walker retired. He ain't so young as he was. Things have changed since he first come to the islands and he ain't changed with them."

"He'll go too far," said the old chiefess. "The natives aren't satisfied."

"That was a good joke about the road," laughed the trader. "When I told them about it in Apia they fair split their sides with laughing. Good old Walker."

Mackintosh looked at him savagely. What did he mean by talking of him in that fashion? To a half-caste trader he was Mr. Walker. It was on his tongue to utter a harsh rebuke for the impertinence. He did not know what held him back.

"When he goes I hope you'll take his place, Mr. Mackintosh," said Jervis. "We all like you on the island. You understand the natives. They're educated now, they must be treated differently to the old days. It wants an educated man to be administrator now. Walker was only a trader same as I am."

Teresa's eyes glistened.

"When the time comes if there's anything anyone can do here, you bet your bottom dollar we'll do it. I'd get all the chiefs to go over to Apia and make a petition."

Mackintosh felt horribly sick. It had not struck him that if anything happened to Walker it might be he who would succeed him. It was true that no one in his official position knew the island so well. He got up suddenly and scarcely taking his leave walked back to the compound. And now he went straight to his room. He took a quick look at his desk. He rummaged among the papers.

The revolver was not there.

His heart thumped violently against his ribs. He looked for the revolver everywhere. He hunted in the chairs and in the drawers. He looked desperately, and all the time he knew he would not find it. Suddenly he heard Walker's gruff, hearty voice.

"What the devil are you up to, Mac?"

He started. Walker was standing in the doorway and instinctively he turned round to hide what lay upon his desk.

"Tidying up?" quizzed Walker. "I've told 'em to put the grey in the trap. I'm going down to Tafoni to bathe. You'd better come along."

"All right," said Mackintosh.

So long as he was with Walker nothing could happen. The place they were bound for was about three miles away, and there was a fresh-water pool, separated by a thin barrier of rock from the sea, which the administrator had blasted out for the natives to bathe in. He had done this at spots round the island, wherever there was a spring; and the fresh water, compared with the sticky warmth of the sea, was cool and invigorating. They drove along the silent grassy road, splashing now and then through fords, where the sea had forced its way in, past a couple of native villages, the bell-shaped huts spaced out roomily and the white chapel in the middle, and at the third village they got out of the trap, tied up the horse, and walked down to the pool. They were accompanied by four or five girls and a dozen children. Soon they were all splashing about, shouting and laughing, while Walker, in a *lava-lava*, swam to and fro like an unwieldy porpoise. He made lewd jokes with the girls, and they amused themselves by diving under him and wriggling away when he tried to catch them. When he was tired he lay down a rock, while the girls and children surrounded him; it was a happy family; and the old man, huge, with his crescent of white hair and his shining bald crown, looked like some old sea god. Once Mackintosh caught a queer soft look in his eyes.

"They're dear children," he said. "They look upon me as their father."

And then without a pause he turned to one of the girls and made an obscene remark which sent them all into fits of laughter. Mackintosh started to dress. With his thin legs and thin arms he made a grotesque figure, a sinister Don Quixote, and Walker began to make coarse jokes about him. They were acknowledged with little smothered laughs. Mackintosh struggled with his shirt. He knew he looked absurd, but he hated being laughed at. He stood silent and glowering.

"If you want to get back in time for dinner you ought to come soon."

"You're not a bad fellow, Mac. Only you're a fool. When you're doing one thing you always want to do another. That's not the way to live."

But all the same he raised himself slowly to his feet and began to put on his clothes. They sauntered back to the village, drank a bowl of *kava* with the chief, and then, after a joyful farewell from all the lazy villagers, drove home.

After dinner, according to his habit, Walker, lighting his cigar, prepared to go for a stroll. Mackintosh was suddenly seized with fear.

"Don't you think it's rather unwise to go out at night by yourself just now?"

Walker stared at him with his round blue eyes.

"What the devil do you mean?"

"Remember the knife the other night. You've got those fellows' backs up."

"Pooh! They wouldn't dare."

"Someone dared before."

"That was only a bluff. They wouldn't hurt me. They look upon me as a father. They know that whatever I do is for their own good."

Mackintosh watched him with contempt in his heart. The man's self-complacency outraged him, and yet something, he knew not what, made him insist.

"Remember what happened this morning. It wouldn't hurt you to stay at home just to-night. I'll play piquet with you."

"I'll play piquet with you when I come back. The Kanaka isn't born yet who can make me alter my plans."

"You'd better let me come with you."

"You stay where you are."

Mackintosh shrugged his shoulders. He had given the man full warning. If he did not heed it that was his own lookout. Walker put on his hat and went out. Mackintosh began to read; but then he thought of something; perhaps it would be as well to have his own whereabouts quite clear. He crossed over to the kitchen and, inventing some pretext, talked for a few minutes with the cook. Then he got out the gramophone and put a record on it, but while it ground out its melancholy tune, some comic song of a London music-hall, his ear was strained for a sound away there in the night. At his elbow the record reeled out its loudness, the words were raucous, but notwithstanding he seemed to be surrounded by an unearthly silence. He heard the dull roar of the breakers against the reef. He heard the breeze sigh, far up, in the leaves of the coconut trees. How long would it be? It was awful.

He heard a hoarse laugh.

"Wonders will never cease. It's not often you play yourself a tune, Mac."

Walker stood at the window, red-faced, bluff and jovial.

"Well, you see I'm alive and kicking. What were you playing for?"

Walker came in.

"Nerves a bit dicky, eh? Playing a tune to keep your pecker up?"

"I was playing your requiem."

"What the devil's that?"

"'Alf o' bitter an' a pint of stout."

"A rattling good song too. I don't mind how often I hear it. Now I'm ready to take your money off you at piquet."

They played and Walker bullied his way to victory, bluffing his opponent, chaffing him, jeering at his mistakes, up to every dodge, browbeating him, exulting. Presently Mackintosh recovered his coolness, and standing outside himself, as it were, he was able to take a detached pleasure in watching the overbearing old man and in his own cold reserve. Somewhere Manuma sat quietly and awaited his opportunity.

Walker won game after game and pocketed his winnings at the end of the evening in high good humour.

"You'll have to grow a little bit older before you stand much chance against me, Mac. The fact is I have a natural gift for cards."

"I don't know that there's much gift about it when I happen to deal you fourteen aces."

"Good cards come to good players," retorted Walker. "I'd have won if I'd had your hands."

He went on to tell long stories of the various occasions on which he had played cards with notorious sharpers and to their consternation had taken all their money from them. He boasted. He praised himself. And Mackintosh listened with absorption. He wanted now to feed his hatred; and everything Walker said, every gesture, made him more detestable. At last Walker got up.

"Well, I'm going to turn in," he said with a loud yawn. "I've got a long day to-morrow."

"What are you going to do?"

"I'm driving over to the other side of the island. I'll start at five, but I don't expect I shall get back to dinner till late."

They generally dined at seven.

"We'd better make it half-past seven then."

"I guess it would be as well."

Mackintosh watched him knock the ashes out of his pipe. His vitality was rude and exuberant. It was strange to think that death hung over him. A faint smile flickered in Mackintosh's cold, gloomy eyes.

"Would you like me to come with you?"

"What in God's name should I want that for? I'm using the mare and she'll have enough to do to carry me; she don't want to drag you over thirty miles of road."

"Perhaps you don't quite realize what the feeling is at Matautu. I think it would be safer if I came with you."

Walker burst into contemptuous laughter.

"You'd be a fine lot of use in a scrap. I'm not a great hand at getting the wind up."

Now the smile passed from Mackintosh's eyes to his lips. It distorted them painfully.

"*Quem deus vult perdere prius dementat.*"

"What the hell is that?" said Walker.

"Latin," answered Mackintosh as he went out.

And now he chuckled. His mood had changed. He had done all he could and the matter was in the hands of fate. He slept more soundly than he had done for weeks. When he awoke next morning he went out. After a good night he found a pleasant exhilaration in the freshness of the early air. The sea was a more vivid blue, the sky more brilliant, than on most days, the trade wind was fresh, and there was a ripple on the lagoon as the breeze brushed over it like velvet brushed the wrong way. He felt himself stronger and younger. He entered upon the day's work with zest. After luncheon he slept again, and as evening drew on he had the bay saddled and sauntered through the bush. He seemed to see it all with new eyes. He felt more normal. The extraordinary thing was that he was able to put Walker out of his mind altogether. So far as he was concerned he might never have existed.

He returned late, hot after his ride, and bathed again. Then he sat on the verandah, smoking his pipe, and looked at the day declining over the lagoon. In the sunset the lagoon, rosy and purple and green, was very beautiful. He felt at peace with the world and with himself. When the cook came out to say that dinner was ready and to ask whether he should wait, Mackintosh smiled at him with friendly eyes. He looked at his watch.

"It's half-past seven. Better not wait. One can't tell when the boss'll be back."

The boy nodded, and in a moment Mackintosh saw him carry

across the yard a bowl of steaming soup. He got up lazily, went
into the dining-room, and ate his dinner. Had it happened? The
uncertainty was amusing and Mackintosh chuckled in the silence. The food did not seem so monotonous as usual, and even
though there was hamburger steak, the cook's invariable dish
when his poor invention failed him, it tasted by some miracle
succulent and spiced. After dinner he strolled over lazily to his
bungalow to get a book. He liked the intense stillness, and now
that the night had fallen the stars were blazing in the sky. He
shouted for a lamp and in a moment the Chink pattered over on
his bare feet, piercing the darkness with a ray of light. He put the
lamp on the desk and noiselessly slipped out of the room. Mackintosh stood rooted to the floor, for there, half hidden by untidy papers, was his revolver. His heart throbbed painfully, and
he broke into a sweat. It was done then.

He took up the revolver with a shaking hand. Four of the
chambers were empty. He paused a moment and looked suspiciously out into the night, but there was no one there. He
quickly slipped four cartridges into the empty chambers and
locked the revolver in his drawer.

He sat down to wait.

An hour passed, a second hour passed. There was nothing. He
sat at his desk as though he were writing, but he neither wrote
nor read. He merely listened. He strained his ears for a sound
travelling from a far distance. At last he heard hesitating footsteps
and knew it was the Chinese cook.

"Ah-Sung," he called.

The boy came to the door.

"Boss velly late," he said. "Dinner no good."

Mackintosh stared at him, wondering whether he knew what
had happened, and whether, when he knew, he would realize on
what terms he and Walker had been. He went about his work,
sleek, silent, and smiling, and who could tell his thoughts?

"I expect he's had dinner on the way, but you must keep the
soup hot at all events."

The words were hardly out of his mouth when the silence was
suddenly broken into by a confusion, cries, and a rapid patter of
naked feet. A number of natives ran into the compound, men and
women and children; they crowded round Mackintosh and they
all talked at once. They were unintelligible. They were excited

and frightened and some of them were crying. Mackintosh pushed
his way through them and went to the gateway. Though he had
scarcely understood what they said he knew quite well what had
happened. And as he reached the gate the dog-cart arrived. The
old mare was being led by a tall Kanaka, and in the dog-cart
crouched two men, trying to hold Walker up. A little crowd of
natives surrounded it.

The mare was led into the yard and the natives surged in after
it. Mackintosh shouted to them to stand back and the two policemen, sprang suddenly from God knows where, pushed them violently aside. By now he had managed to understand that some
lads who had been fishing, on their way back to their village had
come across the cart on the home side of the ford. The mare
was nuzzling about the herbage and in the darkness they could
just see the great white bulk of the old man sunk between the
seat and the dashboard. At first they thought he was drunk and
they peered in, grinning, but then they heard him groan, and
guessed that something was amiss. They ran to the village and
called for help. It was when they returned, accompanied by half a
hundred people, that they discovered Walker had been shot.

With a sudden thrill of horror Mackintosh asked himself
whether he was already dead. The first thing at all events was to
get him out of the cart, and that, owing to Walker's corpulence,
was a difficult job. It took four strong men to lift him. They jolted
him and he uttered a dull groan. He was still alive. At last they
carried him into the house, up the stairs, and placed him on his
bed. Then Mackintosh was able to see him, for in the yard, lit
only by half a dozen hurricane lamps, everything had been obscured. Walker's white ducks were stained with blood, and the
men who had carried him wiped their hands, red and sticky, on
their *lava-lavas*. Mackintosh held up the lamp. He had not expected the old man to be so pale. His eyes were closed. He was
breathing still, his pulse could be just felt, but it was obvious that
he was dying. Mackintosh had not bargained for the shock of
horror that convulsed him. He saw that the native clerk was
there, and in a voice hoarse with fear told him to go into the
dispensary and get what was necessary for a hypodermic injection. One of the policemen had brought up the whisky, and
Mackintosh forced a little into the old man's mouth. The room
was crowded with natives. They sat about the floor, speechless

now and terrified, and every now and then one wailed aloud. It was very hot, but Mackintosh felt cold, his hands and his feet were like ice, and he had to make a violent effort not to tremble in all his limbs. He did not know what to do. He did not know if Walker was bleeding still, and if he was, how he could stop the bleeding.

The clerk brought the hypodermic needle.

"You give it to him," said Mackintosh. "You're more used to that sort of thing than I am."

His head ached horribly. It felt as though all sorts of little savage things were beating inside it, trying to get out. They watched for the effect of the injection. Presently Walker opened his eyes slowly. He did not seem to know where he was.

"Keep quiet," said Mackintosh. "You're at home. You're quite safe."

Walker's lips outlined a shadowy smile.

"They've got me," he whispered.

"I'll get Jervis to send his motor-boat to Apia at once. We'll get a doctor out by to-morrow afternoon."

There was a long pause before the old man answered,

"I shall be dead by then."

A ghastly expression passed over Mackintosh's pale face. He forced himself to laugh.

"What rot! You keep quiet and you'll be as right as rain."

"Give me a drink," said Walker. "A stiff one."

With shaking hand Mackintosh poured out whisky and water, half and half, and held the glass while Walker drank greedily. It seemed to restore him. He gave a long sigh and a little colour came into his great fleshy face. Mackintosh felt extraordinarily helpless. He stood and stared at the old man.

"If you'll tell me what to do I'll do it," he said.

"There's nothing to do. Just leave me alone. I'm done for."

He looked dreadfully pitiful as he lay on the great bed, a huge, bloated, old man; but so wan, so weak, it was heart-rending. As he rested, his mind seemed to grow clearer.

"You were right, Mac," he said presently. "You warned me."

"I wish to God I'd come with you."

"You're a good chap, Mac, only you don't drink."

There was another long silence, and it was clear that Walker was sinking. There was an internal hæmorrhage and even Mackintosh in his ignorance could not fail to see that his chief had but an hour or two to live. He stood by the side of the bed stock still. For half an hour perhaps Walker lay with his eyes closed, then he opened them.

"They'll give you my job," he said, slowly. "Last time I was in Apia I told them you were all right. Finish my road. I want to think that'll be done. All round the island."

"I don't want your job. You'll get all right."

Walker shook his head wearily.

"I've had my day. Treat them fairly, that's the great thing. They're children. You must always remember that. You must be firm with them, but you must be kind. And you must be just. I've never made a bob out of them. I haven't saved a hundred pounds in twenty years. The road's the great thing. Get the road finished."

Something very like a sob was wrung from Mackintosh.

"You're a good fellow, Mac. I always liked you."

He closed his eyes, and Mackintosh thought that he would never open them again. His mouth was so dry that he had to get himself something to drink. The Chinese cook silently put a chair for him. He sat down by the side of the bed and waited. He did not know how long a time passed. The night was endless. Suddenly one of the men sitting there broke into uncontrollable sobbing, loudly, like a child, and Mackintosh grew aware that the room was crowded by this time with natives. They sat all over the floor on their haunches, men and women, staring at the bed.

"What are all these people doing here?" said Mackintosh. "They've got no right. Turn them out, turn them out, all of them."

His words seemed to rouse Walker, for he opened his eyes once more, and now they were all misty. He wanted to speak, but he was so weak that Mackintosh had to strain his ears to catch what he said.

"Let them stay. They're my children. They ought to be here."

Mackintosh turned to the natives.

"Stay where you are. He wants you. But be silent."

A faint smile came over the old man's white face.

"Come nearer," he said.

Mackintosh bent over him. His eyes were closed and the words he said were like a wind sighing through the fronds of the coconut trees.

"Give me another drink. I've got something to say."

This time Mackintosh gave him his whisky neat. Walker collected his strength in a final effort of will.

"Don't make a fuss about this. In 'ninety-five when there were troubles white men were killed, and the fleet came and shelled the villages. A lot of people were killed who'd had nothing to do with it. They're damned fools at Apia. If they make a fuss they'll only punish the wrong people. I don't want anyone punished."

He paused for a while to rest.

"You must say it was an accident. No one's to blame. Promise me that."

"I'll do anything you like," whispered Mackintosh.

"Good chap. One of the best. They're children. I'm their father. A father don't let his children get into trouble if he can help it."

A ghost of a chuckle came out of his throat. It was astonishingly weird and ghastly.

"You're a religious chap, Mac. What's that about forgiving them? You know."

For a while Mackintosh did not answer. His lips trembled.

"Forgive them, for they know not what they do?"

"That's right. Forgive them. I've loved them, you know, always loved them."

He sighed. His lips faintly moved, and now Mackintosh had to put his ears quite close to them in order to hear.

"Hold my hand," he said.

Mackintosh gave a gasp. His heart seemed wrenched. He took the old man's hand, so cold and weak, a coarse, rough hand, and held it in his own. And thus he sat until he nearly started out of his seat, for the silence was suddenly broken by a long rattle. It was terrible and unearthly. Walker was dead. Then the natives broke out with loud cries. The tears ran down their faces, and they beat their breasts.

Mackintosh disengaged his hand from the dead man's, and staggering like one drunk with sleep he went out of the room. He went to the locked drawer in his writing-desk and took out the revolver. He walked down to the sea and walked into the lagoon; he waded out cautiously, so that he should not trip against a coral rock, till the water came to his armpits. Then he put a bullet through his head.

An hour later half a dozen slim brown sharks were splashing and struggling at the spot where he fell.

The Lotus Eater

Most people, the vast majority in fact, lead the lives that circumstances have thrust upon them, and though some repine, looking upon themselves as round pegs in square holes, and think that if things had been different they might have made a much better showing, the greater part accept their lot, if not with serenity, at all events with resignation. They are like tramcars travelling for ever on the selfsame rails. They go backwards and forwards, backwards and forwards, inevitably, till they can go no longer and then are sold as scrap-iron. It is not often that you find a man who has boldly taken the course of his life into his own hands. When you do, it is worth while having a good look at him.

That was why I was curious to meet Thomas Wilson. It was an interesting and a bold thing he had done. Of course the end was not yet and until the experiment was concluded it was impossible to call it successful. But from what I had heard it seemed he must be an odd sort of fellow and I thought I should like to know him. I had been told he was reserved, but I had a notion that with patience and tact I could persuade him to confide in me. I wanted to hear the facts from his own lips. People exaggerate, they love to romanticise, and I was quite prepared to discover that his story was not nearly so singular as I had been led to believe.

And this impression was confirmed when at last I made his acquaintance. It was on the Piazza in Capri, where I was spending the month of August at a friend's villa, and a little before sunset, when most of the inhabitants, native and foreign, gather together to chat with their friends in the cool of the evening. There is a terrace that overlooks the Bay of Naples, and when the sun sinks slowly into the sea the island of Ischia is silhouetted against a blaze of splendour. It is one of the most lovely sights in the world. I was standing there with my friend and host watching it, when suddenly he said:

"Look, there's Wilson."

"Where?"

"The man sitting on the parapet, with his back to us. He's got a blue shirt on."

I saw an undistinguished back and a small head of grey hair short and rather thin.

"I wish he'd turn round," I said.

"He will presently."

"Ask him to come and have a drink with us at Morgano's."

"All right."

The instant of overwhelming beauty had passed and the sun, like the top of an orange, was dipping into a wine-red sea. We turned round and leaning our backs against the parapet looked at the people who were sauntering to and fro. They were all talking their heads off and the cheerful noise was exhilarating. Then the church bell, rather cracked, but with a fine resonant note, began to ring. The Piazza at Capri, with its clock tower over the footpath that leads up from the harbour, with the church up a flight of steps, is a perfect setting for an opera by Donizetti, and you felt that the voluble crowd might at any moment break out into a rattling chorus. It was charming and unreal.

I was so intent on the scene that I had not noticed Wilson get off the parapet and come towards us. As he passed us my friend stopped him.

"Hulloa, Wilson, I haven't seen you bathing the last few days."

"I've been bathing on the other side for a change."

My friend then introduced me. Wilson shook hands with me politely, but with indifference; a great many strangers come to Capri for a few days, or a few weeks, and I had no doubt he was constantly meeting people who came and went; and then my friend asked him to come along and have a drink with us.

"I was just going back to supper," he said.

"Can't it wait?" I asked.

"I suppose it can," he smiled.

Though his teeth were not very good his smile was attractive. It was gentle and kindly. He was dressed in a blue cotton shirt and a pair of grey trousers, much creased and none too clean, of a thin canvas, and on his feet he wore a pair of very old espadrilles. The get-up was picturesque, and very suitable to the place and the weather, but it did not at all go with his face. It was a lined, long face, deeply sunburned, thin-lipped, with small grey

eyes rather close together and tight, neat features. The grey hair
was carefully brushed. It was not a plain face, indeed in his
youth Wilson might have been good-looking, but a prim one. He
wore the blue shirt, open at the neck, and the grey canvas
trousers, not as though they belonged to him, but as though,
shipwrecked in his pyjamas, he had been fitted out with odd gar-
ments by compassionate strangers. Notwithstanding this careless
attire he looked like the manager of a branch office in an insurance
company, who should by rights be wearing a black coat with
pepper-and-salt trousers, a white collar and an unobjectionable
tie. I could very well see myself going to him to claim the insurance money when I had lost a watch, and being rather discon-
certed while I answered the questions he put to me by his obvious
impression, for all his politeness, that people who made such
claims were either fools or knaves.

Moving off, we strolled across the Piazza and down the street
till we came to Morgano's. We sat in the garden. Around us people
were talking in Russian, German, Italian and English. We ordered
drinks. Donna Lucia, the host's wife, waddled up and in her
low, sweet voice passed the time of day with us. Though
middle-aged now and portly, she had still traces of the wonderful
beauty that thirty years before had driven artists to paint so
many bad portraits of her. Her eyes, large and liquid, were the
eyes of Hera and her smile was affectionate and gracious. We
three gossiped for a while, for there is always a scandal of one sort
or another in Capri to make a topic of conversation, but nothing
was said of particular interest and in a little while Wilson got up
and left us. Soon afterwards we strolled up to my friend's villa
to dine. On the way he asked me what I had thought of Wilson.

"Nothing," I said. "I don't believe there's a word of truth in your
story."

"Why not?"

"He isn't the sort of man to do that sort of thing."

"How does anyone know what anyone is capable of?"

"I should put him down as an absolutely normal man of business
who's retired on a comfortable income from gilt-edged securities.
I think your story's just the ordinary Capri tittle-tattle."

"Have it your own way," said my friend.

We were in the habit of bathing at a beach called the Baths of
Tiberius. We took a fly down the road to a certain point and

then wandered through lemon groves and vineyards, noisy with cicadas and heavy with the hot smell of the sun, till we came to the top of the cliff down which a steep winding path led to the sea. A day or two later, just before we got down my friend said:

"Oh, there's Wilson back again."

We scrunched over the beach, the only drawback to the bathing-place being that it was shingle and not sand, and as we came along Wilson saw us and waved. He was standing up, a pipe in his mouth, and he wore nothing but a pair of trunks. His body was dark brown, thin but not emaciated, and, considering his wrinkled face and grey hair, youthful. Hot from our walk, we undressed quickly and plunged at once into the water. Six feet from the shore it was thirty feet deep, but so clear that you could see the bottom. It was warm, yet invigorating.

When I got out Wilson was lying on his belly, with a towel under him reading a book. I lit a cigarette and went and sat down beside him.

"Had a nice swim?" he asked.

He put his pipe inside his book to mark the place and closing it put it down on the pebbles beside him. He was evidently willing to talk.

"Lovely," I said. "It's the best bathing in the world."

"Of course people think those were the Baths of Tiberius." He waved his hand towards a shapeless mass of masonry that stood half in the water and half out. "But that's all rot. It was just one of his villas, you know."

I did. But it is just as well to let people tell you things when they want to. It disposes them kindly towards you if you suffer them to impart information. Wilson gave a chuckle.

"Funny old fellow, Tiberius. Pity they're saying now there's not a word of truth in all those stories about him."

He began to tell me all about Tiberius. Well, I had read my Suetonius too and I had read histories of the Early Roman Empire, so there was nothing very new to me in what he said. But I observed that he was not ill-read. I remarked on it.

"Oh, well, when I settled down here I was naturally interested, and I have plenty of time for reading. When you live in a place like this, with all its associations, it seems to make history so actual. You might almost be living in historical times yourself."

I should remark here that this was in 1913. The world was an easy, comfortable place and no one could have imagined that anything might happen seriously to disturb the serenity of existence.

"How long have you been here?" I asked.

"Fifteen years." He gave the blue and placid sea a glance, and a strangely tender smile hovered on his thin lips. "I fell in love with the place at first sight. You've heard, I daresay, of the mythical German who came here on the Naples boat just for lunch and a look at the Blue Grotto and stayed forty years; well, I can't say I exactly did that, but it's come to the same thing in the end. Only it won't be forty years in my case. Twenty-five. Still, that's better than a poke in the eye with a sharp stick."

I waited for him to go on. For what he had just said looked indeed as though there might be something after all in the singular story I had heard. But at that moment my friend came dripping out of the water very proud of himself because he had swum a mile, and the conversation turned to other things.

After that I met Wilson several times, either in the Piazza or on the beach. He was amiable and polite. He was always pleased to have a talk and I found out that he not only knew every inch of the island but also the adjacent mainland. He had read a great deal on all sorts of subjects, but his speciality was the history of Rome and on this he was very well informed. He seemed to have little imagination and to be of no more than average intelligence. He laughed a good deal, but with restraint, and his sense of humour was tickled by simple jokes. A commonplace man. I did not forget the odd remark he had made during the first short chat we had had by ourselves, but he never so much as approached the topic again. One day on our return from the beach, dismissing the cab at the Piazza, my friend and I told the driver to be ready to take us up to Anacapri at five. We were going to climb Monte Solaro, dine at a tavern we favoured, and walk down in the moonlight. For it was full moon and the views by night were lovely. Wilson was standing by while we gave the cabman instructions, for we had given him a lift to save him the hot dusty walk, and more from politeness than for any other reason I asked him if he would care to join us.

"It's my party," I said.

"I'll come with pleasure," he answered.

But when the time came to set out my friend was not feeling well, he thought he had stayed too long in the water, and would

not face the long and tiring walk. So I went alone with Wilson. We
climbed the mountain, admired the spacious view, and got back to
the inn as night was falling, hot, hungry and thirsty. We had ordered our dinner beforehand. The food was good, for Antonio was
an excellent cook, and the wine came from his own vineyard. It
was so light that you felt you could drink it like water and we
finished the first bottle with our macaroni. By the time we had
finished the second we felt that there was nothing much wrong
with life. We sat in a little garden under a great vine laden with
grapes. The air was exquisitely soft. The night was still and we
were alone. The maid brought us *bel paese* cheese and a plate
of figs. I ordered coffee and strega, which is the best liqueur
they make in Italy. Wilson would not have a cigar, but lit his
pipe.

"We've got plenty of time before we need start," he said, "the
moon won't be over the hill for another hour."

"Moon or no moon," I said briskly, "of course we've got plenty
of time. That's one of the delights of Capri, that there's never any
hurry."

"Leisure," he said. "If people only knew! It's the most priceless
thing a man can have and they're such fools they don't even know
it's something to aim at. Work? They work for work's sake. They
haven't got the brains to realise that the only object of work is to
obtain leisure."

Wine has the effect on some people of making them indulge
in general reflections. These remarks were true, but no one could
have claimed that they were original. I did not say anything,
but struck a match to light my cigar.

"It was full moon the first time I came to Capri," he went on
reflectively. "It might be the same moon as to-night."

"It was, you know," I smiled.

He grinned. The only light in the garden was what came from
an oil lamp that hung over our heads. It had been scanty to eat
by, but it was good now for confidences.

"I didn't mean that. I mean, it might be yesterday. Fifteen years
it is, and when I look back it seems like a month. I'd never been
to Italy before. I came for my summer holiday. I went to Naples
by boat from Marseilles and I had a look round, Pompeii, you
know, and Paestum and one or two places like that; then I came
here for a week. I liked the look of the place right away, from the

sea, I mean, as I watched it come closer and closer; and then when we got into the little boats from the steamer and landed at the quay, with all that crowd of jabbering people who wanted to take your luggage, and the hotel touts, and the tumbledown houses on the Marina and the walk up to the hotel, and dining on the terrace—well, it just got me. That's the truth. I didn't know if I was standing on my head or my heels. I'd never drunk Capri wine before, but I'd heard of it; I think I must have got a bit tight. I sat on that terrace after they'd all gone to bed and watched the moon over the sea, and there was Vesuvius with a great red plume of smoke rising up from it. Of course I know now that wine I drank was ink, Capri wine my eye, but I thought it all right then. But it wasn't the wine that made me drunk, it was the shape of the island and those jabbering people, the moon and the sea and the oleander in the hotel garden. I'd never seen an oleander before."

It was a long speech and it had made him thirsty. He took up his glass, but it was empty. I asked him if he would have another strega.

"It's sickly stuff. Let's have a bottle of wine. That's sound, that is, pure juice of the grape and can't hurt anyone."

I ordered more wine, and when it came filled the glasses. He took a long drink and after a sigh of pleasure went on.

"Next day I found my way to the bathing-place we go to. Not bad bathing, I thought. Then I wandered about the island. As luck would have it, there was a *festa* up at Punta di Timberio and I ran straight into the middle of it. An image of the Virgin and priests, acolytes swinging censers, and a whole crowd of jolly, laughing, excited people, a lot of them all dressed up. I ran across an Englishman there and asked him what it was all about. 'Oh, it's the feast of the Assumption,' he said, 'at least that's what the Catholic Church says it is, but that's just their hanky-panky. It's the festival of Venus. Pagan, you know. Aphrodite rising from the sea and all that.' It gave me quite a funny feeling to hear him. It seemed to take one a long way back, if you know what I mean. After that I went down one night to have a look at the Faraglioni by moonlight. If the fates had wanted me to go on being a bank manager they oughtn't to have let me take that walk."

"You were a bank manager, were you?" I asked.

I had been wrong about him, but not far wrong.

"Yes. I was manager of the Crawford Street branch of the York and City. It was convenient for me because I lived up Hendon way. I could get from door to door in thirty-seven minutes."

He puffed at his pipe and relit it.

"That was my last night, that was. I'd got to be back at the bank on Monday morning. When I looked at those two great rocks sticking out of the water, with the moon above them, and all the little lights of the fishermen in their boats catching cuttle-fish, all so peaceful and beautiful, I said to myself, well, after all, why should I go back? It wasn't as if I had anyone dependent on me. My wife had died of bronchial pneumonia four years before and the kid went to live with her grandmother, my wife's mother. She was an old fool, she didn't look after the kid properly and she got blood-poisoning, they amputated her leg, but they couldn't save her and she died, poor little thing."

"How terrible," I said.

"Yes, I was cut up at the time, though of course not so much as if the kid had been living with me, but I dare say it was a mercy. Not much chance for a girl with only one leg. I was sorry about my wife too. We got on very well together. Though I don't know if it would have continued. She was the sort of woman who was always bothering about what other people'd think. She didn't like travelling. Eastbourne was her idea of a holiday. D'you know, I'd never crossed the Channel till after her death."

"But I suppose you've got other relations, haven't you?"

"None. I was an only child. My father had a brother, but he went to Australia before I was born. I don't think anyone could easily be more alone in the world than I am. There wasn't any reason I could see why I shouldn't do exactly what I wanted. I was thirty-four at that time."

He had told me he had been on the island for fifteen years. That would make him forty-nine. Just about the age I should have given him.

"I'd been working since I was seventeen. All I had to look forward to was doing the same old thing day after day till I retired on my pension. I said to myself, is it worth it? What's wrong with chucking it all up and spending the rest of my life down here? It was the most beautiful place I'd ever seen. But I'd had a business training, I was cautious by nature. 'No,' I said, 'I won't be carried away like this, I'll go to-morrow like I said I would and think it over. Perhaps when I get back to London I'll think quite differently.' Damned fool, wasn't I? I lost a whole year that way."

"You didn't change your mind, then?"

"You bet I didn't. All the time I was working I kept thinking of the bathing here and the vineyards and the walks over the hills and the moon and the sea, and the Piazza in the evening when everyone walks about for a bit of a chat after the day's work is over. There was only one thing that bothered me: I wasn't sure if I was justified in not working like everybody else did. Then I read a sort of history book, by a man called Marion Crawford it was, and there was a story about Sybaris and Crotona. There were two cities; and in Sybaris they just enjoyed life and had a good time, and in Crotona they were hardy and industrious and all that. And one day the men of Crotona came over and wiped Sybaris out, and then after a while a lot of other fellows came over from somewhere else and wiped Crotona out. Nothing remains of Sybaris, not a stone, and all that's left of Crotona is just one column. That settled the matter for me."

"Oh?"

"It came to the same in the end, didn't it? And when you look back now, who were the mugs?"

I did not reply and he went on.

"The money was rather a bother. The bank didn't pension one off till after thirty years' service, but if you retired before that they gave you a gratuity. With that and what I'd got for the sale of my house and the little I'd managed to save, I just hadn't enough to buy an annuity to last the rest of my life. It would have been silly to sacrifice everything so as to lead a pleasant life and not have a sufficient income to make it pleasant. I wanted to have a little place of my own, a servant to look after me, enough to buy tobacco, decent food, books now and then, and something over for emergencies. I knew pretty well how much I needed. I found I had just enough to buy an annuity for twenty-five years."

"You were thirty-five at the time?"

"Yes. It would carry me on till I was sixty. After all, no one can be certain of living longer than that, a lot of men die in their fifties, and by the time a man's sixty he's had the best of life."

"On the other hand no one can be sure of dying at sixty," I said.

"Well, I don't know. It depends on himself, doesn't it?"

"In your place I should have stayed on at the bank till I was entitled to my pension."

"I should have been forty-seven then. I shouldn't have been too old to enjoy my life here, I'm older than that now and I enjoy it as much as I ever did, but I should have been too old to experience the particular pleasure of a young man. You know, you can have just as good a time at fifty as you can at thirty, but it's not the same sort of good time. I wanted to live the perfect life while I still had the energy and the spirit to make the most of it. Twenty-five years seemed a long time to me, and twenty-five years of happiness seemed worth paying something pretty substantial for. I'd made up my mind to wait a year and I waited a year. Then I sent in my resignation and as soon as they paid me my gratuity I bought the annuity and came on here."

"An annuity for twenty-five years?"

"That's right.

"Have you never regretted?"

"Never. I've had my money's worth already. And I've got ten years more. Don't you think after twenty-five years of perfect happiness one ought to be satisfied to call it a day?"

"Perhaps."

He did not say in so many words what he would do then, but his intention was clear. It was pretty much the story my friend had told me, but it sounded different when I heard it from his own lips. I stole a glance at him. There was nothing about him that was not ordinary. No one, looking at that neat, prim face, could have thought him capable of an unconventional action. I did not blame him. It was his own life that he had arranged in this strange manner, and I did not see why he should not do what he liked with it. Still, I could not prevent the little shiver that ran down my spine.

"Getting chilly?" he smiled. "We might as well start walking down. The moon'll be up by now."

Before we parted Wilson asked me if I would like to go and see his house one day; and two or three days later, finding out where he lived, I strolled up to see him. It was a peasant's cottage, well away from the town, in a vineyard, with a view of the sea. By the side of the door grew a great oleander in full flower. There were only two small rooms, a tiny kitchen and a lean-to in which firewood could be kept. The bedroom was furnished like a monk's cell, but the sitting-room, smelling agreeably of tobacco, was comfortable enough, with two large arm-chairs that he had brought from England, a large roll-top desk, a cottage piano and crowded bookshelves. On the walls were framed engravings of pictures by G. F. Watts and Lord Leighton. Wilson told me that the house belonged to the owner of the vineyard who lived in another cottage higher up the hill, and his wife came in every day to do the rooms and the cooking. He had found the place on his first visit to Capri, and taking it on his return for good had been there ever since. Seeing the piano and music open on it, I asked him if he would play.

"I'm no good, you know, but I've always been fond of music and I get a lot of fun out of strumming."

He sat down at the piano and played one of the movements from a Beethoven sonata. He did not play very well. I looked at his music, Schumann and Schubert, Beethoven, Bach and Chopin. On the table on which he had his meals was a greasy pack of cards. I asked him if he played patience.

"A lot."

From what I saw of him then and from what I heard from other people I made for myself what I think must have been a fairly accurate picture of the life he had led for the last fifteen years. It was certainly a very harmless one. He bathed; he walked a great deal, and he seemed never to lose his sense of the beauty of the island which he knew so intimately; he played the piano and he played patience; he read. When he was asked to a party he went and, though a trifle dull, was agreeable. He was not affronted if he was neglected. He liked people, but with an aloofness that prevented intimacy. He lived thriftily, but with sufficient comfort. He never owed a penny. I imagine he had never been a man whom sex had greatly troubled, and if in his younger days he had had now and then a passing affair with a visitor to the island whose head was turned by the atmosphere, his emotion, while it lasted, remained, I am pretty sure, well under his control. I think he was determined that nothing should interfere with his independence of spirit. His only passion was for the beauty of nature, and he sought felicity in the simple and natural things that life offers to everyone. You may say that it was a grossly selfish existence. It was. He was of no use to anybody, but on the other hand he did nobody any harm. His only object was his own happiness, and it

looked as though he had attained it. Very few people know where
to look for happiness; fewer still find it. I don't know whether he
was a fool or a wise man. He was certainly a man who knew his
own mind. The odd thing about him to me was that he was so
immensely commonplace. I should never have given him a second
thought but for what I knew, that on a certain day, ten years from
then, unless a chance illness cut the thread before, he must deliberately take leave of the world he loved so well. I wondered
whether it was the thought of this, never quite absent from his
mind, that gave him the peculiar zest with which he enjoyed every
moment of the day.

I should do him an injustice if I omitted to state that he was
not at all in the habit of talking about himself. I think the friend I
was staying with was the only person in whom he had con-
fided. I believe he only told me the story because he suspected I
already knew it, and on the evening on which he told it me he
had drunk a good deal of wine.

My visit drew to a close and I left the island. The year after,
war broke out. A number of things happened to me, so that the
course of my life was greatly altered, and it was thirteen years
before I went to Capri again. My friend had been back some time,
but he was no longer so well off, and had moved into a house
that had no room for me; so I was putting up at the hotel. He
came to meet me at the boat and we dined together. During
dinner I asked him where exactly his house was.

"You know it," he answered. "It's the little place Wilson had.
I've built on a room and made it quite nice."

With so many other things to occupy my mind I had not
given Wilson a thought for years; but now, with a little shock, I
remembered. The ten years he had before him when I made his
acquaintance must have elapsed long ago.

"Did he commit suicide as he said he would?"

"It's rather a grim story."

Wilson's plan was all right. There was only one flaw in it and
this, I suppose, he could not have foreseen. It had never occurred to him that after twenty-five years of complete happiness,
in this quiet backwater, with nothing in the world to disturb his
serenity, his character would gradually lose its strength. The will
needs obstacles in order to exercise its power; when it is never
thwarted, when no effort is needed to achieve one's desires,

because one has placed one's desires only in the things that can be obtained by stretching out one's hand, the will grows impotent. If you walk on a level all the time the muscles you need to climb a mountain will atrophy. These observations are trite, but there they are. When Wilson's annuity expired he had no longer the resolution to make the end which was the price he had agreed to pay for that long period of happy tranquillity. I do not think, as far as I could gather, both from what my friend told me and afterwards from others, that he wanted courage. It was just that he couldn't make up his mind. He put it off from day to day.

He had lived on the island for so long and had always settled his accounts so punctually that it was easy for him to get credit; never having borrowed money before, he found a number of people who were willing to lend him small sums when now he asked for them. He had paid his rent regularly for so many years that his landlord, whose wife Assunta still acted as his servant, was content to let things slide for several months. Everyone believed him when he said that a relative had died and that he was temporarily embarrassed because owing to legal formalities he could not for some time get the money that was due to him. He managed to hang on after this fashion for something over a year. Then he could get no more credit from the local tradesmen, and there was no one to lend him any more money. His landlord gave him notice to leave the house unless he paid up the arrears of rent before a certain date.

The day before this he went into his tiny bedroom, closed the door and the window, drew the curtain and lit a brazier of charcoal. Next morning when Assunta came to make his breakfast she found him insensible but still alive. The roof was draughty, and though he had done this and that to keep out the fresh air he had not done it very thoroughly. It almost looked as though at the last moment, and desperate though his situation was, he had suffered from a certain infirmity of purpose. Wilson was taken to the hospital, and though very ill for some time he at last recovered. But as a result either of the charcoal poisoning or of the shock he was no longer in complete possession of his faculties. He was not insane, at all events not insane enough to be put in an asylum, but he was quite obviously no longer in his right mind.

"I went to see him," said my friend. "I tried to get him to talk, but he kept looking at me in a funny sort of way, as though he couldn't quite make out where he'd seen me before. He looked rather awful lying there in bed, with a week's growth of grey beard on his chin; but except for that funny look in his eyes he seemed quite normal."

"What funny look in his eyes?"

"I don't know exactly how to describe it. Puzzled. It's an absurd comparison, but suppose you threw a stone up into the air and it didn't come down but just stayed there . . ."

"It would be rather bewildering," I smiled.

"Well, that's the sort of look he had."

It was difficult to know what to do with him. He had no money and no means of getting any. His effects were sold, but for too little to pay what he owed. He was English, and the Italian authorities did not wish to make themselves responsible for him. The British Consul in Naples had no funds to deal with the case. He could of course be sent back to England, but no one seemed to know what could be done with him when he got there. Then Assunta, the servant, said that he had been a good master and a good tenant, and as long as he had the money had paid his way; he could sleep in the woodshed in the cottage in which she and her husband lived, and he could share their meals. This was suggested to him. It was difficult to know whether he understood or not. When Assunta came to take him from the hospital he went with her without remark. He seemed to have no longer a will of his own. She had been keeping him now for two years.

"It's not very comfortable, you know," said my friend. "They've rigged him up a ramshackle bed and given him a couple of blankets, but there's no window, and it's icy cold in winter and like an oven in summer. And the food's pretty rough. You know how these peasants eat: macaroni on Sundays and meat once in a blue moon."

"What does he do with himself all the time?"

"He wanders about the hills. I've tried to see him two or three times, but it's no good; when he sees you coming he runs like a hare. Assunta comes down to have a chat with me now and then and I give her a bit of money so that she can buy him tobacco, but God knows if he ever gets it."

"Do they treat him all right?" I asked.

"I'm sure Assunta's kind enough. She treats him like a child. I'm afraid her husband's not very nice to him. He grudges the cost of his keep. I don't believe he's cruel or anything like that, but I think he's a bit sharp with him. He makes him fetch water and clean the cow-shed and that sort of thing."

"It sounds pretty rotten," I said.

"He brought it on himself. After all, he's only got what he deserved."

"I think on the whole we all get what we deserve," I said. "But that doesn't prevent its being rather horrible."

Two or three days later my friend and I were taking a walk. We were strolling along a narrow path through an olive grove.

"There's Wilson," said my friend suddenly. "Don't look, you'll only frighten him. Go straight on."

I walked with my eyes on the path, but out of the corners of them I saw a man hiding behind an olive tree. He did not move as we approached, but I felt that he was watching us. As soon as we had passed I heard a scamper. Wilson, like a hunted animal, had made for safety. That was the last I ever saw of him.

He died last year. He had endured that life for six years. He was found one morning on the mountainside lying quite peacefully as though he had died in his sleep. From where he lay he had been able to see those two great rocks called the Faraglioni which stand out of the sea. It was full moon and he must have gone to see them by moonlight. Perhaps he died of the beauty of that sight.

The Yellow Streak

The two prahus were dropping easily down-stream, one a few yards ahead of the other, and in the first sat the two white men. After seven weeks on the rivers they were glad to know that they would lodge that night in a civilized house. To Izzart, who had been in Borneo since the war, the Dyak houses and their feasts were of course an old story; but Campion, though new to the country and at first amused by the strangeness, hankered too now for chairs to sit on and a bed to sleep in. The Dyaks were hospitable, but no one could say that there was much comfort to be found in their houses, and there was a monotony in the entertainment they offered a guest which presently grew somewhat wearisome. Every evening, as the travellers reached the landing-place, the headman, bearing a flag, and the more important members of the household, came down to the river to fetch them. They were led up to the long-house—a village really under one roof, built on piles, to which access was obtained by climbing up the trunk of a tree rudely notched into steps—and to the beating of drums and gongs walked up and down the whole length of it in long procession. On both sides serried throngs of brown people sat on their haunches and stared silently as the white men passed. Clean mats were unrolled and the guests seated themselves. The headman brought a live chicken and, holding it by the legs, waved it three times over their heads, called the spirits loudly to witness and uttered an invocation. Then various persons brought eggs. Arak was drunk. A girl, a very small shy thing with the grace of a flower but with something hieratic in her immobile face, held a cup to the white man's lips till it was empty and then a great shout arose. The men began to dance, one after the other, each treading his little measure, with his shield and his parang, to the accompaniment of drum and gong. After this had gone on for some time the visitors were taken into one of the rooms that led off the long platform on which was led the common life of the household and found their supper prepared for them. The girls fed them with Chinese spoons. Then everyone grew a little drunk and they all talked till the early hours of the morning.

But now their journey was done and they were on their way to the coast. They had started at dawn. The river then was very shallow and ran clear and bright over a shingly bottom; the trees leaned over it so that above there was only a strip of blue sky; but now it had broadened out, and the men were poling no longer but paddling. The trees, bamboos, wild sago like huge bunches of ostrich feathers, trees with enormous leaves and trees with feathery foliage like the acacia, coconut trees and areca palms, with their long straight white stems, the trees on the banks were immensely and violently luxuriant. Here and there, gaunt and naked, was the bare skeleton of a tree struck by lightning or dead of old age, and its whiteness against all that green was vivid. Here and there, rival kings of the forest, tall trees soared above the common level of the jungle. Then there were the parasites; in the fork of two branches great tufts of lush green leaves, or flowering creepers that covered the spreading foliage like a bride's veil; sometimes they wound round a tall trunk, a sheath of splendour, and threw long flowering arms from branch to branch. There was something thrilling in the passionate wildness of that eager growth; it had the daring abandon of the nomad rioting in the train of the god.

The day wore on and now the heat was no longer so oppressive. Campion looked at the shabby silver watch on his wrist. It could not be long now before they reached their destination.

"What sort of a chap is Hutchinson?" he asked.

"I don't know him. I believe he's a very good sort."

Hutchinson was the Resident in whose house they were to spend the night and they had sent on a Dyak in a canoe to announce their arrival.

"Well, I hope he's got some whisky. I've drunk enough Arak to last me a lifetime."

Campion was a mining engineer, whom the Sultan on his way to England had met at Singapore and finding him at a loose end had commissioned to go to Sembulu and see whether he could discover any mineral which might be profitably worked. He sent Willis, the Resident at Kuala Solor, instructions to afford him every facility and Willis had put him in the care of Izzart because Izzart spoke both Malay and Dyak like a native. This was the third trip they had made into the interior and now Campion was to go home with his reports. They were to catch the Sultan Ahmed which was due to pass the mouth of the river at dawn on the next day but one, and with any luck should reach Kuala Solor on the same afternoon. They were both glad to get back to it. There was tennis and golf there, and the club with its billiard tables, food which was relatively good, and the comforts of civilization. Izzart was glad too that he would have other society than Campion's. He gave him a sidelong glance. He was a little man with a big, bald head, and though certainly fifty, strong and wiry; he had quick, shining blue eyes and a stubbly, grey moustache. He was seldom without an old briar pipe between his broken and discoloured teeth. He was neither clean nor neat, his khaki shorts were ragged and his singlet torn; he was wearing now a battered topee. He had knocked about the world since he was eighteen and had been in South Africa, in China and in Mexico. He was good company; he could tell a story well, and he was prepared to drink and drink again with any one he met. They had got on very well together, but Izzart had never felt quite at home with him. Though they joked and laughed together, got drunk together, Izzart felt that there was no intimacy between them: for all the cordiality of their relations they remained nothing but acquaintances. He was very sensitive to the impression he made on others, and behind Campion's joviality he had felt a certain coolness; those shining blue eyes had summed him up; and it vaguely irritated Izzart that Campion had formed an opinion of him, and he did not quite know what it was. He was exasperated by the possibility that this common little man did not think entirely well of him. He desired to be liked and admired. He wanted to be popular. He wished the people he met to take an inordinate fancy to him so that he could either reject them or a trifle condescendingly bestow his friendship on them. His inclination was to be familiar with all and sundry, but he was held back by the fear of a rebuff; sometimes he had been uneasily conscious that his effusiveness surprised the persons he lavished it on.

By some chance he had never met Hutchinson, though of course he knew all about him just as Hutchinson knew all about *him*, and they would have many common friends to talk of. Hutchin-

son had been at Winchester, and Izzart was glad that he could
tell him that he had been at Harrow.

The prahu rounded a bend in the river and suddenly, standing
on a slight eminence, they saw the bungalow. In a few minutes
they caught sight of the landing-stage and on it, among a little
group of natives, a figure in white waving to them.

Hutchinson was a tall, stout man with a red face. His appearance led you to expect that he was breezy and self-confident, so
that it was not a little surprising to discover quickly that he was
diffident and even a trifle shy. When he shook hands with his
guests—Izzart introduced himself and then Campion—and led them
up the pathway to the bungalow, though he was plainly anxious
to be civil it was not hard to see that he found it difficult to make
conversation. He took them out on to the verandah and here they
found on the table glasses and whisky and soda. They made themselves comfortable on long chairs. Izzart, conscious of Hutchinson's
slight embarrassment with strangers, expanded; he was very hearty
and voluble. He began to speak of their common acquaintances at
Kuala Solor, and he managed very soon to slip in casually the information that he had been at Harrow.

"You were at Winchester, weren't you?" he asked.

"Yes."

"I wonder if you knew George Parker. He was in my regiment.
He was at Winchester. I daresay he was younger than you."

Izzart felt that it was a bond between them that they had
been at these particular schools and it excluded Campion, who
obviously had enjoyed no such advantage. They drank two or three
whiskies. Izzart in half an hour began to call his host Hutchie. He
talked a good deal about "my regiment" in which he had got
his company during the war, and what good fellows his brother
officers were. He mentioned two or three names which could
hardly be unknown to Hutchinson. They were not the sort of
people that Campion was likely to have come across and he was
not sorry to administer to him a neat snub when he claimed
acquaintance with some one he spoke of.

"Billie Meadows? I knew a fellow called Billie Meadows in
Sinaloa many years ago," said Campion

"Oh, I shouldn't think it could be the same," said Izzart, with
a smile. "Billie's by way of being a peer of the realm. He's the

Lord Meadows who races. Don't you remember, he owned Spring Carrots?"

Dinner-time was approaching and after a wash and brushup they drank a couple of gin pahits. They sat down. Hutchinson had not been to Kuala Solor for the best part of a year, and had not seen another white man for three months. He was anxious to make the most of his visitors. He could give them no wine, but there was plenty of whisky and after dinner he brought out a precious bottle of Benedictine. They were very gay. They laughed and talked a great deal. Izzart was getting on famously. He thought he had never liked a fellow more than Hutchinson and he pressed him to come down to Kuala Solor as soon as he could. They would have a wonderful beano. Campion was left out of the conversation by Izzart with the faintly malicious intention of putting him in his place, and by Hutchinson through shyness; and presently, after yawning a good deal, he said he would go to bed. Hutchinson showed him to his room and when he returned Izzart said to him:

"You don't want to turn in yet, do you?"

"Not on your life. Let's have another drink."

They sat and talked. They both grew a little drunk. Presently Hutchinson told Izzart that he lived with a Malay girl and had a couple of children by her. He had told them to keep out of sight while Campion was there.

"I expect she's asleep now," said Hutchinson, with a glance at the door which Izzart knew led into his room, "but I'd like you to see the kiddies in the morning."

Just then a faint wail was heard and Hutchinson, with a "Hulloa, the little devil's awake," went to the door and opened it. In a moment or two he came out of the room with a child in his arms. A woman followed him.

"He's cutting his teeth," said Hutchinson. "It makes him restless."

The woman wore a sarong and a thin white jacket and she was barefoot. She was young, with fine dark eyes, and she gave Izzart when he spoke to her a bright and pleasant smile. She sat down and lit a cigarette. She answered the civil questions Izzart put to her without embarrassment but also without effusion. Hutchinson asked her if she would have a whisky and soda, but she refused. When the two men began to talk again in English she sat on quite quietly, faintly rocking herself in her chair, and occupied with none could tell what calm thoughts.

"She's a very good girl," said Hutchinson. "She looks after the house and she's no trouble. Of course it's the only thing to do in a place like this."

"I shall never do it myself," said Izzart. "After all, one may want to get married and then it means all sorts of botherations."

"But who wants to get married? What a life for a white woman. I wouldn't ask a white woman to live here for anything in the world."

"Of course it's a matter of taste. If I have any kiddies I'm going to see that they have a white mother."

Hutchinson looked down at the little dark-skinned child he held in his arms. He gave a faint smile.

"It's funny how you get to like them," he said. "When they're your own it doesn't seem to matter that they've got a touch of the tar-brush."

The woman gave the child a look and getting up said she would take it back to bed.

"I should think we'd better all turn in," said Hutchinson. "God knows what the time is."

Izzart went to his room and threw open the shutters which his boy Hassan, whom he was travelling with, had closed. Blowing out the candle so that it should not attract the mosquitoes, he sat down at the window and looked at the soft night. The whisky he had drunk made him feel very wide awake, and he was not inclined to go to bed. He took off his ducks, put on a sarong and lit a cheroot. His good-humour was gone. It was the sight of Hutchinson looking fondly at the half-caste child which had upset him.

"They've got no right to have them," he said to himself. "They've got no chance in the world. Ever."

He passed his hands reflectively along his bare and hairy legs. He shuddered a little. Though he had done everything he could to develop the calves, his legs were like broomsticks. He hated them. He was uneasily conscious of them all the time. They were like a native's. Of course they were the very legs for a top-boot. In his uniform he had looked very well. He was a tall, powerful man, over six feet high, and he had a neat black moustache and neat black hair. His dark eyes were fine and mobile. He was a good-looking fellow and he knew it, and he dressed well, shabbily when shabbiness was good form, and smartly when the occasion demanded. He had loved the army, and it was a bitter blow to him when, at the end of the war, he could not remain in it. His ambitions were simple. He wanted to have two thousand a year, give smart little dinners, go to parties and wear a uniform. He hankered after London.

Of course his mother lived there, and his mother cramped his style. He wondered how on earth he could produce her if ever he got engaged to the girl of good family (with a little money) whom he was looking for to make his wife. Because his father had been dead so long and during the later part of his career was stationed in the most remote of the Malay States, Izzart felt fairly sure that no one in Sembulu knew anything about her, but he lived in terror lest some one, running across her in London, should write over to tell people that she was a half-caste. She had been a beautiful creature when Izzart's father, an engineer in the Government Service, had married her; but now she was a fat old woman with grey hair who sat about all day smoking cigarettes. Izzart was twelve years old when his father died and then he could speak Malay much more fluently than English. An aunt offered to pay for his education and Mrs. Izzart accompanied her son to England. She lived habitually in furnished apartments, and her rooms with their Oriental draperies and Malay silver were overheated and stuffy. She was for ever in trouble with her land-ladies because she would leave cigarette-ends about. Izzart hated the way she made friends with them: she would be shockingly familiar with them for a time, then there would be a falling-out, and after a violent scene she would flounce out of the house. Her only amusement was the pictures, and to these she went every day in the week. At home she wore an old and tawdry dressing-gown, but when she went out she dressed herself—but, oh, how untidily—in extravagant colours, so that it was a mortification to her dapper son. He quarrelled with her frequently, she made him impatient and he was ashamed of her; and yet he felt for her a deep tenderness; it was almost a physical bond between them, something stronger than the ordinary feeling of mother and son, so that notwithstanding the failings that exasperated him she was the only person in the world with whom he felt entirely at home.

It was owing to his father's position and his own knowledge of Malay, for his mother always spoke it to him, that after the war, finding himself with nothing to do, he had managed to enter the service of the Sultan of Sembulu. He had been a success. He played games well, he was strong and a good athlete; in the rest-house at Kuala Solor were the cups which he had won at Harrow for running and jumping, and to these he had added since others for golf and tennis. With his abundant fund of small-talk he was an asset at parties and his cheeriness made things go. He ought to have been happy and he was wretched. He wanted so much to be popular, and he had an impression, stronger than ever at this moment, that popularity escaped him. He wondered whether by any chance the men at Kuala Solor with whom he was so hail fellow well met suspected that he had native blood in him. He knew very well what to expect if they ever found out. They wouldn't say he was gay and friendly then, they would say he was damned familiar; and they would say he was inefficient and careless, as the half-castes were, and when he talked of marrying a white woman they would snigger. Oh, it was so unfair! What difference could it make, that drop of native blood in his veins, and yet because of it they would always be on the watch for the expected failure at the critical moment. Every one knew that you couldn't rely on Eurasians, sooner or later they would let you down; he knew it too, but now he asked himself whether they didn't fail because failure was expected of them. They were never given a chance, poor devils.

But a cock crew loudly. It must be very late and he was be-ginning to feel chilly. He got into bed. When Hassan brought him his tea next morning he had a racking headache and when he went in to breakfast he could not look at the porridge and the bacon and eggs which were set before him. Hutchinson too was feeling none too well.

"I fancy we made rather a night of it," said his host, with a smile to conceal his faint embarrassment.

"I feel like hell," said Izzart.

"I'm going to breakfast off a whisky and soda myself," added Hutchinson.

Izzart asked for nothing better, and it was with distaste that they watched Campion eat with healthy appetite a substantial meal. Campion chaffed them.

"By God, Izzart, you're looking green about the gills," he said. "I never saw such a filthy colour."

Izzart flushed. His swarthiness was always a sensitive point with him. But he forced himself to give a cheery laugh.

"You see, I had a Spanish grandmother," he answered, "and when I'm under the weather it always comes out. I remember at Harrow I fought a boy and licked him because he called me a damned half-caste."

"You are dark," said Hutchinson. "Do Malays ever ask you if you have any native blood in you?"

"Yes, damn their impudence."

A boat with their kit had started early in the morning in order to get to the mouth of the river before them and tell the skipper of the Sultan Ahmed, if by chance he arrived before he was due, that they were on their way. Campion and Izzart were to set out immediately after tiffin in order to arrive at the place where they were to spend the night before the Bore passed. A Bore is a tidal wave that, by reason of a peculiarity in the lie of the land, surges up certain rivers, and there happened to be one on the river on which they were travelling. Hutchinson had talked to them of it the night before and Campion, who had never seen such a thing, was much interested.

"This is one of the best in Borneo. It's worth looking at," said Hutchinson.

He told them how the natives, waiting the moment, rode it and were borne up the river on its crest at a breathless and terrifying speed. He had done it once himself.

"Never no more for me," he said. "I was scared out of my wits."

"I should like to try it once," said Izzart.

"It's exciting enough, but my word, when you're in a flimsy dug-out and you know that if the native doesn't get the right moment you'll be flung out in that seething torrent and you won't have a chance in a million . . . no, it's not my idea of sport."

"I've shot a good many rapids in my day," said Campion.

"Rapids be damned. You wait till you see the Bore. It's one of the most terrifying things I know. D'you know that at least a dozen natives are drowned in it in this river alone every year?"

They lounged about on the verandah most of the morning and Hutchinson showed them the court-house. Then gin pahits were served. They drank two or three. Izzart began to feel himself, and when at length tiffin was ready he found that he had an excellent appetite. Hutchinson had boasted of his Malay curry and when the steaming, succulent dishes were placed before them they all set to ravenously. Hutchinson pressed them to drink.

"You've got nothing to do but sleep. Why shouldn't you get drunk?"

He could not bear to let them go so soon, it was good after so long to have white men to talk to, and he lingered over the meal. He urged them to eat. They would have a filthy meal that night at the long-house and nothing to drink but Arak. They had better make hay while the sun shone. Campion suggested once or twice that they should start, but Hutchinson, and Izzart too, for now he was feeling very happy and comfortable, assured him there was plenty of time. Hutchinson sent for his precious bottle of Benedictine. They had made a hole in it last night; they might as well finish it before they went.

When at last he walked down with them to the river they were all very merry and none of them was quite steady on his legs. Over the middle of the boat was an attap awning and under this Hutchinson had had a mattress laid. The crew were prisoners who had been marched down from the jail to row the white men, and they wore dingy sarongs with the prison mark. They waited at their oars. Izzart and Campion shook hands with Hutchinson and threw themselves down on the mattress. The boat pushed off. The turbid river, wide and placid, glistened in the heat of that brilliant afternoon like polished brass. In the distance ahead of them they could see the bank with its tangle of green trees. They felt drowsy, but Izzart at least found a curious enjoyment in resisting for a little while the heaviness that was creeping over him, and he made up his mind that he would not let himself fall asleep till he had finished his cheroot. At last the stub began to burn his fingers and he flung it into the river.

"I'm going to have a wonderful snooze," he said.

"What about the Bore?" asked Campion.

"Oh, that's all right. We needn't worry about that."

He gave a long and noisy yawn. His limbs felt like lead. He had one moment in which he was conscious of his delicious drowsiness and then he knew nothing more. Suddenly he was awakened by Campion shaking him.

"I say, what's that?"

"What's what?"

He spoke irritably, for sleep was still heavy upon him, but with his eyes he followed Campion's gesture. He could hear nothing, but a good way off he saw two or three white-crested waves following one another. They did not look very alarming.

"Oh, I suppose that's the Bore."

"What are we going to do about it?" cried Campion.

Izzart was scarcely yet quite awake. He smiled at the concern in Campion's voice.

"Don't worry. These fellows know all about it. They know exactly what to do. We may get a bit splashed."

But while they were saying these few words the Bore came nearer, very quickly, with a roar like the roar of an angry sea, and Izzart saw that the waves were much higher than he had thought. He did not like the look of them and he tightened his belt so that his shorts should not slip down if the boat were upset. In a moment the waves were upon them. It was a great wall of water that seemed to tower over them, and it might have been ten or twelve feet high, but you could measure it only with your horror. It was quite plain that no boat could weather it. The first wave dashed over them, drenching them all, half filling the boat with water, and then immediately another wave struck them. The boatmen began to shout. They pulled madly at their oars and the steersman yelled an order. But in that surging torrent they were helpless, and it was frightening to see how soon they lost all control of the boat. The force of the water turned it broadside on and it was carried along, helter-skelter, upon the crest of the Bore. Another great wave dashed over them and the boat began to sink. Izzart and Campion scrambled out of the covered place in which they had been lying and suddenly the boat gave way under their feet and they found themselves struggling in the water. It surged and stormed around them. Izzart's first impulse was to swim for the shore, but his boy, Hassan, shouted to him to cling to the boat. For a minute or two they all did this.

"Are you all right?" Campion shouted to him.

"Yes, enjoying the bath," said Izzart.

He imagined that the waves would pass by as the Bore ascended the river and in a few minutes at the outside they would find themselves in calm water once more. He forgot that they were being carried along on its crest. The waves dashed over them. They clung to the gunwale and the base of the structure which supported the attap awning. Then a larger wave caught the boat and it turned over, falling upon them so that they lost their hold; there seemed nothing but a slippery bottom to cling to and Izzart's hands slithered helplessly on the greasy surface. But the boat continued to turn and he made a desperate grab at the gunwale, only to feel it slip out of his hands as the turn went on, then he caught the framework of the awning, and still it turned, turned slowly right round and once more he sought for a hand-hold on the bottom. The boat went round and round with a horrible regularity. He thought this must be because everyone was clinging to one side of it, and he tried to make the crew go round to the other. He could not make them understand. Every one was shouting and the waves beat against them with a dull and angry roar. Each time the boat rolled over on them Izzart was pushed under water, only to come up again as the gunwale and the framework of the awning gave him something to cling to. The struggle was awful. Presently he began to get terribly out of breath, and he felt his strength leaving him. He knew that he could not hold on much longer, but he did not feel frightened, for his fatigue by now was so great that he did not very much care what happened. Hassan was by his side and he told him he was growing very tired. He thought the best thing was to make a dash for the shore, it did not look more than sixty yards away, but Hassan begged him not to. Still they were being carried along amid those seething, pounding waves. The boat went round and round and they scrambled over it like squirrels in a cage. Izzart swallowed a lot of water. He felt he was very nearly done. Hassan could not help him, but it was a comfort that he was there, for Izzart knew that his boy, used to the water all his life, was a powerful swimmer. Then, Izzart did not know why, for a minute or two the boat held bottom downwards, so that he was able to hold on to the gunwale. It was a precious thing to be able to get his breath. At that moment two dug-outs, with Malays in them riding the Bore, passed swiftly by them. They shouted for help, but the Malays averted their faces and went on. They saw the white men and did not want to be concerned in any trouble that might befall them. It was agonizing to see them go past, callous and indifferent in their safety. But on a sudden the boat rolled round again, round and round, slowly, and the miserable, exhausting scramble repeated itself. It took the heart out of you. But the short respite had helped Izzart and he was able to struggle a little longer. Then once more he found himself so terribly out of breath that he thought his chest would burst. His strength was all gone and he did not know now whether he had enough to try to swim for the shore. Suddenly he heard a cry.

"Izzart, Izzart. Help. Help."

It was Campion's voice. It was a scream of agony. It sent a shock all through Izzart's nerves. Campion, Campion, what did he care for Campion? Fear seized him, a blind, animal fear, and it gave him a new strength. He did not answer.

"Help me, quick, quick," he said to Hassan.

Hassan understood him at once. By a miracle one of the oars was floating quite close to them and he pushed it into Izzart's reach. He placed a hand under Izzart's arm and they struck away from the boat. Izzart's heart was pounding and his breath came with difficulty. He felt horribly weak. The waves beat in his face. The bank looked dreadfully far away. He did not think he could ever reach it. Suddenly the boy cried that he could touch bottom and Izzart put down his legs; but he could feel nothing; he swam a few more exhausted strokes, his eyes fixed on the bank, and then, trying again, felt his feet sink into thick mud. He was thankful. He floundered on and there was the bank within reach of his hands, black mud in which he sank to his knees; he scrambled up, desperate to get out of the cruel water, and when he came to the top he found a little flat with tall rank grass all about it. He and Hassan sank down on it and lay for a while stretched out like dead men. They were so tired that they could not move. They were covered with black mud from head to foot.

But presently Izzart's mind began to work, and a pang of anguish on a sudden shook him. Campion was drowned. It was awful. He did not know how he was going to explain the disaster when he got back to Kuala Solor. They would blame him for it; he ought to have remembered the Bore and told the steersman to make for the bank and tie up the boat when he saw it coming. It wasn't his fault, it was the steersman's, he knew the river: why in God's name hadn't he had the sense to get into safety? How could he have expected that it was possible to ride that horrible torrent? Izzart's limbs shook as he remembered the wall of seething water that rushed down upon them. He must get the body and take it back to Kuala Solor. He wondered whether any of the crew were drowned too. He felt too weak to move, but Hassan now rose and wrung the water out of his sarong; he looked over the river and quickly turned to Izzart.

"Tuan, a boat is coming."

The lalang grass prevented Izzart from seeing anything.

"Shout to them," he said.

Hassan slipped out of view and made his way along the branch of a tree that overhung the water; he cried out and waved. Presently Izzart heard voices. There was a rapid conversation between the boy and the occupants of the boat and then the boy came back.

"They saw us capsize, Tuan," he said, "and they came as soon as the Bore passed. There's a long-house on the other side. If you will cross the river they will give us sarongs and food and we can sleep there."

Izzart for a moment felt that he could not again trust himself on the face of the treacherous water.

"What about the other tuan?" he asked.

"They do not know."

"If he's drowned they must find the body."

"Another boat has gone up-stream."

Izzart did not know what to do. He was numb. Hassan put his arm round his shoulder and raised him to his feet. He made his way through the thick grass to the edge of the water and there he saw a dug-out with two Dyaks in it. The river now once more was calm and sluggish; the great wave had passed and no one would have dreamed that so short a while before the placid surface was like a stormy sea. The Dyaks repeated to him what they had already told the boy. Izzart could not bring himself to speak. He felt that if he said a word he would burst out crying. Hassan helped him to get in, and the Dyaks began to pull across. He fearfully wanted something to smoke but his cigarettes and his matches, both in a hip-pocket, were soaking. The passage of the river seemed endless. The night fell and when they reached the bank the first stars were shining. He stepped ashore and one of the Dyaks took him up to the long-house. But Hassan seized the paddle he had dropped and with the other pushed out into the stream. Two or three men and some children came down to meet

Izzart and he climbed to the house amid a babel of conversation. He went up the ladder and was led with greetings and excited comment to the space where the young men slept. Rattan mats were hurriedly laid to make him a couch and he sank down on them. Some one brought him a jar of Arak and he took a long drink; it was rough and fiery, burning his throat, but it warmed his heart. He slipped off his shirt and trousers and put on a dry sarong which some one lent him. By chance he caught sight of the yellow new moon lying on her back, and it gave him a keen, almost a sensual, pleasure. He could not help thinking that he might at that moment be a corpse floating up the river with the tide. The moon had never looked to him more lovely. He began to feel hungry and he asked for rice. One of the women went into a room to prepare it. He was more himself now and he began to think again of the explanations he would make at Kuala Solor. No one could really blame him because he had gone to sleep; he certainly wasn't drunk, Hutchinson would bear him out there, and how was he to suspect that the steersman would be such a damned fool? It was just rotten luck. But he couldn't think of Campion without a shudder. At last a platter of rice was brought him and he was just about to start eating when a man ran hurriedly along and came up to him.

"The tuan's come," he cried.

"What tuan?"

He jumped up. There was a commotion about the doorway and he stepped forward. Hassan was coming quickly towards him out of the darkness, and then he heard a voice.

"Izzart: Are you there?"

Campion advanced towards him.

"Well, here we are again. By God, that was a pretty near thing, wasn't it? You seem to have made yourself nice and comfortable. My heavens, I could do with a drink."

His dank clothes clung round him and he was muddy and dishevelled. But he was in excellent spirits.

"I didn't know where the hell they were bringing me. I'd made up my mind that I should have to spend the night on the bank. I thought you were drowned."

"Here's some Arak," said Izzart.

Campion put his mouth to the jar and drank and spluttered and drank again.

"Muck, but by God it's strong." He looked at Izzart with a grin of his broken and discoloured teeth. "I say, old man, you look as though you'd be all the better for a wash."

"I'll wash later."

"All right, so will I. Tell them to get me a sarong. How did you get out?" He did not wait for an answer. "I thought I was done for. I owe my life to these two sportsmen here." He indicated with a cheery nod two of the Dyak prisoners whom Izzart vaguely recognized as having been part of their crew. "They were hanging on to that blasted boat on each side of me and somehow they cottoned on to it that I was down and out. I couldn't have lasted another minute. They made signs to me that we could risk having a shot at getting to the bank, but I didn't think I had the strength. By George, I've never been so blown in all my life. I don't know how they managed it, but somehow they got hold of the mattress we'd been lying on, and they made it into a roll. They're sportsmen, they are. I don't know why they didn't just save themselves without bothering about me. They gave it to me. I thought it a damned poor lifebelt, but I saw the force of the proverb about a drowning man clutching at a straw. I caught hold of the damned thing and between them somehow or other they dragged me ashore."

The danger from which he had escaped made Campion excited and voluble; but Izzart hardly listened to what he said. He heard once more, as distinctly as though the words rang now through the air, Campion's agonized cry for help, and he felt sick with terror. The blind panic raced down his nerves. Campion was talking still, but was he talking to conceal his thoughts? Izzart looked into those bright blue eyes and sought to read the sense behind the flow of words. Was there a hard glint in them or something of cynical mockery? Did he know that Izzart, leaving him to his fate, had cut and run? He flushed deeply. After all, what was there that he could have done? At such a moment it was each for himself and the devil take the hindmost. But what would they say in Kuala Solor if Campion told them that Izzart had deserted him? He ought to have stayed, he wished now with all his heart that he had, but then, then it was stronger than himself, he couldn't. Could any one blame him? No one who had seen that fierce and seething torrent. Oh, the water and the exhaustion, so that he could have cried!

"If you're as hungry as I am you'd better have a tuck in at this rice," he said.

Campion ate voraciously, but when Izzart had taken a mouthful or two he found that he had no appetite. Campion talked and talked. Izzart listened suspiciously. He felt that he must be alert and he drank more Arak. He began to feel a little drunk.

"I shall get into the devil of a row at K.S.," he said tentatively.

"I don't know why."

"I was told off to look after you. They won't think it was very clever of me to let you get nearly drowned."

"It wasn't your fault. It was the fault of the damned fool of a steersman. After all, the important thing is that we're saved. By George, I thought I was finished once. I shouted out to you. I don't know if you heard me."

"No, I didn't hear anything. There was such a devil of a row, wasn't there?"

"Perhaps you'd got away before. I don't know exactly when you did get away."

Izzart looked at him sharply. Was it his fancy that there was an odd look in Campion's eyes?

"There was such an awful confusion," he said. "I was just about down and out. My boy threw me over an oar. He gave me to understand you were all right. He told me you'd got ashore."

The oar! He ought to have given Campion the oar and told Hassan, the strong swimmer, to give *him* his help. Was it his fancy again that Campion gave him a quick and searching glance?

"I wish I could have been of more use to you," said Izzart.

"Oh, I'm sure you had enough to do to look after yourself," answered Campion.

The headman brought them cups of Arak, and they both drank a great deal. Izzart's head began to spin and he suggested that they should turn in. Beds had been prepared for them and mosquito nets fixed. They were to set out at dawn on the rest of their journey down the river. Campion's bed was next to his, and in a few minutes he heard him snoring. He had fallen asleep the moment he lay down. The young men of the long-house and the prisoners of the boat's crew went on talking late into the night. Izzart's head now was aching horribly and he could not think. When Hassan roused him as day broke it seemed to him that he had not slept at all. Their clothes had been washed and dried, but they were bedraggled objects as they walked along the narrow pathway to the river where the prahu was waiting for them. They rowed leisurely. The morning was lovely and the great stretch of placid water gleamed in the early light.

"By George, it's fine to be alive," said Campion.

He was grubby and unshaved. He took long breaths and his twisted mouth was half open with a grin. You could tell that he found the air singularly good to breathe. He was delighted with the blue sky and the sunshine and the greenness of the trees. Izzart hated him. He was sure that this morning there was a difference in his manner. He did not know what to do. He had a mind to throw himself on his mercy. He had behaved like a cad, but he was sorry, he would give anything to have the chance again, but any one might have done what he did, and if Campion gave him away he was ruined. He could never stay in Sembulu; his name would be mud in Borneo and the Straits Settlements. If he made his confession to Campion he could surely get Campion to promise to hold his tongue. But would he keep his promise? He looked at him, a shifty little man; how could he be relied on? Izzart thought of what he had said the night before. It wasn't the truth, of course, but who could know that? At all events who could prove that he hadn't honestly thought that Campion was safe? Whatever Campion said it was only his word against Izzart's; he could laugh and shrug his shoulders and say that Campion had lost his head and didn't know what he was talking about. Besides, it wasn't certain that Campion hadn't accepted his story; in that frightful struggle for life he could be very sure of nothing. He had a temptation to go back to the subject, but was afraid if he did that he would excite suspicion in Campion's mind. He *must* hold his tongue. That was his only chance of safety. And when they got to K.S. he would get in his story first.

"I should be completely happy now," said Campion, "if I only had something to smoke."

"We shall be able to get some stinkers on board."

Campion gave a little laugh.

"Human beings are very unreasonable," he said. "At the first moment I was so glad to be alive that I thought of nothing else, but now I'm beginning to regret the loss of my notes and my photographs and my shaving tackle."

Izzart formulated the thought which had lurked at the back of his mind, but which all through the night he had refused to admit into his consciousness.

"I wish to God he'd been drowned. Then I'd have been safe."

"There she is," cried Campion suddenly.

Izzart looked round. They were at the mouth of the river and there was the Sultan Ahmed waiting for them. Izzart's heart sank: he had forgotten that she had an English skipper and that he would have to be told the story of their adventure. What would Campion say? The skipper was called Bredon and Izzart had met him often at Kuala Solor. He was a little bluff man, with a black moustache, and a breezy manner.

"Hurry up," he called out to them, as they rowed up, "I've been waiting for you since dawn." But when they climbed on board his face fell. "Hulloa, what's the matter with you?"

"Give us a drink and you shall hear all about it," said Campion, with his crooked grin.

"Come along."

They sat down under the awning. On a table were glasses, a bottle of whisky and soda water. The skipper gave an order and in a few minutes they were noisily under way.

"We were caught in the Bore," said Izzart.

He felt he must say something. His mouth was horribly dry notwithstanding the drink.

"Were you, by Jove? You're lucky not to have been drowned. What happened?"

He addressed himself to Izzart because he knew him, but it was Campion who answered. He related the whole incident, accurately, and Izzart listened with strained attention. Campion spoke in the plural when he told the early part of the story, and then, as he came to the moment when they were thrown into the water, changed to the singular. At first it was what *they* had done and now it was what happened to *him*. He left Izzart out of it. Izzart did not know whether to be relieved or alarmed. Why did he not mention him? Was it because in that mortal struggle for life he had thought of nothing but himself or—did he *know*?

"And what happened to you?" said Captain Bredon, turning to Izzart.

Izzart was about to answer when Campion spoke.

"Until I got over to the other side of the river I thought he was drowned. I don't know how he got out. I expect he hardly knows himself."

"It was touch and go," said Izzart, with a laugh.

Why had Campion said that? He caught his eye. He was sure now that there was a gleam of amusement in it. It was awful not to be certain. He was frightened. He was ashamed. He wondered if he could not so guide the conversation, either now or later, as to ask Campion whether that was the story he was going to tell in Kuala Solor. There was nothing in it to excite any one's suspicions. But if nobody else knew, Campion knew. He could have killed him.

"Well, I think you're both of you damned lucky to be alive," said the skipper.

It was but a short run to Kuala Solor, and as they steamed up the Sembulu River Izzart moodily watched the banks. On each side were the mangroves and the nipas washed by the water, and behind, the dense green of the jungle; here and there, among fruit trees, were Malay houses on piles. Night fell as they docked. Goring, of the police, came on board and shook hands with them. He was living at the rest-house just then, and as he set about his work of seeing the native passengers he told them that they would find another man, Porter by name, staying there too. They would all meet at dinner. The boys took charge of their kit, and Campion and Izzart strolled along. They bathed and changed and at half-past eight the four of them assembled in the common-room for gin pahits.

"I say, what's this Bredon tells me about your being nearly drowned?" said Goring as he came in.

Izzart felt himself flush, but before he could answer Campion broke in, and it seemed certain to Izzart that he spoke in order to give the story as he chose. He felt hot with shame. Not a word was spoken in disparagement of him, not a word was said of him at all; he wondered if those two men who listened, Goring and Porter, thought it strange that he should be left out. He looked at Campion intently as he proceeded with his narration; he told it rather humorously; he did not disguise the danger in which they had been, but he made a joke of it, so that the two listeners laughed at the quandary in which they had found themselves.

"A thing that's tickled me since," said Campion, "is that when I got over to the other bank I was black with mud from head to foot. I felt I really ought to jump in the river and have a wash, but you know I felt I'd been in that damned river as much as ever I wanted, and I said to myself: No, by George, I'll go dirty. And when I got into the long-house and saw Izzart as black as I was, I knew he'd felt just like I did."

They laughed and Izzart forced himself to laugh too. He noticed that Campion had told the story in precisely the same words as he had used when he told it to the skipper of the Sultan Ahmed. There could be only one explanation of that; he knew, he knew everything, and had made up his mind exactly what story to tell. The ingenuity with which Campion gave the facts and yet left out what must be to Izzart's discredit was devilish. But why was he holding his hand? It wasn't in him not to feel contempt and resentment for the man who had callously deserted him in that moment of dreadful peril. Suddenly, in a flash of inspiration Izzart understood: he was keeping the truth to tell to Willis, the Resident. Izzart had gooseflesh as he thought of confronting Willis. He could deny, but would his denials serve him? Willis was no fool and he would get at Hassan; Hassan could not be trusted to be silent; Hassan would give him away. Then he would be done for. Willis would suggest that he had better go home.

He had a racking headache and after dinner he went to his room, for he wanted to be alone so that he could devise a plan of action. And then a thought came to him which made him go hot and cold; he knew that the secret which he had guarded so long was a secret to nobody. He was on a sudden certain of it. Why should he have those bright eyes and that swarthy skin? Why should he speak Malay with such ease and have learned Dyak so quickly? Of course they knew. What a fool he was ever to think that they believed that story of his, about the Spanish grandmother! They must have laughed up their sleeves when he told it, and behind his back they had called him a damned nigger. And now another thought came to him, torturing, and he asked himself whether it was on account of that wretched drop of native blood in him that when he heard Campion cry out his nerve failed him. After all, any one might at that moment have been seized with panic; and why in God's name should he sacrifice his life to save a man's whom he cared nothing for? It was insane. But of course in K.S. they would say it was only what they expected; they would make no allowances.

At last he went to bed, but when, after tossing about restlessly
for God knows how long, he fell asleep, he was awakened by a
fearful dream; he seemed to be once more in that raging torrent,
with the boat turning, turning; and then there was the desperate
clutching at the gunwale, and the agony as it slipped out of his
hands, and the water that roared over him. He was wide awake
before dawn. His only chance was to see Willis and get his story in
first; and he thought over carefully what he was going to say and
chose the very words he meant to use.

He got up early, and in order not to see Campion went out
without breakfast. He walked along the highroad till such time
as he knew the Resident would be in his office and then walked
back again. He sent in his name and was ushered into Willis's
room. He was a little elderly man with thin grey hair and a long
yellow face.

"I'm glad to see you back safe and sound," he said, shaking
hands with Izzart. "What's this I hear about your being nearly
drowned?"

Izzart, in clean ducks, his topee spotless, was a fine figure of
a man. His black hair was neatly brushed and his moustache was
trimmed. He had an upright and soldierly bearing.

"I thought I'd better come and tell you at once, sir, as you
told me to look after Campion."

"Fire away."

Izzart told his story. He made light of the danger. He gave
Willis to understand that it had not been very great. They would
never have been upset if they had not started so late.

"I tried to get Campion away earlier, but he'd had two or
three drinks and the fact is, he didn't want to move."

"Was he tight?"

"I don't know about that," smiled Izzart good-humouredly. "I
shouldn't say he was cold sober."

He went on with his story. He managed to insinuate that Campion had lost his head a little. Of course it was a very frightening
business to a man who wasn't a decent swimmer: he, Izzart, had
been more concerned for Campion than for himself; he knew the
only chance was to keep cool, and the moment they were upset
he saw that Campion had got the wind up.

"You can't blame him for that," said the Resident.

"Of course I did everything I possibly could for him, sir, but the fact is, there wasn't anything much I could do."

"Well, the great thing is that you both escaped. It would have been very awkward for all of us if he'd been drowned."

"I thought I'd better come and tell you the facts before you saw Campion, sir. I fancy he's inclined to talk rather wildly about it. There's no use exaggerating."

"On the whole your stories agree pretty well," said Willis, with a little smile.

Izzart looked at him blankly.

"Haven't you see Campion this morning? I heard from Goring that there'd been some trouble and I looked in last night on my way home from the Fort after dinner. You'd already gone to bed."

Izzart felt himself trembling and he made a great effort to preserve his composure.

"By the way, you got away first, didn't you?"

"I don't really know, sir. You see, there was a lot of confusion."

"You must have if you got over to the other side before he did."

"I suppose I did then."

"Well, thanks for coming to tell me," said Willis, rising from his chair.

As he did so he knocked some books on the floor. They fell with a sudden thud. The unexpected sound made Izzart start violently and he gave a gasp. The Resident looked at him quickly.

"I say, your nerves are in a pretty state."

Izzart could not control his trembling.

"I'm very sorry, sir," he murmured.

"I expect it's been a shock. You'd better take it easy for a few days. Why don't you get the doctor to give you something?"

"I didn't sleep very well last night."

The Resident nodded as though he understood. Izzart left the room, and as he passed out some man he knew stopped and congratulated him on his escape. They all knew of it. He walked back to the rest-house. And as he walked he repeated to himself the story he had told the Resident. Was it really the same story that Campion had told? He had never suspected that the Resident had already heard it from Campion. What a fool he had been to go to bed! He should never have let Campion out of his sight. Why had the Resident listened without telling him that he already knew? Now Izzart cursed himself for having suggested that Campion was drunk and had lost his head. He had said this in order to discredit him, but he knew now that it was a stupid thing to do. And why had Willis said that about his having got away first? Perhaps he was holding his hand too; perhaps he was going to make enquiries; Willis was very shrewd. But what exactly had Campion said? He must know that; at whatever cost he must know. Izzart's mind was seething so that he felt he could hardly keep a hold on his thoughts, but he must keep calm. He felt like a hunted animal. He did not believe that Willis liked him; once or twice in the office he had blamed him because he was careless; perhaps he was just waiting till he got all the facts. Izzart was almost hysterical.

He entered the rest-house and there, sitting on a long chair, with his legs stretched out, was Campion. He was reading the papers which had arrived during their absence in the jungle. Izzart felt a blind rush of hatred well up in him as he looked at the little, shabby man who held him in the hollow of his hand.

"Hulloa," said Campion, looking up. "Where have you been?"

To Izzart it seemed that there was in his eyes a mocking irony. He clenched his hands and his breath came fast.

"What have you been saying to Willis about me?" he asked abruptly.

The tone in which he put the unexpected question was so harsh that Campion gave him a glance of faint surprise.

"I don't think I've been saying anything very much about you. Why?"

"He came here last night."

Izzart looked at him intently. His brows were drawn together in an angry frown as he tried to read Campion's thoughts.

"I told him you'd gone to bed with a headache. He wanted to know about our mishap."

"I've just seen him."

Izzart walked up and down the large and shaded room; now, though it was still early, the sun was hot and dazzling. He felt himself in a net. He was blind with rage; he could have seized Campion by the throat and strangled him, and yet, because he did not know what he had to fight against, he felt himself powerless. He was tired and ill, and his nerves were shaken. On a sudden the anger which had given him a sort of strength left him and he was filled with despondency. It was as though water and not blood ran through his veins; his heart sank and his knees seemed to give way. He felt that if he did not take care he would begin to cry. He was dreadfully sorry for himself.

"Damn you, I wish to God I'd never set eyes on you," he cried pitifully.

"What on earth's the matter?" asked Campion, with astonishment.

"Oh, don't pretend. We've been pretending for two days and I'm fed up with it." His voice rose shrilly, it sounded odd in that robust and powerful man. "I'm fed up with it. I cut and run. I left you to drown. I know I behaved like a skunk. I couldn't help it."

Campion rose slowly from his chair.

"What *are* you talking about?"

His tone was so genuinely surprised that it gave Izzart a start. A cold shiver ran down his spine.

"When you called for help I was panic-stricken. I just caught hold of an oar and got Hassan to help me get away."

"That was the most sensible thing you could do."

"I couldn't help you. There wasn't a thing I could do."

"Of course not. It was damned silly of me to shout. It was waste of breath, and breath was the very thing I wanted."

"Do you mean to say you didn't know?"

"When those fellows got me the mattress I thought you were still clinging to the boat. I had an idea that I got away before you did."

Izzart put both his hands to his head and gave a hoarse cry of despair.

"My God, what a fool I've been."

The two men stood for a while staring at one another. The silence seemed endless.

"What are you going to do now?" asked Izzart at last.

"Oh, my dear fellow, don't worry. I've been frightened too often myself to blame any one who shows the white feather. I'm not going to tell a soul."

"Yes, but you *know*."

"I promise you, you can trust me. Besides, my job's done here and I'm going home. I want to catch the next boat to Singapore." There was a pause, and Campion looked for a while reflectively at Izzart. "There's only one thing I'd like to ask you: I've made a good many friends here, and there are one or two things I'm a little sensitive about; when you tell the story of our upset I should be grateful if you wouldn't make out that I had behaved badly. I wouldn't like the fellows here to think that I'd lost my nerve."

Izzart flushed darkly. He remembered what he had said to the Resident. It almost looked as though Campion had been listening over his shoulder. He cleared his throat.

"I don't know why you think I should do that."

Campion chuckled good-naturedly, and his blue eyes were gay with amusement.

"The yellow streak," he replied, and then, with a grin that showed his broken and discoloured teeth: "Have a cheroot, dear boy."

Before the Party

Mrs. Skinner liked to be in good time. She was already dressed, in black silk as befitted her age and the mourning she wore for her son-in-law, and now she put on her toque. She was a little uncertain about it, since the egrets' feathers which adorned it might very well arouse in some of the friends she would certainly meet at the party acid expostulations; and of course it was shocking to kill those beautiful white birds, in the mating season too, for the sake of their feathers; but there they were, so pretty and stylish, and it would have been silly to refuse them, and it would have hurt her son-in-law's feelings. He had brought them all the way from Borneo and he expected her to be so pleased with them. Kathleen had made herself rather unpleasant about them, she must wish she hadn't now, after what had happened, but Kathleen had never really liked Harold. Mrs. Skinner, standing at her dressing-table, placed the toque on her head, it was after all the only nice hat she had, and put in a pin with a large jet knob. If anybody spoke to her about the ospreys she had her answer.

"I know it's dreadful," she would say, "and I wouldn't dream of buying them, but my poor son-in-law brought them back the last time he was home on leave."

That would explain her possession of them and excuse their use. Every one had been very kind. Mrs. Skinner took a clean handkerchief from a drawer and sprinkled a little *Eau de Cologne* on it. She never used scent, and she had always thought it rather fast, but *Eau de Cologne* was so refreshing. She was very nearly ready now and her eyes wandered out of the window behind her looking-glass. Canon Heywood had a beautiful day for his garden-party. It was warm and the sky was blue; the trees had not yet lost the fresh green of the spring. She smiled as she saw her little granddaughter in the strip of garden behind the house busily raking her very own flower-bed. Mrs. Skinner wished Joan were not quite so pale, it was a mistake to have kept her so long in the tropics; and she was so grave for her age, you never saw her run about; she played quiet games of her own invention and watered her garden. Mrs. Skinner gave the front of her dress a little pat, took up her gloves, and went down-stairs.

Kathleen was at the writing-table in the window busy with lists she was making, for she was honorary secretary of the Ladies' Golf Club and when there were competitions had a good deal to do. But she too was ready for the party.

"I see you've put on your jumper after all," said Mrs. Skinner. They had discussed at luncheon whether Kathleen should wear her jumper or her black chiffon. The jumper was black and white, and Kathleen thought it rather smart, but it was hardly mourning. Millicent, however, was in favour of it.

"There's no reason why we should all look as if we'd just come from a funeral," she said. "Harold's been dead eight months."

To Mrs. Skinner it seemed rather unfeeling to talk like that. Millicent was strange since her return from Borneo.

"You're not going to leave off your weeds yet, darling?" she asked.

Millicent did not give a direct answer.

"People don't wear mourning in the way they used," she said. She paused a little and when she went on there was a tone in her voice which Mrs. Skinner thought quite peculiar. It was plain that Kathleen noticed it too, for she gave her sister a curious look. "I'm sure Harold wouldn't wish me to wear mourning for him indefinitely."

"I dressed early because I wanted to say something to Millicent," said Kathleen in reply to her mother's observation.

"Oh?"

Kathleen did not explain. But she put her lists aside and with knitted brows read for the second time a letter from a lady who complained that the committee had most unfairly marked down her handicap from twenty-four to eighteen. It requires a good deal of tact to be Honorary Secretary to a ladies' golf club. Mrs. Skinner began to put on her new gloves. The sun-blinds kept the room cool and dark. She looked at the great wooden hornbill, gaily painted, which Harold had left in her safe-keeping; and it seemed a little odd and barbaric to her, but he had set much store on it. It had some religious significance and Canon Heywood had been greatly struck by it. On the wall, over the sofa, were Malay weapons, she forgot what they were called, and here and there on occasional tables pieces of silver and brass which Harold at various times had sent to them. She had liked Harold and involuntarily her eyes sought his photograph which stood on the piano with photographs of her two daughters, her grandchild, her sister and her sister's son.

"Why, Kathleen, where's Harold's photograph?" she asked.

Kathleen looked round. It no longer stood in its place.

"Some one's taken it away," said Kathleen.

Surprised and puzzled, she got up and went over to the piano. The photographs had been rearranged so that no gap should show.

"Perhaps Millicent wanted to have it in her bedroom," said Mrs. Skinner.

"I should have noticed it. Besides, Millicent has several photographs of Harold. She keeps them locked up."

Mrs. Skinner had thought it very peculiar that her daughter should have no photographs of Harold in her room. Indeed she had spoken of it once, but Millicent had made no reply. Millicent had been strangely silent since she came back from Borneo, and had not encouraged the sympathy Mrs. Skinner would have been so willing to show her. She seemed unwilling to speak of her great loss. Sorrow took people in different ways. Her husband had said the best thing was to leave her alone. The thought of him turned her ideas to the party they were going to.

"Father asked if I thought he ought to wear a top-hat," she said. "I said I thought it was just as well to be on the safe side."

It was going to be quite a grand affair. They were having ices, strawberry and vanilla, from Boddy, the confectioner, but the Heywoods were making the iced coffee at home. Every one would be there. They had been asked to meet the Bishop of Hong-Kong, who was staying with the Canon, an old college friend of his, and he was going to speak on the Chinese missions. Mrs. Skinner, whose daughter had lived in the East for eight years and whose son-in-law had been Resident of a district in Borneo, was in a flutter of interest. Naturally it meant more to her than to people who had never had anything to do with the Colonies and that sort of thing.

"What can they know of England who only England know?" as Mr. Skinner said.

He came into the room at that moment. He was a lawyer, as his father had been before him, and he had offices in Lincoln's Inn Fields. He went up to London every morning and came down every evening. He was only able to accompany his wife and daughters to the Canon's garden-party because the Canon had very wisely chosen a Saturday to have it on. Mr. Skinner looked very well in his tail-coat and pepper-and-salt trousers. He was not exactly dressy, but he was neat. He looked like a respectable family solicitor, which indeed he was; his firm never touched work that was not perfectly above board, and if a client went to him with some trouble that was not quite nice, Mr. Skinner would look grave.

"I don't think this is the sort of case that we very much care to undertake," he said. "I think you'd do better to go elsewhere."

He drew towards him his writing-block and scribbled a name and address on it. He tore off a sheet of paper and handed it to his client.

"If I were you I think I would go and see these people. If you mention my name I believe they'll do anything they can for you."

Mr. Skinner was clean-shaven and very bald. His pale lips were tight and thin, but his blue eyes were shy. He had no colour in his cheeks and his face was much lined.

"I see you've put on your new trousers," said Mrs. Skinner.

"I thought it would be a good opportunity," he answered. "I was wondering if I should wear a buttonhole."

"I wouldn't, father," said Kathleen. "I don't think it's awfully good form."

"A lot of people will be wearing them," said Mrs. Skinner.

"Only clerks and people like that," said Kathleen. "The Heywoods have had to ask everybody, you know. And besides, we are in mourning."

"I wonder if there'll be a collection after the Bishop's address," said Mr. Skinner.

"I should hardly think so," said Mrs. Skinner.

"I think it would be rather bad form," agreed Kathleen.

"It's as well to be on the safe side," said Mr. Skinner. "I'll give for all of us. I was wondering if ten shillings would be enough or if I must give a pound."

"If you give anything I think you ought to give a pound, father," said Kathleen.

"I'll see when the time comes. I don't want to give less than any one else, but on the other hand I see no reason to give more than I need."

Kathleen put away her papers in the drawer of the writing-table and stood up. She looked at her wrist-watch.

"Is Millicent ready?" asked Mrs. Skinner.

"There's plenty of time. We're only asked at four and I don't think we ought to arrive much before half-past. I told Davis to bring the car round at four-fifteen."

Generally Kathleen drove the car, but on grand occasions like this Davis, who was the gardener, put on his uniform and acted as chauffeur. It looked better when you drove up and naturally Kathleen didn't much want to drive herself when she was wearing her new jumper. The sight of her mother forcing her fingers one by one into her new gloves reminded her that she must put on her own. She smelt them to see if any odour of the cleaning still clung to them. It was very slight. She didn't believe any one would notice.

At last the door opened and Millicent came in. She wore her widow's weeds. Mrs. Skinner never could get used to them, but of course she knew that Millicent must wear them for a year. It was a pity they didn't suit her; they suited some people. She had tried on Millicent's bonnet once, with its white band and long veil, and thought she looked very well in it. Of course she hoped dear Alfred would survive her, but if he didn't she would never go out of weeds. Queen Victoria never had. It was different for Millicent; Millicent was a much younger woman; she was only thirty-six; it was very sad to be a widow at thirty-six. And there wasn't much chance of her marrying again. Kathleen wasn't very likely to marry now, she was thirty-five; last time Millicent and Harold had come home she had suggested that they should have Kathleen to stay with them; Harold had seemed willing enough, but Millicent said it wouldn't do. Mrs. Skinner didn't know why not. It would give her a chance. Of course they didn't want to get rid of her, but a girl ought to marry, and somehow all the men they knew at home were married already. Millicent said the climate was trying. It was true she was a bad colour. No one would think now that Millicent had been the prettier of the two.

Kathleen had fined down as she grew older (of course some people said she was too thin) but now that she had cut her hair, with her cheeks red from playing golf in all weathers, Mrs. Skinner thought her quite pretty. No one could say that of poor Millicent; she had lost her figure completely; she had never been tall and now that she had filled out she looked stocky. She was a good deal too fat; Mrs. Skinner supposed it was due to the tropical heat that prevented her from taking exercise. Her skin was sallow and muddy; and her blue eyes, which had been her best feature, had gone quite pale.

"She ought to do something about her neck," Mrs. Skinner reflected. "She's becoming dreadfully jowly."

She had spoken of it once or twice to her husband. He remarked that Millicent wasn't as young as she was: that might be, but she needn't let herself go altogether. Mrs. Skinner made up her mind to talk to her daughter seriously, but of course she must respect her grief and she would wait till the year was up. She was just as glad to have this reason to put off a conversation the thought of which made her slightly nervous. For Millicent was certainly changed. There was something sullen in her face which made her mother not quite at home with her. Mrs. Skinner liked to say aloud all the thoughts that passed through her head, but Millicent when you made a remark (just to say something, you know), had an awkward habit of not answering so that you wondered whether she had heard. Sometimes Mrs. Skinner found it so irritating, that not to be quite sharp with Millicent she had to remind herself that poor Harold had only been dead eight months.

The light from the window fell on the widow's heavy face as she advanced silently, but Kathleen stood with her back to it. She watched her sister for a moment.

"Millicent, there's something I want to say to you," she said. "I was playing golf with Gladys Heywood this morning."

"Did you beat her?" asked Millicent.

Gladys Heywood was the Canon's only unmarried daughter.

"She told me something about you which I think you ought to know."

Millicent's eyes passed beyond her sister to the little girl watering flowers in the garden.

"Have you told Annie to give Joan her tea in the kitchen, mother?" she said.

"Yes, she'll have it when the servants have theirs."

Kathleen looked at her sister coolly.

"The Bishop spent two or three days at Singapore on his way home," she went on. "He's very fond of travelling. He's been to Borneo and he knows a good many of the people that you know."

"He'll be interested to see you, dear," said Mrs. Skinner. "Did he know poor Harold?"

"Yes, he met him at Kuala Solor. He remembers him very well. He says he was shocked to hear of his death."

Millicent sat down and began to put on her black gloves. It seemed strange to Mrs. Skinner that she received these remarks with complete silence.

"Oh, Millicent," she said, "Harold's photo has disappeared. Have you taken it?"

"Yes, I put it away."

"I should have thought you'd like to have it out."

Once more Millicent said nothing. It really was an exasperating habit.

Kathleen turned slightly in order to face her sister.

"Millicent, why did you tell us that Harold died of fever?"

The widow made no gesture, she looked at Kathleen with steady eyes, but her sallow skin darkened with a flush. She did not reply.

"What *do* you mean, Kathleen?" asked Mr. Skinner, with surprise.

"The Bishop says that Harold committed suicide."

Mrs. Skinner gave a startled cry, but her husband put out a deprecating hand.

"Is it true, Millicent?"

"It is."

"But why didn't you tell us?"

Millicent paused for an instant. She fingered idly a piece of Brunei brass which stood on the table by her side. That too had been a present from Harold.

"I thought it better for Joan that her father should be thought to have died of fever. I didn't want her to know anything about it."

"You've put us in an awfully awkward position," said Kathleen, frowning a little. "Gladys Heywood said she thought it rather nasty of me not to have told her the truth. I had the greatest difficulty in getting her to believe that I knew absolutely nothing about it. She said her father was rather put out. He says, after all the years we've known one another, and considering that he married you, and the terms we've been on, and all that, he does think we might have had confidence in him. And at all events if we didn't want to tell him the truth we needn't have told him a lie."

"I must say I sympathize with him there," said Mr. Skinner acidly.

"Of course I told Gladys that we weren't to blame. We only told them what you told us."

"I hope it didn't put you off your game," said Millicent.

"Really, my dear, I think that is a most improper observation," exclaimed her father.

He rose from his chair, walked over to the empty fireplace, and from force of habit stood in front of it with parted coat-tails.

"It was my business," said Millicent, "and if I chose to keep it to myself I didn't see why I shouldn't."

"It doesn't look as if you had any affection for your mother if you didn't even tell her," said Mrs. Skinner.

Millicent shrugged her shoulders.

"You might have known it was bound to come out," said Kathleen.

"Why? I didn't expect that two gossiping old parsons would have nothing else to talk about than me."

"When the Bishop said he'd been to Borneo it's only natural that the Heywoods should ask him if he knew you and Harold."

"All that's neither here nor there," said Mr. Skinner. "I think you should certainly have told us the truth and we could have decided what was the best thing to do. As a solicitor I can tell you that in the long run it only makes things worse if you attempt to hide them."

"Poor Harold," said Mrs. Skinner, and the tears began to trickle down her raddled cheeks. "It seems dreadful. He was always a good son-in-law to me. Whatever induced him to do such a dreadful thing?"

"The climate."

"I think you'd better give us all the facts, Millicent," said her father.

"Kathleen will tell you."

Kathleen hesitated. What she had to say really was rather dreadful. It seemed terrible that such things should happen to a family like theirs.

"The Bishop says he cut his throat."

Mrs. Skinner gasped and she went impulsively up to her bereaved daughter. She wanted to fold her in her arms.

"My poor child," she sobbed.

But Millicent withdrew herself.

"Please don't fuss me, mother. I really can't stand being mauled about."

"Really, Millicent," said Mr. Skinner, with a frown.

He did not think she was behaving very nicely.

Mrs. Skinner dabbed her eyes carefully with her handkerchief and with a sigh and a little shake of the head returned to her chair. Kathleen fidgeted with the long chain she wore round her neck.

"It does seem rather absurd that I should have to be told the details of my brother-in-law's death by a friend. It makes us all look such fools. The Bishop wants very much to see you, Millicent; he wants to tell you how much he feels for you." She paused, but Millicent did not speak. "He says that Millicent had been away with Joan and when she came back she found poor Harold lying dead on his bed."

"It must have been a great shock," said Mr. Skinner.

Mrs. Skinner began to cry again, but Kathleen put her hand gently on her shoulder.

"Don't cry, mother," she said. "It'll make your eyes red and people will think it so funny."

They were all silent while Mrs. Skinner, drying her eyes, made a successful effort to control herself. It seemed very strange to her that at this very moment she should be wearing in her toque the ospreys that poor Harold had given her.

"There's something else I ought to tell you," said Kathleen.

Millicent looked at her sister again, without haste, and her eyes were steady, but watchful. She had the look of a person who is waiting for a sound which he is afraid of missing.

"I don't want to say anything to wound you, dear," Kathleen

went on, "but there's something else and I think you ought to know it. The Bishop says that Harold drank."

"Oh, my dear, how dreadful!" cried Mrs. Skinner. "What a shocking thing to say. Did Gladys Heywood tell you? What did you say?"

"I said it was entirely untrue."

"This is what comes of making secrets of things," said Mr. Skinner irritably. "It's always the same. If you try and hush a thing up all sorts of rumours get about which are ten times worse than the truth."

"They told the Bishop in Singapore that Harold had killed himself while he was suffering from *delirium tremens*. I think for all our sakes you ought to deny that, Millicent."

"It's such a dreadful thing to have said about any one who's dead," said Mrs. Skinner. "And it'll be so bad for Joan when she grows up."

"But what is the foundation of this story, Millicent?" asked her father. "Harold was always very abstemious."

"Here," said the widow.

"Did he drink?"

"Like a fish."

The answer was so unexpected, and the tone so sardonic, that all three of them were startled.

"Millicent, how can you talk like that of your husband when he's dead?" cried her mother, clasping her neatly gloved hands. "I can't understand you. You've been so strange since you came back. I could never have believed that a girl of mine could take her husband's death like that."

"Never mind about that, mother," said Mr. Skinner. "We can go into all that later."

He walked to the window and looked out at the sunny little garden, and then walked back into the room. He took his pince-nez out of his pocket and, though he had no intention of putting them on, wiped them with his handkerchief. Millicent looked at him and in her eyes, unmistakably, was a look of irony which was quite cynical. Mr. Skinner was vexed. He had finished his week's work and he was a free man till Monday morning. Though he had told his wife that this garden-party was a great nuisance and he would much sooner have tea quietly in his own garden, he had been looking forward to it. He did not care very much about Chinese missions, but it would be interesting to meet the Bishop. And now this! It was not the kind of thing he cared to be mixed up in; it was most unpleasant to be told on a sudden that his son-in-law was a drunkard and a suicide. Millicent was thoughtfully smoothing her white cuffs. Her coolness irritated him; but instead of addressing her he spoke to his younger daughter.

"Why don't you sit down, Kathleen? Surely there are plenty of chairs in the room."

Kathleen drew forward a chair and without a word seated herself. Mr. Skinner stopped in front of Millicent and faced her.

"Of course I see why you told us Harold had died of fever. I think it was a mistake, because that sort of thing is bound to come out sooner or later. I don't know how far what the Bishop has told the Heywoods coincides with the facts, but if you will take my advice you will tell us everything as circumstantially as you can, then we can see. We can't hope that it will go no further now that Canon Heywood and Gladys know. In a place like this people are bound to talk. It will make it easier for all of us if we at all events know the exact truth."

Mrs. Skinner and Kathleen thought he put the matter very well. They waited for Millicent's reply. She had listened with an impassive face; that sudden flush had disappeared and it was once more, as usual, pasty and sallow.

"I don't think you'll much like the truth if I tell it to you," she said.

"You must know that you can count on our sympathy and understanding," said Kathleen gravely.

Millicent gave her a glance and the shadow of a smile flickered across her set mouth. She looked slowly at the three of them. Mrs. Skinner had an uneasy impression that she looked at them as though they were mannequins at a dressmaker's. She seemed to live in a different world from theirs and to have no connection with them.

"You know, I wasn't in love with Harold when I married him," she said reflectively.

Mrs. Skinner was on the point of making an exclamation when a rapid gesture of her husband, barely indicated, but after so many years of married life perfectly significant, stopped her. Millicent went on. She spoke with a level voice, slowly, and there was little change of expression in her tone.

"I was twenty-seven, and no one else seemed to want to marry me. It's true he was forty-four, and it seemed rather old, but he had a very good position, hadn't he? I wasn't likely to get a better chance."

Mrs. Skinner felt inclined to cry again, but she remembered the party.

"Of course I see now why you took his photograph away," she said dolefully.

"Don't, mother," exclaimed Kathleen.

It had been taken when he was engaged to Millicent and was a very good photograph of Harold. Mrs. Skinner had always thought him quite a fine man. He was heavily built, tall and perhaps a little too fat, but he held himself well, and his presence was imposing. He was inclined to be bald, even then, but men did go bald very early nowadays, and he said that topees, sun-helmets, you know, were very bad for the hair. He had a small dark moustache and his face was deeply burned by the sun. Of course his best feature was his eyes; they were brown and large, like Joan's. His conversation was interesting. Kathleen said he was pompous, but Mrs. Skinner didn't think him so, she didn't mind it if a man laid down the law; and when she saw, as she very soon did, that he was attracted by Millicent she began to like him very much. He was always very attentive to Mrs. Skinner and she listened as though she were really interested when he spoke of his district and told her of the big game he had killed. Kathleen said he had a pretty good opinion of himself, but Mrs. Skinner came of a generation which accepted without question the good opinion that men had of themselves. Millicent saw very soon which way the wind blew and, though she said nothing to her mother, her mother knew that if Harold asked her she was going to accept him.

Harold was staying with some people who had been thirty years in Borneo and they spoke well of the country. There was no reason why a woman shouldn't live there comfortably; of course the children had to come home when they were seven; but Mrs. Skinner thought it unnecessary to trouble about that yet. She asked Harold to dine and she told him they were always in to tea. He seemed to be at a loose end and when his visit to his old friends was drawing to a close she told him they would be very much pleased if he would come and spend a fortnight with them.

It was towards the end of this that Harold and Millicent became engaged. They had a very pretty wedding, they went to Venice for their honeymoon, and then they started for the East. Millicent wrote from the various ports at which the ship touched. She seemed happy.

"People were very nice to me at Kuala Solor," she said. Kuala Solor was the chief town of the state of Sembulu. "We stayed with the Resident and every one asked us to dinner. Once or twice I heard men ask Harold to have a drink but he refused; he said he had turned over a new leaf now he was a married man. I didn't know why they laughed. Mrs. Gray, the Resident's wife, told me they were all so glad Harold was married. She said it was dreadfully lonely for a bachelor on one of the out-stations. When we left Kuala Solor Mrs. Gray said good-bye to me so funnily that I was quite surprised. It was as if she was solemnly putting Harold in my charge."

They listened to her in silence. Kathleen never took her eyes off her sister's impassive face, but Mr. Skinner stared straight in front of him at the Malay arms, krises and parangs, which hung on the wall above the sofa on which his wife sat.

"It wasn't till I went back to Kuala Solor a year and a half later that I found out why their manner had seemed so odd." Millicent gave a queer little sound like the echo of a scornful laugh. "I knew then a good deal that I hadn't known before. Harold came to England that time in order to marry. He didn't much mind who it was. Do you remember how we spread ourselves out to catch him, mother? We needn't have taken so much trouble."

"I don't know what you mean, Millicent," said Mrs. Skinner, not without acerbity, for the insinuation of scheming did not please her. "I saw he was attracted by you."

Millicent shrugged her heavy shoulders.

"He was a confirmed drunkard. He used to go to bed every night with a bottle of whisky and empty it before morning. The Chief Secretary told him he'd have to resign unless he stopped drinking. He said he'd give him one more chance. He could take his leave then and go to England. He advised him to marry so that when he got back he'd have some one to look after him. Harold married me because he wanted a keeper. They took bets in Kuala Solor on how long I'd make him stay sober."

"But he was in love with you," Mrs. Skinner interrupted. "You don't know how he used to speak to me about you, and at that time you're speaking of, when you went to Kuala Solor to have Joan, he wrote me such a charming letter about you."

Millicent looked at her mother again and a deep colour dyed her sallow skin. Her hands, lying on her lap, began to tremble a little. She thought of those first months of her married life. The Government launch took them to the mouth of the river and they spent the night at the bungalow which Harold said jokingly was their seaside residence. Next day they went up-stream in a prahu. From the novels she had read she expected the rivers of Borneo to be dark and strangely sinister, but the sky was blue, dappled with little white clouds, and the green of the mangroves and the nipas, washed by the flowing water, glistened in the sun. On each side stretched the pathless jungle, and in the distance, silhouetted against the sky, was the rugged outline of a mountain. The air in the early morning was fresh and buoyant. She seemed to enter upon a friendly, fertile land, and she had a sense of spacious freedom. They watched the banks for monkeys sitting on the branches of the tangled trees and once Harold pointed out something that looked like a log and said it was a crocodile. The Assistant Resident, in ducks and a topee, was at the landing-stage to meet them, and a dozen trim little soldiers were lined up to do them honour. The Assistant Resident was introduced to her. His name was Simpson.

"By Jove, sir," he said to Harold, "I'm glad to see you back. It's been deuced lonely without you."

The Resident's bungalow, surrounded by a garden in which grew wildly all manner of gay flowers, stood on the top of a low hill. It was a trifle shabby and the furniture was sparse, but the rooms were cool and of generous size.

"The kampong is down there," said Harold, pointing.

Her eyes followed his gesture, and from among the coconut trees rose the beating of a gong. It gave her a queer little sensation in the heart.

Though she had nothing much to do the days passed easily enough. At dawn a boy brought them their tea and they lounged about the verandah, enjoying the fragrance of the morning (Harold in a singlet and a sarong, she in a dressing-gown), till it was time to dress for breakfast. Then Harold went to his office and she spent an hour or two learning Malay. After tiffin

he went back to his office while she slept. A cup of tea revived
them both and they went for a walk or played golf on the nine-
hole links which Harold had made on a level piece of cleared
jungle below the bungalow. Night fell at six and Mr. Simpson
came along to have a drink. They chatted till their late dinner
hour, and sometimes Harold and Mr. Simpson played chess. The
balmy evenings were enchanting. The fireflies turned the bushes
just below the verandah into coldly sparkling, tremulous beacons,
and flowering trees scented the air with sweet odours. After dinner
they read the papers which had left London six weeks before and
presently went to bed. Millicent enjoyed being a married woman,
with a house of her own, and she was pleased with the native
servants, in their gay sarongs, who went about the bungalow,
with bare feet, silent but friendly. It gave her a pleasant sense
of importance to be the wife of the Resident. Harold impressed
her by the fluency with which he spoke the language, by his air
of command, and by his dignity. She went into the court-house
now and then to hear him try cases. The multifariousness of his
duties and the competent way in which he performed them
aroused her respect. Mr. Simpson told her that Harold understood
the natives as well as any man in the country. He had the combination of firmness, tact, and good humour which was essential in deal-
ing with that timid, revengeful, and suspicious race. Millicent began to feel a certain admiration for her husband.

They had been married nearly a year when two English
naturalists came to stay with them for a few days on their way to
the interior. They brought a pressing recommendation from the
Governor and Harold said he wanted to do them proud. Their
arrival was an agreeable change. Millicent asked Mr. Simpson to
dinner (he lived at the Fort and only dined with them on Sunday
nights) and after dinner the men sat down to play bridge. Millicent left them presently and went to bed, but they were so noisy
that for some time she could not get to sleep. She did not know at
what hour she was awakened by Harold staggering into the
room. She kept silent. He made up his mind to have a bath before
getting into bed; the bath-house was just below their room and he
went down the steps that led to it. Apparently he slipped, for
there was a great clatter, and he began to swear. Then he was
violently sick. She heard him sluice the buckets of water over
himself and in a little while, walking very cautiously this time, he

crawled up the stairs and slipped into bed. Millicent pretended to
be asleep. She was disgusted. Harold was drunk. She made up
her mind to speak about it in the morning. What would the
naturalists think of him? But in the morning Harold was so
dignified that she hadn't quite the determination to refer to the
matter. At eight Harold and she, with their two guests, sat down
to breakfast. Harold looked round the table.

"Porridge," he said. "Millicent, your guests might manage a little Worcester Sauce for breakfast, but I don't think they'll much
fancy anything else. Personally I shall content myself with a whisky
and soda."

The naturalists laughed, but shamefacedly.

"Your husband's a terror," said one of them.

"I should not think I had properly performed the duties of
hospitality if I sent you sober to bed on the first night of your
visit," said Harold, with his round, stately way of putting things.

Millicent, smiling acidly, was relieved to think that her guests
had been as drunk as her husband. The next evening she sat up
with them and the party broke up at a reasonable hour. But she
was glad when the strangers went on with their journey. Their
life resumed its placid course. Some months later Harold went on a
tour of inspection of his district and came back with a bad attack
of malaria. This was the first time she had seen the disease of
which she had heard so much, and when he recovered it did not
seem strange to her that Harold was very shaky. She found his
manner peculiar. He would come back from the office and stare at
her with glazed eyes; he would stand on the verandah, swaying
slightly, but still dignified, and make long harangues about the
political situation in England; losing the thread of his discourse,
he would look at her with an archness which his natural stateliness
made somewhat disconcerting and say:

"Pulls you down dreadfully, this confounded malaria. Ah, little
woman, you little know the strain it puts upon a man to be an
empire builder."

She thought that Mr. Simpson began to looked worried, and
once or twice, when they were alone, he seemed on the point of
saying something to her which his shyness at the last moment
prevented. The feeling grew so strong that it made her nervous
and one evening when Harold, she knew not why, had remained
later than usual at the office she tackled him.

"What have you got to say to me, Mr. Simpson?" she broke out suddenly.

He blushed and hesitated.

"Nothing. What makes you think I have anything in particular to say to you?"

Mr. Simpson was a thin, weedy youth of four and twenty, with a fine head of waving hair which he took great pains to plaster down very flat. His wrists were swollen and scarred with mosquito bites. Millicent looked at him steadily.

"If it's something to do with Harold, don't you think it would be kinder to tell me frankly?"

He grew scarlet now. He shuffled uneasily on his rattan chair. She insisted.

"I'm afraid you'll think it awful cheek," he said at last. "It's rotten of me to say anything about my chief behind his back. Malaria's a rotten thing and after one's had a bout of it one feels awfully down and out."

He hesitated again. The corners of his mouth sagged as if he were going to cry. To Millicent he seemed like a little boy.

"I'll be as silent as the grave," she said with a smile, trying to conceal her apprehension. "Do tell me."

"I think it's a pity your husband keeps a bottle of whisky at the office. He's apt to take a nip more often than he otherwise would."

Mr. Simpson's voice was hoarse with agitation. Millicent felt a sudden coldness shiver through her. She controlled herself, for she knew that she must not frighten the boy if she were to get out of him all there was to tell. He was unwilling to speak. She pressed him, wheedling, appealing to his sense of duty, and at last she began to cry. Then he told her that Harold had been drunk more or less for the last fortnight, the natives were talking about it, and they said that soon he would be as bad as he had been before his marriage. He had been in the habit of drinking a good deal too much then, but details of that time, notwithstanding all her attempts, Mr. Simpson resolutely declined to give her.

"Do you think he's drinking now?" she asked.

"I don't know."

Millicent felt herself on a sudden hot with shame and anger. The Fort, as it was called because the rifles and the ammunition were kept there, was also the court-house. It stood opposite the

Resident's bungalow in a garden of its own. The sun was just about to set and she did not need a hat. She got up and walked across. She found Harold sitting in the office behind the large hall in which he administered justice. There was a bottle of whisky in front of him. He was smoking cigarettes and talking to three or four Malays who stood in front of him listening with obsequious and at the same time scornful smiles. His face was red.

The natives vanished.

"I came to see what you were doing," she said.

He rose, for he always treated her with elaborate politeness, and lurched. Feeling himself unsteady he assumed an elaborate stateliness of demeanour.

"Take a seat, my dear, take a seat. I was detained by press of work."

She looked at him with angry eyes.

"You're drunk," she said.

He stared at her, his eyes bulging a little, and a haughty look gradually traversed his large and fleshy face.

"I haven't the remotest idea what you mean," he said.

She had been ready with a flow of wrathful expostulation, but suddenly she burst into tears. She sank into a chair and hid her face. Harold looked at her for an instant, then the tears began to trickle down his cheeks; he came towards her with outstretched arms and fell heavily on his knees. Sobbing, he clasped her to him.

"Forgive me, forgive me," he said. "I promise you it shall not happen again. It was that damned malaria."

"It's so humiliating," she moaned.

He wept like a child. There was something very touching in the self-abasement of that big dignified man. Presently Millicent looked up. His eyes, appealing and contrite, sought hers.

"Will you give me your word of honour that you'll never touch liquor again?"

"Yes, yes. I hate it."

It was then she told him that she was with child. He was overjoyed.

"That is the one thing I wanted. That'll keep me straight."

They went back to the bungalow. Harold bathed himself and had a nap. After dinner they talked long and quietly. He admitted that before he married her he had occasionally drunk more than was good for him: in out-stations it was easy to fall into bad habits. He agreed to everything that Millicent asked. And during the months before it was necessary for her to go to Kuala Solor for her confinement Harold was an excellent husband, tender, thoughtful, proud and affectionate: he was irreproachable. A launch came to fetch her, she was to leave him for six weeks, and he promised faithfully to drink nothing during her absence. He put his hands on her shoulders.

"I never break a promise," he said in his dignified way. "But even without it, can you imagine that while you are going through so much, I should do anything to increase your troubles?"

Joan was born. Millicent stayed at the Resident's and Mrs. Gray, his wife, a kindly creature of middle age, was very good to her. The two women had little to do during the long hours they were alone but to talk, and in course of time Millicent learnt everything there was to know of her husband's alcoholic past. The fact which she found most difficult to reconcile herself to was that Harold had been told that the only condition upon which he would be allowed to keep his post was that he should bring back a wife. It caused in her a dull feeling of resentment. And when she discovered what a persistent drunkard he had been she felt vaguely uneasy. She had a horrid fear that during her absence he would not have been able to resist the craving. She went home with her baby and a nurse. She spent a night at the mouth of the river and sent a messenger in a canoe to announce her arrival. She scanned the landing-stage anxiously as the launch approached it. Harold and Mr. Simpson were standing there. The trim little soldiers were lined up. Her heart sank, for Harold was swaying slightly, like a man who seeks to keep his balance on a rolling ship, and she knew he was drunk.

It wasn't a very pleasant home-coming. She had almost forgotten her mother and father and her sister who sat there silently listening to her. Now she roused herself and became once more aware of their presence. All that she spoke of seemed very far away.

"I knew that I hated him then," she said. "I could have killed him."

"Oh, Millicent, don't say that," cried her mother. "Don't forget that he's dead, poor man."

Millicent looked at her mother, and for a moment a scowl darkened her impassive face. Mr. Skinner moved uneasily.

"Go on," said Kathleen.

"When he found out that I knew all about him he didn't bother very much more. In three months he had another attack of D. T.'s."

"Why didn't you leave him?" said Kathleen.

"What would have been the good of that? He would have been dismissed from the service in a fortnight. Who was to keep me and Joan? I had to stay. And when he was sober I had nothing to complain of. He wasn't in the least in love with me, but he was fond of me: I hadn't married him because I was in love with him but because I wanted to be married. I did everything I could to keep liquor from him; I managed to get Mr. Gray to prevent whisky being sent from Kuala Solor, but he got it from the Chinese. I watched him as a cat watches a mouse. He was too cunning for me. In a little while he had another outbreak. He neglected his duties. I was afraid complaints would be made. We were two days from Kuala Solor and that was our safeguard, but I suppose something was said, for Mr. Gray wrote a private letter of warning to me. I showed it to Harold. He stormed and blustered, but I saw he was frightened, and for two or three months he was quite sober. Then he began again. And so it went on till our leave became due.

"Before we came to stay here I begged and prayed him to be careful. I didn't want any of you to know what sort of a man I had married. All the time he was in England he was all right and before we sailed I warned him. He'd grown to be very fond of Joan, and very proud of her, and she was devoted to him. She always liked him better than she liked me. I asked him if he wanted to have his child grow up knowing that he was a drunkard, and I found out that at last I'd got a hold on him. The thought terrified him. I told him that *I* wouldn't allow it, and if he ever let Joan see him drunk I'd take her away from him at once. Do you know, he grew quite pale when I said it. I fell on my knees that night and thanked God because I'd found a way of saving my husband.

"He told me that if I would stand by him he would have another try. We made up our minds to fight the thing together. And he tried so hard. When he felt as though he *must* drink he came to me. You know he was inclined to be rather pompous: with me he was so humble, he was like a child; he depended on me. Perhaps he didn't love me when he married me, but he loved me then, me and Joan. I'd hated him, because of the humiliation, because when he was drunk and tried to be dignified and impressive he was loathsome; but now I got a strange feeling in my heart. It wasn't love, but it was a queer, shy tenderness. He was something more than my husband, he was like a child that I'd carried under my heart for long and weary months. He was so proud of me and you know, I was proud too. His long speeches didn't irritate me any more and I only thought his stately ways rather funny and charming. At last we won. For two years he never touched a drop. He lost his craving entirely. He was even able to joke about it.

"Mr. Simpson had left us then and we had another young man called Francis.

"'I'm a reformed drunkard you know, Francis,' Harold said to him once. 'If it hadn't been for my wife I'd have been sacked long ago. I've got the best wife in the world, Francis.'

"You don't know what it meant to me to hear him say that. I felt that all I'd gone through was worth while. I was so happy."

She was silent. She thought of the broad, yellow and turbid river on whose banks she had lived so long. The egrets, white and gleaming in the tremulous sunset, flew down the stream in a flock, flew low and swift, and scattered. They were like a ripple of snowy notes, sweet and pure and spring-like, which an unseen hand drew forth, a divine arpeggio, from an unseen harp. They fluttered along between the green banks, wrapped in the shadows of evening, like the happy thoughts of a contented mind.

"Then Joan fell ill. For three weeks we were very anxious. There was no doctor nearer than Kuala Solor and we had to put up with the treatment of a native dispenser. When she grew well again I took her down to the mouth of the river in order to give her a breath of sea air. We stayed there a week. It was the first time I had been separated from Harold since I went away to have Joan. There was a fishing village, on piles, not far from us, but really we were quite alone. I thought a great deal about Harold, so tenderly, and all at once I knew that I loved him. I was so glad when the prahu came to fetch us back, because I wanted to tell him. I thought it would mean a good deal to him. I can't tell you how happy I was. As we rowed up-stream the headman told me that Mr. Francis had had to go up-country to arrest a woman who had murdered her husband. He had been gone a couple of days.

"I was surprised that Harold was not on the landing-stage to meet me; he was always very punctilious about that sort of thing; he used to say that husband and wife should treat one another as politely as they treated acquaintances; and I could not imagine what business had prevented him. I walked up the little hill on which the bungalow stood. The ayah brought Joan behind me. The bungalow was strangely silent. There seemed to be no servants about and I could not make it out; I wondered if Harold hadn't expected me so soon and was out. I went up the steps. Joan was thirsty and the ayah took her to the servants' quarters to give her something to drink. Harold was not in the sitting-room. I called him, but there was no answer. I was disappointed, because I should have liked him to be there. I went into our bedroom. Harold wasn't out after all: he was lying on the bed asleep. I was really very much amused because he always pretended he never slept in the afternoon. He said it was an unnecessary habit that we white people got into. I went up to the bed softly. I thought I would have a joke with him. I opened the mosquito curtains. He was lying on his back, with nothing on but a sarong, and there was an empty whisky bottle by his side. He was drunk.

"It had begun again. All my struggles for so many years were wasted. My dream was shattered. It was all hopeless. I was seized with rage."

Millicent's face grew once again darkly red and she clenched the arms of the chair she sat in.

"I took him by the shoulders and shook him with all my might. 'You beast,' I cried, 'you beast.' I was so angry I don't know what I did, I don't know what I said. I kept on shaking him. You don't know how loathsome he looked, that large fat man, half naked; he hadn't shaved for days, and his face was bloated and purple. He was breathing heavily. I shouted at him, but he took no notice. I tried to drag him out of bed, but he was too heavy. He lay there like log. 'Open your eyes,' I screamed. I shook him again. I hated him. I hated him all the more because for a week I'd loved him with all my heart. He'd let me down.

He'd let me down. I wanted to tell him what a filthy beast he was. I could make no impression on him. 'You shall open your eyes,' I cried. I was determined to make him look at me."

The widow licked her dry lips. Her breath seemed hurried. She was silent.

"If he was in that state I should have thought it best to have let him go on sleeping," said Kathleen.

"There was a parang on the wall by the side of the bed. You know how fond Harold was of curios."

"What's a parang?" said Mrs. Skinner.

"Don't be silly, mother," her husband replied irritably. "There's one on the wall immediately behind you."

He pointed to the Malay sword on which for some reason his eyes had been unconsciously resting. Mrs. Skinner drew quickly into the corner of the sofa, with a little frightened gesture, as though she had been told that a snake lay curled up beside her.

"Suddenly the blood spurted out from Harold's throat. There was a great red gash right across it."

"Millicent," cried Kathleen, springing up and almost leaping towards her, "what in God's name do you mean?"

Mrs. Skinner stood staring at her with wide startled eyes, her mouth open.

"The parang wasn't on the wall any more. It was on the bed. Then Harold opened his eyes. They were just like Joan's."

"I don't understand," said Mr. Skinner. "How could he have committed suicide if he was in the state you describe?"

Kathleen took her sister's arm and shook her angrily.

"Millicent, for God's sake, explain."

Millicent released herself.

"The parang was on the wall, I told you. I don't know what happened. There was all the blood and Harold opened his eyes. He died almost at once. He never spoke, but he gave a sort of gasp."

At last Mr. Skinner found his voice.

"But, you wretched woman, it was murder."

Millicent, her face mottled with red, gave him such a look of scornful hatred that he shrank back. Mrs. Skinner cried out.

"Millicent, you didn't do it, did you?"

Then Millicent did something that made them all feel as though their blood were turned to ice in their veins. She chuckled.

"I don't know who else did," she said.

"My God," muttered Mr. Skinner.

Kathleen had been standing bolt upright, with her hands to her heart, as though its beating were intolerable.

"And what happened then?" she said.

"I screamed. I went to the window and flung it open. I called for the ayah. She came across the compound with Joan. 'Not Joan,' I cried. 'Don't let her come.' She called the cook and told him to take the child. I cried to her to hurry. And when she came I showed her Harold. 'The Tuan's killed himself!' I cried. She gave a scream and ran out of the house.

"No one would come near. They were all frightened out of their wits. I wrote a letter to Mr. Francis, telling him what had happened, and asking him to come at once."

"How do you mean you told him what had happened?"

"I said, on my return from the mouth of the river, I'd found Harold with his throat cut. You know, in the tropics you have to bury people quickly. I got a Chinese coffin, and the soldiers dug a grave behind the Fort. When Mr. Francis came Harold had been buried for nearly two days. He was only a boy. I could do anything I wanted with him. I told him I'd found the parang in Harold's hand and there was no doubt he'd killed himself in an attack of *delirium tremens*. I showed him the empty bottle. The servants said he'd been drinking hard ever since I left to go to the sea. I told the same story at Kuala Solor. Every one was very kind to me, and the Government granted me a pension."

For a little while nobody spoke. At last Mr. Skinner gathered himself together.

"I am a member of the legal profession. I'm a solicitor. I have certain duties. We've always had a most respectable practice. You've put me in a monstrous position."

He fumbled, searching for the phrases that played at hide and seek in his scattered wits. Millicent looked at him with scorn.

"What are you going to do about it?"

"It was murder, that's what it was; do you think I can possibly connive at it?"

"Don't talk nonsense, father," said Kathleen sharply. "You can't give your own daughter up."

"You've put me in a monstrous position," he repeated.

Millicent shrugged her shoulders again.

"You made me tell you. And I've borne it long enough by myself. It was time that all of you bore it too."

At that moment the door was opened by the maid.

"Davis has brought the car round, sir," she said.

Kathleen had the presence of mind to say something, and the maid withdrew.

"We'd better be starting," said Millicent.

"I can't go to the party now," cried Mrs. Skinner, with horror. "I'm far too upset. How can we face the Heywoods? And the Bishop will want to be introduced to you."

Millicent made a gesture of indifference. Her eyes held their ironical expression.

"We must go, mother," said Kathleen. "It would look so funny if we stayed away." She turned on Millicent furiously. "Oh, I think the whole thing is such frightfully bad form."

Mrs. Skinner looked helplessly at her husband. He went to her and gave her his hand to help her up from the sofa.

"I'm afraid we must go, mother," he said.

"And me with the ospreys in my toque that Harold gave me with his own hands," she moaned.

He led her out of the room, Kathleen followed close on their heels, and a step or two behind came Millicent.

"You'll get used to it, you know," she said quietly. "At first I thought of it all the time, but now I forget it for two or three days together. It's not as if there was any danger."

They did not answer. They walked through the hall and out of the front door. The three ladies got into the back of the car and Mr. Skinner seated himself beside the driver. They had no self-starter; it was an old car, and Davis went to the bonnet to crank it up. Mr. Skinner turned round and looked petulantly at Millicent.

"I ought never to have been told," he said. "I think it was most selfish of you."

Davis took his seat and they drove off to the Canon's garden-party.

Rain

It was nearly bed-time and when they awoke next morning land would be in sight. Dr. Macphail lit his pipe and, leaning over the rail, searched the heavens for the Southern Cross. After two years at the front and a wound that had taken longer to heal than it should, he was glad to settle down quietly at Apia for twelve months at least, and he felt already better for the journey. Since some of the passengers were leaving the ship next day at Pago-Pago they had had a little dance that evening and in his ears hammered still the harsh notes of the mechanical piano. But the deck was quiet at last. A little way off he saw his wife in a long chair talking with the Davidsons, and he strolled over to her. When he sat down under the light and took off his hat you saw that he had very red hair, with a bald patch on the crown, and the red, freckled skin which accompanies red hair; he was a man of forty, thin, with a pinched face, precise and rather pedantic; and he spoke with a Scots accent in a very low, quiet voice.

Between the Macphails and the Davidsons, who were missionaries, there had arisen the intimacy of shipboard, which is due to propinquity rather than to any community of taste. Their chief tie was the disapproval they shared of the men who spent their days and nights in the smoking-room playing poker or bridge and drinking. Mrs. Macphail was not a little flattered to think that she and her husband were the only people on board with whom the Davidsons were willing to associate, and even the doctor, shy but no fool, half unconsciously acknowledged the compliment. It was only because he was of an argumentative mind that in their cabin at night he permitted himself to carp.

"Mrs. Davidson was saying she didn't know how they'd have got through the journey if it hadn't been for us," said Mrs. Macphail, as she neatly brushed out her transformation. "She said we were really the only people on the ship they cared to know."

"I shouldn't have thought a missionary was such a big bug that he could afford to put on frills."

"It's not frills. I quite understand what she means. It wouldn't have been very nice for the Davidsons to have to mix with all that rough lot in the smoking-room."

"The founder of their religion wasn't so exclusive," said Dr. Macphail with a chuckle.

"I've asked you over and over again not to joke about religion," answered his wife. "I shouldn't like to have a nature like yours, Alec. You never look for the best in people."

He gave her a sidelong glance with his pale, blue eyes, but did not reply. After many years of married life he had learned that it was more conducive to peace to leave his wife with the last word. He was undressed before she was, and climbing into the upper bunk he settled down to read himself to sleep.

When he came on deck next morning they were close to land. He looked at it with greedy eyes. There was a thin strip of silver beach rising quickly to hills covered to the top with luxuriant vegetation. The coconut trees, thick and green, came nearly to the water's edge, and among them you saw the grass houses of the Samoans; and here and there, gleaming white, a little church. Mrs. Davidson came and stood beside him. She was dressed in black and wore round her neck a gold chain, from which dangled a small cross. She was a little woman, with brown, dull hair very elaborately arranged, and she had prominent blue eyes behind invisible *pince-nez*. Her face was long, like a sheep's, but she gave no impression of foolishness, rather of extreme alertness; she had the quick movements of a bird. The most remarkable thing about her was her voice, high, metallic, and without inflection; it fell on the ear with a hard monotony, irritating to the nerves like the pitiless clamour of the pneumatic drill.

"This must seem like home to you," said Dr. Macphail, with his thin, difficult smile.

"Ours are low islands, you know, not like these. Coral. These are volcanic. We've got another ten days' journey to reach them."

"In these parts that's almost like being in the next street at home," said Dr. Macphail facetiously.

"Well, that's rather an exaggerated way of putting it, but one does look at distances differently in the South Seas. So far you're right."

Dr. Macphail sighed faintly.

"I'm glad we're not stationed here," she went on. "They say this is a terribly difficult place to work in. The steamers' touching makes the people unsettled; and then there's the naval station; that's bad for the natives. In our district we don't have difficulties like that to contend with. There are one or two traders, of course, but we take care to make them behave, and if they don't we make the place so hot for them they're glad to go."

Fixing the glasses on her nose she looked at the green island with a ruthless stare.

"It's almost a hopeless task for the missionaries here. I can never be sufficiently thankful to God that we are at least spared that."

Davidson's district consisted of a group of islands to the North of Samoa; they were widely separated and he had frequently to go long distances by canoe. At these times his wife remained at their headquarters and managed the mission. Dr. Macphail felt his heart sink when he considered the efficiency with which she certainly managed it. She spoke of the depravity of the natives in a voice which nothing could hush, but with a vehemently unctuous horror. Her sense of delicacy was singular. Early in their acquaintance she had said to him:

"You know, their marriage customs when we first settled in the islands were so shocking that I couldn't possibly describe them to you. But I'll tell Mrs. Macphail and she'll tell you."

Then he had seen his wife and Mrs. Davidson, their deck-chairs close together, in earnest conversation for about two hours. As he walked past them backwards and forwards for the sake of exercise, he had heard Mrs. Davidson's agitated whisper, like the distant flow of a mountain torrent, and he saw by his wife's open mouth and pale face that she was enjoying an alarming experience. At night in their cabin she repeated to him with bated breath all she had heard.

"Well, what did I say to you?" cried Mrs. Davidson, exultant, next morning. "Did you ever hear anything more dreadful? You don't wonder that I couldn't tell you myself, do you? Even though you are a doctor."

Mrs. Davidson scanned his face. She had a dramatic eagerness to see that she had achieved the desired effect.

"Can you wonder that when we first went there our hearts

sank? You'll hardly believe me when I tell you it was impossible to find a single good girl in any of the villages."

She used the word *good* in a severely technical manner.

"Mr. Davidson and I talked it over, and we made up our minds the first thing to do was to put down the dancing. The natives were crazy about dancing."

"I was not averse to it myself when I was a young man," said Dr. Macphail.

"I guessed as much when I heard you ask Mrs. Macphail to have a turn with you last night. I don't think there's any real harm if a man dances with his wife, but I was relieved that she wouldn't. Under the circumstances I thought it better that we should keep ourselves to ourselves."

"Under what circumstances?"

Mrs. Davidson gave him a quick look through her *pince-nez*, but did not answer his question.

"But among white people it's not quite the same," she went on, "though I must say I agree with Mr. Davidson, who says he can't understand how a husband can stand by and see his wife in another man's arms, and as far as I'm concerned I've never danced a step since I married. But the native dancing is quite another matter. It's not only immoral in itself, but it distinctly leads to immorality. However, I'm thankful to God that we stamped it out, and I don't think I'm wrong in saying that no one has danced in our district for eight years."

But now they came to the mouth of the harbour and Mrs. Macphail joined them. The ship turned sharply and steamed slowly in. It was a great land-locked harbour big enough to hold a fleet of battleships; and all around it rose, high and steep, the green hills. Near the entrance, getting such breeze as blew from the sea, stood the governor's house in a garden. The Stars and Stripes dangled languidly from a flagstaff. They passed two or three trim bungalows, and a tennis court, and then they came to the quay with its warehouses. Mrs. Davidson pointed out the schooner, moored two or three hundred yards from the side, which was to take them to Apia. There was a crowd of eager, noisy, and good-humoured natives come from all parts of the island, some from curiosity, others to barter with the travellers on their way to Sydney; and they brought pineapples and huge bunches of bananas, *tapa* cloths, necklaces of shells or sharks' teeth, *kava-*

bowls, and models of war canoes. American sailors, neat and trim, clean-shaven and frank of face, sauntered among them, and there was a little group of officials. While their luggage was being landed the Macphails and Mrs. Davidson watched the crowd. Dr. Macphail looked at the yaws from which most of the children and the young boys seemed to suffer, disfiguring sores like torpid ulcers, and his professional eyes glistened when he saw for the first time in his experience cases of elephantiasis, men going about with a huge, heavy arm or dragging along a grossly disfigured leg. Men and women wore the *lava-lava.*

"It's a very indecent costume," said Mrs. Davidson. "Mr. Davidson thinks it should be prohibited by law. How can you expect people to be moral when they wear nothing but a strip of red cotton round their loins?"

"It's suitable enough to the climate," said the doctor, wiping the sweat off his head.

Now that they were on land the heat, though it was so early in the morning, was already oppressive. Closed in by its hills, not a breath of air came in to Pago-Pago.

"In our islands," Mrs. Davidson went on in her high-pitched tones, "we've practically eradicated the *lava-lava.* A few old men still continue to wear it, but that's all. The women have all taken to the Mother Hubbard, and the men wear trousers and singlets. At the very beginning of our stay Mr. Davidson said in one of his reports: the inhabitants of these islands will never be thoroughly Christianized till every boy of more than ten years is made to wear a pair of trousers."

But Mrs. Davidson had given two or three of her birdlike glances at heavy grey clouds that came floating over the mouth of the harbour. A few drops began to fall.

"We'd better take shelter," she said.

They made their way with all the crowd to a great shed of corrugated iron, and the rain began to fall in torrents. They stood there for some time and then were joined by Mr. Davidson. He had been polite enough to the Macphails during the journey, but he had not his wife's sociability, and had spent much of his time reading. He was a silent, rather sullen man, and you felt that his affability was a duty that he imposed upon himself Christianly; he was by nature reserved and even morose. His appearance was singular. He was very tall and thin, with

long limbs loosely jointed; hollow cheeks and curiously high cheek-
bones; he had so cadaverous an air that it surprised you to notice
how full and sensual were his lips. He wore his hair very long.
His dark eyes, set deep in their sockets, were large and tragic;
and his hands with their big, long fingers, were finely shaped;
they gave him a look of great strength. But the most striking thing
about him was the feeling he gave you of suppressed fire. It was
impressive and vaguely troubling. He was not a man with whom
any intimacy was possible.

He brought now unwelcome news. There was an epidemic of
measles, a serious and often fatal disease among the Kanakas,
on the island, and a case had developed among the crew of the
schooner which was to take them on their journey. The sick man
had been brought ashore and put in hospital on the quarantine
station, but telegraphic instructions had been sent from Apia to
say that the schooner would not be allowed to enter the harbour
till it was certain no other member of the crew was affected.

"It means we shall have to stay here for ten days at least."

"But I'm urgently needed at Apia," said Dr. Macphail.

"That can't be helped. If no more cases develop on board,
the schooner will be allowed to sail with white passengers, but
all native traffic is prohibited for three months."

"Is there a hotel here?" asked Mrs. Macphail.

Davidson gave a low chuckle.

"There's not."

"What shall we do then?"

"I've been talking to the governor. There's a trader along the
front who has rooms that he rents, and my proposition is that
as soon as the rain lets up we should go along there and see
what we can do. Don't expect comfort. You've just got to be thankful if we get a bed to sleep on and a roof over our heads."

But the rain showed no sign of stopping, and at length with
umbrellas and waterproofs they set out. There was no town, but
merely a group of official buildings, a store or two, and at the
back, among the coconut trees and plantains, a few native dwellings. The house they sought was about five minutes' walk from
the wharf. It was a frame house of two storeys, with broad verandahs on both floors and a roof of corrugated iron. The owner was
a half-caste named Horn, with a native wife surrounded by little
brown children, and on the ground-floor he had a store where he

sold canned goods and cottons. The rooms he showed them were almost bare of furniture. In the Macphails' there was nothing but a poor, worn bed with a ragged mosquito net, a rickety chair, and a washstand. They looked round with dismay. The rain poured down without ceasing.

"I'm not going to unpack more than we actually need," said Mrs. Macphail.

Mrs. Davidson came into the room as she was unlocking a portmanteau. She was very brisk and alert. The cheerless surroundings had no effect on her.

"If you'll take my advice you'll get a needle and cotton and start right in to mend the mosquito net," she said, "or you'll not be able to get a wink of sleep to-night."

"Will they be very bad?" asked Dr. Macphail.

"This is the season for them. When you're asked to a party at Government House at Apia you'll notice that all the ladies are given a pillow-slip to put their—their lower extremities in."

"I wish the rain would stop for a moment," said Mrs. Macphail. "I could try to make the place comfortable with more heart if the sun were shining."

"Oh, if you wait for that, you'll wait a long time. Pago-Pago is about the rainiest place in the Pacific. You see, the hills, and that bay, they attract the water, and one expects rain at this time of year anyway."

She looked from Macphail to his wife, standing helplessly in different parts of the room, like lost souls, and she pursed her lips. She saw that she must take them in hand. Feckless people like that made her impatient, but her hands itched to put everything in order which came so naturally to her.

"Here, you give me a needle and cotton and I'll mend that net of yours, while you go on with your unpacking. Dinner's at one. Dr. Macphail, you'd better go down to the wharf and see that your heavy luggage has been put in a dry place. You know what these natives are, they're quite capable of storing it where the rain will beat in on it all the time."

The doctor put on his waterproof again and went downstairs. At the door Mr. Horn was standing in conversation with the quartermaster of the ship they had just arrived in and a second-class passenger whom Dr. Macphail had seen several times on board. The quartermaster, a little, shrivelled man, extremely dirty, nodded to him as he passed.

"This is a bad job about the measles, doc," he said. "I see you've fixed yourself up already."

Dr. Macphail thought he was rather familiar, but he was a timid man and he did not take offence easily.

"Yes, we've got a room upstairs."

"Miss Thompson was sailing with you to Apia, so I've brought her along here."

The quartermaster pointed with his thumb to the woman standing by his side. She was twenty-seven perhaps, plump, and in a coarse fashion pretty. She wore a white dress and a large white hat. Her fat calves in white cotton stockings bulged over the tops of long white boots in glacé kid. She gave Macphail an ingratiating smile.

"The feller's tryin' to soak me a dollar and a half a day for the meanest sized room," she said in a hoarse voice.

"I tell you she's a friend of mine, Jo," said the quartermaster. "She can't pay more than a dollar, and you've sure got to take her for that."

The trader was fat and smooth and quietly smiling.

"Well, if you put it like that, Mr. Swan, I'll see what I can do about it. I'll talk to Mrs. Horn and if we think we can make a reduction we will."

"Don't try to pull that stuff with me," said Miss Thompson. "We'll settle this right now. You get a dollar a day for the room and not one bean more."

Dr. Macphail smiled. He admired the effrontery with which she bargained. He was the sort of man who always paid what he was asked. He preferred to be over-charged than to haggle. The trader sighed.

"Well, to oblige Mr. Swan I'll take it."

"That's the goods," said Miss Thompson. "Come right in and have a shot of hooch. I've got some real good rye in that grip if you'll bring it along, Mr. Swan. You come along too, doctor."

"Oh, I don't think I will, thank you," he answered. "I'm just going down to see that our luggage is all right."

He stepped out into the rain. It swept in from the opening of the harbour in sheets and the opposite shore was all blurred. He passed two or three natives clad in nothing but the *lava-lava*, with huge umbrellas over them. They walked finely, with leisurely movements, very upright; and they smiled and greeted him in a strange tongue as they went by.

It was nearly dinner-time when he got back, and their meal was laid in the trader's parlour. It was a room designed not to live in but for purposes of prestige, and it had a musty, melancholy air. A suite of stamped plush was arranged neatly round the walls, and from the middle of the ceiling, protected from the flies by yellow tissue paper, hung a gilt chandelier. Davidson did not come.

"I know he went to call on the governor," said Mrs. Davidson, "and I guess he's kept him to dinner."

A little native girl brought them a dish of hamburger steak, and after a while the trader came up to see that they had everything they wanted.

"I see we have a fellow lodger, Mr. Horn," said Dr. Macphail.

"She's taken a room, that's all," answered the trader. "She's getting her own board."

He looked at the two ladies with an obsequious air.

"I put her downstairs so she shouldn't be in the way. She won't be any trouble to you."

"Is it someone who was on the boat?" asked Mrs. Macphail.

"Yes, ma'am, she was in the second cabin. She was going to Apia. She has a position as cashier waiting for her."

"Oh!"

When the trader was gone Macphail said:

"I shouldn't think she'd find it exactly cheerful having her meals in her room."

"If she was in the second cabin I guess she'd rather," answered Mrs. Davidson. "I don't exactly know who it can be."

"I happened to be there when the quartermaster brought her along. Her name's Thompson."

"It's not the woman who was dancing with the quartermaster last night?" asked Mrs. Davidson.

"That's who it must be," said Mrs. Macphail. "I wondered at the time what she was. She looked rather fast to me."

"Not good style at all," said Mrs. Davidson.

They began to talk of other things, and after dinner, tired with their early rise, they separated and slept. When they awoke, though the sky was still grey and the clouds hung low, it was not raining and they went for a walk on the high road which the Americans had built along the bay.

On their return they found that Davidson had just come in.

"We may be here for a fortnight," he said irritably. "I've argued it out with the governor, but he says there is nothing to be done."

"Mr. Davidson's just longing to get back to his work," said his wife, with an anxious glance at him.

"We've been away for a year," he said, walking up and down the verandah. "The mission has been in charge of native missionaries and I'm terribly nervous that they've let things slide. They're good men, I'm not saying a word against them, God-fearing, devout, and truly Christian men—their Christianity would put many so-called Christians at home to the blush—but they're pitifully lacking in energy. They can make a stand once, they can make a stand twice, but they can't make a stand all the time. If you leave a mission in charge of a native missionary, no matter how trustworthy he seems, in course of time you'll find he's let abuses creep in."

Mr. Davidson stood still. With his tall, spare form, and his great eyes flashing out of his pale face, he was an impressive figure. His sincerity was obvious in the fire of his gestures and in his deep, ringing voice.

"I expect to have my work cut out for me. I shall act and I shall act promptly. If the tree is rotten it shall be cut down and cast into the flames."

And in the evening after the high tea which was their last meal, while they sat in the stiff parlour, the ladies working and Dr. Macphail smoking his pipe, the missionary told them of his work in the islands.

"When we went there they had no sense of sin at all," he said. "They broke the commandments one after the other and never knew they were doing wrong. And I think that was the most difficult part of my work, to instil into the natives the sense of sin."

The Macphails knew already that Davidson had worked in the Solomons for five years before he met his wife. She had been a missionary in China, and they had become acquainted in Boston, where they were both spending part of their leave to attend a missionary congress. On their marriage they had been appointed to the islands in which they had laboured ever since.

In the course of all the conversations they had had with Mr. Davidson one thing had shone out clearly and that was the man's unflinching courage. He was a medical missionary, and he was liable to be called at any time to one or other of the islands in the group. Even the whaleboat is not so very safe a conveyance in the stormy Pacific of the wet season, but often he would be sent for in a canoe, and then the danger was great. In cases of illness or accident he never hesitated. A dozen times he had spent the whole night baling for his life, and more than once Mrs. Davidson had given him up for lost.

"I'd beg him not to go sometimes," she said, "or at least to wait till the weather was more settled, but he'd never listen. He's obstinate, and when he's once made up his mind, nothing can move him."

"How can I ask the natives to put their trust in the Lord if I am afraid to do so myself?" cried Davidson. "And I'm not, I'm not. They know that if they send for me in their trouble I'll come if it's humanly possible. And do you think the Lord is going to abandon me when I am on his business? The wind blows at his bidding and the waves toss and rage at his word."

Dr. Macphail was a timid man. He had never been able to get used to the hurtling of the shells over the trenches, and when he was operating in an advanced dressing-station the sweat poured from his brow and dimmed his spectacles in the effort he made to control his unsteady hand. He shuddered a little as he looked at the missionary.

"I wish I could say that I've never been afraid," he said.

"I wish you could say that you believed in God," retorted the other.

But for some reason, that evening the missionary's thoughts travelled back to the early days he and his wife had spent on the islands.

"Sometimes Mrs. Davidson and I would look at one another and the tears would stream down our cheeks. We worked without ceasing, day and night, and we seemed to make no progress. I don't know what I should have done without her then. When I felt my heart sink, when I was very near despair, she gave me courage and hope."

Mrs. Davidson looked down at her work, and a slight colour

rose to her thin cheeks. Her hands trembled a little. She did not
trust herself to speak.

"We had no one to help us. We were alone, thousands of miles
from any of our own people, surrounded by darkness. When I
was broken and weary she would put her work aside and take the
Bible and read to me till peace came and settled upon me like
sleep upon the eyelids of a child, and when at last she closed the
book she'd say: 'We'll save them in spite of themselves.' And I felt
strong again in the Lord, and I answered: 'Yes, with God's help
I'll save them. I must save them.'"

He came over to the table and stood in front of it as though it
were a lectern.

"You see, they were so naturally depraved that they couldn't
be brought to see their wickedness. We had to make sins out of
what they thought were natural actions. We had to make it a sin,
not only to commit adultery and to lie and thieve, but to expose
their bodies, and to dance and not to come to church. I made it a
sin for a girl to show her bosom and a sin for a man not to wear
trousers."

"How?" asked Dr. Macphail, not without surprise.

"I instituted fines. Obviously the only way to make people realize that an action is sinful is to punish them if they commit it. I
fined them if they didn't come to church, and I fined them if
they danced. I fined them if they were improperly dressed. I had
a tariff, and every sin had to be paid for either in money or work.
And at last I made them understand."

"But did they never refuse to pay?"

"How could they?" asked the missionary.

"It would be a brave man who tried to stand up against Mr.
Davidson," said his wife, tightening her lips.

Dr. Macphail looked at Davidson with troubled eyes. What he
heard shocked him, but he hesitated to express his disapproval.

"You must remember that in the last resort I could expel them
from their church membership."

"Did they mind that?"

Davidson smiled a little and gently rubbed his hands.

"They couldn't sell their copra. When the men fished they got
no share of the catch. It meant something very like starvation.
Yes, they minded quite a lot."

"Tell him about Fred Ohlson," said Mrs. Davidson.

The missionary fixed his fiery eyes on Dr. Macphail.

"Fred Ohlson was a Danish trader who had been in the islands a good many years. He was a pretty rich man as traders go, and he wasn't very pleased when we came. You see, he'd had things very much his own way. He paid the natives what he liked for their copra, and he paid in goods and whiskey. He had a native wife, but he was flagrantly unfaithful to her. He was a drunkard. I gave him a chance to mend his ways, but he wouldn't take it. He laughed at me."

Davidson's voice fell to a deep bass as he said the last words, and he was silent for a minute or two. The silence was heavy with menace.

"In two years he was a ruined man. He'd lost everything he'd saved in a quarter of a century. I broke him, and at last he was forced to come to me like a beggar and beseech me to give him a passage back to Sydney."

"I wish you could have seen him when he came to see Mr. Davidson," said the missionary's wife. "He had been a fine, powerful man, with a lot of fat on him, and he had a great big voice, but now he was half the size, and he was shaking all over. He'd suddenly become an old man."

With abstracted gaze Davidson looked out into the night. The rain was falling again.

Suddenly from below came a sound, and Davidson turned and looked questioningly at his wife. It was the sound of a gramophone, harsh and loud, wheezing out a syncopated tune.

"What's that?" he asked.

Mrs. Davidson fixed her *pince-nez* more firmly on her nose.

"One of the second-class passengers has a room in the house. I guess it comes from there."

They listened in silence, and presently they heard the sound of dancing. Then the music stopped, and they heard the popping of corks and voices raised in animated conversation.

"I daresay she's giving a farewell party to her friends on board," said Dr. Macphail. "The ship sails at twelve, doesn't it?"

Davidson made no remark, but he looked at his watch.

"Are you ready?" he asked his wife.

She got up and folded her work.

"Yes, I guess I am," she answered.

"It's early to go to bed yet, isn't it?" said the doctor.

"We have a good deal of reading to do," explained Mrs. Davidson. "Wherever we are, we read a chapter of the Bible before retiring for the night and we study it with the commentaries, you
know, and discuss it thoroughly. It's a wonderful training for the
mind."

The two couples bade one another good-night. Dr. and Mrs.
Macphail were left alone. For two or three minutes they did not
speak.

"I think I'll go and fetch the cards," the doctor said at last.

Mrs. Macphail looked at him doubtfully. Her conversation with
the Davidsons had left her a little uneasy, but she did not like to
say that she thought they had better not play cards when the
Davidsons might come in at any moment. Dr. Macphail brought
them and she watched him, though with a vague sense of guilt,
while he laid out his patience. Below the sound of revelry continued.

It was fine enough next day, and the Macphails, condemned to
spend a fortnight of idleness at Pago-Pago, set about making the
best of things. They went down to the quay and got out of their
boxes a number of books. The doctor called on the chief surgeon
of the naval hospital and went round the beds with him. They
left cards on the governor. They passed Miss Thompson on the
road. The doctor took off his hat, and she gave him a "Good morning, doc," in a loud, cheerful voice. She was dressed as on the
day before, in a white frock, and her shiny white boots with their
high heels, her fat legs bulging over the tops of them, were strange
things on that exotic scene.

"I don't think she's very suitably dressed, I must say," said Mrs.
Macphail. "She looks extremely common to me."

When they got back to their house, she was on the verandah
playing with one of the trader's dark children.

"Say a word to her," Dr. Macphail whispered to his wife. "She's
all alone here, and it seems rather unkind to ignore her."

Mrs. Macphail was shy, but she was in the habit of doing what
her husband bade her.

"I think we're fellow lodgers here," she said, rather foolishly.

"Terrible, ain't it, bein' cooped up in a one-horse burg like this?"
answered Miss Thompson. "And they tell me I'm lucky to have
gotten a room. I don't see myself livin' in a native house, and

that's what some have to do. I don't know why they don't have a hotel."

They exchanged a few more words. Miss Thompson, loud-voiced and garrulous, was evidently quite willing to gossip, but Mrs. Macphail had a poor stock of small talk and presently she said:

"Well, I think we must go upstairs."

In the evening when they sat down to their high-tea Davidson on coming in said:

"I see that woman downstairs has a couple of sailors sitting there. I wonder how she's gotten acquainted with them."

"She can't be very particular," said Mrs. Davidson.

They were all rather tired after the idle, aimless day.

"If there's going to be a fortnight of this I don't know what we shall feel like at the end of it," said Dr. Macphail.

"The only thing to do is to portion out the day to different activities," answered the missionary. "I shall set aside a certain number of hours to study and a certain number to exercise, rain or fine—in the wet season you can't afford to pay any attention to the rain—and a certain number to recreation."

Dr. Macphail looked at his companion with misgiving. Davidson's programme oppressed him. They were eating hamburger steak again. It seemed the only dish the cook knew how to make. Then below the gramophone began. Davidson started nervously when he heard it, but said nothing. Men's voices floated up. Miss Thompson's guests were joining in a well-known song and presently they heard her voice too, hoarse and loud. There was a good deal of shouting and laughing. The four people upstairs, trying to make conversation, listened despite themselves to the clink of glasses and the scrape of chairs. More people had evidently come. Miss Thompson was giving a party.

"I wonder how she gets them all in," said Mrs. Macphail, suddenly breaking into a medical conversation between the missionary and her husband.

It showed whither her thoughts were wandering. The twitch of Davidson's face proved that, though he spoke of scientific things, his mind was busy in the same direction. Suddenly, while the doctor was giving some experience of practice on the Flanders front, rather prosily, he sprang to his feet with a cry.

"What's the matter, Alfred?" asked Mrs. Davidson.

"Of course! It never occurred to me. She's out of Iwelei."

"She can't be."

"She came on board at Honolulu. It's obvious. And she's carrying on her trade here. Here."

He uttered the last word with a passion of indignation.

"What's Iwelei?" asked Mrs. Macphail.

He turned his gloomy eyes on her and his voice trembled with horror.

"The plague spot of Honolulu. The Red Light district. It was a blot on our civilization."

Iwelei was on the edge of the city. You went down side streets by the harbour, in the darkness, across a rickety bridge, till you came to a deserted road, all ruts and holes, and then suddenly you came out into the light. There was parking room for motors on each side of the road, and there were saloons, tawdry and bright, each one noisy with its mechanical piano, and there were barbers' shops and tobacconists. There was a stir in the air and a sense of expectant gaiety. You turned down a narrow alley, either to the right or to the left, for the road divided Iwelei into two parts, and you found yourself in the district. There were rows of little bungalows, trim and neatly painted in green, and the pathway between them was broad and straight. It was laid out like a garden-city. In its respectable regularity, its order and spruceness, it gave an impression of sardonic horror; for never can the search for love have been so systematized and ordered. The pathways were lit by a rare lamp, but they would have been dark except for the lights that came from the open windows of the bungalows. Men wandered about, looking at the women who sat at their windows, reading or sewing, for the most part taking no notice of the passers-by; and like the women they were of all nationalities. There were Americans, sailors from the ships in port, enlisted men off the gunboats, sombrely drunk, and soldiers from the regiments, white and black, quartered on the island; there were Japanese, walking in twos and threes; Hawaiians, Chinese in long robes, and Filipinos in preposterous hats. They were silent and as it were oppressed. Desire is sad.

"It was the most crying scandal of the Pacific," exclaimed Davidson vehemently. "The missionaries had been agitating against it for years, and at last the local press took it up. The police refused to stir. You know their argument. They say that vice is inevitable and consequently the best thing is to localize and control it. The truth is, they were paid. Paid. They were paid by the saloon-keepers, paid by the bullies, paid by the women themselves. At last they were forced to move."

"I read about it in the papers that came on board in Honolulu," said Dr. Macphail.

"Iwelei, with its sin and shame, ceased to exist on the very day we arrived. The whole population was brought before the justices. I don't know why I didn't understand at once what that woman was."

"Now you come to speak of it," said Mrs. Macphail, "I remember seeing her come on board only a few minutes before the boat sailed. I remember thinking at the time she was cutting it rather fine."

"How dare she come here!" cried Davidson indignantly. "I'm not going to allow it."

He strode towards the door.

"What are you going to do?" asked Macphail.

"What do you expect me to do? I'm going to stop it. I'm not going to have this house turned into—into . . ."

He sought for a word that should not offend the ladies' ears. His eyes were flashing and his pale face was paler still in his emotion.

"It sounds as though there were three or four men down there," said the doctor. "Don't you think it's rather rash to go in just now?"

The missionary gave him a contemptuous look and without a word flung out of the room.

"You know Mr. Davidson very little if you think the fear of personal danger can stop him in the performance of his duty," said his wife.

She sat with her hands nervously clasped, a spot of colour on her high cheek bones, listening to what was about to happen below. They all listened. They heard him clatter down the wooden stairs and throw open the door. The singing stopped suddenly, but the gramophone continued to bray out its vulgar tune. They heard Davidson's voice and then the noise of something heavy falling. The music stopped. He had hurled the gramophone on the floor. Then again they heard Davidson's voice, they could not make out the words, then Miss Thompson's, loud and shrill, then a confused clamour as though several people were shouting together at the top of their lungs. Mrs. Davidson gave a little gasp, and she clenched her hands more tightly. Dr. Macphail looked uncertainly from her to his wife. He did not want to go down, but he wondered if they expected him to. Then there was something that sounded like a scuffle. The noise now was more distinct. It might be that Davidson was being thrown out of the room. The door was slammed. There was a moment's silence and they heard Davidson come up the stairs again. He went to his room.

"I think I'll go to him," said Mrs. Davidson.

She got up and went out.

"If you want me, just call," said Mrs. Macphail, and then when the other was gone: "I hope he isn't hurt."

"Why couldn't he mind his own business?" said Dr. Macphail.

They sat in silence for a minute or two and then they both started, for the gramophone began to play once more, defiantly, and mocking voices shouted hoarsely the words of an obscene song.

Next day Mrs. Davidson was pale and tired. She complained of headache, and she looked old and wizened. She told Mrs. Macphail that the missionary had not slept at all; he had passed the night in a state of frightful agitation and at five had got up and gone out. A glass of beer had been thrown over him and his clothes were stained and stinking. But a sombre fire glowed in Mrs. Davidson's eyes when she spoke of Miss Thompson.

"She'll bitterly rue the day when she flouted Mr. Davidson," she said. "Mr. Davidson has a wonderful heart and no one who is in trouble has ever gone to him without being comforted, but he has no mercy for sin, and when his righteous wrath is excited he's terrible."

"Why, what will he do?" asked Mrs. Macphail.

"I don't know, but I wouldn't stand in that creature's shoes for anything in the world."

Mrs. Macphail shuddered. There was something positively alarming in the triumphant assurance of the little woman's manner. They were going out together that morning, and they went down the stairs side by side. Miss Thompson's door was open, and they saw her in a bedraggled dressing-gown, cooking something in a chafing-dish.

"Good morning," she called. "Is Mr. Davidson better this morning?"

They passed her in silence, with their noses in the air, as if she did not exist. They flushed, however, when she burst into a shout of derisive laughter. Mrs. Davidson turned on her suddenly.

"Don't you dare to speak to me," she screamed. "If you insult me I shall have you turned out of here."

"Say, did I ask Mr. Davidson to visit with me?"

"Don't answer her," whispered Mrs. Macphail hurriedly.

They walked on till they were out of earshot.

"She's brazen, brazen," burst from Mrs. Davidson.

Her anger almost suffocated her.

And on their way home they met her strolling towards the quay. She had all her finery on. Her great white hat with its vulgar, showy flowers was an affront. She called out cheerily to them as she went by, and a couple of American sailors who were standing there grinned as the ladies set their faces to an icy stare. They got in just before the rain began to fall again.

"I guess she'll get her fine clothes spoilt," said Mrs. Davidson with a bitter sneer.

Davidson did not come in till they were half way through dinner. He was wet through, but he would not change. He sat, morose and silent, refusing to eat more than a mouthful, and he stared at the slanting rain. When Mrs. Davidson told him of their two encounters with Miss Thompson he did not answer. His deepening frown alone showed that he had heard.

"Don't you think we ought to make Mr. Horn turn her out of here?" asked Mrs. Davidson. "We can't allow her to insult us."

"There doesn't seem to be any other place for her to go," said Macphail.

"She can live with one of the natives."

"In weather like this a native hut must be a rather uncomfortable place to live in."

"I lived in one for years," said the missionary.

When the little native girl brought in the fried bananas which formed the sweet they had every day, Davidson turned to her.

"Ask Miss Thompson when it would be convenient for me to see her," he said.

The girl nodded shyly and went out.

"What do you want to see her for, Alfred?" asked his wife.

"It's my duty to see her. I won't act till I've given her every chance."

"You don't know what she is. She'll insult you."

"Let her insult me. Let her spit on me. She has an immortal soul, and I must do all that is in my power to save it."

Mrs. Davidson's ears rang still with the harlot's mocking laughter.

"She's gone too far."

"Too far for the mercy of God?" His eyes lit up suddenly and his voice grew mellow and soft. "Never. The sinner may be deeper in sin than the depth of hell itself, but the love of the Lord Jesus can reach him still."

The girl came back with the message.

"Miss Thompson's compliments and as long as Rev. Davidson don't come in business hours she'll be glad to see him any time."

The party received it in stony silence, and Dr. Macphail quickly effaced from his lips the smile which had come upon them. He knew his wife would be vexed with him if he found Miss Thompson's effrontery amusing.

They finished the meal in silence. When it was over the two ladies got up and took their work, Mrs. Macphail was making another of the innumerable comforters which she had turned out since the beginning of the war, and the doctor lit his pipe. But Davidson remained in his chair and with abstracted eyes stared at the table. At last he got up and without a word went out of the room. They heard him go down and they heard Miss Thompson's defiant "Come in" when he knocked at the door. He remained with her for an hour. And Dr. Macphail watched the rain. It was beginning to get on his nerves. It was not like our soft English rain that drops gently on the earth; it was unmerciful and somehow terrible; you felt in it the malignancy of the primitive powers of nature. It did not pour, it flowed. It was like a deluge from heaven, and it rattled on the roof of corrugated iron with a steady persistence that was maddening. It seemed to have a fury of its own. And sometimes you felt that you must scream if it did not stop, and then suddenly you felt powerless, as though your bones had suddenly become soft; and you were miserable and hopeless.

Macphail turned his head when the missionary came back. The two women looked up.

"I've given her every chance. I have exhorted her to repent. She is an evil woman."

He paused, and Dr. Macphail saw his eyes darken and his pale face grow hard and stern.

"Now I shall take the whips with which the Lord Jesus drove the usurers and the money changers out of the Temple of the Most High."

He walked up and down the room. His mouth was close set, and his black brows were frowning.

"If she fled to the uttermost parts of the earth I should pursue her."

With a sudden movement he turned round and strode out of the room. They heard him go downstairs again.

"What is he going to do?" asked Mrs. Macphail.

"I don't know." Mrs. Davidson took off her *pince-nez* and wiped them. "When he is on the Lord's work I never ask him questions."

She sighed a little.

"What is the matter?"

"He'll wear himself out. He doesn't know what it is to spare himself."

Dr. Macphail learnt the first results of the missionary's activity from the half-caste trader in whose house they lodged. He stopped the doctor when he passed the store and came out to speak to him on the stoop. His fat face was worried.

"The Rev. Davidson has been at me for letting Miss Thompson have a room here," he said, "but I didn't know what she was when I rented it to her. When people come and ask if I can rent them a room all I want to know is if they've the money to pay for it. And she paid me for hers a week in advance."

Dr. Macphail did not want to commit himself.

"When all's said and done it's your house. We're very much obliged to you for taking us in at all."

Horn looked at him doubtfully. He was not certain yet how definitely Macphail stood on the missionary's side.

"The missionaries are in with one another," he said, hesitatingly. "If they get it in for a trader he may just as well shut up his store and quit."

"Did he want you to turn her out?"

"No, he said so long as she behaved herself he couldn't ask me to do that. He said he wanted to be just to me. I promised she shouldn't have no more visitors. I've just been and told her."

"How did she take it?"

"She gave me Hell."

The trader squirmed in his old ducks. He had found Miss Thompson a rough customer.

"Oh, well, I daresay she'll get out. I don't suppose she wants to stay here if she can't have anyone in."

"There's nowhere she can go, only a native house, and no native'll take her now, not now that the missionaries have got their knife in her."

Dr. Macphail looked at the falling rain.

"Well, I don't suppose it's any good waiting for it to clear up."

In the evening when they sat in the parlour Davidson talked to them of his early days at college. He had had no means and had worked his way through by doing odd jobs during the vacations. There was silence downstairs. Miss Thompson was sitting in her little room alone. But suddenly the gramophone began to play. She had set it on in defiance, to cheat her loneliness, but there was no one to sing, and it had a melancholy note. It was like a cry for help. Davidson took no notice. He was in the middle of a long anecdote and without change of expression went on. The gramophone continued. Miss Thompson put on one reel after another. It looked as though the silence of the night were getting on her nerves. It was breathless and sultry. When the Macphails went to bed they could not sleep. They lay side by side with their eyes wide open, listening to the cruel singing of the mosquitoes outside their curtain.

"What's that?" whispered Mrs. Macphail at last.

They heard a voice, Davidson's voice, through the wooden partition. It went on with a monotonous, earnest insistence. He was praying aloud. He was praying for the soul of Miss Thompson.

Two or three days went by. Now when they passed Miss Thompson on the road she did not greet them with ironic cordiality or smile; she passed with her nose in the air, a sulky look on her painted face, frowning, as though she did not see them. The trader told Macphail that she had tried to get lodging elsewhere, but had failed. In the evening she played through the various reels of her gramophone, but the pretence of mirth was obvious now. The ragtime had a cracked, heartbroken rhythm as though it were a one-step of despair. When she began to play on Sunday Davidson sent Horn to beg her to stop at once since it was the Lord's day. The reel was taken off and the house was silent except for the steady pattering of the rain on the iron roof.

"I think she's getting a bit worked up," said the trader next day to Macphail. "She don't know what Mr. Davidson's up to and it makes her scared."

Macphail had caught a glimpse of her that morning and it struck him that her arrogant expression had changed. There was in her face a hunted look. The half-caste gave him a sidelong glance.

"I suppose you don't know what Mr. Davidson is doing about it?" he hazarded.

"No, I don't."

It was singular that Horn should ask him that question, for he also had the idea that the missionary was mysteriously at work. He had an impression that he was weaving a net around the woman, carefully, systematically, and suddenly, when everything was ready, would pull the strings tight.

"He told me to tell her," said the trader, "that if at any time she wanted him she only had to send and he'd come."

"What did she say when you told her that?"

"She didn't say nothing. I didn't stop. I just said what he said I was to and then I beat it. I thought she might be going to start weepin'."

"I have no doubt the loneliness is getting on her nerves," said the doctor. "And the rain—that's enough to make anyone jumpy," he continued irritably. "Doesn't it ever stop in this confounded place?"

"It goes on pretty steady in the rainy season. We have three hundred inches in the year. You see, it's the shape of the bay. It seems to attract the rain from all over the Pacific."

"Damn the shape of the bay," said the doctor.

He scratched his mosquito bites. He felt very short-tempered. When the rain stopped and the sun shone, it was like a hot-house, seething, humid, sultry, breathless, and you had a strange feeling that everything was growing with a savage violence. The natives, blithe and childlike by reputation, seemed then, with their tattooing and their dyed hair, to have something sinister in their appearance; and when they pattered along at your heels with their naked feet you looked back instinctively. You felt they might at any moment come behind you swiftly and thrust a long knife between your shoulder blades. You could not tell what dark thoughts lurked behind their wide-set eyes. They had a little the look of ancient Egyptians painted on a temple wall, and there was about them the terror of what is immeasurably old.

The missionary came and went. He was busy, but the Macphails did not know what he was doing. Horn told the doctor that he saw the governor every day, and once Davidson mentioned him.

"He looks as if he had plenty of determination," he said, "but when you come down to brass tacks he has no backbone."

"I suppose that means he won't do exactly what you want," suggested the doctor facetiously.

The missionary did not smile.

"I want him to do what's right. It shouldn't be necessary to persuade a man to do that."

"But there may be differences of opinion about what is right."

"If a man had a gangrenous foot would you have patience with anyone who hesitated to amputate it?"

"Gangrene is a matter of fact."

"And Evil?"

What Davidson had done soon appeared. The four of them had just finished their midday meal, and they had not yet separated for the siesta which the heat imposed on the ladies and on the doctor. Davidson had little patience with the slothful habit. The door was suddenly flung open and Miss Thompson came in. She looked round the room and then went up to Davidson.

"You low-down skunk, what have you been saying about me to the governor?"

She was spluttering with rage. There was a moment's pause. Then the missionary drew forward a chair.

"Won't you be seated, Miss Thompson? I've been hoping to have another talk with you."

"You poor low-life bastard."

She burst into a torrent of insult, foul and insolent. Davidson kept his grave eyes on her.

"I'm indifferent to the abuse you think fit to heap on me, Miss Thompson," he said, "but I must beg you to remember that ladies are present."

Tears by now were struggling with her anger. Her face was red and swollen as though she were choking.

"What has happened?" asked Dr. Macphail.

"A feller's just been in here and he says I gotter beat it on the next boat."

Was there a gleam in the missionary's eyes? His face remained impassive.

"You could hardly expect the governor to let you stay here under the circumstances."

"You done it," she shrieked. "You can't kid me. You done it."

"I don't want to deceive you. I urged the governor to take the only possible step consistent with his obligations."

"Why couldn't you leave me be? I wasn't doin' you no harm."

"You may be sure that if you had I should be the last man to resent it."

"Do you think I want to stay on in this poor imitation of a burg? I don't look no busher, do I?"

"In that case I don't see what cause of complaint you have," he answered.

She gave an inarticulate cry of rage and flung out of the room. There was a short silence.

"It's a relief to know that the governor has acted at last," said Davidson finally. "He's a weak man and he shilly-shallied. He said she was only here for a fortnight anyway, and if she went on to Apia that was under British jurisdiction and had nothing to do with him."

The missionary sprang to his feet and strode across the room.

"It's terrible the way the men who are in authority seek to evade their responsibility. They speak as though evil that was out of sight ceased to be evil. The very existence of that woman is a scandal and it does not help matters to shift it to another of the islands. In the end I had to speak straight from the shoulder."

Davidson's brow lowered, and he protruded his firm chin. He looked fierce and determined.

"What do you mean by that?"

"Our mission is not entirely without influence at Washington. I pointed out to the governor that it wouldn't do him any good if there was a complaint about the way he managed things here."

"When has she got to go?" asked the doctor, after a pause.

"The San Francisco boat is due here from Sydney next Tuesday. She's to sail on that."

That was in five days' time. It was next day, when he was coming back from the hospital where for want of something better to do Macphail spent most of his mornings, that the half-caste stopped him as he was going upstairs.

"Excuse me, Dr. Macphail, Miss Thompson's sick. Will you have a look at her?"

"Certainly."

Horn led him to her room. She was sitting in a chair idly, neither reading nor sewing, staring in front of her. She wore her white dress and the large hat with the flowers on it. Macphail noticed that her skin was yellow and muddy under her powder, and her eyes were heavy.

"I'm sorry to hear you're not well," he said.

"Oh, I ain't sick really. I just said that, because I just had to see you. I've got to clear on a boat that's going to 'Frisco."

She looked at him and he saw that her eyes were suddenly startled. She opened and clenched her hands spasmodically. The trader stood at the door, listening.

"So I understand," said the doctor.

She gave a little gulp.

"I guess it ain't very convenient for me to go to 'Frisco just now. I went to see the governor yesterday afternoon, but I couldn't get to him. I saw the secretary, and he told me I'd got to take that boat and that was all there was to it. I just had to see the governor, so I waited outside his house this morning, and when he come out I spoke to him. He didn't want to speak to me, I'll say, but I wouldn't let him shake me off, and at last he said he hadn't no objection to my staying here till the next boat to Sydney if the Rev. Davidson will stand for it."

She stopped and looked at Dr. Macphail anxiously.

"I don't know exactly what I can do," he said.

"Well, I thought maybe you wouldn't mind asking him. I swear to God I won't start anything here if he'll just only let me stay. I won't go out of the house if that'll suit him. It's no more'n a fortnight."

"I'll ask him."

"He won't stand for it," said Horn. "He'll have you out on Tuesday, so you may as well make up your mind to it."

"Tell him I can get work in Sydney, straight stuff, I mean. 'Tain't asking very much."

"I'll do what I can."

"And come and tell me right away, will you? I can't set down to a thing till I get the dope one way or the other."

It was not an errand that much pleased the doctor, and, characteristically perhaps, he went about it indirectly. He told his wife what Miss Thompson had said to him and asked her to speak to Mrs. Davidson. The missionary's attitude seemed rather arbitrary and it could do no harm if the girl were allowed to stay in Pago-Pago another fortnight. But he was not prepared for the result of his diplomacy. The missionary came to him straightway.

"Mrs. Davidson tells me that Thompson has been speaking to you."

Dr. Macphail, thus directly tackled, had the shy man's resentment at being forced out into the open. He felt his temper rising, and he flushed.

"I don't see that it can make any difference if she goes to Sydney rather than to San Francisco, and so long as she promises to behave while she's here it's dashed hard to persecute her."

The missionary fixed him with his stern eyes.

"Why is she unwilling to go back to San Francisco?"

"I didn't enquire," answered the doctor with some asperity. "And I think one does better to mind one's own business."

Perhaps it was not a very tactful answer.

"The governor has ordered her to be deported by the first boat that leaves the island. He's only done his duty and I will not interfere. Her presence is a peril here."

"I think you're very harsh and tyrannical."

The two ladies looked up at the doctor with some alarm, but they need not have feared a quarrel, for the missionary smiled gently.

"I'm terribly sorry you should think that of me, Dr. Macphail. Believe me, my heart bleeds for that unfortunate woman, but I'm only trying to do my duty."

The doctor made no answer. He looked out of the window sullenly. For once it was not raining and across the bay you saw nestling among the trees the huts of a native village.

"I think I'll take advantage of the rain stopping to go out," he said.

"Please don't bear me malice because I can't accede to your wish," said Davidson, with a melancholy smile. "I respect you very much, doctor, and I should be sorry if you thought ill of me."

"I have no doubt you have a sufficiently good opinion of yourself to bear mine with equanimity," he retorted.

"That's one on me," chuckled Davidson.

When Dr. Macphail, vexed with himself because he had been uncivil to no purpose, went downstairs, Miss Thompson was waiting for him with her door ajar.

"Well," she said, "have you spoken to him?"

"Yes, I'm sorry, he won't do anything," he answered, not looking at her in his embarrassment.

But then he gave her a quick glance, for a sob broke from her. He saw that her face was white with fear. It gave him a shock of dismay. And suddenly he had an idea.

"But don't give up hope yet. I think it's a shame the way they're treating you and I'm going to see the governor myself."

"Now?"

He nodded. Her face brightened.

"Say, that's real good of you. I'm sure he'll let me stay if you speak for me. I just won't do a thing I didn't ought all the time I'm here."

Dr. Macphail hardly knew why he had made up his mind to appeal to the governor. He was perfectly indifferent to Miss Thompson's affairs, but the missionary had irritated him, and with him temper was a smouldering thing. He found the governor at home. He was a large, handsome man, a sailor, with a grey toothbrush moustache; and he wore a spotless uniform of white drill.

"I've come to see you about a woman who's lodging in the same house as we are," he said. "Her name's Thompson."

"I guess I've heard nearly enough about her, Dr. Macphail," said the governor, smiling. "I've given her the order to get out next Tuesday and that's all I can do."

"I wanted to ask you if you couldn't stretch a point and let her stay here till the boat comes in from San Francisco so that she can go to Sydney. I will guarantee her good behaviour."

The governor continued to smile, but his eyes grew small and serious.

"I'd be very glad to oblige you, Dr. Macphail, but I've given the order and it must stand."

The doctor put the case as reasonably as he could, but now the governor ceased to smile at all. He listened sullenly, with averted gaze. Macphail saw that he was making no impression.

"I'm sorry to cause any lady inconvenience, but she'll have to sail on Tuesday and that's all there is to it."

"But what difference can it make?"

"Pardon me, doctor, but I don't feel called upon to explain my official actions except to the proper authorities."

Macphail looked at him shrewdly. He remembered Davidson's hint that he had used threats, and in the governor's attitude he read a singular embarrassment.

"Davidson's a damned busybody," he said hotly.

"Between ourselves, Dr. Macphail, I don't say that I have formed a very favourable opinion of Mr. Davidson, but I am bound to confess that he was within his rights in pointing out to me the danger that the presence of a woman of Miss Thompson's character was to a place like this where a number of enlisted men are stationed among a native population."

He got up and Dr. Macphail was obliged to do so too.

"I must ask you to excuse me. I have an engagement. Please give my respects to Mrs. Macphail."

The doctor left him crest-fallen. He knew that Miss Thompson would be waiting for him, and unwilling to tell her himself that he had failed, he went into the house by the back door and sneaked up the stairs as though he had something to hide.

At supper he was silent and ill-at-ease, but the missionary was jovial and animated. Dr. Macphail thought his eyes rested on him now and then with triumphant good-humour. It struck him suddenly that Davidson knew of his visit to the governor and of its ill success. But how on earth could he have heard of it? There was something sinister about the power of that man. After supper he saw Horn on the verandah and, as though to have a casual word with him, went out.

"She wants to know if you've seen the governor," the trader whispered.

"Yes. He wouldn't do anything. I'm awfully sorry, I can't do anything more."

"I knew he wouldn't. They daren't go against the missionaries."

"What are you talking about?" said Davidson affably, coming out to join them.

"I was just saying there was no chance of your getting over to Apia for at least another week," said the trader glibly.

He left them, and the two men returned into the parlour. Mr.

Davidson devoted one hour after each meal to recreation. Presently a timid knock was heard at the door.

"Come in," said Mrs. Davidson, in her sharp voice.

The door was not opened. She got up and opened it. They saw Miss Thompson standing at the threshold. But the change in her appearance was extraordinary. This was no longer the flaunting hussy who had jeered at them in the road, but a broken, frightened woman. Her hair, as a rule so elaborately arranged, was tumbling untidily over her neck. She wore bedroom slippers and a skirt and blouse. They were unfresh and bedraggled. She stood at the door with the tears streaming down her face and did not dare to enter.

"What do you want?" said Mrs. Davidson harshly.

"May I speak to Mr. Davidson?" she said in a choking voice.

The missionary rose and went towards her.

"Come right in, Miss Thompson," he said in cordial tones. "What can I do for you?"

She entered the room.

"Say, I'm sorry for what I said to you the other day an' for—for everythin' else. I guess I was a bit lit up. I beg pardon."

"Oh, it was nothing. I guess my back's broad enough to bear a few hard words."

She stepped towards him with a movement that was horribly cringing.

"You've got me beat. I'm all in. You won't make me go back to 'Frisco?"

His genial manner vanished and his voice grew on a sudden hard and stern.

"Why don't you want to go back there?"

She cowered before him.

"I guess my people live there. I don't want them to see me like this. I'll go anywhere else you say."

"Why don't you want to go back to San Francisco?"

"I've told you."

He leaned forward, staring at her, and his great, shining eyes seemed to try to bore into her soul. He gave a sudden gasp.

"The penitentiary."

She screamed, and then she fell at his feet, clasping his legs.

"Don't send me back there. I swear to you before God I'll be a good woman. I'll give all this up."

She burst into a torrent of confused supplication and the tears coursed down her painted cheeks. He leaned over her and, lifting her face, forced her to look at him.

"Is that it, the penitentiary?"

"I beat it before they could get me," she gasped. "If the bulls grab me it's three years for mine."

He let go his hold of her and she fell in a heap on the floor, sobbing bitterly. Dr. Macphail stood up.

"This alters the whole thing," he said. "You can't make her go back when you know this. Give her another chance. She wants to turn over a new leaf."

"I'm going to give her the finest chance she's ever had. If she repents let her accept her punishment."

She misunderstood the words and looked up. There was a gleam of hope in her heavy eyes.

"You'll let me go?"

"No. You shall sail for San Francisco on Tuesday."

She gave a groan of horror and then burst into low, hoarse shrieks which sounded hardly human, and she beat her head passionately on the ground. Dr. Macphail sprang to her and lifted her up.

"Come on, you mustn't do that. You'd better go to your room and lie down. I'll get you something."

He raised her to her feet and partly dragging her, partly carrying her, got her downstairs. He was furious with Mrs. Davidson and with his wife because they made no effort to help. The half-caste was standing on the landing and with his assistance he managed to get her on the bed. She was moaning and crying. She was almost insensible. He gave her a hypodermic injection. He was hot and exhausted when he went upstairs again.

"I've got her to lie down."

The two women and Davidson were in the same positions as when he had left them. They could not have moved or spoken since he went.

"I was waiting for you," said Davidson, in a strange, distant voice. "I want you all to pray with me for the soul of our erring sister."

He took the Bible off a shelf, and sat down at the table at which they had supped. It had not been cleared, and he pushed the tea-pot out of the way. In a powerful voice, resonant and

deep, he read to them the chapter in which is narrated the meeting of Jesus Christ with the woman taken in adultery.

"Now kneel with me and let us pray for the soul of our dear
sister, Sadie Thompson."

He burst into a long, passionate prayer in which he implored
God to have mercy on the sinful woman. Mrs. Macphail and Mrs.
Davidson knelt with covered eyes. The doctor, taken by surprise,
awkward and sheepish, knelt too. The missionary's prayer had a
savage eloquence. He was extraordinarily moved, and as he spoke
the tears ran down his cheeks. Outside, the pitiless rain fell, fell
steadily, with a fierce malignity that was all too human.

At last he stopped. He paused for a moment and said:

"We will now repeat the Lord's prayer."

They said it and then, following him, they rose from their knees.
Mrs. Davidson's face was pale and restful. She was comforted
and at peace, but the Macphails felt suddenly bashful. They did
not know which way to look.

"I'll just go down and see how she is now," said Dr. Macphail.

When he knocked at her door it was opened for him by Horn.
Miss Thompson was in a rocking-chair, sobbing quietly.

"What are you doing there?" exclaimed Macphail. "I told you
to lie down."

"I can't lie down. I want to see Mr. Davidson."

"My poor child, what do you think is the good of it? You'll
never move him."

"He said he'd come if I sent for him."

Macphail motioned to the trader.

"Go and fetch him."

He waited with her in silence while the trader went upstairs.
Davidson came in.

"Excuse me for asking you to come here," she said, looking at
him sombrely.

"I was expecting you to send for me. I knew the Lord would
answer my prayer."

They stared at one another for a moment and then she looked
away. She kept her eyes averted when she spoke.

"I've been a bad woman. I want to repent."

"Thank God! thank God! He has heard our prayers."

He turned to the two men.

"Leave me alone with her. Tell Mrs. Davidson that our prayers have been answered."

They went out and closed the door behind them.

"Gee whizz," said the trader.

That night Dr. Macphail could not get to sleep till late, and when he heard the missionary come upstairs he looked at his watch. It was two o'clock. But even then he did not go to bed at once, for through the wooden partition that separated their rooms he heard him praying aloud, till he himself, exhausted, fell asleep.

When he saw him next morning he was surprised at his appearance. He was paler than ever, tired, but his eyes shone with an inhuman fire. It looked as though he were filled with an overwhelming joy.

"I want you to go down presently and see Sadie," he said. "I can't hope that her body is better, but her soul—her soul is transformed."

The doctor was feeling wan and nervous.

"You were with her very late last night," he said.

"Yes, she couldn't bear to have me leave her."

"You look as pleased as Punch," the doctor said irritably.

Davidson's eyes shone with ecstasy.

"A great mercy has been vouchsafed me. Last night I was privileged to bring a lost soul to the loving arms of Jesus."

Miss Thompson was again in the rocking-chair. The bed had not been made. The room was in disorder. She had not troubled to dress herself, but wore a dirty dressing-gown, and her hair was tied in a sluttish knot. She had given her face a dab with a wet towel, but it was all swollen and creased with crying. She looked a drab.

She raised her eyes dully when the doctor came in. She was cowed and broken.

"Where's Mr. Davidson?" she asked.

"He'll come presently if you want him," answered Macphail acidly. "I came here to see how you were."

"Oh, I guess I'm O.K. You needn't worry about that."

"Have you had anything to eat?"

"Horn brought me some coffee."

She looked anxiously at the door.

"D'you think he'll come down soon? I feel as if it wasn't so terrible when he's with me."

"Are you still going on Tuesday?"

"Yes, he says I've got to go. Please tell him to come right along. You can't do me any good. He's the only one as can help me now."

"Very well," said Dr. Macphail.

During the next three days the missionary spent almost all his time with Sadie Thompson. He joined the others only to have his meals. Dr. Macphail noticed that he hardly ate.

"He's wearing himself out," said Mrs. Davidson pitifully. "He'll have a breakdown if he doesn't take care, but he won't spare himself."

She herself was white and pale. She told Mrs. Macphail that she had had no sleep. When the missionary came upstairs from Miss Thompson he prayed till he was exhausted, but even then he did not sleep for long. After an hour or two he got up and dressed himself, and went for a tramp along the bay. He had strange dreams.

"This morning he told me that he'd been dreaming about the mountains of Nebraska," said Mrs. Davidson.

"That's curious," said Dr. Macphail.

He remembered seeing them from the windows of the train when he crossed America. They were like huge mole-hills, rounded and smooth, and they rose from the plain abruptly. Dr. Macphail remembered how it struck him that they were like a woman's breasts.

Davidson's restlessness was intolerable even to himself. But he was buoyed up by a wonderful exhilaration. He was tearing out by the roofs the last vestiges of sin that lurked in the hidden corners of that poor woman's heart. He read with her and prayed with her.

"It's wonderful," he said to them one day at supper. "It's a true rebirth. Her soul, which was black as night, is now pure and white like the new-fallen snow. I am humble and afraid. Her remorse for all her sins is beautiful. I am not worthy to touch the hem of her garment."

"Have you the heart to send her back to San Francisco?" said the doctor. "Three years in an American prison. I should have thought you might have saved her from that."

"Ah, but don't you see? It's necessary. Do you think my heart doesn't bleed for her? I love her as I love my wife and my sister. All the time that she is in prison I shall suffer all the pain that she suffers."

"Bunkum," cried the doctor impatiently.

"You don't understand because you're blind. She's sinned, and she must suffer. I know what she'll endure. She'll be starved and tortured and humiliated. I want her to accept the punishment of man as a sacrifice to God. I want her to accept it joyfully. She has an opportunity which is offered to very few of us. God is very good and very merciful."

Davidson's voice trembled with excitement. He could hardly articulate the words that tumbled passionately from his lips.

"All day I pray with her and when I leave her I pray again, I pray with all my might and main, so that Jesus may grant her this great mercy. I want to put in her heart the passionate desire to be punished so that at the end, even if I offered to let her go, she would refuse. I want her to feel that the bitter punishment of prison is the thank-offering that she places at the feet of our Blessed Lord, who gave his life for her."

The days passed slowly. The whole household, intent on the wretched, tortured woman downstairs, lived in a state of unnatural excitement. She was like a victim that was being prepared for the savage rites of a bloody idolatry. Her terror numbed her. She could not bear to let Davidson out of her sight; it was only when he was with her that she had courage, and she hung upon him with a slavish dependence. She cried a great deal, and she read the Bible, and prayed. Sometimes she was exhausted and apathetic. Then she did indeed look forward to her ordeal, for it seemed to offer an escape, direct and concrete, from the anguish she was enduring. She could not bear much longer the vague terrors which now assailed her. With her sins she had put aside all personal vanity, and she slopped about her room, unkempt and dishevelled, in her tawdry dressing-gown. She had not taken off her night-dress for four days, nor put on stockings. Her room was littered and untidy. Meanwhile the rain fell with a cruel persistence. You felt that the heavens must at last be empty of water, but still it poured down, straight and heavy, with a maddening iteration, on the iron roof. Everything was damp and clammy. There was mildew on the walls and on the boots that stood on the floor. Through the sleepless nights the mosquitoes droned their angry chant.

"If it would only stop raining for a single day it wouldn't be so bad," said Dr. Macphail.

They all looked forward to the Tuesday when the boat for San Francisco was to arrive from Sydney. The strain was intolerable. So far as Dr. Macphail was concerned, his pity and his resentment were alike extinguished by his desire to be rid of the unfortunate woman. The inevitable must be accepted. He felt he would breathe more freely when the ship had sailed. Sadie Thompson was to be escorted on board by a clerk in the governor's office. This person called on the Monday evening and told Miss Thompson to be prepared at eleven in the morning. Davidson was with her.

"I'll see that everything is ready. I mean to come on board with her myself."

Miss Thompson did not speak.

When Dr. Macphail blew out his candle and crawled cautiously under his mosquito curtains, he gave a sigh of relief.

"Well, thank God that's over. By this time tomorrow she'll be gone."

"Mrs. Davidson will be glad too. She says he's wearing himself to a shadow," said Mrs. Macphail. "She's a different woman."

"Who?"

"Sadie. I should never have thought it possible. It makes one humble."

Dr. Macphail did not answer, and presently he fell asleep. He was tired out, and he slept more soundly than usual.

He was awakened in the morning by a hand placed on his arm, and, starting up, saw Horn by the side of his bed. The trader put his finger on his mouth to prevent any exclamation from Dr. Macphail and beckoned to him to come. As a rule he wore shabby ducks, but now he was barefoot and wore only the *lava-lava* of the natives. He looked suddenly savage, and Dr. Macphail, getting out of bed, saw that he was heavily tattooed. Horn made him a sign to come on to the verandah. Dr. Macphail got out of bed and followed the trader out.

"Don't make a noise," he whispered. "You're wanted. Put on a coat and some shoes. Quick."

Dr. Macphail's first thought was that something had happened to Miss Thompson.

"What is it? Shall I bring my instruments?"

"Hurry, please, hurry."

Dr. Macphail crept back into the bedroom, put on a waterproof over his pyjamas, and a pair of rubber-soled shoes. He rejoined the trader, and together they tiptoed down the stairs. The door leading out to the road was open and at it were standing half a dozen natives.

"What is it?" repeated the doctor.

"Come along with me," said Horn.

He walked out and the doctor followed him. The natives came after them in a little bunch. They crossed the road and came on to the beach. The doctor saw a group of natives standing round some object at the water's edge. They hurried along, a couple of dozen yards perhaps, and the natives opened out as the doctor came up. The trader pushed him forwards. Then he saw, lying half in the water and half out, a dreadful object, the body of Davidson. Dr. Macphail bent down—he was not a man to lose his head in an emergency—and turned the body over. The throat was cut from ear to ear, and in the right hand was still the razor with which the deed was done.

"He's quite cold," said the doctor. "He must have been dead some time."

"One of the boys saw him lying there on his way to work just now and came and told me. Do you think he did it himself?"

"Yes. Someone ought to go for the police."

Horn said something in the native tongue, and two youths started off.

"We must leave him here till they come," said the doctor.

"They mustn't take him into my house. I won't have him in my house."

"You'll do what the authorities say," replied the doctor sharply. "In point of fact I expect they'll take him to the mortuary."

They stood waiting where they were. The trader took a cigarette from a fold in his *lava-lava* and gave one to Dr. Macphail. They smoked while they stared at the corpse. Dr. Macphail could not understand.

"Why do you think he did it?" asked Horn.

The doctor shrugged his shoulders. In a little while native police came along, under the charge of a marine, with a stretcher, and immediately afterwards a couple of naval officers and a naval doctor. They managed everything in a businesslike manner.

"What about the wife?" said one of the officers.

"Now that you've come I'll go back to the house and get some things on. I'll see that it's broken to her. She'd better not see him till he's been fixed up a little."

"I guess that's right," said the naval doctor.

When Dr. Macphail went back he found his wife nearly dressed.

"Mrs. Davidson's in a dreadful state about her husband," she said to him as soon as he appeared. "He hasn't been to bed all night. She heard him leave Miss Thompson's room at two, but he went out. If he's been walking about since then he'll be absolutely dead."

Dr. Macphail told her what had happened and asked her to break the news to Mrs. Davidson.

"But why did he do it?" she asked, horror-stricken.

"I don't know."

"But I can't. I can't."

"You must."

She gave him a frightened look and went out. He heard her go into Mrs. Davidson's room. He waited a minute to gather himself together and then began to shave and wash. When he was dressed he sat down on the bed and waited for his wife. At last she came.

"She wants to see him," she said.

"They've taken him to the mortuary. We'd better go down with her. How did she take it?"

"I think she's stunned. She didn't cry. But she's trembling like a leaf."

"We'd better go at once."

When they knocked at her door Mrs. Davidson came out. She was very pale, but dry-eyed. To the doctor she seemed unnaturally composed. No word was exchanged, and they set out in silence down the road. When they arrived at the mortuary Mrs. Davidson spoke.

"Let me go in and see him alone."

They stood aside. A native opened a door for her and closed it behind her. They sat down and waited. One or two white men came and talked to them in undertones. Dr. Macphail told them again what he knew of the tragedy. At last the door was quietly opened and Mrs. Davidson came out. Silence fell upon them.

"I'm ready to go back now," she said.

Her voice was hard and steady. Dr. Macphail could not understand the look in her eyes. Her pale face was very stern. They walked back slowly, never saying a word, and at last they came round the bend on the other side of which stood their house. Mrs. Davidson gave a gasp, and for a moment they stopped still. An incredible sound assaulted their ears. The gramophone which had been silent for so long was playing, playing ragtime loud and harsh.

"What's that?" cried Mrs. Macphail with horror.

"Let's go on," said Mrs. Davidson.

They walked up the steps and entered the hall. Miss Thompson was standing at her door, chatting with a sailor. A sudden change had taken place in her. She was no longer the cowed drudge of the last days. She was dressed in all her finery, in her white dress, with the high shiny boots over which her fat legs bulged in their cotton stockings; her hair was elaborately arranged; and she wore that enormous hat covered with gaudy flowers. Her face was painted, her eyebrows were boldly black, and her lips were scarlet. She held herself erect. She was the flaunting queen that they had known at first. As they came in she broke into a loud, jeering laugh; and then, when Mrs. Davidson involuntarily stopped, she collected the spittle in her mouth and spat. Mrs. Davidson cowered back, and two red spots rose suddenly to her cheeks. Then, covering her face with her hands, she broke away and ran quickly up the stairs. Dr. Macphail was outraged. He pushed past the woman into her room.

"What the devil are you doing?" he cried. "Stop that damned machine."

He went up to it and tore the record off. She turned on him.

"Say, doc, you can that stuff with me. What the hell are you doin' in my room?"

"What do you mean?" he cried. "What d'you mean?"

She gathered herself together. No one could describe the scorn of her expression or the contemptuous hatred she put into her answer.

"You men! You filthy, dirty pigs! You're all the same, all of you. Pigs! Pigs!"

Dr. Macphail gasped. He understood.

Mr. Harrington's Washing

When Ashenden went on deck and saw before him a low-lying coast and a white town he felt a pleasant flutter of excitement. It was early and the sun had not long risen, but the sea was glassy and the sky was blue; it was warm already and one knew that the day would be sweltering. Vladivostok. It really gave one the sensation of being at the end of the world. It was a long journey that Ashenden had made from New York to San Francisco, across the Pacific in a Japanese boat to Yokohama, then from Tsuruki in a Russian boat, he the only Englishman on board, up the Sea of Japan. From Vladivostok he was to take the Trans-Siberian to Petrograd. It was the most important mission that he had ever had and he was pleased with the sense of responsibility that it gave him. He had no one to give him orders, unlimited funds (he carried in a belt next to his skin bills of exchange for a sum so enormous that he was staggered when he thought of them), and though he had been sent to do something that was beyond human possibility he did not know this and was prepared to set about his task with confidence. He believed in his own astuteness. Though he had both esteem and admiration for the sensibility of the human race he had little respect for their intelligence: man has always found it easier to sacrifice his life than to learn the multiplication table.

Ashenden did not much look forward to ten days on a Russian train and in Yokohama he had heard rumours that in one or two places bridges had been blown up and the line cut. He was told that the soldiers, completely out of hand, would rob him of everything he possessed and turn him out on the steppe to shift for himself. It was a cheerful prospect. But the train was certainly starting and whatever happened later (and Ashenden had always a feeling that things never turned out as badly as you expected) he was determined to get a place on it. His intention on landing was to go at once to the British Consulate and find out what arrangements had been made for him; but as they neared the shore and he was able to discern the untidy and bedraggled town he felt not a little forlorn. He knew but a few words of Russian. The only man on the ship who spoke English was the purser and though he promised Ashenden to do anything he could to help him Ashenden had the impression that he must not too greatly count upon him. It was a relief then, when they docked, to have a young man, small and with a mop of untidy hair, obviously a Jew, come up to him and ask if his name was Ashenden.

"Mine is Benedict. I'm the interpreter at the British Consulate. I've been told to look after you. We've got you a place on the train to-night."

Ashenden's spirits went up. They landed. The little Jew looked after his luggage and had his passport examined and then, getting into a car that waited for them, they drove off to the Consulate.

"I've had instructions to offer you every facility," said the Consul, "and you've only got to tell me what you want. I've fixed you up all right on the train, but God knows if you'll ever get to Petrograd. Oh, by the way, I've got a travelling companion for you. He's a man called Harrington, an American, and he's going to Petrograd for a firm in Philadelphia. He's trying to fix up some deal with the Provisional Government."

"What's he like?" asked Ashenden.

"Oh, he's all right. I wanted him to come with the American Consul to luncheon, but they've gone for an excursion in the country. You must get to the station a couple of hours before the train starts. There's always an awful scrimmage and if you're not there in good time someone will pinch your seat."

The train started at midnight and Ashenden dined with Benedict at the station restaurant which was, it appeared, the only place in that slatternly town where you could get a decent meal. It was crowded. The service was intolerably slow. Then they went on to the platform, where, though they had still two hours to spare, there was already a seething mob. Whole families, sitting on piles of luggage, seemed to be camped there. People rushed to and fro, or stood in little groups violently arguing. Women screamed. Others were silently weeping. Here two men were engaged in a fierce quarrel. It was a scene of indescribable confusion. The light in the station was wan and cold and the white faces of all those people were like the white faces of the dead waiting, patient or anxious, distraught or penitent, for the judgment of the last day. The train was made up and most of the carriages were already filled to overflowing. When at last Benedict found that in which Ashenden had his place a man sprang out of it excitedly.

"Come in and sit down," he said. "I've had the greatest difficulty in keeping your seat. A fellow wanted to come in here with a wife and two children. My Consul has just gone off with him to see the station-master."

"This is Mr. Harrington," said Benedict.

Ashenden stepped into the carriage. It had two berths in it. The porter stowed his luggage away. He shook hands with his travelling companion.

Mr. John Quincy Harrington was a very thin man of somewhat less than middle height, he had a yellow, bony face, with large, pale-blue eyes and when he took off his hat to wipe his brow wet from the perturbation he had endured he showed a large, bald skull; it was very bony and the ridges and protuberances stood out disconcertingly. He wore a bowler hat, a black coat and waistcoat, and a pair of striped trousers; a very high white collar and a neat, unobtrusive tie. Ashenden did not know precisely how you should dress in order to take a ten days' journey across Siberia, but he could not but think that Mr. Harrington's costume was eccentric. He spoke with precision in a high-pitched voice and in an accent that Ashenden recognized as that of New England.

In a minute the station-master came accompanied by a bearded Russian, suffering evidently from profound emotion, and followed by a lady holding two children by the hand. The Russian, tears running down his face, was talking with quivering lips to the station-master and his wife between her sobs was apparently telling him the story of her life. When they arrived at the carriage the altercation became more violent and Benedict joined in with his fluent Russian. Mr. Harrington did not know a word of the language, but being obviously of an excitable turn broke in and explained in voluble English that these seats had been booked by the Consuls of Great Britain and the United States respectively, and though he didn't know about the King of England, he could tell them straight and they could take it from him that the President of the United States would never permit an American citizen to be done out of a seat on the train that he had duly paid for. He would yield to force, but to nothing else, and if they touched him he would register a complaint with the Consul at once. He said all this and a great deal more to the station-master, who of course had no notion what he was talking about, but with much emphasis and a good deal of gesticulation made him in reply a passionate speech. This roused Mr. Harrington to the utmost pitch of indignation, for shaking his fist in the station-master's face, his own pale with fury, he cried out:

"Tell him I don't understand a word he says and I don't want to understand. If the Russians want us to look upon them as a civilized people why don't they talk a civilized language? Tell him that I am Mr. John Quincy Harrington and I'm travelling on behalf of Messrs Crewe and Adams of Philadelphia with a special letter of introduction to Mr. Kerensky and if I'm not left in peaceful possession of this carriage, Mr. Crewe will take the matter up with the Administration in Washington."

Mr. Harrington's manner was so truculent and his gestures so menacing that the station-master, throwing up the sponge, turned on his heel without another word and walked moodily away. He was followed by the bearded Russian and his wife arguing heatedly with him and the two apathetic children. Mr. Harrington jumped back into the carriage.

"I'm terribly sorry to have to refuse to give up my seat to a lady with two children," he said. "No one knows better than I the respect due to a woman and a mother, but I've got to get to Petrograd by this train if I don't want to lose a very important order and I'm not going to spend ten days in a corridor for all the mothers in Russia."

"I don't blame you," said Ashenden.

"I am a married man and I have two children myself. I know that travelling with your family is a difficult matter, but there's nothing that I know to prevent you from staying at home."

When you are shut up with a man for ten days in a railway carriage you can hardly fail to learn most of what there is to know about him, and for ten days (for eleven to be exact) Ashenden spent twenty-four hours a day with Mr. Harrington. It is true that they went into the dining-room three times a day for their meals, but they sat opposite to one another; it is true that the train stopped for an hour morning and afternoon so that

they were able to have a tramp up and down the platform, but
they walked side by side. Ashenden made acquaintance with some
of his fellow-travellers and sometimes they came into the compartment to have a chat, but if they only spoke French or German Mr. Harrington would watch them with acidulous disapproval
and if they spoke English he would never let them get a word in.
For Mr. Harrington was a talker. He talked as though it were a
natural function of the human being, automatically, as men breathe
or digest their food; he talked not because he had something to
say, but because he could not help himself, in a high-pitched,
nasal voice, without inflection, at one dead level of tone. He talked
with precision, using a copious vocabulary and forming his sentences with deliberation; he never used a short word when a
longer one would do; he never paused. He went on and on. It
was not a torrent, for there was nothing impetuous about it, it
was like a stream of lava pouring irresistibly down the side of a
volcano. It flowed with a quiet and steady force that overwhelmed
everything that was in its path.

Ashenden thought he had never known as much about anyone as he knew about Mr. Harrington, and not only about him,
with all his opinions, habits and circumstances, but about his wife
and his wife's family, his children and their schoolfellows, his employers and the alliances they had made for three or four genera-
tions with the best families of Philadelphia. His own family had
come from Devonshire early in the eighteenth century and Mr.
Harrington had been to the village where the graves of his fore-
bears were still to be seen in the churchyard. He was proud of
his English ancestry, but proud too of his American birth, though
to him America was a little strip of land along the Atlantic coast
and Americans were a small number of persons of English or
Dutch origin whose blood had never been sullied by foreign ad-
mixture. He looked upon the Germans, Swedes, Irish and the
inhabitants of Central and Eastern Europe who for the last hundred years have descended upon the United States as interlopers.
He turned his attention away from them as a maiden lady who
lived in a secluded manor might avert her eyes from the factory
chimneys that had trespassed upon her retirement.

When Ashenden mentioned a man of vast wealth who owned
some of the finest pictures in America Mr. Harrington said:

"I've never met him. My great-aunt Maria Penn Warmington

always said his grandmother was a very good cook. My great-aunt Maria was terribly sorry when she left her to get married. She said she never knew anyone who could make an apple pancake as she could."

Mr. Harrington was devoted to his wife and he told Ashenden at unbelievable length how cultivated and what a perfect mother she was. She had delicate health and had undergone a great number of operations all of which he described in detail. He had had two operations himself, one on his tonsils and one to remove his appendix and he took Ashenden day by day through his experiences. All his friends had had operations and his knowledge of surgery and encyclopædic. He had two sons, both at school, and he was seriously considering whether he would not be well-advised to have them operated on. It was curious that one of them should have enlarged tonsils, and he was not at all happy about the appendix of the other. They were more devoted to one another than he had ever seen two brothers be and a very good friend of his, the brightest surgeon in Philadelphia, had offered to operate on them both together so that they should not be separated. He showed Ashenden photographs of the boys and their mother. This journey of his to Russia was the first time in their lives that he had been separated from them and every morning he wrote a long letter to his wife telling her everything that had happened and a good deal of what he had said during the day. Ashenden watched him cover sheet after sheet of paper with his neat, legible and precise handwriting.

Mr. Harrington had read all the books on conversation and knew its technique to the last detail. He had a little book in which he noted down the stories he heard and he told Ashenden that when he was going out to dinner he always looked up half a dozen so that he should not be at a loss. They were marked with a G if they could be told in general society and with an M (for men) if they were more fit for rough masculine ears. He was a specialist in that peculiar form of anecdote that consists in narrating a long serious incident, piling detail upon detail, till a comic end is reached. He spared you nothing and Ashenden foreseeing the point long before it arrived would clench his hands and knit his brows in the strenuous effort not to betray his impatience and at last force from his unwilling mouth a grim and hollow laugh. If

someone came into the compartment in the middle Mr. Harrington would greet him with cordiality.

"Come right in and sit down. I was just telling my friend a
story. You must listen to it, it's one of the funniest things you ever
heard."

Then he would begin again from the very beginning and repeat it word for word, without altering a single apt epithet, till
he reached the humorous end. Ashenden suggested once that they
should see whether they could find two people on the train who
played cards so that they might while away the time with a game
of bridge, but Mr. Harrington said he never touched cards and
when Ashenden in desperation began to play patience he pulled
a wry face.

"It beats me how an intelligent man can waste his time card
playing, and of all the unintellectual pursuits I have ever seen
it seems to me that solitaire is the worst. It kills conversation.
Man is a social animal and he exercises the highest part of his
nature when he takes part in social intercourse."

"There is a certain elegance in wasting time," said Ashenden.
"Any fool can waste money, but when you waste time you waste
what is priceless. Besides," he added with bitterness, "you can still
talk."

"How can I talk when your attention is taken up by whether
you are going to get a black seven to put on a red eight? Conversation calls forth the highest powers of the intellect and if
you have made a study of it you have the right to expect that
the person you're talking to will give you the fullest attention he
is capable of."

He did not say this acrimoniously, but with the good-humoured
patience of a man who has been much tried. He was just stating
a plain fact and Ashenden could take it or leave it. It was the
claim of the artist to have his work taken seriously.

Mr. Harrington was a diligent reader. He read pencil in hand,
underlining passages that attracted his attention and on the mar-
gin making in his neat writing comments on what he read. This
he was fond of discussing and when Ashenden himself was reading and felt on a sudden that Mr. Harrington, book in one hand
and pencil in the other, was looking at him with his large pale
eyes he began to have violent palpitations of the heart. He dared
not look up, he dared not even turn the page, for he knew that

Mr. Harrington would regard this as ample excuse to break into a discourse, but remained with his eyes fixed desperately on a single word, like a chicken with its beak to a chalk line, and only ventured to breathe when he realized that Mr. Harrington, having given up the attempt, had resumed his reading. He was then engaged on a History of the American Constitution in two volumes and for recreation was perusing a stout volume that purported to contain all the great speeches of the world. For Mr. Harrington was an after-dinner speaker and had read all the best books on speaking in public. He knew exactly how to get on good terms with his audience, just where to put in the serious words that touched their hearts, how to catch their attention by a few apt stories and finally with what degree of eloquence, suiting the occasion, to deliver his peroration.

Mr. Harrington was very fond of reading aloud. Ashenden had had frequent occasion to observe the distressing propensity of Americans for this pastime. In hotel drawing-rooms at night after dinner he had often seen the father of a family seated in a retired corner and surrounded by his wife, his two sons and his daughter, reading to them. On ships crossing the Atlantic he had sometimes watched with awe the tall, spare gentleman of commanding aspect who sat in the centre of fifteen ladies no longer in their first youth and in a resonant voice read to them the history of Art. Walking up and down the promenade deck he had passed honeymooning couples lying on deck-chairs and caught the unhurried tones of the bride as she read to her young husband the pages of a popular novel. It had always seemed to him a curious way of showing affection. He had had friends who had offered to read to him and he had known women who had said they loved being read to, but he had always politely refused the invitation and firmly ignored the hint. He liked neither reading aloud nor being read aloud to. In his heart he thought the national predilection for this form of entertainment the only flaw in the perfection of the American character. But the immortal gods love a good laugh at the expense of human beings and now delivered him, bound and helpless, to the knife of the high priest. Mr. Harrington flattered himself that he was a very good reader and he explained to Ashenden the theory and practice of the art. Ashenden learned that there were two schools, the dramatic and the natural: in the first you imitated the voices of those who spoke (if you were reading a novel) and when the heroine wailed you wailed and when emotion choked her you choked too; but in the other you read as impassively as though you were reading the price-list of a mail-order house in Chicago. This was the school Mr. Harrington belonged to. In the seventeen years of his married life he had read aloud to his wife, and to his sons as soon as they were old enough to appreciate them, the novels of Sir Walter Scott, Jane Austen, Dickens, the Brontë Sisters, Thackeray, George Eliot, Nathaniel Hawthorne and W. J. Howells. Ashenden came to the conclusion that it was second nature with Mr. Harrington to read aloud and to prevent him from doing so made him as uneasy as cutting off his tobacco made the confirmed smoker. He would take you unawares.

"Listen to this," he would say, "you must listen to this," as though he were suddenly struck by the excellence of a maxim or the neatness of a phrase. "Now just tell me if you don't think this is remarkably well put. It's only three lines."

He read them and Ashenden was willing to give him a moment's attention, but having finished them, without pausing for a moment to take breath, he went on. He went right on. On and on. In his measured high-pitched voice, without emphasis or expression, he read page after page. Ashenden fidgeted, crossed and uncrossed his legs, lit cigarettes and smoked them, sat first in one position, then in another. Mr. Harrington went on and on. The train went leisurely through the interminable steppes of Siberia. They passed villages and crossed rivers. Mr. Harrington went on and on. When he finished a great speech by Edmund Burke he put down the book in triumph.

"Now that in my opinion is one of the finest orations in the English language. It is certainly a part of our common heritage that we can look upon with genuine pride."

"Doesn't it seem to you a little ominous that the people to whom Edmund Burke made that speech are all dead?" asked Ashenden gloomily.

Mr. Harrington was about to reply that this was hardly to be wondered at since the speech was made in the eighteenth century when it dawned upon him that Ashenden (bearing up wonderfully under affliction as any unprejudiced person could not fail to admit) was making a joke. He slapped his knee and laughed heartily.

"Gee, that's a good one," he said. "I'll write that down in my little book. I see exactly how I can bring it in one time when I have to speak at our luncheon club."

Mr. Harrington was a highbrow; but that appellation, invented by the vulgar as a term of abuse, he had accepted like the instrument of a saint's martyrdom, the gridiron of Saint Laurence for instance or the wheel of Saint Catherine, as an honorific title. He gloried in it.

"Emerson was a highbrow," he said. "Longfellow was a high-brow. Oliver Wendell Holmes was a highbrow. James Russell Lowell was a highbrow."

Mr. Harrington's study of American literature had taken him no further down the years than the period during which those eminent, but not precisely thrilling, authors flourished.

Mr. Harrington was a bore. He exasperated Ashenden, and enraged him; he got on his nerves, and drove him to frenzy. But Ashenden did not dislike him. His self-satisfaction was enormous but so ingenuous that you could not resent it; his conceit was so childlike that you could only smile at it. He was so well-meaning, so thoughtful, so deferential, so polite that though Ashenden would willingly have killed him he could not but own that in that short while he had conceived for Mr. Harrington something very like affection. His manners were exquisite, formal, a trifle elaborate perhaps (there is no harm in that, for good manners are the product of an artificial state of society and so can bear a touch of the powdered wig and the lace ruffle) but though natural to his good breeding they gained a pleasant significance from his good heart. He was ready to do anyone a kindness and seemed to find nothing too much trouble if he could thereby oblige his fellow man. He was eminently *serviable*. And it may be that this is a word for which there is no exact translation because the charming quality it denotes is not very common among our practical people. When Ashenden was ill for a couple of days Mr. Harrington nursed him with devotion. Ashenden was embarrassed by the care he took of him and though racked with pain could not help laughing at the fussy attention with which Mr. Harrington took his temperature, from his neatly packed valise extracted a whole regiment of tabloids and firmly doctored him; and he was touched by the trouble he gave himself to get from the dining-car the things that he thought Ashenden could eat. He did everything in the world for him but stop talking.

It was only when he was dressing that Mr. Harrington was silent, for then his maidenly mind was singly occupied with the problem of changing his clothes before Ashenden without indelicacy. He was extremely modest. He changed his linen every day, neatly taking it out of his suit-case and neatly putting back what was soiled; but he performed miracles of dexterity in order during the process not to show an inch of bare skin. After a day or two Ashenden gave up the struggle to keep neat and clean in that dirty train, with one lavatory for the whole carriage, and soon was as grubby as the rest of the passengers; but Mr. Harrington refused to yield to the difficulties. He performed his toilet with deliberation, notwithstanding the impatient persons who rattled the door-handle, and returned from the lavatory every morning washed, shining and smelling of soap. Once dressed, in his black coat, striped trousers and well-polished shoes, he looked as spruce as though he had just stepped out of his tidy little red-brick house in Philadelphia and was about to board the street-car that would take him down town to his office. At one point of the journey it was announced that an attempt had been made to blow up a bridge and that there were disturbances at the next station over the river; it might be that the train would be stopped and the passengers turned adrift or taken prisoners. Ashenden, thinking he might be separated from his luggage, took the precaution to change into his thickest clothes so that if he had to pass the winter in Siberia he need suffer as little as necessary from the cold; but Mr. Harrington would not listen to reason; he made no preparations for the possible experience and Ashenden had the conviction that if he spent three months in a Russian prison he would still preserve that smart and natty appearance. A troop of Cossacks boarded the train and stood on the platform of each carriage with their guns loaded, and the train rattled gingerly over the damaged bridge; then they came to the station at which they had been warned of danger, put on steam and dashed straight through it. Mr. Harrington was mildly satirical when Ashenden changed back into a light summer suit.

Mr. Harrington was a keen business man. It was obvious that it would need someone very astute to over reach him and Ashenden was sure that his employers had been well-advised to send him on this errand. He would safeguard their interests with all his might and if he succeeded in driving a bargain with the Russians it would be a hard one. His loyalty to his firm demanded that. He spoke of the partners with affectionate reverence. He loved them and was proud of them; but he did not envy them because their wealth was great. He was quite content to work on a salary and thought himself adequately paid; so long as he could educate his boys and leave his widow enough to live on what was money to him? He thought it a trifle vulgar to be rich. He looked upon culture as more important than money. He was careful of it and after every meal put down in his note-book exactly what it had cost him. His firm might be certain that he would not charge a penny more for his expenses than he had spent. But having discovered that poor people came to the station at the stopping places of the train to beg and seeing that the war had really brought them to destitution he took care before each halt to supply himself with ample small change and in a shame-faced way, mocking himself for being taken in by such impostors, distributed everything in his pocket.

"Of course I know they don't deserve it," he said, "and I don't do it for them. I do it entirely for my own peace of mind. I should feel so terribly badly if I thought some man really was hungry and I'd refused to give him the price of a meal."

Mr. Harrington was absurd, but lovable. It was inconceivable that anyone should be rude to him, it would have seemed as dreadful as hitting a child; and Ashenden, chafing inwardly but with a pretence of amiability, suffered meekly and with a truly Christian spirit the affliction of the gentle, ruthless creature's society. It took eleven days at that time to get from Vladivostok to Petrograd and Ashenden felt that he could not have borne another day. If it had been twelve he would have killed Mr. Harrington.

When at last (Ashenden tired and dirty, Mr. Harrington neat, sprightly and sententious) they reached the outskirts of Petrograd and stood at the window looking at the crowded houses of the city, Mr. Harrington turned to Ashenden and said:

"Well, I never would have thought that eleven days in the train would pass so quickly. We've had a wonderful time. I've enjoyed your company and I know you've enjoyed mine. I'm not going to pretend I don't know that I'm a pretty good conversa-

tionalist. But now we've come together like this we must take care
to stay together. We must see as much of one another as we can
while I'm in Petrograd."

"I shall have a great deal to do," said Ashenden. "I'm afraid
my time won't be altogether my own."

"I know," answered Mr. Harrington cordially. "I expect to be
pretty busy myself, but we can have breakfast together anyway
and we'll meet in the evening and compare notes. It would be
too bad if we drifted apart now."

"Too bad," sighed Ashenden.

When Ashenden found himself alone in his bedroom for the
first time, he sat down and looked about him. It had seemed an
age. He had not the energy to start immediately to unpack. How
many of these hotel bedrooms had he known since the beginning
of the war, grand or shabby, in one place and one land after
another! It seemed to him that he had been living in his luggage
for as long as he could remember. He was weary. He asked himself how he was going to set about the work that he had been sent
to do. He felt lost in the immensity of Russia and very solitary.
He had protested when he was chosen for this mission, it looked
too large an order, but his protests were ignored. He was chosen
not because those in authority thought him particularly suited for
the job, but because there was no one to be found who was more
suited. There was a knock at the door and Ashenden, pleased to
make use of the few words of the language he knew, called out in
Russian. The door was opened. He sprang to his feet.

"Come in, come in," he cried. "I'm awfully glad to see you."

Three men entered. He knew them by sight, since they had
travelled on the same boat with him from San Francisco to Yokohama, but following their instructions no communications had
passed between them and Ashenden. They were Czechs, exiled
from their country for their revolutionary activity and long settled
in America, who had been sent over to Russia to help Ashenden
in his mission and put him in touch with Professor Z. whose
authority over the Czechs in Russia was absolute. Their chief was
a certain Dr. Egon Orth, a tall thin man, with a little grey head;
he was minister to some church in the Middle West and a doctor
of divinity; but had abandoned his cure to work for the liberation
of his country, and Ashenden had the impression that he was an
intelligent fellow who would not put too fine a point on matters

of conscience. A parson with a fixed idea has this advantage over
common men that he can persuade himself of the Almighty's ap-
proval for almost any goings on. Dr. Orth had a merry twinkle
in his eye and a dry humour.

Ashenden had had two secret interviews with him in Yokohama
and had learnt that Professor Z., though eager to free his country
from the Austrian rule and since he knew that this could only
come about by the downfall of the Central Powers with the allies
body and soul, yet had scruples; he would not do things that
outraged his conscience, all must be straightforward and above
board, and so some things that it was necessary to do had to be
done without his knowledge. His influence was so great that his
wishes could not be disregarded, but on occasion it was felt better
not to let him know too much of what was going on.

Dr. Orth had arrived in Petrograd a week before Ashenden and
now put before him what he had learned of the situation. It
seemed to Ashenden that it was critical and if anything was to
be done it must be done quickly. The army was dissatisfied and
mutinous, the Government under the weak Kerensky was tottering
and held power only because no one else had the courage to
seize it, famine was staring the country in the face and already
the possibility had to be considered that the Germans would march
on Petrograd. The ambassadors of Great Britain and the United
States had been apprised of Ashenden's coming, but his mission
was secret even from them, and there were particular reasons
why he could demand no assistance from them. He arranged with
Dr. Orth to make an appointment with Professor Z. so that he
could learn his views and explain to him that he had the financial
means to support any scheme that seemed likely to prevent the
catastrophe that the Allied governments foresaw of Russia's making a separate peace. But he had to get in touch with influential
persons in all classes. Mr. Harrington with his business proposition and his letters to Ministers of State would be thrown in
contact with members of the Government and Mr. Harrington
wanted an interpreter. Dr. Orth spoke Russian almost as well as
his own language and it struck Ashenden that he would be admirably suited to the post. He explained the circumstances to him
and it was arranged that while Ashenden and Mr. Harrington
were at luncheon Dr. Orth should come in, greeting Ashenden as
though he had not seen him before, and be introduced to Mr.

Harrington; then Ashenden, guiding the conversation, would suggest to Mr. Harrington that the heavens had sent in Dr. Orth the ideal man for his purpose.

But there was another person on whom Ashenden had fixed as possibly useful to him and now he said:

"Have you ever heard of a woman called Anastasia Alexandrovna Leonidov? She's the daughter of Alexander Denisiev."

"I know all about him of course."

"I have reason to believe she's in Petrograd. Will you find out where she lives and what she's doing."

"Certainly."

Dr. Orth spoke in Czech to one of the two men who accompanied him. They were sharp-looking fellows both of them, one was tall and fair and the other was short and dark, but they were younger than Dr. Orth and Ashenden understood that they were there to do as he bade them. The man nodded, got up, shook hands with Ashenden and went out.

"You shall have all the information possible this afternoon."

"Well, I think there's nothing more we can do for the present," said Ashenden. "To tell you the truth I haven't had a bath for eleven days and I badly want one."

Ashenden had never quite made up his mind whether the pleasure of reflection was better pursued in a railway carriage or in a bath. So far as the act of invention was concerned he was inclined to prefer a train that went smoothly and not too fast, and many of his best ideas had come to him when he was thus traversing the plains of France; but for the delight of reminiscence or the entertainment of embroidery upon a theme already in his head he had no doubt that nothing could compare with a hot bath. He considered now, wallowing in soapy water like a water-buffalo in a muddy pond, the grim pleasantry of his relations with Anastasia Alexandrovna Leonidov.

In these stories no more than the barest suggestion has been made that Ashenden was capable on occasions of the passion ironically called tender. The specialists in this matter, those charming creatures who make a business of what philosophers know is but a diversion, assert that writers, painters and musicians, all in short who are connected with the arts, in the relation of love cut no very conspicuous figure. There is much cry but little wool. They rave or sigh, make phrases and strike many a romantic at-

titude, but in the end, loving art or themselves (which with
them is one and the same thing) better than the object of their
emotion offer a shadow when the said object, with the practical
common sense of the sex, demands a substance. It may be so and
this may be the reason (never before suggested) why women in
their souls look upon art with such a virulent hatred. Be this as it
may Ashenden in the last twenty years had left his heart go pit-
a-pat because of one charming person after another. He had had
a good deal of fun and had paid for it with a great deal of misery,
but even when suffering most acutely from the pangs of unrequited love he had been able to say to himself, albeit with a
wry face, after all, it's grist to the mill.

Anastasia Alexandrovna Leonidov was the daughter of a revolutionary who had escaped from Siberia after being sentenced to
penal servitude for life and had settled in England. He was an
able man and had supported himself for thirty years by the activity of a restless pen and had even made himself a distinguished
position in English letters. When Anastasia Alexandrovna reached
a suitable age she married Vladimir Semenovich Leonidov, also
an exile from his native country, and it was after she had been
married to him for some years that Ashenden made her acquaintance. It was at the time when Europe discovered Russia. Everyone
was reading the Russian novelists, the Russian dancers captivated
the civilized world, and the Russian composers set shivering the
sensibility of persons who were beginning to want a change from
Wagner. Russian art seized upon Europe with the virulence of an
epidemic of influenza. New phrases became the fashion, new
colours, new emotions, and the highbrows described themselves
without a moment's hesitation as members of the intelligentsia. It
was a difficult word to spell but an easy one to say. Ashenden
fell like the rest, changed the cushions of his sitting-room, hung
an eikon on the wall, read Chekoff and went to the ballet.

Anastasia Alexandrovna was by birth, circumstances and education very much a member of the intelligentsia. She lived with
her husband in a tiny house near Regent's Park and here all the
literary folk in London might gaze with humble reverence at pale-
faced bearded giants who leaned against the wall like caryatids
taking a day off; they were revolutionaries to a man and it was
a miracle that they were not in the mines of Siberia. Women of
letters tremulously put their lips to a glass of vodka. If you were

lucky and greatly favoured you might shake hands there with Diaghileff and now and again, like a peach-blossom wafted by the breeze, Pavlova herself hovered in and out. At this time Ashenden's success had not been so great as to affront the highbrows, he had very distinctly been one of them in his youth, and though some already looked askance, others (optimistic creatures with a faith in human nature) still had hopes of him. Anastasia Alexandrovna told him to his face that he was a member of the intelligentsia. Ashenden was quite ready to believe it. He was in a state when he was ready to believe anything. He was thrilled and excited. It seemed to him that at last he was about to capture that illusive spirit of romance that he had so long been chasing. Anastasia Alexandrovna had fine eyes and a good, though for these days, too voluptuous figure, high cheek bones and a snub nose (this was very Tartar), a wide mouth full of large square teeth and a pale skin. She dressed somewhat flamboyantly. In her dark melancholy eyes Ashenden saw the boundless steppes of Russia, and the Kremlin with its pealing bells, and the solemn ceremonies of Easter at St. Isaac's, and forests of silver beeches and the Nevsky Prospekt; it was astonishing how much he saw in her eyes. They were round and shining and slightly protuberant like those of a Pekinese. They talked together of Alyosha in the *Brothers Karamazov*, of Natasha in *War and Peace*, of Anna Karenina and of *Fathers and Sons*.

Ashenden soon discovered that her husband was quite unworthy of her and presently learned that she shared his opinion. Vladimir Semenovich was a little man with a large, long head that looked as though it had been pulled like a piece of liquorice, and he had a great shock of unruly Russian hair. He was a gentle, unobtrusive creature and it was hard to believe that the Czarist government had really feared his revolutionary activities. He taught Russian and wrote for papers in Moscow. He was amiable and obliging. He needed these qualities for Anastasia Alexandrovna was a woman of character: when she had a toothache Vladimir Semenovich suffered the agonies of the damned and when her heart was wrung by the suffering of her unhappy country Vladimir Semenovich might well have wished he had never been born. Ashenden could not help admitting that he was a poor thing, but he was so harmless that he conceived quite a liking for him, and when in due course he had disclosed his passion to

Anastasia Alexandrovna and to his joy found it was returned he was puzzled to know what to do about Vladimir Semenovich. Neither Anastasia Alexandrovna nor he felt that they could live another minute out of one another's pockets, and Ashenden feared that with her revolutionary views and all that she would never consent to marry him; but somewhat to his surprise, and very much to his relief, she accepted the suggestion with alacrity.

"Would Vladimir Semenovich let himself be divorced, do you think?" he asked, as he sat on the sofa, leaning against cushions the colour of which reminded him of raw meat just gone bad, and held her hand.

"Vladimir adores me," she answered. "It'll break his heart."

"He's a nice fellow, I shouldn't like him to be very unhappy. I hope he'll get over it."

"He'll never get over it. That is the Russian spirit. I know that when I leave him he'll feel that he has lost everything that made life worth living for him. I've never known anyone so wrapped up in a woman as he is in me. But of course he wouldn't want to stand in the way of my happiness. He's far too great for that. He'll see that when it's a question of my own self-development I haven't the right to hesitate. Vladimir will give me my freedom without question."

At that time the divorce law in England was even more complicated and absurd than it is now and in case she was not acquainted with its peculiarities Ashenden explained to Anastasia Alexandrovna the difficulties of the case. She put her hand gently on his.

"Vladimir would never expose me to the vulgar notoriety of the divorce court. When I tell him that I have decided to marry you he will commit suicide."

"That would be terrible," said Ashenden.

He was startled, but thrilled. It was really very much like a Russian novel and he saw the moving and terrible pages, pages and pages, in which Dostoievsky would have described the situation. He knew the lacerations his characters would have suffered, the broken bottles of champagne, the visits to the gipsies, the vodka, the swoonings, the catalepsy and the long, long speeches everyone would have made. It was all very dreadful and wonderful and shattering.

"It would make us horribly unhappy," said Anastasia Alexan-

drovna, "but I don't know what else he could do. I couldn't ask
him to live without me. He would be like a ship without a rudder
or a car without a carburettor. I know Vladimir so well. He will
commit suicide."

"How?" asked Ashenden, who had the realist's passion for the
exact detail.

"He will blow his brains out."

Ashenden remembered *Rosmerholm.* In his day he had been
an ardent Ibsenite and had even flirted with the notion of learning Norwegian so that he might, by reading the master in the
original, get at the secret essence of his thought. He had once
seen Ibsen in the flesh drink a glass of Munich beer.

"But do you think we could ever pass another easy hour if we
had the death of that man on our conscience?" he asked. "I have
a feeling that he would always be between us."

"I know we shall suffer, we shall suffer dreadfully," said Anastasia Alexandrovna, "but how can we help it? Life is like that.
We must think of Vladimir. There is his happiness to be considered
too. He will prefer to commit suicide."

She turned her face away and Ashenden saw that the heavy
tears were coursing down her cheeks. He was much moved. For
he had a soft heart and it was dreadful to think of poor Vladimir
lying there with a bullet in his brain.

These Russians, what fun they have!

But when Anastasia Alexandrovna had mastered her emotion
she turned to him gravely. She looked at him with her humid,
round and slightly protuberant eyes.

"We must be quite sure that we're doing the right thing,"
she said. "I should never forgive myself if I'd allowed Vladimir to
commit suicide and then found I'd made a mistake. I think we
ought to make sure that we really love one another."

"But don't you know?" exclaimed Ashenden in a low, tense
voice. "I know."

"Let's go over to Paris for a week and see how we get on.
Then we shall know."

Ashenden was a trifle conventional and the suggestion took
him by surprise. But only for a moment. Anastasia was wonderful. She was very quick and she saw the hesitation that for an
instant troubled him.

"Surely you have no bourgeois prejudices?" she said.

"Of course not," he assured her hurriedly, for he would much sooner have been thought knavish than bourgeois, "I think it's a splendid idea."

"Why should a woman hazard her whole life on a throw? It's impossible to know what a man is really like till you've lived with him. It's only fair to give her the opportunity to change her mind before it's too late."

"Quite so," said Ashenden.

Anastasia Alexandrovna was not a woman to let the grass grow under her feet and so having made their arrangements forthwith on the following Saturday they started for Paris.

"I shall not tell Vladimir that I am going with you," she said. "It would only distress him."

"It would be a pity to do that," said Ashenden.

"And if at the end of the week I come to the conclusion that we've made a mistake he need never know anything about it."

"Quite so," said Ashenden.

They met at Victoria station.

"What class have you got?" she asked him.

"First."

"I'm glad of that. Father and Vladimir travel third on account of their principles, but I always feel sick on a train and I like to be able to lean my head on somebody's shoulder. It's easier in a first-class carriage."

When the train started Anastasia Alexandrovna said she felt dizzy, so she took off her hat and leaned her head on Ashenden's shoulder. He put his arm round her waist.

"Keep quite still, won't you?" she said.

When they got on to the boat she went down to the ladies' cabin and at Calais was able to eat a very hearty meal, but when they got into the train she took off her hat again and rested her head on Ashenden's shoulder. He thought he would like to read and took up a book.

"Do you mind not reading?" she said. "I have to be held and when you turn the pages it makes me feel all funny."

Finally they reached Paris and went to a little hotel on the Left Bank that Anastasia Alexandrovna knew of. She said it had atmosphere. She could not bear those great big grand hotels on the other side; they were hopelessly vulgar and bourgeois.

"I'll go anywhere you like," said Ashenden, "as long as there's a bathroom."

She smiled and pinched his cheek.

"How adorably English you are. Can't you do without a bath-room for a week? My dear, my dear, you have so much to learn."

They talked far into the night about Maxim Gorki and Karl Marx, human destiny, love and the brotherhood of man; and drank innumerable cups of Russian tea, so that in the morning Ashenden would willingly have breakfasted in bed and got up for luncheon; but Anastasia Alexandrovna was an early riser. When life was so short and there was so much to do it was a sinful thing to have breakfast a minute after half-past eight. They sat down in a dingy little dining-room the windows of which showed no signs of having been opened for a month. It was full of atmo-sphere. Ashenden asked Anastasia Alexandrovna what she would have for breakfast.

"Scrambled eggs," she said.

She ate heartily. Ashenden had already noticed that she had a healthy appetite. He supposed it was a Russian trait: you could not picture Anna Karenina making her midday meal off a bath-bun and a cup of coffee, could you?

After breakfast they went to the Louvre and in the afternoon they went to the Luxembourg. They dined early in order to go to the Comédie Française; then they went to a Russian cabaret where they danced. When next morning at eight-thirty they took their places in the dining-room and Ashenden asked Anastasia Alexandrovna what she fancied, her reply was:

"Scrambled eggs."

"But we had scrambled eggs yesterday," he expostulated.

"Let's have them again to-day," she smiled.

"All right."

They spent the day in the same manner except that they went to the Carnavalet instead of the Louvre and the Musée Guimet in-stead of the Luxembourg. But when the morning after in answer to Ashenden's enquiry Anastasia Alexandrovna again asked for scrambled eggs, his heart sank.

"But we had scrambled eggs yesterday and the day before," he said.

"Don't you think that's a very good reason to have them again to-day?"

"No, I don't."

"Is it possible that your sense of humour is a little deficient this morning?" she asked. "I eat scrambled eggs every day. It's the only way I like them."

"Oh, very well. In that case of course we'll have scrambled eggs."

But the following morning he could not face them.

"Will you have scrambled eggs as usual?" he asked her.

"Of course," she smiled affectionately, showing him two rows of large square teeth.

"All right, I'll order them for you, I shall have mine fried."

The smile vanished from her lips.

"Oh?" She paused a moment. "Don't you think that's rather inconsiderate? Do you think it's fair to give the cook unnecessary work? You English, you're all the same, you look upon servants as machines. Does it occur to you that they have hearts like yours, the same feelings and the same emotions? How can you be surprised that the proletariat are seething with discontent when the bourgeoisie like you are so monstrously selfish?"

"Do you really think that there'll be a revolution in England if I have my eggs in Paris fried rather than scrambled?"

She tossed her pretty head in indignation.

"You don't understand. It's the principle of the thing. You think it's a jest, of course I know you're being funny, I can laugh at a joke as well as anyone, Chekoff was well-known in Russia as a humorist; but don't you see what is involved? Your whole attitude is wrong. It's a lack of feeling. You wouldn't talk like that if you had been through the events of 1905 in Petersburg. When I think of the crowds in front of the Winter Palace kneeling in the snow while the Cossacks charged them, women and children! No, no, no."

Her eyes filled with tears and her face was all twisted with pain. She took Ashenden's hand.

"I know you have a good heart. It was just thoughtless on your part and we won't say anything more about it. You have imagination. You're very sensitive. I know. You'll have your eggs done in the same way as mine, won't you?"

"Of course," said Ashenden.

He ate scrambled eggs for breakfast every morning after that. The waiter said: "*Monsieur aime les œufs brouillés.*" At the end of the week they returned to London. He held Anastasia Alexandrovna in his arms, her head resting on his shoulder, from Paris to Calais and again from Dover to London. He reflected that the journey from New York to San Francisco took five days. When they arrived at Victoria and stood on the platform waiting for a cab she looked at him with her round, shining and slightly protuberant eyes.

"We've had a wonderful time, haven't we?" she said.

"Wonderful."

"I've quite made up my mind. The experiment has justified itself. I'm willing to marry you whenever you like."

But Ashenden saw himself eating scrambled eggs every morning for the rest of his life. When he had put her in a cab, he called another for himself, went to the Cunard office and took a berth on the first ship that was going to America. No immigrant, eager for freedom and a new life, ever looked upon the statue of Liberty with more heartfelt thankfulness than did Ashenden, when on that bright and sunny morning his ship steamed into the harbour of New York.

Some years had passed since then and Ashenden had not seen Anastasia Alexandrovna again. He knew that on the outbreak of the revolution in March she and Vladimir Semenovich had gone to Russia. It might be that they would be able to help him, in a way Vladimir Semenovich owed him his life, and he made up his mind to write to Anastasia Alexandrovna to ask if he might come to see her.

When Ashenden went down to lunch he felt somewhat rested. Mr. Harrington was waiting for him and they sat down. They ate what was put before them.

"Ask the waiter to bring us some bread," said Mr. Harrington.

"Bread?" replied Ashenden. "There's no bread."

"I can't eat without bread," said Mr. Harrington.

"I'm afraid you'll have to. There's no bread, no butter, no sugar, no eggs, no potatoes. There's fish and meat and green vegetables, and that's all."

Mr. Harrington's jaw dropped.

"But this is war," he said.

"It looks very much like it."

Mr. Harrington was for a moment speechless; then he said: "I'll tell you what I'm going to do, I'm going to get through with my business as quick as I can and then I'm going to get out of this country. I'm sure Mrs. Harrington wouldn't like me to go without sugar or butter. I've got a very delicate stomach. The firm would never have sent me here if they'd thought I wasn't going to have the best of everything."

In a little while Dr. Egon Orth came in and gave Ashenden an envelope. On it was written Anastasia Alexandrovna's address. He introduced him to Mr. Harrington. It was soon clear that he was pleased with Dr. Egon Orth and so without further to do he suggested that here was the perfect interpreter for him.

"He talks Russian like a Russian. But he's an American citizen so that he won't do you down. I've known him a considerable time and I can assure you that he's absolutely trustworthy."

Mr. Harrington was pleased with the notion and after luncheon Ashenden left them to settle the matter by themselves. He wrote a note to Anastasia Alexandrovna and presently received an answer to say that she was going to a meeting, but would look in at his hotel about seven. He awaited her with apprehension. Of course he knew now that he had not loved her, but Tolstoi and Dostoievsky, Rimsky-Korsakoff, Stravinsky and Bakst; but he was not quite sure if the point had occurred to her. When between eight and half-past she arrived he suggested that she should join Mr. Harrington and him at dinner. The presence of a third party, he thought, would prevent any awkwardness their meeting might have; but he need not have had any anxiety, for five minutes after they had sat down to a plate of soup it was borne in upon him that the feelings of Anastasia Alexandrovna towards him were as cool as were his towards her. It gave him a momentary shock. It is very hard for a man, however modest, to grasp the possibility that a woman who has once loved him may love him no longer, and though of course he did not imagine that Anastasia Alexandrovna had languished for five years with a hopeless passion for him, he did think that by a heightening of colour, a flutter of the eyelashes, or a quiver of the lips she would betray the fact that she had still a soft place in her heart for him. Not at all. She talked to him as though he were a friend she was very glad to see again after an absence of a few days, but whose intimacy with her was purely social. He asked after Vladimir Semenovich.

"He has been a disappointment to me," she said. "I never

'thought he was a clever man, but I thought he was an honest one. He's going to have a baby."

Mr. Harrington who was about to put a piece of fish into his mouth, stopped, his fork in the air, and stared at Anastasia Alexandrovna with astonishment. In extenuation it must be explained that he had never read a Russian novel in his life. Ashenden, slightly perplexed too, gave her a questioning look.

"I'm not the mother," she said with a laugh. "I am not interested in that sort of thing. The mother is a friend of mine and a well-known writer on Political Economy. I do not think her views are sound, but I should be the last to deny that they deserve consideration. She has a good brain, quite a good brain." She turned to Mr. Harrington. "Are you interested in Political Economy?"

For once in his life Mr. Harrington was speechless. Anastasia Alexandrovna gave them her views on the subject and they began to speak on the situation in Russia. She seemed to be on intimate terms with the leaders of the various political parties and Ashenden made up his mind to sound her on the possibility of her working with him. His infatuation had not blinded him to the fact that she was an extremely intelligent woman. After dinner he told Mr. Harrington that he wished to talk business with Anastasia Alexandrovna and took her to a retired corner of the lounge. He told her all he thought necessary and found her interested and anxious to help. She had a passion for intrigue and a desire for power. When he hinted that he had command of large sums of money she saw at once that through him she might acquire an influence in the affairs of Russia. It tickled her vanity. She was immensely patriotic, but like many patriots she had an impression that her own aggrandisement tended to the good of her country. When they parted they had come to a working agreement.

"That was a very remarkable woman," said Mr. Harrington next morning when they met at breakfast.

"Don't fall in love with her," smiled Ashenden.

This, however, was not a matter on which Mr. Harrington was prepared to jest.

"I have never looked at a woman since I married Mrs. Harrington," he said. "That husband of hers must be a bad man."

"I could do with a plate of scrambled eggs," said Ashenden, irrelevantly, for their breakfast consisted of a cup of tea without milk and a little jam instead of sugar.

With Anastasia Alexandrovna to help him and Dr. Orth in the background, Ashenden set to work. Things in Russia were going from bad to worse. Kerensky, the head of the Provisional Government, was devoured by vanity and dismissed any minister who gave evidence of a capacity that might endanger his own position. He made speeches. He made endless speeches. At one moment there was a possibility that the Germans would make a dash for Petrograd. Kerensky made speeches. The food shortage grew more serious, the winter was approaching and there was no fuel. Kerensky made speeches. In the background the Bolsheviks were active, Lenin was hiding in Petrograd, it was said that Kerensky knew where he was, but dared not arrest him. He made speeches.

It amused Ashenden to see the unconcern with which Mr. Harrington wandered through this turmoil. History was in the making and Mr. Harrington minded his own business. It was uphill work. He was made to pay bribes to secretaries and underlings under the pretence that the ear of great men would be granted to him. He was kept waiting for hours in antechambers and then sent away without ceremony. When at last he saw the great men he found they had nothing to give him but idle words. They made him promises and in a day or two he discovered that the promises meant nothing. Ashenden advised him to throw in his hand and return to America; but Mr. Harrington would not hear of it; his firm had sent him to do a particular job, and by gum, he was going to do it or perish in the attempt. Then Anastasia Alexandrovna took him in hand. A singular friendship had arisen between the pair. Mr. Harrington thought her a very remarkable and deeply wronged woman; he told her all about his wife and his two sons, he told her all about the Constitution of the United States; she on her side told him all about Vladimir Semenovich, and she told him about Tolstoi, Turgenieff and Dostoievsky. They had great times together. He said he couldn't manage to call her Anastasia Alexandrovna, it was too much of a mouthful; so he called her Delilah. And now she placed her inexhaustible energy at his service and they went together to the persons who might be useful to him. But things were coming to a head. Riots broke out and the streets were growing dangerous. Now and then armoured cars filled with discontented reservists careered wildly along the Nevsky Prospekt and in order to show that they were not happy took pot-shots at the passers-by. On one occasion when Mr. Harrington and Anastasia Alexandrovna were in a tram together shots peppered the windows and they had to lie down on the floor for safety. Mr. Harrington was highly indignant.

"An old fat woman was lying right on top of me and when I wriggled to get out Delilah caught me a clip on the side of the head and said, stop still, you fool. I don't like your Russian ways, Delilah."

"Anyhow you stopped still," she giggled.

"What you want in this country is a little less art and a little more civilization."

"You are bourgeoisie, Mr. Harrington, you are not a member of the intelligentsia."

"You are the first person who's ever said that, Delilah. If I'm not a member of the intelligentsia I don't know who is," retorted Mr. Harrington with dignity.

Then one day when Ashenden was working in his room there was a knock at the door and Anastasia Alexandrovna stalked in followed, somewhat sheepishly, by Mr. Harrington. Ashenden saw that she was excited.

"What's the matter?" he asked.

"Unless this man goes back to America he'll get killed. You really must talk to him. If I hadn't been there something very unpleasant might have happened to him."

"Not at all, Delilah," said Mr. Harrington, with asperity. "I'm perfectly capable of taking care of myself and I wasn't in the smallest danger."

"What is it all about?" asked Ashenden.

"I'd taken Mr. Harrington to the Lavra of Alexander Nevsky to see Dostoievsky's grave," said Anastasia Alexandrovna, "and on our way back we saw a soldier being rather rough with an old woman."

"Rather rough!" cried Mr. Harrington. "There was an old woman walking along the side-walk with a basket of provisions on her arm. Two soldiers came up behind her and one of them snatched the basket from her and walked off with it. She burst out screaming and crying, I don't know what she was saying, but I can guess, and the other soldier took his gun and with the butt-end of it hit her over the head. Isn't that right, Delilah?"

"Yes," she answered, unable to help smiling. "And before I could prevent it Mr. Harrington jumped out of the cab and ran up to the soldier who had the basket, wrenched it from him and began to abuse the pair of them like pickpockets. At first they were so taken aback they didn't know what to do and then they got in a rage. I ran after Mr. Harrington and explained to them that he was a foreigner and drunk."

"Drunk?" cried Mr. Harrington.

"Yes, drunk. Of course a crowd collected. It looked as though it wasn't going to be very nice."

Mr. Harrington smiled with those large, pale-blue eyes of his.

"It sounded to me as though you were giving them a piece of your mind, Delilah. It was as good as a play to watch you."

"Don't be stupid, Mr. Harrington," cried Anastasia, in a sudden fury, stamping her foot. "Don't you know that those soldiers might very easily have killed you and me too, and not one of the by-standers would have raised a finger to help us?"

"Me? I'm an American citizen, Delilah. They wouldn't dare touch a hair of my head."

"They'd have difficulty in finding one," said Anastasia Alexandrovna, who when she was in a temper had no manners. "But if you think Russian soldiers are going to hesitate to kill you because you're an American citizen you'll get a big surprise one of these days."

"Well, what happened to the old woman?" asked Ashenden.

"The soldiers went off after a little and we went back to her."

"Still with the basket?"

"Yes. Mr. Harrington clung on to that like grim death. She was lying on the ground with the blood pouring from her head. We got her into the cab and when she could speak enough to tell us where she lived we drove her home. She was bleeding dreadfully and we had some difficulty in staunching the blood."

Anastasia Alexandrovna gave Mr. Harrington an odd look and to his surprise Ashenden saw him turn scarlet.

"What's the matter now?"

"You see, we had nothing to bind her up with. Mr. Harrington's handkerchief was soaked. There was only one thing about me that I could get off quickly and so I took off my . . ."

But before she could finish Mr. Harrington interrupted her.

"You need not tell Mr. Ashenden what you took off. I'm a married man and I know ladies wear them, but I see no need to refer to them in general society."

Anastasia Alexandrovna giggled.

"Then you must kiss me, Mr. Harrington. If you don't I shall say."

Mr. Harrington hesitated a moment, considering evidently the pros and cons of the matter, but he saw that Anastasia Alexandrovna was determined.

"Go on then, you may kiss me, Delilah, though I'm bound to say I don't see what pleasure it can be to you."

She put her arms round his neck and kissed him on both cheeks, then without a word of warning burst into a flood of tears.

"You're a brave little man, Mr. Harrington. You're absurd but magnificent," she sobbed.

Mr. Harrington was less surprised than Ashenden would have expected him to be. He looked at Anastasia with a thin, quizzical smile and gently patted her.

"Come, come, Delilah, pull yourself together. It gave you a nasty turn, didn't it? You're quite upset. I shall have terrible rheumatism in my shoulder if you go on weeping all over it."

The scene was ridiculous and touching, Ashenden laughed, but he had the beginnings of a lump in his throat.

When Anastasia Alexandrovna had left them Mr. Harrington sat in a brown study.

"They're very queer, these Russians. Do you know what Delilah did?" he said, suddenly. "She stood up in the cab, in the middle of the street, with people passing on both sides, and took her pants off. She tore them in two and gave me one to hold while she made a bandage of the other. I was never so embarrassed in my life."

"Tell me what gave you the idea of calling her Delilah?" smiled Ashenden.

Mr. Harrington reddened a little.

"She's a very fascinating woman, Mr. Ashenden. She's been deeply wronged by her husband and I naturally felt a great deal of sympathy for her. These Russians are very emotional people and I did not want her to mistake my sympathy for anything else. I told her I was very much attached to Mrs. Harrington."

"You're not under the impression that Delilah was Potiphar's wife?" asked Ashenden.

"I don't know what you mean by that, Mr. Ashenden," replied Mr. Harrington. "Mrs. Harrington has always given me to understand that I'm very fascinating to women, and I thought if I called our little friend Delilah it would make my position quite clear."

"I don't think Russia's any place for you, Mr. Harrington," said Ashenden smiling. "If I were you I'd get out of it as quick as I could."

"I can't go now. I've got them to agree to my terms at last and we're going to sign next week. Then I shall pack my grip and go."

"I wonder if your signatures will be worth the paper they're written on," said Ashenden.

He had at length devised a plan of campaign. It took him twenty-four hours' hard work to code a telegram in which he put his scheme before the persons who had sent him to Petrograd. It was accepted and he was promised all the money he needed. Ashenden knew he could do nothing unless the Provisional Government remained in power for another three months; but winter was at hand and food was getting scarcer every day. The army was mutinous. The people clamoured for peace. Every evening at the Europe Ashenden drank a cup of chocolate with Professor Z. and discussed with him how best to make use of his devoted Czechs. Anastasia Alexandrovna had a flat in a retired spot and here he had meetings with all manner of persons. Plans were drawn up. Measures were taken. Ashenden argued, persuaded, promised. He had to overcome the vacillation of one and wrestle with the fatalism of another. He had to judge who was resolute and who was self-sufficient, who was honest and who was infirm of purpose. He had to curb his impatience with the Russian verbosity; he had to be good-tempered with people who were willing to talk of everything but the matter in hand; he had to listen sympathetically to ranting and rhodomontade. He had to beware of treachery. He had to humour the vanity of fools and elude the greed of the ambitious. Time was pressing. The rumours grew hot and many of the activities of the Bolsheviks. Kerensky ran hither and thither like a frightened hen.

Then the blow fell. On the night of November 7th, 1917, the Bolsheviks rose, Kerensky's ministers were arrested and the Winter Palace was sacked by the mob; the reins of power were seized by Lenin and Trotsky.

Anastasia Alexandrovna came to Ashenden's room at the hotel early in the morning. Ashenden was coding a telegram. He had been up all night, first at the Smolny, and then at the Winter

Palace. He was tired out. Her face was white and her shining brown eyes were tragic.

"Have you heard?" she asked Ashenden.

He nodded.

"It's all over then. They say Kerensky has fled. They never even showed fight." Rage seized her. "The buffoon!" she screamed.

At that moment there was a knock at the door and Anastasia Alexandrovna looked at it with sudden apprehension.

"You know the Bolsheviks have got a list of people they've decided to execute. My name is on it, and it may be that yours is too."

"If it's they and they want to come in they only have to turn the handle," said Ashenden, smiling, but with ever so slightly odd a feeling at the pit of his stomach. "Come in."

The door was opened and Mr. Harrington stepped into the room. He was as dapper as ever, in his short black coat and striped trousers, his shoes neatly polished and a derby on his bald head. He took it off when he saw Anastasia Alexandrovna.

"Oh, fancy finding you here so early. I looked in on my way out, I wanted to tell you my news. I tried to find you yesterday evening, but couldn't. You didn't come in to dinner."

"No, I was at a meeting," said Ashenden.

"You must both congratulate me, I got my signatures yesterday, and my business is done."

Mr. Harrington beamed on them, the picture of self-satisfaction, and he arched himself like a bantam-cock who has chased away all rivals. Anastasia Alexandrovna burst into a sudden shriek of hysterical laughter. He stared at her in perplexity.

"Why, Delilah, what is the matter?" he said.

Anastasia laughed till the tears ran from her eyes and then began to sob in earnest. Ashenden explained.

"The Bolsheviks have overthrown the Government. Kerensky's ministers are in prison. The Bolsheviks are out to kill. Delilah says her name is on the list. Your minister signed your documents yesterday because he knew it did not matter what he did then. Your contracts are worth nothing. The Bolsheviks are going to make peace with Germany as soon as they can."

Anastasia Alexandrovna had recovered her self-control as quickly as she had lost it.

"You had better get out of Russia as soon as you can, Mr. Harrington. It's no place for a foreigner now and it may be that in a few days you won't be able to."

Mr. Harrington looked from one to the other.

"O my," he said. "O my!" It seemed inadequate. "Are you going to tell me that that Russian minister was just making a fool of me?"

Ashenden shrugged his shoulders.

"How can one tell what he was thinking of? He may have a keen sense of humour and perhaps he thought it funny to sign a fifty million dollar contract yesterday when there was every chance of his being stood against the wall and shot to-day. Anastasia Alexandrovna's right, Mr. Harrington, you'd better take the first train that'll get you to Sweden."

"And what about you?"

"There's nothing for me to do here any more. I'm cabling for instructions and I shall go as soon as I get leave. The Bolsheviks have got in ahead of us and the people I was working with will have their work cut out to save their lives."

"Boris Petrovich was shot this morning," said Anastasia Alexandrovna with a frown.

They both looked at Mr. Harrington and he stared at the floor. His pride in this achievement of his was shattered and he sagged like a pricked balloon. But in a minute he looked up. He gave Anastasia Alexandrovna a little smile and for the first time Ashenden noticed how attractive and kindly his smile was. There was something peculiarly disarming about it.

"If the Bolsheviks are after you, Delilah, don't you think you'd better come with me? I'll take care of you and if you'd like to come to America I'm sure Mrs. Harrington would be glad to do anything she could for you."

"I can see Mrs. Harrington's face if you arrived in Philadelphia with a Russian refugee," laughed Anastasia Alexandrovna. "I'm afraid it would need more explaining than you could ever manage. No, I shall stay here."

"But if you're in danger?"

"I'm a Russian. My place is here. I will not leave my country when most my country needs me."

"That is the bunk, Delilah," said Mr. Harrington very quietly.

Anastasia Alexandrovna had spoken with deep emotion, but now with a little start she shot a sudden quizzical look at him.

"I know it is, Samson," she answered. "To tell you the truth
I think we're all going to have a hell of a time, God knows what's
going to happen, but I want to see; I wouldn't miss a minute of
it for the world."

Mr. Harrington shook his head.

"Curiosity is the bane of your sex, Delilah," he said.

"Go along and do your packing, Mr. Harrington," said Ashenden,
smiling, "and then we'll take you to the station. The train will be
besieged."

"Very well, I'll go. And I shan't be sorry either. I haven't had a
decent meal since I came here and I've done a thing I never
thought I should have to do in my life, I've drunk my coffee without sugar and when I've been lucky enough to get a little piece
of black bread I've had to eat it without butter. Mrs. Harrington
will never believe me when I tell her what I've gone through.
What this country wants is organization."

When he left them Ashenden and Anastasia Alexandrovna
talked over the situation. Ashenden was depressed because all his
careful schemes had come to nothing, but Anastasia Alexandrovna
was excited and she hazarded every sort of guess about the out-
come of this new revolution. She pretended to be very serious,
but in her heart she looked upon it all very much as a thrilling
play. She wanted more and more things to happen. Then there
was another knock at the door and before Ashenden could answer Mr. Harrington burst in.

"Really the service at this hotel is a scandal," he cried heatedly,
"I've been ringing my bell for fifteen minutes and I can't get anyone to pay the smallest attention to me."

"Service?" exclaimed Anastasia Alexandrovna. "There is not a
servant left in the hotel."

"But I want my washing. They promised to let me have it back
last night."

"I'm afraid you haven't got much chance of getting it now," said
Ashenden.

"I'm not going to leave without my washing. Four shirts, two
union suits, a pair of pyjamas, and four collars. I wash my hand-
kerchiefs and socks in my room. I want my washing and I'm not
going to leave this hotel without it."

"Don't be a fool," cried Ashenden. "What you've got to do is to get out of here while the going's good. If there are no servants to get it you'll just have to leave your washing behind you."

"Pardon me, sir, I shall do nothing of the kind. I'll go and fetch it myself. I've suffered enough at the hands of this country and I'm not going to leave four perfectly good shirts to be worn by a lot of dirty Bolsheviks. No, sir. I do not leave Russia till I have my washing."

Anastasia Alexandrovna stared at the floor for a moment; then with a little smile looked up. It seemed to Ashenden that there was something in her that responded to Mr. Harrington's futile obstinacy. In her Russian way she understood that Mr. Harrington could not leave Petrograd without his washing. His insistence had given it the value of a symbol.

"I'll go downstairs and see if I can find anybody about who knows where the laundry is and if I can, I'll go with you and you can bring your washing away with you."

Mr. Harrington unbent. He answered with that sweet and disarming smile of his.

"That's terribly kind of you, Delilah. I don't mind if it's ready or not, I'll take it just as it is."

Anastasia Alexandrovna left them.

"Well, what do you think of Russia and the Russians now?" Mr. Harrington asked Ashenden.

"I'm fed up with them. I'm fed up with Tolstoi, I'm fed up with Turgeniev and Dostoievski, I'm fed up with Chekov. I'm fed up with the Intelligentsia. I hanker after people who know their mind from one minute to another, who mean what they say an hour after they've said it, whose word you can rely on; I'm sick of fine phrases, and oratory and attitudinizing."

Ashenden, bitten by the prevailing ill, was about to make a speech when he was interrupted by a rattle as of peas on a drum. In the city, so strangely silent, it sounded abrupt and odd.

"What's that?" asked Mr. Harrington.

"Rifle firing. On the other side of the river I should think."

Mr. Harrington gave a funny little look. He laughed, but his face was a trifle pale; he did not like it, and Ashenden did not blame him.

"I think it's high time I got out. I shouldn't so much mind for myself, but I've got a wife and children to think of. I haven't had a letter from Mrs. Harrington for so long I'm a bit worried." He paused an instant. "I'd like you to know Mrs. Harrington, she's a very wonderful woman. She's the best wife a man ever had. Until I came here I'd not been separated from her for more than three days since we were married."

Anastasia Alexandrovna came back and told them that she had found the address.

"It's about forty minutes' walk from here and if you'll come now I'll go with you," she said.

"I'm ready."

"You'd better look out," said Ashenden. "I don't believe the streets are very healthy to-day."

Anastasia Alexandrovna looked at Mr. Harrington.

"I must have my washing, Delilah," he said. "I should never rest in peace if I left it behind me and Mrs. Harrington would never let me hear the last of it."

"Come on then."

They set out and Ashenden went on with the dreary business of translating into a very complicated code the shattering news he had to give. It was a long message, and then he had to ask for instructions upon his own movements. It was a mechanical job and yet it was one in which you could not allow your attention to wander. The mistake of a single figure might make a whole sentence incomprehensible.

Suddenly his door was burst open and Anastasia Alexandrovna flung into the room. She had lost her hat and was dishevelled. She was panting. Her eyes were starting out of her head and she was obviously in a state of great excitement.

"Where's Mr. Harrington?" she cried. "Isn't he here?"

"No."

"Is he in his bedroom?"

"I don't know. Why, what's the matter? We'll go and look if you like. Why didn't you bring him along with you?"

They walked down the passage and knocked at Mr. Harrington's door; there was no answer; they tried the handle; the door was locked.

"He's not there."

They went back to Ashenden's room. Anastasia Alexandrovna sank into a chair.

"Give me a glass of water, will you. I'm out of breath. I've been running."

She drank the water Ashenden poured out for her. She gave a sudden sob.

"I hope he's all right. I should never forgive myself if he was hurt. I was hoping he would have got here before me. He got his washing all right. We found the place. There was only an old woman there and they didn't want to let us take it, but we insisted. Mr. Harrington was furious because it hadn't been touched. It was exactly as he had sent it. They'd promised it last night and it was still in the bundle that Mr. Harrington had made himself. I said that was Russia and Mr. Harrington said he preferred coloured people. I'd led him by side streets because I thought it was better, and we started to come back again. We passed at the top of a street and at the bottom of it I saw a little crowd. There was a man addressing them.

"'Let's go and hear what he's saying,' I said.

"I could see they were arguing. It looked exciting. I wanted to know what was happening.

"'Come along, Delilah,' he said. 'Let us mind our own business.'

"'You go back to the hotel and do your packing. I'm going to see the fun,' I said.

"I ran down the street and he followed me. There were about two or three hundred people there and a student was addressing them. There were some working men and they were shouting at him. I love a row and I edged my way into the crowd. Suddenly we heard the sound of shots and before you could realize what was happening two armoured cars came dashing down the street. There were soldiers in them and they were firing as they went. I don't know why. For fun, I suppose, or because they were drunk. We all scattered like a lot of rabbits. We just ran for our lives. I lost Mr. Harrington. I can't make out why he isn't here. Do you think something has happened to him?"

Ashenden was silent for a while.

"We'd better go out and look for him," he said. "I don't know why the devil he couldn't leave his washing."

"I understand, I understand so well."

"That's a comfort," said Ashenden irritably. "Let's go."

He put on his hat and coat, and they walked downstairs. The hotel seemed strangely empty. They went out into the street. There was hardly anyone to be seen. They walked along. The trams were not running and the silence in the great city was uncanny. The shops were closed. It was quite startling when a motor car dashed by at breakneck speed. The people they passed looked frightened and downcast. When they had to go through a main thoroughfare they hastened their steps. A lot of people were there and they stood about irresolutely as though they did not know what to do next. Reservists in their shabby grey were walking down the middle of the roadway in little bunches. They did not speak. They looked like sheep looking for their shepherd. Then they came to the street down which Anastasia Alexandrovna had run, but they entered it from the opposite end. A number of windows had been broken by the wild shooting. It was quite empty. You could see where the people had scattered, for strewn about were articles they had dropped in their haste, books, a man's hat, a lady's bag and a basket. Anastasia Alexandrovna touched Ashenden's arm to draw his attention: sitting on the pavement, her head bent right down to her lap, was a woman and she was dead. A little way on two men had fallen together. They were dead too. The wounded, one supposed, had managed to drag themselves away or their friends had carried them. Then they found Mr. Harrington. His derby had rolled in the gutter. He lay on his face, in a pool of blood, his bald head, with its prominent bones, very white; his neat black coat smeared and muddy. But his hand was clenched tight on the parcel that contained four shirts, two union suits, a pair of pyjamas and four collars. Mr. Harrington had not let his washing go.

The Force of Circumstance

She was sitting on the verandah waiting for her husband to come in for luncheon. The Malay boy had drawn the blinds when the morning lost its freshness, but she had partly raised one of them so that she could look at the river. Under the breathless sun of midday it had the white pallor of death. A native was paddling along in a dug-out so small that it hardly showed above the surface of the water. The colours of the day were ashy and wan. They were but the various tones of the heat. (It was like an Eastern melody, in the minor key, which exacerbates the nerves by its ambiguous monotony; and the ear awaits impatiently a resolution, but waits in vain.) The cicadas sang their grating song with a frenzied energy: it was as continual and monotonous as the rustling of a brook over the stones; but on a sudden it was drowned by the loud singing of a bird, mellifluous and rich; and for an instant, with a catch at her heart, she thought of the English blackbird.

Then she heard her husband's step on the gravel path behind the bungalow, the path that led to the court-house in which he had been working, and she rose from her chair to greet him. He ran up the short flight of steps, for the bungalow was built on piles, and at the door the boy was waiting to take his topee. He came into the room which served them as dining-room and parlour, and his eyes lit up with pleasure as he saw her.

"Hulloa, Doris. Hungry?"

"Ravenous."

"It'll only take me a minute to have a bath and then I'm ready."

"Be quick," she smiled.

He disappeared into his dressing-room and she heard him whistling cheerily while, with the carelessness with which she was always remonstrating, he tore off his clothes and flung them on the floor. He was twenty-nine, but he was still a schoolboy; he would never grow up. That was why she had fallen in love with him, perhaps, for no amount of affection could persuade her that he was good-looking. He was a little round man, with a red face like the full moon, and blue eyes. He was rather pimply. She had examined him carefully and had been forced to confess to him that he had not a single feature which she could praise. She had told him often that he wasn't her type at all.

"I never said I was a beauty," he laughed.

"I can't think what it is I see in you."

But of course she knew perfectly well. He was a gay, jolly little man, who took nothing very solemnly, and he was constantly laughing. He made her laugh too. He found life an amusing rather than a serious business, and he had a charming smile. When she was with him she felt happy and good-tempered. And the deep affection which she saw in those merry blue eyes of his touched her. It was very satisfactory to be loved like that. Once, sitting on his knees, during their honeymoon she had taken his face in her hands and said to him:

"You're an ugly, little fat man, Guy, but you've got charm. I can't help loving you."

A wave of emotion swept over her and her eyes filled with tears. She saw his face contorted for a moment with the extremity of his feeling and his voice was a little shaky when he answered.

"It's a terrible thing for me to have married a woman who's mentally deficient," he said.

She chuckled. It was the characteristic answer which she would have liked him to make.

It was hard to realize that nine months ago she had never even heard of him. She had met him at a small place by the seaside where she was spending a month's holiday with her mother. Doris was secretary to a member of parliament. Guy was home on leave. They were staying at the same hotel, and he quickly told her all about himself. He was born in Sembulu, where his father had served for thirty years under the second Sultan, and on leaving school he had entered the same service. He was devoted to the country.

"After all, England's a foreign land to me," he told her. "My home's Sembulu."

And now it was her home too. He asked her to marry him at the end of the month's holiday. She had known he was going to, and had decided to refuse him. She was her widowed mother's only child and she could not go so far away from her, but when the moment came she did not quite know what happened to her, she was carried off her feet by an unexpected emotion, and she accepted him. They had been settled now for four months in the little outstation of which he was in charge. She was very happy.

She told him once that she had quite made up her mind to refuse him.

"Are you sorry you didn't?" he asked, with a merry smile in his twinkling blue eyes.

"I should have been a perfect fool if I had. What a bit of luck that fate or chance or whatever it was stepped in and took the matter entirely out of my hands!"

Now she heard Guy clatter down the steps to the bath-house. He was a noisy fellow and even with bare feet he could not be quiet. But he uttered an exclamation. He said two or three words in the local dialect and she could not understand. Then she heard some one speaking to him, not aloud, but in a sibilant whisper. Really it was too bad of people to waylay him when he was going to have his bath. He spoke again and though his voice was low she could hear that he was vexed. The other voice was raised now; it was a woman's. Doris supposed it was some one who had a complaint to make. It was like a Malay woman to come in that surreptitious way. But she was evidently getting very little from Guy, for she heard him say: get out. That at all events she understood, and then she heard him bolt the door. There was a sound of the water he was throwing over himself (the bathing arrangements still amused her, the bath-houses were under the bedrooms, on the ground; you had a large tub of water and you sluiced yourself with a little tin pail) and in a couple of minutes he was back again in the dining-room. His hair was still wet. They sat down to luncheon.

"It's lucky I'm not a suspicious or a jealous person," she laughed. "I don't know that I should altogether approve of your having animated conversations with ladies while you're having your bath."

His face, usually so cheerful, had borne a sullen look when he came in, but now it brightened.

"I wasn't exactly pleased to see her."

"So I judged by the tone of your voice. In fact, I thought you were rather short with the young person."

"Damned cheek, waylaying me like that!"

"What did she want?"

"Oh, I don't know. It's a woman from the kampong. She's had a row with her husband or something."

"I wonder if it's the same one who was hanging about this morning."

He frowned a little.

"Was there some one hanging about?"

"Yes, I went into your dressing-room to see that everything was nice and tidy, and then I went down to the bath-house. I saw some one slink out of the door as I went down the steps and when I looked out I saw a woman standing there."

"Did you speak to her?"

"I asked her what she wanted and she said something, but I couldn't understand."

"I'm not going to have all sorts of stray people prowling about here," he said. "They've got no right to come."

He smiled, but Doris, with the quick perception of a woman in love, noticed that he smiled only with his lips, not as usual with his eyes also, and wondered what it was that troubled him.

"What have you been doing this morning?" he asked.

"Oh, nothing much. I went for a little walk."

"Through the kampong?"

"Yes. I saw a man send a chained monkey up a tree to pick coconuts, which rather thrilled me."

"It's rather a lark, isn't it?"

"Oh, Guy, there were two little boys watching him who were much whiter than the others. I wondered if they were half-castes. I spoke to them, but they didn't know a word of English."

"There are two or three half-caste children in the kampong," he answered.

"Who do they belong to?"

"Their mother is one of the village girls."

"Who is their father?"

"Oh, my dear, that's the sort of question we think it a little dangerous to ask out here." He paused. "A lot of fellows have native wives, and then when they go home or marry, they pension them off and send them back to their village."

Doris was silent. The indifference with which he spoke seemed a little callous to her. There was almost a frown on her frank, open, pretty English face when she replied.

"But what about the children?"

"I have no doubt they're properly provided for. Within his means, a man generally sees that there's enough money to have them decently educated. They get jobs as clerks in a Government office, you know; they're all right."

She gave him a slightly rueful smile.

"You can't expect me to think it's a very good system."

"You mustn't be too hard," he smiled back.

"I'm not hard. But I'm thankful you never had a Malay wife. I should have hated it. Just think if those two little brats were yours."

The boy changed their plates. There was never much variety in their menu. They started luncheon with river fish, dull and insipid, so that a good deal of tomato ketchup was needed to make it palatable, and then went on to some kind of stew. Guy poured Worcester Sauce over it.

"The old Sultan didn't think it was a white woman's country," he said presently. "He rather encouraged people to—keep house with native girls. Of course things have changed now. The country's perfectly quiet and I suppose we know better how to cope with the climate."

"But, Guy, the eldest of those boys wasn't more than seven or eight and the other was about five."

"It's awfully lonely on an outstation. Why, often one doesn't see another white man for six months on end. A fellow comes out here when he's only a boy." He gave her that charming smile of his which transfigured his round, plain face. "There are excuses, you know."

She always found that smile irresistible. It was his best argument. Her eyes grew once more soft and tender.

"I'm sure there are." She stretched her hand across the little table and put it on his. "I'm very lucky to have caught you so young. Honestly, it would upset me dreadfully if I were told that you had lived like that."

He took her hand and pressed it.

"Are you happy here, darling?"

"Desperately."

She looked very cool and fresh in her linen frock. The heat did not distress her. She had no more than the prettiness of youth, though her brown eyes were fine; but she had a pleasing frankness of expression, and her dark, short hair was neat and glossy. She gave you the impression of a girl of spirit and you felt sure that the member of parliament for whom she had worked had in her a very competent secretary.

"I loved the country at once," she said. "Although I'm alone so much I don't think I've ever once felt lonely."

Of course she had read novels about the Malay Archipelago and she had formed an impression of a sombre land with great ominous rivers and a silent, impenetrable jungle. When the little coasting steamer set them down at the mouth of the river, where a large boat, manned by a dozen Dyaks, was waiting to take them to the station, her breath was taken away by the beauty, friendly rather than awe-inspiring, of the scene. It had a gaiety, like the joyful singing of birds in the trees, which she had never expected. On each bank of the river were mangroves and nipa palms, and behind them the dense green of the forest. In the distance stretched blue mountains, range upon range, as far as the eye could see. She had no sense of confinement nor of gloom, but rather of openness and wide spaces where the exultant fancy could wander with delight. The green glittered in the sunshine and the sky was blithe and cheerful. The gracious land seemed to offer her a smiling welcome.

They rowed on, hugging a bank, and high overhead flew a pair of doves. A flash of colour, like a living jewel, dashed across their path. It was a kingfisher. Two monkeys, with their dangling tails, sat side by side on a branch. On the horizon, over there on the other side of the broad and turbid river, beyond the jungle, was a row of little white clouds, the only clouds in the sky, and they looked like a row of ballet-girls, dressed in white, waiting at the back of the stage, alert and merry, for the curtain to go up. Her heart was filled with joy; and now, remembering it all, her eyes rested on her husband with a grateful, assured affection.

And what fun it had been to arrange their living-room! It was very big. On the floor, when she arrived, was a torn and dirty matting; on the walls of unpainted wood hung (much too high up) photogravures of Academy pictures, Dyak shields and parangs. The tables were covered with Dyak cloth in sombre colours, and on them stood pieces of Brunei brassware, much in need of cleaning, empty cigarette tins and bits of Malay silver. There was a rough wooden shelf with cheap editions of novels and a number of old travel books in battered leather; and another shelf was crowded with empty bottles. It was a bachelor's room, untidy but stiff; and though it amused her she found it intolerably pathetic. It was a dreary, comfortless life that Guy had led there, and she threw her arms round his neck and kissed him.

"You poor darling," she laughed.

She had deft hands and she soon made the room habitable. She arranged this and that, and what she could not do with she turned out. Her wedding-presents helped. Now the room was friendly and comfortable. In glass vases were lovely orchids and in great bowls huge masses of flowering shrubs. She felt an inordinate pride because it was her house (she had never in her life lived in anything but a poky flat) and she had made it charming for him.

"Are you pleased with me?" she asked when she had finished.

"Quite," he smiled.

The deliberate understatement was much to her mind. How jolly it was that they should understand each other so well! They were both of them shy of displaying emotion, and it was only at rare moments that they used with one another anything but ironic banter.

They finished luncheon and he threw himself into a long chair to have a sleep. She went towards her room. She was a little surprised that he drew her to him as she passed and, making her bend down, kissed her lips. They were not in the habit of exchanging embraces at odd hours of the day.

"A full tummy is making you sentimental, my poor lamb," she chaffed him.

"Get out and don't let me see you again for at least two hours."

"Don't snore."

She left him. They had risen at dawn and in five minutes were fast asleep.

Doris was awakened by the sound of her husband's splashing in the bath-house. The walls of the bungalow were like a sounding-board and not a thing that one of them did escaped the other. She felt too lazy to move, but she heard the boy bring the tea things in, so she jumped up and ran down into her own bath-house. The water, not cold but cool, was deliciously refreshing. When she came into the sitting-room Guy was taking the rackets out of the press, for they played tennis in the short cool of the evening. The night fell at six.

The tennis-court was two or three hundred yards from the bungalow and after tea, anxious not to lose time, they strolled down to it.

"Oh, look," said Doris, "there's that girl that I saw this morning."

Guy turned quickly. His eyes rested for a moment on a native woman, but he did not speak.

"What a pretty sarong she's got," said Doris. "I wonder where it comes from."

They passed her. She was slight and small, with the large, dark, starry eyes of her race and a mass of raven hair. She did not stir as they went by, but stared at them strangely. Doris saw then that she was not quite so young as she had at first thought. Her features were a trifle heavy and her skin was dark, but she was very pretty. She held a small child in her arms. Doris smiled a little as she saw it, but no answering smile moved the woman's lips. Her face remained impassive. She did not look at Guy, she looked only at Doris, and he walked on as though he did not see her. Doris turned to him.

"Isn't that baby a duck?"

"I didn't notice."

She was puzzled by the look of his face. It was deathly white, and the pimples which not a little distressed her were more than commonly red.

"Did you notice her hands and feet? She might be a duchess."

"All natives have good hands and feet," he answered, but not jovially as was his wont; it was as though he forced himself to speak.

But Doris was not intrigued.

"Who is she, d'you know?"

"She's one of the girls in the kampong."

They had reached the court now. When Guy went up to the net to see that it was taut he looked back. The woman was still standing where they had passed her. Their eyes met.

"Shall I serve?" said Doris.

"Yes, you've got the balls on your side."

He played very badly. Generally he gave her fifteen and beat her, but to-day she won easily. And he played silently. Generally he was a noisy player, shouting all the time, cursing his foolishness when he missed a ball and chaffing her when he placed one out of her reach.

"You're off your game, young man," she cried.

"Not a bit," he said.

He began to slam the balls, trying to beat her, and sent one after the other into the net. She had never seen him with that set face. Was it possible that he was a little out of temper because he was not playing well? The light fell, and they ceased to play. The woman whom they had passed stood in exactly the same position as when they came and once more, with expressionless face, she watched them go.

The blinds on the verandah were raised now and on the table between their two long chairs were bottles and soda-water. This was the hour at which they had the first drink of the day and Guy mixed a couple of gin slings. The river stretched widely before them and on the further bank the jungle was wrapped in the mystery of the approaching night. A native was silently rowing up-stream, standing at the bow of the boat, with two oars.

"I played like a fool," said Guy, breaking a silence. "I'm feeling a bit under the weather."

"I'm sorry. You're not going to have fever, are you?"

"Oh, no. I shall be all right to-morrow."

Darkness closed in upon them. The frogs croaked loudly and now and then they heard a few short notes from some singing bird of the night. Fireflies flitted across the verandah and they made the trees that surrounded it look like Christmas trees lit with tiny candles. They sparkled softly. Doris thought she heard a little sigh. It vaguely disturbed her. Guy was always so full of gaiety.

"What is it, old man?" she said gently. "Tell mother."

"Nothing. Time for another drink," he answered breezily.

Next day he was as cheerful as ever and the mail came. The coasting steamer passed the mouth of the river twice a month, once on its way to the coal-fields and once on its way back. On the outward journey it brought mail, which Guy sent a boat down to fetch. Its arrival was the excitement of their uneventful lives. For the first day or two they skimmed rapidly all that had come, letters, English papers and papers from Singapore, magazines and books, leaving for the ensuing weeks a more exact perusal. They snatched the illustrated papers from one another. If Doris had not been so absorbed she might have noticed that there was a change in Guy. She would have found it hard to describe and harder still to explain. There was in his eyes a sort of watchfulness and in his mouth a slight droop of anxiety.

Then, perhaps a week later, one morning when she was sitting in the shaded room studying a Malay grammar, for she was industriously learning the language, she heard a commotion in the compound. She heard the house-boy's voice, he was speaking angrily, the voice of another man, perhaps it was the water-carrier's, and then a woman's, shrill and vituperative. There was a scuffle. She went to the window and opened the shutters. The water-carrier had hold of a woman's arm and was dragging her along, while the house-boy was pushing her from behind with both hands. Doris recognized her at once as the woman she had seen one morning loitering in the compound and later in the day outside the tennis-court. She was holding a baby against her breast. All three were shouting angrily.

"Stop," cried Doris. "What are you doing?"

At the sound of her voice the water-carrier let go suddenly and the woman, still pushed from behind, fell to the ground. There was a sudden silence and the house-boy looked sullenly into space. The water-carrier hesitated a moment and then slunk away. The woman raised herself slowly to her feet, arranged the baby on her arm, and stood impassive, staring at Doris. The boy said something to her which Doris could not have heard even if she had understood; the woman by no change of face showed that his words meant anything to her; but she slowly strolled away. The boy followed her to the gate of the compound. Doris called to him as he walked back, but he pretended not to hear. She was growing angry now and she called more sharply.

"Come here at once," she cried.

Sullenly, avoiding her wrathful glance, he came towards the bungalow. He came in and stood at the door. He looked at her sulkily.

"What were you doing with that woman?" she asked abruptly.

"Tuan say she no come here."

"You mustn't treat a woman like that. I won't have it. I shall tell the tuan exactly what I saw."

The boy did not answer. He looked away, but she felt that

he was watching her through his long eyelashes. She dismissed him.

"That'll do."

Without a word he turned and went back to the servants' quarters. She was exasperated and she found it impossible to give her attention once more to the Malay exercises. In a little while the boy came in to lay the cloth for luncheon. On a sudden he went to the door.

"What is it?" she asked.

"Tuan just coming."

He went out to take Guy's hat from him. His quick ears had caught the footsteps before they were audible to her. Guy did not as usual come up the steps immediately; he paused, and Doris at once surmised that the boy had gone down to meet him in order to tell him of the morning's incident. She shrugged her shoulders. The boy evidently wanted to get his story in first. But she was astonished when Guy came in. His face was ashy.

"Guy, what on earth's the matter?"

He flushed a sudden hot red.

"Nothing. Why?"

She was so taken aback that she let him pass into his room without a word of what she had meant to speak of at once. It took him longer than usual to have his bath and change his clothes, and luncheon was served when he came in.

"Guy," she said, as they sat down, "that woman we saw the other day was here again this morning."

"So I've heard," he answered.

"The boys were treating her brutally. I had to stop them. You must really speak to them about it."

Though the Malay understood every word she said, he made no sign that he heard. He handed her the toast.

"She's been told not to come here. I gave instructions that if she showed herself again she was to be turned out."

"Were they obliged to be so rough?"

"She refused to go. I don't think they were any rougher than they could help."

"It was horrible to see a woman treated like that. She had a baby in her arms."

"Hardly a baby. It's three years old."

"How d'you know?"

"I know all about her. She hasn't the least right to come here pestering everybody."

"What does she want?"

"She wants to do exactly what she did. She wants to make a disturbance."

For a little while Doris did not speak. She was surprised at her husband's tone. He spoke tersely. He spoke as though all this were no concern of hers. She thought him a little unkind. He was nervous and irritable.

"I doubt if we shall be able to play tennis this afternoon," he said. "It looks to me as though we were going to have a storm."

The rain was falling when she awoke and it was impossible to go out. During tea Guy was silent and abstracted. She got her sewing and began to work. Guy sat down to read such of the English papers as he had not yet gone through from cover to cover; but he was restless; he walked up and down the large room and then went out on the verandah. He looked at the steady rain. What was he thinking of? Doris was vaguely uneasy.

It was not till after dinner that he spoke. During the simple meal he had exerted himself to be his usual gay self, but the exertion was apparent. The rain had ceased and the night was starry. They sat on the verandah. In order not to attract insects they had put out the lamp in the sitting-room. At their feet, with a mighty, formidable sluggishness, silent, mysterious and fatal, flowed the river. It had the terrible deliberation and the relentlessness of destiny.

"Doris, I've got something to say to you," he said suddenly.

His voice was very strange. Was it her fancy that he had difficulty in keeping it quite steady? She felt a little pang in her heart because he was in distress, and she put her hand gently into his. He drew it away.

"It's rather a long story. I'm afraid it's not a very nice one and I find it rather difficult to tell. I'm going to ask you not to interrupt me, or to say anything, till I've finished."

In the darkness she could not see his face, but she felt that it was haggard. She did not answer. He spoke in a voice so low that it hardly broke the silence of the night.

"I was only eighteen when I came out here. I came straight from school. I spent three months in Kuala Solor, and then I was sent to a station up the Sembulu River. Of course there was a Resident there and his wife. I lived in the court-house, but I used to have my meals with them and spend the evening with them. I had an awfully good time. Then the fellow who was here fell ill and had to go home. We were short of men on account of the war and I was put in charge of this place. Of course I was very young, but I spoke the language like a native, and they remembered my father. I was as pleased as Punch to be on my own."

He was silent while he knocked the ashes out of his pipe and refilled it. When he lit a match Doris, without looking at him, noticed that his hand was unsteady.

"I'd never been alone before. Of course at home there'd been father and mother and generally an assistant. And then at school naturally there were always fellows about. On the way out, on the boat, there were people all the time, and at K.S., and the same at my first post. The people there were almost like my own people. I seemed always to live in a crowd. I like people. I'm a noisy blighter. I like to have a good time. All sorts of things make me laugh and you must have somebody to laugh with. But it was different here. Of course it was all right in the daytime; I had my work and I could talk to the Dyaks. Although they were head-hunters in those days and now and then I had a bit of trouble with them, they were an awfully decent lot of fellows. I got on very well with them. Of course I should have liked a white man to gas to, but they were better than nothing, and it was easier for me because they didn't look upon me quite as a stranger. I like the work too. It was rather lonely in the evening to sit on the verandah and drink a gin and bitters by myself, but I could read. And the boys were about. My own boy was called Abdul. He'd known my father. When I got tired of reading I could give him a shout and have a bit of a jaw with him.

"It was the nights that did for me. After dinner the boys shut up and went away to sleep in the kampong. I was all alone. There wasn't a sound in the bungalow except now and then the croak of the chik-chak. It used to come out of the silence, suddenly, so that it made me jump. Over in the kampong I heard the sound of a gong or fire-crackers. They were having a good time, they weren't so far away, but I had to stay where I was. I was tired of reading. I couldn't have been more of a prisoner if I'd been in jail. Night after night it was the same. I tried drinking three or four whiskies, but it's poor fun drinking alone, and it didn't cheer me up; it only made me feel rather rotten next day. I tried going to bed immediately after dinner, but I couldn't sleep. I used to lie in bed, getting hotter and hotter, and more wide awake, till I didn't know what to do with myself. By George, those nights were long. D'you know, I got so low, I was so sorry for myself that sometimes—it makes me laugh now when I think of it, but I was only nineteen and a half—sometimes I used to cry.

"Then, one evening, after dinner, Abdul had cleared away and was just going off, when he gave a little cough. He said, wasn't I lonely in the house all night by myself? 'Oh, no, that's all right,' I said. I didn't want him to know what a damned fool I was, but I expect he knew all right. He stood there without speaking, and I knew he wanted to say something to me. 'What is it?' I said. 'Spit it out.' Then he said that if I'd like to have a girl to come and live with me he knew one who was willing. She was a very good girl and he could recommend her. She'd be no trouble and it would be some one to have about the bungalow. She'd mend my things for me. . . . I felt awfully low. It had been raining all day and I hadn't been able to get any exercise. I knew I shouldn't go to sleep for hours. It wouldn't cost me very much money, he said, her people were poor and they'd be quite satisfied with a small present. Two hundred Straits dollars. 'You look,' he said. 'If you don't like her you send her away.' I asked him where she was. 'She's here,' he said. 'I call her.' He went to the door. She'd been waiting on the steps with her mother. They came in and sat down on the floor. I gave them some sweets. She was shy, of course, but cool enough, and when I said something to her she gave me a smile. She was very young, hardly more than a child, they said she was fifteen. She was awfully pretty, and she had her best clothes on. We began to talk. She didn't say much, but she laughed a lot when I chaffed her. Abdul said I'd find she had plenty to say for herself when she got to know me. He told her to come and sit by me. She giggled and refused, but her mother told her to come, and I made room for her on the chair. She blushed and laughed, but she came, and then she snuggled up to me. The boy laughed too. 'You see, she's taken to you already,' he said. 'Do you want her to stay?' he asked. 'Do you want to?' I said to her. She hid her face, laughing, on my shoulder. She was very soft and small. 'Very well,' I said, 'let her stay.'"

Guy leaned forward and helped himself to a whisky and soda.

"May I speak now?" asked Doris.

"Wait a minute, I haven't finished yet. I wasn't in love with her, not even at the beginning. I only took her so as to have somebody about the bungalow. I think I should have gone mad if I hadn't, or else taken to drink. I was at the end of my tether. I was too young to be quite alone. I was never in love with any one but you." He hesitated a moment. "She lived here till I went home last year on leave. It's the woman you've seen hanging about."

"Yes, I guessed that. She had a baby in her arms. Is that your child?"

"Yes. It's a little girl."

"Is it the only one?"

"You saw the two small boys the other day in the kampong. You mentioned them."

"She has three children then?"

"Yes."

"It's quite a family you've got."

She felt the sudden gesture which her remark forced from him, but he did not speak.

"Didn't she know that you were married till you suddenly turned up here with a wife?" asked Doris.

"She knew I was going to be married."

"When?"

"I sent her back to the village before I left here. I told her it was all over. I gave her what I'd promised. She always knew it was only a temporary arrangement. I was fed up with it. I told her I was going to marry a white woman."

"But you hadn't even seen me then."

"No, I know. But I'd made up my mind to marry when I was home." He chuckled in his old manner. "I don't mind telling you that I was getting rather despondent about it when I met you. I fell in love with you at first sight and then I knew it was either you or nobody."

"Why didn't you tell me? Don't you think it would have been only fair to give me a chance of judging for myself? It might have occurred to you that it would be rather a shock to a girl to find out that her husband had lived for ten years with another girl and had three children."

"I couldn't expect you to understand. The circumstances out here are peculiar. It's the regular thing. Five men out of six do it. I thought perhaps it would shock you and I didn't want to lose you. You see, I was most awfully in love with you. I am now, darling. There was no reason that you should ever know. I didn't expect to come back here. One seldom goes back to the same station after home leave. When we came here I offered her money if she'd go to some other village. First she said she would and then she changed her mind."

"Why have you told me now?"

"She's been making the most awful scenes. I don't know how she found out that you knew nothing about it. As soon as she did she began to blackmail me. I've had to give her an awful lot of money. I gave orders that she wasn't to be allowed in the compound. This morning she made that scene just to attract your attention. She wanted to frighten me. I couldn't go on like that. I thought the only thing was to make a clean breast of it."

There was a long silence as he finished. At last he put his hand on hers.

"You do understand, Doris, don't you? I know I've been to blame."

She did not move her hand. He felt it cold beneath his.

"Is she jealous?"

"I daresay there were all sorts of perks when she was living here, and I don't suppose she much likes not getting them any longer. But she was never in love with me any more than I was in love with her. Native women never do really care for white men, you know."

"And the children?"

"Oh, the children are all right. I've provided for them. As soon as the boys are old enough I shall send them to school at Singapore."

"Do they mean nothing to you at all?"

He hesitated.

"I want to be quite frank with you. I should be sorry if anything happened to them. When the first one was expected I thought I'd be much fonder of it than I ever had been of its mother. I suppose I should have been if it had been white. Of course, when it was a baby it was rather funny and touching, but I had no particular feeling that it was mine. I think that's what it is; you see, I have no sense of their belonging to me. I've reproached myself sometimes, because it seemed rather unnatural, but the honest truth is that they're no more to me than if they were somebody else's children. Of course a lot of slush is talked about children by people who haven't got any."

Now she had heard everything. He waited for her to speak, but she said nothing. She sat motionless.

"Is there anything more you want to ask me, Doris?" he said at last.

"No, I've got rather a headache. I think I shall go to bed." Her voice was as steady as ever. "I don't quite know what to say. Of course it's been all very unexpected. You must give me a little time to think."

"Are you very angry with me?"

"No. Not at all. Only—only I must be left to myself for a while. Don't move. I'm going to bed."

She rose from her long chair and put her hand on his shoulder.

"It's so very hot to-night. I wish you'd sleep in your dressing-room. Good night."

She was gone. He heard her lock the door of her bedroom.

She was pale next day and he could see that she had not slept. There was no bitterness in her manner, she talked as usual, but without ease; she spoke of this and that as though she were making conversation with a stranger. They had never had a quarrel, but it seemed to Guy that so would she talk if they had had a disagreement and the subsequent reconciliation had left her still wounded. The look in her eyes puzzled him; he seemed to read in them a strange fear. Immediately after dinner she said:

"I'm not feeling very well to-night. I think I shall go straight to bed."

"Oh, my poor darling, I'm so sorry," he cried.

"It's nothing. I shall be all right in a day or two."

"I shall come in and say good night to you later."

"No, don't do that. I shall try and get straight off to sleep."

"Well, then, kiss me before you go."

He saw that she flushed. For an instant she seemed to hesitate; then, with averted eyes, she leaned towards him. He took her in his arms and sought her lips, but she turned her face away and he kissed her cheek. She left him quickly and again he heard the key turn softly in the lock of her door. He flung himself heavily on the chair. He tried to read, but his ear was attentive to the smallest sound in his wife's room. She had said she was going to bed, but he did not hear her move. The silence in there made him unaccountably nervous. Shading the lamp with his hand he saw that there was a glimmer under her door; she had not put out her light. What on earth was she doing? He put down his book. It would not have surprised him if she had been angry and had made him a scene, or if she had cried; he could have coped with that; but her calmness frightened him. And then what was that fear which he had seen so plainly in her eyes? He thought once more over all he had said to her on the previous night. He didn't know how else he could have put it. After all, the chief point was that he'd done the same as everybody else, and it was all over long before he met her. Of course as things turned out he had been a fool, but any one could be wise after the event. He put his hand to his heart. Funny how it hurt him there!

"I suppose that's the sort of thing people mean when they say they're heart-broken," he said to himself. "I wonder how long it's going on like this?"

Should he knock at the door and tell her he must speak to her? It was better to have it out. He *must* make her understand. But the silence scared him. Not a sound! Perhaps it was better to leave her alone. Of course it had been a shock. He must give her as long as she wanted. After all, she knew how devotedly he loved her. Patience, that was the only thing; perhaps she was fighting it out with herself; he must give her time; he must have patience.

Next morning he asked her if she had slept better.

"Yes, much," she said.

"Are you very angry with me?" he asked piteously.

She looked at him with candid, open eyes.

"Not a bit."

"Oh, my dear, I'm so glad. I've been a brute and a beast. I know it's been hateful for you. But do forgive me. I've been so miserable."

"I do forgive you. I don't even blame you."

He gave her a little rueful smile, and there was in his eyes the look of a whipped dog.

"I haven't much liked sleeping by myself the last two nights." She glanced away. Her face grew a trifle paler.

"I've had the bed in my room taken away. It took up so much space. I've had a little camp bed put there instead."

"My dear, what are you talking about?"

Now she looked at him steadily.

"I'm not going to live with you as your wife again."

"Never?"

She shook her head. He looked at her in a puzzled way. He could hardly believe he had heard aright and his heart began to beat painfully.

"But that's awfully unfair to me, Doris."

"Don't you think it was a little unfair to me to bring me out here in the circumstances?"

"But you just said you didn't blame me."

"That's quite true. But the other's different. I can't do it."

"But how are we going to live together like that?"

She stared at the floor. She seemed to ponder deeply.

"When you wanted to kiss me on the lips last night I—it almost made me sick."

"Doris."

She looked at him suddenly and her eyes were cold and hostile.

"That bed I slept on, is that the bed in which she had her children?" She saw him flush deeply. "Oh, it's horrible. How could you?" She wrung her hands, and her twisting, tortured fingers looked like little writhing snakes. But she made a great effort and controlled herself. "My mind is quite made up. I don't want to be unkind to you, but there are some things that you can't ask me to do. I've thought it all over. I've been thinking of nothing else since you told me, night and day, till I'm exhausted. My first instinct was to get up and go. At once. The steamer will be here in two or three days."

"Doesn't it mean anything to you that I love you?"

"Oh, I know you love me. I'm not going to do that. I want to give us both a chance. I have loved you so, Guy." Her voice broke, but she did not cry. "I don't want to be unreasonable. Heaven knows, I don't want to be unkind. Guy, will you give me time?"

"I don't know quite what you mean."

"I just want you to leave me alone. I'm frightened by the feelings that I have."

He had been right then; she was afraid.

"What feelings?"

"Please don't ask me. I don't want to say anything to wound you. Perhaps I shall get over them. Heaven knows, I want to. I'll try, I promise you. I'll try. Give me six months. I'll do everything in the world for you, but just that one thing." She made a little gesture of appeal. "There's no reason why we shouldn't be happy enough together. If you really love me you'll—you'll have patience."

He sighed deeply.

"Very well," he said. "Naturally I don't want to force you to do anything you don't like. It shall be as you say."

He sat heavily for a little, as though, on a sudden grown old, it was an effort to move; then he got up.

"I'll be getting along to the office."

He took his topee and went out.

A month passed. Women conceal their feelings better than men and a stranger visiting them would never have guessed that Doris was in any way troubled. But in Guy the strain was obvious; his round, good-natured face was drawn, and in his eyes was a hungry, harassed look. He watched Doris. She was gay and she chaffed him as she had been used to do; they played tennis together; they chatted about one thing and another. But it was evident that she was merely playing a part, and at last, unable to contain himself, he tried to speak again of his connection with the Malay woman.

"Oh, Guy, there's no object in going back on all that," she answered breezily. "We've said all we had to say about it and I don't blame you for anything."

"Why do you punish me then?"

"My poor boy, I don't want to punish you. It's not my fault if . . ." She shrugged her shoulders. "Human nature is very odd."

"I don't understand."

"Don't try."

The words might have been harsh, but she softened them with a pleasant, friendly smile. Every night when she went to bed she leaned over Guy and lightly kissed his cheek. Her lips only touched it. It was as though a moth had just brushed his face in its flight.

A second month passed, then a third, and suddenly the six months which had seemed so interminable were over. Guy asked himself whether she remembered. He gave a strained attention now to everything she said, to every look on her face and to every gesture of her hands. She remained impenetrable. She had asked him to give her six months; well, he had.

The coasting steamer passed the mouth of the river, dropped their mail, and went on its way. Guy busily wrote the letters which it would pick up on the return journey. Two or three days passed by. It was a Tuesday and the prahu was to start at dawn on Thursday to await the steamer. Except at mealtime when Doris exerted herself to make conversation they had not of late talked very much together; and after dinner as usual they took their books and began to read; but when the boy had finished clearing away and was gone for the night Doris put down hers.

"Guy, I have something I want to say to you," she murmured.

His heart gave a sudden thud against his ribs and he felt himself change colour.

"Oh, my dear, don't look like that, it's not so very terrible," she laughed.

But he thought her voice trembled a little.

"Well?"

"I want you to do something for me."

"My darling, I'll do anything in the world for you."

He put out his hand to take hers, but she drew it away.

"I want you to let me go home."

"You?" he cried, aghast. "When? Why?"

"I've borne it as long as I can. I'm at the end of my tether."

"How long do you want to go for? For always?"

"I don't know. I think so." She gathered determination. "Yes, for always."

"Oh, my God!"

His voice broke and she thought he was going to cry.

"Oh, Guy, don't blame me. It really is not my fault. I can't help myself."

"You asked me for six months. I accepted your terms. You can't say I've made a nuisance of myself."

"No, no."

"I've tried not to let you see what a rotten time I was having."

"I know. I'm very grateful to you. You've been awfully kind to me. Listen, Guy, I want to tell you again that I don't blame you for a single thing you did. After all, you were only a boy, and you did no more than the others; I know what the loneliness is here. Oh, my dear, I'm so dreadfully sorry for you. I knew all that from the beginning. That's why I asked you for six months. My common sense tells me that I'm making a mountain out of a mole-hill. I'm unreasonable; I'm being unfair to you. But, you see, common sense has nothing to do with it; my whole soul is in revolt. When I see the woman and her children in the village I just feel my legs shaking. Everything in this house; when I think of that bed I slept in, it gives me gooseflesh. . . . You don't know what I've endured."

"I think I've persuaded her to go away. And I've applied for a transfer."

"That wouldn't help. She'd be there always. You belong to them, you don't belong to me. I think perhaps I could have stood it if there'd only been one child, but three; and the boys are quite big boys. For ten years you lived with her." And now she came out with what she had been working up to. She was desperate. "It's a physical thing, I can't help it, it's stronger than I am. I think of those thin, black arms of hers round you and it fills me with a physical nausea. I think of you holding those little black babies in your arms. Oh, it's loathsome. The touch of you is odious to me. Each night, when I've kissed you, I've had to brace myself up to it. I've had to clench my hands and force myself to touch your cheek." Now she was clasping and unclasping her fingers in a nervous agony and her voice was out of control. "I know it's I who am to blame now. I'm a silly, hysterical woman. I thought I'd get over it. I can't, and now I never shall. I've brought it all on myself; I'm willing to take the consequences; if you say I must stay here, I'll stay, but if I stay I shall die. I beseech you to let me go."

And now the tears which she had restrained so long overflowed and she wept broken-heartedly. He had never seen her cry before.

"Of course I don't want to keep you here against your will," he said hoarsely.

Exhausted, she leaned back in her chair. Her features were

all twisted and awry. It was horribly painful to see the abandon-
ment of grief on that face which was habitually so placid.

"I'm so sorry, Guy. I've broken your life, but I've broken mine
too. And we might have been so happy."

"When do you want to go? On Thursday?"

"Yes."

She looked at him piteously. He buried his face in his hands.
At last he looked up.

"I'm tired out," he muttered.

"May I go?"

"Yes."

For two minutes perhaps they sat there without a word. She
started when the chik-chak gave its piercing, hoarse and strangely
human cry. Guy rose and went out on to the verandah. He
leaned against the rail and looked at the softly flowing water. He
heard Doris go into her room.

Next morning, up earlier than usual, he went to her door and
knocked.

"Yes?"

"I have to go up-river to-day. I shan't be back till late."

"All right."

She understood. He had arranged to be away all day in order
not to be about while she was packing. It was heart-breaking
work. When she had packed her clothes she looked round the
sitting-room at the things that belonged to her. It seemed dreadful to take them. She left everything but the photograph of her
mother. Guy did not come in till ten o'clock at night.

"I'm sorry I couldn't get back to dinner," he said. "The headman
at the village I had to go to had a lot of things for me to attend
to."

She saw his eyes wander about the room and notice that her
mother's photograph no longer stood in its place.

"Is everything quite ready?" he asked. "I've ordered the boatman
to be at the steps at dawn."

"I told the boy to wake me at five."

"I'd better give you some money." He went to his desk and
wrote out a cheque. He took some notes from a drawer. "Here's
some cash to take you as far as Singapore and at Singapore you'll
be able to change the cheque."

"Thank you."

"Would you like me to come to the mouth of the river with you?"

"Oh, I think it would be better if we said good-bye here."

"All right. I think I shall turn in. I've had a long day and I'm dead beat."

He did not even touch her hand. He went into his room. In a few minutes she heard him throw himself on his bed. For a little while she sat looking for the last time around that room in which she had been so happy and so miserable. She sighed deeply. She got up and went into her own room. Everything was packed except the one or two things she needed for the night.

It was dark when the boy awakened them. They dressed hurriedly and when they were ready breakfast was waiting for them. Presently they heard the boat row up to the landing-stage below the bungalow, and then the servants carried down her luggage. It was a poor pretence they made at eating. The darkness thinned away and the river was ghostly. It was not yet day, but it was no longer night. In the silence the voices of the natives at the landing-stage were very clear. Guy glanced at his wife's untouched plate.

"If you've finished we might stroll down. I think you ought to be starting."

She did not answer. She rose from the table. She went into her room to see that nothing had been forgotten and then side by side with him walked down the steps. A little winding path led them to the river. At the landing-stage the native guards in their smart uniforms were lined up and they presented arms as Guy and Doris passed. The head boatman gave her his hand as she stepped into the boat. She turned and looked at Guy. She wanted desperately to say one last word of comfort, once more to ask for his forgiveness, but she seemed to be struck dumb.

He stretched out his hand.

"Well, good-bye, I hope you'll have a jolly journey."

They shook hands.

Guy nodded to the head boatman and the boat pushed off. The dawn now was creeping along the river mistily, but the night lurked still in the dark trees of the jungle. He stood at the landing-stage till the boat was lost in the shadows of the morning. With a sigh he turned away. He nodded absentmindedly when the guard once more presented arms. But when he reached the bungalow he called the boy. He went round the room picking out everything that had belonged to Doris.

"Pack all these things up," he said. "It's no good leaving them about."

Then he sat down on the verandah and watched the day advance gradually like a bitter, an unmerited and an overwhelming sorrow. At last he looked at his watch. It was time for him to go to the office.

In the afternoon he could not sleep, his head ached miserably, so he took his gun and went for a tramp in the jungle. He shot nothing, but he walked in order to tire himself out. Towards sunset he came back and had two or three drinks, and then it was time to dress for dinner. There wasn't much use in dressing now; he might just as well be comfortable; he put on a loose native jacket and a sarong. That was what he had been accustomed to wear before Doris came. He was barefoot. He ate his dinner listlessly and the boy cleared away and went. He sat down to read The Tatler. The bungalow was very silent. He could not read and let the paper fall on his knees. He was exhausted. He could not think and his mind was strangely vacant. The chik-chak was noisy that night and its hoarse and sudden cry seemed to mock him. You could hardly believe that this reverberating sound came from so small a throat. Presently he heard a discreet cough.

"Who's there?" he cried.

There was a pause. He looked at the door. The chik-chak laughed harshly. A small boy sidled in and stood on the threshold. It was a little half-caste boy in a tattered singlet and a sarong. It was the elder of his two sons.

"What do you want?" said Guy.

The boy came forward into the room and sat down, tucking his legs away under him.

"Who told you to come here?"

"My mother sent me. She says, do you want anything?"

Guy looked at the boy intently. The boy said nothing more. He sat and waited, his eyes cast down shyly. Then Guy in deep and bitter reflection buried his face in his hands. What was the use? It was finished. Finished! He surrendered. He sat back in his chair and sighed deeply.

"Tell your mother to pack up her things and yours. She can come back."

"When?" asked the boy impassively.

Hot tears trickled down Guy's funny, round, spotty face.

"To-night."

Footprints in the Jungle

There is no place in Malaya that has more charm than Tanah Merah. It lies on the sea and the sandy shore is fringed with casuarinas. The government offices are still in the old Raad Huis that the Dutch built when they owned the land, and on the hill stand the grey ruins of the fort by aid of which the Portuguese maintained their hold over the unruly natives. Tanah Merah has a history and in the vast labyrinthine houses of the Chinese merchants, backing on the sea so that in the cool of the evening they may sit in their loggias and enjoy the salt breeze, families dwell that have been settled in the country for three centuries. Many have forgotten their native language and hold intercourse with one another in Malay and pidgin English. The imagination lingers here gratefully, for in the Federated Malay States the only past is within the memory for the most part of the fathers of living men.

Tanah Merah was for long the busiest mart of the Middle East and its harbour was crowded with shipping when the clipper and the junk still sailed the China seas. But now it is dead. It has the sad and romantic air of all places that have once been of importance and live now on the recollection of a vanished grandeur. It is a sleepy little town and strangers that come to it, losing their native energy, insensibly drop into its easy and lethargic ways. Successive rubber booms bring it no prosperity and the ensuing slumps hasten its decay.

The European quarter is very silent. It is trim and neat and clean. The houses of the white men—Government servants and agents of companies—stand round an immense padang, agreeable and roomy bungalows shaded by great cassias, and the padang is vast and green and well cared for, like the lawn of a cathedral close, and indeed there is in the aspect of this corner of Tanah Merah something quiet and delicately secluded that reminds you of the procincts of Canterbury.

The Club faces the sea; it is a spacious but shabby building;

it has an air of neglect and when you enter you feel that you intrude. It gives you the impression that it is closed really, for alterations and repairs, and that you have taken indiscreet advantage of an open door to go where you are not wanted. In the morning you may find there a couple of planters who have come in from their estates on business and are drinking a gin-sling before starting back again; and latish in the afternoon a lady or two may perhaps be seen looking with a furtive air through old numbers of the Illustrated London News. At nightfall a few men saunter in and sit about the billiard-room watching the play and drinking sukus. But on Wednesdays there is a little more animation. On that day the gramophone is set going in the large room upstairs and people come in from the surrounding country to dance. There are sometimes no less than a dozen couples and it is even possible to make up two tables of bridge.

It was on one of these occasions that I met the Cartwrights. I was staying with a man called Gaze who was head of the police and he came into the billiard-room, where I was sitting, and asked me if I would make up a four. The Cartwrights were planters and they came in to Tanah Merah on Wednesdays because it gave their girl a chance of a little fun. They were very nice people, said Gaze, quiet and unobtrusive, and played a very pleasant game of bridge. I followed Gaze into the card-room and was introduced to them. They were already seated at a table and Mrs. Cartwright was shuffling the cards. It inspired me with confidence to see the competent way in which she did it. She took half the pack in each hand, and her hands were large and strong, deftly inserted the corners of one half under the corners of the others, and with a click and a neat bold gesture cascaded the cards together.

It had all the effect of a conjuring trick. The card-player knows that it can be done perfectly only after incessant practice. He can be fairly sure that anyone who can so shuffle a pack of cards loves cards for their own sake.

"Do you mind if my husband and I play together?" asked Mrs. Cartwright. "It's no fun for us to win one another's money."

"Of course not."

We cut for deal and Gaze and I sat down.

Mrs. Cartwright drew an ace and while she dealt, quickly and neatly, chatted with Gaze of local affairs. But I was aware that she took stock of me. She looked shrewd but good-natured.

She was a woman somewhere in the fifties (though in the East, where people age quickly, it is difficult to tell their ages), with white hair very untidily arranged, and a constant gesture with her was an impatient movement of the hand to push back a long wisp of hair that kept falling over her forehead. You wondered why she did not, by the use of a hairpin or two, save herself so much trouble. Her blue eyes were large, but pale and a little tired; her face was lined and sallow; I think it was her mouth that gave it the expression which I felt was characteristic of caustic but tolerant irony. You saw that here was a woman who knew her mind and was never afraid to speak it. She was a chatty player (which some people object to strongly, but which does not disconcert me, for I do not see why you should behave at the card-table as though you were at a memorial service) and it was soon apparent that she had an effective knack of badinage. It was pleasantly acid, but it was amusing enough to be offensive only to a fool. If now and then she uttered a remark so sarcastic that you wanted all your sense of humour to see the fun in it, you could not but quickly see that she was willing to take as much as she gave. Her large, thin mouth broke into a dry smile and her eyes shone brightly when by a lucky chance you brought off a repartee that turned the laugh against her.

I thought her a very agreeable person. I liked her frankness. I liked her quick wit. I liked her plain face. I never met a woman who obviously cared so little how she looked. It was not only her head that was untidy, everything about her was slovenly; she wore a high-necked silk blouse, but for coolness had unbuttoned the top buttons and showed a gaunt and withered neck; the blouse was crumpled and none too clean, for she smoked innumerable cigarettes and covered herself with ash. When she got up for a moment to speak to somebody I saw that her blue skirt was rather ragged at the hem and badly needed a brush, and she wore heavy, low-heeled boots. But none of this mattered. Everything she wore was perfectly in character.

And it was a pleasure to play bridge with her. She played very quickly, without hesitation, and she had not only knowledge but flair. Of course she knew Gaze's game, but I was a stranger and she soon took my measure. The team-work between her husband and herself was admirable; he was sound and cautious, but knowing him, she was able to be bold with assurance and brilliant with safety. Gaze was a player who founded a foolish optimism on the hope that his opponents would not have the sense to take advantage of his errors, and the pair of us were no match for the Cartwrights. We lost one rubber after another, and there was nothing to do but smile and look as if we liked it.

"I don't know what's the matter with the cards," said Gaze at last, plaintively. "Even when we have every card in the pack we go down."

"It can't be anything to do with your play," answered Mrs. Cartwright, looking him full in the face with those pale blue eyes of hers, "it must be bad luck pure and simple. Now if you hadn't had your hearts mixed up with your diamonds in that last hand you'd have saved the game."

Gaze began to explain at length how the misfortune, which had cost us dear, occurred, but Mrs. Cartwright, with a deft flick of the hand, spread out the cards in a great circle so that we should cut for deal. Cartwright looked at the time.

"This will have to be the last, my dear," he said.

"Oh, will it?" She glanced at her watch and then called to a young man who was passing through the room. "Oh, Mr. Bullen, if you're going upstairs tell Olive that we shall be going in a few minutes." She turned to me. "It takes us the best part of an hour to get back to the estate and poor Theo has to be up at the crack of dawn."

"Oh, well, we only come in once a week," said Cartwright, "and it's the one chance Olive gets of being gay and abandoned."

I thought Cartwright looked tired and old. He was a man of middle height, with a bald, shiny head, a stubbly grey moustache, and gold-rimmed spectacles. He wore white ducks and a black-and-white tie. He was rather neat and you could see he took much more pains with his clothes than his untidy wife. He talked little, but it was plain that he enjoyed his wife's caustic humour and sometimes he made quite a neat retort. They were evidently very good friends. It was pleasing to see so solid and tolerant an affection between two people who were almost elderly and must have lived together for so many years.

It took but two hands to finish the rubber and we had just ordered a final gin and bitters when Olive came down.

"Do you really want to go already, Mumsey?" she asked.

Mrs. Cartwright looked at her daughter with fond eyes.

"Yes, darling. It's nearly half-past eight. It'll be ten before we get our dinner."

"Damn our dinner," said Olive, gaily.

"Let her have one more dance before we go," suggested Cartwright.

"Not one. You must have a good night's rest."

Cartwright looked at Olive with a smile.

"If your mother has made up her mind, my dear, we may just as well give in without any fuss."

"She's a determined woman," said Olive, lovingly stroking her mother's wrinkled cheek.

Mrs. Cartwright patted her daughter's hand, and kissed it.

Olive was not very pretty, but she looked extremely nice. She was nineteen or twenty, I suppose, and she had still the plumpness of her age; she would be more attractive when she had fined down a little. She had none of the determination that gave her mother's face so much character, but resembled her father; she had his dark eyes and slightly aquiline nose, and his look of rather weak good nature. It was plain that she was strong and healthy. Her cheeks were red and her eyes bright. She had a vitality that he had long since lost. She seemed to be the perfectly normal English girl, with high spirits, a great desire to enjoy herself, and an excellent temper.

When we separated, Gaze and I set out to walk to his house.

"What did you think of the Cartwrights?" he asked me.

"I liked them. They must be a great asset in a place like this."

"I wish they came oftener. They live a very quiet life."

"It must be dull for the girl. The father and mother seem very well satisfied with one another's company."

"Yes, it's been a great success."

"Olive is the image of her father, isn't she?"

Gaze gave me a sidelong glance.

"Cartwright isn't her father. Mrs. Cartwright was a widow when he married her. Olive was born four months after her father's death."

"Oh!"

I drew out the sound in order to put in it all I could of surprise, interest and curiosity. But Gaze said nothing and we walked

the rest of the way in silence. The boy was waiting at the door
as we entered the house and after a last gin pahit we sat down to
dinner.

At first Gaze was inclined to be talkative. Owing to the re-
striction of the output of rubber there had sprung up a considerable activity among the smugglers and it was part of his
duty to circumvent their knavishness. Two junks had been cap-
tured that day and he was rubbing his hands over his success.
The go-downs were full of confiscated rubber and in a little while
it was going to be solemnly burnt. But presently he fell into
silence and we finished without a word. The boys brought in
coffee and brandy and we lit our cheroots. Gaze leaned back in
his chair. He looked at me reflectively and then looked at his
brandy. The boys had left the room and we were alone.

"I've known Mrs. Cartwright for over twenty years," he said
slowly. "She wasn't a bad-looking woman in those days. Always
untidy, but when she was young it didn't seem to matter so much.
It was rather attractive. She was married to a man called Bronson. Reggie Bronson. He was a planter. He was manager of an
estate up in Selantan and I was stationed at Alor Lipis. It was a
much smaller place than it is now; I don't suppose there were
more than twenty people in the whole community, but they had a
jolly little club, and we used to have a very good time. I remember
the first time I met Mrs. Bronson as though it was yesterday.
There were no cars in those days and she and Bronson had ridden
in on their bicycles. Of course then she didn't look so determined
as she looks now. She was much thinner, she had a nice colour,
and her eyes were very pretty—blue, you know—and she had a
lot of dark hair. If she'd only taken more trouble with herself she'd
have been rather stunning. As it was she was the best-looking
woman there."

I tried to construct in my mind a picture of what Mrs. Cartwright—Mrs. Bronson as she was then—looked like from what she
was now and from Gaze's not very graphic description. In the
solid woman, with her well-covered bones, who sat rather heavily
at the bridge-table, I tried to see a slight young thing with
buoyant movements and graceful, easy gestures. Her chin now
was square and her nose decided, but the roundness of youth
must have masked this: she must have been charming with a pink
and white skin and her hair carelessly dressed, brown and abun-

dant. At that period she wore a long skirt, a tight waist and a picture hat. Or did women in Malaya still wear the topis that you see in old numbers of the illustrated papers?

"I hadn't seen her for—oh, nearly twenty years," Gaze went on. "I knew she was living somewhere in the F.M.S., but it was a surprise when I took this job and came here to run across her in the club just as I had up in Selantan so many years before. Of course she's an elderly woman now and she's changed out of all recognition. It was rather a shock to see her with a grown-up daughter, it made me realize how the time had passed; I was a young fellow when I met her last and now, by Jingo, I'm due to retire on the age limit in two or three years. Bit thick, isn't it?"

Gaze, a rueful grin on his ugly face, looked at me with faint indignation, as though I could help the hurrying march of the years as they trod upon one another's heels.

"I'm no chicken myself," I replied.

"You haven't lived out East all your life. It ages one before one's time. One's an elderly man at fifty and at fifty-five one's good for nothing but the scrap heap."

But I did not want Gaze to wander off into a disquisition on old age.

"Did you recognize Mrs. Cartwright when you saw her again?" I asked.

"Well, I did and I didn't. At the first glance I thought I knew her, but couldn't quite place her. I thought perhaps she was some-one I'd met on board ship when I was going on leave and had known only by sight. But the moment she spoke I remembered at once. I remembered the dry twinkle in her eyes and the crisp sound of her voice. There was something in her voice that seemed to mean: you're a bit of a damned fool, my lad, but you're not a bad sort and upon my soul I rather like you."

"That's a good deal to read into the sound of a voice," I smiled.

"She came up to me in the club and shook hands with me. 'How do you do, Major Gaze? Do you remember me?' she said.

" 'Of course I do.'

" 'A lot of water has passed under the bridge since we met last. We're none of us as young as we were. Have you seen Theo?'

"For a moment I couldn't think whom she meant. I suppose I looked rather stupid, because she gave a little smile, that chaffing smile that I knew so well, and explained.

" 'I married Theo, you know. It seemed the best thing to do. I was lonely and he wanted it.'

" 'I heard you married him,' I said. 'I hope you've been very happy.'

" 'Oh, very. Theo's a perfect duck. He'll be here in a minute. He'll be so glad to see you.'

"I wondered. I should have thought I was the last man Theo would wish to see. I shouldn't have thought she would wish it very much either. But women are funny."

"Why shouldn't she wish to see you?" I asked.

"I'm coming to that later," said Gaze. "Then Theo turned up. I don't know why I call him Theo; I never called him anything but Cartwright, I never thought of him as anything but Cartwright. Theo was a shock. You know what he looks like now; I remembered him as a curly-headed youngster, very fresh and clean looking; he was always neat and dapper, he had a good figure and he held himself well, like a man who's used to taking a lot of exercise. Now I come to think of it he wasn't bad looking, not in a big, massive way, but graceful, you know, and lithe. When I saw this bowed, cadaverous, bald-headed old buffer with spectacles I could hardly believe my eyes. I shouldn't have known him from Adam. He seemed pleased to see me, at least, interested; he wasn't effusive, but he'd always been on the quiet side and I didn't expect him to be.

" 'Are you surprised to find us here?' he asked me.

" 'Well, I hadn't the faintest notion where you were.'

" 'We've kept track of your movements more or less. We've seen your name in the paper every now and then. You must come out one day and have a look at our place. We've been settled there a good many years, and I suppose we shall stay there till we go home for good. Have you ever been back to Alor Lipis?'

" 'No, I haven't,' I said.

" 'It was a nice little place. I'm told it's grown. I've never been back.'

" 'It hasn't got the pleasantest recollections for us,' said Mrs. Cartwright.

"I asked them if they'd have a drink and we called the boy. I daresay you noticed that Mrs. Cartwright likes her liquor; I don't mean that she gets tight or anything like that, but she drinks her stengah like a man. I couldn't help looking at them

with a certain amount of curiosity. They seemed perfectly happy;
I gathered that they hadn't done at all badly, and I found out
later that they were quite well off. They had a very nice car,
and when they went on leave they denied themselves nothing.
They were on the best of terms with one another. You know
how jolly it is to see two people who've been married a great
many years obviously better pleased with their own company than
anyone else's. Their marriage had evidently been a great success.
And they were both of them devoted to Olive and very proud
of her, Theo especially."

"Although she was only his step-daughter?" I said.

"Although she was only his step-daughter," answered Gaze.
"You'd think that she would have taken his name. But she hadn't.
She called him Daddy, of course, he was the only father she'd
ever known, but she signed her letters, Olive Bronson."

"What was Bronson like, by the way?"

"Bronson? He was a great big fellow, very hearty, with a loud
voice and a bellowing laugh, beefy, you know, and a fine athlete.
There was not very much to him but he was as straight as a die.
He had a red face and red hair. Now I come to think of it I
remember that I never saw a man sweat as much as he did.
Water just poured off him, and when he played tennis he always
used to bring a towel on the court with him."

"It doesn't sound very attractive."

"He was a handsome chap. He was always fit. He was keen
on that. He hadn't much to talk about but rubber and games,
tennis, you know, and golf and shooting; and I don't suppose he
read a book from year's end to year's end. He was the typical
public-school boy. He was about thirty-five when I first knew him,
but he had the mind of a boy of eighteen. You know how many
fellows when they come out East seem to stop growing."

I did indeed. One of the most disconcerting things to the travel-
ler is to see stout, middle-aged gentlemen, with bald heads, speaking and acting like schoolboys. You might almost think that no
idea has entered their heads since they first passed through the
Suez Canal. Though married and the fathers of children, and perhaps in control of a large business, they continue to look upon life
from the standpoint of the sixth form.

"But he was no fool," Gaze went on. "He knew his work from
A to Z. His estate was one of the best managed in the country

and he knew how to handle his labour. He was a damned good
sort, and if he did get on your nerves a little you couldn't help
liking him. He was generous with his money, and always ready
to do anybody a good turn. That's how Cartwright happened to
turn up in the first instance."

"Did the Bronsons get on well together?"

"Oh, yes, I think so. I'm sure they did. He was good natured
and she was very jolly and gay. She was very outspoken, you
know. She can be very amusing when she likes even now, but
there's generally a sting lurking in the joke; when she was a young
woman and married to Bronson it was just pure fun. She had
high spirits and liked having a good time. She never cared a hang
what she said, but it went with her type, if you understand what
I mean; there was something so open and frank and careless about
her that you didn't care what she said to you. They seemed very
happy.

"Their estate was about five miles from Alor Lipis. They had a
trap and they used to drive in most evenings about five. Of course
it was a very small community and men were in the majority.
There were only about six women. The Bronsons were a god-send.
They bucked things up the moment they arrived. We used to have
very jolly times in that little club. I've often thought of them since
and I don't know that on the whole I've ever enjoyed myself
more than I did when I was stationed there. Between six and
eight-thirty the club at Alor Lipis twenty years ago was about as
lively a place as you could find between Aden and Yokohama.

"One day Mrs. Bronson told us that they were expecting a friend
to stay with them and a few days later they brought Cartwright
along. It appeared that he was an old friend of Bronson's, they'd
been at school together, Marlborough, or some place like that, and
they'd first come out East on the same ship. Rubber had taken
a toss and a lot of fellows had lost their jobs. Cartwright was one
of them. He'd been out of work for the greater part of a year
and he hadn't anything to fall back on. In those days planters
were even worse paid than they are now and a man had to be
very lucky to put by something for a rainy day. Cartwright had
gone to Singapore. They all go there when there's a slump, you
know. It's awful then, I've seen it; I've known of planters sleeping
in the street because they hadn't the price of a night's lodging.
I've known them stop strangers outside the Europe and ask for

a dollar to get a meal, and I think Cartwright had had a pretty rotten time.

"At last he wrote to Bronson and asked him if he couldn't do something for him. Bronson asked him to come and stay till things got better, at least it would be free board and lodging, and Cartwright jumped at the chance, but Bronson had to send him the money to pay his railway fare. When Cartwright arrived at Alor Lipis he hadn't ten cents in his pocket. Bronson had a little money of his own, two or three hundred a year, I think, and though his salary had been cut, he'd kept his job, so that he was better off than most planters. When Cartwright came Mrs. Bronson told him that he was to look upon the place as his home and stay as long as he liked."

"It was very nice of her, wasn't it?" I remarked.

"Very."

Gaze lit himself another cheroot and filled his glass. It was very still and but for the occasional croak of the chik-chak the silence was intense. We seemed to be alone in the tropical night and heaven only knows how far from the habitations of men. Gaze did not speak for so long that at last I was forced to say something.

"What sort of a man was Cartwright at that time?" I asked. "Younger, of course, and you told me rather nice looking; but in himself?"

"Well, to tell you the truth, I never paid much attention to him. He was pleasant and unassuming. He's very quiet now, as I daresay you noticed; well, he wasn't exactly lively then. But he was perfectly inoffensive. He was fond of reading and he played the piano rather nicely. You never minded having him about, he was never in the way, but you never bothered very much about him. He danced well and the women rather liked that, but he also played billiards quite decently and he wasn't bad at tennis. He fell into our little groove very naturally. I wouldn't say that he ever became wildly popular, but everybody liked him. Of course we were sorry for him, as one is for a man who's down and out, but there was nothing we could do, and, well, we just accepted him and then forgot that he hadn't always been there. He used to come in with the Bronsons every evening and pay for his drinks like everyone else, I suppose Bronson had lent a bit of money for current expenses, and he was always very civil. I'm rather vague about him, because really he didn't make any particular impression on me; in the East one meets such a lot of people, and he seemed very much like anybody else. He did everything he could to get something to do, but he had no luck; the fact is, there were no jobs going, and sometimes he seemed rather depressed about it. He was with the Bronsons for over a year. I remember his saying to me once:

"'After all I can't live with them for ever. They've been most awfully good to me, but there are limits.'

"'I should think the Bronsons would be very glad to have you,' I said. 'It's not particularly gay on a rubber estate, and as far as your food and drink go, it must make precious little difference if you're there or not.'"

Gaze stopped once more and looked at me with a sort of hesitation.

"What's the matter?" I asked.

"I'm afraid I'm telling you this story very badly," he said. "I seem to be just rambling on. I'm not a damned novelist, I'm a policeman, and I'm just telling you the facts as I saw them at the time; and from my point of view all the circumstances are important; it's important, I mean, to realize what sort of people they were."

"Of course. Fire away."

"I remember someone, a woman, I think it was, the doctor's wife, asking Mrs. Bronson if she didn't get tired sometimes of having a stranger in the house. You know, in places like Alor Lipis there isn't very much to talk about, and if you didn't talk about your neighbours there'd be nothing to talk about at all.

"'Oh, no,' she said. 'Theo's no trouble.' She turned to her husband who was sitting there mopping his face. 'We like having him, don't we?'

"'He's all right,' said Bronson.

"'What does he do with himself all day long?'

"'Oh, I don't know,' said Mrs. Bronson. 'He walks round the estate with Reggie sometimes, and he shoots a bit. He talks to me.'

"'He's always glad to make himself useful,' said Bronson. 'The other day when I had a go of fever, he took over my work and I just lay in bed and had a good time.'"

"Hadn't the Bronsons any children?" I asked.

"No," Gaze answered. "I don't know why, they could well have afforded it."

Gaze leant back in his chair. He took off his glasses and wiped them. They were very strong and hideously distorted his eyes. Without them he wasn't so homely. The chik-chak on the ceiling gave its strangely human cry. It was like the cackle of an idiot child.

"Bronson was killed," said Gaze suddenly.

"Killed?"

"Yes, murdered. I shall never forget that night. We'd been playing tennis, Mrs. Bronson and the doctor's wife, Theo Cartwright and I; and then we played bridge. Cartwright had been off his game and when we sat down at the bridge-table Mrs. Bronson said to him: 'Well, Theo, if you play bridge as rottenly as you played tennis we shall lose our shirts.'

"We'd just had a drink, but she called the boy and ordered another round.

" 'Put that down your throat,' she said to him, 'and don't call without top honours and an outside trick.'

"Bronson hadn't turned up, he'd cycled in to Kabulong to get the money to pay his coolies their wages and was to come along to the club when he got back. The Bronsons' estate was nearer Alor Lipis than it was to Kabulong, but Kabulong was a more important place commercially, and Bronson banked there.

" 'Reggie can cut in when he turns up,' said Mrs. Bronson.

" 'He's late, isn't he?' said the doctor's wife.

" 'Very. He said he wouldn't get back in time for tennis, but would be here for a rubber. I have a suspicion that he went to the club at Kabulong instead of coming straight home and is having drinks, the ruffian.'

" 'Oh, well, he can put away a good many without their having much effect on him,' I laughed.

" 'He's getting fat, you know. He'll have to be careful.'

"We sat by ourselves in the card-room and we could hear the crowd in the billiard-room talking and laughing. They were all on the merry side. It was getting on to Christmas Day and we were all letting ourselves go a little. There was going to be a dance on Christmas Eve.

"I remembered afterwards that when we sat down the doctor's wife asked Mrs. Bronson if she wasn't tired.

"'Not a bit,' she said. 'Why should I be?'

"I didn't know why she flushed.

"'I was afraid the tennis might have been too much for you,' said the doctor's wife.

"'Oh, no,' answered Mrs. Bronson, a trifle abruptly, I thought, as though she didn't want to discuss the matter.

"I didn't know what they meant, and indeed it wasn't till later that I remembered the incident.

"We played three or four rubbers and still Bronson didn't turn up.

"'I wonder what's happened to him,' said his wife. 'I can't think why he should be so late.'

"Cartwright was always silent, but this evening he had hardly opened his mouth. I thought he was tired and asked him what he'd been doing.

"'Nothing very much,' he said. 'I went out after tiffin to shoot pigeon.'

"'Did you have any luck?' I asked.

"'Oh, I got half a dozen. They were very shy.'

"But now he said: 'If Reggie got back late, I daresay he thought it wasn't worth while to come here. I expect he's had a bath and when we get in we shall find him asleep in his chair.'

"'It's a good long ride from Kabulong,' said the doctor's wife.

"'He doesn't take the road, you know,' Mrs. Bronson explained. 'He takes the short cut through the jungle.'

"'Can he get along on his bicycle?' I asked.

"'Oh, yes, it's a very good track. It saves about a couple of miles.'

"We had just started another rubber when the barboy came in and said there was a police-sergeant outside who wanted to speak to me.

"'What does he want?' I asked.

"The boy said he didn't know, but he had two coolies with him.

"'Curse him,' I said. 'I'll give him hell if I find he's disturbed me for nothing.'

"I told the boy I'd come and I finished playing the hand. Then I got up.

"'I won't be a minute,' I said. 'Deal for me, will you?' I added to Cartwright.

"I went out and found the sergeant with two Malays waiting for me on the steps. I asked him what the devil he wanted. You can imagine my consternation when he told me that the Malays had come to the police-station and said there was a white man lying dead on the path that led through the jungle to Kabulong. I immediately thought of Bronson.

" 'Dead?' I cried.

" 'Yes, shot. Shot through the head. A white man with red hair.'

"Then I knew it was Reggie Bronson, and indeed, one of them naming his estate said he'd recognized him as the tuan. It was an awful shock. And there was Mrs. Bronson in the card-room waiting impatiently for me to sort my cards and make a bid. For a moment I really didn't know what to do. I was frightfully upset. It was dreadful to give her such a terrible and unexpected blow without a word of preparation, but I found myself quite unable to think of any way to soften it. I told the sergeant and the coolies to wait and went back into the club. I tried to pull myself together. As I entered the card-room Mrs. Bronson said: 'You've been an awful long time.' Then she caught sight of my face. 'Is anything the matter?' I saw her clench her fists and go white. You'd have thought she had a presentiment of evil.

" 'Something dreadful has happened,' I said, and my throat was all closed up so that my voice sounded even to myself hoarse and uncanny. 'There's been an accident. Your husband's been wounded.'

"She gave a long gasp, it was not exactly a scream, it reminded me oddly of a piece of silk torn in two.

" 'Wounded?'

"She leapt to her feet and with her eyes starting from her head stared at Cartwright. The effect on him was ghastly, he fell back in his chair and went as white as death.

" 'Very, very badly, I'm afraid,' I added.

"I knew that I must tell her the truth, and tell it then, but I couldn't bring myself to tell it all at once.

" 'Is he,' her lips trembled so that she could hardly form the words, 'is he—conscious?'

"I looked at her for a moment without answering. I'd have given a thousand pounds not to have to.

" 'No, I'm afraid he isn't.'

"Mrs. Bronson stared at me as though she were trying to see right into my brain.

"'Is he dead?'

"I thought the only thing was to get it out and have done with it.

"'Yes, he was dead when they found him.'

"Mrs. Bronson collapsed into her chair and burst into tears.

"'Oh, my God,' she muttered. 'Oh, my God.'

"The doctor's wife went to her and put her arms round her. Mrs. Bronson with her face in her hands swayed to and fro weeping hysterically. Cartwright, with that livid face, sat quite still, his mouth open, and stared at her. You might have thought he was turned to stone.

"'Oh, my dear, my dear,' said the doctor's wife, 'you must try and pull yourself together.' Then, turning to me, 'Get her a glass of water and fetch Harry.'

"Harry was her husband and he was playing billiards. I went in and told him what had happened.

"'A glass of water be damned,' he said. 'What she wants is a good long peg of brandy.'

"We took it in to her and forced her to drink it and gradually the violence of her emotion exhausted itself. In a few minutes the doctor's wife was able to take her into the ladies' lavatory to wash her face. I'd made up my mind now what had better be done. I could see that Cartwright wasn't good for much; he was all to pieces. I could understand that it was a fearful shock to him, for after all Bronson was his greatest friend and had done everything in the world for him.

"'You look as though you'd be all the better for a drop of brandy yourself, old man,' I said to him.

"He made an effort.

"'It's shaken me, you know,' he said. 'I . . . I didn't . . .' He stopped as though his mind was wandering; he was still fearfully pale; he took out a packet of cigarettes and struck a match, but his hand was shaking so that he could hardly manage it.

"'Yes, I'll have a brandy.'

"'Boy,' I shouted, and then to Cartwright: 'Now, are you fit to take Mrs. Bronson home?'

"'Oh, yes,' he answered.

"'That's good. The doctor and I will go along with the coolies and some police to where the body is.'

"'Will you bring him back to the bungalow?' asked Cartwright.

"'I think he'd better be taken straight to the mortuary,' said the doctor before I could answer. 'I shall have to do a P.M.'

"When Mrs. Bronson, now so much calmer that I was amazed, came back, I told her what I suggested. The doctor's wife, kind woman, offered to go with her and spend the night at the bungalow, but Mrs. Bronson wouldn't hear of it. She said she would be perfectly all right, and when the doctor's wife insisted—you know how bent some people are on forcing their kindness on those in trouble—she turned on her almost fiercely.

"'No, no, I must be alone,' she said. 'I really must. And Theo will be there.'

"They got into the trap. Theo took the reins and they drove off. We started after them, the doctor and I, while the sergeant and the coolies followed. I had sent my seis to the police-station with instructions to send two men to the place where the body was lying. We soon passed Mrs. Bronson and Cartwright.

"'All right?' I called.

"'Yes,' he answered.

"For some time the doctor and I drove without saying a word; we were both of us deeply shocked. I was worried as well. Somehow or other I'd got to find the murderers and I foresaw that it would be no easy matter.

"'Do you suppose it was gang robbery?' said the doctor at last.

"He might have been reading my thoughts.

"'I don't think there's a doubt of it,' I answered. 'They knew he'd gone into Kabulong to get the wages and lay in wait for him on the way back. Of course he should never have come alone through the jungle when everyone knew he had a packet of money with him.'

"'He'd done it for years,' said the doctor. 'And he's not the only one.'

"'I know. The question is, how we're going to get hold of the fellows that did it.'

"'You don't think the two coolies who say they found him could have had anything to do with it?'

"'No. They wouldn't have the nerve. I think a pair of Chinks might think out a trick like that, but I don't believe Malays would. They'd be much too frightened. Of course we'll keep an eye on them. We shall soon see if they seem to have any money to fling about.'

"'It's awful for Mrs. Bronson,' said the doctor. 'It would have been bad enough at any time, but now she's going to have a baby . . .'

"'I didn't know that,' I said, interrupting him.

"'No, for some reason she wanted to keep it dark. She was rather funny about it, I thought.'

"I recollected then that little passage between Mrs. Bronson and the doctor's wife. I understood why that good woman had been so anxious that Mrs. Bronson should not overtire herself.

"'It's strange her having a baby after being married so many years.'

"'It happens, you know. But it was a surprise to her. When first she came to see me and I told her what was the matter she fainted, and then she began to cry. I should have thought she'd be as pleased as Punch. She told me that Bronson didn't like children and he'd be awfully bored at the idea, and she made me promise to say nothing about it till she had had a chance of breaking it to him gradually.'

"I reflected for a moment.

"'He was the kind of breezy, hearty cove whom you'd expect to be as keen as mustard on having kids.'

"'You never can tell. Some people are very selfish and just don't want the bother.'

"'Well, how did he take it when she did tell him? Wasn't he rather bucked?'

"'I don't know that she ever told him. Though she couldn't have waited much longer; unless I'm very much mistaken she ought to be confined in about five months.'

"'Poor devil,' I said. 'You know, I've got a notion that he'd have been most awfully pleased to know.'

"We drove in silence for the rest of the way and at last came to the point at which the short cut to Kabulong branched off from the road. Here we stopped and in a minute or two my trap, in which were the police-sergeant and the two Malays, came up. We took the head-lamps to light us on our way. I left the doctor's seis to look after the ponies and told him that when the policemen came they were to follow the path till they found us. The two coolies, carrying the lamps, walked ahead and we followed them. It was a fairly broad track, wide enough for a small cart to pass, and before the road was built it had been the highway between Kabulong and Alor Lipis. It was firm to the foot and good walking. The surface here and there was sandy and in places you could see quite plainly the mark of a bicycle wheel. It was the track Bronson had left on his way to Kabulong.

"We walked twenty minutes, I should think, in single file, and on a sudden the coolies, with a cry, stopped sharply. The sight had come upon them so abruptly that notwithstanding they were expecting it they were startled. There, in the middle of the pathway lit dimly by the lamps the coolies carried, lay Bronson; he'd fallen over his bicycle and lay across it in an ungainly heap. I was too shocked to speak, and I think the doctor was, too. But in our silence the din of the jungle was deafening; those damned cicadas and the bull-frogs were making enough row to wake the dead. Even under ordinary circumstances the noise of the jungle at nights always seems to me uncanny; because you feel that at that hour there should be an utter silence it has an odd effect on you, that ceaseless and invisible uproar that beats upon your nerves. It surrounds you and hems you in. But just then, believe me, it was terrifying. That poor fellow lay dead and all round him the restless life of the jungle pursued its indifferent and ferocious course.

"He was lying face downwards. The sergeant and the coolies looked at me as though awaiting an order. I was a young fellow then and I'm afraid I felt a little frightened. Though I couldn't see the face I had no doubt that it was Bronson, but I felt that I ought to turn the body over to make sure. I suppose we all have our little squeamishnesses; you know, I've always had a horrible distaste for touching dead bodies. I've had to do it fairly often now, but it still makes me feel slightly sick.

"'It's Bronson, all right,' I said.

"The doctor—by George, it was lucky for me he was there—the doctor bent down and turned the head. The sergeant directed the lamp on the dead face.

"'My God, half his head's been shot away,' I cried.

"'Yes.'

"The doctor stood up straight and wiped his hands on the leaves of a tree that grew beside the path.

"'Is he quite dead?' I asked.

"'Oh, yes. Death must have been instantaneous. Whoever shot him must have fired at pretty close range.'

"'How long has he been dead, d'you think?'

"'Oh, I don't know, several hours.'

"'He would have passed here about five o'clock, I suppose, if he was expecting to get to the club for a rubber at six.'

"'There's no sign of any struggle,' said the doctor.

"'No, there wouldn't be. He was shot as he was riding along.'

"I looked at the body for a little while. I couldn't help thinking how short a time ago it was since Bronson, noisy and loud-voiced, had been so full of hearty life.

"'You haven't forgotten that he had the coolies' wages on him,' said the doctor.

"'No, we'd better search him.'

"'Shall we turn him over?'

"'Wait a minute. Let us just have a look at the ground first.'

"I took the lamp and as carefully as I could looked all about me. Just where he had fallen the sandy pathway was trodden and confused; there were our footprints and the footprints of the coolies who had found him. I walked two or three paces and then saw quite clearly the mark of his bicycle wheels; he had been riding straight and steadily. I followed it to the spot where he had fallen, to just before that rather, and there saw very distinctly the prints on each side of the wheels of his heavy boots. He had evidently stopped there and put his feet to the ground, then he'd started off again, there was a great wobble of the wheel, and he'd crashed.

"'Now let's search him,' I said.

"The doctor and the sergeant turned the body over and one of the coolies dragged the bicycle away. They laid Bronson on his back. I supposed he would have had the money partly in notes and partly in silver. The silver would have been in a bag attached to the bicycle and a glance told me that it was not there. The notes he would have put in a wallet. It would have been a good thick bundle. I felt him all over, but there was nothing; then I turned out the pockets, they were all empty except the right trouser pocket, in which there was a little small change.

"'Didn't he always wear a watch?' asked the doctor.

"'Yes, of course he did.'

"I remembered that he wore the chain through the buttonhole in the lapel of his coat and the watch and some seals and things in his handkerchief pocket. But watch and chain were gone.

"'Well, there's not much doubt now, is there?' I said.

"It was clear that he had been attacked by gang robbers who knew he had money on him. After killing him they had stripped him of everything. I suddenly remembered the footprints that proved that for a moment he had stood still. I saw exactly how it had been done. One of them had stopped him on some pretext and then, just as he started off again, another, slipping out of the jungle behind him, had emptied the two barrels of a gun into his head.

"'Well,' I said to the doctor, 'it's up to me to catch them, and I'll tell you what, it'll be a real pleasure to me to see them hanged.'

"Of course there was an inquest. Mrs. Bronson gave evidence, but she had nothing to say that we didn't know already. Bronson had left the bungalow about eleven, he was to have tiffin at Kabulong and was to be back between five and six. He asked her not to wait for him, he said he would just put the money in the safe and come straight to the club. Cartwright confirmed this. He had lunched alone with Mrs. Bronson and after a smoke had gone out with a gun to shoot pigeon. He had got in about five, a little before perhaps, had a bath and changed to play tennis. He was shooting not far from the place where Bronson was killed, but never heard a shot. That, of course, meant nothing; what with the cicadas and the frogs, and the other sounds of the jungle he would have had to be very near to hear anything; and besides, Cartwright was probably back in the bungalow before Bronson was killed. We traced Bronson's movements. He had lunched at the club, he had got money at the bank just before it closed, had gone back to the club and had one more drink, and then started off on his bicycle. He had crossed the river by the ferry, the ferryman re-membered distinctly seeing him, but was positive that no one else with a bicycle had crossed. That looked as though the murderers were not following, but lying in wait for him. He rode along the main road for a couple of miles and then took the path which was a short cut to his bungalow.

"It looked as though he had been killed by men who knew his habits, and suspicion, of course, fell immediately on the coolies of his estate. We examined them all—pretty carefully—but there was not a scrap of evidence to connect any of them with the crime. In fact, most of them were able satisfactorily to account for their actions and those who couldn't seemed to me for one reason and another out of the running. There were a few bad characters among the Chinese at Alor Lipis and I had them looked up. But somehow I didn't think it was the work of the Chinese; I had a feeling that Chinese would have used revolvers and not a shot gun. Anyhow, I could find out nothing there. So then we offered a reward of a thousand dollars to anyone who could put us in the way of discovering the murderers. I thought there were a good many people to whom it would appeal to do a public service and at the same time earn a tidy sum. But I knew that an informer would take no risks, he wouldn't want to tell what he knew till he knew he could tell it safely, and I armed myself with patience. The reward had brightened the interest of my police and I knew they would use every means they had to bring the criminals to trial. In a case like this they could do more than I.

"But it was strange, nothing happened; the reward seemed to tempt no one. I cast my net a little wider. There were two or three kampongs along the road and I wondered if the murderers were there; I saw the headmen, but got no help from them. It was not that they would tell me nothing, I was sure they had nothing to tell. I talked to the bad hats, but there was absolutely nothing to connect them with the murder. There was not the shadow of a clue.

"'Very well, my lads,' I said to myself, as I drove back to Alor Lipis, 'there's no hurry; the rope won't spoil by keeping.'

"The scoundrels had got away with a considerable sum, but money is no good unless you spend it. I felt I knew the native temperament enough to be sure that the possession of it was a constant temptation. The Malays are an extravagant race, and a race of gamblers, and the Chinese are gamblers, too; sooner or later someone would start flinging his money about, and then I should want to know where it came from. With a few well-directed questions I thought I could put the fear of God into the fellow and then, if I knew my business, it shouldn't be hard to get a full confession.

"The only thing now was to sit down and wait till the hue and cry had died down and the murderers thought the affair was forgotten. The itch to spend those ill-gotten dollars would grow more and more intolerable till at last it could be resisted no longer. I would go about my business, but I meant never to relax my watch, and one day, sooner or later, my time must come.

"Cartwright took Mrs. Bronson down to Singapore. The company Bronson had worked for asked him if he would care to take Bronson's place, but he said, very naturally, that he didn't like the idea of it; so they put another man in and told Cartwright that he could have the job that Bronson's successor had vacated. It was the management of the estate that Cartwright lives on now. He moved in at once. Four months after this Olive was born at Singapore, and a few months later, when Bronson had been dead just over a year, Cartwright and Mrs. Bronson were married. I was surprised; but on thinking it over I couldn't help confessing that it was very natural. After the trouble Mrs. Bronson had leant much on Cartwright and he had arranged everything for her; she must have been lonely, and rather lost, and I daresay she was grateful for his kindness, he did behave like a brick; and so far as he was concerned I imagined he was sorry for her, it was a dreadful position for a woman, she had nowhere to go, and all they'd gone through must have been a tie between them. There was every reason for them to marry and it was probably the best thing for them both.

"It looked as though Bronson's murderers would never be caught, for that plan of mine didn't work; there was no one in the district who spent more money than he could account for, and if anyone had that hoard buried away under his floor he was showing a self-control that was super-human. A year had passed and to all intents and purposes the thing was forgotten. Could anyone be so prudent as after so long not to let a little money dribble out? It was incredible. I began to think that Bronson had been killed by a couple of wandering Chinese who had got away, to Singapore perhaps, where there would be small chance of catching them. At last I gave it up. If you come to think of it, as a rule, it's just those crimes, crimes of robbery, in which there is least chance of getting the culprit; for there's nothing to attach suspicion to him, and if he's caught it can only be by his own carelessness. It's different with crimes of passion or vengeance, then you can find out who had a motive to put the victim out of the way.

"It's no use grizzling over one's failures, and bringing my com-

mon sense to bear I did my best to put the matter out of my
mind. No one likes to be beaten, but beaten I was and I had to
put as good a face on it as I could. And then a Chinaman was
caught trying to pawn poor Bronson's watch.

"I told you that Bronson's watch and chain had been taken,
and of course Mrs. Bronson was able to give us a fairly accurate
description of it. It was a half-hunter, by Benson, there was a
gold chain, three or four seals and a sovereign purse. The pawnbroker was a smart fellow and when the Chinaman brought the
watch he recognized it at once. On some pretext he kept the
man waiting and sent for a policeman. The man was arrested
and immediately brought to me. I greeted him like a long-lost
brother. I was never so pleased to see anyone in my life. I have
no feeling about criminals, you know; I'm rather sorry for them,
because they're playing a game in which their opponents hold
all the aces and kings; but when I catch one it gives me a little
thrill of satisfaction, like bringing off a neat finesse at bridge.
At last the mystery was going to be cleared up, for if the Chinaman hadn't done the thing himself we were pretty sure through
him to trace the murderers. I beamed on him.

"I asked him to account for his possession of the watch. He
said he had bought it from a man he didn't know. That was very
thin. I explained the circumstances briefly and told him he would
be charged with murder. I meant to frighten him and I did. He
said then that he'd found the watch.

"'Found it?' I said. 'Fancy that. Where?'

"His answer staggered me; he said he'd found it in the jungle;
I laughed at him; I asked him if he thought watches were likely
to be left lying about in the jungle; then he said he'd been
coming along the pathway that led from Kabulong to Alor Lipis,
and had gone into the jungle and caught sight of something gleaming and there was the watch. That was odd. Why should he have
said he found the watch just there? It was either true or exces-
sively astute. I asked him where the chain and the seals were,
and he produced them immediately. I'd got him scared, and he
was pale and shaking; he was a knock-kneed little fellow and I
should have been a fool not to see that I hadn't got hold of the
murderer there. But his terror suggested that he knew something

"I asked him when he'd found the watch.

"'Yesterday,' he said.

"I asked him what he was doing on the short-cut from Kabu-long to Alor Lipis. He said that he'd been working in Singapore and had gone to Kabulong because his father was ill, and that he himself had come to Alor Lipis to work. A friend of his father, a carpenter by trade, had given him a job. He gave me the name of the man with whom he had worked in Singapore and the name of the man who had engaged him at Alor Lipis. All he said seemed plausible and could so easily be verified that it was hardly likely to be false. Of course it occurred to me that if he had found the watch as he said it must have been lying in the jungle for more than a year. It could hardly be in very good condition; I tried to open it, but couldn't. The pawnbroker had come to the police-station and was waiting in the next room. Luckily he was also something of a watchmaker. I sent for him and asked him to look at the watch; when he opened it he gave a little whistle, the works were thick with rust.

"'This watch no good,' he said, shaking his head. 'Him never go now.'

"I asked him what had put it in such a state, and without a word from me he said that it had been long exposed to wet. For the moral effect I had the prisoner put in a cell and I sent for his employer. I sent a wire to Kabulong and another to Singapore. While I waited I did my best to put two and two to-gether. I was inclined to believe the man's story true; his fear might be ascribed to no more guilt than consisted in his having found something and tried to sell it. Even quite innocent persons are apt to be nervous when they're in the hands of the police; I don't know what there is about a policeman, people are never very much at their ease in his company. But if he really had found the watch where he said, someone had thrown it there. Now that was funny. Even if the murderers had thought the watch a dangerous thing to possess, one would have expected them to melt down the gold case; that would be a very simple thing for any native to do; and the chain was of so ordinary a pattern they could hardly have thought it possible to trace that. There were chains like it in every jeweller's shop in the country. Of course there was the possibility that they had plunged into the jungle and having dropped the watch in their hurry had been afraid to go back and look for it. I didn't think that very likely: the Malays are used to keeping things tucked away in their sarongs, and the

Chinese have pockets in their coats. Besides, the moment they got into the jungle they knew there was no hurry; they probably waited and divided the swag then and there.

"In a few minutes the man I had sent for came to the police-station and confirmed what the prisoner had said, and in an hour I got an answer from Kabulong. The police had seen his father who told them that the boy had gone to Alor Lipis to get a job with a carpenter. So far everything he had said seemed true. I had him brought in again, and told him I was going to take him to the place where he said he had found the watch and he must show me the exact spot. I handcuffed him to a policeman, though it was hardly necessary, for the poor devil was shaking with fright, and took a couple of men besides. We drove out to where the track joined the road and walked along it; within five yards of the place where Bronson was killed the Chinaman stopped.

"'Here,' he said.

"He pointed to the jungle and we followed him in. We went in about ten yards and he pointed to a chink between two large boulders and said that he found the watch there. It could only have been by the merest chance that he noticed it, and if he really had found it there it looked very much as though some-one had put it there to hide it."

Gaze stopped and gave me a reflective look.

"What would you have thought then?" he asked.

"I don't know," I answered.

"Well, I'll tell you what I thought. I thought that if the watch was there the money might be there, too. It seemed worth while having a look. Of course, to look for something in the jungle makes looking for a needle in a bundle of hay a drawing-room pastime. I couldn't help that. I released the Chinaman, I wanted all the help I could get, and set him to work. I set my three men to work and I started in myself. We made a line—there were five of us—and we searched from the road; for fifty yards on each side of the place at which Bronson was murdered and for a hundred yards in we went over the ground foot by foot. We routed among dead leaves and peered in bushes, we looked under boulders and in the hollows of trees. I knew it was a foolish thing to do, for the chances against us were a thousand to one; my only hope was that anyone who had just committed a murder would be rattled and if he wanted to hide anything would hide it quickly; he would choose the first obvious hiding-place that offered itself. That is what he had done when he hid the watch. My only reason for looking in so circumscribed an area was that as the watch had been found so near the road, the person who wanted to get rid of the things must have wanted to get rid of them quickly.

"We worked on. I began to grow tired and cross. We were sweating like pigs. I had a maddening thirst and nothing in the world to drink. At last I came to the conclusion that we must give it up as a bad job, for that day at least, when suddenly the Chinaman—he must have had sharp eyes, that young man—uttered a guttural cry. He stooped down and from under the winding root of a tree drew out a messy, mouldering, stinking thing. It was a pocket-book that had been out in the rain for a year, that had been eaten by ants and beetles and God knows what, that was sodden and foul, but it was a pocket-book all right, Bronson's, and inside were the shapeless, mushed-up, fetid remains of the Singapore notes he had got from the bank at Kabulong. There was still the silver and I was convinced that it was hidden somewhere about, but I wasn't going to bother about that. I had found out something very important; whoever had murdered Bronson had made no money out of it.

"Do you remember my telling you that I'd noticed the print of Bronson's feet on each side of the broad line of the pneumatic tyre, where he had stopped, and presumably spoken to someone? He was a heavy man and the prints were well marked. He hadn't just put his feet on the soft sand and taken them off, but must have stopped at least for a minute or two. My explanation was that he had stopped to chat with a Malay or a Chinaman, but the more I thought of it the less I liked it. Why the devil should he? Bronson wanted to get home, and though a jovial chap, he certainly was not hail-fellow-well-met with the natives. His relations towards them were those of master and servants. Those footprints had always puzzled me. And now the truth flashed across me. Whoever had murdered Bronson hadn't murdered him to rob and if he'd stopped to talk with someone it could only be with a friend. I knew at last who the murderer was."

I have always thought the detective story a most diverting and ingenious variety of fiction, and have regretted that I never had the skill to write one, but I have read a good many, and I flatter myself it is rarely that I have not solved the mystery before it was disclosed to me; and now for some time I had foreseen what Gaze was going to say, but when at last he said it I confess that it gave me, notwithstanding, somewhat of a shock.

"The man he met was Cartwright. Cartwright was pigeon-shooting. He stopped and asked him what sport he had had, and as he rode on Cartwright raised his gun and discharged both barrels into his head. Cartwright took the money and the watch in order to make it look like the work of gang robbers and hurriedly hid them in the jungle, then made his way along the edge till he got to the road, went back to the bungalow, changed into his tennis things and drove with Mrs. Bronson to the club.

"I remembered how badly he'd played tennis, and how he'd collapsed when, in order to break the news more gently to Mrs. Bronson, I said Bronson was wounded and not dead. If he was only wounded he might have been able to speak. By George, I bet that was a bad moment. The child was Cartwright's. Look at Olive: why, you saw the likeness yourself. The doctor had said that Mrs. Bronson was upset when he told her she was going to have a baby and made him promise not to tell Bronson. Why? Because Bronson knew that he couldn't be the father of the child."

"Do you think that Mrs. Bronson knew what Cartwright had done?" I asked.

"I'm sure of it. When I look back on her behaviour that evening at the club I am convinced of it. She was upset, but not because Bronson was killed; she was upset because I said he was wounded; on my telling her that he was dead when they found him she burst out crying, but from relief. I know that woman. Look at that square chin of hers and tell me that she hasn't got the courage of the devil. She has a will of iron. She made Cartwright do it. She planned every detail and every move. He was completely under her influence; he is now."

"But do you mean to tell me that neither you nor anyone else ever suspected that there was anything between them?"

"Never. Never."

"If they were in love with one another and knew that she was going to have a baby, why didn't they just bolt?"

"How could they? It was Bronson who had the money; she hadn't a bean and neither had Cartwright. He was out of a job. Do you think he would have got another with that story round his neck? Bronson had taken him in when he was starving and he'd stolen his wife from him. They wouldn't have had a dog's chance. They couldn't afford to let the truth come out, their only chance was to get Bronson out of the way, and they got him out of the way."

"They might have thrown themselves on his mercy."

"Yes, but I think they were ashamed. He'd been so good to them, he was such a decent chap, I don't think they had the heart to tell him the truth. They preferred to kill him."

There was a moment's silence while I reflected over what Gaze said.

"Well, what did you do about it?" I asked.

"Nothing. What was there to do? What was the evidence? That the watch and notes had been found? They might easily have been hidden by someone who was afterwards afraid to come and get them. The murderer might have been quite content to get away with the silver. The footprints? Bronson might have stopped to light a cigarette or there might have been a tree trunk across the path and he waited while the coolies he met there by chance moved it away. Who could prove that the child that a perfectly decent, respectable woman had had four months after her husband's death was not his child? No jury would have convicted Cartwright. I held my tongue and the Bronson murder was forgotten."

"I don't suppose the Cartwrights have forgotten," I suggested.

"I shouldn't be surprised. Human memory is astonishingly short and if you want my professional opinion I don't mind telling you that I don't believe remorse for a crime ever sits very heavily on a man when he's absolutely sure he'll never be found out."

I thought once more of the pair I had met that afternoon, the thin, elderly, bald man with gold-rimmed spectacles, and that white-haired untidy woman with her frank speech and kindly, caustic smile. It was almost impossible to imagine that in the distant past they had been swayed by so turbulent a passion, for that alone made their behaviour explicable, that it had brought them in the end to such a pass that they could see no other issue than a cruel and cold-blooded murder.

"Doesn't it make you feel a little uncomfortable to be with them?" I asked Gaze. "For, without wishing to be censorious, I'm bound to say that I don't think they can be very nice people."

"That's where you're wrong. They are very nice people; they're about the pleasantest people here. Mrs. Cartwright is a thoroughly good sort and a very amusing woman. It's my business to prevent crime and to catch the culprit when crime is committed, but I've known far too many criminals to think that on the whole they're worse than anybody else. A perfectly decent fellow may be driven by circumstances to commit a crime and if he's found out he's punished; but he may very well remain a perfectly decent fellow. Of course society punishes him if he breaks its laws, and it's quite right, but it's not always his actions that indicate the essential man. If you'd been a policeman as long as I have, you'd know it's not what people do that really matters, it's what they are. Luckily a policeman has nothing to do with their thoughts, only with their deeds; if he had, it would be a very different, a much more difficult matter."

Gaze flicked the ash from his cheroot and gave me his wry, sardonic, but agreeable smile.

"I'll tell you what, there's one job I *shouldn't* like," he said.

"What is that?" I asked.

"God's, at the Judgment Day," said Gaze. "No, sir."

A Man With a Conscience

St. Laurent de Maroni is a pretty little place. It is neat and clean. It has an Hôtel de Ville and a Palais de Justice of which many a town in France would be proud. The streets are wide, and the fine trees that border them give a grateful shade. The houses look as though they had just had a coat of paint. Many of them nestle in little gardens, and in the gardens are palm trees and flame of the forest; cannas flaunt their bright colours and crotons their variety; the bougainvillæas, purple or red, riot profusely, and the elegant hibiscus offers its gorgeous flowers with a negligence that seems almost affected. St. Laurent de Maroni is the centre of the French penal settlements of Guiana, and a hundred yards from the quay at which you land is the great gateway of the prison camp. These pretty little houses in their tropical gardens are the residence of the prison officials, and if the streets are neat and clean it is because there is no lack of convicts to keep them so. One day, walking with a casual acquaintance, I came upon a young man, in the round straw hat and the pink and white stripes of the convict's uniform, who was standing by the road-side with a pick. He was doing nothing.

"Why are you idling?" my companion asked him.

The man gave his shoulders a scornful shrug.

"Look at the blade of grass there," he answered. "I've got twenty years to scratch it away."

St. Laurent de Maroni exists for the group of prison camps of which it is the centre. Such trade as it has depends on them; its shops, kept by Chinese, are there to satisfy the wants of the warders, the doctors and the numerous officials who are connected with the penal settlements. The streets are silent and deserted. You pass a convict with a dispatch-case under his arm; he has some job in the administration; or another with a basket; he is a servant in somebody's house. Sometimes you come upon a little group in the charge of a warder; often you see them strolling to or from the prison unguarded. The prison gates are open all day long and the prisoners freely saunter in and out. If you see a man not in the prison uniform he is probably a freed man who is condemned to spend a number of years in the colony and who, unable to get work, living on the edge of starvation, is drinking himself to death on the cheap strong rum which is called tafia.

There is an hotel at St. Laurent de Maroni and here I had my meals. I soon got to know by sight the habitual frequenters. They came in and sat each at his little table, ate their meals in silence and went out again. The hotel was kept by a coloured woman, and the man she lived with, an ex-convict, was the only waiter. But the Governor of the colony, who lives at Cayenne, had put at my disposal his own bungalow and it was there I slept. An old Arab looked after it; he was a devout Mohammedan, and at intervals during the day I heard him say his prayers. To make my bed, keep my rooms tidy and run errands for me, the commandant of the prison had assigned me another convict. Both were serving life sentences for murder; the commandant told me that I could place entire confidence in them; they were as honest as the day, and I could leave anything about without the slightest risk. But I will not conceal from the reader that when I went to bed at night I took the precaution to lock my door and to bolt my shutters. It was foolish no doubt, but I slept more comfortably.

I had come with letters of introduction, and both the Governor of the prison settlements and the commandant of the camp at St. Laurent did everything they could to make my visit agreeable and instructive. I will not here narrate all I heard and saw. I am not a reporter. It is not my business to attack or to defend the system which the French have thought fit to adopt in regard to their criminals. Besides, the system is now condemned; prisoners will soon cease to be sent out to French Guiana, to suffer the illnesses incidental to the climate and the work in malarial jungles to which so many are relegated, to endure nameless degradations, to lose hope, to rot, to die. I will only say that I saw no physical cruelty. On the other hand I saw no attempt to make the criminal on the expiration of his sentence a useful citizen. I saw nothing done for his spiritual welfare. I heard nothing of classes that he could attend in order to improve his education or organised games that might distract his mind. I saw no library where he could get books to read when his day's work was done. I saw a condition of affairs that only the strongest character could hope to surmount. I saw a brutishness that must reduce all but a very few to apathy and despair.

All this has nothing to do with me. It is vain to torment oneself over sufferings that one cannot alleviate. My object here is to tell a story. As I am well aware, one can never know everything there is to be known about human nature. One can be sure only of one thing, and that is that it will never cease to have a surprise in store for you. When I had got over the impression of bewilderment, surprise and horror to which my first visit to the prison camp gave rise, I bethought myself that there were certain matters that I was interested to enquire into. I should inform the reader that three-quarters of the convicts at St. Laurent de Maroni are there for murder. This is not official information and it may be that I exaggerate; every prisoner has a little book in which are set down his crime, his sentence, his punishments, and whatever else the authorities think necessary to keep note of; and it was from an examination of a considerable number of these that I formed my estimate. It gave me something of a shock to realise that in England far, far the greater number of these men whom I saw working in shops, lounging about the verandahs of their dormitories or sauntering through the streets would have suffered capital punishment. I found them not at all disinclined to speak of the crime for which they had been convicted, and in pursuance of my purpose I spent the better part of one day enquiring into crimes of passion. I wanted to know exactly what was the motive that had made a man kill his wife or his girl. I had a notion that jealousy and wounded honour might not perhaps tell the whole story. I got some curious replies, and among them one that was not to my mind lacking in humour. This was from a man working in the carpenter's shop who had cut his wife's throat; when I asked him why he had done it, he answered with a shrug of the shoulders: *Manque d'entente*. His casual tone made the best translation of this: We didn't get on very well. I could not help observing that if men in general looked upon this as an adequate reason for murdering their wives, the mortality in the female sex would be alarming. But after putting a good many questions to a good many men I arrived at the conclusion that at the bottom of nearly all these crimes was an economic motive; they had killed their wives or mistresses not only from jealousy, because they were unfaithful to them, but also because somehow it affected their pockets. A woman's infidelity was sometimes an occasion of financial loss, and it was this in the end that drove a man to his desperate act; or, himself in need of money to gratify other passions, he murdered because his victim was an obstacle to his exclusive possession of it. I do not conclude that a man never kills his woman because his love is spurned or his honour tarnished, I only offer my observation on these particular cases as a curious sidelight on human nature. I should not venture to deduce from it a general rule.

I spent another day enquiring into the matter of conscience. Moralists have sought to persuade us that it is one of the most powerful agents in human behaviour. Now that reason and pity have agreed to regard hell-fire as a hateful myth, many good men have seen in conscience the chief safeguard that shall induce the human race to walk in the way of righteousness. Shakespeare has told us that it makes cowards of us all. Novelists and playwrights have described for us the pangs that assail the wicked; they have vividly pictured the anguish of a stricken conscience and the sleepless nights it occasions; they have shown it poisoning every pleasure till life is so intolerable that discovery and punishment come as a welcome relief. I had often wondered how much of all this was true. Moralists have an axe to grind; they must draw a moral. They think that if they say a thing often enough people will believe it. They are apt to state that a thing is so when they consider it desirable that it should be. They tell us that the wages of sin is death; we know very well that it is not always. And so far as the authors of fiction are concerned, the playwrights and the novelists, when they got hold of an effective theme they are disposed to make use of it without bothering very much whether it agrees with the facts of life. Certain statements about human nature become, as it were, common property and so are accepted as self-evident. In the same way painters for ages painted shadows black, and it was not till the impressionists looked at them with unprejudiced eyes and painted what they saw that we discovered that shadows were coloured. It had sometimes struck me that perhaps conscience was the expression of a high moral development, so that its influence was strong only in those whose virtue was so shining that they were unlikely to commit any action for which they could seriously reproach themselves. It is generally accepted that murder is a shocking crime, and it is the murderer above all other criminals who is supposed to suffer remorse. His victim, we have been led to believe, haunts his dreams in horrifying nightmares, and the recollection of his dreadful deed tortures his waking hours. I could not miss the opportunity to enquire into the truth of this. I had no intention of insisting if I encountered reticence or distress, but I found in none of those with whom I talked any such thing. Some said that in the same circumstances they would do as they had done before. Determinists without knowing it, they seemed to look upon their action as ordained by a fate over which they had no control. Some appeared to think that their crime was committed by someone with whom they had no connection.

"When one's young, one's foolish," they said, with a careless gesture or a deprecating smile.

Others told me that if they had known what the punishment was they would suffer, they would certainly have held their hands. I found in none any regret for the human being they had violently bereft of life. It seemed to me that they had no more feeling for the creature they had killed than if it had been a pig whose throat they had cut in the way of business. Far from feeling pity for their victim, they were more inclined to feel anger because he had been the occasion of their imprisonment in that distant land. In only one man did I discern anything that might appropriately be called a conscience, and his story was so remarkable that I think it well worth narrating. For in this case it was, so far as I can understand, remorse that was the motive of the crime. I noticed the man's number, which was printed on the chest of the pink and white pyjamas of his prison uniform, but I have forgotten it. Anyhow it is of no consequence. I never knew his name. He did not offer to tell me and I did not like to ask it. I will call him Jean Charvin.

I met him on my first visit to the camp with the commandant. We were walking through a courtyard round which were cells, not punishment cells, but individual cells which are given to well-behaved prisoners who ask for them. They are sought after by those to whom the promiscuity of the dormitories is odious. Most of them were empty, for their occupants were engaged in their various employments. Jean Charvin was at work in his cell, writing at a small table, and the door was open. The commandant called

him and he came out. I looked into the cell. It contained a fixed
hammock, with a dingy mosquito-net; by the side of this was a
small table on which were his bits and pieces, a shaving-mop
and a razor, a hairbrush and two or three battered books. On
the walls were photographs of persons of respectable appearance
and illustrations from picture papers. He had been sitting on his
bed to write and the table on which he had been writing was
covered with papers. They looked like accounts. He was a handsome man, tall, erect and lean, with flashing dark eyes and clean-
cut, strong features. The first thing I noticed about him was that
he had a fine head of long, naturally-waving dark brown hair.
This at once made him look different from the rest of the prisoners,
whose hair is close-cropped, but cropped so badly, in ridges, that
it gives them a sinister look. The commandant spoke to him of
some official business, and then as we were leaving added in a
friendly way:

"I see your hair is growing well."

Jean Charvin reddened and smiled. His smile was boyish and
engaging.

"It'll be some time yet before I get it right again."

The commandant dismissed him and we went on.

"He's a very decent fellow," he said. "He's in the accountant's
department, and he's had leave to let his hair grow. He's delighted."

"What is he here for?" I asked.

"He killed his wife. But he's only got six years. He's clever and
a good worker. He'll do well. He comes from a very decent family
and he's had an excellent education."

I thought no more of Jean Charvin, but by chance I met him
next day on the road. He was coming towards me. He carried a
black dispatch-case under his arm, and except for the pink and
white stripes of his uniform and the ugly round straw hat that
concealed his handsome head of hair, you might have taken him
for a young lawyer on his way to court. He walked with a long,
leisurely stride, and he had an easy, you might almost say a gallant, bearing. He recognised me, and taking off his hat bade me
good-morning. I stopped, and for something to say asked him
where he was going. He told me he was taking some papers from
the Governor's office to the bank. There was a pleasing frankness
in his face, and his eyes, his really beautiful eyes, shone with

good will. I supposed that the vigour of his youth was such that it made life, notwithstanding his position and his surroundings, more than tolerable, even pleasant. You would have said that here was a young man without a care in the world.

"I hear you're going to St. Jean to-morrow," he said.

"Yes. It appears I must start at dawn."

St. Jean is a camp seventeen kilometres from St. Laurent, and it is here that are interned the habitual criminals who have been sentenced to transportation after repeated terms of imprisonment. They are petty thieves, confidence men, forgers, tricksters and suchlike; the prisoners of St. Laurent, condemned for more serious offences, look upon them with contempt.

"You should find it an interesting experience," Jean Charvin said, with his frank and engaging smile. "But keep your pocket-book buttoned up, they'd steal the shirt off your back if they had half a chance. They're a dirty lot of scoundrels!"

That afternoon, waiting till the heat of the day was less, I sat on the verandah outside my bedroom and read: I had drawn the jalousies and it was tolerably cool. My old Arab came up the stairs on his bare feet, and in his halting French told me that there was a man from the commandant who wanted to see me.

"Send him up," I said.

In a moment the man came, and it was Jean Charvin. He told me that the commandant had sent him to give me a message about my excursion next day to St. Jean. When he had delivered it I asked him if he would not sit down and have a cigarette with me. He wore a cheap wrist-watch and he looked at it.

"I have a few minutes to spare. I should be glad to." He sat down and lit the cigarette I offered him. He gave me a smiling look of his soft eyes. "Do you know, this is the first time I've ever been asked to sit down since I was sentenced." He inhaled a long whiff of his cigarette. "Egyptian. I haven't smoked an Egyptian cigarette for three years."

The convicts make their own cigarettes out of a coarse, strong tobacco that is sold in square blue packets. Since one is not allowed to pay them for the services they may render you, but may give them tobacco, I had bought a good many packets of this.

"How does it taste?"

"One gets accustomed to everything and, to tell you the truth, my palate is so vitiated, I prefer the stuff we get here."

"I'll give you a couple of packets."

I went into my room and fetched them. When I returned he was looking at some books that were lying on the table.

"Are you fond of reading?" I asked.

"Very. I think the want of books is what I most suffer from now. The few I can get hold of I'm forced to read over and over again."

To so great a reader as myself no deprivation seems more insupportable than the lack of books.

"I have several French ones in my bag. I'll look them out and if you care to have them I'll give them to you if you can come along again."

My offer was due only in part to kindness; I wanted to have another chance of a talk with him.

"I should have to show them to the commandant. He would only let me keep them if there was no doubt they couldn't possibly corrupt my morals. But he's a good-natured man, I don't think he'll make any difficulties."

There was a hint of slyness in the smile with which he said this, and I suspected that he had taken the measure of the well-meaning, conscientious chief of the camp and knew pretty well how to get on the right side of him. It would have been unjust to blame him if he exercised tact, and even cunning, to render his lot as tolerable as might be.

"The commandant has a very good opinion of you."

"He's a fine man. I'm very grateful to him, he's done a great deal for me. I'm an accountant by profession and he's put me in the accountant's department. I love figures, it gives me an intense satisfaction to deal with them, they're living things to me, and now that I can handle them all day long I feel myself again."

"And are you glad to have a cell of your own?"

"It's made all the difference. To be herded with fifty men, the scum of the earth, and never to be alone for a minute—it was awful. That was the worst of all. At home, at Le Havre, that is where I lived, I had an apartment, modest of course, but my own, and we had a maid who came in by the day. We lived decently. It made it ten times harder for me than for the rest, most of them, who have never known anything but squalor, filth and promiscuity."

I had asked him about the cell in the hope that I could get him to talk about the life that is led in those vast dormitories in which the men are locked from five in the evening till five next morning. During these twelve hours they are their own masters. A warder can enter, they told me, only at the risk of his life. They have no light after eight o'clock, but from sardine-tins, a little oil, and a rag they make lamps by the light of which they can see enough to play cards. They gamble furiously, not for love, but for the money they keep secreted on their bodies; they are unscrupulous ruthless men, and naturally enough bitter quarrels often arise. They are settled with knives. Often in the morning, when the dormitory is opened, a man is found dead, but no threats, no promises, will induce anyone to betray the slayer. Other things Jean Charvin told me which I cannot narrate. He told me of one young fellow who had come out from France on the same ship with himself and with whom he had made friends. He was a good-looking boy. One day he went to the commandant and asked him if he could have a cell to himself. The commandant asked him why he wanted one. He explained. The commandant looked through his list and told him that at the moment all were occupied, but that as soon as there was a vacancy he should have one. Next morning when the dormitory was opened, he was found dead on his hammock with his belly ripped open to the breast-bone.

"They're savage brutes, and if one isn't a brute by the time one arrives only a miracle can save one from becoming as brutal as the rest."

Jean Charvin looked at his watch and got up. He walked away from me and then, with his charming smile, turned and faced me.

"I must go now. If the commandant gives me permission I will come and get the books you were kind enough to offer me."

In Guiana you do not shake hands with a convict, and a tactful man, taking leave of you, puts himself in such a position that there can be no question of your offering him your hand or of refusing his should he, forgetting for a moment, instinctively tender it. Heaven knows, it would have meant nothing to me to shake hands with Jean Charvin; it gave me a pang to see the care he had taken to spare me embarrassment.

I saw him twice more during my stay at St. Laurent. He told me his story, but I will tell it now in my words rather than in his, for I had to piece it together from what he said at one time and another, and what he left out I have had to supply out of my own imagination. I do not believe it has led me astray. It was as though he had given me three letters out of a number of five-letter words; the chances are that I have guessed most of the words correctly.

Jean Charvin was born and bred in the great seaport of Le Havre. His father had a good post in the Customs. Having finished his education, he did his military service, and then looked about for a job. Like a great many other young Frenchmen he was prepared to sacrifice the hazardous chance of wealth for a respectable security. His natural gift for figures made it easy for him to get a place in the accountant's department of a large exporting house. His future was assured. He could look forward to earning a sufficient income to live in the modest comfort of the class to which he belonged. He was industrious and well-behaved. Like most young Frenchmen of his generation he was athletic. He swam and played tennis in summer, and in winter he bicycled. On two evenings a week to keep himself fit he spent a couple of hours in a gymnasium. Through his childhood, his adolescence and his young manhood, he lived in the constant companionship of a boy called, shall we say for the purposes of this narrative, Henri Renard, whose father was also an official in the Customs. Jean and Riri went to school together, played together, worked for their examinations together, spent their holidays together, for the two families were intimate, had their first affairs with girls together, partnered one another in the local tennis tournaments, and did their military service together. They never quarrelled. They were never so happy as in one another's society. They were inseparable. When the time came for them to start working they decided that they would go into the same firm; but that was not so easy; Jean tried to get Riri a job in the exporting house that had engaged him, but could not manage it, and it was not till a year later that Riri got something to do. But by then trade was as bad at Le Havre as everywhere else, and in a few months he found himself once more without employment.

Riri was a light-hearted youth, and he enjoyed his leisure. He danced, bathed and played tennis. It was thus that he made the acquaintance of a girl who had recently come to live at Le Havre. Her father had been a captain in the colonial army and on his death her mother had returned to Le Havre, which was her native place. Marie-Louise was then eighteen. She had spent almost all her life in Tonkin. This gave her an exotic attraction for the young men who had never been out of France in their lives, and first Riri, then Jean, fell in love with her. Perhaps that was inevitable; it was certainly unfortunate. She was a well-brought-up girl, an only child, and her mother, besides her pension, had a little money of her own. It was evident that she could be pursued only with a view to marriage. Of course Riri, dependent for the while entirely on his father, could not make an offer that there was the least chance of Madame Meurice, Marie-Louise's mother, accepting; but having the whole day to himself he was able to see a great deal more of Marie-Louise than Jean could. Madame Meurice was something of an invalid, so that Marie-Louise had more liberty than most French girls of her age and station. She knew that both Riri and Jean were in love with her, she liked them both and was pleased by their attentions, but she gave no sign that she was in love with either. It was impossible to tell which she preferred. She was well aware that Riri was not in a position to marry her.

"What did she look like?" I asked Jean Charvin.

"She was small, with a pretty little figure, with large grey eyes, a pale skin and soft, mouse-coloured hair. She was rather like a little mouse. She was not beautiful, but pretty, in a quaint demure way; there was something very appealing about her. She was easy to get on with. She was simple and unaffected. You couldn't help feeling that she was reliable and would make anyone a good wife."

Jean and Riri hid nothing from one another and Jean made no secret of the fact that he was in love with Marie-Louise, but Riri had met her first and it was an understood thing between them that Jean should not stand in his way. At length she made her choice. One day Riri waited for Jean to come away from his office and told him that Marie-Louise had consented to marry him. They had arranged that as soon as he got a job his father should go to her mother and make the formal offer. Jean was hard hit. It was not easy to listen with eager sympathy to the plans that the excitable and enchanted Riri made for the future. But he was too much attached to Riri to feel sore with him; he knew how lovable he was and he could not blame Marie-Louise.

He tried with all his might to accept honestly the sacrifice he made on the altar of friendship.

"Why did she choose him rather than you?" I asked.

"He had immense vitality. He was the gayest, most amusing lad you ever met. His high spirits were infectious. You couldn't be dull in his company."

"He had pep," I smiled.

"And an incredible charm."

"Was he good-looking?"

"No, not very. He was shorter than me, slight and wiry; but he had a nice, good-humoured face." Jean Charvin smiled rather pleasantly. "I think without any vanity I can say that I was better-looking than Riri."

But Riri did not get a job. His father, tired of keeping him in idleness, wrote to everyone he could think of, the members of his family and his friends in various parts of France, asking them if they could not find something, however modest, for Riri to do; and at last he got a letter from a cousin in Lyons who was in the silk business to say that his firm were looking for a young man to go out to Phnom-Penh, in Cambodia, where they had a branch, to buy native silk for them. If Riri was willing to take the job he could get it for him.

Though like all French parents Riri's hated him to emigrate, there seemed no help for it, and it was determined, although the salary was small, that he must go. He was not disinclined. Cambodia was not so far from Tonkin, and Marie-Louise must be familiar with the life. She had so often talked of it that he had come to the conclusion that she would be glad to go back to the East. To his dismay she told him that nothing would induce her to. In the first place she could not desert her mother, whose health was obviously declining; and then, after having at last settled down in France, she was determined never again to leave it. She was sympathetic to Riri, but resolute. With nothing else in prospect his father would not hear of his refusing the offer; there was no help for it, he had to go. Jean hated losing him, but from the moment Riri told him his bad news, he had realised with an exulting heart that fate was playing into his hands. With Riri out of his way for five years at least, and unless he were incompetent with the probability that he would settle in the East for good, Jean could not doubt that after a while Marie-Louise would

marry him. His circumstances, his settled, respectable position in
Le Havre, where she could be near her mother, would make her
think it very sensible; and when she was no longer under the
spell of Riri's charm there was no reason why her great liking for
him should not turn to love. Life changed for him. After months
of misery he was happy again, and though he kept them to himself he too now made great plans for the future. There was no
need any longer to try not to love Marie-Louise.

Suddenly his hopes were shattered. One of the shipping firms
at Le Havre had a vacancy, and it looked as though the applica-
tion that Riri had quickly made would be favourably considered.
A friend in the office told him that it was a certainty. It would
settle everything. It was an old and conservative house, and it was
well known that when you once got into it you were there for
life. Jean Charvin was in despair, and the worst of it was that
he had to keep his anguish to himself. One day the director of
his own firm sent for him.

When he reached this point Jean stopped. A harassed look came
into his eyes.

"I'm going to tell you something now that I've never told to
anyone before. I'm an honest man, a man of principle; I'm going
to tell you of the only discreditable action I've ever done in my
life."

I must remind the reader here that Jean Charvin was wearing
the pink and white stripes of the convict's uniform, with his number stencilled on his chest, and that he was serving a term of
imprisonment for the murder of his wife.

"I couldn't imagine what the director wanted with me. He was
sitting at his desk when I went into his office, and he gave me a
searching look.

" 'I want to ask you a question of great importance,' he said.
'I wish you to treat it as confidential. I shall of course treat your
answer as equally so.'

"I waited. He went on:

" 'You've been with us for a considerable time. I am very well
satisfied with you, there is no reason why you shouldn't reach a
very good position in the firm. I put implicit confidence in you.'

" 'Thank you, sir,' I said. 'I will always try to merit your good
opinion.'

" 'The question at issue is this. Monsieur Untel is proposing to engage Henri Renard. He is very particular about the character of his employees, and in this case it is essential that he shouldn't make a mistake. Part of Henri Renard's duties would be to pay the crews of the firm's ships, and many hundreds of thousand francs will pass through his hands. I know that Henri Renard is your great friend and that your families have always been very intimate. I put you on your honour to tell me whether Monsieur Untel would be justified in engaging this young man.'

"I saw at once what the question meant. If Riri got the job he would stay and marry Marie-Louise, if he didn't he would go out to Cambodia and I should marry her. I swear to you it was not I who answered, it was someone who stood in my shoes and spoke with my voice, I had nothing to do with the words that came from my mouth.

"'*Monsieur le directeur,*' I said, 'Henri and I have been friends all our lives. We have never been separated for a week. We went to school together; we shared our pocket-money and our mistresses when we were old enough to have them; we did our military service together.'

"'I know. You know him better than anyone in the world. That is why I ask you these questions.'

"'It is not fair, *Monsieur le directeur*. You are asking me to betray my friend. I cannot, and I will not answer your questions.'

"The director gave me a shrewd smile. He thought himself much cleverer than he really was.

"'Your answer does you credit, but it has told me all I wished to know.' Then he smiled kindly. I suppose I was pale, I dare say I was trembling a little. 'Pull yourself together, my dear boy; you're upset and I can understand it. Sometimes in life one is faced by a situation where honesty stands on the one side and loyalty on the other. Of course one mustn't hesitate, but the choice is bitter. I shall not forget your behaviour in this case and on behalf of Monsieur Untel I thank you.'

"I withdrew. Next morning Riri received a letter informing him that his services were not required, and a month later he sailed for the far East."

Six months after this Jean Charvin and Marie-Louise were married. The marriage was hastened by the increasing gravity of Madame Meurice's illness. Knowing that she could not live long, she was anxious to see her daughter settled before she died. Jean wrote to Riri telling him the facts and Riri wrote back warmly congratulating him. He assured him that he need have no compunctions on his behalf; when he had left France he realised that *he* could never marry Marie-Louise, and he was glad that Jean was going to. He was finding consolation at Phnom-Penh. His letter was very cheerful. From the beginning Jean had told himself that Riri, with his mercurial temperament, would soon forget Marie-Louise, and his letter looked as if he had already done so. He had done him no irreparable injury. It was a justification. For if *he* had lost Marie-Louise he would have died; with him it was a matter of life and death.

For a year Jean and Marie-Louise were extremely happy. Madame Meurice died, and Marie-Louise inherited a couple of hundred thousand francs; but with the depression and the unstable currency they decided not to have a child till the economic situation was less uncertain. Marie-Louise was a good and frugal housekeeper. She was an affectionate, amiable and satisfactory wife. She was placid. This before he married her had seemed to Jean a rather charming trait, but as time wore on it was borne in upon him that her placidity came from a certain lack of emotional ardour. It concealed no depth. He had always thought she was like a little mouse; there was something mouse-like in her furtive reticences; she was oddly serious about trivial matters and could busy herself indefinitely with things that were of no consequence. She had her own tiny little set of interests and they left no room in her pretty sleek head for any others. She sometimes began a novel, but seldom cared to finish it. Jean was obliged to admit to himself that she was rather dull. The uneasy thought came to him that perhaps it had not been worth while to do a dirty trick for her sake. It began to worry him. He missed Riri. He tried to persuade himself that what was done was done and that he had really not been a free agent, but he could not quite still the prickings of his conscience. He wished now that when the director of his firm spoke to him he had answered differently.

Then a terrible thing happened. Riri contracted typhoid fever and died. It was a frightful shock for Jean. It was a shock to Marie-Louise too; she paid Riri's parents the proper visit of condolence, but she neither ate less heartily nor slept less soundly. Jean was exasperated by her composure.

"Poor chap, he was always so gay," she said, "he must have hated dying. But why did he go out there? I told him the climate was bad; it killed my father and I knew what I was talking about."

Jean felt that he had killed him. If he had told the director all the good he knew of Riri, knew as no one else in the world did, he would have got the post and would now be alive and well.

"I shall never forgive myself," he thought. "I shall never be happy again. Oh, what a fool I was, and what a cad!"

He wept for Riri. Marie-Louise sought to comfort him. She was a kind little thing and she loved him.

"You mustn't take it too hardly. After all, you wouldn't have seen him for five years, and you'd have found him so changed that there wouldn't have been anything between you any more. He would have been a stranger to you. I've seen that sort of thing happen so often. You'd have been delighted to see him, and in half an hour you'd have discovered that you had nothing to say to one another."

"I dare say you're right," he sighed.

"He was too scatter-brained ever to have amounted to anything very much. He never had your firmness of character and your clear, solid intellect."

He knew what she was thinking. What would have been her position now if she had followed Riri to Indo-China and found herself at twenty-one a widow with nothing but her own two hundred thousand francs to live on? It was a lucky escape and she congratulated herself on her good sense. Jean was a husband of whom she could be proud. He was earning good money. Jean was tortured by remorse. What he had suffered before was nothing to what he suffered now. The anguish that the recollection of his treachery caused him was worse than a physical pain gnawing at his vitals. It would assail him suddenly when he was in the middle of his work and twist his heartstrings with a violent pang. His agony was such that he craved for relief, and it was only by an effort of all his will that he prevented himself from making a full confession to Marie-Louise. But he knew how she would take it; she would not be shocked, she would think it rather a clever trick and be even subtly flattered that for her sake he had been guilty of a despicable act. She could not help him. He began to dislike her. For it was for her that he had done the shameful

thing, and what was she? An ordinary, commonplace, rather cal-
culating little woman.

"What a fool I've been," he repeated.

He did not even find her pretty any more. He knew now that
she was terribly stupid. But of course she was not to blame for
that, she was not to blame because he had been false to his
friend; and he forced himself to be as sweet and tender to her as
he had always been. He did whatever she wanted. She had only
to express a wish for him to fulfil it if it was in his power. He
tried to pity her, he tried to be tolerant; he told himself that
from her own petty standpoint she was a good wife, methodical,
saving, and in her manner, dress and appearance a credit to a
respectable young man. All that was true; but it was on her
account that Riri had died, and he loathed her. She bored him
to distraction. Though he said nothing, though he was kind, amiable and indulgent, he could often have killed her. When he did,
however, it was almost without meaning to. It was ten months
after Riri's death, and Riri's parents, Monsieur and Madame Renard, gave a party to celebrate the engagement of their daughter.
Jean had seen little of them since Riri's death and he did not want
to go. But Marie-Louise said they must; he had been Riri's greatest friend and it would be a grave lack of politeness on Jean's part
not to attend an important celebration in the family. She had a
keen sense of social obligation.

"Besides, it'll be a distraction for you. You've been in poor spirits
for so long, a little amusement will do you good. There'll be champagne, won't there? Madame Renard doesn't like spending money,
but on an occasion like this she'll have to sacrifice herself."

Marie-Louise chuckled slyly when she thought what a wrench
it would be to Madame Renard to unloose her purse-strings.

The party had been very gay. It gave Jean a nasty turn when
he found that they were using Riri's old room for the women to
put their wraps in and the men their coats. There was plenty of
champagne. Jean drank a great deal to drown the bitter remorse
that tormented him. He wanted to deaden the sound in his ears
of Riri's laugh and to shut his eyes to the good-humour of his
shining glance. It was three o'clock when they got home. Next day
was Sunday, so Jean had no work to go to. They slept late. The
rest I can tell in Jean Charvin's own words.

"I had a headache when I woke. Marie-Louise was not in bed.

She was sitting at the dressing-table brushing her hair. I've always been very keen on physical culture, and I was in the habit of doing exercises every morning. I didn't feel very much inclined to do them that morning, but after all that champagne I thought I'd better. I got out of bed and took up my Indian clubs. Our bedroom was fairly large and there was plenty of room to swing them between the bed and the dressing-table where Marie-Louise was sitting. I did my usual exercises. Marie-Louise had started a little while before having her hair cut differently, quite short, and I thought it repulsive. From the back she looked like a boy, and the stubble of cropped hair on her neck made me feel rather sick. She put down her brushes and began to powder her face. She gave a nasty little laugh.

"'What are you laughing at?' I asked.

"'Madame Renard. That was the same dress she wore at our wedding, she'd had it dyed and done over; but it didn't deceive me. I'd have known it anywhere.'

"It was such a stupid remark, it infuriated me. I was seized with rage, and with all my might I hit her over the head with my Indian club. I broke her skull, apparently, and she died two days later in hospital without recovering consciousness."

He paused for a moment. I handed him a cigarette and lit another myself.

"I was glad she did. We could never have lived together again, and it would have been very hard to explain my action."

"Very."

"I was arrested and tried for murder. Of course I swore it was an accident, I said the club had slipped out of my hand, but the medical evidence was against me. The prosecution proved that such an injury as Marie-Louise had suffered could only have been caused by a violent and deliberate blow. Fortunately for me they could find no motive. The public prosecutor tried to make out that I had been jealous of the attentions some man had paid her at the party and that we had quarrelled on that account, but the man he mentioned swore that he had done nothing to arouse my suspicions and others at the party testified that we had left the best of friends. They found on the dressing-table an unpaid dressmaker's bill and the prosecutor suggested that we had quarrelled about that, but I was able to prove that Marie-Louise paid for her clothes out of her own money, so that the bill could not possibly have been the cause of a dispute. Witnesses came forward and said that I had always been kind to Marie-Louise. We are generally looked upon as a devoted couple. My character was excellent and my employer spoke in the highest terms of me. I was never in danger of losing my head, and at one moment I thought I had a chance of getting off altogether. In the end I was sentenced to six years. I don't regret what I did, for from that day, all the time I was in prison awaiting my trial, and since, while I've been here, I've ceased to worry about Riri. If I believed in ghosts I'd be inclined to say that Marie-Louise's death had laid Riri's. Anyhow, my conscience is at rest, and after all the torture I suffered I can assure you that everything I've gone through since is worth it; I feel I can now look the world in the face again."

I know that this is a fantastic story; I am by way of being a realist, and in the stories I write I seek verisimilitude. I eschew the bizarre as scrupulously as I avoid the whimsical. If this had been a tale that I was inventing I would certainly have made it more probable. As it is, unless I had heard it with my own ears I am not sure that I should believe it. I do not know whether Jean Charvin told me the truth, and yet the words with which he closed his final visit to me had a convincing ring. I had asked him what were his plans for the future.

"I have friends working for me in France," he answered. "A great many people thought at the time that I was the victim of a grave miscarriage of justice; the director of my firm is convinced that I was unjustly condemned; and I may get a reduction of my sentence. Even if I don't, I think I can count upon getting back to France at the end of my six years. You see, I'm making myself very useful here. The accounts were very badly kept when I took them over, and I've got them in apple-pie order. There have been leakages, and I am convinced that if they'll give me a free hand, I can stop them. The commandant likes me and I'm certain that he'll do everything he can for me. At the worst I shan't be much over thirty when I get back."

"But won't you find it rather difficult to get work?"

"A clever accountant like me, and a man who's honest and industrious, can always get work. Of course I shan't be able to live in Le Havre, but the director of my firm has business connections at Lille and Lyons and Marseilles. He's promised to do something for me. No, I look forward to the years to come with a good deal of confidence. I shall settle down somewhere, and as soon as I'm comfortably fixed up I shall marry. After what I've been through I want a home."

We were sitting in one of the corners of the verandah that surrounded my house in order to get any draught there might be, and on the north side I had left a jalousie undrawn. The strip of sky you saw with a single coconut tree on one side, its green foliage harsh against the blue, looked like an advertisement for a tropical cruise. Jean Charvin's eyes searched the distance as though he sought to see the future.

"But next time I marry," he said thoughtfully, "I shan't marry for love, I shall marry for money."

P. & O.

Mrs. Hamlyn lay on her long chair and lazily watched the passengers come along the gangway. The ship had reached Singapore in the night and since dawn had been taking on cargo; the winches had been grinding away all day, but by now her ears were accustomed to their insistent clamour. She had lunched at the Europe and for lack of anything better to do had driven in a rickshaw through the gay, multitudinous streets of the city. Singapore is the meeting-place of many races. The Malays, though natives of the soil, dwell uneasily in towns, and are few; and it is the Chinese, supple, alert and industrious, who throng the streets, the dark-skinned Tamils walk on their silent, naked feet as though they were but brief sojourners in a strange land, but the Bengalis, sleek and prosperous, are easy in their surroundings and self-assured; the sly and obsequious Japanese seem busy with pressing and secret affairs; and the English in their topees and white ducks, speeding past in motor-cars or at leisure in their rickshaws, wear a nonchalant and careless air. The rulers of these teeming peoples take their authority with a smiling unconcern. And now, tired and hot, Mrs. Hamlyn waited for the ship to set out again on her long journey across the Indian Ocean.

She waved a rather large hand, for she was a big woman, to the doctor and Mrs. Linsell as they came on board. She had been on the ship since she left Yokohama, and had watched with acid amusement the intimacy which had sprung up between the two. Linsell was a naval officer who had been attached to the British Embassy at Tokio, and she had wondered at the indifference with which he took the attentions that the doctor paid his wife. Two men came along the gangway, new passengers, and she amused herself by trying to discover from their demeanour whether they were married or single. Close by, a group of men were sitting together on rattan chairs, planters she judged by their khaki suits and wide-brimmed double felt hats, and they kept the deck-steward busy with their orders. They were talking loudly and laughing, for they had all drunk enough to make them somewhat foolishly hilarious, and they were evidently giving one of their number a send-off; but Mrs. Hamlyn could not tell which it was that was to be a fellow-passenger. The time was growing short. More passengers arrived, and then Mr. Jephson with dignity strolled up the gangway. He was a consul and was going home on leave. He had joined the ship at Shanghai and had immediately set about making himself agreeable to Mrs. Hamlyn. But just then she was disinclined for anything in the nature of a flirtation. She frowned as she thought of the reason which was taking her back to England. She would be spending Christmas at sea, far from anyone who cared two straws for her, and for a moment she felt a little twist at her heartstrings; it vexed her that a subject which she was so resolute to put away from her should so constantly intrude on her unwilling mind.

But a warning bell clanged loudly and there was a general movement among the men who sat beside her.

"Well, if we don't want to be taken on we'd better be toddling," said one of them.

They rose and walked towards the gangway. Now that they were all shaking hands she saw who it was that they had come to see the last of. There was nothing very interesting about the man on whom Mrs. Hamlyn's eyes rested, but because she had nothing better to do she gave him more than a casual glance. He was a big fellow, well over six feet high, broad and stout; he was dressed in a bedraggled suit of khaki drill and his hat was battered and shabby. His friends left him, but they bandied chaff from the quay, and Mrs. Hamlyn noticed that he had a strong Irish brogue; his voice was full, loud and hearty.

Mrs. Linsell had gone below and the doctor came and sat down beside Mrs. Hamlyn. They told one another their small adventures of the day. The bell sounded again and presently the ship slid away from the wharf. The Irishman waved a last farewell to his friends and then sauntered towards the chair on which he had left papers and magazines. He nodded to the doctor.

"Is that some one you know?" asked Mrs. Hamlyn.

"I was introduced to him at the club before tiffin. His name is Gallagher. He's a planter."

After the hubbub of the port and the noisy bustle of departure,

the silence of the ship was marked and grateful. They steamed
slowly past green-clad, rocky cliffs (the P. & O. anchorage was in
a charming and secluded cove), and came out into the main harbour. Ships of all nations lay at anchor, a great multitude, passenger boats, tugs, lighters, tramps; and beyond, behind the break-
water, you saw the crowded masts, a bare straight forest, of the
native junks. In the soft light of the evening the busy scene was
strangely touched with mystery, and you felt that all those vessels,
their activity for the moment suspended, waited for some event
of a peculiar significance.

Mrs. Hamlyn was a bad sleeper and when the dawn broke she
was in the habit of going on deck. It rested her troubled heart to
watch the last faint stars fade before the encroaching day and at
that early hour the glassy sea had often an immobility which
seemed to make all earthly sorrows of little consequence. The
light was wan, and there was a pleasant shiver in the air. But
next morning when she went to the end of the promenade deck,
she found that some one was up before her. It was Gallagher. He
was watching the low coast of Sumatra which the sunrise like a
magician seemed to call forth from the dark sea. She was startled
and a little vexed, but before she could turn away he had seen her
and nodded.

"Up early," he said. "Have a cigarette?"

He was in pyjamas and slippers. He took his case from his coat
pocket and handed it to her. She hesitated. She had on nothing
but a dressing-gown and a little lace cap which she had put over
her tousled hair, and she knew that she must look a sight; but
she had her reasons for scourging her soul.

"I suppose a woman of forty has no right to mind how she
looks," she smiled, as though he must know what vain thoughts
occupied her. She took the cigarette. "But you're up early too."

"I'm a planter. I've had to get up at five in the morning for so
many years that I don't know how I'm going to get out of the
habit."

"You'll not find it will make you very popular at home."

She saw his face better now that it was not shadowed by a hat.
It was agreeable without being handsome. He was of course much
too fat, and his features which must have been good enough when
he was a young man were thickened. His skin was red and
bloated. But his dark eyes were merry; and though he could not

have been less than five and forty his hair was black and thick. He gave you an impression of great strength. He was a heavy, ungraceful, commonplace man, and Mrs. Hamlyn, except for the promiscuity of shipboard, would never have thought it worth while to talk to him.

"Are you going home on leave?" she hazarded.

"No, I'm going home for good."

His black eyes twinkled. He was of a communicative turn, and before it was time for Mrs. Hamlyn to go below in order to have her bath he had told her a good deal about himself. He had been in the Federated Malay States for twenty-five years, and for the last ten had managed an estate in Selantan. It was a hundred miles from anything that could be described as civilization and the life had been lonely; but he had made money; during the rubber boom he had done very well and with an astuteness which was unexpected in a man who looked so happy-go-lucky he had invested his savings in Government stock. Now that the slump had come he was prepared to retire.

"What part of Ireland do you come from?" asked Mrs. Hamlyn.

"Galway."

Mrs. Hamlyn had once motored through Ireland and she had a vague recollection of a sad and moody town with great stone warehouses, deserted and crumbling, which faced the melancholy sea. She had a sensation of greenness and of soft rain, of silence and of resignation. Was it here that Mr. Gallagher meant to spend the rest of his life? He spoke of it with boyish eagerness. The thought of his vitality in that grey world of shadows was so incongruous that Mrs. Hamlyn was intrigued.

"Does your family live there?" she asked.

"I've got no family. My mother and father are dead. So far as I know I haven't a relation in the world."

He had made all his plans, he had been making them for twenty-five years, and he was pleased to have some one to talk to of all these things that he had been obliged for so long only to talk to himself about. He meant to buy a house and he would keep a motor-car. He was going to breed horses. He didn't much care about shooting; he had shot a lot of big game during his first years in the F.M.S.; but now he had lost his zest. He didn't see why the beasts of the jungle should be killed; he had lived in the jungle so long. But he could hunt.

"Do you think I'm too heavy?" he asked.

Mrs. Hamlyn, smiling, looked him up and down with appraising eyes.

"You must weigh a ton," she said.

He laughed. The Irish horses were the best in the world, and he'd always kept pretty fit. You had a devil of a lot of walking exercise on a rubber estate and he'd played a good deal of tennis. He'd soon get thin in Ireland. Then he'd marry. Mrs. Hamlyn looked silently at the sea, coloured now with the tenderness of the sunrise. She sighed.

"Was it easy to drag up all your roots? Is there no one you regret leaving behind? I should have thought after so many years, however much you'd looked forward to going home, when the time came at last to go it must have given you a pang."

"I was glad to get out. I was fed up. I never want to see the country again or any one in it."

One or two early passengers now began to walk round the deck and Mrs. Hamlyn, remembering that she was scantily clad, went below.

During the next day or two she saw little of Mr. Gallagher who passed his time in the smoking-room. Owing to a strike the ship was not touching at Colombo and the passengers settled down to a pleasant voyage across the Indian Ocean. They played deck games, they gossiped about one another, they flirted. The approach of Christmas gave them an occupation, for some one had suggested that there should be a fancy-dress dance on Christmas day, and the ladies set about making their dresses. A meeting was held of the first-class passengers to decide whether the second-class passengers should be invited, and notwithstanding the heat the discussion was animated. The ladies said that the second-class passengers would only feel ill-at-ease. On Christmas day it was to be expected that they would drink more than was good for them and unpleasantness might ensue. Every one who spoke insisted that there was in his (or her) mind no idea of class distinction, no one would be so snobbish as to think there was any difference between first- and second-class passengers as far as that went, but it would really be kinder to the second-class passengers not to put them in a false position. They would enjoy themselves much more if they had a party of their own in the second-class cabin. On the other hand, no one wanted to hurt their feelings, and of course

one had to be more democratic nowadays (this was in reply to
the wife of a missionary in China who said she had travelled on
the P. & O. for thirty-five years and she had never heard of the
second-class passengers being invited to a dance in the first-class
saloon) and even though they wouldn't enjoy it, they might like
to come. Mr. Gallagher, dragged unwillingly from the card-table,
because it had been foreseen that the voting would be close, was
asked his opinion by the consul. He was taking home in the second-class a man who had been employed on his estate. He raised
his massive bulk from the couch on which he sat.

"As far as I'm concerned I've only got this to say: I've got the
man who was looking after our engines with me. He's a rattling
good fellow and he's just as fit to come to your party as I am. But
he won't come because I'm going to make him so drunk on Christmas day that by six o'clock he'll be fit for nothing but to be put
to bed."

Mr. Jephson, the consul, gave a distorted smile. On account of
his official position he had been chosen to preside at the meeting
and he wished the matter to be taken seriously. He was a man
who often said that if a thing was worth doing it was worth doing
well.

"I gather from your observations," he said, not without acidity,
"that the question before the meeting does not seem to you of
great importance."

"I don't think it matters a tinker's curse," said Gallagher, with
twinkling eyes.

Mrs. Hamlyn laughed. The scheme was at last devised to invite
the second-class passengers, but to go to the captain privily and
point out to him the advisability of withholding his consent to
their coming into the first-class saloon. It was on the evening of
the day on which this happened that Mrs. Hamlyn, having dressed
for dinner, came on deck at the same time as Mr. Gallagher.

"Just in time for a cocktail, Mrs. Hamlyn," he said jovially.

"I'd like one. To tell you the truth I need cheering up."

"Why?" he smiled.

Mrs. Hamlyn thought his smile attractive, but she did not want
to answer his question.

"I told you the other morning," she answered cheerfully. "I'm
forty."

"I never met a woman who insisted on the fact so much."

They went into the lounge and the Irishman ordered a dry
Martini for her and a gin pahit for himself. He had lived too long
in the East to drink anything else.

"You've got hiccups," said Mrs. Hamlyn.

"Yes, I've had them all the afternoon," he answered carelessly.
"It's rather funny, they came on just as we got out of sight of land."

"I daresay they'll pass off after dinner."

They drank, the second bell rang, and they went into the dining-saloon.

"You don't play bridge?" he said, as they parted.

"No."

Mrs. Hamlyn did not notice that she saw nothing of Gallagher
for two or three days. She was occupied with her own thoughts.
They crowded upon her when she was sewing; they came between
her and the novel with which she sought to cheat their insistence.
She had hoped that as the ship took her further away from the
scene of her unhappiness the torment of her mind would be eased;
but contrariwise, each day that brought her nearer England increased her distress. She looked forward with dismay to the bleak
emptiness of the life that awaited her; and then, turning her exhausted wits from a prospect that made her flinch, she considered,
as she had done she knew not how many times before, the situation from which she had fled.

She had been married for twenty years. It was a long time and
of course she could not expect her husband to be still madly in
love with her; she was not madly in love with him; but they were
good friends and they understood one another. Their marriage, as
marriages go, might very well have been looked upon as a success. Suddenly she discovered that he had fallen in love. She
would not have objected to a flirtation, he had had those before,
and she had chaffed him about them; he had not minded that, it
somewhat flattered him, and they had laughed together at an inclination which was neither deep nor serious. But this was different. He was in love as passionately as a boy of eighteen. He was
fifty-two. It was ridiculous. It was indecent. And he loved without
sense or prudence: by the time the hideous fact was forced upon
her all the foreigners in Yokohama knew it. After the first shock
of astonished anger, for he was the last man from whom such a
folly might have been expected, she tried to persuade herself that
she could have understood, and so have forgiven, if he had fallen

in love with a girl. Middle-aged men often make fools of themselves with flappers, and after twenty years in the Far East she
knew that the fifties were the dangerous age for men. But he had
no excuse. He was in love with a woman eight years older than
herself. It was grotesque, and it made her, his wife, perfectly
absurd. Dorothy Lacom was hard on fifty. He had known her for
eighteen years, for Lacom, like her own husband, was a silk merchant in Yokohama. Year in, year out, they had seen one another
three or four times a week, and once, when they happened to be
in England together, had shared a house at the seaside. But nothing! Not till a year ago had there been anything between them
but a chaffing friendship. It was incredible. Of course Dorothy
was a handsome woman; she had a good figure, overdeveloped,
perhaps, but still comely; with bold black eyes and a red mouth
and lovely hair; but all that she had had years before. She was
forty-eight. Forty-eight!

Mrs. Hamlyn tackled her husband at once. At first he swore
that there was not a word of truth in what she accused him of, but
she had her proofs; he grew sulky; and at last he admitted what
he could no longer deny. Then he said an astonishing thing.

"Why should you care?" he asked.

It maddened her. She answered him with angry scorn. She was
voluble, finding in the bitterness of her heart wounding things to
say. He listened to her quietly.

"I've not been such a bad husband to you for the twenty years
we've been married. For a long time now we've only been friends.
I have a great affection for you and this hasn't altered it in the
very smallest degree. I'm giving Dorothy nothing that I take away
from you."

"But what have you to complain of in me?"

"Nothing. No man could want a better wife."

"How can you say that when you have the heart to treat me so
cruelly?"

"I don't want to be cruel to you. I can't help myself."

"But what on earth made you fall in love with her?"

"How can I tell? You don't think I wanted to, do you?"

"Couldn't you have resisted?"

"I tried. I think we both tried."

"You talk as though you were twenty. Why, you're both middle-aged people. She's eight years older than I am. It makes me look such a perfect fool."

He did not answer. She did not know what emotions seethed in her heart. Was it jealousy that seemed to clutch at her throat, anger, or was it merely wounded pride?

"I'm not going to let it go on. If only you and she were concerned I would divorce you, but there's her husband and then there are the children. Good heavens, does it occur to you that if they were girls instead of boys she might be a grandmother by now?"

"Easily."

"What a mercy that we have no children!"

He put out an affectionate hand as though to caress her, but she drew back with horror.

"You've made me the laughing-stock of all my friends. For all our sakes I'm willing to hold my tongue, but only on the condition that everything stops now, at once, and for ever."

He looked down and played reflectively with a Japanese knick-knack that was on the table.

"I'll tell Dorothy what you say," he replied at last.

She gave him a little bow, silently, and walked past him out of the room. She was too angry to observe that she was somewhat melodramatic.

She waited for him to tell her the result of his interview with Dorothy Lacom, but he made no further reference to the scene. He was quiet, polite, and silent; and at last she was obliged to ask him.

"Have you forgotten what I said to you the other day?" she enquired frigidly.

"No. I talked to Dorothy. She wishes me to tell you that she is desperately sorry that she has caused you so much pain. She would like to come and see you, but she is afraid you wouldn't like it."

"What decision have you come to?"

He hesitated. He was very grave, but his voice trembled a little.

"I'm afraid there's no use in our making a promise we shouldn't be able to keep."

"That settles it then," she answered.

"I think I should tell you that if you brought an action for divorce we should have to contest it. You would find it impossible to get the necessary evidence and you would lose your case."

"I wasn't thinking of doing that. I shall go back to England and consult a lawyer. Nowadays these things can be managed fairly easily and I shall throw myself on your generosity. I daresay you will enable me to get my freedom without bringing Dorothy Lacom into the matter."

He sighed.

"It's an awful muddle, isn't it? I don't want you to divorce me, but of course I'll do anything I can to meet your wishes."

"What on earth do you expect me to do?" she cried, her anger rising again. "Do you expect me to sit still and be made a damned fool of?"

"I'm awfully sorry to put you in a humiliating position." He looked at her with harassed eyes. "I'm quite sure we didn't want to fall in love with one another. We're both of us very conscious of our age. Dorothy, as you say, is old enough to be a grandmother and I'm a baldish, stoutish gentleman of fifty-two. When you fall in love at twenty you think your love will last for ever, but at fifty you know so much, about life and about love, and you know that it will last so short a time." His voice was low and rueful. It was as though before his mind's eye he saw the sadness of autumn and the leaves falling from the trees. He looked at her gravely. "And at that age you feel that you can't afford to throw away the chance of happiness which a freakish destiny has given you. In five years it will certainly be over, and perhaps in six months. Life is rather drab and grey, and happiness is so rare. We shall be dead so long."

It gave Mrs. Hamlyn a bitter sensation of pain to hear her husband, a matter-of-fact and practical man, speak in a strain which was quite new to her. He had gained on a sudden a wistful and tragic personality of which she knew nothing. The twenty years during which they had lived together had no power over him and she was helpless in face of his determination. She could do nothing but go, and now, resentfully determined to get the divorce with which she had threatened him, she was on her way to England.

The smooth sea, upon which the sun beat down so that it shone like a sheet of glass, was as empty and hostile as life in which there was no place for her. For three days no other craft had broken in upon the solitariness of that expanse. Now and again its even surface was scattered for the twinkling of an eye by the

scurry of flying fish. The heat was so great that even the most
energetic of passengers had given up deck games and now (it
was after luncheon) such as were not resting in their cabins lay
about on chairs. Linsell strolled towards her and sat down.

"Where's Mrs. Linsell?" asked Mrs. Hamlyn.

"Oh, I don't know. She's about somewhere."

His indifference exasperated her. Was it possible that he did
not see that his wife and the surgeon were falling in love with
one another? Yet, not so very long ago, he must have cared. Their
marriage had been romantic. They had become engaged when
Mrs. Linsell was still at school and he little more than a boy. They
must have been a charming, handsome pair, and their youth and
their mutual love must have been touching. And now, after so
short a time, they were tired of one another. It was heartbreaking.
What had her husband said?

"I suppose you're going to live in London when you get home?"
asked Linsell lazily, for something to say.

"I suppose so," said Mrs. Hamlyn.

It was hard to reconcile herself to the fact that she had nowhere to go and where she lived mattered not in the least to
any one alive. Some association of ideas made her think of Gallagher. She envied the eagerness with which he was returning to
his native land, and she was touched, and at the same time
amused, when she remembered the exuberant imagination he
showed in describing the house he meant to live in and the wife
he meant to marry. Her friends in Yokohama, apprised in confidence of her determination to divorce her husband, had assured
her that she would marry again. She did not much want to enter
a second time upon a state which had once so disappointed her,
and besides, most men would think twice before they suggested
marriage to a woman of forty. Mr. Gallagher wanted a buxom
young person.

"Where is Mr. Gallagher?" she asked the submissive Linsell. "I
haven't seen him for the last day or two."

"Didn't you know? He's ill."

"Poor thing. What's the matter with him?"

"He's got hiccups."

Mrs. Hamlyn laughed.

"Hiccups don't make one ill, do they?"

"The surgeon is rather worried. He's tried all sorts of things, but he can't stop them."

"How very odd."

She thought no more about it, but next morning, chancing upon the surgeon, she asked him how Mr. Gallagher was. She was surprised to see his boyish, cheerful face darken and grow perplexed.

"I'm afraid he's very bad, poor chap."

"With hiccups?" she cried in amazement.

It was a disorder that really it was impossible to take seriously.

"You see, he can't keep any food down. He can't sleep. He's fearfully exhausted. I've tried everything I can think of." He hesitated. "Unless I can stop them soon—I don't quite know what'll happen."

Mrs. Hamlyn was startled.

"But he's so strong. He seemed so full of vitality."

"I wish you could see him now."

"Would he like me to go and see him?"

"Come along."

Gallagher had been moved from his cabin into the ship's hospital, and as they approached it they heard a loud hiccup. The sound, perhaps owing to its connection with insobriety, had in it something ludicrous. But Gallagher's appearance gave Mrs. Hamlyn a shock. He had lost flesh and the skin hung about his neck in loose folds; under the sunburn his face was pale. His eyes, before, full of fun and laughter, were haggard and tormented. His great body was shaken incessantly by the hiccups, and now there was nothing ludicrous in the sound; to Mrs. Hamlyn, for no reason that she knew, it seemed strangely terrifying. He smiled when she came in.

"I'm sorry to see you like this," she said.

"I shan't die of it, you know," he gasped. "I shall reach the green shores of Erin all right."

There was a man sitting beside him and he rose as they entered.

"This is Mr. Pryce," said the surgeon. "He was in charge of the machinery on Mr. Gallagher's estate."

Mrs. Hamlyn nodded. This was the second-class passenger to whom Gallagher had referred when they had discussed the party which was to be given on Christmas day. He was a very small man, but sturdy, with a pleasantly impudent countenance and an air of self-assurance.

"Are you glad to be going home?" asked Mrs. Hamlyn.

"You bet I am, lady," he answered.

The intonation of the few words told Mrs. Hamlyn that he was a cockney and, recognizing the cheerful, sensible, good-humoured and careless type, her heart warmed to him.

"You're not Irish?" she smiled.

"Not me, miss. London's my 'ome and I shan't be sorry to see it again, I can tell you."

Mrs. Hamlyn never thought it offensive to be called miss.

"Well, sir, I'll be getting along," he said to Gallagher, with the beginning of a gesture as though he were going to touch a cap which he hadn't got on.

Mrs. Hamlyn asked the sick man whether she could do anything for him and in a minute or two left him with the doctor. The little cockney was waiting outside the door.

"Can I speak to you a minute or two, miss?" he asked.

"Of course."

The hospital cabin was aft and they stood, leaning against the rail, and looked down on the well-deck where lascars and stewards off duty were lounging about on the covered hatches.

"I don't know exactly 'ow to begin," said Pryce, uncertainly, a serious look strangely changing his lively, puckered face. "I've been with Mr. Gallagher for four years now and a better gentleman you wouldn't find in a week of Sundays."

He hesitated again.

"I don't like it and that's the truth."

"What don't you like?"

"Well, if you ask me 'e's for it, and the doctor don't know it. I told 'im, but 'e won't listen to a word I say."

"You mustn't be too depressed, Mr. Pryce. Of course the doctor's young, but I think he's quite clever, and people don't die of hiccups, you know. I'm sure Mr. Gallagher will be all right in a day or two."

"You know when it come on? Just as we was out of sight of land. She said 'e'd never see 'is 'ome."

Mrs. Hamlyn turned and faced him. She stood a good three inches taller than he.

"What do you mean?"

"My belief is, it's a spell been put on 'im, if you understand what I mean. Medicine's going to do 'im no good. You don't know them Malay women like what I do."

For a moment Mrs. Hamlyn was startled, and because she was startled she shrugged her shoulders and laughed.

"Oh, Mr. Pryce, that's nonsense."

"That's what the doctor said when I told 'im. But you mark my words, 'e'll die before we see land again."

The man was so serious that Mrs. Hamlyn, vaguely uneasy, was against her will impressed.

"Why should any one cast a spell on Mr. Gallagher?" she asked.

"Well, it's a bit awkward speakin' of it to a lady."

"Please tell me."

Pryce was so embarrassed that at another time Mrs. Hamlyn would have had difficulty in concealing her amusement.

"Mr. Gallagher's lived a long time up-country, if you understand what I mean, and of course it's lonely, and you know what men are, miss."

"I've been married for twenty years," she replied, smiling.

"I beg your pardon, ma'am. The fact is he had a Malay girl living with him. I don't know 'ow long, ten or twelve years, I think. Well, when he made up 'is mind to come 'ome for good she didn't say nothing. She just sat there. He thought she'd carry on no end, but she didn't. Of course 'e provided for 'er all right, 'e gave 'er a little 'ouse for herself, an' 'e fixed it up so as so much should be paid 'er every month; 'e wasn't mean, I will say that for 'im, an' she knew all along as 'e'd be going some time. She didn't cry or anything. When 'e packed up all 'is things and sent them off she just sat there an' watched 'em go. And when 'e sold 'is furniture to the Chinks she never said a word. He'd give 'er all she wanted. And when it was time for 'im to go so as to catch the boat she just kep' on sitting, on the steps of the bungalow, you know, and she just looked an' said nothing. He wanted to say good-bye to 'er, same as any one would, an', would you believe it? she never even moved. 'Aren't you going to say good-bye to me?' he says. A rare funny look came over 'er face. And do you know what she says? 'You go,' she says; they 'ave a funny way of talking, them natives, not like we 'ave, 'you go,' she says, 'but I tell you that you will never come to your own country. When the land sinks into the sea death will come upon you, an' before them as goes with you sees the land again, death will have took you.' It gave me quite a turn."

"What did Mr. Gallagher say?" asked Mrs. Hamlyn.

"Oh, well, you know what 'e is. He just laughed. 'Always merry an' bright,' he says and he jumps into the motor, an' off we go."

Mrs. Hamlyn saw the bright and sunny road that ran through the rubber estates, with their trim green trees, carefully spaced, and their silence, and then wound its way up hill and down through the tangled jungle. The car raced on, driven by a reckless Malay, with its white passengers, past Malay houses that stood away from the road among the coconut trees, sequestered and taciturn, and through busy villages where the market-place was crowded with dark-skinned little people in gay sarongs. Then towards evening it reached the trim, modern town, with its clubs and its golf links, its well-ordered rest-house, its white people, and its railway station, from which the two men could take the train to Singapore. And the woman sat on the steps of the bungalow, empty till the new manager moved in, and watched the road down which the car had panted, watched the car as it sped on, and watched till at last it was lost in the shadow of the night.

"What was she like?" Mrs. Hamlyn asked.

"Oh, well, to my way of thinking them Malay women are all very much alike, you know," Pryce answered. "Of course she wasn't so young any more and you know what they are, them natives, they run to fat something terrible."

"Fat?"

The thought, absurdly enough, filled Mrs. Hamlyn with dismay.

"Mr. Gallagher was always one to do himself well, if you understand what I mean."

The idea of corpulence at once brought Mrs. Hamlyn back to common sense. She was impatient with herself because for an instant she had seemed to accept the little cockney's suggestion.

"It's perfectly absurd, Mr. Pryce. Fat women can't throw spells on people at a distance of a thousand miles. In fact life is very difficult for a fat woman anyway."

"You can laugh, miss, but unless something's done, you mark my words, the governor's for it. And medicine ain't goin' to save him, not white man's medicine."

"Pull yourself together, Mr. Pryce. This fat lady had no particular grievance against Mr. Gallagher. As these things are done

in the East he seems to have treated her very well. Why should
she wish him any harm?"

"We don't know 'ow they look at things. Why, a man can live
there for twenty years with one of them natives, and d'you think
'e knows what's goin' on in that black heart of hers? Not 'im!"

She could not smile at his melodramatic language, for his in-
tensity was impressive. And she knew, if any one did, that the
hearts of men, whether their skins are yellow or white or brown,
are incalculable.

"But even if she felt angry with him, even if she hated him
and wanted to kill him, what could she do?" It was strange that
Mrs. Hamlyn with her questions was trying now, unconsciously,
to reassure herself. "There's no poison that could start working
after six or seven days."

"I never said it was poison."

"I'm sorry, Mr. Pryce," she smiled, "but I'm not going to believe
in a magic spell, you know."

"You've lived in the East."

"Off and on for twenty years."

"Well, if you can say what they can do and what they can't,
it's more than I can." He clenched his fist and beat it on the rail
with sudden, angry violence. "I'm fed up with the bloody country. It's got on my nerves, that's what it is. We're no match for
them, us white men, and that's a fact. If you'll excuse me I think
I'll go an' 'ave a tiddley. I've got the jumps."

He nodded abruptly and left her. Mrs. Hamlyn watched him,
a sturdy, shuffling little man in shabby khaki, slither down the
companion into the waist of the ship, walk across it with bent
head, and disappear into the second-class saloon. She did not
know why he left with her a vague uneasiness. She could not
get out of her mind that picture of a stout woman, no longer
young, in a sarong, a coloured jacket and gold ornaments, who
sat on the steps of a bungalow looking at an empty road. Her
heavy face was painted, but in her large, tearless eyes there was
no expression. The men who drove in the car were like schoolboys
going home for the holidays. Gallagher gave a sigh of relief. In
the early morning, under the bright sky, his spirits bubbled. The
future was like a sunny road that wandered through a wide-flung,
wooded plain.

Later in the day Mrs. Hamlyn asked the doctor how his patient did. The doctor shook his head.

"I'm done. I'm at the end of my tether." He frowned unhappily. "It's rotten luck, striking a case like this. It would be bad enough at home, but on board ship . . ."

He was an Edinburgh man, but recently qualified, and he was taking this voyage as a holiday before settling down to practice. He felt himself aggrieved. He wanted to have a good time and, faced with this mysterious illness, he was worried to death. Of course he was inexperienced, but he was doing everything that could be done and it exasperated him to suspect that the passengers thought him an ignorant fool.

"Have you heard what Mr. Pryce thinks?" asked Mrs. Hamlyn.

"I never heard such rot. I told the captain and he's right up in the air. He doesn't want it talked about. He thinks it'll upset the passengers."

"I'll be as silent as the grave."

The surgeon looked at her sharply.

"Of course you don't believe that there can be any truth in nonsense of that sort?" he asked.

"Of course not." She looked out at the sea which shone, blue and oily and still, all round them. "I've lived in the East a long time," she added. "Strange things happen there."

"This is getting on my nerves," said the doctor.

Near them two little Japanese gentlemen were playing deck quoits. They were trim and neat in their tennis shirts, white trousers and buckram shoes. They looked very European, they even called the score to one another in English, and yet somehow to look at them filled Mrs. Hamlyn at that moment with a vague disquiet. Because they seemed to wear so easily a disguise there was about them something sinister. Her nerves too were on edge.

And presently, no one quite knew how, the notion spread through the ship that Gallagher was bewitched. While the ladies sat about on their deck-chairs, stitching away at the costumes they were making for the fancy-dress party on Christmas day, they gossiped about it in undertones, and the men in the smoking-room talked of it over their cocktails. A good many of the passengers had lived long in the East and from the recesses of their memory they produced strange and inexplicable stories. Of course it was absurd to think seriously that Gallagher was suffering from a malignant spell, such things were impossible, and yet this and that was a fact and no one had been able to explain it. The doctor had to confess that he could suggest no cause for Gallagher's condition, he was able to give a physiological explanation, but why these terrible spasms should have suddenly assailed him he did not say. Feeling vaguely to blame, he tried to defend himself.

"Why, it's the sort of case you might never come across in the whole of your practice," he said. "It's rotten luck."

He was in wireless communication with passing ships and suggestions for treatment came from here and there.

"I've tried everything they tell me," he said irritably. "The doctor of the Japanese boat advised adrenalin. How the devil does he expect me to have adrenalin in the middle of the Indian Ocean?"

There was something impressive in the thought of this ship speeding through a deserted sea while to her from all parts came unseen messages. She seemed at that moment strangely alone and yet the centre of the world. In the lazaret the sick man, shaken by the cruel spasms, gasped for life. Then the passengers became conscious that the ship's course was altered and they heard that the captain had made up his mind to put in at Aden. Gallagher was to be landed there and taken to the hospital where he could have attention which on board was impossible. The chief engineer received orders to force his engines. The ship was an old one and she throbbed with the greater effort. The passengers had grown used to the sound and feel of her engines and now the greater vibration shook their nerves with a new sensation. It would not pass into each one's unconsciousness, but beat on their sensibilities so that each felt a personal concern. And still the wide sea was empty of traffic so that they seemed to traverse an empty world. And now the uneasiness which had descended upon the ship, but which no one had been willing to acknowledge, became a definite malaise. The passengers grew irritable, and people quarrelled over trifles which at another time would have seemed insignificant. Mr. Jephson made his hackneyed jokes, but no one any longer repaid him with a smile. The Linsells had an altercation and Mrs. Linsell was heard late at night walking round the deck with her husband, and uttering in a low, tense voice a stream of vehement reproaches. There was a violent scene in the smoking-room one night over a game of bridge, and the reconciliation which followed it was attended with general intoxication. People talked little of Gallagher, but he was seldom absent from their thoughts. They examined the route map. The doctor said now that Gallagher could not live more than three or four days and they discussed acrimoniously what was the shortest time in which Aden could be reached. What happened to him after he was landed was no affair of theirs; they did not want him to die on board.

Mrs. Hamlyn saw Gallagher every day. With the suddenness with which after tropical rain in the spring you seem to see the herbage grow before your very eyes, she saw him go to pieces. Already his skin hung loosely on his bones and his double chin was like the wrinkled wattle of a turkey-cock. His cheeks were sunken. You saw now how large his frame was and through the sheet under which he lay his bony structure was like the skeleton of a prehistoric giant. For the most part he lay with his eyes closed, torpid with morphia, but shaken still with terrible spasms and when now and again he opened his eyes they were preternaturally large; they looked at you vaguely, perplexed and troubled, from the depths of their bony sockets. But when, emerging from his stupor, he recognized Mrs. Hamlyn he forced a gallant smile to his lips.

"How are you, Mr. Gallagher?" she said.

"Getting along, getting along. I shall be all right when we get out of this confounded heat. Lord, how I look forward to a dip in the Atlantic. I'd give anything for a good long swim. I want to feel the cold grey sea of Galway beating against my chest."

Then the hiccup shook him from the crown of his head to the sole of his foot. Mr. Pryce and the stewardess shared the care of him. The little cockney's face wore no longer its look of impudent gaiety, but instead was sullen.

"The captain sent for me yesterday," he told Mrs. Hamlyn when they were alone. "He gave me a rare talking to."

"What about?"

"He said 'e wouldn't 'ave all this hoodoo stuff. He said it was frightening the passengers and I'd better keep a watch on me tongue or I'd 'ave 'im to reckon with. It's not my doing. I never said a word except to you and the doctor."

"It's all over the ship."

"I know it is. D'you think it's only me that's saying it? All

them lascars and the Chinese, they all know what's the matter
with him. You don't think you can teach them much, do you?
They know it ain't a natural illness."

Mrs. Hamlyn was silent. She knew through the amahs of some
of the passengers that there was no one on the ship, except the
whites, who doubted that the woman whom Gallagher had left in
distant Selantan was killing him with her magic. All were convinced that as they sighted the barren rocks of Arabia his soul
would be parted from his body.

"The captain says if he hears of me trying any hanky-panky
he'll confine me to my cabin for the rest of the voyage," said
Pryce suddenly, a surly frown on his puckered face.

"What do you mean by hanky-panky?"

He looked at her for a moment fiercely as though she too were
an object of the anger he felt against the captain.

"The doctor's tried every damned thing he knows, and he's
wirelessed all over the place, and what good 'as 'e done? Tell
me that. Can't 'e see the man's dying? There's only one way to
save him now."

"What do you mean?"

"It's magic what's killing 'im, and it's only magic what'll save
him. Oh, don't you say it can't be done. I've seen it with me own
eyes." His voice rose, irritable and shrill. "I've seen a man dragged
from the jaws of death, as you might say, when they got in a
pawang, what we call a witch-doctor, an' 'e did 'is little tricks.
I seen it with me own eyes, I tell you."

Mrs. Hamlyn did not speak. Pryce gave her a searching look.

"One of them lascars on board, he's a witch-doctor, same as
the *pawang* thet we 'ave in the F.M.S. An' 'e says he'll do it.
Only he must 'ave a live animal. A cock would do."

"What do you want a live animal for?" Mrs. Hamlyn asked,
frowning a little.

The cockney looked at her with quick suspicion.

"If you take my advice you won't know anything about it. But
I tell you what, I'm going to leave no stone unturned to save
my governor. An' if the captain 'ears of it and shuts me up in
me cabin, well, let 'im."

At that moment Mrs. Linsell came up and Pryce with his quaint
gesture of salute left them. Mrs. Linsell wanted Mrs. Hamlyn to
fit the dress she had been making herself for the fancy-dress

ball, and on the way down to the cabin she spoke to her anxiously about the possibility that Mr. Gallagher might die on Christmas day. They could not possibly have the dance if he did. She had told the doctor that she would never speak to him again if this happened, and the doctor had promised her faithfully that he would keep the man alive over Christmas day somehow.

"It would be nice for him, too," said Mrs. Linsell.

"For whom?" asked Mrs. Hamlyn.

"For poor Mr. Gallagher. Naturally no one likes to die on Christmas day. Do they?"

"I don't really know," said Mrs. Hamlyn.

That night, after she had been asleep a little while, she awoke weeping. It dismayed her that she should cry in her sleep. It was as though then the weakness of the flesh mastered her, and, her will broken, she was defenceless against a natural sorrow. She turned over in her mind, as so often before, the details of the disaster which had so profoundly affected her; she repeated the conversations with her husband, wishing she had said this and blaming herself because she had said the other. She wished with all her heart that she had remained in comfortable ignorance of her husband's infatuation, and asked herself whether she would not have been wiser to pocket her pride and shut her eyes to the unwelcome truth. She was a woman of the world and she knew too well how much more she lost in separating herself from her husband than his love; she lost the settled establishment and the assured position, the ample means and the support of a recognized background. She had known of many separated wives, living equivocally on smallish incomes, and knew how quickly their friends found them tiresome. And she was lonely. She was as lonely as the ship that throbbed her hasting way through an unpeopled sea, and lonely as the friendless man who lay dying in the ship's lazaret. Mrs. Hamlyn knew that her thoughts had got the better of her now and that she would not easily sleep again. It was very hot in her cabin. She looked at the time; it was between four and half-past; she must pass two mortal hours before broke the reassuring day.

She slipped into a kimono and went on deck. The night was sombre and although the sky was unclouded no stars were visible. Panting and shaking, the old ship under full steam lumbered through the darkness. The silence was uncanny. Mrs. Hamlyn with bare feet groped her way slowly along the deserted deck. It was so black that she could see nothing. She came to the end of the promenade deck and leaned against the rail. Suddenly she started and her attention was fixed, for on the lower deck she caught a fitful glow. She leaned forward cautiously. It was a little fire, and she saw only the glow because the naked backs of men, crouched round, hid the flame. At the edge of the circle she divined, rather than saw, a stocky figure in pyjamas. The rest were natives, but this was a European. It must be Pryce and she guessed immediately that some dark ceremony of exorcism was in progress. Straining her ears she heard a low voice muttering a string of secret words. She began to tremble. She was aware that they were too intent upon their business to think that any one was watching them, but she dared not move. Suddenly, rending the sultry silence of the night like a piece of silk violently torn in two, came the crowing of a cock. Mrs. Hamlyn almost shrieked. Mr. Pryce was trying to save the life of his friend and master by a sacrifice to the strange gods of the East. The voice went on, low and insistent. Then in the dark circle there was a movement, something was happening, she knew not what; there was a cluck-cluck from the cock, angry and frightened, and then a strange, indescribable sound; the magician was cutting the cock's throat; then silence; there were vague doings that she could not follow, and in a little while it looked as though some one was stamping out the fire. The figures she had dimly seen were dissolved in the night and all once more was still. She heard again the regular throbbing of the engines.

Mrs. Hamlyn stood still for a little while, strangely shaken, and then walked slowly along the deck. She found a chair and lay down in it. She was trembling still. She could only guess what had happened. She did not know how long she lay there, but at last she felt that the dawn was approaching. It was not yet day, but it was no longer night. Against the darkness of the sky she could now see the ship's rail. Then she saw a figure come towards her. It was a man in pyjamas.

"Who's that?" she cried nervously.

"Only the doctor," came a friendly voice.

"Oh! What are you doing here at this time of night?"

"I've been with Gallagher." He sat down beside her and lit a cigarette. "I've given him a good strong hypodermic and he's quiet now."

"Has he been very ill?"

"I thought he was going to pass out. I was watching him, and suddenly he started up on his bed and began to talk Malay. Of course I couldn't understand a thing. He kept on saying one word over and over again."

"Perhaps it was a name, a woman's name."

"He wanted to get out of bed. He's a damned powerful man even now. By George, I had a struggle with him. I was afraid he'd throw himself overboard. He seemed to think some one was calling him."

"When was that?" asked Mrs. Hamlyn slowly.

"Between four and half-past. Why?"

"Nothing."

She shuddered.

Later in the morning when the ship's life was set upon its daily round, Mrs. Hamlyn passed Pryce on the deck, but he gave her a brief greeting and walked on with quickly averted gaze. He looked tired and overwrought. Mrs. Hamlyn thought again of that fat woman, with golden ornaments in her thick, black hair, who sat on the steps of the deserted bungalow and looked at the road which ran through the trim lines of the rubber trees.

It was fearfully hot. She knew now why the night had been so dark. The sky was no longer blue, but a dead, level white; its surface was too even to give the effect of cloud; it was as though in the upper air the heat hung like a pall. There was no breeze and the sea, as colourless as the sky, was smooth and shining like the dye in a dyer's vat. The passengers were listless; when they walked round the deck they panted and beads of sweat broke out on their foreheads. They spoke in undertones. Something uncanny and disquieting brooded over the ship, and they could not bring themselves to laugh. A feeling of resentment arose in their hearts; they were alive and well, and it exasperated them that, so near, a man should be dying and by the fact (which was after all no concern of theirs) so mysteriously affect them. A planter in the smoking-room over a gin sling said brutally what most of them felt, though none had confessed.

"Well, if he's going to peg out," he said, "I wish he'd hurry up and get it over. It gives me the creeps."

The day was interminable. Mrs. Hamlyn was thankful when the dinner hour arrived. So much time, at all events, was passed. She sat at the doctor's table.

"When do we reach Aden?" she asked.

"Some time to-morrow. The captain says we shall sight land between five and six in the morning."

She gave him a sharp look. He stared at her for a moment, then dropped his eyes and reddened. He remembered that the woman, the fat woman sitting on the bungalow steps, had said that Gallagher would never see the land. Mrs. Hamlyn wondered whether he, the sceptical, matter-of-fact young doctor, was wavering at last. He frowned a little, and then, as though he sought to pull himself together, looked at her once more.

"I shan't be sorry to hand over my patient to the hospital people at Aden, I can tell you," he said.

Next day was Christmas eve. When Mrs. Hamlyn awoke from a troubled sleep the dawn was breaking. She looked out of her porthole and saw that the sky was clear and silvery; during the night the haze had melted, and the morning was brilliant. With a lighter heart she went on deck. She walked as far forward as she could go. A late star twinkled palely close to the horizon. There was a shimmer on the sea as though a loitering breeze passed playful fingers over its surface. The light was exquisitely soft, tenuous like a budding wood in spring, and crystalline so that it reminded you of the bubbling of water in a mountain brook. She turned to look at the sun rising rosy in the east, and saw coming towards her the doctor. He wore his uniform; he had not been to bed all night; he was dishevelled and he walked, with bowed shoulders, as though he were dog-tired. She knew at once that Gallagher was dead. When he came up to her she saw that he was crying. He looked so young then that her heart went out to him. She took his hand.

"You poor dear," she said. "You're tired out."

"I did all I could," he said. "I wanted so awfully to save him." His voice shook and she saw that he was almost hysterical.

"When did he die?" she asked.

He closed his eyes, trying to control himself, and his lips trembled.

"A few minutes ago."

Mrs. Hamlyn sighed. She found nothing to say. Her gaze wandered across the calm, dispassionate and ageless sea. It stretched on all sides of them as infinite as human sorrow. But on a sudden her eyes were held, for there, ahead of them, on the horizon was something which looked like a precipitous and massy cloud. But its outline was too sharp to be a cloud's. She touched the doctor on the arm.

"What's that?"

He looked at it for a moment and under his sunburn she saw him grow white.

"Land."

Once more Mrs. Hamlyn thought of the fat Malay woman who sat silent on the steps of Gallagher's bungalow. Did she know?

They buried him when the sun was high in the heavens. They stood on the lower deck and on the hatches, the first- and second-class passengers, the white stewards and the European officers. The missionary read the burial service.

"Man that is born of woman hath but a short time to live, and is full of misery. He cometh up, and is cut down, like a flower; he fleeth as it were a shadow, and never continueth in one stay."

Pryce looked down at the deck with knit brows. His teeth were tightly clenched. He did not grieve, for his heart was hot with anger. The doctor and the consul stood side by side. The consul bore to a nicety the expression of an official regret, but the doctor, clean-shaven now, in his neat fresh uniform and his gold braid, was pale and harassed. From him Mrs. Hamlyn's eyes wandered to Mrs. Linsell. She was pressed against her husband, weeping, and he was holding her hand tenderly. Mrs. Hamlyn did not know why this sight singularly affected her. At that moment of grief, her nerves distraught, the little woman went by instinct to the protection and support of her husband. But then Mrs. Hamlyn felt a little shudder pass through her and she fixed her eyes on the seams in the deck, for she did not want to see what was toward. There was a pause in the reading. There were various movements. One of the officers gave an order. The missionary's voice continued.

"Forasmuch as it has pleased Almighty God of his great mercy to take unto himself the soul of our dear brother here departed; we therefore commend his body to the deep, to be turned into corruption, looking for the resurrection of the body when the sea shall give up its dead."

Mrs. Hamlyn felt the hot tears flow down her cheeks. There was a dull splash. The missionary's voice went on.

When the service was finished the passengers scattered; the second-class passengers returned to their quarters and a bell rang to summon them to luncheon. But the first-class passengers sauntered aimlessly about the promenade deck. Most of the men made for the smoking-room and sought to cheer themselves with whiskies and sodas and with gin slings. But the consul put up a notice on the board outside the dining-saloon summoning the passengers to a meeting. Most of them had an idea for what purpose it was called and at the appointed hour they assembled. They were more cheerful than they had been for a week and they chattered with a gaiety which was only subdued by a mannerly reserve. The consul, an eye-glass in his eye, said that he had gathered them together to discuss the question of the fancy-dress ball on the following day. He knew they all had the deepest sympathy for Mr. Gallagher and he would have proposed that they should combine to send an appropriate message to the deceased's relatives; but his papers had been examined by the purser and no trace could be found of any relative or friend with whom it was possible to communicate. The late Mr. Gallagher appeared to be quite alone in the world. Meanwhile he (the consul) ventured to offer his sincere sympathy to the doctor who, he was quite sure, had done everything that was possible in the circumstances.

"Hear, hear," said the passengers.

They had all passed through a very trying time, proceeded the consul, and to some it might seem that it would be more respectful to the deceased's memory if the fancy-dress ball were postponed till New Year's eve. This, however, he told them frankly was not his view, and he was convinced that Mr. Gallagher himself would not have wished it. Of course it was a question for the majority to decide. The doctor got up and thanked the consul and the passengers for the kind things that had been said of him, it had of course been a very trying time, but he was authorized by the captain to say that the captain expressly wished all the festivities to be carried out on Christmas day as though nothing had happened. He (the doctor) told them in confidence that the captain felt the passengers had got into a rather morbid state and thought it would do them all good if they had a jolly good time on Christmas day. Then the missionary's wife rose and said they mustn't think only of themselves; it had been arranged by the Entertainment Committee that there should be a Christmas tree for the children immediately after the first-class passengers' dinner, and the children had been looking forward to seeing every one in fancy dress; it would be too bad to disappoint them; she yielded to no one in her respect for the dead and she sympathized with any one who felt too sad to think of dancing just then. Her own heart was very heavy, but she did feel it would be merely selfish to give way to a feeling which could do no good to any one. Let them think of the little ones. This very much impressed the passengers. They wanted to forget the brooding terror which had hung over the boat for so many days, they were alive and they wanted to enjoy themselves; but they had an uneasy notion that it would be decent to exhibit a certain grief. It was quite another matter if they could do as they wished from altruistic motives. When the consul called for a show of hands every one, but Mrs. Hamlyn and one old lady who was rheumatic, held up an eager arm.

"The ayes have it," said the consul. "And I venture to congratulate the meeting on a very sensible decision."

It was just going to break up when one of the planters got on his feet and said he wished to offer a suggestion. In the circumstances didn't they all think it would be as well to invite the second-class passengers? They had all come to the funeral that morning. The missionary jumped up and seconded the motion. The events of the last few days had drawn them all together, he said, and in the presence of death all men were equal. The consul again addressed them. This matter had been discussed at a previous meeting and the conclusion had been reached that it would be pleasanter for the second-class passengers to have their own party, but circumstances alter cases, and he was distinctly of opinion that their previous decision should be reversed.

"Hear, hear," said the passengers.

A wave of democratic feeling swept over them and the motion was carried by acclamation. They separated light-heartedly, they felt charitable and kindly. Every one stood every one else drinks in the smoking-room.

And so, on the following evening, Mrs. Hamlyn put on her fancy-dress. She had no heart for the gaiety before her, and for a moment had thought of feigning illness, but she knew no one

would believe her, and was afraid to be thought affected. She
was dressed as Carmen and she could not resist the vanity of
making herself as attractive as possible. She darkened her eyelashes and rouged her cheeks. The costume suited her. When the
bugle sounded and she went into the saloon she was received
with flattering surprise. The consul (always a humorist) was
dressed as a ballet-girl and was greeted with shouts of delighted
laughter. The missionary and his wife, self-conscious but pleased
with themselves, were very grand as Manchus. Mrs. Linsell, as
Columbine, showed all that was possible of her very pretty legs.
Her husband was an Arab sheik and the doctor was a Malay sultan.

A subscription had been collected to provide champagne at
dinner and the meal was hilarious. The company had provided
crackers in which were paper hats of various shapes and these
the passengers put on. There were paper streamers too which they
threw at one another and little balloons which they beat from
one to the other across the room. They laughed and shouted.
They were very gay. No one could say that they were not having
a good time. As soon as dinner was finished they went into the
saloon where the Christmas tree, with candles lit, was ready, and
the children were brought in, shrieking with delight, and given
presents. Then the dance began. The second-class passengers stood
about shyly round the part of the deck reserved for dancing and
occasionally danced with one another.

"I'm glad we had them," said the consul, dancing with Mrs.
Hamlyn. "I'm all for democracy, and I think they're very sensible
to keep themselves to themselves."

But he noticed that Pryce was not to be seen, and when an
opportunity presented asked one of the second-class passengers
where he was.

"Blind to the world," was the answer. "We put him to bed in
the afternoon and locked him up in his cabin."

The consul claimed her for another dance. He was very facetious. Suddenly Mrs. Hamlyn felt that she could not bear it any
more, the noise of the amateur band, the consul's jokes, the gaiety
of the dancers. She knew not why, but the merriment of those
people passing on their ship through the night and the solitary
sea affected her on a sudden with horror. When the consul released her she slipped away and, with a look to see that no one

had noticed her, ascended the companion to the boat-deck. Here everything was in darkness. She walked softly to a spot where she knew she would be safe from all intrusion. But she heard a faint laugh and she caught sight in a hidden corner of a Columbine and a Malay sultan. Mrs. Linsell and the doctor had resumed already the flirtation which the death of Gallagher had interrupted.

Already all those people had put out of their minds with a kind of ferocity the thought of that poor lonely man who had so strangely died in their midst. They felt no compassion for him, but resentment rather, because on his account they had been ill-at-ease. They seized upon life avidly. They made their jokes, they flirted, they gossiped. Mrs. Hamlyn remembered what the consul had said, that among Mr. Gallagher's papers no letter could be found, not the name of a single friend to whom the news of his death might be sent, and she knew not why this seemed to her unbearably tragic. There was something mysterious in a man who could pass through the world in such solitariness. When she remembered how he had come on deck in Singapore, so short a while since, in such rude health, full of vitality, and his arrogant plans for the future, she was seized with dismay. Those words of the burial service filled her with a solemn awe: *Man that is born of woman hath but a short time to live, and is full of misery. He cometh up, and is cut down, like a flower.* . . . Year in, year out, he had made his plans for the future, he wanted to live so much and he had so much to live for, and then just when he stretched out his hand—oh, it was pitiful; it made all the other distresses of the world of small account. Death with its mystery was the only thing that really mattered. Mrs. Hamlyn leaned over the rail and looked at the starry sky. Why did people make themselves unhappy? Let them weep for the death of those they loved, death was terrible always, but for the rest, was it worth while to be wretched, to harbour malice, to be vain and uncharitable? She thought again of herself and her husband and the woman he so strangely loved. He too had said that we live to be happy so short a time and we are so long dead. She pondered long and intently, and suddenly, as summer lightning flashes across the darkness of the night, she made a discovery which filled her with tremulous surprise; for she found that in her heart was no longer anger with her husband nor jealousy of her rival. A notion dawned on some remote horizon of her consciousness and like the morning sun suffused her soul with a tender, blissful glow. Out of the tragedy of that unknown Irishman's death she gathered elatedly the courage for a desperate resolution. Her heart beat quickly, she was impatient to carry it into effect. A passion for self-sacrifice seized her.

The music had stopped, the ball was over; most of the passengers would have gone to bed and the rest would be in the smoking-room. She went down to her cabin and met no one on the way. She took her writing-pad and wrote a letter to her husband.

My dear. It is Christmas day and I want to tell you that my heart is filled with kindly thoughts towards both of you. I have been foolish and unreasonable. I think we should allow those we care for to be happy in their own way, and we should care for them enough not to let it make us unhappy. I want you to know that I grudge you none of the joy that has so strangely come into your life. I am no longer jealous, nor hurt, nor vindictive. Do not think I shall be unhappy or lonely. If ever you feel that you need me, come to me, and I will welcome you with a cheerful spirit and without reproach or ill-will. I am most grateful for all the years of happiness and of tenderness that you gave me, and in return I wish to offer you an affection which makes no claim on you and is, I hope, utterly disinterested. Think kindly of me and be happy, happy, happy.

She signed her name and put the letter into an envelope. Though it would not go till they reached Port Said she wanted to place it at once in the letter-box. When she had done this, beginning to undress, she looked at herself in the glass. Her eyes were shining and under her rouge her colour was bright. The future was no longer desolate, but bright with a fair hope. She slipped into bed and fell at once into a sound and dreamless sleep.

Virtue

There are few things better than a good Havana. When I was young and very poor and smoked a cigar only when somebody gave me one, I determined that if ever I had money I would smoke a cigar every day after luncheon and after dinner. This is the only resolution of my youth that I have kept. It is the only ambition I have achieved that has never been embittered by disillusion. I like a cigar that is mild, but full-flavoured, neither so small that it is finished before you have become aware of it nor so large as to be irksome, rolled so that it draws without consciousness of effort on your part, with a leaf so firm that it doesn't become messy on your lips and in such condition that it keeps its savour to the very end. But when you have taken the last pull and put down the shapeless stump and watched the final cloud of smoke dwindle blue in the surrounding air it is impossible, if you have a sensitive nature, not to feel a certain melancholy at the thought of all the labour, the care and pains that have gone, the thought, the trouble, the complicated organization that have been required, to provide you with half an hour's delight. For this men have sweltered long years under tropical suns and ships have scoured the seven seas. These reflections become more poignant still when you are eating a dozen oysters (with half a bottle of dry white wine) and they become almost unbearable when it comes to a lamb cutlet. For these are animals, and there is something that inspires awe in the thought that since the surface of the earth became capable of supporting life from generation to generation for millions upon millions of years creatures have come into existence, to end at last upon a plate of crushed ice or on a silver grill. It may be that a sluggish fancy cannot grasp the dreadful solemnity of eating an oyster and evolution has taught us that the bivalve has through the ages kept itself to itself in a manner that inevitably alienates sympathy. There is an aloofness in it that is offensive to the aspiring spirit of man, and a self-complacency that is obnoxious to his vanity. But I do not know how anyone can look upon a lamb cutlet without thoughts too deep for tears: here man himself has taken a hand, and the history of the race is bound up with the tender morsel on your plate.

And sometimes even the fate of human beings is curious to consider. It is strange to look upon this man or that, the quiet ordinary persons of every day, the bank clerk, the dustman, the middle-aged girl in the second row of the chorus, and think of the interminable history behind them and of the long, long series of hazards by which from the primeval slime the course of events has brought them at this moment to such and such a place. When such tremendous vicissitudes have been needed to get them here at all, one would have thought some huge significance must be attached to them; one would have thought that what befell them must matter a little to the Life Spirit or whatever else it is that has produced them. An accident befalls them. The thread is broken. The story that began with the world is finished abruptly, and it looks as though it meant nothing at all. A tale told by an idiot. And is it not odd that this event, of an importance so dramatic, may be brought about by a cause so trivial?

An incident of no moment, that might easily not have happened, has consequences that are incalculable. It looks as though blind chance ruled all things. Our smallest actions may affect profoundly the whole lives of people who have nothing to do with us. The story I have to tell would never have happened if one day I had not walked across the street. Life is really very fantastic, and one has to have a peculiar sense of humour to see the fun of it.

I was strolling down Bond Street one spring morning and, having nothing much to do till lunch time, thought I would look in at Sotheby's, the auction rooms, to see whether there was anything on show that interested me. There was a block in the traffic and I threaded my way through the cars. When I reached the other side I ran into a man I had known in Borneo coming out of a hatter's.

"Hullo, Morton," I said. "When did you come home?"

"I've been back about a week."

He was a District Officer. The Governor had given me a letter of introduction to him, and I wrote and told him I meant to spend a week at the place he lived at and should like to put up at the government rest-house. He met me on the ship when I arrived and asked me to stay with him. I demurred. I did not see how I could spend a week with a total stranger, I did not want to put him to the expense of my board, and besides I thought I should have more freedom if I were on my own. He would not listen to me.

"I've got plenty of room," he said, "and the rest-house is beastly. I haven't spoken to a white man for six months and I'm fed to the teeth with my own company."

But when Morton had got me and his launch had landed us at the bungalow and he had offered me a drink, he did not in the least know what to do with me. He was seized on a sudden with shyness, and his conversation, which had been fluent and ready, ran dry. I did my best to make him feel at home (it was the least I could do, considering that it was his own house) and asked him if he had any new records. He turned on the gramophone, and the sound of ragtime gave him confidence.

His bungalow overlooked the river, and his living-room was a large verandah. It was furnished in the impersonal fashion that characterized the dwellings of government officials who were moved here and there at little notice according to the exigencies of the service. There were native hats as ornaments on the walls and the horns of animals, blow-pipes and spears. In the book-shelf were detective novels and old magazines. There was a cottage piano with yellow keys. It was very untidy, but not uncomfortable.

Unfortunately I cannot very well remember what he looked like. He was young, twenty-eight, I learnt later, and he had a boyish and attractive smile. I spent an agreeable week with him. We went up and down the river and we climbed a mountain. We had tiffin one day with some planters who lived twenty miles away, and every evening we went to the club. The only members were the manager of a kutch factory and his assistants, but they were not on speaking terms with one another and it was only on Morton's representations that they must not let him down when he had a visitor that we could get up a rubber of bridge. The atmosphere was strained. We came back to dinner, listened to the gramophone and went to bed. Morton had little office work, and one would have thought the time hung heavy on his hands, but he had energy and high spirits; it was his first post of the sort and he was happy to be independent. His only anxiety was lest he should be transferred before he had finished a road he was building. This was the joy of his heart. It was his own idea and he had wheedled the government into giving him the money to make it; he had surveyed the country himself and traced the path. He had solved unaided the technical problems that presented themselves. Every morning, before he went to his office, he drove out in a rickety old Ford to where the coolies were working and watched the progress that had been made since the day before. He thought of nothing else. He dreamt of it at night. He reckoned that it would be finished in a year and he did not want to take his leave till then. He could not have worked with more zest if he had been a painter or a sculptor creating a work of art. I think it was this eagerness that made me take a fancy to him. I liked his zeal. I liked his ingenuousness. And I was impressed by the passion for achievement that made him indifferent to the solitariness of his life, to promotion and even to the thought of going home. I forget how long the road was, fifteen or twenty miles, I think, and I forget what purpose it was to serve. I don't believe Morton cared very much. His passion was the artist's and his triumph was the triumph of man over nature. He learnt as he went along. He had the jungle to contend against, torrential rains that destroyed the labour of weeks, accidents of topography; he had to collect his labour and hold it together; he had inadequate funds. His imagination sustained him. His labours gained a sort of epic quality, and the vicissitudes of the work were a great saga that unrolled itself with an infinity of episodes.

His only complaint was that the day was too short. He had office duties, he was judge and tax collector, father and mother (at twenty-eight) of the people in his district; he had now and then to make tours that took him away from home. Unless he were on the spot nothing was done. He would have liked to be there twenty-four hours a day driving the reluctant coolies to further effort. It so happened that shortly before I arrived an incident had occurred that filled him with jubilation. He had offered a contract to a Chinese to make a certain section of the road, and the Chinese had asked more than Morton could afford to pay. Notwithstanding interminable discussions they had been unable to arrive at an agreement, and Morton with rage in his heart saw his work held up. He was at his wit's end. Then, going down to his office one morning, he heard that there had been a row in one of the Chinese gambling houses the night before. A coolie had been badly wounded and his assailant was under arrest. This assailant was the contractor. He was brought into court, the evidence was clear and Morton sentenced him to eighteen months' hard labour.

"Now he'll have to build the blasted road for nothing," said Morton, his eyes glistening when he told me the story.

We saw the fellow at work one morning, in the prison sarong, unconcerned. He was taking his misfortunes in good part.

"I've told him I'll remit the rest of his sentence when the road's finished," said Morton, "and he's as pleased as Punch. Bit of a snip for me, eh, what?"

When I left Morton I asked him to let me know when he came to England, and he promised to write to me as soon as he landed. On the spur of the moment one gives these invitations and one is perfectly sincere about them. But when one is taken at one's word a slight dismay seizes one. People are so different at home from what they are abroad. There they are easy, cordial and natural. They have interesting things to tell you. They are immensely kind. You are anxious, when your turn comes, to do something in return for the hospitality you have received. But it is not easy. The persons who were so entertaining in their own surroundings are very dull in yours. They are constrained and shy. You introduce them to your friends, and your friends find them a crashing bore. They do their best to be civil, but sigh with relief when the strangers go and the conversation can once more run easily in its accustomed channels. I think the residents in far places early in their careers understand the situation pretty well, as the result maybe of bitter and humiliating experiences, for I have found that they seldom take advantage of the invitation which on some out-station on the edge of the jungle has been so cordially extended to them and by them as cordially accepted. But Morton was different. He was a young man and single. It is generally the wives that are the difficulty; other women look at their drab clothes, in a glance take in their provincial air, and freeze them with their indifference. But a man can play bridge and tennis, and dance. Morton had charm. I had no doubt that in a day or two he would find his feet.

"Why didn't you let me know you were back?" I asked him.

"I thought you wouldn't want to be bothered with me," he smiled.

"What nonsense!"

Of course now as we stood in Bond Street on the curb and chatted for a minute he looked strange to me. I had never seen him in anything but khaki shorts and a tennis shirt, except when we got back from the club at night and he put on a pajama jacket and a sarong for dinner. It is as comfortable a form of evening dress as has ever been devised. He looked a bit awkward in his blue serge suit. His face against a white collar was very brown.

"How about the road?" I asked him.

"Finished. I was afraid I'd have to postpone my leave. We struck one or two snags towards the end, but I made 'em hustle and the day before I left I drove the Ford to the end and back without stopping."

I laughed. His pleasure was charming.

"What have you been doing with yourself in London?"

"Buying clothes."

"Been having a good time?"

"Marvellous. A bit lonely, you know, but I don't mind that. I've been to a show every night. The Palmers, you know—I think you met them in Sarawak—were going to be in town and we were going to do the plays together, but they had to go to Scotland because her mother's ill."

His words, said so breezily, cut me to the quick. His was the common experience. It was heart-breaking. For months, for long months before it was due, these people planned their leave, and when they got off the ship they were in such spirits they could hardly contain themselves. London. Shops and clubs and theatres and restaurants. London. They were going to have the time of their lives. London. It swallowed them. A strange, turbulent city, not hostile but indifferent, and they were lost in it. They had no friends. They had nothing in common with the acquaintances they made. They were more lonely than in the jungle. It was a relief when at a theatre they ran across someone they had known in the East (and perhaps been bored stiff by or disliked) and they could fix up an evening together and have a good laugh and tell one another what a grand time they were having and talk of common friends and at last confide to one another a little shyly that they would not be sorry when their leave was up and they were once again in harness. They went to see their families and of course they were glad to see them, but it wasn't the same as it had been; they did feel a bit out of it, and when you came down to brass tacks the life people led in England was deadly. It was grand fun to come home, but you couldn't live there any more, and sometimes you thought of your bungalow overlooking the river and your tours of the district and what a lark it was to run over once in a blue moon to Sandakan or Kuching or Singapore.

And because I remembered what Morton had looked forward to when, the road finished and off his chest, he went on leave, I could not but feel a pang when I thought of him dining by himself in a dismal club where he knew nobody, or alone in a restaurant in Soho and then going off to see a play with no one by his side with whom he could enjoy it, and no one to have a drink with during the interval. And at the same time I reflected that even if I had known he was in London I could have done nothing much for him, for during the last week I had not had a moment free. That very evening I was dining with friends and going to a play, and the next day I was going abroad.

"What are you doing to-night?" I asked him.

"I'm going to the Pavilion. It's packed jammed full, but there's a fellow over the road who's wonderful and he's got me a ticket that had been returned. You can often get one seat, you know, when you can't get two."

"Why don't you come and have supper with me? I'm taking some people to the Haymarket and we're going on to Ciro's afterwards."

"I'd love to."

We arranged to meet at eleven, and I left him to keep an engagement.

I was afraid the friends I had asked him to meet would not amuse Morton very much, for they were distinctly middle-aged, but I could not think of anyone young that at this season of the year I should be likely to get hold of at the last moment. None of the girls I knew would thank me for asking her to supper to dance with a shy young man from Malaya. I could trust the Bishops to do their best for him, and after all it must be jollier for him to have supper in a club with a good band where he could see pretty women dancing than to go home to bed at eleven because he had nowhere else in the world to go. I had known Charlie Bishop first when I was a medical student. He was then a thin little fellow with sandy hair and blunt features; he had fine eyes, dark and gleaming, but he wore spectacles. He had a round, merry, red face. He was very fond of the girls. I suppose he had a way with him, for with no money and no looks, he managed to pick up a succession of young persons who gratified his roving desires. He was clever and bumptious, argumentative and quick-tempered. He had a caustic tongue. Looking back, I should say he was a rather disagreeable young man, but I do not think he was a bore. Now, halfway through the fifties, he was inclined to be stout and he was very bald, but his eyes behind the gold-rimmed spectacles were still bright and alert. He was dogmatic and somewhat conceited, argumentative still and caustic, but he was good-natured and amusing. After you have known a person so long his idiosyncrasies cease to trouble you. You accept them as you accept your own physical defects. He was by profession a pathologist, and now and then he sent me a slim book he had just published. It was severe and extremely technical and grimly illustrated with photographs of bacteria. I did not read it. I gathered from what I sometimes heard that Charlie's views on the subjects with which he dealt were unsound. I do not believe that he was very popular with the other members of his profession—he made no secret of the fact that he looked upon them as a set of incompetent idiots—but he had his job, it brought him in six or eight hundred a year, I think, and he was completely indifferent to other people's opinion of him.

I liked Charlie Bishop because I had known him for thirty years, but I liked Margery, his wife, because she was very nice. I was extremely surprised when he told me he was going to be married. He was hard on forty at the time, and so fickle in his affections that I had made up my mind he would remain single. He was very fond of women, but he was not in the least sentimental, and his aims were loose. His views on the female sex would in these idealistic days be thought crude. He knew what he wanted and he asked for it, and if he couldn't get it for love or money he shrugged his shoulders and went his way. To be brief, he did not look to women to gratify his ideal but to provide him with fornication. It was odd that, though small and plain, he found so many who were prepared to grant his wishes. For his spiritual needs he found satisfaction in unicellular organisms. He had always been a man who spoke to the point, and when he told me he was going to marry a young woman called Margery Hobson I did not hesitate to ask him why. He grinned.

"Three reasons. First, she won't let me go to bed with her without. Second, she makes me laugh like a hyena. And third, she's alone in the world, without a single relation, and she must have someone to take care of her."

"The first reason is just swank and the second is eyewash. The third is the real one and it means that she's got you by the short hairs."

His eyes gleamed softly behind his large spectacles.

"I shouldn't be surprised if you weren't dead right."

"She's not only got you by the short hairs but you're as pleased as Punch that she has."

"Come and lunch to-morrow and have a look at her. She's easy on the eye."

Charlie was a member of a cock-and-hen club which at that time I used a good deal, and we arranged to lunch there. I found Margery a very attractive young woman. She was then just under thirty. She was a lady. I noticed the fact with satisfaction, but with a certain astonishment, for it had not escaped my notice that Charlie was attracted as a rule by women whose breeding left something to be desired. She was not beautiful, but comely, with fine dark hair and fine eyes, a good colour and a look of health. She had a pleasant frankness and an air of candour that was very taking. She looked honest, simple and dependable. I took an immediate liking to her. She was easy to talk to, and though she did not say anything very brilliant she understood what other people were talking about; she was quick to see a joke and she was not shy. She gave you the impression of being competent and businesslike. She had a happy placidity that suggested a good temper and an excellent digestion.

They seemed extremely pleased with one another. I had asked myself when I first saw her why Margery was marrying this irritable little man, baldish already and by no means young, but I discovered very soon that it was because she was in love with him. They chaffed one another a good deal and laughed a lot, and every now and then their eyes met more significantly and they seemed to exchange a little private message. It was really rather touching.

A week later they were married at a registrar's office. It was a very successful marriage. Looking back now after sixteen years I could not but chuckle sympathetically at the thought of the lark they had made of their life together. I had never known a more devoted couple. They had never had very much money. They never seemed to want any. They had no ambitions. Their life was a picnic that never came to an end. They lived in the smallest flat I ever saw, in Panton Street, a small bedroom, a small sitting-room and a bathroom that served also as a kitchen. But they had no sense of home, they ate their meals in restaurants, and only had breakfast in the flat. It was merely a place to sleep in. It was comfortable, though a third person coming in for a whisky and soda crowded it, and Margery with the help of a charwoman kept it as neat as Charlie's untidiness permitted, but there was not a single thing in it that had a personal note. They had a tiny car, and whenever Charlie had a holiday they took it across the Channel and started off, with a bag each for all their luggage, to drive wherever the fancy took them. Breakdowns never disturbed them, bad weather was part of the fun, a puncture was no end of a joke, and if they lost their way and had to sleep out in the open they thought they were having the time of their lives.

Charlie continued to be irascible and contentious, but nothing he did ever disturbed Margery's lovely placidity. She could calm him with a word. She still made him laugh. She typed his monographs on obscure bacteria and corrected the proofs of his articles in the scientific magazines. Once I asked them if they ever quarrelled.

"No," she said, "we never seem to have anything to quarrel about. Charlie has the temper of an angel."

"Nonsense," I said, "he's an overbearing, aggressive, and cantankerous fellow. He always has been."

She looked at him and giggled, and I saw that she thought I was being funny.

"Let him rave," said Charlie. "He's an ignorant fool and he uses words of whose meaning he hasn't the smallest idea."

They were sweet together. They were very happy in one another's company and were never apart if they could help it. Even after the long time they had been married Charlie used to get into the car every day at luncheon time to come west and meet Margery at a restaurant. People used to laugh at them, not unkindly, but perhaps with a little catch in the throat, because when they were asked to go and spend a weekend in the country Margery would write to the hostess and say they would like to come if they could be given a double bed. They had slept together for so many years that neither of them could sleep alone. It was often a trifle awkward. Husbands and wives as a rule not only demanded separate rooms, but were inclined to be peevish if asked to share the same bathroom. Modern houses were not arranged for domestic couples, but among their friends it became an understood thing that if you wanted the Bishops you must give them a room with a double bed. Some people of course thought it a little indecent and it was never convenient, but they were a pleasant pair to have to stay and it was worth while to put up with their crankiness. Charlie was always full of spirits and in his caustic way extremely amusing, and Margery was peaceful and easy. They were no trouble to entertain. Nothing pleased them more than to be left to go out together for a long ramble in the country.

When a man marries, his wife sooner or later estranges him from his old friends, but Margery on the contrary increased Charlie's intimacy with them. By making him more tolerant she made him a more agreeable companion. They gave you the impression not of a married couple, but, rather amusingly, of two middle-aged bachelors living together; and when Margery, as was the rule, found herself the only woman among half a dozen men, ribald, argumentative and gay, she was not a bar to good-fellowship but an asset. Whenever I was in England I saw them. They generally dined at the club of which I have spoken, and if I happened to be alone I joined them.

When we met that evening for a snack before going to the play I told them I had asked Morton to come to supper.

"I'm afraid you'll find him rather dull," I said. "But he's a very decent sort of boy and he was awfully kind to me when I was in Borneo."

"Why didn't you let me know sooner?" cried Margery. "I'd have brought a girl along."

"What do you want a girl for?" said Charlie. "There'll be you."

"I don't think it can be much fun for a young man to dance with a woman of my advanced years," said Margery.

"Rot. What's your age got to do with it?" He turned to me. "Have you ever danced with anyone who danced better?"

I had, but she certainly danced very well. She was light on her feet and she had a good sense of rhythm.

"Never," I said heartily.

Morton was waiting for us when we reached Ciro's. He looked very sunburned in his evening clothes. Perhaps it was because I knew that they had been wrapped away in a tin box with moth balls for four years that I felt he did not look quite at home in them. He was certainly more at ease in khaki shorts. Charlie Bishop was a good talker and liked to hear himself speak. Morton was shy. I gave him a cocktail and ordered some champagne. I had a feeling that he would be glad to dance, but was not quite sure whether it would occur to him to ask Margery. I was acutely conscious that we all belonged to another generation.

"I think I should tell you that Mrs. Bishop is a beautiful dancer," I said.

"Is she?" He flushed a little. "Will you dance with me?"

She got up and they took the floor. She was looking peculiarly nice that evening, not at all smart, and I do not think her plain black dress had cost more than six guineas, but she looked a lady. She had the advantage of having extremely good legs, and at that time skirts were still being worn very short. I suppose she had a little make-up on, but in contrast with the other women there she looked very natural. Shingled hair suited her; it was not even touched with white and it had an attractive sheen. She was not a pretty woman, but her kindliness, her wholesome air, her good health, gave you, if not the illusion that she was, at least the feeling that it didn't at all matter. When she came back to the table her eyes were bright and she had a heightened colour.

"How does he dance?" asked her husband.

"Divinely."

"You're very easy to dance with," said Morton.

Charlie went on with his discourse. He had a sardonic humour and he was interesting because he was himself so interested in what he said. But he spoke of things that Morton knew nothing about, and though he listened with a civil show of interest I could see that he was too much excited by the gaiety of the scene, the music and the champagne to give his attention to conversation.

When the music struck up again his eyes immediately sought
Margery's. Charles caught the look and smiled.

"Dance with him, Margery. Good for my figure to see you take
exercise."

They set off again, and for a moment Charlie watched her with
fond eyes.

"Margery's having the time of her life. She loves dancing, and
it makes me puff and blow. Not a bad youth."

My little party was quite a success, and when Morton and I,
having taken leave of the Bishops, walked together towards Piccadilly Circus he thanked me warmly. He had really enjoyed
himself. I said good-bye to him. Next morning I went abroad.

I was sorry not to have been able to do more for Morton, and
I knew that when I returned he would be on his way back to
Borneo. I gave him a passing thought now and then, but by the
autumn when I got home he had slipped my memory. After I
had been in London a week or so I happened to drop in one night
at the club to which Charlie Bishop also belonged. He was sitting
with three or four men I knew and I went up. I had not seen
any of them since my return. One of them, a man called Bill
Marsh, whose wife, Janet, was a great friend of mine, asked me
to have a drink.

"Where have you sprung from?" asked Charlie. "Haven't seen
you about lately."

I noticed at once that he was drunk. I was astonished. Charlie
had always liked his liquor, but he carried it well and never ex-
ceeded. In years gone by, when we were very young, he got tight
occasionally, but probably more than anything to show what a
great fellow he was, and it is unfair to bring up against a man the
excesses of his youth. But I remembered that Charlie had never
been very nice when he was drunk: his natural aggressiveness
was exaggerated then and he talked too much and too loud; he
was very apt to be quarrelsome. He was very dogmatic now, laying down the law and refusing to listen to any of the objections
his rash statements called forth. The others knew he was drunk
and were struggling between the irritation his cantankerousness
aroused in them and the good-natured tolerance which they felt
his condition demanded. He was not an agreeable object. A man
of that age, bald and fattish, with spectacles, is disgusting drunk.

He was generally rather dapper, but he was untidy now and there was tobacco ash all over him. Charlie called the waiter and ordered another whisky. The waiter had been at the club for thirty years.

"You've got one in front of you, sir."

"Mind your own damned business," said Charlie Bishop. "Bring me a double whisky right away or I'll report you to the secretary for insolence."

"Very good, sir," said the waiter.

Charlie emptied his glass at a gulp, but his hand was unsteady and he spilled some of the whisky over himself.

"Well, Charlie, old boy, we'd better be toddling along," said Bill Marsh. He turned to me. "Charlie's staying with us for a bit."

I was more surprised still. But I felt that something was wrong and thought it safer not to say anything.

"I'm ready," said Charlie. "I'll just have another drink before I go. I shall have a better night if I do."

It did not look to me as though the party would break up for some time, so I got up and announced that I meant to stroll home.

"I say," said Bill, as I was about to go, "you wouldn't come and dine with us to-morrow night, would you, just me and Janet and Charlie?"

"Yes, I'll come with pleasure," I said.

It was evident that something was up.

The Marshes lived in a terrace on the east side of Regent's Park. The maid who opened the door for me asked me to go in to Mr. Marsh's study. He was waiting for me there.

"I thought I'd better have a word with you before you went upstairs," he said as he shook hands with me. "You know Margery's left Charlie?"

"No?"

"He's taken it very hard. Janet thought it was so awful for him alone in that beastly little flat that we asked him to stay here for a bit. We've done everything we could for him. He's been drinking like a fish. He hasn't slept a wink for a fortnight."

"But she hasn't left him for good?"

"Yes. She's crazy about a fellow called Morton."

I was astounded.

"Morton. Who's he?"

It never struck me it was my friend from Borneo.

"Damn it all, you introduced him, and a pretty piece of work you did. Let's go upstairs. I thought I'd better put you wise."

He opened the door and we went out. I was thoroughly confused.

"But look here——" I said.

"Ask Janet. She knows the whole thing. It beats me. I've got no patience with Margery, and he must be a mess."

He preceded me into the drawing-room. Janet Marsh rose as I entered, and came forward to greet me. Charlie was sitting at the window, reading the evening paper; he put it aside as I went up to him and shook his hand. He was quite sober and he spoke in his usual rather perky manner, but I noticed that he looked very ill. We had a glass of sherry and went down to dinner. Janet was a woman of spirit. She was tall and fair and good to look at. She kept the conversation going with alertness. When she left us to drink a glass of port it was with instructions not to stay more than ten minutes. Bill, as a rule somewhat taciturn, exerted himself now to talk. I tumbled to the game. I was hampered by my ignorance of what exactly had happened, but it was plain that the Marshes wanted to prevent Charlie from brooding, and I did my best to interest him. He seemed willing to play his part, he was always fond of holding forth, and he discussed, from the pathologist's standpoint, a murder that was just then absorbing the public. But he spoke without life. He was an empty shell, and one had the feeling that though for the sake of his host he forced himself to speak, his thoughts were elsewhere. It was a relief when a knocking on the floor above indicated to us that Janet was getting impatient. This was an occasion when a woman's presence eased the situation. We went upstairs and played family bridge. When it was time for me to go Charlie said he would walk with me as far as the Marylebone Road.

"Oh, Charlie, it's so late, you'd much better go to bed," said Janet.

"I shall sleep better if I have a stroll before turning in," he replied.

She gave him a worried look. You cannot forbid a middle-aged professor of pathology from going for a little walk if he wants to. She glanced brightly at her husband.

"I daresay it'll do Bill no harm."

I think the remark was tactless. Women are often a little too managing. Charlie gave her a sullen look.

"There's absolutely no need to drag Bill out," he said with some firmness.

"I haven't the smallest intention of coming," said Bill, smiling. "I'm tired out and I'm going to hit the hay."

I fancy we left Bill Marsh and his wife to a little argument.

"They've been frightfully kind to me," said Charlie, as we walked along by the railings. "I don't know what I should have done without them. I haven't slept for a fortnight."

I expressed regret but did not ask the reason, and we walked for a little in silence. I presumed that he had come with me in order to talk to me of what had happened, but I felt that he must take his own time. I was anxious to show my sympathy, but afraid of saying the wrong thing; I did not want to seem eager to extract confidences from him. I did not know how to give him a lead. I was sure he did not want one. He was not a man given to beating about the bush. I imagined that he was choosing his words. We reached the corner.

"You'll be able to get a taxi at the church," he said. "I'll walk on a bit farther. Good-night."

He nodded and slouched off. I was taken aback. There was nothing for me to do but to stroll on till I found a cab. I was having my bath next morning when a telephone call dragged me out of it, and with a towel round my wet body I took up the receiver. It was Janet.

"Well, what do you think of it all?" she said. "You seem to have kept Charlie up pretty late last night. I heard him come home at three."

"He left me at the Marylebone Road," I answered. "He said nothing to me at all."

"Didn't he?"

There was something in Janet's voice that suggested that she was prepared to have a long talk with me. I suspected she had a telephone by the side of her bed.

"Look here," I said quickly, "I'm having my bath."

"Oh, have you got a telephone in your bathroom?" she answered eagerly, and I think with envy.

"No, I haven't." I was abrupt and firm. "And I'm dripping all over the carpet."

"Oh," I felt disappointment in her tone and a trace of irritation. "Well, when can I see you? Can you come here at twelve?"

It was inconvenient, but I was not prepared to start an argument.

"Yes, good-bye."

I rang off before she could say anything more. In heaven when the blessed use the telephone they will say what they have to say and not a word besides.

I was devoted to Janet, but I knew that there was nothing that thrilled her more than the misfortunes of her friends. She was only too anxious to help them, but she wanted to be in the thick of their difficulties. She was the friend in adversity. Other people's business was meat and drink to her. You could not enter upon a love affair without finding her somehow your confidante, nor be mixed up in a divorce case without discovering that she too had a finger in the pie. Withal she was a very nice woman. I could not help, then, chuckling in my heart when at noon I was shown in to Janet's drawing-room and observed the subdued eagerness with which she received me. She was very much upset by the catastrophe that had befallen the Bishops, but it was exciting, and she was tickled to death to have someone fresh to whom she could tell all about it. Janet had just that businesslike expectancy that a mother has when she is discussing with the family doctor her married daughter's first confinement. Janet was conscious that the matter was very serious, and she would not for a moment have been thought to regard it flippantly, but she was determined to get every ounce of value out of it.

"I mean, no one could have been more horrified than I was when Margery told me she'd finally made up her mind to leave Charlie," she said, speaking with the fluency of a person who has said the same thing in the same words a dozen times at least. "They were the most devoted couple I'd ever known. It was a perfect marriage. They got on like a house on fire. Of course Bill and I are devoted to one another, but we have awful rows now and then. I mean, I could kill him sometimes."

"I don't care a hang about your relations with Bill," I said. "Tell me about the Bishops. That's what I've come here for."

"I simply felt I must see you. After all, you're the only person who can explain it."

"Oh, God, don't go on like that. Until Bill told me last night I didn't know a thing about it."

"That was my idea. It suddenly dawned on me that perhaps you didn't know and I thought you might put your foot in it too awfully."

"Supposing you begin at the beginning," I said.

"Well, you're the beginning. After all you started the trouble. You introduced the young man. That's why I was so crazy to see you. You know all about him. I never saw him. All I know is what Margery has told me about him."

"At what time are you lunching?" I asked.

"Half-past one."

"So am I. Get on with the story."

But my remark had given Janet an idea.

"Look here, will you get out of your luncheon if I get out of mine? We could have a snack here. I'm sure there's some cold meat in the house, and then we needn't hurry. I don't have to be at the hair-dresser's till three."

"No, no, no," I said. "I hate the notion of that. I shall leave here at twenty minutes past one at the latest."

"Then I shall just have to race through it. What do *you* think of Gerry?"

"Who's Gerry?"

"Gerry Morton. His name's Gerald."

"How should I know that?"

"You stayed with him. Weren't there any letters lying about?"

"I daresay, but I didn't happen to read them," I answered somewhat tartly.

"Oh, don't be so stupid. I meant the envelopes. What's he like?"

"All right. Rather the Kipling type, you know. Very keen on his work. Hearty. Empire-builder and all that sort of thing."

"I don't mean that," cried Janet, not without impatience. "I mean, what does he look like?"

"More or less like everybody else, I think. Of course I should recognize him if I saw him again, but I can't picture him to myself very distinctly. He looks clean."

"Oh, my God," said Janet. "Are you a novelist or are you not? What's the colour of his eyes?"

"I don't know."

"You must know. You can't spend a week with anyone without knowing if their eyes are blue or brown. Is he fair or dark?"

"Neither."

"Is he tall or short?"

"Average, I should say."

"Are you trying to irritate me?"

"No. He's just ordinary. There's nothing in him to attract your attention. He's neither plain nor good-looking. He looks quite decent. He looks a gentleman."

"Margery says he has a charming smile and a lovely figure."

"I daresay."

"He's absolutely crazy about her."

"What makes you think that?" I asked dryly.

"I've seen his letters."

"Do you mean to say she's shown them to you?"

"Why, of course."

It is always difficult for a man to stomach the want of reticence that women betray in their private affairs. They have no shame. They will talk to one another without embarrassment of the most intimate matters. Modesty is a masculine virtue. But though a man may know this theoretically, each time he is confronted with women's lack of reserve he suffers a new shock. I wondered what Morton would think if he knew that not only were his letters read by Janet Marsh as well as by Margery, but that she had been kept posted from day to day with the progress of his infatuation. According to Janet he had fallen in love with Margery at first sight. The morning after they had met at my little supper party at Ciro's he had rung up and asked her to come and have tea with him at some place where they could dance. While I listened to Janet's story I was conscious of course that she was giving me Margery's view of the circumstances, and I kept an open mind. I was interested to observe that Janet's sympathies were with Margery. It was true that when Margery left her husband it was her idea that Charlie should come to them for two or three weeks rather than stay on in miserable loneliness in the deserted flat, and she had been extraordinarily kind to him. She lunched with him almost every day, because he had been accustomed to lunch every day with Margery; she took him for walks in Regent's Park and made Bill play golf with him on Sundays. She listened with wonderful patience to the story of his unhappiness and did what she could to console him. She was terribly sorry for him. But all the same she was definitely on Margery's side, and when I expressed my disapproval of her she came down on me like a thousand of bricks. The affair thrilled her. She had been in it from the beginning, when Margery, smiling, flattered and a little doubtful, came and told her that she had a young man, to the final scene when Margery, exasperated and distraught, announced that she could not stand the strain any more and had packed her things and moved out of the flat.

"Of course, at first I couldn't believe my ears," she said. "You know how Charlie and Margery were. They simply lived in one another's pockets. One couldn't help laughing at them, they were so devoted to one another. I never thought him a very nice little man, and heavens knows he wasn't very attractive physically, but one couldn't help liking him because he was so awfully nice to Margery. I rather envied her sometimes. They had no money and they lived in a hugger-mugger sort of way, but they were frightfully happy. Of course I never thought anything would come of it. Margery was rather amused. 'Naturally I don't take it very seriously,' she told me, 'but it is rather fun to have a young man at my time of life. I haven't had any flowers sent me for years. I had to tell him not to send any more because Charlie would think it so silly. He doesn't know a soul in London and he loves dancing and he says I dance like a dream. It's miserable for him going to the theatre by himself all the time, and we've done two or three matinees together. It's pathetic to see how grateful he is when I say I'll go out with him.' 'I must say,' I said, 'he sounds rather a lamb.' 'He is,' she said. 'I knew you'd understand. You don't blame me, do you?' 'Of course not, darling,' I said, 'surely you know me better than that. I'd do just the same in your place.'"

Margery made no secret of her outings with Morton, and her husband chaffed her good-naturedly about her beau. But he thought him a very civil, pleasant-spoken young man and was glad that Margery had someone to play with while he was busy. It never occurred to him to be jealous. The three of them dined together several times and went to a show. But presently Gerry Morton begged Margery to spend an evening with him alone; she said it was impossible, but he was persuasive, he gave her no peace; and at last she went to Janet and asked her to ring up Charlie one day and ask him to come to dinner and make a fourth at bridge. Charlie would never go anywhere without his wife, but the Marshes were old friends, and Janet made a point of it. She invented some cock-and-bull story that made it seem important that he should consent. Next day Margery and she met. The evening had been wonderful. They had dined at Maidenhead and danced there and then had driven home through the summer night.

"He says he's crazy about me," Margery told her.

"Did he kiss you?" asked Janet.

"Of course," Margery chuckled. "Don't be silly, Janet. He is awfully sweet and, you know, he has such a nice nature. Of course I don't believe half the things he says to me."

"My dear, you're not going to fall in love with him."

"I have," said Margery.

"Darling, isn't it going to be rather awkward?"

"Oh, it won't last. After all, he's going back to Borneo in the autumn."

"Well, one can't deny that it's made you look years younger."

"I know, and I feel years younger."

Soon they were meeting every day. They met in the morning and walked in the park together or went to a picture gallery. They separated for Margery to lunch with her husband and after lunch met again and motored into the country or to some place on the river. Margery did not tell her husband. She very naturally thought he would not understand.

"How was it you never met Morton?" I asked Janet.

"Oh, she didn't want me to. You see, we belong to the same generation, Margery and I. I quite understand that."

"I see."

"Of course I did everything I could. When she went out with Gerry she was always supposed to be with me."

I am a person who likes to cross a t and dot an i.

"Were they having an affair?" I asked.

"Oh, no. Margery isn't that sort of woman at all."

"How do you know?"

"She would have told me."

"I suppose she would."

"Of course I asked her. But she denied it point-blank and I'm sure she was telling me the truth. There's never been anything of that sort between them at all."

VIRTUE

"It seems rather odd to me."

"Well, you see, Margery is a very good woman."

I shrugged my shoulders.

"She was absolutely loyal to Charlie. She wouldn't have deceived him for anything in the world. She couldn't bear the thought of having any secret from him. As soon as she knew she was in love with Gerry she wanted to tell Charlie. Of course I begged her not to. I told her it wouldn't do any good and it would only make Charlie miserable. And after all, the boy was going away in a couple of months; it didn't seem much good to make a lot of fuss about a thing that couldn't possibly last."

But Gerry's imminent departure was the cause of the crash. The Bishops had arranged to go abroad as usual and proposed to motor through Belgium, Holland and the north of Germany. Charlie was busy with maps and guides. He collected information from friends about hotels and roads. He looked forward to his holiday with the bubbling excitement of a schoolboy. Margery listened to him discussing it with a sinking heart. They were to be away four weeks, and in September Gerry was sailing. She could not bear to lose so much of the short time that remained to them, and the thought of the motor tour filled her with exasperation. As the interval grew shorter and shorter she grew more and more nervous. At last she decided that there was only one thing to do.

"Charlie, I don't want to come on this trip," she interrupted him suddenly, one day when he was talking to her of some restaurant he had just heard of. "I wish you'd get someone else to go with you."

He looked at her blankly. She was startled at what she had said, and her lips trembled a little.

"Why, what's the matter?"

"Nothing's the matter. I don't feel like it. I want to be by myself for a bit."

"Are you ill?"

She saw the sudden fear in his eyes. His concern drove her beyond her endurance.

"No. I've never been better in my life. I'm in love."

"You? Who with?"

"Gerry."

He looked at her in amazement. He could not believe his ears. She mistook his expression.

"It's no good blaming me. I can't help it. He's going away in a few weeks. I'm not going to waste the little time he has left."

He burst out laughing.

"Margery, how can you make such a damned fool of yourself? You're old enough to be his mother."

She flushed.

"He's just as much in love with me as I am with him."

"Has he told you so?"

"A thousand times."

"He's a bloody liar, that's all."

He chuckled. His fat stomach rippled with mirth. He thought it a huge joke. I daresay Charlie did not treat his wife in the proper way. Janet seemed to think he should have been tender and compassionate. *He should have understood.* I saw the scene that was in her mind's eye, the stiff upper lip, the silent sorrow, and the final renunciation. Women are always sensitive to the beauty of the self-sacrifice of others. Janet would have sympathized also if he had flown into a violent passion, broken one or two pieces of furniture (which he would have had to replace), or given Margery a sock in the jaw. But to laugh at her was unpardonable. I did not point out that it is very difficult for a rather stout and not very tall professor of pathology, aged fifty-five, to act all of a sudden like a caveman. Anyhow, the excursion to Holland was given up and the Bishops stayed in London through August. They were not very happy. They lunched and dined together every day because they had been in the habit of doing so for so many years, and the rest of the time Margery spent with Gerry. The hours she passed with him made up for all she had to put up with, and she had to put up with a good deal. Charlie had a ribald and sarcastic humour and he made himself very funny at her expense and at Gerry's. He persisted in refusing to take the matter seriously. He was vexed with Margery for being so silly, but apparently it never occurred to him that she might have been unfaithful to him. I commented upon this to Janet.

"He never suspected it even," she said. "He knew Margery much too well."

The weeks passed and at last Gerry sailed. He went from Tilbury and Margery saw him off. When she came back she cried for

forty-eight hours. Charlie watched her with increasing exasperation. His nerves were much frayed.

"Look here, Margery," he said at last, "I've been very patient
with you, but now you must pull yourself together. This is getting
past a joke."

"Why can't you leave me alone?" she cried. "I've lost everything
that made life lovely to me."

"Don't be such a fool," he said.

I do not know what else he said. But he was unwise enough to
tell her what he thought of Gerry, and I gather that the picture
he drew was virulent. It started the first violent scene they had
ever had. She had borne Charlie's jibes when she knew that she
would see Gerry in an hour or next day, but now that she had lost
him for ever she could bear them no longer. She had held herself in for weeks: now she flung her self-control to the winds. Perhaps she never knew exactly what she said to Charlie. He had
always been irascible, and at last he hit her. They were both
frightened when he had. He seized a hat and flung out of the
flat. During all that miserable time they had shared the same bed,
but when he came back, in the middle of the night, he found that
she had made herself up a shake-down on the sofa in the sitting-
room.

"You can't sleep there," he said. "Don't be so silly. Come to bed."

"No, I won't, let me alone."

For the rest of the night they wrangled, but she had her way
and now made up her bed every night on the sofa. But in that
tiny flat they could not get away from one another; they could
not even get out of sight or out of hearing of one another. They
had lived in such intimacy for so many years that it was an instinct
for them to be together. He tried to reason with her. He thought
her incredibly stupid and argued with her interminably in the
effort to show her how wrong-headed she was. He could not leave
her alone. He would not let her sleep, and he talked half through
the night till they were both exhausted. He thought he could
talk her out of love. For two or three days at a time they would
not speak to one another. Then one day, coming home, he found
her crying bitterly; the sight of her tears distracted him; he told
her how much he loved her and sought to move her by the recollection of all the happy years they had spent together. He wanted
to let bygones be bygones. He promised never to refer to Gerry

again. Could they not forget the nightmare they had been through? But the thought of all that a reconciliation implied revolted her. She told him she had a racking headache and asked him to give her a sleeping draught. She pretended to be still asleep when he went out next morning, but the moment he was gone she packed up her things and left. She had a few trinkets that she had inherited, and by selling them she got a little money. She took a room at a cheap boarding-house and kept her address a secret from Charlie.

It was when he found she had left him that he went all to pieces. The shock of her flight broke him. He told Janet that his loneliness was intolerable. He wrote to Margery imploring her to come back, and asked Janet to intercede for him; he was willing to promise anything; he abased himself. Margery was obdurate.

"Do you think she'll ever go back?" I asked Janet.

"She says not."

I had to leave then, for it was nearly half-past one and I was bound for the other end of London.

Two or three days later I got a telephone message from Margery asking if I could see her. She suggested coming to my rooms. I asked her to tea. I tried to be nice to her; her affairs were no business of mine, but in my heart I thought her a very silly woman and I daresay my manner was cold. She had never been handsome and the passing years had changed her little. She had still those fine dark eyes and her face was astonishingly unlined. She was very simply dressed, and if she wore make-up it was so cunningly put on that I did not perceive it. She had still the charm she had always had of perfect naturalness and of a kindly humour.

"I want you to do something for me if you will," she began without beating about the bush.

"What is it?"

"Charlie is leaving the Marshes to-day and going back to the flat. I'm afraid his first few days there will be rather difficult; it would be awfully nice of you if you'd ask him to dinner or something."

"I'll have a look at my book."

"I'm told he's been drinking heavily. It's such a pity. I wish you could give him a hint."

"I understand he's had some domestic worries of late," I said perhaps acidly.

Margery flushed. She gave me a pained look. She winced as though I had struck her.

"Of course you've known him ever so much longer than you've known me. It's natural that you should take his part."

"My dear, to tell you the truth I've known him all these years chiefly on your account. I have never very much liked him, but I thought you were awfully nice."

She smiled at me and her smile was very sweet. She knew that I meant what I said.

"Do you think I was a good wife to him?"

"Perfect."

"He used to put people's backs up. A lot of people didn't like him, but I never found him difficult."

"He was awfully fond of you."

"I know. We had a wonderful time together. For sixteen years we were perfectly happy." She paused and looked down. "I had to leave him. It became quite impossible. That cat-and-dog life we were leading was too awful."

"I never see why two persons should go on living together if they don't want to."

"You see, it was awful for us. We'd always lived in such close intimacy. We could never get away from one another. At the end I hated the sight of him."

"I don't suppose the situation was easy for either of you."

"It wasn't my fault that I fell in love. You see, it was quite a different love from the one I'd felt for Charlie. There was always something maternal in that and protective. I was so much more reasonable than he was. He was unmanageable, but I could always manage him. Gerry was different." Her voice grew soft and her face was transfigured with glory. "He gave me back my youth. I was a girl to him and I could depend on his strength and be safe in his care."

"He seemed to me a very nice lad," I said slowly. "I imagine he'll do well. He was very young for the job he had when I ran across him. He's only twenty-nine now, isn't he?"

She smiled softly. She knew quite well what I meant.

"I never made any secret of my age to him. He says it doesn't matter."

I knew this was true. She was not the woman to have lied about her age. She had found a sort of fierce delight in telling him the truth about herself.

"How old are you?"

"Forty-four."

"What are you going to do now?"

"I've written to Gerry and told him I've left Charlie. As soon as I hear from him I'm going out to join him."

I was staggered.

"You know, it's a very primitive little colony he's living in. I'm afraid you'll find your position rather awkward."

"He made me promise that if I found my life impossible after he left I'd go to him."

"Are you sure you're wise to attach so much importance to the things a young man says when he's in love?"

Again that really beautiful look of exaltation came into her face.

"Yes, when the young man happens to be Gerry."

My heart sank. I was silent for a moment. Then I told her the story of the road Gerry Morton had built. I dramatized it, and I think I made it rather effective.

"What did you tell me that for?" she asked when I finished.

"I thought it rather a good story."

She shook her head and smiled.

"No, you wanted to show me that he was very young and enthusiastic, and so keen on his work that he hadn't much time to waste on other interests. I wouldn't interfere with his work. You don't know him as I do. He's incredibly romantic. He looks upon himself as a pioneer. I've caught from him something of his excitement at the idea of taking part in the opening up of a new country. It *is* rather splendid, isn't it? It makes life here seem very humdrum and commonplace. But of course it's very lonely there. Even the companionship of a middle-aged woman may be worth having."

"Are you proposing to marry him?" I asked.

"I leave myself in his hands. I want to do nothing that he does not wish."

She spoke with so much simplicity, there was something so touching in her self-surrender, that when she left me I no longer felt angry with her. Of course I thought her very foolish, but if the folly of men made one angry one would pass one's life in a state of chronic ire. I thought all would come right. She said Gerry was romantic. He was, but the romantics in this workaday world only get away with their nonsense because they have at bottom a shrewd sense of reality: the mugs are the people who take their vapourings at their face value. The English are romantic; that is why other nations think them hypocritical; they are not: they set out in all sincerity for the Kingdom of God, but the journey is arduous and they have reason to pick up any gilt-edged investment that offers itself by the way. The British soul, like Wellington's armies, marches on its belly. I supposed that Gerry would go through a bad quarter of an hour when he received Margery's letter. My sympathies were not deeply engaged in the matter and I was only curious to see how he would extricate himself from the pass he was in. I thought Margery would suffer a bitter disappointment—well, that would do her no great harm, and then she would go back to her husband and I had no doubt the pair of them, chastened, would live in peace, quiet and happiness for the rest of their lives.

The event was different. It happened that it was quite impossible for me to make any sort of engagement with Charlie Bishop for some days, but I wrote to him and asked him to dine with me one evening in the following week. I proposed, though with misgiving, that we should go to a play; I knew he was drinking like a fish, and when tight he was noisy. I hoped he would not make a nuisance of himself in the theatre. We arranged to meet at our club and dine at seven because the piece we were going to began at a quarter past eight. I arrived. I waited. He did not come. I rang up his flat, but could get no reply, so concluded that he was on his way. I hate missing the beginning of a play and I waited impatiently in the hall so that when he came we could go straight upstairs. To save time I had ordered dinner. The clock pointed to half-past seven, then a quarter to eight; I did not see why I should wait for him any longer, so walked up to the dining-room and ate my dinner alone. He did not appear. I put a call through from the dining-room to the Marshes and presently was told by a waiter that Bill Marsh was at the end of the wire.

"I say, do you know anything about Charlie Bishop?" I said. "We were dining together and going to a play and he hasn't turned up."

"He died this afternoon."

"What?"

My exclamation was so startled that two or three people within earshot looked up. The dining-room was full and the waiters were hurrying to and fro. The telephone was on the cashier's desk, and a wine waiter came up with a bottle of hock and two long-stemmed glasses on a tray and gave the cashier a chit. The portly steward showing two men to a table jostled me.

"Where are you speaking from?" asked Bill.

I suppose he heard the clatter that surrounded me. When I told him he asked me if I could come round as soon as I had finished my dinner. Janet wanted to speak to me.

"I'll come at once," I said.

I found Janet and Bill sitting in the drawing-room. He was reading the paper and she was playing patience. She came forward swiftly when the maid showed me in. She walked with a sort of spring, crouching a little, on silent feet, like a panther stalking his prey. I saw at once that she was in her element. She gave me her hand and turned her face away to hide her eyes brimming with tears. Her voice was low and tragic.

"I brought Margery here and put her to bed. The doctor has given her a sedative. She's all in. Isn't it awful?" She gave a sound that was something between a gasp and a sob. "I don't know why these things always happen to me."

The Bishops had never kept a servant, but a charwoman went in every morning, cleaned the flat and washed up the breakfast things. She had her own key. That morning she had gone in as usual and done the sitting-room. Since his wife had left him Charlie's hours had been irregular and she was not surprised to find him asleep. But the time passed and she knew he had his work to go to. She went to the bedroom door and knocked. There was no answer. She thought she heard him groaning. She opened the door softly. He was lying in bed, on his back, and was breathing stertorously. He did not wake. She called him. Something about him frightened her. She went to the flat on the same landing. It was occupied by a journalist. He was still in bed when she rang, and opened the door to her in pajamas.

"Beg pardon, sir," she said, "but would you just come and 'ave a look at my gentleman? I don't think he's well."

The journalist walked across the landing and into Charlie's flat. There was an empty bottle of veronal by the bed.

"I think you'd better fetch a policeman," he said.

A policeman came and rang through to the police station for an ambulance. They took Charlie to Charing Cross Hospital. He never recovered consciousness. Margery was with him at the end.

"Of course there'll have to be an inquest," said Janet. "But it's quite obvious what happened. He'd been sleeping awfully badly for the last three or four weeks and I suppose he'd been taking veronal. He must have taken an overdose by accident."

"Is that what Margery thinks?" I asked.

"She's too upset to think anything, but I told her I was positive he hadn't committed suicide. I mean, he wasn't that sort of a man. Am I right, Bill?"

"Yes, dear," he answered.

"Did he leave any letter?"

"No, nothing. Oddly enough Margery got a letter from him this morning—well, hardly a letter, just a line. 'I'm so lonely without you, darling.' That's all. But of course that means nothing and she's promised to say nothing about it at the inquest. I mean, what is the use of putting ideas in people's heads? Everyone knows that you never can tell with veronal—I wouldn't take it myself for anything in the world—and it was quite obviously an accident. Am I right, Bill?"

"Yes, dear," he answered.

I saw that Janet was quite determined to believe that Charlie Bishop had not committed suicide, but how far in her heart she believed what she wanted to believe I was not sufficiently expert in female psychology to know. And of course it might be that she was right. It is unreasonable to suppose that a middle-aged scientist should kill himself because his middle-aged wife leaves him, and it is extremely plausible that, exasperated by sleeplessness, and in all probability far from sober, he took a larger dose of the sleeping draught than he realized. Anyhow that was the view the coroner took of the matter. It was indicated to him that of late Charles Bishop had given way to habits of intemperance which had caused his wife to leave him, and it was quite obvious that nothing was further from his thoughts than to put an end to himself. The coroner expressed his sympathy with the widow and commented very strongly on the dangers of sleeping draughts.

I hate funerals, but Janet begged me to go to Charlie's. Several of his colleagues at the hospital had intimated their desire to

come, but at Margery's wish they were dissuaded; and Janet and
Bill, Margery and I were the only persons who attended it. We
were to fetch the hearse from the mortuary, and they offered to
call for me on their way. I was on the lookout for the car, and
when I saw it drive up went downstairs, but Bill got out and met
me just inside the door.

"Half a minute," he said. "I've got something to say to you.
Janet wants you to come back afterwards and have tea. She says
it's no good Margery moping and after tea we'll play a few rubbers of bridge. Can you come?"

"Like this?" I asked.

I had a tail coat on and a black tie and my evening dress
trousers.

"Oh, that's all right. It'll take Margery's mind off."

"Very well."

But we did not play bridge after all. Janet, with her fair hair,
was very smart in her deep mourning and she played the part of
the sympathetic friend with amazing skill. She cried a little, wiping her eyes delicately so as not to disturb the black on her eyelashes, and, when Margery sobbed broken-heartedly, put her arm
tenderly through hers. She was a very present help in trouble.
We returned to the house. There was a telegram for Margery.
She took it and went upstairs. I presumed it was a message of
condolence from one of Charlie's friends who had just heard of his
death. Bill went to change and Janet and I went up to the drawing-room and got the bridge table out. She took off her hat and
put it on the piano.

"It's no good being hypocritical," she said. "Of course Margery
has been frightfully upset, but she must pull herself together now.
A rubber of bridge will help her to get back to her normal
state. Naturally I'm dreadfully sorry about poor Charlie, but as
far as he was concerned I don't believe he'd ever have got over
Margery's leaving him, and one can't deny that it has made
things much easier for her. She wired to Gerry this morning."

"What about?"

"To tell him about poor Charlie."

At that moment the maid came to the room.

"Will you go up to Mrs. Bishop, please, ma'am. She wants to see
you."

"Yes, of course."

She went out of the room quickly and I was left alone. Bill joined me presently and we had a drink. At last Janet came back. She handed a telegram to me. It read as follows:

FOR GOD'S SAKE AWAIT LETTER. GERRY.

"What do you think it means?" she asked me.

"What it says," I replied.

"Idiot! Of course I've told Margery that it doesn't mean anything, but she's rather worried. It must have crossed her cable telling him that Charles was dead. I don't think she feels very much like bridge after all. I mean, it would be rather bad form to play on the very day her husband has been buried."

"Quite," I said.

"Of course he may wire in answer to the cable. He's sure to do that, isn't he? The only thing we can do now is to sit tight and wait for his letter."

I saw no object in continuing the conversation. I left. In a couple of days Janet rang me up to tell me that Margery had recieved a telegram of condolence from Morton. She repeated it to me:

DREADFULLY DISTRESSED TO HEAR SAD NEWS. DEEPLY SYMPATHIZE WITH YOUR GREAT GRIEF. LOVE. GERRY.

"What do you think of it?" she asked me.

"I think it's very proper."

"Of course he couldn't say he was as pleased as Punch, could he?"

"Not with any delicacy."

"And he did put in *love*."

I imagined how those women had examined the two telegrams from every point of view and scrutinized every word to press from it every possible shade of meaning. I almost heard their interminable conversations.

"I don't know what'll happen to Margery if he lets her down now," Janet went on. "Of course it remains to be seen if he's a gentleman."

"Rot," I said and rang off quickly.

In the course of the following days I dined with the Marshes a couple of times. Margery looked tired. I guess that she awaited the letter that was on the way with sickening anxiety. Grief and fear had worn her to a shadow; she seemed very fragile now, and she had acquired a spiritual look that I had never seen in her before. She was very gentle, very grateful for every kindness shown her, and in her smile, unsure and a little timid, was an infinite pathos. Her helplessness was very appealing. But Morton was several thousand miles away. Then one morning Janet rang me up.

"The letter has come. Margery says I can show it to you. Will you come round?"

Her tense voice told me everything. When I arrived Janet gave it to me. I read it. It was a very careful letter and I guessed that Morton had written it a good many times. It was very kind and he had evidently taken great pains to avoid saying anything that could possibly wound Margery; but what transpired was his terror. It was obvious that he was shaking in his shoes. He had felt apparently that the best way to cope with the situation was to be mildly facetious, and he made very good fun of the white people in the colony. What would they say if Margery suddenly turned up? He would be given the order of the boot pretty damn quick. People thought the East was free and easy; it wasn't, it was more suburban than Clapham. He loved Margery far too much to bear the thought of those horrible women out there turning up their noses at her. And besides he had been sent to a station ten days from anywhere; she couldn't live in his bungalow exactly, and of course there wasn't a hotel, and his work took him out into the jungle for days at a time. It was no place for a woman anyhow. He told her how much she meant to him, but she mustn't bother about him and he couldn't help thinking it would be better if she went back to her husband. He would never forgive himself if he thought he had come between her and Charlie. Yes, I am quite sure it had been a difficult letter to write.

"Of course he didn't know then that Charlie was dead. I've told Margery that changes everything."

"Does she agree with you?"

"I think she's being rather unreasonable. What do you make of the letter?"

"Well, it's quite plain that he doesn't want her."

"He wanted her badly enough two months ago."

"It's astonishing what a change of air and a change of scene will do for you. It must seem to him already like a year since he left London. He's back among his old friends and his old interests. My

VIRTUE

dear, it's no good Margery kidding herself, the life there has taken him back and there's no place for her."

"I've advised her to ignore the letter and go straight out to him."

"I hope she's too sensible to expose herself to a very terrible rebuff."

"But then what's to happen to her? Oh, it's too cruel. She's the best woman in the world. She has real goodness."

"It's funny, if you come to think of it, it's her goodness that has caused all the trouble. Why on earth didn't she have an affair with Morton? Charlie would have known nothing about it and wouldn't have been a penny the worse. She and Morton could have had a grand time and when he went away they could have parted with the consciousness that a pleasant episode had come to a graceful end. It would have been a jolly recollection, and she could have gone back to Charlie satisfied and rested and continued to make him the excellent wife she had always been."

Janet pursed her lips. She gave me a look of disdain.

"There is such a thing as virtue, you know."

"Virtue be damned. A virtue that only causes havoc and unhappiness is worth nothing. You can call it virtue if you like. I call it cowardice."

"The thought of being unfaithful to Charlie while she was living with him revolted her. There are women like that, you know."

"Good gracious, she could have remained faithful to him in spirit while she was being unfaithful to him in the flesh. That is a feat of legerdemain that women find it easy to accomplish."

"What an odious cynic you are."

"If it's cynical to look truth in the face and exercise common-sense in the affairs of life, then certainly I'm a cynic and odious, if you like. Let's face it: Margery's a middle-aged woman, Charlie was fifty-five and they'd been married for sixteen years. It was natural enough that she should lose her head over a young man who made a fuss of her. But don't call it love. It was physiology. She was a fool to take anything he said seriously. It wasn't himself speaking, it was his starved sex; he'd suffered from sexual starvation, at least as far as white women are concerned, for four years; it's monstrous that she should seek to ruin his life by holding him to the wild promises he made then. It was an accident that Margery took his fancy; he wanted her, and because he couldn't get her wanted her more. I daresay he thought it love; believe me, it was only letch. If they'd gone to bed together Charlie would be alive to-day. It's her damned virtue that caused the whole trouble."

"How stupid you are. Don't you see that she couldn't help herself? She just doesn't happen to be a loose woman."

"I prefer a loose woman to a selfish one and a wanton to a fool."

"Oh, shut up. I didn't ask you to come here in order to make yourself absolutely beastly."

"What did you ask me to come here for?"

"Gerry is your friend. You introduced him to Margery. If she's in the soup it's on his account. But *you* are the cause of the whole trouble. It's your duty to write to him and tell him he must do the right thing by her."

"I'm damned if I will," I said.

"Then you'd better go."

I started to do so.

"Well, at all events it's a mercy that Charlie's life was insured," said Janet.

Then I turned on her.

"And you have the nerve to call me a cynic."

I will not repeat the opprobrious word I flung at her as I slammed the door behind me. But Janet is all the same a very nice woman. I often think it would be great fun to be married to her.

Cakes and Ale

CHAPTER I

I have noticed that when someone asks for you on the telephone and, finding you out, leaves a message begging you to call him up the moment you come in, and it's important, the matter is more often important to him than to you. When it comes to making you a present or doing you a favour most people are able to hold their impatience within reasonable bounds. So when I got back to my lodgings with just enough time to have a drink, a cigarette, and to read my paper before dressing for dinner, and was told by Miss Fellows, my landlady, that Mr. Alroy Kear wished me to ring him up at once, I felt that I could safely ignore his request.

"Is that the writer?" she asked me.

"It is."

She gave the telephone a friendly glance.

"Shall I get him?"

"No, thank you."

"What shall I say if he rings again?"

"Ask him to leave a message."

"Very good, sir."

She pursed her lips. She took the empty siphon, swept the room with a look to see that it was tidy, and went out. Miss Fellows was a great novel reader. I was sure that she had read all Roy's books. Her disapproval of my casualness suggested that she had read them with admiration. When I got home again, I found a note in her bold, legible writing on the sideboard.

Mr. Kear rang up twice. Can you lunch with him to-morrow? If not what day will suit you?

I raised my eyebrows. I had not seen Roy for three months and then only for a few minutes at a party; he had been very friendly, he always was, and when we separated he had expressed his hearty regret that we met so seldom.

"London's awful," he said. "One never has time to see any of the people one wants to. Let's lunch together one day next week, shall we?"

"I'd like to," I replied.

"I'll look at my book when I get home and ring you up."

"All right."

I had not known Roy for twenty years without learning that he always kept in the upper left-hand pocket of his waistcoat the little book in which he put down his engagements; I was therefore not surprised when I heard from him no further. It was impossible for me now to persuade myself that this urgent desire of his to dispense hospitality was disinterested. As I smoked a pipe before going to bed I turned over in my mind the possible reasons for which Roy might want me to lunch with him. It might be that an admirer of his had pestered him to introduce me to her or that an American editor, in London for a few days, had desired Roy to put me in touch with him; but I could not do my old friend the injustice of supposing him so barren of devices as not to be able to cope with such a situation. Besides, he told me to choose my own day, so it could hardly be that he wished me to meet anyone else.

Than Roy no one could show a more genuine cordiality to a fellow novelist whose name was on everybody's lips, but no one could more genially turn a cold shoulder on him when idleness, failure, or someone else's success had cast a shade on his notoriety. The writer has his ups and downs, and I was but too conscious that at the moment I was not in the public eye. It was obvious that I might have found excuses without affront to refuse Roy's invitation, though he was a determined fellow and if he was resolved for purposes of his own to see me, I well knew that nothing short of a downright "Go to hell" would check his persistence; but I was beset by curiosity. I had also a considerable affection for Roy.

I had watched with admiration his rise in the world of letters. His career might well have served as a model for any young man entering upon the pursuit of literature. I could think of no one among my contemporaries who had achieved so considerable a position on so little talent. This, like the wise man's daily dose of Bemax, might have gone into a heaped-up tablespoon. He was perfectly aware of it, and it must have seemed to him sometimes little short of a miracle that he had been able with it to

compose already some thirty books. I cannot but think that he saw
the white light of revelation when first he read that Thomas Carlyle in an after-dinner speech had stated that genius was an infinite capacity for taking pains. He pondered the saying. If that
was all, he must have told himself, he could be a genius like the
rest; and when the excited reviewer of a lady's paper, writing a
notice of one of his works, used the word (and of late the critics
have been doing it with agreeable frequency) he must have
sighed with the satisfaction of one who after long hours of toil has
completed a cross-word puzzle. No one who for years had observed his indefatigable industry could deny that at all events he
deserved to be a genius.

Roy started with certain advantages. He was the only son of a
civil servant who after being Colonial Secretary for many years in
Hong-Kong ended his career as Governor of Jamaica. When you
looked up Alroy Kear in the serried pages of *Who's Who* you saw
o.s. of Sir Raymond Kear, K.C.M.G., K.C.V.O. *q.v.* and of Emily,
y.d. of the late Major-General Percy Camperdown, Indian Army.
He was educated at Winchester and at New College, Oxford. He
was President of the Union and but for an unfortunate attack of
measles might very well have got his rowing blue. His academic
career was respectable rather than showy, and he left the university without a debt in the world. Roy was even then of a thrifty
habit, without any inclination to unprofitable expense, and he was
a good son. He knew that it had been a sacrifice to his parents to
give him so costly an education. His father, having retired, lived
in an unpretentious, but not mean, house near Stroud in Glouces-
tershire, but at intervals went to London to attend official dinners
connected with the colonies he had administered, and on these
occasions was in the habit of visiting the Athenæum, of which he
was a member. It was through an old crony at this club that he
was able to get his boy, when he came down from Oxford, appointed tutor to the delicate and only son of a very noble lord.
This gave Roy a chance to become acquainted at an early age
with the great world. He made good use of his opportunities. You
will never find in his works any of the solecisms that disfigure
the productions of those who have studied the upper circles of
society only in the pages of the illustrated papers. He knew
exactly how dukes spoke to one another, and the proper way they
should be addressed respectively by a member of Parliament, an

attorney, a bookmaker and a valet. There is something captivating in the jauntiness with which in his early novels he handles viceroys, ambassadors, prime ministers, royalties and great ladies. He is friendly without being patronising and familiar without being impertinent. He does not let you forget their rank, but shares with you his comfortable feeling that they are of the same flesh as you and I. I always think it a pity that, fashion having decided that the doings of the aristocracy are no longer a proper subject for serious fiction, Roy, always keenly sensitive to the tendency of the age, should in his later novels have confined himself to the spiritual conflicts of solicitors, chartered accountants and produce brokers. He does not move in these circles with his old assurance.

I knew him first soon after he resigned his tutorship to devote himself exclusively to literature, and he was then a fine, upstanding young man, six feet high in his stockinged feet and of an athletic build, with broad shoulders and a confident carriage. He was not handsome, but in a manly way agreeable to look at, with wide blue frank eyes and curly hair of a lightish brown; his nose was rather short and broad, his chin square. He looked honest, clean, and healthy. He was something of an athlete. No one who has read in his early books the descriptions of a run with the hounds, so vivid and so accurate, can doubt that he wrote from personal experience; and until quite lately he was willing now and then to desert his desk for a day's hunting. He published his first novel at the period when men of letters, to show their virility, drank beer and played cricket, and for some years there was seldom a literary eleven in which his name did not figure. This particular school, I hardly know why, has lost its bravery, their books are neglected and, cricketers though they have remained, they find difficulty in placing their articles. Roy ceased playing cricket a good many years ago and he has developed a fine taste for claret.

Roy was very modest about his first novel. It was short, neatly written, and, as is everything he has produced since, in perfect taste. He sent it with a pleasant letter to all the leading writers of the day, and in this he told each one how greatly he admired his works, how much he had learned from his study of them, and how ardently he aspired to follow, albeit at a humble distance, the trail his correspondent had blazed. He laid his book at the feet of a great artist as the tribute of a young man entering upon the profession of letters to one whom he would always look up to as his master. Deprecatingly, fully conscious of his audacity in asking so busy a man to waste his time on a neophyte's puny effort, he begged for criticism and guidance. Few of the replies were perfunctory. The authors he wrote to, flattered by his praise, answered at length. They commended his book; many of them asked him to luncheon. They could not fail to be charmed by his frankness and warmed by his enthusiasm. He asked for their advice with a humility that was touching and promised to act upon it with a sincerity that was impressive. Here, they felt, was someone worth taking a little trouble over.

His novel had a considerable success. It made him many friends in literary circles and in a very short while you could not go to a tea-party in Bloomsbury, Campden Hill, or Westminster without finding him handing round bread and butter or disembarrassing an elderly lady of an empty cup. He was so young, so bluff, so gay, he laughed so merrily at other people's jokes that no one could help liking him. He joined dining clubs where in the basement of a hotel in Victoria Street or Holborn men of letters, young barristers and ladies in Liberty silks and strings of beads ate a three-and-sixpenny dinner and discussed art and literature. It was soon discovered that he had a pretty gift for after-dinner speaking. He was so pleasant that his fellow writers, his rivals and contemporaries, forgave him even the fact that he was a gentleman. He was generous in his praise of their fledgeling works, and when they sent him manuscripts to criticise could never find a thing amiss. They thought him not only a good sort, but a sound judge.

He wrote a second novel. He took great pains with it and he profited by the advice his elders in the craft had given him. It was only just that more than one should at his request write a review for a paper with whose editor Roy had got into touch and only natural that the review should be flattering. His second novel was successful, but not so successful as to arouse the umbrageous susceptibilities of his competitors. In fact it confirmed them in their suspicions that he would never set the Thames on fire. He was a jolly good fellow, no side, or anything like that: they were quite content to give a leg up to a man who would never climb so

high as to be an obstacle to themselves. I know some who smile
bitterly now when they reflect on the mistake they made.

But when they say that he is swollen-headed they err. Roy has
never lost the modesty which in his youth was his most engaging
trait.

"I know I'm not a great novelist," he will tell you. "When I
compare myself with the giants I simply don't exist. I used to think
that one day I should write a really great novel, but I've long
ceased even to hope for that. All I want people to say is that I do
my best. I do work. I never let anything slipshod get past me. I
think I can tell a good story and I can create characters that ring
true. And, after all, the proof of the pudding is in the eating: *The
Eye of the Needle* sold thirty-five thousand in England and eighty
thousand in America, and for the serial rights of my next book
I've got the biggest terms I've ever had yet."

And what, after all, can it be other than modesty that makes
him even now write to the reviewers of his books, thanking them
for their praise, and ask them to luncheon? Nay, more: when someone has written a stinging criticism and Roy, especially since his
reputation became so great, has had to put up with some very
virulent abuse, he does not, like most of us, shrug his shoulders,
fling a mental insult at the ruffian who does not like our work, and
then forget about it; he writes a long letter to his critic, telling him
that he is very sorry he thought his book bad, but his review was
so interesting in itself and, if he might venture to say so, showed
so much critical sense and so much feeling for words, that he felt
bound to write to him. No one is more anxious to improve himself
than he, and he hopes he is still capable of learning. He does not
want to be a bore, but if the critic has nothing to do on Wednes-
day or Friday will he come and lunch at the Savoy and tell him
why exactly he thought his book so bad? No one can order a lunch
better than Roy, and generally by the time the critic has eaten
half a dozen oysters and a cut from a saddle of baby lamb, he has
eaten his words too. It is only poetic justice that when Roy's next
novel comes out the critic should see in the new work a very great
advance.

One of the difficulties that a man has to cope with as he goes
through life is what to do about the persons with whom he has
once been intimate and whose interest for him has in due course
subsided. If both parties remain in a modest station the break

comes about naturally, and no ill-feeling subsists, but if one of them achieves eminence the position is awkward. He makes a multitude of new friends, but the old ones are inexorable; he has a thousand claims on his time, but they feel that they have the first right to it. Unless he is at their beck and call they sigh and with a shrug of the shoulders say:

"Ah, well, I suppose you're like everyone else. I must expect to be dropped now that you're a success."

That of course is what he would like to do if he had the courage. For the most part he hasn't. He weakly accepts an invitation to supper on Sunday evening. The cold roast beef is frozen and comes from Australia and was over-cooked at middle day; and the burgundy—ah, why will they call it burgundy? Have they never been to Beaune and stayed at the Hôtel de la Poste? Of course it is grand to talk of the good old days when you shared a crust of bread in a garret together, but it is a little disconcerting when you reflect how near to a garret is the room you are sitting in. You feel ill at ease when your friend tells you that his books don't sell and that he can't place his short stories; the managers won't even read his plays, and when he compares them with some of the stuff that's put on (here he fixes you with an accusing eye) it really does seem a bit hard. You are embarrassed and you look away. You exaggerate the failures you have had in order that he may realise that life has its hardships for you too. You refer to your work in the most disparaging way you can and are a trifle taken aback to find that your host's opinion of it is the same as yours. You speak of the fickleness of the public so that he may comfort himself by thinking that your popularity cannot last. He is a friendly but severe critic.

"I haven't read your last book," he says, "but I read the one before. I've forgotten its name."

You tell him.

"I was rather disappointed in it. I didn't think it was quite so good as some of the things you've done. Of course you know which my favourite is."

And you, having suffered from other hands than his, answer at once with the name of the first book you ever wrote: you were twenty then, and it was crude and ingenuous, and on every page was written your inexperience.

"You'll never do anything so good as that," he says heartily, and you feel that your whole career has been a long decadence from that one happy hit. "I always think you've never *quite* fulfilled the promise you showed then."

The gas fire roasts your feet, but your hands are icy. You look at your wrist-watch surreptitiously and wonder whether your old friend would think it offensive if you took your leave as early as ten. You have told your car to wait round the corner so that it should not stand outside the door and by its magnificence affront his poverty, but at the door he says:

"You'll find a bus at the bottom of the street. I'll just walk down with you."

Panic seizes you and you confess that you have a car. He finds it very odd that the chauffeur should wait round the corner. You answer that this is one of his idiosyncrasies. When you reach it your friend looks at it with tolerant superiority. You nervously ask him to dinner with you one day. You promise to write to him and you drive away wondering whether when he comes he will think you are swanking if you ask him to Claridge's or mean if you suggest Soho.

Roy Kear suffered from none of these tribulations. It sounds a little brutal to say that when he had got all he could get of people he dropped them; but it would take so long to put the matter more delicately, and would need so subtle an adjustment of hints, half-tones and allusions, playful or tender, that, such being at bottom the fact, I think it as well to leave it at that. Most of us when we do a caddish thing harbour resentment against the person we have done it to, but Roy's heart, always in the right place, never permitted him such pettiness. He could use a man very shabbily without afterward bearing him the slightest ill-will.

"Poor old Smith," he would say. "He is a dear; I'm so fond of him. Pity he's growing so bitter. I wish one could do something for him. No, I haven't seen him for years. It's no good trying to keep up old friendships. It's painful for both sides. The fact is, one grows out of people, and the only thing is to face it."

But if he ran across Smith at some gathering like the private view of the Royal Academy no one could be more cordial. He wrung his hand and told him how delighted he was to see him. His face beamed. He shed good fellowship as the kindly sun its rays. Smith rejoiced in the glow of this wonderful vitality and it was damned decent of Roy to say he'd give his eye-teeth to have

written a book half as good as Smith's last. On the other hand, if
Roy thought Smith had not seen him, he looked the other way; but
Smith *had* seen him, and Smith resented being cut. Smith was very
acid. He said that in the old days Roy had been glad enough to
share a steak with him in a shabby restaurant and spend a
month's holiday in a fisherman's cottage at St. Ives. Smith said
that Roy was a time-server. He said he was a snob. He said he
was a humbug.

Smith was wrong here. The most shining characteristic of Alroy
Kear was his sincerity. No one can be a humbug for five-and-
twenty years. Hypocrisy is the most difficult and nerve-racking
vice that any man can pursue; it needs an unceasing vigilance and
a rare detachment of spirit. It cannot, like adultery or gluttony, be
practised at spare moments; it is a whole-time job. It needs also
a cynical humour; although Roy laughed so much, I never thought
he had a very quick sense of humour, and I am quite sure that
he was incapable of cynicism. Though I have finished few of his
novels, I have begun a good many, and to my mind his sincerity
is stamped on every one of their multitudinous pages. This is
clearly the chief ground of his stable popularity. Roy has always
sincerely believed what everyone else believed at the moment.
When he wrote novels about the aristocracy he sincerely believed
that its members were dissipated and immoral, and yet had a certain nobility and an innate aptitude for governing the British
Empire; when later he wrote of the middle classes he sincerely
believed that they were the backbone of the country. His villains
have always been villainous, his heroes heroic, and his maidens
chaste.

When Roy asked the author of a flattering review to lunch it
was because he was sincerely grateful to him for his good opinion,
and when he asked the author of an unflattering one it was because he was sincerely concerned to improve himself. When unknown admirers from Texas or Western Australia came to London
it was not only to cultivate his public that he took them to the
National Gallery, it was because he was sincerely anxious to observe their reactions to art. You had only to hear him lecture to be
convinced of his sincerity.

When he stood on the platform, in evening dress admirably
worn, or in a loose, much used but perfectly cut lounge suit if
it better fitted the occasion, and faced his audience seriously,

frankly, but with an engaging diffidence you could not but realise
that he was giving himself up to his task with complete earnest-
ness. Though now and then he pretended to be at a loss for a
word, it was only to make it more effective when he uttered it.
His voice was full and manly. He told a story well. He was never
dull. He was fond of lecturing upon the younger writers of England and America, and he explained their merits to his audience
with an enthusiasm that attested his generosity. Perhaps he told
almost too much, for when you had heard his lecture you felt that
you really knew all you wanted to about them and it was quite
unnecessary to read their books. I suppose that is why when Roy
had lectured in some provincial town not a single copy of the
books of the authors he had spoken of was ever asked for, but
there was always a run on his own. His energy was prodigious.
Not only did he make successful tours of the United States, but he
lectured up and down Great Britain. No club was so small, no
society for the self-improvement of its members so insignificant,
that Roy disdained to give it an hour of his time. Now and then
he revised his lectures and issued them in neat little books. Most
people who are interested in these things have at least looked
through the works entitled *Modern Novelists, Russian Fiction,* and
Some Writers; and few can deny that they exhibit a real feeling
for literature and a charming personality.

But this by no means exhausted his activities. He was an active
member of the organisations that have been founded to further
the interests of authors or to alleviate their hard lot when sickness
or old age has brought them to penury. He was always willing to
give his help when matters of copyright were the subject of legis-
lation and he was never unprepared to take his place in those
missions to a foreign country which are devised to establish amica-
ble relations between writers of different nationalities. He could
be counted on to reply for literature at a public dinner and he
was invariably on the reception committee formed to give a proper
welcome to a literary celebrity from overseas. No bazaar lacked
an autographed copy of at least one of his books. He never refused to grant an interview. He justly said that no one knew better than he the hardships of the author's trade and if he could help
a struggling journalist to earn a few guineas by having a pleasant
chat with him he had not the inhumanity to refuse. He generally
asked his interviewer to luncheon and seldom failed to make a

good impression on him. The only stipulation he made was that he should see the article before it was published. He was never impatient with the persons who call up the celebrated on the telephone at inconvenient moments to ask them, for the information of newspaper readers, whether they believe in God or what they eat for breakfast. He figured in every symposium and the public knew what he thought of prohibition, vegetarianism, jazz, garlic, exercise, marriage, politics and the place of women in the home.

His views on marriage were abstract, for he had successfully evaded the state which so many artists have found difficult to reconcile with the arduous pursuit of their calling. It was generally known that he had for some years cherished a hopeless passion for a married woman of rank, and though he never spoke of her but with chivalrous admiration, it was understood that she had treated him with harshness. The novels of his middle period reflected in their unwonted bitterness the strain to which he had been put. The anguish of spirit he had passed through then enabled him without offence to elude the advances of ladies of little reputation, frayed ornaments of a hectic circle, who were willing to exchange an uncertain present for the security of marriage with a successful novelist. When he saw in their bright eyes the shadow of the registry office he told them that the memory of his one great love would always prevent him from forming any permanent tie. His quixotry might exasperate, but could not affront, them. He sighed a little when he reflected that he must be for ever denied the joys of domesticity and the satisfaction of parenthood, but it was a sacrifice that he was prepared to make not only to his ideal, but also to the possible partner of his joys. He had noticed that people really do not want to be bothered with the wives of authors and painters. The artist who insisted on taking his wife wherever he went only made himself a nuisance and indeed was in consequence often not asked to places he would have liked to go to; and if he left his wife at home, he was on his return exposed to recriminations that shattered the repose so essential for him to do the best that was in him. Alroy Kear was a bachelor and now at fifty was likely to remain one.

He was an example of what an author can do, and to what heights he can rise, by industry, commonsense, honesty and the efficient combination of means and ends. He was a good fellow and none but a cross-grained carper could grudge him his success. I felt that to fall asleep with his image in my mind would insure me a good night. I scribbled a note to Miss Fellows, knocked the ashes out of my pipe, put out the light in my sitting-room and went to bed.

CHAPTER II

When I rang for my letters and the papers next morning a message was delivered to me, in answer to my note to Miss Fellows, that Mr. Alroy Kear expected me at one-fifteen at his club in St. James's Street; so a little before one I strolled round to my own and had the cocktail, which I was pretty sure Roy would not offer me. Then I walked down St. James's Street, looking idly at the shop windows, and since I had still a few minutes to spare (I did not want to keep my appointment too punctually) I went into Christie's to see if there was anything I liked the look of. The auction had already begun and a group of dark, small men were passing round to one another pieces of Victorian silver, while the auctioneer, following their gestures with bored eyes, muttered in a drone: "Ten shillings offered, eleven, eleven and six" . . . It was a fine day, early in June, and the air in King Street was bright. It made the pictures on the walls of Christie's look very dingy. I went out. The people in the street walked with a kind of nonchalance, as though the ease of the day had entered into their souls and in the midst of their affairs they had a sudden and surprised inclination to stop and look at the picture of life.

Roy's club was sedate. In the ante-chamber were only an ancient porter and a page; and I had a sudden and melancholy feeling that the members were all attending the funeral of the head-waiter. The page, when I had uttered Roy's name, led me into an empty passage to leave my hat and stick and then into an empty hall hung with life-sized portraits of Victorian statesmen. Roy got up from a leather sofa and warmly greeted me.

"Shall we go straight up?" he said.

I was right in thinking that he would not offer me a cocktail and I commended my prudence. He led me up a noble flight of heavily carpeted stairs, and we passed nobody on the way; we entered the strangers' dining-room, and we were its only occupants. It was a room of some size, very clean and white, with an Adam window. We sat down by it and a demure waiter handed us the bill of fare. Beef, mutton and lamb, cold salmon, apple tart, rhubarb tart, gooseberry tart. As my eye travelled down the inevitable list I sighed as I thought of the restaurants round the corner where there were French cooking, the clatter of life and pretty painted women in summer frocks.

"I can recommend the veal-and-ham pie," said Roy.

"All right."

"I'll mix the salad myself," he told the waiter in an off-hand and yet commanding way, and then, casting his eye once more on the bill of fare, generously: "And what about some asparagus to follow?"

"That would be very nice."

His manner grew a trifle grander.

"Asparagus for two and tell the chef to choose them himself. Now what would you like to drink? What do you say to a bottle of hock? We rather fancy our hock here."

When I had agreed to this he told the waiter to call the wine-steward. I could not but admire the authoritative and yet perfectly polite manner in which he gave his orders. You felt that thus would a well-bred king send for one of his field-marshals. The wine-steward, portly in black, with the silver chain of his office round his neck, bustled in with the wine-list in his hand. Roy nodded to him with curt familiarity.

"Hulloa, Armstrong, we want some of the Liebfraumilch, the '21."

"Very good, sir."

"How's it holding up? Pretty well? We shan't be able to get any more of it, you know."

"I'm afraid not, sir."

"Well, it's no good meeting trouble half-way, is it, Armstrong?"

Roy smiled at the steward with breezy cordiality. The steward saw from his long experience of members that the remark needed an answer.

"No, sir."

Roy laughed and his eye sought mine. Quite a character, Armstrong.

"Well, chill it, Armstrong; not too much, you know, but just right. I want my guest to see that we know what's what here."

He turned to me. "Armstrong's been with us for eight-and-forty years." And when the wine-steward had left us: "I hope you don't mind coming here. It's quiet and we can have a good talk. It's ages since we did. You're looking very fit."

This drew my attention to Roy's appearance.

"Not half so fit as you," I answered.

"The result of an upright, sober and godly life," he laughed. "Plenty of work. Plenty of exercise. How's the golf? We must have a game one of these days."

I knew that Roy was scratch and that nothing would please him less than to waste a day with so indifferent a player as myself. But I felt I was quite safe in accepting so vague an invitation. He looked the picture of health. His curly hair was getting very grey, but it suited him and made his frank, sun-burned face look younger. His eyes, which looked upon the world with such a hearty candour, were bright and clear. He was not so slim as in his youth and I was not surprised that when the waiter offered us rolls he asked for Ryvita. His slight corpulence only added to his dignity. It gave weight to his observations. Because his movements were a little more deliberate than they had been you had a comfortable feeling of confidence in him; he filled his chair with so much solidity that you had almost the impression that he sat upon a monument.

I do not know whether, as I wished, I have indicated by my report of his dialogue with the waiter that his conversation was not as a rule brilliant or witty, but it was fluent and he laughed so much that you sometimes had the illusion that what he said was funny. He was never at a loss for a remark and he could discourse on the topics of the day with an ease that prevented his hearers from experiencing any sense of strain.

Many authors from their preoccupation with words have the bad habit of choosing those they use in conversation too carefully. They form their sentences with unconscious care and say neither more nor less than they mean. It makes intercourse with them somewhat formidable to persons in the upper ranks of society whose vocabulary is limited by their simple spiritual needs, and their company consequently is sought only with hesitation. No constraint of this sort was ever felt with Roy. He could talk with a dancing guardee in terms that were perfectly comprehensible to him and with a racing countess in the language of her stable boys.

They said of him with enthusiasm and relief that he was not a bit like an author. No compliment pleased him better. The wise always use a number of ready-made phrases (at the moment I write "nobody's business" is the most common), popular adjectives (like "divine" or "shy-making"), verbs that you only know the meaning of if you live in the right set (like "dunch"), which give a homely sparkle to small talk and avoid the necessity of thought. The Americans, who are the most efficient people on the earth, have carried this device to such a height of perfection and have invented so wide a range of pithy and hackneyed phrases that they can carry on an amusing and animated conversation without giving a moment's reflection to what they are saying and so leave their minds free to consider the more important matters of big business and fornication. Roy's repertory was extensive and his scent for the word of the minute unerring; it peppered his speech, but aptly, and he used it each time with a sort of bright eagerness, as though his fertile brain had just minted it.

Now he talked of this and that, of our common friends and the latest books, of the opera. He was very breezy. He was always cordial, but to-day his cordiality took my breath away. He lamented that we saw one another so seldom and told me with the frankness that was one of his pleasantest characteristics how much he liked me and what a high opinion he had of me. I felt I must not fail to meet this friendliness half-way. He asked me about the book I was writing, I asked him about the book he was writing. We told one another that neither of us had had the success he deserved. We ate the veal-and-ham pie and Roy told me how he mixed a salad. We drank the hock and smacked appreciative lips.

And I wondered when he was coming to the point.

I could not bring myself to believe that at the height of the London season Alroy Kear would waste an hour on a fellow-writer who was not a reviewer and had no influence in any quarter whatever in order to talk of Matisse, the Russian Ballet and Marcel Proust. Besides, at the back of his gaiety I vaguely felt a slight apprehension. Had I not known that he was in a prosperous state I should have suspected that he was going to borrow a hundred pounds from me. It began to look as though luncheon would end without his finding the opportunity to say what he had in mind. I knew he was cautious. Perhaps he thought that this meeting, the first after so long a separation, had better be employed in establishing friendly relations, and was prepared to look upon the pleasant, substantial meal merely as ground bait.

"Shall we go and have our coffee in the next room?" he said.

"If you like."

"I think it's more comfortable."

I followed him into another room, much more spacious, with great leather arm-chairs and huge sofas; there were papers and magazines on the tables. Two old gentlemen in a corner were talking in undertones. They gave us a hostile glance, but this did not deter Roy from offering them a cordial greeting.

"Hullo, General," he cried, nodding breezily.

I stood for a moment at the window, looking at the gaiety of the day, and wished I knew more of the historical associations of St. James's Street. I was ashamed that I did not even know the name of the club across the way and was afraid to ask Roy lest he should despise me for not knowing what every decent person knew. He called me back by asking me whether I would have a brandy with my coffee, and when I refused, insisted. The club's brandy was famous. We sat side by side on a sofa by the elegant fireplace and lit cigars.

"The last time Edward Driffield ever came to London he lunched with me here," said Roy casually. "I made the old man try our brandy and he was delighted with it. I was staying with his widow over last week-end."

"Were you?"

"She sent you all sorts of messages."

"That's very kind of her. I shouldn't have thought she remembered me."

"Oh, yes, she does. You lunched there about six years ago, didn't you? She says the old man was so glad to see you."

"I didn't think *she* was."

"Oh, you're quite wrong. Of course she had to be very careful. The old man was pestered with people who wanted to see him and she had to husband his strength. She was always afraid he'd do too much. It's a wonderful thing if you come to think of it that she should have kept him alive and in possession of all his faculties to the age of eighty-four. I've been seeing a good deal of her since he died. She's awfully lonely. After all, she devoted

herself to looking after him for twenty-five years. Othello's occupation, you know. I really feel sorry for her."

"She's still comparatively young. I dare say she'll marry again."

"Oh, no, she couldn't do that. That would be dreadful."

There was a slight pause while we sipped our brandy.

"You must be one of the few persons still alive who knew Driffield when he was unknown. You saw quite a lot of him at one
time, didn't you?"

"A certain amount. I was almost a small boy and he was a
middle-aged man. We weren't boon companions, you know."

"Perhaps not, but you must know a great deal about him that
other people don't."

"I suppose I do."

"Have you ever thought of writing your recollections of him?"

"Good heavens, no!"

"Don't you think you ought to? He was one of the greatest
novelists of our day. The last of the Victorians. He was an enormous figure. His novels have as good a chance of surviving as
any that have been written in the last hundred years."

"I wonder. I've always thought them rather boring."

Roy looked at me with eyes twinkling with laughter.

"How like you that is! Anyhow you must admit that you're in
the minority. I don't mind telling you that I've read his novels
not once or twice, but half a dozen times, and every time I read
them I think they're finer. Did you read the articles that were
written about him at his death?"

"Some of them."

"The consensus of opinion was absolutely amazing. I read every
one."

"If they all said the same thing, wasn't that rather unnecessary?"

Roy shrugged his massive shoulders good-humouredly, but did
not answer my question.

"I thought the *Times Lit. Sup.*, was splendid. It would have
done the old man good to read it. I hear that the *Quarterly* is
going to have an article in its next number."

"I still think his novels rather boring."

Roy smiled indulgently.

"Doesn't it make you slightly uneasy to think that you dis-
agree with everyone whose opinion matters?"

"Not particularly. I've been writing for thirty-five years now, and you can't think how many geniuses I've seen acclaimed, enjoy their hour or two of glory and vanish into obscurity. I wonder what's happened to them. Are they dead, are they shut up in mad-houses, are they hidden away in offices? I wonder if they furtively lend their books to the doctor and the maiden lady in some obscure village. I wonder if they are still great men in some Italian pension."

"Oh, yes, they're the flash-in-the-pans. I've known them."

"You've even lectured about them."

"One has to. One wants to give them a leg up if one can and one knows they won't amount to anything. Hang it all, one can afford to be generous. But after all, Driffield wasn't anything like that. The collected edition of his works is in thirty-seven volumes and the last set that came up at Sotheby's sold for seventy-eight pounds. That speaks for itself. His sales have increased steadily every year and last year was the best he ever had. You can take my word for that. Mrs. Driffield showed me his accounts last time I was down there. Driffield has come to stay all right."

"Who can tell?"

"Well, you think you can," replied Roy acidly.

I was not put out. I knew I was irritating him and it gave me a pleasant sensation.

"I think the instinctive judgments I formed when I was a boy were right. They told me Carlyle was a great writer and I was ashamed that I found the *French Revolution* and *Sartor Resartus* unreadable. Can anyone read them now? I thought the opinions of others must be better than mine and I persuaded myself that I thought George Meredith magnificent. In my heart I found him affected, verbose and insincere. A good many people think so too now. Because they told me that to admire Walter Pater was to prove myself a cultured young man, I admired Walter Pater, but heavens, how *Marius* bored me!"

"Oh, well, I don't suppose anyone reads Pater now, and of course Meredith has gone all to pot and Carlyle was a pretentious windbag."

"You don't know how secure of immortality they all looked thirty years ago."

"And have you never made mistakes?"

"One or two. I didn't think half as much of Newman as I do now, and I thought a great deal more of the tinkling quatrains of

Fitzgerald. I could not read Goethe's *Wilhelm Meister;* now I
think it his masterpiece."

"And what did you think much of then that you think much of
still?"

"Well, *Tristram Shandy* and *Amelia* and *Vanity Fair. Madame
Bovary, La Chartreuse de Parme,* and *Anna Karenina.* And Wordsworth and Keats and Verlaine."

"If you don't mind my saying so, I don't think that's particularly
original."

"I don't mind your saying so at all. I don't think it is. But you
asked me why I believed in my own judgment, and I was trying
to explain to you that, whatever I said out of timidity and in def-
erence to the cultured opinion of the day, I didn't really admire
certain authors who were then thought admirable and the event
seems to show that I was right. And what I honestly and instinctively liked then has stood the test of time with me and
with critical opinion in general."

Roy was silent for a moment. He looked in the bottom of his
cup, but whether to see if there were any more coffee in it or to
find something to say, I did not know. I gave the clock on the
chimney-piece a glance. In a minute it would be fitting for me to
take my leave. Perhaps I had been wrong and Roy had invited
me only that we might idly chat of Shakespeare and the musical
glasses. I chid myself for the uncharitable thoughts I had had of
him. I looked at him with concern. If that was his only object it
must be that he was feeling tired or discouraged. If he was
disinterested it could only be that for the moment at least the
world was too much for him. But he caught my look at the clock
and spoke.

"I don't see how you can deny that there must be something in
a man who's able to carry on for sixty years, writing book after
book, and who's able to hold an ever-increasing public. After all,
at Ferne Court there are shelves filled with the translations of
Driffield's books into every language of civilised people. Of course
I'm willing to admit that a lot he wrote seems a bit old-fashioned
nowadays. He flourished in a bad period and he was inclined to
be long-winded. Most of his plots are melodramatic; but there's
one quality you must allow him: beauty."

"Yes?" I said.

"When all's said and done, that's the only thing that counts and Driffield never wrote a page that wasn't instinct with beauty."

"Yes?" I said.

"I wish you'd been there when we went down to present him with his portrait on his eightieth birthday. It really was a memorable occasion."

"I read about it in the papers."

"It wasn't only writers, you know, it was a thoroughly representative gathering—science, politics, business, art, the world; I think you'd have to go a long way to find gathered together such a collection of distinguished people as got out from that train at Blackstable. It was awfully moving when the P.M. presented the old man with the Order of Merit. He made a charming speech. I don't mind telling you there were tears in a good many eyes that day."

"Did Driffield cry?"

"No, he was singularly calm. He was like he always was, rather shy, you know, and quiet, very well-mannered, grateful, of course, but a little dry. Mrs. Driffield didn't want him to get overtired and when we went into lunch he stayed in his study, and she sent him something in on a tray. I slipped away while the others were having their coffee. He was smoking his pipe and looking at the portrait. I asked him what he thought of it. He wouldn't tell me, he just smiled a little. He asked me if I thought he could take his teeth out and I said, No, the deputation would be coming in presently to say good-bye to him. Then I asked him if he didn't think it was a wonderful moment. 'Rum,' he said, 'very rum.' The fact is, I suppose, he was shattered. He was a messy eater in his later days and a messy smoker—he scattered the tobacco all over himself when he filled his pipe; Mrs. Driffield didn't like people to see him when he was like that, but of course she didn't mind me; I tidied him up a bit and then they all came in and shook hands with him, and we went back to town."

I got up.

"Well, I really must be going. It's been awfully nice seeing you."

"I'm just going along to the private view at the Leicester Galleries. I know the people there. I'll take you in if you like."

"It's very kind of you, but they sent me a card. No, I don't think I'll come."

We walked down the stairs and I got my hat. When we came
out into the street and I turned toward Piccadilly, Roy said:

"I'll just walk up to the top with you." He got into step with
me. "You knew his first wife, didn't you?"

"Whose?"

"Driffield's."

"Oh!" I had forgotten him. "Yes."

"Well?"

"Fairly."

"I suppose she was awful."

"I don't recollect that."

"She must have been dreadfully common. She was a barmaid,
wasn't she?"

"Yes."

"I wonder why the devil he married her. I've always been given
to understand that she was extremely unfaithful to him."

"Extremely."

"Do you remember at all what she was like?"

"Yes, very distinctly," I smiled. "She was sweet."

Roy gave a short laugh.

"That's not the general impression."

I did not answer. We had reached Piccadilly, and stopping I
held out my hand to Roy. He shook it, but I fancied without his
usual heartiness. I had the impression that he was disappointed
with our meeting. I could not imagine why. Whatever he had
wanted of me I had not been able to do, for the reason that he
had given me no inkling of what it was, and as I strolled under
the arcade of the Ritz Hotel and along the park railings till I
came opposite Half Moon Street I wondered if my manner had
been more than ordinarily forbidding. It was quite evident that
Roy had felt the moment inopportune to ask me to grant him a
favour.

I walked up Half Moon Street. After the gay tumult of Piccadilly it had a pleasant silence. It was sedate and respectable.
Most of the houses let apartments, but this was not advertised by
the vulgarity of a card; some had a brightly polished brass plate,
like a doctor's, to announce the fact and others the word *Apartments* neatly painted on the fanlight. One or two with an added
discretion merely gave the name of the proprietor, so that if you
were ignorant you might have thought it a tailor's or a money-

lender's. There was none of the congested traffic of Jermyn Street, where also they let rooms, but here and there a smart car, unattended, stood outside a door and occasionally at another a taxi deposited a middle-aged lady. You had the feeling that the people who lodged here were not gay and a trifle disreputable as in Jermyn Street, racing men who rose in the morning with headaches and asked for a hair of the dog that bit them, but respectable women from the country who came up for six weeks for the London season and elderly gentlemen who belonged to exclusive clubs. You felt that they came year after year to the same house and perhaps had known the proprietor when he was still in private service. My own Miss Fellows had been cook in some very good places, but you would never have guessed it had you seen her walking along to do her shopping in Shepherd's Market. She was not stout, red-faced and blowsy as one expects a cook to be; she was spare and very upright, neatly but fashionably dressed, a woman of middle age with determined features; her lips were rouged and she wore an eye-glass. She was businesslike, quiet, coolly cynical and very expensive.

The rooms I occupied were on the ground floor. The parlour was papered with an old marbled paper and on the walls were water-colours of romantic scenes, cavaliers bidding good-bye to their ladies and knights of old banqueting in stately halls; there were large ferns in pots, and the arm-chairs were covered with faded leather. There was about the room an amusing air of the eighteen-eighties, and when I looked out of the window I expected to see a private hansom rather than a Chrysler. The curtains were of a heavy red rep.

CHAPTER III

I had a good deal to do that afternoon, but my conversation with Roy and the impression of the day before yesterday, the sense of a past that still dwelt in the minds of men not yet old, that my room, I could not tell why, had given me even more strongly than usual as I entered it, inveigled my thoughts to saunter down the road of memory. It was as though all the people who had at one time and another inhabited my lodging pressed upon me with their old-fashioned ways and odd clothes, men with mutton-chop whiskers in frock-coats and women in bustles and flounced skirts. The rumble of London, which I did not know if I imagined or heard (my house was at the top of Half Moon Street), and the beauty of the sunny June day (*le vierge, le vivace et le bel aujour-d'hui*), gave my reverie a poignancy which was not quite painful. The past I looked at seemed to have lost its reality and I saw it as though it were a scene in a play and I a spectator in the back row of a dark gallery. But it was all very clear as far as it went. It was not misty like life as one leads it when the ceaseless throng of impressions seems to rob them of outline, but sharp and definite like a landscape painted in oils by a painstaking artist of the middle-Victorian era.

I fancy that life is more amusing now than it was forty years ago and I have a notion that people are more amiable. They may have been worthier then, possessed of more solid virtue as, I am told, they were possessed of more substantial knowledge; I do not know. I know they were more cantankerous; they ate too much, many of them drank too much, and they took too little exercise. Their livers were out of order and their digestions often impaired. They were irritable. I do not speak of London, of which I knew nothing till I was grown up, nor of grand people who hunted and shot, but of the countryside and of the modest persons, gentlemen of small means, clergymen, retired officers and such-like who made up the local society. The dullness of their lives was almost incredible. There were no golf links; at a few houses was an ill-kept tennis court, but it was only the very young who played; there was a dance once a year in the Assembly Rooms; carriage folk went for a drive in the afternoon; the others went for a "constitutional"! You may say that they did not miss amusements they had never thought of, and that they created excitement for themselves from the small entertainment (tea when you were asked to bring your music and you sang the songs of Maude Valérie White and Tosti) which at infrequent intervals they offered one another; the days were very long; they were bored. People who were condemned to spend their lives within a mile of one another quarrelled bitterly and, seeing each other every day in the town, cut one another for twenty years. They were vain, pig-headed and odd. It was a life that perhaps formed queer characters; people were not so like one another as now and they acquired a small celebrity by their idiosyncrasies, but they were not easy to get on with. It may be that we are flippant and careless, but we accept one another without the old suspicion; our manners, rough and ready, are kindly; we are more prepared to give and take and we are not so crabbed.

I lived with an uncle and aunt on the outskirts of a little Kentish town by the sea. It was called Blackstable and my uncle was the vicar. My aunt was a German. She came of a very noble but impoverished family, and the only portion she brought her husband was a marquetry writing-desk, made for an ancestor in the seventeenth century, and a set of tumblers. Of these only a few remained when I entered upon the scene and they were used as ornaments in the drawing-room. I liked the grand coat-of-arms with which they were heavily engraved. There were I don't know how many quarterings, which my aunt used demurely to explain to me, and the supporters were fine and the crest emerging from a crown incredibly romantic. She was a simple old lady, of a meek and Christian disposition, but she had not, though married for more than thirty years to a modest parson with very little income beyond his stipend, forgotten that she was *hochwohlgeboren*. When a rich banker from London, with a name that in these days is famous in financial circles, took a neighbouring house for the summer holidays, though my uncle called on him (chiefly, I surmise, to get a subscription to the Additional Curates Society), she refused to do so because he was in trade. No one thought her a snob. It was accepted as perfectly reasonable. The banker had a little boy of my own age, and, I forget how, I became acquainted with him. I still remember the discussion that ensued when I asked if I might bring him to the vicarage; permission was reluctantly given me, but I was not allowed to go in return to his house. My aunt said I'd be wanting to go to the coal merchant's next, and my uncle said:

"Evil communications corrupt good manners."

The banker used to come to church every Sunday morning, and he always put half a sovereign in the plate, but if he thought his generosity made a good impression he was much mistaken. All Blackstable knew, but only thought him purse-proud.

Blackstable consisted of a long winding street that led to the sea, with little two-storey houses, many of them residential but with a good many shops; and from this ran a certain number of short

streets, recently built, that ended on one side in the country and
on the other in the marshes. Round about the harbour was a
congeries of narrow winding alleys. Colliers brought coal from
Newcastle to Blackstable and the harbour was animated. When I
was old enough to be allowed out by myself I used to spend hours
wandering about there looking at the rough grimy men in their
jerseys and watching the coal being unloaded.

It was at Blackstable that I first met Edward Driffield. I was
fifteen and had just come back from school for the summer holidays. The morning after I got home I took a towel and bathing
drawers and went down to the beach. The sky was unclouded
and the air hot and bright, but the North Sea gave it a pleasant
tang so that it was a delight just to live and breathe. In winter
the natives of Blackstable walked down the empty street with a
hurried gait, screwing themselves up in order to expose as little
surface as possible to the bitterness of the east wind, but now
they dawdled; they stood about in groups in the space between
the "Duke of Kent" and the "Bear and Key". You heard a hum
of their East-Anglian speech, drawling a little with an accent that
may be ugly, but in which from old association I still find a leisurely charm. They were fresh-complexioned, with blue eyes and
high cheek-bones, and their hair was light. They had a clean,
honest and ingenuous look. I do not think they were very intelligent, but they were guileless. They looked healthy, and though
not tall for the most part were strong and active. There was little
wheeled traffic in Blackstable in those days and the groups that
stood about the road chatting seldom had to move for anything
but the doctor's dogcart or the baker's trap.

Passing the bank, I called in to say how-do-you-do to the manager, who was my uncle's churchwarden, and when I came out
met my uncle's curate. He stopped and shook hands with me.
He was walking with a stranger. He did not introduce me to him.
He was a smallish man with a beard and he was dressed rather
loudly in a bright brown knickerbocker suit, the breeches very
tight, with navy-blue stockings, black boots and a billycock hat.
Knickerbockers were uncommon then, at least in Blackstable, and
being young and fresh from school I immediately set the fellow
down as a cad. But while I chatted with the curate he looked
at me in a friendly way, with a smile in his pale blue eyes.
I felt that for two pins he would have joined in the conversation

and I assumed a haughty demeanour. I was not going to run the risk of being spoken to by a chap who wore knickerbockers like a gamekeeper and I resented the familiarity of his good-humoured expression. I was myself faultlessly dressed in white flannel trousers, a blue blazer with the arms of my school on the breast pocket, and a black-and-white straw hat with a very wide brim. The curate said that he must be getting on (fortunately, for I never knew how to break away from a meeting in the street and would endure agonies of shyness while I looked in vain for an opportunity), but said that he would be coming up to the vicarage that afternoon and would I tell my uncle. The stranger nodded and smiled as we parted, but I gave him a stony stare. I supposed he was a summer visitor and in Blackstable we did not mix with the summer visitors. We thought London people vulgar. We said it was horrid to have all that rag-tag and bob-tail down from town every year, but of course it was all right for the tradespeople. Even they, however, gave a faint sigh of relief when September came to an end and Blackstable sank back into its usual peace.

When I went home to dinner, my hair insufficiently dried and clinging dankly to my head, I remarked that I had met the curate and he was coming up that afternoon.

"Old Mrs. Shepherd died last night," said my uncle in explanation.

The curate's name was Galloway; he was a tall, thin, ungainly man with untidy black hair and a small sallow dark face. I suppose he was quite young, but to me he seemed middle-aged. He talked very quickly and gesticulated a great deal. This made people think him rather queer and my uncle would not have kept him but that he was very energetic, and my uncle, being extremely lazy, was glad to have someone to take so much work off his shoulders. After he had finished the business that had brought him to the vicarage Mr. Galloway came in to say how-do-you-do to my aunt and she asked him to stay to tea.

"Who was that you were with this morning?" I asked him as he sat down.

"Oh, that was Edward Driffield. I didn't introduce him. I wasn't sure if your uncle would wish you to know him."

"I think it would be most undesirable," said my uncle.

"Why, who is he? He's not a Blackstable man, is he?"

"He was born in the parish," said my uncle. "His father was old Miss Wolfe's bailiff at Ferne Court. But they were chapel people."

"He married a Blackstable girl," said Mr. Galloway.

"In church, I believe," said my aunt. "Is it true that she was a barmaid at the 'Railway Arms'?"

"She looks as if she might have been something like that," said Mr. Galloway with a smile.

"Are they going to stay long?"

"Yes, I think so. They've taken one of those houses in that street where the Congregational chapel is," said the curate.

At that time in Blackstable, though the new streets doubtless had names, nobody knew or used them.

"Is he coming to church?" asked my uncle.

"I haven't actually talked to him about it yet," answered Mr. Galloway. "He's quite an educated man, you know."

"I can hardly believe that," said my uncle.

"He was at Haversham School, I understand, and he got any number of scholarships and prizes. He got a scholarship at Wadham, but he ran away to sea instead."

"I'd heard he was rather a harum-scarum," said my uncle.

"He doesn't look much like a sailor," I remarked.

"Oh, he gave up the sea many years ago. He's been all sorts of things since then."

"Jack of all trades and master of none," said my uncle.

"Now, I understand, he's a writer."

"That won't last long," said my uncle.

I had never known a writer before; I was interested.

"What does he write?" I asked. "Books?"

"I believe so," said the curate, "and articles. He had a novel published last spring. He's promised to lend it me."

"I wouldn't waste my time on rubbish in your place," said my uncle, who never read anything but *The Times* and the *Guardian*.

"What's it called?" I asked.

"He told me the title, but I forget it."

"Anyhow, it's quite unnecessary that you should know," said my uncle. "I should very much object to your reading trashy novels. During your holidays the best thing you can do is to keep out in the open air. And you have a holiday task, I presume?"

I had. It was *Ivanhoe*. I had read it when I was ten, and the notion of reading it again and writing an essay on it bored me to distraction.

When I consider the greatness that Edward Driffield afterward achieved I cannot but smile as I remember the fashion in which he was discussed at my uncle's table. When he died a little while ago and an agitation arose among his admirers to have him buried in Westminster Abbey the present incumbent at Blackstable, my uncle's successor twice removed, wrote to the *Daily Mail* pointing out that Driffield was born in the parish and not only had passed long years, especially the last twenty-five of his life, in the neighbourhood, but had laid there the scene of some of his most famous books; it was only becoming then that his bones should rest in the churchyard where under the Kentish elms his father and mother dwelt in peace. There was relief in Blackstable when, the Dean of Westminster having somewhat curtly refused the Abbey, Mrs. Driffield sent a dignified letter to the Press in which she expressed her confidence that she was carrying out the dearest wishes of her dead husband in having him buried among the simple people he knew and loved so well. Unless the notabilities of Blackstable have very much changed since my day I do not believe they vastly liked that phrase about "simple people", but, as I afterward learnt, they had never been able to "abide" the second Mrs. Driffield.

CHAPTER IV

To my surprise, two or three days after I lunched with Alroy Kear I received a letter from Edward Driffield's widow. It ran as follows:

Dear Friend,

I hear that you had a long talk with Roy last week about Edward Driffield and I am so glad to know that you spoke of him so nicely. He often talked to me of you. He had the greatest admiration for your talent and he was so very pleased to see you when you came to lunch with us. I wonder if you have in your possession any letters that he wrote to you and if so whether you would let me have copies of them. I should be very pleased if I could persuade you to come down for two or three days and

stay with me. I live very quietly now and have no one here,
so please choose your own time. I shall be delighted to see you
again and have a talk of old times. I have a particular service
I want you to do me and I am sure that for the sake of my
dear dead husband you will not refuse.

Yours ever sincerely,
Amy Driffield.

I had seen Mrs. Driffield only once and she but mildly interested me; I do not like being addressed as "dear friend"; that
alone would have been enough to make me decline her invitation;
and I was exasperated by its general character which, however ingenious an excuse I invented, made the reason I did not go quite
obvious, namely, that I did not want to. I had no letters of Driffield's. I suppose years ago he had written to me several times,
brief notes, but he was then an obscure scribbler and even if I
ever kept letters it would never have occurred to me to keep his.
How was I to know that he was going to be acclaimed as the
greatest novelist of our day? I hesitated only because Mrs. Driffield said she wanted me to do something for her. It would certainly be a nuisance, but it would be churlish not to do it if I
could, and after all her husband was a very distinguished man.

The letter came by the first post and after breakfast I rang up
Roy. As soon as I mentioned my name I was put through to him
by his secretary. If I were writing a detective story I should immediately have suspected that my call was awaited, and Roy's
virile voice calling hullo would have confirmed my suspicion. No
one could naturally be quite so cheery so early in the morning.

"I hope I didn't wake you," I said.

"Good God, no." His healthy laugh rippled along the wires.
"I've been up since seven. I've been riding in the park. I'm just
going to have breakfast. Come along and have it with me."

"I have a great affection for you, Roy," I answered, "but I don't
think you're the sort of person I'd care to have breakfast with.
Besides, I've already had mine. Look here, I've just had a letter
from Mrs. Driffield asking me to go down and stay."

"Yes, she told me she was going to ask you. We might go down
together. She's got quite a good grass court and she does one very
well. I think you'd like it."

"What is it that she wants me to do?"

"Ah, I think she'd like to tell you that herself."

There was a softness in Roy's voice such as I imagined he would use if he were telling a prospective father that his wife was about to gratify his wishes. It cut no ice with me.

"Come off it, Roy," I said. "I'm too old a bird to be caught with chaff. Spit it out."

There was a moment's pause at the other end of the telephone. I felt that Roy did not like my expression.

"Are you busy this morning?" he asked suddenly. "I'd like to come and see you."

"All right, come on. I shall be in till one."

"I'll be round in about an hour."

I replaced the receiver and relit my pipe. I gave Mrs. Driffield's letter a second glance.

I remembered vividly the luncheon to which she referred. I happened to be staying for a long week-end not far from Tercanbury with a certain Lady Hodmarsh, the clever and handsome American wife of a sporting baronet with no intelligence and charming manners. Perhaps to relieve the tedium of domestic life she was in the habit of entertaining persons connected with the arts. Her parties were mixed and gay. Members of the nobility and gentry mingled with astonishment and an uneasy awe with painters, writers and actors. Lady Hodmarsh neither read the books nor looked at the pictures of the people to whom she offered hospitality, but she liked their company and enjoyed the feeling it gave her of being in the artistic know. When on this occasion the conversation happened to dwell for a moment on Edward Driffield, her most celebrated neighbour, and I mentioned that I had at one time known him very well she proposed that we should go over and lunch with him on Monday when a number of her guests were going back to London. I demurred, for I had not seen Driffield for five-and-thirty years and I could not believe that he would remember me; and if he did (though this I kept to myself) I could not believe that it would be with pleasure. But there was a young peer there, a certain Lord Scallion, with literary inclinations so violent that, instead of ruling this country as the laws of man and nature have decreed, he devoted his energy to the composition of detective novels. His curiosity to see Driffield was boundless and the moment Lady Hodmarsh made her suggestion he said it would be too divine. The star guest of the party was a big young fat duchess and it appeared that her admiration for the famous writer was so intense that she was prepared to cut an engagement in London and not go up till the afternoon.

"That would make four of us," said Lady Hodmarsh. "I don't think they could manage more than that. I'll wire to Mrs. Driffield at once."

I could not see myself going to see Driffield in that company and tried to throw cold water on the scheme.

"It'll only bore him to death," I said. "He'll hate having a lot of strangers barging in on him like this. He's a very old man."

"That's why if they want to see him they'd better see him now. He can't last much longer. Mrs. Driffield says he likes to meet people. They never see anybody but the doctor and the parson and it's a change for them. Mrs. Driffield said I could always bring anyone interesting. Of course she has to be very careful. He's pestered by all sorts of people who want to see him just out of idle curiosity, and interviewers and authors who want him to read their books, and silly hysterical women. But Mrs. Driffield is wonderful. She keeps everyone away from him but those she thinks he ought to see. I mean, he'd be dead in a week if he saw everyone who wants to see him. She has to think of his strength. Naturally we're different."

Of course I thought I was; but as I looked at them I perceived that the duchess and Lord Scallion thought they were too; so it seemed best to say no more.

We drove over in a bright yellow Rolls. Ferne Court was three miles from Blackstable. It was a stucco house built, I suppose, about 1840, plain and unpretentious, but substantial; it was the same back and front, with two large bows on each side of a flat piece in which was the front door, and there were two large bows on the first floor. A plain parapet hid the low roof. It stood in about an acre of garden, somewhat overgrown with trees, but neatly tended, and from the drawing-room window you had a pleasant view of woods and green downland. The drawing-room was furnished so exactly as you felt a drawing-room in a country house of modest size should be furnished that it was slightly disconcerting. Clean bright chintzes covered the comfortable chairs and the large sofa, and the curtains were of the same bright clean chintz. On little Chippendale tables stood large Oriental bowls filled with pot-pourri. On the cream-coloured walls were pleasant water-colours by painters well known at the beginning of this century. There were great masses of flowers charmingly arranged, and on the grand piano in silver frames photographs of celebrated actresses, deceased authors and minor royalties.

It was no wonder that the duchess cried out that it was a lovely room. It was just the kind of room in which a distinguished writer should spend the evening of his days. Mrs. Driffield received us with modest assurance. She was a woman of about five-and-forty, I judged, with a small sallow face and neat sharp features. She had a black cloche hat pressed tight down on her head and wore a grey coat and skirt. Her figure was slight and she was neither tall nor short, and she looked trim, competent and alert. She might have been the squire's widowed daughter, who ran the parish and had a peculiar gift for organisation. She introduced us to a clergyman and a lady, who got up as we were shown in. They were the Vicar of Blackstable and his wife. Lady Hodmarsh and the duchess immediately assumed the cringing affability that persons of rank assume with their inferiors in order to show them that they are not in the least conscious of any difference in station between them.

Then Edward Driffield came in. I had seen portraits of him from time to time in the illustrated papers but it was with dismay that I saw him in the flesh. He was smaller than I remembered and very thin, his head was barely covered with fine silvery hair, he was clean-shaven and his skin was almost transparent. His blue eyes were very pale and the rims of his eyelids red. He looked an old, old man, hanging on to mortality by a thread; he wore very white false teeth and they made his smile seem forced and stiff. I had never seen him but bearded, and his lips were thin and pallid. He was dressed in a new, well-cut suit of blue serge and his low collar, two or three sizes too large for him, showed a wrinkled, scraggy neck. He wore a neat black tie with a pearl in it. He looked a little like a dean in mufti on his summer holiday in Switzerland.

Mrs. Driffield gave him a quick glance as he came in and smiled encouragingly; she must have been satisfied with the neatness of his appearance. He shook hands with his guests and to each said something civil. When he came to me he said:

"It's very good of a busy and successful man like you to come all this way to see an old fogey."

I was a trifle taken aback, for he spoke as though he had never seen me before, and I was afraid my friends would think I had been boasting when I claimed at one time to have known him intimately. I wondered if he had completely forgotten me.

"I don't know how many years it is since we last met," I said, trying to be hearty.

He looked at me for what I suppose was no more than a few seconds, but for what seemed to me quite a long time, and then I had a sudden shock; he gave me a little wink. It was so quick that nobody but I could have caught it, and so unexpected in that distinguished old face that I could hardly believe my eyes. In a moment his face was once more composed, intelligently benign and quietly observant. Luncheon was announced and we trooped into the dining-room.

This also was in what can only be described as the acme of good taste. On the Chippendale sideboard were silver candlesticks. We sat on Chippendale chairs and ate off a Chippendale table. In a silver bowl in the middle were roses and round this were silver dishes with chocolates in them and peppermint creams; the silver salt-cellars were brightly polished and evidently Georgian. On the cream-coloured walls were mezzotints of ladies painted by Sir Peter Lely and on the chimney-piece a garniture of blue delf. The service was conducted by two maids in brown uniform and Mrs. Driffield in the midst of her fluent conversation kept a wary eye on them. I wondered how she had managed to train these buxom Kentish girls (their healthy colour and high cheek-bones betrayed the fact that they were "local") to such a pitch of efficiency. The lunch was just right for the occasion, smart but not showy, fillets of sole rolled up and covered with a white sauce, roast chicken, with new potatoes and green peas, asparagus and gooseberry fool. It was the dining-room and the lunch and the manner which you felt exactly fitted a literary gent of great celebrity but moderate wealth.

Mrs. Driffield, like the wives of most men of letters, was a great talker and she did not let the conversation at her end of the table flag; so that, however much we might have wanted to hear what her husband was saying at the other, we had no opportunity. She was gay and sprightly. Though Edward Driffield's indifferent health and great age obliged her to live most of the year in the country, she managed notwithstanding to run up to town often enough to keep abreast of what was going on and she was soon engaged with Lord Scallion in an animated discussion of the plays in the London theatres and the terrible crowd at the Royal Academy. It had taken her two visits to look at all the pictures and even then she had not had time to see the water-colours. She liked water-colours so much; they were unpretentious; she hated things to be pretentious.

So that host and hostess should sit at the head and foot of the table, the vicar sat next to Lord Scallion and his wife next to the duchess. The duchess engaged her in conversation on the subject of working-class dwellings, a subject on which she seemed to be much more at home than the parson's lady, and my attention being thus set free I watched Edward Driffield. He was talking to Lady Hodmarsh. She was apparently telling him how to write a novel and giving him a list of a few that he really ought to read. He listened to her with what looked like polite interest, putting in now and then a remark in a voice too low for me to catch, and when she made a jest (she made them frequently and often good ones) he gave a little chuckle and shot her a quick look that seemed to say: This woman isn't such a damned fool after all. Remembering the past, I asked myself curiously what he thought of this grand company, his neatly turned-out wife, so competent and discreetly managing, and the elegant surroundings in which he lived. I wondered if he regretted his early days of adventure. I wondered if all this amused him or if the amiable civility of his manner masked a hideous boredom. Perhaps he felt my eyes upon him, for he raised his. They rested on me for a while with a thoughtful look, mild and yet oddly scrutinising, and then suddenly, unmistakably this time, he gave me another wink. The frivolous gesture in that old, withered face was more than startling, it was embarrassing; I did not know what to do. My lips outlined a dubious smile.

But the duchess joining in the conversation at the head of the table, the vicar's wife turned to me.

"You knew him many years ago, didn't you?" she asked me in a low tone.

"Yes."

She gave the company a glance to see that no one was attending to us.

"His wife is anxious that you shouldn't call up old memories that might be painful to him. He's very frail, you know, and the least thing upsets him."

"I'll be very careful."

"The way she looks after him is simply wonderful. Her devotion is a lesson to all of us. She realises what a precious charge it is. Her unselfishness is beyond words." She lowered her voice a little more. "Of course he's a very old man and old men sometimes are a little trying; I've never seen her out of patience. In her way she's just as wonderful as he is."

These were the sort of remarks to which it was difficult to find a reply, but I felt that one was expected of me.

"Considering everything I think he looks very well," I murmured.

"He owes it all to her."

At the end of luncheon we went back into the drawing-room and after we had been standing about for two or three minutes Edward Driffield joined me. I was talking with the vicar and for want of anything better to say was admiring the charming view. I turned to my host.

"I was just saying how picturesque that little row of cottages is down there."

"From here." Driffield looked at their broken outline and an ironic smile curled his thin lips. "I was born in one of them. Rum, isn't it?"

But Mrs. Driffield came up to us with bustling geniality. Her voice was brisk and melodious.

"Oh, Edward, I'm sure the duchess would like to see your writing-room. She has to go almost immediately."

"I'm so sorry, but I must catch the three-eighteen from Tercanbury," said the duchess.

We filed into Driffield's study. It was a large room on the other side of the house, looking out on the same view as the dining-room, with a bow window. It was the sort of room that a devoted wife would evidently arrange for her literary husband. It was scrupulously tidy and large bowls of flowers gave it a feminine touch.

"This is the desk at which he's written all his later works," said
Mrs. Driffield, closing a book that was open face-downward on it.
"It's the frontispiece in the third volume of the *édition de luxe*.
It's a period piece."

We all admired the writing-table, and Lady Hodmarsh, when
she thought no one was looking, ran her fingers along its under
edge to see if it was genuine. Mrs. Driffield gave us a quick,
bright smile.

"Would you like to see one of his manuscripts?"

"I'd love to," said the duchess, "and then I simply must bolt."

Mrs. Driffield took from a shelf a manuscript bound in blue
morocco, and while the rest of the party reverently examined it
I had a look at the books with which the room was lined. As
authors will, I ran my eye round quickly to see if there were any
of mine, but could not find one; I saw, however, a complete set
of Alroy Kear's and a great many novels in bright bindings, which
looked suspiciously unread; I guessed that they were the works of
authors who had sent them to the master in homage to his talent
and perhaps the hope of a few words of eulogy that could be used
in the publisher's advertisements. But all the books were so neatly
arranged, they were so clean, that I had the impression they were
very seldom read. There was the Oxford Dictionary and there
were standard editions in grand bindings of most of the English
classics, Fielding, Boswell, Hazlitt and so on, and there were a
great many books on the sea; I recognised the variously coloured,
untidy volumes of the sailing directions issued by the Admiralty,
and there were a number of works on gardening. The room had
the look not of a writer's workshop, but of a memorial to a great
name, and you could almost see already the desultory tripper
wandering in for want of something better to do and smell the
rather musty, close smell of a museum that few visited. I had
a suspicion that nowadays if Driffield read anything at all it was
the *Gardener's Chronicle* or the *Shipping Gazette*, of which I saw
a bundle on a table in the corner.

When the ladies had seen all they wanted we bade our hosts
farewell. But Lady Hodmarsh was a woman of tact and it must
have occurred to her that I, the excuse for the party, had scarcely
had a word with Edward Driffield, for at the door, enveloping me
with a friendly smile, she said to him:

"I was so interested to hear that you and Mr. Ashenden had known one another years and years ago. Was he a nice little boy?"

Driffield looked at me for a moment with that level, ironic gaze of his. I had the impression that if there had been nobody there he would have put his tongue out at me.

"Shy," he replied. "I taught him to ride a bicycle."

We got once more into the huge yellow Rolls and drove off.

"He's too sweet," said the duchess. "I'm so glad we went."

"He has such nice manners, hasn't he?" said Lady Hodmarsh.

"You didn't really expect him to eat his peas with a knife, did you?" I asked.

"I wish he had," said Scallion. "It would have been so picturesque."

"I believe it's very difficult," said the duchess. "I've tried over and over again and I can never get them to stay on."

"You have to spear them," said Scallion.

"Not at all," retorted the duchess. "You have to balance them on the flat, and they roll like the devil."

"What did you think of Mrs. Driffield?" asked Lady Hodmarsh.

"I suppose she serves her purpose," said the duchess.

"He's so old, poor darling, he must have someone to look after him. You know she was a hospital nurse?"

"Oh, was she?" said the duchess. "I thought perhaps she'd been his secretary or typist or something."

"She's quite nice," said Lady Hodmarsh, warmly defending a friend.

"Oh, quite."

"He had a long illness about twenty years ago, and she was his nurse then, and after he got well he married her."

"Funny how men will do that. She must have been years younger than him. She can't be more than—what?—forty or forty-five."

"No, I shouldn't think so. Forty-seven, say. I'm told she's done a great deal for him. I mean, she's made him quite presentable. Alroy Kear told me that before that he was almost too bohemian."

"As a rule authors' wives are odious."

"It's such a bore having to have them, isn't it?"

"Crashing. I wonder they don't see that themselves."

"Poor wretches, they often suffer from the delusion that people find them interesting," I murmured.

We reached Tercanbury, dropped the duchess at the station and drove on.

CHAPTER V

It was true that Edward Driffield had taught me to bicycle. That was indeed how I first made his acquaintance. I do not know how long the safety bicycle had been invented, but I know that it was not common in the remote part of Kent in which I lived and when you saw someone speeding along on solid tyres you turned round and looked till he was out of sight. It was still a matter for jocularity on the part of middle-aged gentlemen who said Shank's pony was good enough for them, and for trepidation on the part of elderly ladies who made a dash for the side of the road when they saw one coming. I had been for some time filled with envy of the boys whom I saw riding into the school grounds on their bicycles. It gave a pretty opportunity for showing off when you entered the gateway without holding on to the handles. I had persuaded my uncle to let me have one at the beginning of the summer holidays, and though my aunt was against it, since she said I should only break my neck, he had yielded to my pertinacity more willingly because I was of course paying for it out of my own money. I ordered it before school broke up and a few days later the carrier brought it over from Tercanbury.

I was determined to learn to ride it by myself and chaps at school had told me that they had learned in half an hour. I tried and tried and at last came to the conclusion that I was abnormally stupid, but even after my pride was sufficiently humbled for me to allow the gardener to hold me up I seemed at the end of the first morning no nearer to being able to get on by myself than at the beginning. Next day, however, thinking that the carriage drive at the vicarage was too winding to give a fellow a proper chance, I wheeled the bicycle to a road not far away which I knew was perfectly flat and straight and so solitary that no one would see me making a fool of myself. I tried several times to mount, but fell off each time. I barked my shins against the pedals and got very hot and bothered. After I had been doing this for about an hour, though I began to think that God did not intend me to ride a bicycle, but was determined (unable to bear the thought of the sarcasms of my uncle, his representative at Blackstable) to do so all the same, to my disgust I saw two people on bicycles coming along the deserted road. I immediately wheeled my machine to the side and sat down on a stile, looking out to sea in a nonchalant way as though I had been for a ride and were just sitting there wrapped in contemplation of the vasty ocean. I kept my eyes dreamily averted from the two persons who were advancing towards me, but I felt that they were coming nearer, and through the corner of my eye I saw that they were a man and a woman. As they passed me the woman swerved violently to my side of the road and, crashing against me, fell to the ground.

"Oh, I'm sorry," she said. "I knew I should fall off the moment I saw you."

It was impossible under the circumstances to preserve my appearance of abstraction and, blushing furiously, I said that it didn't matter at all.

The man had got off as she fell.

"You haven't hurt yourself?" he asked.

"Oh, no."

I recognised him then as Edward Driffield, the author I had seen walking with the curate a few days before.

"I'm just learning to ride," said his companion. "And I fall off whenever I see anything in the road."

"Aren't you the vicar's nephew?" said Driffield. "I saw you the other day. Galloway told me who you were. This is my wife."

She held out her hand with an oddly frank gesture and when I took it gave mine a warm and hearty pressure. She smiled with her lips and with her eyes and there was in her smile something that even then I recognised as singularly pleasant. I was confused. People I did not know made me dreadfully self-conscious, and I could not take in any of the details of her appearance. I just had an impression of a rather large blonde woman. I do not know if I noticed then or only remembered afterward that she wore a full skirt of blue serge, a pink shirt with a starched front and a starched collar, and a straw hat, called in those days, I think, a boater, perched on the top of a lot of golden hair.

"I think bicycling's lovely, don't you?" she said, looking at my beautiful new machine which leaned against the stile. "It must be wonderful to be able to ride well."

I felt that this inferred an admiration for my proficiency.

"It's only a matter of practice," I said.

"This is only my third lesson. Mr. Driffield says I'm coming on wonderful, but I feel so stupid I could kick myself. How long did it take you before you could ride?"

I blushed to the roots of my hair. I could hardly utter the shameful words.

"I can't ride," I said. "I've only just got this bike and this is the first time I've tried."

I equivocated a trifle there, but I made it all right with my conscience by adding the mental reservation: except yesterday at home in the garden.

"I'll give you a lesson if you like," said Driffield in his good-humoured way. "Come on."

"Oh, no," I said. "I wouldn't dream of it."

"Why not?" asked his wife, her blue eyes still pleasantly smiling. "Mr. Driffield would like to and it'll give me a chance to rest."

Driffield took my bicycle, and I, reluctant but unable to withstand his friendly violence, clumsily mounted. I swayed from side to side, but he held me with a firm hand.

"Faster," he said.

I pedalled and he ran by me as I wobbled from side to side. We were both very hot when, notwithstanding his efforts, I at last fell off. It was very hard under such circumstances to preserve the standoffishness befitting the vicar's nephew with the son of Miss Wolfe's bailiff, and when I started back again and for thirty or forty thrilling yards actually rode by myself and Mrs. Driffield ran into the middle of the road with her arms akimbo shouting: "Go it, go it, two to one on the favourite," I was laughing so much that I positively forgot all about my social status. I got off of my own accord, my face no doubt wearing an air of immodest triumph, and received without embarrassment the Driffields' congratulation on my cleverness in riding a bicycle the very first day I tried.

"I want to see if I can get on by myself," said Mrs. Driffield, and I sat down again on the stile while her husband and I watched her unavailing struggles.

Then, wanting to rest again, disappointed but cheerful, she sat down beside me. Driffield lit his pipe. We chatted. I did not of course realise it then, but I know now that there was a disarming frankness in her manner that put one at one's ease. She talked with a kind of eagerness, like a child bubbling over with the zest of life, and her eyes were lit all the time by her engaging smile. I did not know why I liked it. I should say it was a little sly, if slyness were not a displeasing quality; it was too innocent to be sly. It was mischievous rather, like that of a child who has done something that he thinks funny, but is quite well aware that you will think rather naughty; he knows all the same that you won't be really cross and if you don't find out about it quickly he'll come and tell you himself. But of course then I only knew that her smile made me feel at home.

Presently Driffield, looking at his watch, said that they must be going and suggested that we should all ride back together in style. It was just the time that my aunt and uncle would be coming home from their daily walk down the town and I did not like to run the risk of being seen with people whom they would not at all approve of; so I asked them to go on first, as they would go more quickly than I. Mrs. Driffield would not hear of it, but Driffield gave me a funny, amused little look, which made me think that he saw through my excuse, so that I blushed scarlet, and he said:

"Let him go by himself, Rosie. He can manage better alone."

"All right. Shall you be here to-morrow? We're coming."

"I'll try to," I answered.

They rode off, and in a few minutes I followed. Feeling very much pleased with myself, I rode all the way to the vicarage gates without falling. I think I boasted a good deal at dinner, but I did not say that I had met the Driffields.

Next day at about eleven I got my bicycle out of the coach-house. It was so called though it held not even a pony trap and was used by the gardener to keep the mower and the roller, and by Mary-Ann for her sack of meal for the chickens. I wheeled it down to the gate and, mounting none too easily, rode along the Tercanbury Road till I came to the old turnpike and turned into Joy Lane.

The sky was blue and the air, warm and yet fresh, crackled, as it were, with the heat. The light was brilliant without harshness.

The sun's beams seemed to hit the white road with a directed energy and bounce back like a rubber ball.

I rode backward and forward, waiting for the Driffields, and presently saw them come. I waved to them and turned round (getting off to do so) and we pedalled along together. Mrs. Driffield and I complimented one another on our progress. We rode anxiously, clinging like grim death to the handle-bars, but exultant, and Driffield said that as soon as we felt sure of ourselves we must go for rides all over the country.

"I want to get rubbings of one or two brasses in the neighbourhood," he said.

I did not know what he meant, but he would not explain.

"Wait and I'll show you," he said. "Do you think you could ride fourteen miles to-morrow, seven there and seven back?"

"Rather," I said.

"I'll bring a sheet of paper for you and some wax and you can make a rubbing. But you'd better ask your uncle if you can come."

"I needn't do that."

"I think you'd better all the same."

Mrs. Driffield gave me that peculiar look of hers, mischievous and yet friendly, and I blushed scarlet. I knew that if I asked my uncle he would say no. It would be much better to say nothing about it. But as we rode along I saw coming towards us the doctor in his dogcart. I looked straight in front of me as he passed in the vain hope that if I did not look at him he would not look at me. I was uneasy. If he had seen me the fact would quickly reach the ears of my uncle or my aunt and I considered whether it would not be safer to disclose myself a secret that could no longer be concealed. When we parted at the vicarage gates (I had not been able to avoid riding as far as this in their company) Driffield said that if I found I could come with them next day I had better call for them as early as I could.

"You know where we live, don't you? Next door to the Congregational Church. It's called Lime Cottage."

When I sat down to dinner I looked for an opportunity to slip in casually the information that I had by accident run across the Driffields; but news travelled fast in Blackstable.

"Who were those people you were bicycling with this morning?" asked my aunt. "We met Dr. Anstey in the town and he said he'd seen you."

My uncle, chewing his roast beef with an air of disapproval, looked sullenly at his plate.

"The Driffields," I said with nonchalance. "You know, the author. Mr. Galloway knows them."

"They're most disreputable people," said my uncle. "I don't wish you to associate with them."

"Why not?" I asked.

"I'm not going to give you my reasons. It's enough that I don't wish it."

"How did you ever get to know them?" asked my aunt.

"I was just riding along and they were riding along, and they asked me if I'd like to ride with them," I said, distorting the truth a little.

"I call it very pushing," said my uncle.

I began to sulk. And to show my indignation when the sweet was put on the table, though it was raspberry tart which I was extremely fond of, I refused to have any. My aunt asked me if I was not feeling very well.

"Yes," I said, as haughtily as I could, "I'm feeling all right."

"Have a little bit," said my aunt.

"I'm not hungry," I answered.

"Just to please me."

"He must know when he's had enough," said my uncle.

I gave him a bitter look.

"I don't mind having a small piece," I said.

My aunt gave me a generous helping, which I ate with the air of one who, impelled by a stern sense of duty, performs an act that is deeply distasteful to him. It was a beautiful raspberry tart. Mary-Ann made short pastry that melted in the mouth. But when my aunt asked me whether I could not manage a little more I refused with cold dignity. She did not insist. My uncle said grace and I carried my outraged feelings into the drawing-room.

But when I reckoned that the servants had finished their dinner I went into the kitchen. Emily was cleaning the silver in the pantry. Mary-Ann was washing up.

"I say, what's wrong with the Driffields?" I asked her.

Mary-Ann had come to the vicarage when she was eighteen. She had bathed me when I was a small boy, given me powders in plum jam when I needed them, packed my box when I went to school, nursed me when I was ill, read to me when I was bored and scolded me when I was naughty. Emily, the housemaid, was a flighty young thing, and Mary-Ann didn't know whatever would become of me if *she* had the looking after of me. Mary-Ann was a Blackstable girl. She had never been to London in her life and I do not think she had been to Tercanbury more than three or four times. She was never ill. She never had a holiday. She was paid twelve pounds a year. One evening a week she went down the town to see her mother, who did the vicarage washing; and on Sunday evenings she went to church. But Mary-Ann knew everything that went on in Blackstable. She knew who everybody was, who had married whom, what anyone's father had died of, and how many children, and what they were called, any woman had had.

I asked Mary-Ann my question and she slopped a wet clout noisily into the sink.

"I don't blame your uncle," she said. "I wouldn't let you go about with them, not if you was my nephew. Fancy their askin' you to ride your bicycle with them! Some people will do anything."

I saw that the conversation in the dining-room had been repeated to Mary-Ann.

"I'm not a child," I said.

"That makes it all the worse. The inpudence of their comin' 'ere at all!" Mary-Ann dropped her aitches freely. "Takin' a house and pretendin' to be ladies and gentlemen. Now leave that pie alone."

The raspberry tart was standing on the kitchen table and I broke off a piece of crust with my fingers and put it in my mouth.

"We're goin' to eat that for our supper. If you'd wanted a second 'elpin' why didn't you 'ave one when you was 'avin' your dinner? Ted Driffield never could stick to anything. He 'ad a good education, too. The one I'm sorry for is his mother. He's been a trouble to 'er from the day he was born. And then to go an' marry Rosie Gann. They tell me that when he told his mother what he was goin' to do she took to 'er bed and stayed there for three weeks and wouldn't talk to anybody."

"Was Mrs. Driffield Rosie Gann before she married? Which Ganns were those?"

Gann was one of the commonest names at Blackstable. The churchyard was thick with their graves.

"Oh, you wouldn't 'ave known them. Old Josiah Gann was her father. He was a wild one, too. He went for a soldier and when he come back he 'ad a wooden leg. He used to go out doing painting, but he was out of work more often than not. They lived in the next 'ouse to us in Rye Lane. Me an' Rosie used to go to Sunday School together."

"But she's not as old as you are," I said with the bluntness of my age.

"She'll never see thirty again."

Mary-Ann was a little woman with a snub nose and decayed teeth, but fresh-coloured, and I do not suppose she could have been more than thirty-five.

"Rosie ain't more than four or five years younger than me, whatever she may pretend she is. They tell me you wouldn't know her now all dressed up and everything."

"Is it true that she was a barmaid?" I asked.

"Yes, at the 'Railway Arms' and then at the 'Prince of Wales's Feathers' at Haversham. Mrs. Reeves 'ad her to 'elp in the bar at the 'Railway Arms', but it got so bad she had to get rid of her."

The "Railway Arms" was a very modest little public-house just opposite the station of the London, Chatham & Dover Railway. It had a sort of sinister gaiety. On a winter's night as you passed by you saw through the glass doors men lounging about the bar. My uncle very much disapproved of it, and had for years been trying to get its licence taken away. It was frequented by the railway porters, colliers and farm labourers. The respectable residents of Blackstable would have disdained to enter it and, when they wanted a glass of bitter, went to the "Bear and Key" or the "Duke of Kent".

"Why, what did she do?" I asked, my eyes popping out of my head.

"What didn't she do?" said Mary-Ann. "What d'you think your uncle would say if he caught me tellin' you things like that? There wasn't a man who come in to 'ave a drink what she didn't carry on with. No matter who they was. She couldn't stick to anybody, it was just one man after another. They tell me it was simply 'orrible. That was when it begun with Lord George. It wasn't the sort of place he was likely to go to, he was too grand for that, but they say he went in accidental-like one day when his train was late, and he saw her. And after that he was never out of the place, mixin' with all them common rough people, and of course they all knew what he was there for, and him with a wife and three children. Oh, I was sorry for her! And the talk it made. Well, it got so Mrs. Reeves said she wasn't going to put up with it another day and she give her her wages and told her to pack her box and go. Good riddance to bad rubbish, that's what I said."

I knew Lord George very well. His name was George Kemp and the title by which he was always known had been given him ironically owing to his grand manner. He was our coal merchant, but he also dabbled in house property, and he owned a share in one or two colliers. He lived in a new brick house that stood in its own grounds and he drove his own trap. He was a stoutish man with a pointed beard, florid, with a high colour and bold blue eyes. Remembering him, I think he must have looked like some jolly rubicund merchant in an old Dutch picture. He was always very flashily dressed and when you saw him driving at a smart pace down the middle of the High Street in a fawn-coloured covert-coat with large buttons, his brown bowler on the side of his head and a red rose in his buttonhole, you could not but look at him. On Sunday he used to come to church in a lustrous topper and a frock-coat. Everyone knew that he wanted to be made churchwarden, and it was evident that his energy would have made him useful, but my uncle said not in his time, and though Lord George as a protest went to chapel for a year my uncle remained obdurate. He cut him dead when he met him in the town. A reconciliation was effected and Lord George came to church again, but my uncle only yielded so far as to appoint him sidesman. The gentry thought him vulgar and I have no doubt that he was vain and boastful. They complained of his loud voice and his strident laugh—when he was talking to somebody on one side of the street you heard every word he said from the other—and they thought his manners dreadful. He was much too friendly; when he talked to them it was as though he were not in trade at all; they said he was very pushing. But if he thought his hail-fellow-well-met air, his activity in public works, his open purse when subscriptions were needed for the annual regatta or for the harvest festival, his willingness to do anyone a good turn were going to break the barriers at Blackstable he was mistaken. His efforts at sociability were met with blank hostility.

I remember once that the doctor's wife was calling on my aunt and Emily came in to tell my uncle that Mr. George Kemp would like to see him.

"But I heard the front door ring, Emily," said my aunt.

"Yes'm, he came to the front door."

There was a moment's awkwardness. Everyone was at a loss to know how to deal with such an unusual occurrence, and even Emily, who knew who should come to the front door, who should go to the side door, and who to the back, looked a trifle flustered. My aunt, who was a gentle soul, I think felt honestly embarrassed that anyone should put himself in such a false position; but the doctor's wife gave a little sniff of contempt. At last my uncle collected himself.

"Show him into the study, Emily," he said. "I'll come as soon as I've finished my tea."

But Lord George remained exuberant, flashy, loud and boisterous. He said the town was dead and he was going to wake it up. He was going to get the company to run excursion trains. He didn't see why it shouldn't become another Margate. And why shouldn't they have a mayor? Ferne Bay had one.

"I suppose he thinks he'd be mayor himself," said the people of Blackstable. They pursed their lips. "Pride goeth before a fall," they said.

And my uncle remarked that you could take a horse to the water but you couldn't make him drink.

I should add that I looked upon Lord George with the same scornful derision as everyone else. It outraged me that he should stop me in the street and call me by my Christian name and talk to me as though there were no social difference between us. He even suggested that I should play cricket with his sons, who were of about the same age as myself. But they went to the grammar school at Haversham and of course I couldn't possibly have anything to do with them.

I was shocked and thrilled by what Mary-Ann told me, but I had difficulty in believing it. I had read too many novels and had learnt too much at school not to know a good deal about love, but I thought it was a matter that only concerned young people. I could not conceive that a man with a beard, who had sons as old as I, could have any feelings of that sort. I thought when you married all that was finished. That people over thirty should make love seemed to me rather disgusting.

"You don't mean to say they did anything?" I asked Mary-Ann.

"From what I hear there's very little that Rosie Gann didn't do. And Lord George wasn't the only one."

"But, look here, why didn't she have a baby?"

In the novels I had read whenever lovely woman stooped to folly she had a baby. The cause was put with infinite precaution, sometimes indeed suggested only by a row of asterisks, but the result was inevitable.

"More by good luck than by good management, I lay," said Mary-Ann. Then she recollected herself and stopped drying the plates she was busy with. "It seems to me you know a lot more than you ought to," she said.

"Of course I know," I said importantly. "Hang it all, I'm practically grown up, aren't I?"

"All I can tell you," said Mary-Ann, "is that when Mrs. Reeves give her the sack Lord George got her a job at the 'Prince of Wales's Feathers' at Haversham and he was always poppin' over there in his trap. You can't tell me the ale's any different over there from what it is here."

"Then why did Ted Driffield marry her?" I asked.

"Ask me another," said Mary-Ann. "It was at the 'Feathers' he saw her. I suppose he couldn't get no one else to marry him. No respectable girl would 'ave 'ad 'im."

"Did he know about her?"

"You'd better ask him."

I was silent. It was all very puzzling.

"What does she look like now?" asked Mary-Ann. "I never seen her since she married. I never even speak to 'er after I 'eard what was goin' on at the 'Railway Arms'."

"She looks all right," I said.

"Well, you ask her if she remembers me and see what she says."

CHAPTER VI

I had quite made up my mind that I was going out with the Driffields next morning, but knew that it was no good asking my uncle if I might. If he found out that I had been and made a row it couldn't be helped, and if Ted Driffield asked me whether I had got my uncle's permission I was quite prepared to say I had. But I had after all no need to lie. In the afternoon, the tide being high, I walked down to the beach to bathe and my uncle, having something to do in the town, walked part of the way with me. Just as we were passing the "Bear and Key", Ted Driffield stepped out of it. He saw us and came straight up to my uncle. I was startled at his coolness.

"Good-afternoon, Vicar," he said. "I wonder if you remember me. I used to sing in the choir when I was a boy. Ted Driffield. My old governor was Miss Wolfe's bailiff."

My uncle was a very timid man, and he was taken aback.

"Oh, yes, how do you do? I was sorry to hear your father died."

"I've made the acquaintance of your young nephew. I was wondering if you'd let him come for a ride with me to-morrow. It's rather dull for him riding alone, and I'm going to do a rubbing of one of the brasses at Ferne Church."

"It's very kind of you, but——"

My uncle was going to refuse, but Driffield interrupted him.

"I'll see he doesn't get up to any mischief. I thought he might like to make a rubbing himself. It would be an interest for him. I'll give him some paper and wax so that it won't cost him anything."

My uncle had not a consecutive mind and the suggestion that Ted Driffield should pay for my paper and wax offended him so much that he quite forgot his intention to forbid me to go at all.

"He can quite well get his own paper and wax," he said. "He has plenty of pocket money, and he'd much better spend it on something like that than on sweets and make himself sick."

"Well, if he goes to Hayward, the stationer's, and says he wants the same paper as I got and the wax they'll let him have it."

"I'll go now," I said, and to prevent any changes of mind on my uncle's part dashed across the road.

CHAPTER VII

I do not know why the Driffields bothered about me unless it was from pure kindness of heart. I was a dull little boy, not very talkative, and if I amused Ted Driffield at all it must have been unconsciously. Perhaps he was tickled by my attitude of superiority. I was under the impression that it was condescension on my part to consort with the son of Miss Wolfe's bailiff, and he what my uncle called a penny-a-liner; and when, perhaps with a trace of superciliousness, I asked him to lend me one of his books and he said it wouldn't interest me I took him at his word and did not insist. After my uncle had once consented to my going out with the Driffields he made no further objection to my association with them. Sometimes we went for sails together, sometimes we went to some picturesque spot and Driffield painted a little water-colour. I do not know if the English climate was better in those days or if it is only an illusion of youth, but I seem to remember that all through that summer the sunny days followed one another in an unbroken line. I began to feel a curious affection for the undulating, opulent and gracious country. We went far afield, to one church after another, taking rubbings of brasses, knights in armour and ladies in stiff farthingales. Ted Driffield fired me with his own enthusiasm for this simple pursuit and I rubbed with passion. I showed my uncle proudly the results of my industry, and I suppose he thought that, whatever my company, I could not come to much harm when I was occupied in church. Mrs. Driffield used to remain in the churchyard while we were at work, not reading or sewing, but just mooning about; she seemed able to do nothing for an indefinite time without feeling bored. Sometimes I would go out and sit with her for a little on the grass. We chattered about my school, my friends there and my masters, about the people at Blackstable and about nothing at all. She gratified me by calling me Mr. Ashenden. I think she was the first person who had ever done so and it made me feel grown up. I resented it vastly when people called me Master Willie. I thought it a ridiculous name for anyone to have. In fact I did not like either of my names and spent much time inventing others that would have suited me better. The ones I preferred were Roderic Ravensworth and I covered sheets of paper with this signature in a suitably dashing hand. I did not mind Ludovic Montgomery either.

I could not get over what Mary-Ann had told me about Mrs. Driffield. Though I knew theoretically what people did when they were married, and was capable of putting the facts in the bluntest language, I did not really understand it. I thought it indeed rather disgusting and I did not quite, quite believe it. After all, I was aware that the earth was round, but I *knew* it was flat. Mrs. Driffield seemed so frank, her laugh was so open, there was in her demeanour something so young and childlike, that I could not see her "going with" sailors and above all anyone so gross and horrible as Lord George. She was not at all the type of the wicked woman I had read of in novels. Of course I knew she wasn't "good form" and she spoke with the Blackstable accent, she dropped an aitch now and then, and sometimes her grammar gave me a shock, but I couldn't help liking her. I came to the conclusion that what Mary-Ann had told me was a pack of lies.

One day I happened to tell her that Mary-Ann was our cook.

"She says she lived next door to you in Rye Lane," I added, quite prepared to hear Mrs. Driffield say that she had never even heard of her.

But she smiled and her blue eyes gleamed.

"That's right. She used to take me to Sunday School. She used to have a rare job keeping me quiet. I heard she'd gone to service at the vicarage. Fancy her being there still! I haven't seen her for donkey's years. I'd like to see her again and have a chat about old days. Remember me to her, will you, and ask her to look in on her evening out. I'll give her a cup of tea."

I was taken aback at this. After all, the Driffields lived in a house that they were talking of buying and they had a "general". It wouldn't be at all the thing for them to have Mary-Ann to tea, and it would make it very awkward for me. They seemed to have no sense of the things one could do and the things one simply couldn't. It never ceased to embarrass me, the way in which they talk of incidents in their past that I should have thought they would not dream of mentioning. I do not know that the people I lived among were pretentious in the sense of making themselves out to be richer or grander than they really were, but looking back it does seem to me that they lived a life full of pretences. They dwelt behind a mask of respectability. You never caught them in their shirt-sleeves with their feet on the table. The ladies put on afternoon dresses and were not visible till then; they lived privately with rigid economy so that you could not drop in for a casual meal, but when they entertained their tables groaned with food. Though catastrophe overwhelmed the family, they held their heads high and ignored it. One of the sons might have married an actress, but they never referred to the calamity, and though the neighbours said it was dreadful, they took ostentatious care not to mention the theatre in the presence of the afflicted. We all knew that the wife of Major Greencourt who had taken the Three Gables was connected with trade, but neither she nor the major ever so much as hinted at the discreditable secret; and though we sniffed at them behind their backs, we were too polite even to mention crockery (the source of Mrs. Greencourt's adequate income) in their presence. It was still not unheard of for an angry parent to cut off his son with a shilling or to tell his daughter (who like my own mother had married a solicitor) never to darken his doors again. I was used to all this and it seemed to me natural. What did shock me was to hear Ted Driffield speak of being a waiter in a restaurant in Holborn as though it were the most ordinary thing in the world. I knew he had run away to sea; that was romantic; I knew that boys, in books at all events, often did this and had thrilling adventures before they married a fortune and an earl's daughter; but Ted Driffield had driven a cab at Maidstone and had been clerk in a booking-office at Birmingham. Once when we bicycled past the "Railway Arms", Mrs. Driffield mentioned quite casually, as though it were something that anyone might have done, that she had worked there for three years.

"It was my first place," she said. "After that I went to the 'Feathers' at Haversham. I only left there to get married."

She laughed as though she enjoyed the recollection. I did not know what to say; I did not know which way to look; I blushed scarlet. Another time when we were going through Ferne Bay on our way back from a long excursion, it being a hot day and all of us thirsty, she suggested that we should go into the "Dolphin" and have a glass of beer. She began talking to the girl behind the bar and I was horrified to hear her remark that she had been in the business herself for five years. The landlord joined us and Ted Driffield offered him a drink, and Mrs. Driffield said that the barmaid must have a glass of port, and for some time they all chatted amiably about trade and tied houses and how the price of everything was going up. Meanwhile, I stood, hot and cold all over and not knowing what to do with myself. As we went out Mrs. Driffield remarked:

"I took quite a fancy to that girl, Ted. She ought to do well for herself. As I said to her, it's a hard life but a merry one. You do see a bit of what's going on and if you play your cards right you ought to marry well. I noticed she had an engagement ring on, but she told me she just wore that because it gave the fellows a chance to tease her."

Driffield laughed. She turned to me.

"I had a rare old time when I was a barmaid, but of course you can't go on for ever. You have to think of your future."

But a great jolt awaited her. It was half-way through September and my holidays were drawing to an end. I was very full of the Driffields, but my desire to talk about them at home was snubbed by my uncle.

"We don't want your friends pushed down our throats all day long," said he. "There are other topics of conversation that are more suitable. But I do think that, as Ted Driffield was born in the parish and is seeing you almost every day, he might come to church occasionally."

One day I told Driffield: "My uncle wants you to come to church."

"All right. Let's go to church next Sunday night, Rosie."

"I don't mind," she said.

I told Mary-Ann they were going. I sat in the vicarage pew just behind the squire's and I could not look round, but I was conscious by the behaviour of my neighbours on the other side of the aisle that they were there, and as soon as I had a chance next day I asked Mary-Ann if she had seen them.

"I see 'er all right," said Mary-Ann grimly.

"Did you speak to her afterwards?"

"Me?" She suddenly burst into anger. "You get out of my kitchen. What d'you want to come bothering me all day long? How d'you expect me to do my work with you getting in my way all the time?"

"All right," I said. "Don't get in a wax."

"I don't know what your uncle's about, lettin' you go all over the place with the likes of them. All them flowers in her 'at. I wonder she ain't ashamed to show her face. Now run along, I'm busy."

I did not know why Mary-Ann was so cross. I did not mention Mrs. Driffield again. But two or three days later I happened to go into the kitchen to get something I wanted. There were two kitchens at the vicarage, a small one in which the cooking was done and a large one, built I suppose for a time when country clergymen had large families and gave grand dinners to the surrounding gentry, where Mary-Ann sat and sewed when her day's work was over. We had cold supper at eight, so that after tea she had little to do. It was getting on for seven and the day was drawing in. It was Emily's evening out and I expected to find Mary-Ann alone, but as I went along the passage I heard voices and the sound of laughter. I supposed Mary-Ann had someone in to see her. The lamp was lit, but it had a thick green shade and the kitchen was almost in darkness. I saw a teapot and cups on the table. Mary-Ann was having a late cup of tea with her friend. The conversation stopped as I opened the door, then I heard a voice.

"Good-evening."

With a start I saw that Mary-Ann's friend was Mrs. Driffield. Mary-Ann laughed a little at my surprise.

"Rosie Gann dropped in to have a cup of tea with me," she said.

"We've been having a talk about old times."

Mary-Ann was a little shy at my finding her thus, but not half so shy as I. Mrs. Driffield gave me that childlike, mischievous smile of hers; she was perfectly at her ease. For some reason I noticed her dress. I suppose because I had never seen her so grand before. It was of pale-blue cloth, very tight at the waist, with high sleeves and a long skirt with a flounce at the bottom. She wore a large black straw hat with a great quantity of roses and leaves and bows on it. It was evidently the hat she had worn in church on Sunday.

"I thought if I went on waiting till Mary-Ann came to see me I'd have to wait till doomsday, so I thought the best thing I could do was to come and see her myself."

Mary-Ann grinned self-consciously, but did not look displeased. I asked for whatever it was I wanted and as quickly as I could left them. I went out into the garden and wandered about aimlessly. I walked down to the road and looked over the gate. The night had fallen. Presently I saw a man strolling along. I paid no attention to him, but he passed backward and forward and it looked as though he were waiting for someone. At first I thought it might be Ted Driffield and I was on the point of going out when he stopped and lit a pipe; I saw it was Lord George. I wondered what he was doing there and at the same moment it struck me that he was waiting for Mrs. Driffield. My heart began to beat fast, and though I was hidden by the darkness I withdrew into the shade of the bushes. I waited a few minutes longer, then I saw the side door open and Mrs. Driffield let out by Mary-Ann. I heard her footsteps on the gravel. She came to the gate and opened it. It opened with a little click. At the sound Lord George stepped across the road and before she could come out slipped in. He took her in his arms and gave her a great hug. She gave a little laugh.

"Take care of my hat," she whispered.

I was not more than three feet away from them and I was terrified lest they should notice me. I was so ashamed for them. I was trembling with agitation. For a minute he held her in his arms.

"What about the garden?" he said, still in a whisper.

"No, there's that boy. Let's go in the fields."

They went out by the gate, he with his arm round her waist, and were lost in the night. Now I felt my heart pounding against my chest so that I could hardly breathe. I was so astonished at what I had seen that I could not think sensibly. I would have given anything to be able to tell someone, but it was a secret and I must keep it. I was thrilled with the importance it gave me. I walked slowly up to the house and let myself in by the side door. Mary-Ann, hearing it open, called me.

"Is that you, Master Willie?"

"Yes."

I looked in the kitchen. Mary-Ann was putting the supper on a tray to take it into the dining-room.

"I wouldn't say anything to your uncle about Rosie Gann 'avin' been here," she said.

"Oh, no."

"It was a surprisement to me. When I 'eard a knock at the side door and opened it and saw Rosie standing there, you could 'ave knocked me down with a feather. 'Mary-Ann,' she says, an' before I knew what she was up to she was kissing me all over me face. I couldn't but ask 'er in and when she was in I couldn't but ask her to 'ave a nice cup of tea."

Mary-Ann was anxious to excuse herself. After all she had said of Mrs. Driffield it must seem strange to me that I should find them sitting there together chatting away and laughing. I did not want to crow.

"She's not so bad, is she?" I said.

Mary-Ann smiled. Notwithstanding her black decayed teeth her smile was sweet and touching.

"I don't 'ardly know what it is, but there's somethin' you can't 'elp likin' about her. She was 'ere the best part of an hour and I will say that for 'er, she never once give 'erself airs. And she told me with 'er own lips the material of that dress she 'ad on cost thirteen and eleven a yard and I believe it. She remembers everything, how I used to brush her 'air for her when she was a tiny tot and how I used to make her wash her little 'ands before tea. You see, sometimes her mother used to send 'er in to 'ave her tea with us. She was as pretty as a picture in them days."

Mary-Ann looked back into the past and her funny crumpled face grew wistful.

"Oh, well," she said after a pause, "I dare say she's been no worse than plenty others if the truth was only known. She 'ad more temptation than most, and I dare say a lot of them as blame her would 'ave been no better than what she was if they'd 'ad the opportunity."

CHAPTER VIII

The weather broke suddenly; it grew chilly and heavy rain fell. It put an end to our excursions. I was not sorry, for I did not know how I could look Mrs. Driffield in the face now that I had seen her meeting with George Kemp. I was not so much shocked as astonished. I could not understand how it was possible for her to like being kissed by an old man, and the fantastic notion passed through my mind, filled with the novels I had read, that somehow Lord George held her in his power and forced her by his knowledge of some fearful secret to submit to his loathsome embraces. My imagination played with terrible possibilities. Bigamy, murder and forgery. Very few villains in books failed to hold the threat of exposure of one of these crimes over some hapless female. Perhaps Mrs. Driffield had backed a bill; I never could quite understand what this meant, but I knew that the consequences were disastrous. I toyed with the fancy of her anguish (the long sleepless nights when she sat at her window in her nightdress, her fair hair hanging to her knees, and watched hopelessly for the dawn) and saw myself (not a boy of fifteen with sixpence a week pocket money, but a tall man with a waxed moustache and muscles of steel in faultless evening dress) with a happy blend of heroism and dexterity rescuing her from the toils of the rascally blackmailer. On the other hand, it had not looked as though she had yielded quite unwillingly to Lord George's fondling and I could not get out of my ears the sound of her laugh. It had a note that I had never heard before. It gave me a queer feeling of breathlessness.

During the rest of my holidays I only saw the Driffields once more. I met them by chance in the town and they stopped and spoke to me. I suddenly felt very shy again, but when I looked at Mrs. Driffield I could not help blushing with embarrassment, for there was nothing in her countenance that indicated a guilty secret. She looked at me with those soft blue eyes of hers in which there was a child's playful naughtiness. She often held her mouth a little open, as though it were just going to break into a smile, and her lips were full and red. There was honesty and innocence in her face and an ingenuous frankness and though then I could not have expressed this, I felt it quite strongly. If I had put it into words at all I think I should have said: She looks as straight as a die. It was impossible that she could be "carrying on" with Lord George. There must be an explanation; I did not believe what my eyes had seen.

Then the day came when I had to go back to school. The carter had taken my trunk and I walked to the station by myself. I had refused to let my aunt see me off, thinking it more manly to go alone, but I felt rather low as I walked down the street. It was a small branch line to Tercanbury and the station was at the other end of the town near the beach. I took my ticket and settled myself in the corner of a third-class carriage. Suddenly I heard a voice: There he is; and Mr. and Mrs. Driffield bustled gaily up.

"We thought we must come and see you off," she said. "Are you feeling miserable?"

"No, of course not."

"Oh, well, it won't last long. We'll have no end of a time when you come back for Christmas. Can you skate?"

"No."

"I can. I'll teach you."

Her high spirits cheered me, and at the same time the thought that they had come to the station to say good-bye to me gave me a lump in my throat. I tried hard not to let the emotion I felt appear on my face.

"I expect I shall be playing a lot of rugger this term," I said. "I ought to get into the second fifteen."

She looked at me with kindly shining eyes, smiling with her full red lips. There was something in her smile I had always rather liked, and her voice seemed almost to tremble with a laugh or a tear. For one horrible moment I was afraid that she was going to kiss me. I was scared out of my wits. She talked on, she was mildly facetious as grown-up people are with schoolboys, and Driffield stood there without saying anything. He looked at me with a smile in his eyes and pulled his beard. Then the guard blew a cracked whistle and waved a red flag. Mrs. Driffield took my hand and shook it. Driffield came forward.

"Good-bye," he said. "Here's something for you."

He pressed a tiny packet into my hand and the train steamed off. When I opened it I found two half-crowns wrapped in a piece of toilet-paper. I blushed to the roots of my hair. I was glad enough to have an extra five shillings, but the thought that Ted Driffield had dared to give me a tip filled me with rage and humiliation. I could not possibly accept anything from him. It was true that I had bicycled with him and sailed with him, but he wasn't a sahib (I had got that from Major Greencourt) and it was an insult to give me five shillings. At first I thought of returning the money without a word, showing by my silence how outraged I was at the solecism he had committed, then I composed in my head a dignified and frigid letter in which I thanked him for his generosity, but said that he must see how impossible it was for a gentleman to accept a tip from someone who was practically a stranger. I thought it over for two or three days and every day it seemed more difficult to part with the two half-crowns. I felt sure that Driffield had meant it kindly, and of course he was very bad form and didn't know about things; it would be rather hard to hurt his feelings by sending the money back, and finally I spent it. But I assuaged my wounded pride by not writing to thank Driffield for his gift.

When Christmas came, however, and I went back to Blackstable for the holidays, it was the Driffields I was most eager to see. In that stagnant little place they alone seemed to have a connection with the outside world which already was beginning to touch my day-dreams with anxious curiosity. But I could not overcome my shyness enough to go to their house and call, and I hoped that I should meet them in the town. But the weather was dreadful, a boisterous wind whistled down the street, piercing you to the bone, and the few women who had an errand were swept along by their full skirts like fishing boats in half a gale. The cold rain scudded in sudden squalls and the sky, which in summer had enclosed the friendly country so snugly, now was a great pall that pressed upon the earth with awful menace. There was small hope of meeting the Driffields by chance and at last I took my courage in both hands and one day after tea slipped out. As far as the station the road was pitch dark, but there the street lamps, few and dim, made it easier to keep to the pavement. The Driffields lived in a little two-storey house in a side-street; it was of dingy yellow brick and had a bow window. I knocked and presently a little maid opened the door; I asked if Mrs. Driffield was in. She gave me an uncertain look and, saying she would go and see, left me standing in the passage. I had already heard voices in the next room, but they were stilled as she opened the door and, entering, shut it behind her. I had a faint impression of mystery; in the houses of my uncle's friends, even if there was no fire and the gas had to be lit as you went in, you were shown into the drawing-room when you called. But the door was opened and Driffield came out. There was only a speck of light in the passage and at first he could not see who it was; but in an instant he recognised me.

"Oh, it's you. We wondered when we were going to see you." Then he called out: "Rosie, it's young Ashenden."

There was a cry and before you could say knife Mrs. Driffield had come into the passage and was shaking my hands.

"Come in, come in. Take off your coat. Isn't it awful, the weather? You must be perishing."

She helped me with my coat and took off my muffler and snatched my cap out of my hand and drew me into the room. It was hot and stuffy, a tiny room full of furniture, with a fire burning in the grate; they had gas there, which we hadn't at the vicarage, and the three burners in round globes of frosted glass filled the room with harsh light. The air was grey with tobacco smoke. At first, dazzled and then taken aback by my effusive welcome, I did not see who the two men were who got up as I came in. Then I saw they were the curate, Mr. Galloway, and Lord George Kemp. I fancied that the curate shook my hand with constraint.

"How are you? I just came in to return some books that Mr.

Driffield had lent me and Mrs. Driffield very kindly asked me to stay to tea."

I felt rather than saw the quizzical look that Driffield gave him. He said something about the mammon of unrighteousness, which I recognised as a quotation, but did not gather the sense of. Mr. Galloway laughed.

"I don't know about that," he said. "What about the publicans and sinners?"

I thought the remark in very bad taste, but I was immediately seized upon by Lord George. There was no constraint about him.

"Well, young fellow, home for the holidays? My word, what a big chap you're growing."

I shook hands with him rather coldly. I wished I had not come.

"Let me give you a nice strong cup of tea," said Mrs. Driffield.

"I've already had tea."

"Have some more," said Lord George, speaking as though he owned the place (that was just like him). "A big fellow like you can always tuck away another piece of bread and butter and jam and Mrs. D. will cut you a slice with her own fair hands."

The tea things were still on the table and they were sitting round it. A chair was brought up for me and Mrs. Driffield gave me a piece of cake.

"We were just trying to persuade Ted to sing us a song," said Lord George. "Come on, Ted."

"Sing, 'All Through Stickin' to a Soljer', Ted," said Mrs. Driffield. "I love that."

"No, sing 'First We Mopped the Floor with Him'."

"I'll sing 'em both if you're not careful," said Driffield.

He took his banjo, which was lying on the top of the cottage piano, tuned it and began to sing. He had a rich baritone voice. I was quite used to people singing songs. When there was a tea party at the vicarage, or I went to one at the major's or the doctor's, people always brought their music with them. They left it in the hall, so that it should not seem that they wanted to be asked to play or sing; but after tea the hostess asked them if they had brought it. They shyly admitted that they had, and if it was at the vicarage I was sent to fetch it. Sometimes a young lady would say that she had quite given up playing and hadn't brought anything with her, and then her mother would break in and say that *she* had brought it. But when they sang it was not comic songs;

it was "I'll Sing Thee Songs of Araby", or "Good-Night, Beloved", or "Queen of My Heart". Once at the annual concert at the Assembly Rooms, Smithson, the draper, had sung a comic song, and though the people at the back of the hall had applauded a great deal, the gentry had seen nothing funny in it. Perhaps there wasn't. Anyhow, before the next concert he was asked to be a little more careful about what he sang ("Remember there are ladies present, Mr. Smithson") and so gave "The Death of Nelson". The next ditty that Driffield sang had a chorus and the curate and Lord George joined in lustily. I heard it a good many times afterward, but I can only remember four lines:

> *First we mopped the floor with him,*
> *Dragged him up and down the stairs;*
> *Then we lugged him round the room,*
> *Under tables, over chairs.*

When it was finished, assuming my best company manners, I turned to Mrs. Driffield.

"Don't you sing?" I asked.

"I do, but it always turns the milk, so Ted doesn't encourage me."

Driffield put down his banjo and lit a pipe.

"Well, how's the old book getting along, Ted?" said Lord George heartily.

"Oh, all right. I'm working away, you know."

"Good old Ted and his books," Lord George laughed. "Why don't you settle down and do something respectable for a change? I'll give you a job in my office."

"Oh, I'm all right."

"You let him be, George," said Mrs. Driffield. "He likes writing, and what I say is, as long as it keeps him happy, why shouldn't he?"

"Well, I don't pretend to know anything about books," began George Kemp.

"Then don't talk about them," interrupted Driffield with a smile.

"I don't think anyone need be ashamed to have written *Fairhaven*," said Mr. Galloway, "and I don't care what the critics said."

"Well, Ted, I've known you since I was a boy and I couldn't read it, try as I would."

"Oh, come on, we don't want to start talking about books," said Mrs. Driffield. "Sing us another song, Ted."

"I must be going," said the curate. He turned to me. "We might walk along together. Have you got anything for me to read, Driffield?"

Driffield pointed to a pile of new books that were heaped up on a table in the corner.

"Take your pick."

"By Jove, what a lot!" I said, looking at them greedily.

"Oh, it's all rubbish. They're sent down for review."

"What d'you do with them?"

"Take 'em into Tercanbury and sell 'em for what they'll fetch. It all helps to pay the butcher."

When we left, the curate and I, he with several books under his arm, he asked me:

"Did you tell your uncle you were coming to see the Driffields?"

"No, I just went out for a walk and it suddenly occurred to me that I might look in."

This of course was some way from the truth, but I did not care to tell Mr. Galloway that, though I was practically grown up, my uncle realised the fact so little that he was quite capable of trying to prevent me from seeing people he objected to.

"Unless you have to I wouldn't say anything about it in your place. The Driffields are perfectly all right, but your uncle doesn't quite approve of them."

"I know," I said. "It's such rot."

"Of course they're rather common, but he doesn't write half badly, and when you think what he came from it's wonderful that he writes at all."

I was glad to know how the land lay. Mr. Galloway did not wish my uncle to know that he was on friendly terms with the Driffields. I could feel sure at all events that he would not give me away.

The patronising manner in which my uncle's curate spoke of one who has been now so long recognised as one of the greater of the later Victorian novelists must arouse a smile; but it was the manner in which he was generally spoken of at Blackstable. One day we went to tea at Mrs. Greencourt's, who had staying with her a cousin, the wife of an Oxford don, and we had been told that she was very cultivated. She was a Mrs. Encombe, a little woman with an eager wrinkled face; she surprised us very much because she wore her grey hair short and a black serge skirt that only just came down below the tops of her square-toed boots. She was the first example of the New Woman that had ever been seen in Blackstable. We were staggered and immediately on the defensive, for she looked intellectual, and it made us feel shy. (Afterward we all scoffed at her, and my uncle said to my aunt: "Well, my dear, I'm thankful you're not clever, at least I've been spared that"; and my aunt in a playful mood put my uncle's slippers which were warming for him by the fire over her boots and said: "Look, I'm the new woman." And then we all said: "Mrs. Greencourt is very funny; you never know what she'll do next. But of course she isn't quite quite." We could hardly forget that her father made china and that her grandfather had been a factory hand.)

But we all found it very interesting to hear Mrs. Encombe talk of the people she knew. My uncle had been at Oxford, but everyone he asked about seemed to be dead. Mrs. Encombe knew Mrs. Humphry Ward and admired *Robert Elsmere*. My uncle considered it a scandalous work, and he was surprised that Mr. Gladstone, who at least called himself a Christian, had found a good word to say for it. They had quite an argument about it. My uncle said he thought it would unsettle people's opinions and give them all sorts of ideas that they were much better without. Mrs. Encombe answered that he wouldn't think that if he knew Mrs. Humphry Ward. She was a woman of the very highest character, a niece of Mr. Matthew Arnold, and whatever you might think of the book itself (and she, Mrs. Encombe, was quite willing to admit that there were parts which had better have been omitted) it was quite certain that she had written it from the very highest motives. Mrs. Encombe knew Miss Broughton too. She was of very good family and it was strange that she wrote the books she did.

"I don't see any harm in them," said Mrs. Hayforth the doctor's wife. "I enjoy them, especially *Red as a Rose is She*."

"Would you like your girls to read them?" asked Mrs. Encombe.

"Not just yet perhaps," said Mrs. Hayforth. "But when they're married I should have no objection."

"Then it might interest you to know," said Mrs. Encombe, "that when I was in Florence last Easter I was introduced to Ouida."

"That's quite another matter," returned Mrs. Hayforth. "I can't believe that any lady would read a book by Ouida."

"I read one out of curiosity," said Mrs. Encombe. "I must say, it's more what you'd expect from a Frenchman than from an English gentlewoman."

"Oh, but I understand she isn't really English. I've always heard her real name is Mademoiselle de la Ramée."

It was then that Mr. Galloway mentioned Edward Driffield. "You know we have an author living here," he said.

"We're not very proud of him," said the major. "He's the son of old Miss Wolfe's bailiff and he married a barmaid."

"Can he write?" asked Mrs. Encombe.

"You can tell at once that he's not a gentleman," said the curate, "but when you consider the disadvantages he's had to struggle against it's rather remarkable that he should write as well as he does."

"He's a friend of Willie's," said my uncle.

Everyone looked at me, and I felt very uncomfortable.

"They bicycled together last summer, and after Willie had gone back to school I got one of his books from the library to see what it was like. I read the first volume and then I sent it back. I wrote a pretty stiff letter to the librarian and I was glad to hear that he'd withdrawn it from circulation. If it had been my own property I should have put it promptly in the kitchen stove."

"I looked through one of his books myself," said the doctor. "It interested me because it was set in this neighbourhood and I recognised some of the people. But I can't say I liked it; I thought it unnecessarily coarse."

"I mentioned that to him," said Mr. Galloway, "and he said the men in the colliers that run up to Newcastle and the fishermen and farm hands don't behave like ladies and gentlemen and don't talk like them."

"But why write about people of that character?" said my uncle.

"That's what I say," said Mrs. Hayforth. "We all know that there are coarse and wicked and vicious people in the world, but I don't see what good it does to write about them."

"I'm not defending him," said Mr. Galloway. "I'm only telling you what explanation he gives himself. And then of course he brought up Dickens."

"Dickens is quite different," said my uncle. "I don't see how anyone can object to the *Pickwick Papers.*"

"I suppose it's a matter of taste," said my aunt. "I always found Dickens very coarse. I don't want to read about people who drop their aitches. I must say I'm very glad the weather's so bad now and Willie can't take any more rides with Mr. Driffield. I don't think he's quite the sort of person he ought to associate with."

Both Mr. Galloway and I looked down our noses.

CHAPTER IX

As often as the mild Christmas gaieties of Blackstable allowed me I went to the Driffields' little house next door to the Congregational chapel. I always found Lord George and often Mr. Galloway. Our conspiracy of silence had made us friends and when we met at the vicarage or in the vestry after church we looked at one another archly. We did not talk about our secret, but we enjoyed it; I think it gave us both a great deal of satisfaction to know that we were making a fool of my uncle. But once it occurred to me that George Kemp, meeting my uncle in the street, might remark casually that he had been seeing a lot of me at the Driffields'.

"What about Lord George?" I said to Mr. Galloway.

"Oh, I made that all right."

We chuckled. I began to like Lord George. At first I was very cold with him and scrupulously polite, but he seemed so unconscious of the social difference between us that I was forced to conclude that my haughty courtesy failed to put him in his place. He was always cordial, breezy, even boisterous; he chaffed me in his common way and I answered him back with schoolboy wit; we made the others laugh and this disposed me kindly toward him. He was forever bragging about the great schemes he had in mind, but he took in good part my jokes at the expense of his grandiose imaginations. It amused me to hear him tell stories about the swells of Blackstable that made them look foolish and when he mimicked their oddities I roared with laughter. He was blatant and vulgar and the way he dressed was always a shock to me (I had never been to Newmarket nor seen a trainer, but that was my idea of how a Newmarket trainer dressed), and his table manners were offensive, but I found myself less and less affronted by him. He gave me the *Pink 'Un* every week and I took it home, carefully tucked away in my greatcoat pocket, and read it in my bedroom.

I never went to the Driffields' till after tea at the vicarage, but I always managed to make a second tea when I got there. Afterward Ted Driffield sang comic songs, accompanying himself sometimes on the banjo and sometimes on the piano. He would sing, peering at the music with his rather short-sighted eyes, for an hour at a time; there was a smile on his lips and he liked us all to join in the chorus. We played whist. I had learned the game when I was a child and my uncle and aunt and I used to play at the vicarage during the long winter evenings. My uncle always took dummy, and though of course we played for love, when my aunt and I lost I used to retire under the dining-room table and cry. Ted Driffield did not play cards, he said he had no head for them, and when we started a game he would sit down by the fire and, pencil in hand, read one of the books that had been sent down to him from London to review. I had never played with three people before and of course I did not play well, but Mrs. Driffield had a natural card sense. Her movements as a rule were rather deliberate, but when it came to playing cards she was quick and alert. She played the rest of us right off our heads. Ordinarily she did not speak very much and then slowly, but when, after a hand was played, she took the trouble good-humouredly to point out to me my mistakes, she was not only lucid but voluble. Lord George chaffed her as he chaffed everybody; she would smile at his banter, for she very seldom laughed, and sometimes make a neat retort. They did not behave like lovers, but like familiar friends, and I should have quite forgotten what I had heard about them and what I had seen but that now and then she gave him a look that embarrassed me. Her eyes rested on him quietly, as though he were not a man but a chair or a table, and in them was a mischievous, childlike smile. Then I would notice that his face seemed suddenly to swell and he moved uneasily in his chair. I looked quickly at the curate, afraid that he would notice something, but he was intent on the cards or else was lighting his pipe.

The hour or two I spent nearly every day in that hot, poky, smoke-laden room passed like lightning, and as the holidays drew nearer to their end I was seized with dismay at the thought that I must spend the next three months dully at school.

"I don't know what we shall do without you," said Mrs. Driffield. "We shall have to play dummy."

I was glad that my going would break up the game. While I was doing prep I did not want to think that they were sitting in that little room and enjoying themselves just as if I did not exist.

"How long do you get at Easter?" asked Mr. Galloway.

"About three weeks."

"We'll have a lovely time then," said Mrs. Driffield. "The weather ought to be all right. We can ride in the mornings and then after tea we'll play whist. You've improved a lot. If we play three or four times a week during your Easter holidays you won't need to be afraid to play with anybody."

CHAPTER X

But the term came to an end at last. I was in high spirits when once more I got out of the train at Blackstable. I had grown a little and I had had a new suit made at Tercanbury, blue serge and very smart, and I had bought a new tie. I meant to go and see the Driffields immediately I had swallowed my tea and I was full of hope that the carrier would have brought my box in time for me to put the new suit on. It made me look quite grown up. I had already begun putting vaseline on my upper lip every night to make my moustache grow. On my way through the town I looked down the street in which the Driffields lived in the hope of seeing them. I should have liked to go in and say how-do-you-do, but I knew that Driffield wrote in the morning and Mrs. Driffield was not "presentable". I had all sorts of exciting things to tell them. I had won a heat in the hundred-yard race in the sports and I had been second in the hurdles. I meant to have a shot for the history prize in the summer and I was going to swot up my English history during the holidays. Though there was an east wind blowing, the sky was blue and there was a feeling of spring in the air. The High Street, with its colours washed clean by the wind and its lines sharp as though drawn with a new pen, looked like a picture by Samuel Scott, quiet and naïve and cosy—now, looking back; then it looked like nothing but High Street, Blackstable. When I came to the railway bridge I noticed that two or three houses were being built.

"By Jove," I said, "Lord George *is* going it."

In the fields beyond little white lambs were frisking. The elm trees were just beginning to turn green. I let myself in by the side door. My uncle was sitting in his arm-chair by the fire reading *The Times.* I shouted to my aunt and she came downstairs, a pink spot from the excitement of seeing me on each of her withered cheeks, and threw her thin old arms round my neck. She said all the right things:

"How you've grown!" and "Good gracious me, you'll be getting a moustache soon!"

I kissed my uncle on his bald forehead and I stood in front of the fire, with my legs well apart and my back to it, and was extremely grown up and rather condescending. Then I went upstairs to say how-do-you-do to Emily, and into the kitchen to shake hands with Mary-Ann, and out into the garden to see the gardener.

When I sat down hungrily to dinner and my uncle carved the leg of mutton I asked my aunt:

"Well, what's happened at Blackstable since I was here?"

"Nothing very much. Mrs. Greencourt went down to Mentone for six weeks, but she came back a few days ago. The major had an attack of gout."

"And your friends the Driffields have bolted," added my uncle.

"They've done what?" I cried.

"Bolted. They took their luggage away one night and just went up to London. They've left bills all over the place. They hadn't paid their rent and they hadn't paid for their furniture. They owed Harris the butcher the best part of thirty pounds."

"How awful," I said.

"That's bad enough," said my aunt, "but it appears they hadn't even paid the wages of the maid they had for three months."

I was flabbergasted. I thought I felt a little sick.

"I think in future," said my uncle, "you would be wiser not to consort with people whom your aunt and I don't think proper associates for you."

"One can't help feeling sorry for all those tradesmen they cheated," said my aunt.

"It serves them right," said my uncle. "Fancy giving credit to people like that! I should have thought anyone could see they were nothing but adventurers."

"I always wonder why they came down here at all."

"They just wanted to show off, and I suppose they thought as people knew who they were here it would be easier to get things on credit."

I did not think this quite logical, but was too much crushed to argue.

As soon as I had the chance I asked Mary-Ann what she knew of the incident. To my surprise she did not take it at all in the same way as my uncle and aunt. She giggled.

"They let everyone in proper," she said. "They was as free as you like with their money and everyone thought they 'ad plenty. It was always the best end of the neck for them at the butcher's and when they wanted a steak nothing would do but the undercut. Asparagus and grapes and I don't know what all. They ran up bills in every shop in the town. I don't know 'ow people can be such fools."

But it was evidently of the tradesmen she was speaking and not of the Driffields.

"But how did they manage to bunk without anyone knowing?" I asked.

"Well, that's what everybody's askin'. They do say it was Lord George 'elped them. How did they get their boxes to the station, I ask you, if 'e didn't take them in that there trap of 'is?"

"What does he say about it?"

"He says 'e knows no more about it than the man in the moon. There was a rare to-do all over the town when they found out the Driffields had shot the moon. It made me laugh. Lord George says 'e never knew they was broke, and 'e makes out 'e was as surprised as anybody. But I for one don't believe a word of it. We all know about 'im and Rosie before she was married, and between you and me and the gatepost I don't know that it ended there. They do say they was seen walkin' about the fields together last summer and 'e was in and out of the 'ouse pretty near every day."

"How did people find out?"

"Well, it's like this. They 'ad a girl there and they told 'er she could go 'ome and spend the night with her mother, but she wasn't to be back later than eight o'clock in the morning. Well, when she come back she couldn't get in. She knocked and she rung but nobody answered, and so she went in next door and asked the lady there what she'd better do, and the lady said she'd better go to the police station. The sergeant come back with 'er and 'e knocked and 'e rung, but 'e couldn't get no answer. Then he asked the girl 'ad they paid 'er 'er wages, and she said no, not for three months, and then 'e said: You take my word for it, they've shot the moon, that's what they've done. An' when they come to get inside they found they'd took all their clothes, an' their books—they say as Ted Driffield 'ad a rare lot of books—an' every blessed thing that belonged to them."

"And has nothing been heard of them since?"

"Well, not exactly, but when they'd been gone about a week the girl got a letter from London, and when she opened it there was no letter or anything, but just a postal order for 'er wages. An' if you ask me, I call that very 'andsome not to do a poor girl out of her wages."

I was much more shocked than Mary-Ann. I was a very respectable youth. The reader cannot have failed to observe that I accepted the conventions of my class as if they were the laws of Nature, and though debts on the grand scale in books had seemed to me romantic, and duns and money-lenders were familiar figures to my fancy, I could not but think it mean and paltry not to pay the tradesmen's books. I listened with confusion when people talked in my presence of the Driffields, and when they spoke of them as my friends I said: "Hang it all, I just knew them"; and when they asked: "Weren't they fearfully common?" I said: "Well, they didn't exactly suggest the Vere de Veres, you know." Poor Mr. Galloway was dreadfully upset.

"Of course I didn't think they were wealthy," he told me, "but I thought they had enough to get along. The house was very nicely furnished and the piano was new. It never struck me that they hadn't paid for a single thing. They never stinted themselves. What hurts me is the deceit. I used to see quite a lot of them and I thought they liked me. They always made one welcome. You'd hardly believe it, but the last time I saw them when they shook hands with me Mrs. Driffield asked me to come next day and Driffied said: 'Muffins for tea to-morrow.' And all the time they

had everything packed upstairs and that very night they took the
last train to London."

"What does Lord George say about it?"

"To tell you the truth I haven't gone out of my way to see him
lately. It's been a lesson to me. There's a little proverb about evil
communications that I've thought well to bear in mind."

I felt very much the same about Lord George, and I was a little
nervous too. If he took it into his head to tell people that at
Christmas I had been going to see the Driffields almost every day,
and it came to my uncle's ears, I foresaw an unpleasant fuss. My
uncle would accuse me of deceit and prevarication and disobedi-
ence and of not behaving like a gentleman, and I did not at
the moment see what answer I could make. I knew him well
enough to be aware that he would not let the matter drop, and
that I should be reminded of my transgression for years. I was
just as glad not to see Lord George. But one day I ran into him
face to face in the High Street.

"Hulloa, youngster," he cried, addressing me in a way I particularly resented. "Back for the holidays, I suppose."

"You suppose quite correctly," I answered with what I thought
withering sarcasm.

Unfortunately he only bellowed with laughter.

"You're so sharp you'll cut yourself if you don't look out," he
answered heartily. "Well, it looks as if there was no more whist
for you and me just yet. Now you see what comes of living
beyond your means. What I always say to my boys is: If you've
got a pound and you spend nineteen and six you're a rich man,
but if you spend twenty shillings and sixpence you're a pauper.
Look after the pence, young fellow, and the pounds'll look after
themselves."

But though he spoke after this fashion there was in his voice
no note of disapproval, but a bubble of laughter as though in his
heart he were tittering at these admirable maxims.

"They say you helped them to bunk," I remarked.

"Me?" His face assumed a look of extreme surprise, but his
eyes glittered with sly mirth. "Why, when they came and told
me the Driffields had shot the moon you could have knocked me
down with a feather. They owed me four pounds seventeen and
six for coal. We've all been let in, even poor old Galloway who
never got his muffins for tea."

I had never thought Lord George more blatant. I should have liked to say something final and crushing, but as I could not think of anything I just said that I must be getting along and with a curt nod left him.

CHAPTER XI

Musing thus over the past, while I waited for Alroy Kear, I chuckled when I considered this shabby incident of Edward Driffield's obscurity in the light of the immense respectability of his later years. I wondered whether it was because in my boyhood he was as a writer held in such small esteem by the people about me that I had never been able to see in him the astonishing merit that the best critical opinion eventually ascribed to him. He was for long thought to write very bad English, and indeed he gave you the impression of writing with the stub of a blunt pencil; his style was laboured, an uneasy mixture of the classical and the slangy, and his dialogue was such as could never have issued from the mouth of a human being. Toward the end of his career, when he dictated his books, his style, acquiring a conversational ease, became flowing and limpid; and then the critics, going back to the novels of his maturity, found that their English had a nervous, racy vigour that eminently suited the matter. His prime belonged to a period when the purple patch was in vogue and there are descriptive passages in his works that have found their way into all the anthologies of English prose. His pieces on the sea, and spring in the Kentish woods, and sunset on the lower reaches of the Thames are famous. It should be a mortification to me that I cannot read them without discomfort.

When I was a young man, though his books sold but little and one or two were banned by the libraries, it was very much a mark of culture to admire him. He was thought boldly realistic. He was a very good stick to beat the Philistines with. Somebody's lucky inspiration discovered that his sailors and peasants were Shakespearean, and when the advanced got together they uttered shrill cries of ecstasy over the dry and spicy humour of his yokels. This was a commodity that Edward Driffield had no difficulty in supplying. My own heart sank when he led me into the fore-castle of a sailing ship or the tap-room of a public-house and I

knew I was in for half a dozen pages in dialect of facetious comment on life, ethics and immortality. But, I admit, I have always
thought the Shakespearean clowns tedious and their innumerable
progeny insupportable.

Driffield's strength lay evidently in his depiction of the class he
knew best, farmers and farm labourers, shopkeepers and bartenders, skippers of sailing ships, mates, cooks and able seamen.
When he introduces characters belonging to a higher station in
life even his warmest admirers, one would have thought, must
experience a certain malaise; his fine gentlemen are so incredibly
fine, his high-born ladies are so good, so pure, so noble that you
are not surprised that they can only express themselves with
polysyllabic dignity. His women hardly come to life. But here
again I must add that this is only my own opinion; the world at
large and the most eminent critics have agreed that they are very
winsome types of English womanhood, spirited, gallant, high-
souled, and they have been often compared with the heroines of
Shakespeare. We know of course that women are habitually constipated, but to represent them in fiction as being altogether
devoid of a back passage seems to me really an excess of chivalry.
I am surprised that they care to see themselves thus limned.

The critics can force the world to pay attention to a very
indifferent writer, and the world may lose its head over one who
has no merit at all, but the result in neither case is lasting; and I
cannot help thinking that no writer can hold the public for as
long as Edward Driffield without considerable gifts. The elect
sneer at popularity; they are inclined even to assert that it is a
proof of mediocrity; but they forget that posterity makes its choice
not from among the unknown writers of a period, but from among
the known. It may be that some great masterpiece which deserves
immortality has fallen still-born from the press, but posterity will
never hear of it; it may be that posterity will scrap all the best
sellers of our day, but it is among them that it must choose. At
all events Edward Driffield is in the running. His novels happen to
bore me; I find them long; the melodramatic incidents with which
he sought to stir the sluggish reader's interest leave me cold; but
he certainly had sincerity. There is in his best books the stir of
life, and in none of them can you fail to be aware of the author's
enigmatic personality. In his earlier days he was praised or blamed
for his realism; according to the idiosyncrasy of his critics he was

extolled for his truth or censured for his coarseness. But realism
has ceased to excite remark, and the library reader will take in his
stride obstacles at which a generation back he would have violently
shied. The cultured reader of these pages will remember the
leading article in the *Literary Supplement* of *The Times* which
appeared at the moment of Driffield's death. Taking the novels
of Edward Driffield as his text, the author wrote what was very
well described as a hymn to beauty. No one who read it could fail
to be impressed by those swelling periods, which reminded one
of the noble prose of Jeremy Taylor, by that reverence and piety,
by all those high sentiments, in short, expressed in a style that was
ornate without excess and dulcet without effeminacy. It was itself
a thing of beauty. If some suggested that Edward Driffield was by
way of being a humorist and that a jest would here and there
have lightened this eulogious article it must be replied that after
all it was a funeral oration. And it is well known that Beauty does
not look with a good grace on the timid advances of Humour.
Roy Kear, when he was talking to me of Driffield, claimed that,
whatever his faults, they were redeemed by the beauty that suffused his pages. Now I come to look back on our conversation,
I think it was this remark that had most exasperated me.

Thirty years ago in literary circles God was all the fashion. It
was good form to believe and journalists used Him to adorn a
phrase or balance a sentence; then God went out (oddly enough
with cricket and beer) and Pan came in. In a hundred novels his
cloven hoof left its imprint on the sward; poets saw him lurking
in the twilight on London commons, and literary ladies in Surrey,
nymphs of an industrial age, mysteriously surrendered their virgin-
ity to his rough embrace. Spiritually they were never the same
again. But Pan went out and now beauty has taken his place.
People find it in a phrase, or a turbot, a dog, a day, a picture, an
action, a dress. Young women in cohorts, each of whom has written so promising and competent a novel, prattle of it in every
manner from allusive to arch, from intense to charming; and the
young men, more or less recently down from Oxford, but still
trailing its clouds of glory, who tell us in the weekly papers what
we should think of art, life and the universe, fling the word with a
pretty negligence about their close-packed pages. It is sadly frayed.
Gosh, they have worked it hard! The ideal has many names and
beauty is but one of them. I wonder if this clamour is anything

more than the cry of distress of those who cannot make themselves at home in our heroic world of machines, and I wonder if their passion for beauty, the Little Nell of this shamefaced day, is anything more than sentimentality. It may be that another generation, accommodating itself more adequately to the stress of life, will look for inspiration not in a flight from reality, but in an eager acceptance of it.

I do not know if others are like myself, but I am conscious that I cannot contemplate beauty long. For me no poet made a falser statement than Keats when he wrote the first line of *Endymion*. When the thing of beauty has given me the magic of its sensation my mind quickly wanders; I listen with incredulity to the persons who tell me that they can look with rapture for hours at a view or a picture. Beauty is an ecstasy; it is as simple as hunger. There is really nothing to be said about it. It is like the perfume of a rose: you can smell it and that is all: that is why the criticism of art, except in so far as it is unconcerned with beauty and therefore with art, is tiresome. All the critic can tell you with regard to Titian's *Entombment of Christ*, perhaps of all the pictures in the world that which has most pure beauty, is to go and look at it. What else he has to say is history, or biography, or what not. But people add other qualities to beauty—sublimity, human interest, tenderness, love—because beauty does not long content them. Beauty is perfect, and perfection (such is human nature) holds our attention but for a little while. The mathematician who after seeing *Phèdre* asked: *"Qu'est-ce que ça prouve?"* was not such a fool as he has been generally made out. No one has ever been able to explain why the Doric temple of Pæstum is more beautiful than a glass of cold beer except by bringing in considerations that have nothing to do with beauty. Beauty is a blind alley. It is a mountain peak which once reached leads nowhere. That is why in the end we find more to entrance us in El Greco than in Titian, in the incomplete achievement of Shakespeare than in the consummate success of Racine. Too much has been written about beauty. That is why I have written a little more. Beauty is that which satisfies the æsthetic instinct. But who wants to be satisfied? It is only to the dullard that enough is as good as a feast. Let us face it: beauty is a bit of a bore.

But of course what the critics wrote about Edward Driffield was eye-wash. His outstanding merit was not the realism that gave vigour to his work, nor the beauty that informed it, nor his graphic portraits of seafaring men, nor his poetic descriptions of salty marshes, of storm and calm and of nestling hamlets; it was his longevity. Reverence for old age is one of the most admirable traits of the human race and I think it may safely be stated that in no other country than ours is this trait more marked. The awe and love with which other nations regard old age is often platonic; but ours is practical. Who but the English would fill Covent Garden to listen to an aged prima donna without a voice? Who but the English would pay to see dancers so decrepit that they can hardly put one foot before the other and say to one another admiringly in the intervals: "By George, sir, d'you know he's a long way past sixty?" But compared with politicians and writers these are but striplings, and I often think that a *jeune premier* must be of a singularly amiable disposition if it does not make him bitter to consider that when at the age of seventy he must end his career the public man and the author are only at their prime. A man who is a politician at forty is a statesman at three score and ten. It is at this age, when he would be too old to be a clerk or a gardener or a police-court magistrate, that he is ripe to govern a country. This is not so strange when you reflect that from the earliest times the old have rubbed it into the young that they are wiser than they, and before the young had discovered what non-sense this was they were old too, and it profited them to carry on the imposture; and besides, no one can have moved in the society of politicians without discovering that (if one may judge by results) it requires little mental ability to rule a nation. But why writers should be more esteemed the older they grow has long perplexed me. At one time I thought that the praise accorded to them when they had ceased for twenty years to write anything of interest was largely due to the fact that the younger men, having no longer to fear their competition, felt it safe to extol their merit; and it is well known that to praise someone whose rivalry you do not dread is often a very good way of putting a spoke in the wheel of someone whose rivalry you do. But this is to take a low view of human nature and I would not for the world lay myself open to a charge of cheap cynicism. After mature consideration I have come to the conclusion that the real reason for the universal applause that comforts the declining years of the author who exceeds the common span of man is that intelligent people after the age of thirty read nothing at all. As they grow older the books they read in their youth are lit with its glamour and with every year that passes they ascribe greater merit to the author that wrote them. Of course he must go on; he must keep in the public eye. It is no good his thinking that it is enough to write one or two masterpieces; he must provide a pedestal for them of forty or fifty works of no particular consequence. This needs time. His production must be such that if he cannot captivate a reader by his charm he can stun him by his weight.

If, as I think, longevity is genius, few in our time have enjoyed it in a more conspicuous degree than Edward Driffield. When he was a young fellow in the sixties (the cultured having had their way with him and passed him by) his position in the world of letters was only respectable; the best judges praised him, but with moderation; the younger men were inclined to be frivolous at his expense. It was agreed that he had talent, but it never occurred to anyone that he was one of the glories of English literature. He celebrated his seventieth birthday; an uneasiness passed over the world of letters, like a ruffling of the waters when on an Eastern sea a typhoon lurks in the distance, and it grew evident that there had lived among us all these years a great novelist and none of us had suspected it. There was a rush for Driffield's books in the various libraries and a hundred busy pens, in Bloomsbury, in Chelsea and in other places where men of letters congregate, wrote appreciations, studies, essays and works, short and chatty or long and intense, on his novels. These were reprinted, in complete editions, in select editions, at a shilling and three and six and five shillings and a guinea. His style was analysed, his philosophy was examined, his technique was dissected. At seventy-five everyone agreed that Edward Driffield had genius. At eighty he was the Grand Old Man of English Letters. This position he held till his death.

Now we look about and think sadly that there is no one to take his place. A few septuagenarians are sitting up and taking notice, and they evidently feel that they could comfortably fill the vacant niche. But it is obvious that they lack something.

Though these recollections have taken so long to narrate they took but a little while to pass through my head. They came to me higgledy-piggledy, an incident and then a scrap of conversation that belonged to a previous time, and I have set them down in order for the convenience of the reader and because I have a neat mind. One thing that surprised me was that even at that far distance I could remember distinctly what people looked like and even the gist of what they said, but only with vagueness what they wore. I knew of course that the dress, especially of women, was quite different forty years ago from what it was now, but if I recalled it at all it was not from life but from pictures and photographs that I had seen much later.

I was still occupied with my idle fancies when I heard a taxi stop at the door, the bell ring, and in a moment Alroy Kear's booming voice telling the butler that he had an appointment with me. He came in, big, bluff and hearty; his vitality shattered with a single gesture the frail construction I had been building out of the vanished past. He brought in with him, like a blustering wind in March, the aggressive and inescapable present.

"I was just asking myself," I said, "who could possibly succeed Edward Driffield as the Grand Old Man of English Letters and you arrive to answer my question."

He broke into a jovial laugh, but into his eyes came a quick look of suspicion.

"I don't think there's anybody," he said.

"How about yourself?"

"Oh, my dear boy, I'm not fifty yet. Give me another twenty-five years." He laughed, but his eyes held mine keenly. "I never know when you're pulling my leg." He looked down suddenly. "Of course one can't help thinking about the future sometimes. All the people who are at the top of the tree now are anything from fifteen to twenty years older than me. They can't last for ever, and when they're gone who is there? Of course there's Aldous; he's a good deal younger than me, but he's not very strong and I don't believe he takes great care of himself. Barring accidents, by which I mean barring some genius who suddenly springs up and sweeps the board, I don't quite see how in another twenty or twenty-five years I can help having the field pretty well to myself. It's just a question of pegging away and living on longer than the others."

Roy sank his virile bulk into one of my landlady's arm-chairs and I offered him a whisky and soda.

"No, I never drink spirits before six o'clock," he said. He looked about him. "Jolly, these digs are."

"I know. What have you come to see me about?"

"I thought I'd better have a little chat with you about Mrs. Driffield's invitation. It was rather difficult to explain over the telephone. The truth of the matter is that I've arranged to write Driffield's life."

"Oh! Why didn't you tell me the other day?"

I felt friendly disposed toward Roy. I was happy to think that I had not misjudged him when I suspected that it was not merely for the pleasure of my company that he had asked me to luncheon.

"I hadn't entirely made up my mind. Mrs. Driffield is very keen on my doing it. She's going to help me in every way she can. She's giving me all the material she has. She's been collecting it for a good many years. It's not an easy thing to do and of course I can't afford not to do it well. But if I can make a pretty good job of it, it can't fail to do me a lot of good. People have so much more respect for a novelist if he writes something serious now and then. Those critical works of mine were an awful sweat, and they sold nothing, but I don't regret them for a moment. They've given me a position I could never have got without them."

"I think it's a very good plan. You've known Driffield more intimately than most people for the last twenty years."

"I think I have. But of course he was over sixty when I first made his acquaintance. I wrote and told him how much I admired his books and he asked me to go and see him. But I know nothing about the early part of his life. Mrs. Driffield used to try to get him to talk about those days and she made very copious notes of all he said, and then there are diaries that he kept now and then, and of course a lot of the stuff in the novels is obviously autobiographical. But there are immense lacunæ. I'll tell you the sort of book I want to write, a sort of intimate life, with a lot of those little details that make people feel warm inside, you know, and then woven in with this a really exhaustive criticism of his literary work, not ponderous, of course, but, although sympathetic, searching and . . . subtle. Naturally it wants doing, but Mrs. Driffield seems to think I can do it."

"I'm sure you can," I put in.

"I don't see why not," said Roy. "I am a critic, and I'm a novelist. It's obvious that I have certain literary qualifications. But I can't do anything unless everyone who can is willing to help me."

I began to see where I came in. I tried to make my face look quite blank. Roy leaned forward.

"I asked you the other day if you were going to write anything about Driffield yourself and you said you weren't. Can I take that as definite?"

"Certainly."

"Then have you got any objection to giving me your material?"

"My dear boy, I haven't got any."

"Oh, that's nonsense," said Roy good-humouredly, with the tone of a doctor who is trying to persuade a child to have its throat examined. "When he was living at Blackstable you must have seen a lot of him."

"I was only a boy then."

"But you must have been conscious of the unusual experience. After all, no one could be for half an hour in Edward Driffield's society without being impressed by his extraordinary personality. It must have been obvious even to a boy of sixteen, and you were probably more observant and sensitive than the average boy of that age."

"I wonder if his personality would have seemed extraordinary without the reputation to back it up. Do you imagine that if you went down to a spa in the west of England as Mr. Atkins, a chartered accountant taking the waters for his liver, you would impress the people you met there as a man of character?"

"I imagine they'd soon realise that I was not quite the common or garden chartered accountant," said Roy, with a smile that took from his remark any appearance of self-esteem.

"Well, all I can tell you is that what chiefly bothered me about Driffield in those days was that the knickerbocker suit he wore was dreadfully loud. We used to bicycle a lot together and it always made me feel a trifle uncomfortable to be seen with him."

"It sounds comic now. What did he talk about?"

"I don't know; nothing very much. He was rather keen on architecture, and he talked about farming, and if a pub looked nice he generally suggested stopping for five minutes and having a glass of bitter, and then he would talk to the landlord about the crops, and the price of coal and things like that."

I rambled on, though I could see by the look of Roy's face that he was disappointed with me; he listened, but he was a trifle bored, and it struck me that when he was bored he looked peevish.

But though I couldn't remember that Driffield had ever said anything significant during those long rides of ours, I had a very acute recollection of the *feel* of them. Blackstable was peculiar in this, that though it was on the sea, with a long shingly beach and marshland at the back, you had only to go about half a mile inland to come into the most rural country in Kent. Winding roads that ran between the great fat green fields and clumps of huge elms, substantial and with a homely stateliness like good old Kentish farmers' wives, high-coloured and robust, who had grown portly on good butter and home-made bread and cream and fresh eggs. And sometimes the road was only a lane, with thick hawthorn hedges, and the green elms overhung it on either side so that when you looked up there was only a strip of blue sky between. And as you rode along in the warm, keen air you had a sensation that the world was standing still and life would last for ever. Although you were pedalling with such energy you had a delicious feeling of laziness. You were quite happy when no one spoke, and if one of the party from sheer high spirits suddenly put on speed and shot ahead it was a joke that everyone laughed at and for a few minutes you pedalled as hard as you could. And we chaffed one another innocently and giggled at our own humour. Now and then one would pass cottages with little gardens in front of them and in the gardens were hollyhocks and tiger lilies; and a little way from the road were farmhouses, with their spacious barns and oasthouses; and one would pass through hop-fields with the ripening hops hanging in garlands. The public-houses were friendly and informal, hardly more important than cottages, and on the porches often honeysuckle would be growing. The names they bore were usual and familiar: the "Jolly Sailor", the "Merry Ploughman", the "Crown and Anchor", the "Red Lion".

But of course all that could matter nothing to Roy, and he interrupted me.

"Did he never talk of literature?" he asked.

"I don't think so. He wasn't that sort of writer. I suppose he thought about his writing, but he never mentioned it. He used to lend the curate books. In the winter, on Christmas holidays, I used to have tea at his house nearly every day and sometimes the curate and he would talk about books, but we used to shut them up."

"Don't you remember anything he said?"

"Only one thing. I remember it because I hadn't ever read the things he was talking about and what he said made me do so. He said that when Shakespeare retired to Stratford-on-Avon and became respectable, if he ever thought of his plays at all, probably the two that he remembered with most interest were *Measure for Measure* and *Troilus and Cressida*."

"I don't think that's very illuminating. Didn't he say anything about anyone more modern than Shakespeare?"

"Well, not then, that I can remember; but when I was lunching with the Driffields a few years ago I overheard him saying that Henry James had turned his back on one of the great events of the world's history, the rise of the United States, in order to report tittle-tattle at tea parties in English country houses. Driffield called it *il gran rifiuto*. I was surprised at hearing the old man use an Italian phrase and amused because a great big bouncing duchess who was there was the only person who knew what the devil he was talking about. He said: 'Poor Henry, he's spending eternity wandering round and round a stately park and the fence is just too high for him to peep over and they're having tea just too far away for him to hear what the countess is saying.'"

Roy listened to my little anecdote with attention. He shook his head reflectively.

"I don't think I could use that. I'd have the Henry James gang down on me like a thousand of bricks. . . . But what used you to do during those evenings?"

"Well, we played whist while Driffield read books for review, and he used to sing."

"That's interesting," said Roy, leaning forward eagerly. "Do you remember what he sang?"

"Perfectly. 'All Through Stickin' to a Soljer' and 'Come Where the Booze Is Cheaper' were his favourites."

"Oh!"

I could see that Roy was disappointed.

"Did you expect him to sing Schumann?" I asked.

"I don't know why not. It would have been rather a good point. But I think I should have expected him to sing sea chanties or old English country airs, you know, the sort of thing they used to sing at fairings—blind fiddlers and the village swains dancing with the girls on the threshing floor and all that sort of thing. I might have made something rather beautiful out of that, but I can't *see* Ed-

ward Driffield singing music-hall songs. After all, when you're
drawing a man's portrait you must get the values right; you only
confuse the impression if you put in stuff that's all out of tone."

"You know that shortly after this he shot the moon. He let
everybody in."

Roy was silent for fully a minute and he looked down at the
carpet reflectively.

"Yes, I knew there'd been some unpleasantness. Mrs. Driffield
mentioned it. I understand everything was paid up later before he
finally bought Ferne Court and settled down in the district. I
don't think it's necessary to dwell on an incident that is not really
of any importance in the history of his development. After all,
it happened nearly forty years ago. You know, there were some
very curious sides to the old man. One would have thought that
after a rather sordid little scandal like that the neighbourhood
of Blackstable would be the last place he'd choose to spend the rest
of his life in when he'd become celebrated, especially when it was
the scene of his rather humble origins; but he didn't seem to mind
a bit. He seemed to think the whole thing rather a good joke. He
was quite capable of telling people who came to lunch about it
and it was very embarrassing for Mrs. Driffield. I should like you
to know Amy better. She's a very remarkable woman. Of course
the old man had written all his great books before he ever set
eyes on her, but I don't think anyone can deny that it was she who
created the rather imposing and dignified figure that the world
saw for the last twenty-five years of his life. She's been very
frank with me. She didn't have such an easy job of it. Old Driffield had some very queer ways and she had to use a good deal of
tact to get him to behave decently. He was very obstinate in some
things and I think a woman of less character would have been discouraged. For instance, he had a habit that poor Amy had a lot of
trouble to break him of: after he'd finished his meat and vegetables he'd take a piece of bread and wipe the plate clean with
it and eat it."

"Do you know what that means?" I said. "It means that for
long he had so little to eat that he couldn't afford to waste any
food he could get."

"Well, that may be, but it's not a very pretty habit for a distinguished man of letters. And then, he didn't exactly tipple, but
he was rather fond of going down to the 'Bear and Key' at Black-

stable and having a few beers in the public bar. Of course there
was no harm in it, but it did make him rather conspicuous, especially in summer when the place was full of trippers. He didn't
mind who he talked to. He didn't seem able to realise that he
had a position to keep up. You can't deny it was rather awkward
after they'd been having a lot of interesting people to lunch—
people like Edmund Gosse, for instance, and Lord Curzon—that
he should go down to a public-house and tell the plumber and the
baker and the sanitary inspector what he thought about them. But
of course that could be explained away. One could say that he
was after local colour and was interested in types. But he had some
habits that really were rather difficult to cope with. Do you know
that it was with the greatest difficulty that Amy Driffield could
ever get him to take a bath?"

"He was born at a time when people thought it unhealthy to
take too many baths. I don't suppose he ever lived in a house
that had a bathroom till he was fifty."

"Well, he said he never had had a bath more than once a week
and he didn't see why he should change his habits at his time of
life. Then Amy said that he must change his under-linen every day,
but he objected to that too. He said he'd always been used to wearing his vest and drawers for a week and it was nonsense, it only
wore them out to have them washed so often. Mrs. Driffield did
everything she could to tempt him to have a bath every day, with
bath salts and perfumes, you know, but nothing would induce him
to, and as he grew older he wouldn't even have one once a week.
She tells me that for the last three years of his life he never had
a bath at all. Of course, all this is between ourselves; I'm merely
telling it to show you that in writing his life I shall have to use a
good deal of tact. I don't see how one can deny that he was just a
wee bit unscrupulous in money matters and he had a kink in him
that made him take a strange pleasure in the society of his inferiors, and some of his personal habits were rather disagreeable,
but I don't think that side of him was the most significant. I don't
want to say anything that's untrue, but I do think there's a certain
amount that's better left unsaid."

"Don't you think it would be more interesting if you went the
whole hog and drew him warts and all?"

"Oh, I couldn't. Amy Driffield would never speak to me again.

She only asked me to do the life because she felt she could trust my discretion. I must behave like a gentleman."

"It's very hard to be a gentleman and a writer."

"I don't see why. And besides, you know what the critics are. If you tell the truth they only say you're cynical and it does an author no good to get a reputation for cynicism. Of course I don't deny that if I were thoroughly unscrupulous I could make a sensation. It would be rather amusing to show the man with his passion for beauty and his careless treatment of his obligations, his fine style and his personal hatred for soap and water, his idealism and his tippling in disreputable pubs; but honestly, would it pay? They'd only say I was imitating Lytton Strachey. No, I think I shall do much better to be allusive and charming and rather subtle, you know the sort of thing, and tender. I think one ought always to *see* a book before one starts it. Well, I see this rather like a portrait by Van Dyck, with a good deal of atmosphere, you know, and a certain gravity, and with a sort of aristocratic distinction. Do you know what I mean? About eighty thousand words."

He was absorbed for a moment in the ecstasy of æsthetic contemplation. In his mind's eye he saw a book, in royal octavo, slim and light in the hand, printed with large margins on handsome paper in a type that was both clear and comely, and I think he saw a binding in smooth black cloth with a decoration in gold and gilt lettering. But being human, Alroy Kear could not, as I suggested a few pages back, hold the ecstasy that beauty yields for more than a little while. He gave me a candid smile.

"But how the devil am I to get over the first Mrs. Driffield?"

"The skeleton in the cupboard," I murmured.

"She is damned awkward to deal with. She was married to Driffield for a good many years. Amy has very decided views on the subject, but I don't see how I can possibly meet them. You see, her attitude is that Rose Driffield exerted a most pernicious influence on her husband, and that she did everything possible to ruin him morally, physically and financially; she was beneath him in every way, at least intellectually and spiritually, and it was only because he was a man of immense force and vitality that he survived. It was of course a very unfortunate marriage. It's true that she's been dead for ages and it seems a pity to rake up old scandals and wash a lot of dirty linen in public; but the fact remains that all Driffield's greatest books were written when he was living with her. Much as I admire the later books, and no one is more conscious of their genuine beauty than I am, and they have a restraint and a sort of classical sobriety which are admirable, I must admit that they haven't the tang and the vigour and the smell and bustle of life of the early ones. It does seem to me that you can't altogether ignore the influence his first wife had on his work."

"What are you going to do about it?" I asked.

"Well, I can't see why all that part of his life shouldn't be treated with the greatest possible reserve and delicacy, so as not to offend the most exacting susceptibility, and yet with a sort of manly frankness, if you understand what I mean, that would be rather moving."

"It sounds a very tall order."

"As I see it, there's no need to dot the i's or to cross the t's. It can only be a question of getting just the right touch. I wouldn't state more than I could help, but I would suggest what was essential for the reader to realise. You know, however gross a subject is you can soften its unpleasantness if you treat it with dignity. But I can do nothing unless I am in complete possession of the facts."

"Obviously you can't cook them unless you have them."

Roy had been speaking with a fluent ease that revealed the successful lecturer. I wished (a) that I could express myself with so much force and aptness, never at a loss for a word, rolling off the sentences without a moment's hesitation; and (b) that I did not feel so miserably incompetent with my one small insignificant person to represent the large and appreciative audience that Roy was instinctively addressing. But now he paused. A genial look came over his face, which his enthusiasm had reddened and the heat of the day caused to perspire, and the eyes that had held me with a dominating brilliance softened and smiled.

"This is where you come in, old boy," he said plesantly.

I have always found it a very good plan in life to say nothing when I had nothing to say and when I do not know how to answer a remark to hold my tongue. I remained silent and looked back at Roy amiably.

"You know more about his life at Blackstable than anybody else."

"I don't know about that. There must be a number of people at Blackstable who saw as much of him in the old days as I did."

"That may be, but after all they're presumably not people of any importance, and I don't think they matter very much."

"Oh, I see. You mean that I'm the only person who might blow the gaff."

"Roughly, that is what I do mean, if you feel that you must put it in a facetious way."

I saw that Roy was not inclined to be amused. I did not mind, for I am quite used to people not being amused at my jokes. I often think that the purest type of artist is the humorist who laughs alone at his own jests.

"And you saw a good deal of him later on in London, I believe."

"Yes."

"That is when he had an apartment somewhere in Lower Belgravia."

"Well, lodgings in Pimlico."

Roy smiled dryly.

"We won't quarrel about the exact designation of the quarter of London in which he lived. You were very intimate with him then."

"Fairly."

"How long did that last?"

"About a couple of years."

"How old were you then?"

"Twenty."

"Now look here, I want you to do me a great favour. It won't take you very long and it will be of quite inestimable value to me. I want you to jot down as fully as you can all your recollections of Driffield, and all you remember about his wife and his relations with her and so on, both at Blackstable and in London."

"Oh, my dear fellow, that's asking a great deal. I've got a lot of work to do just now."

"It needn't take you very long. You can write it quite roughly, I mean. You needn't bother about style, you know, or anything like that. I'll put the style in. All I want are the facts. After all, you know them and nobody else does. I don't want to be pompous or anything like that, but Driffield was a great man and you owe it to his memory and to English literature to tell everything you know. I shouldn't have asked you, but you told me the other day that you weren't going to write anything about him yourself. It would be rather like a dog in a manger to keep to yourself a whole lot of material that you have no intention of using."

Thus Roy appealed at once to my sense of duty, my indolence, my generosity and my rectitude.

"But why does Mrs. Driffield want me to go down and stay at Ferne Court?" I asked.

"Well, we talked it over. It's a very jolly house to stay in. She does one very well, and it ought to be divine in the country just now. She thought it would be very nice and quiet for you if you felt inclined to write your recollections there; of course, I said I couldn't promise that, but naturally being so near Blackstable would remind you of all sorts of things that you might otherwise forget. And then, living in his house, among his books and things, it would make the past seem much more real. We could all talk about him, and you know how in the heat of conversation things come back. Amy's very quick and clever. She's been in the habit of making notes of Driffield's talk for years, and after all it's quite likely that you'll say things on the spur of the moment that you wouldn't think of writing and she can just jot them down afterward. And we can play tennis and bathe."

"I'm not very fond of staying with people," I said. "I hate getting up for a nine-o'clock breakfast to eat things I have no mind to. I don't like going for walks, and I'm not interested in other people's chickens."

"She's a lonely woman now. It would be a kindness to her and it would be a kindness to me too."

I reflected.

"I'll tell you what I'll do: I'll go down to Blackstable, but I'll go down on my own. I'll put up at the 'Bear and Key' and I'll come over and see Mrs. Driffield while you're there. You can both talk your heads off about Edward Driffield, but I shall be able to get away when I'm fed up with you."

Roy laughed good-naturedly.

"All right. That'll do. And will you jot down anything you can remember that you think will be useful to me?"

"I'll try."

"When will you come? I'm going down on Friday."

"I'll come with you if you'll promise not to talk to me in the train."

"All right. The five-ten's the best one. Shall I come and fetch you?"

"I'm capable of getting to Victoria by myself. I'll meet you on the platform."

I don't know if Roy was afraid of my changing my mind, but he got up at once, shook my hand heartily and left. He begged me on no account to forget my tennis racket and bathing suit.

CHAPTER XII

My promise to Roy sent my thoughts back to my first years in London. Having nothing much to do that afternoon, it occurred to me to stroll along and have a cup of tea with my old landlady. Mrs. Hudson's name had been given to me by the secretary of the medical school at St. Luke's when, a callow youth just arrived in town, I was looking for lodgings. She had a house in Vincent Square. I lived there for five years, in two rooms on the ground floor, and over me on the drawing-room floor lived a master at Westminster School. I paid a pound a week for my rooms and he paid twenty-five shillings. Mrs. Hudson was a little, active, bustling woman, with a sallow face, a large aquiline nose and the brightest, the most vivacious black eyes that I ever saw. She had a great deal of very dark hair, in the afternoons and all day on Sunday arranged in a fringe on the forehead with a bun at the nape of the neck as you may see in old photographs of the Jersey Lily. She had a heart of gold (though I did not know it then, for when you are young you take the kindness people show you as your right) and she was an excellent cook. No one could make a better *omelette soufflée* than she. Every morning she was up betimes to get the fire lit in her gentlemen's sitting-rooms so that "they needn't eat their breakfasts simply perishin' with the cold, my word it's bitter this morning"; and if she didn't hear you having your bath, a flat tin bath that slipped under the bed, the water put in the night before to take the chill off, she'd say: "There now, there's my dining-room floor not up yet, 'e'll be late for his lecture again," and she would come tripping upstairs and thump on the door and you would hear her shrill voice: "If you don't get up at once you won't 'ave time to 'ave breakfast, an' I've got a lovely 'addick for you." She worked all day long and she sang at her work and she was gay and happy and smiling. Her husband was much older than she. He had been a butler in very good families, and wore side-whiskers and a perfect manner; he was verger at a neighbouring church, highly respected, and he waited at table and cleaned the boots and helped with the washing-up. Mrs. Hudson's only relaxation was to come up after she had served the dinners (I had mine at half-past six and the schoolmaster at seven) and have a little chat with her gentlemen. I wish to goodness I had had the sense (like Amy Driffield with her celebrated husband) to take notes of her conversation, for Mrs. Hudson was a mistress of Cockney humour. She had a gift of repartee that never failed her, she had a racy style and an apt and varied vocabulary, she was never at a loss for the comic metaphor or the vivid phrase. She was a pattern of propriety and she would never have women in her house, you never knew what they were up to ("It's men, men, men all the time with them, and afternoon tea and thin bread and butter, and openin' the door and ringin' for 'ot water and I don't know what all"); but in conversation she did not hesitate to use what was called in those days the blue bag. One could have said of her what she said of Marie Lloyd: "What I like about 'er is that she gives you a good laugh. She goes pretty near the knuckle sometimes, but she never jumps over the fence." Mrs. Hudson enjoyed her own humour and I think she talked more willingly to her lodgers because her husband was a serious man ("It's as it should be," she said, "'im bein' a verger and attendin' weddings and funerals and what all") and wasn't much of a one for a joke. "Wot I says to 'Udson is, laugh while you've got the chance, you won't laugh much when you're dead and buried."

Mrs. Hudson's humour was cumulative and the story of her feud with Miss Butcher who let lodgings at number fourteen was a great comic saga that went on year in and year out.

"She's a disagreeable old cat, but I give you my word I'd miss 'er if the Lord took 'er one fine day. Though what 'e'd do with 'er when 'e got 'er I can't think. Many's the good laugh she's give me in 'er time."

Mrs. Hudson had very bad teeth and the question whether she should have them taken out and have false ones was discussed by her for two or three years with an unimaginable variety of comic invention.

"But as I said to 'Udson on'y last night, when he said, 'Oh, come on, 'ave 'em out and 'ave done with it,' I shouldn't 'ave anythin' to talk about."

I had not seen Mrs. Hudson for two or three years. My last visit had been in answer to a little letter in which she asked me to come and drink a nice strong cup of tea with her and announced: "Hudson died three months ago next Saturday, aged seventy-nine, and George and Hester send their respectful compliments." George was the issue of her marriage with Hudson. He was now a man approaching middle age who worked at Woolwich Arsenal, and his mother had been repeating for twenty years that George would be bringing a wife home one of these days. Hester was the maid-of-all-work she had engaged toward the end of my stay with her, and Mrs. Hudson still spoke of her as "that dratted girl of mine". Though Mrs. Hudson must have been well over thirty when I first took her rooms, and that was five-and-thirty years ago, I had no feeling as I walked leisurely through the Green Park that I should not find her alive. She was as definitely part of the recollections of my youth as the pelicans that stood at the edge of the ornamental water.

I walked down the area steps and the door was opened to me by Hester, a woman getting on for fifty now and stoutish, but still bearing on her shyly grinning face the irresponsibility of the dratted girl. Mrs. Hudson was darning George's socks when I was shown into the front room of the basement and she took off her spectacles to look at me.

"Well, if that isn't Mr. Ashenden! Who ever thought of seeing you? Is the water boiling, 'Ester? You will 'ave a nice cup of tea, won't you?"

Mrs. Hudson was a little heavier than when I first knew her and her movements were more deliberate, but there was scarcely a white hair on her head, and her eyes, as black and shining as buttons, sparkled with fun. I sat down in a shabby little arm-chair covered with maroon leather.

"How are you getting on, Mrs. Hudson?" I asked.

"Oh, I've got nothin' much to complain of except that I'm not so young as I used to was," she answered. "I can't do so much as I could when you was 'ere. I don't give my gentlemen dinner now, only breakfast."

"Are all your rooms let?"

"Yes, I'm thankful to say."

Owing to the rise of prices Mrs. Hudson was able to get more for her rooms than in my day, and I think in her modest way she was quite well off. But of course people wanted a lot nowadays.

"You wouldn't believe it, first I 'ad to put in a bathroom, and then I 'ad to put in the electric light, and then nothin' would satisfy them but I must 'ave a telephone. What they'll want next I can't think."

"Mr. George says it's pretty near time Mrs. 'Udson thought of retiring," said Hester, who was laying the tea.

"You mind your own business, my girl," said Mrs. Hudson tartly. "When I retire it'll be to the cemetery. Fancy me livin' all alone with George and 'Ester without nobody to talk to."

"Mr. George says she ought to take a little 'ouse in the country an' take care of 'erself," said Hester, unperturbed by the reproof.

"Don't talk to me about the country. The doctor said I was to go there for six weeks last summer. It nearly killed me, I give you my word. The noise of it. All them birds singin' all the time, and the cocks crowin' and the cows mooin'. I couldn't stick it. When you've lived all the years I 'ave in peace and quietness you can't get used to all that racket goin' on all the time."

A few doors away was the Vauxhall Bridge Road and down it trams were clanging, ringing their bells as they went, motor-buses were lumbering along, taxis were tooting their horns. If Mrs. Hudson heard it, it was London she heard, and it soothed her as a mother's crooning soothes a restless child.

I looked round the cosy, shabby, homely little parlour in which Mrs. Hudson had lived so long. I wondered if there was anything I could do for her. I noticed that she had a gramophone. It was the only thing I could think of.

"Is there anything you want, Mrs. Hudson?" I asked.

She fixed her beady eyes on me reflectively.

"I don't know as there is, now you come to speak of it, except me 'ealth and strength for another twenty years so as I can go on workin'."

I do not think I am a sentimentalist, but her reply, unexpected but so characteristic, made a sudden lump come to my throat.

When it was time for me to go I asked if I could see the rooms I had lived in for five years.

"Run upstairs, 'Ester, and see if Mr. Graham's in. If he ain't, I'm sure 'e wouldn't mind you 'aving a look at them."

Hester scurried up, and in a moment, slightly breathless, came down again to say that Mr. Graham was out. Mrs. Hudson came with me. The bed was the same narrow iron bed that I had slept in and dreamed in and there was the same chest-of-drawers and the same washing-stand. But the sitting-room had the grim heartiness of the athlete; on the walls were photographs of cricket elevens and rowing men in shorts; golf clubs stood in the corner and pipes and tobacco jars, ornamented with the arms of a college, were littered on the chimney-piece. In my day we believed in art for art's sake and this I exemplified by draping the chimney-piece with a Moorish rug, putting up curtains of art serge and a bilious green, and hanging on the walls autotypes of pictures by Perugino, Van Dyck and Hobbema.

"Very artistic you was, wasn't you?" Mrs. Hudson remarked, not without irony.

"Very," I murmured.

I could not help feeling a pang as I thought of all the years that had passed since I inhabited that room, and of all that had happened to me. It was at that same table that I had eaten my hearty breakfast and my frugal dinner, read my medical books and written my first novel. It was in that same arm-chair that I had read for the first time Wordsworth and Stendhal, the Elizabethan dramatists and the Russian novelists, Gibbon, Boswell, Voltaire and Rousseau. I wondered who had used them since. Medical students, articled clerks, young fellows making their way in the City and elderly men retired from the colonies or thrown unexpectedly upon the world by the break up of an old home. The room made me, as Mrs. Hudson would have put it, go queer all over. All the hopes that had been cherished there, the bright visions of the future, the flaming passion of youth; the regrets, the disillusion, the weariness, the resignation; so much had been felt in that room, by so many, the whole gamut of human emotion, that it seemed strangely to have acquired a troubling and enigmatic personality of its own. I have no notion why, but it made me think of a woman at a cross-road with a finger on her lips, looking back and with her other hand beckoning. What I obscurely (and rather shamefacedly) felt, communicated itself to

Mrs. Hudson, for she gave a laugh and with a characteristic gesture rubbed her prominent nose.

"My word, people are funny," she said. "When I think of all the gentlemen I've 'ad here, I give you my word you wouldn't believe it if I told you some of the things I know about them. One of them's funnier than the other. Sometimes I lie abed thinkin' of them, and *laugh*. Well, it would be a bad world if you didn't get a good laugh now and then, but, lor', lodgers really are the limit."

CHAPTER XIII

I lived with Mrs. Hudson for nearly two years before I met the Driffields again. My life was very regular. I spent all day at the hospital and about six walked back to Vincent Square. I bought the *Star* at Lambeth Bridge and read it till my dinner was served. Then I read seriously for an hour or two, works to improve my mind, for I was a strenuous, earnest and industrious youth, and after that wrote novels and plays till bedtime. I do not know for what reason it was that one day toward the end of June, happening to leave the hospital early, I thought I would walk down the Vauxhall Bridge Road. I liked it for its noisy bustle. It had a sordid vivacity that was pleasantly exciting and you felt that at any moment an adventure might there befall you. I strolled along in a daydream and was surprised suddenly to hear my name. I stopped and looked, and there to my astonishment stood Mrs. Driffield. She was smiling at me.

"Don't you know me?" she cried.

"Yes. Mrs. Driffield."

And though I was grown up I was conscious that I was blushing as furiously as when I was sixteen. I was embarrassed. With my lamentably Victorian notions of honesty I had been much shocked by the Driffields' behaviour in running away from Blackstable without paying their bills. It seemed to me very shabby. I felt deeply the shame I thought they must feel and I was astounded that Mrs. Driffield should speak to someone who knew of the discreditable incident. If I had seen her coming I should have looked away, my delicacy presuming that she would wish to avoid the mortification of being seen by me; but she held out her hand and shook mine with obvious pleasure.

"I am glad to see a Blackstable face," she said. "You know we left there in a hurry."

She laughed and I laughed too; but her laugh was mirthful and childlike, while mine, I felt, was strained.

"I hear there *was* a to-do when they found out we'd skipped. I thought Ted would never stop laughing when he heard about it. What did your uncle say?"

I was quick to get the right tone. I wasn't going to let her think that I couldn't see a joke as well as anyone.

"Oh, you know what he is. He's very old-fashioned."

"Yes, that's what's wrong with Blackstable. They want waking up." She gave me a friendly look. "You've grown a lot since I saw you last. Why, you're growing a moustache."

"Yes," I said, giving it as much of a twirl as its size allowed me. "I've had that for ages."

"How time does fly, doesn't it? You were just a boy four years ago and now you're a man."

"I ought to be," I replied somewhat haughtily. "I'm nearly twenty-one."

I was looking at Mrs. Driffield. She wore a very small hat with feathers in it, and a pale grey dress with large leg-of-mutton sleeves and a long train. I thought she looked very smart. I had always thought that she had a nice face, but I noticed now, for the first time, that she was pretty. Her eyes were bluer than I remembered and her skin was like ivory.

"You know we live just round the corner," she said.

"So do I."

"We live in Limpus Road. We've been there almost ever since we left Blackstable."

"Well, I've been in Vincent Square for nearly two years."

"I knew you were in London. George Kemp told me so, and I often wondered where you were. Why don't you walk back with me now? Ted will be so pleased to see you."

"I don't mind," I said.

As we walked along she told me that Driffield was now literary editor of a weekly paper; his last book had done much better than any of his others and he was expecting to get quite a bit as an advance on royalties for the next one. She seemed to know most of the Blackstable news, and I remembered how it had been suspected that Lord George had helped the Driffields in their flight. I guessed that he wrote to them now and then. I noticed as we walked along that sometimes the men who passed us stared at Mrs. Driffield. It occurred to me presently that they must think her pretty too. I began to walk with a certain swagger.

Limpus Road was a long, wide, straight street that ran parallel with the Vauxhall Bridge Road. The houses were all alike, of stucco, dingily painted, solid and with substantial porticos. I suppose they had been built to be inhabited by men of standing in the city of London, but the street had gone down in the world or had never attracted the right sort of tenant; and its decayed respectability had an air at once furtive and shabbily dissipated, that made you think of persons who had seen better days and now, genteelly fuddled, talked of the social distinction of their youth. The Driffields lived in a house painted a dull red, and Mrs. Driffield, letting me into a narrow dark hall, opened a door and said:

"Go in. I'll tell Ted you're here."

She walked down the hall and I entered the sitting-room. The Driffields had the basement and the ground floor of the house, which they rented from the lady who lived in the upper part. The room into which I went looked as if it had been furnished with the scourings of auction sales. There were heavy velvet curtains with great fringes, all loops and festoons, and a gilt suite, upholstered in yellow damask, heavily buttoned; and there was a great pouffe in the middle of the room. There were gilt cabinets in which were masses of little articles, pieces of china, ivory figures, wood carvings, bits of Indian brass; and on the walls hung large oil paintings of highland glens and stags and gillies. In a moment Mrs. Driffield brought her husband and he greeted me warmly. He wore a shabby alpaca coat and grey trousers; he had shaved his beard and wore now a moustache and a small imperial. I noticed for the first time how short he was; but he looked more distinguished than he used to. There was something a trifle foreign in his appearance and I thought this was much more what I should expect an author to look like.

"Well, what do you think of our new abode?" he asked. "It looks rich, doesn't it? I think it inspires confidence."

He looked round him with satisfaction.

"And Ted's got his den at the back where he can write, and we've got a dining-room in the basement," said Mrs. Driffield. "Miss Cowley was companion for many years to a lady of title and when she died she left her all her furniture. You can see everything's good, can't you? You can see it came out of a gentleman's house."

"Rosie fell in love with the place the moment we saw it," said Driffield.

"You did too, Ted."

"We've lived in sordid circumstances so long; it's a change to be surrounded by luxury. Madame de Pompadour and all that sort of thing."

When I left them it was with a very cordial invitation to come again. It appeared that they were at home every Saturday afternoon and all sorts of people whom I would like to meet were in the habit of dropping in.

CHAPTER XIV

I went. I enjoyed myself. I went again. When the autumn came and I returned to London for the winter session at St. Luke's I got into the habit of going every Saturday. It was my introduction into the world of art and letters; I kept it a profound secret that in the privacy of my lodgings I was busily writing; I was excited to meet people who were writing also and I listened entranced to their conversation. All sorts of persons came to these parties: at that time week-ends were rare, golf was still a subject for ridicule and few had much to do on Saturday afternoons. I do not think anyone came who was of any great importance; at all events, of all the painters, writers and musicians I met at the Driffields' I cannot remember one whose reputation has endured; but the effect was cultured and animated. You found young actors who were looking for parts and middle-aged singers who deplored the fact that the English were not a musical race, composers who played their compositions on the Driffields' cottage piano and complained in a whispered aside that they sounded nothing except on a concert grand, poets who on pressure consented to read a little thing that they had just written and painters who were looking for commissions. Now and then a person of title added a certain glamour; seldom, however, for in those days the aristocracy had not yet become bohemian and if a person of quality cultivated the society of artists it was generally because a notorious divorce or a little difficulty over cards had made life in his own station (or hers) a bit awkward. We have changed all that. One of the greatest benefits that compulsory education has conferred upon the world is the wide diffusion among the nobility and gentry of the practice of writing. Horace Walpole once wrote a *Catalogue of Royal and Noble Authors;* such a work now would have the dimensions of an encyclopædia. A title, even a courtesy one, can make a well-known author of almost anyone and it may be safely asserted that there is no better passport to the world of letters than rank.

I have indeed sometimes thought that now that the House of Lords must inevitably in a short while be abolished, it would be a very good plan if the profession of literature were by law confined to its members and their wives and children. It would be a graceful compensation that the British people might offer the peers in return for the surrender of their hereditary privileges. It would be a means of support for those (too many) whom devotion to the public cause in keeping chorus girls and race-horses and playing *chemin de fer* has impoverished, and a pleasant occupation for the rest who by the process of natural selection have in the course of time become unfit to do anything but govern the British Empire. But this is an age of specialisation and if my plan is adopted it is obvious that it cannot but be to the greater glory of English literature that its various provinces should be apportioned among the various ranks of the nobility. I would suggest, therefore, that the humbler branches of literature should be practised by the lower orders of the peerage and that the barons and viscounts should devote themselves exclusively to journalism and the drama. Fiction might be the privileged demesne of the earls. They have already shown their aptitude for this difficult art and their numbers are so great that they would very competently supply the demand. To the marquises might safely be left the production of that part of literature which is known (I have never quite seen why) as *belles lettres*. It is perhaps not very profitable from a pecuniary standpoint, but it has a distinction that very well suits the holders of this romantic title.

The crown of literature is poetry. It is its end and aim. It is

the sublimest activity of the human mind. It is the achievement
of beauty. The writer of prose can only step aside when the poet
passes; he makes the best of us look like a piece of cheese. It is
evident then that the writing of poetry should be left to the dukes,
and I should like to see their rights protected by the most severe
pains and penalties, for it is intolerable that the noblest of arts
should be practised by any but the noblest of men. And since
here, too, specialisation must prevail, I foresee that the dukes (like
the successors of Alexander) will divide the realm of poetry between them, each confining himself to that aspect with which
hereditary influence and natural bent have rendered him competent to deal: thus I see the Dukes of Manchester writing poems of
a didactic and moral character, the Dukes of Westminster com-
posing stirring odes on Duty and the Responsibilities of Empire;
whereas I imagine that the Dukes of Devonshire would be more
likely to write love lyrics and elegies in the Propertian manner,
while it is almost inevitable that the Dukes of Marlborough should
pipe in an idyllic strain on such subjects as domestic bliss, con-
scription and content with modest station.

But if you say that this is somewhat formidable and remind me
that the muse does not only stalk with majestic tread, but on
occasion trips on a light fantastic toe; if, recalling the wise person
who said that he did not care who made a nation's laws so long as
he wrote its songs, you ask me (thinking rightly that it would ill
become the dukes to do so) who shall twang those measures on
the lyre that the diverse and inconstant soul of man occasionally
hankers after—I answer (obviously enough, I should have thought)
the duchesses. I recognise that the day is past when the amorous
peasants of the Romagna sang to their sweethearts the verses of
Torquato Tasso and Mrs. Humphry Ward crooned over young
Arnold's cradle the choruses of Œdipus in Colonus. The age
demands something more up-to-date. I suggest, therefore, that
the more domestic duchesses should write our hymns and our
nursery rhymes; while the skittish ones, those who incline to
mingle vine leaves with the strawberry, should write the lyrics for
musical comedies, humorous verse for the comic papers and mot-
toes for Christmas cards and crackers. Thus would they retain in
the hearts of the British public that place which they have held
hitherto only on account of their exalted station.

It was at these parties on Saturday afternoon that I discovered

very much to my surprise that Edward Driffield was a distinguished person. He had written something like twenty books, and
though he had never made more than a pittance out of them his
reputation was considerable. The best judges admired them and
the friends who came to his house were agreed that one of these
days he would be recognised. They upbraided the public because
it would not see that here was a great writer, and since the easiest
way to exalt one man is to kick another in the pants, they reviled
freely all the novelists whose contemporary fame obscured his.
If, indeed, I had known as much of literary circles as I learned
later I should have guessed by the not infrequent visits of Mrs.
Barton Trafford that the time was approaching when Edward
Driffield, like a runner in a long-distance race breaking away suddenly from the little knot of plodding athletes, must forge ahead.
I admit that when first I was introduced to this lady her name
meant nothing to me. Driffield presented me as a young neighbour
of his in the country and told her that I was a medical student.
She gave me a mellifluous smile, murmured in a soft voice something about Tom Sawyer, and, accepting the bread and butter I
offered her, went on talking with her host. But I noticed that her
arrival had made an impression and the conversation, which had
been noisy and hilarious, was hushed. When in an undertone I
asked who she was, I found that my ignorance was amazing; I
was told that she had "made" So-and-So and So-and-So. After
half an hour she rose, shook hands very graciously with such of
the people as she was acquainted with, and with a sort of lithe
sweetness sidled out of the room. Driffield accompanied her to
the door and put her in a hansom.

Mrs. Barton Trafford was then a woman of about fifty; she was
small and slight, but with rather large features, which made her
head look a little too big for her body; she had crisp white hair
which she wore like the Venus of Milo, and she was supposed in
her youth to have been very comely. She dressed discreetly in
black silk, and wore round her neck jangling chains of beads and
shells. She was said to have been unhappily married in early life,
but now for many years had been congenially united to Barton
Trafford, a clerk in the Home Office and a well-known authority
on prehistoric man. She gave you the curious impression of having
no bones in her body and you felt that if you pinched her shin
(which of course my respect for her sex as well as something of

quiet dignity in her appearance would have never allowed me to do) your fingers would meet. When you took her hand it was like taking a fillet of sole. Her face, notwithstanding its large features, had something fluid about it. When she sat it was as though she had no backbone and were stuffed, like an expensive cushion, with swansdown.

Everything was soft about her, her voice, her smile, her laugh; her eyes, which were small and pale, had the softness of flowers; her manner was as soft as the summer rain. It was this extraordinary, and charming, characteristic that made her the wonderful friend she was. It was this that had gained her the celebrity that she now enjoyed. The whole world was aware of her friendship with the great novelist whose death a few years back had come as such a shock to the English-speaking peoples. Everyone had read the innumerable letters which he had written to her and which she was induced to publish shortly after his demise. Every page revealed his admiration for her beauty and his respect for her judgment; he could never say often enough how much he owed to her encouragement, her ready sympathy, her tact, her taste; and if certain of his expressions of passion were such as some persons might think would not be read by Mr. Barton Trafford with unmixed feelings, that only added to the human interest of the work. But Mr. Barton Trafford was above the prejudices of vulgar men (his misfortune, if such it was, was one that the greatest personages in history have endured with philosophy) and, abandoning his studies of aurignacian flints and neolithic axe heads, he consented to write a Life of the deceased novelist in which he showed quite definitely how great a part of the writer's genius was due to his wife's influence.

But Mrs. Barton Trafford's interest in literature, her passion for art, were not dead because the friend for whom she had done so much had become part, with her far from negligible assistance, of posterity. She was a great reader. Little that was noteworthy escaped her attention and she was quick to establish personal relations with any young writer who showed promise. Her fame, especially since the Life, was now such that she was sure that no one would hesitate to accept the sympathy she was prepared to offer. It was inevitable that Mrs. Barton Trafford's genius for friendship should in due course find an outlet. When she read something that struck her, Mr. Barton Trafford, himself no mean

critic, wrote a warm letter of appreciation to the author and asked
him to luncheon. After luncheon, having to get back to the Home
Office, he left him to have a chat with Mrs. Barton Trafford.
Many were called. They all had *something,* but that was not
enough. Mrs. Barton Trafford had a *flair,* and she trusted her
flair; her *flair* bade her wait.

She was so cautious indeed that with Jasper Gibbons she almost
missed the bus. The records of the past tell us of writers who
grew famous in a night, but in our more prudent day this is
unheard of. The critics want to see which way the cat will jump,
and the public has been sold a pup too often to take unnecessary
chances. But in the case of Jasper Gibbons it is almost the exact
truth that he did thus jump into celebrity. Now that he is so
completely forgotten and the critics who praised him would willingly eat their words if they were not carefully guarded in the
files of innumerable newspaper offices, the sensation he made with
his first volume of poems is almost unbelievable. The most important papers gave to reviews of it as much space as they would
have to the report of a prize fight, the most influential critics
fell over one another in their eagerness to welcome him. They
likened him to Milton (for the sonority of his blank verse), to
Keats (for the opulence of his sensuous imagery), and to Shelley
(for his airy fantasy); and, using him as a stick to beat idols
of whom they were weary, they gave in his name many a re-
sounding whack on the emaciated buttocks of Lord Tennyson and
a few good husky smacks on the bald pate of Robert Browning.
The public fell like the walls of Jericho. Edition after edition
was sold, and you saw Jasper Gibbons's handsome volume in the
boudoirs of countesses in Mayfair, in vicarage drawing-rooms from
Land's End to John o' Groats and in the parlours of many an
honest but cultured merchant in Glasgow, Aberdeen and Belfast.
When it became known that Queen Victoria had accepted a
specially bound copy of the book from the hands of the loyal
publisher, and had given him (not the poet, the publisher) a copy
of *Leaves from a Journal in the Highlands* in exchange, the national enthusiasm knew no bounds.

And all this happened as it were in the twinkling of an eye.
Seven cities in Greece disputed the honour of having given birth
to Homer, and though Jasper Gibbons's birthplace (Walsall) was
well known, twice seven critics claimed the honour of having dis-

covered him; eminent judges of literature who for twenty years had written eulogies of one another's works in the weekly papers quarrelled so bitterly over this matter that one cut the other dead in the Athenæum. Nor was the great world remiss in giving him its recognition. Jasper Gibbons was asked to luncheon and invited to tea by dowager duchesses, the wives of cabinet ministers and the widows of bishops. It is said that Harrison Ainsworth was the first English man of letters to move in English society on terms of equality (and I have sometimes wondered that an enterprising publisher on this account has not thought of bringing out a complete edition of his works); but I believe that Jasper Gibbons was the first poet to have his name engraved at the bottom of an At Home card as a draw as enticing as an opera singer or a ventriloquist.

It was out of the question then for Mrs. Barton Trafford to get in on the ground floor. She could only buy in the open market. I do not know what prodigious strategy she employed, what miracles of tact, what tenderness, what exquisite sympathy, what demure blandishments; I can only surmise and admire; she nobbled Jasper Gibbons. In a little while he was eating out of her soft hand. She was admirable. She had him to lunch to meet the right people; she gave At Homes where he recited his poems before the most distinguished persons in England; she introduced him to eminent actors who gave him commissions to write plays; she saw that his poems should only appear in the proper places; she dealt with the publishers and made contracts for him that would have staggered even a cabinet minister; she took care that he should accept only the invitations of which she approved; she even went so far as to separate him from his wife with whom he had lived happily for ten years, since she felt that a poet to be true to himself and his art must not be encumbered with domestic ties. When the crash came Mrs. Barton Trafford, had she chosen, might have said that she had done everything for him that it was humanly possible to do.

For there was a crash. Jasper Gibbons brought out another volume of poetry; it was neither better nor worse than the first; it was very much like the first; it was treated with respect, but the critics made reservations; some of them even carped. The book was a disappointment. Its sale also. And unfortunately Jasper Gibbons was inclined to tipple. He had never been accustomed to

having money to spend, he was quite unused to the lavish enter-
tainments that were offered him, perhaps he missed his homely,
common little wife; once or twice he came to dinner at Mrs. Barton
Trafford's in a condition that anyone less worldly, less simple-
minded than she, would have described as blind to the world. She
told her guests gently that the bard was not quite himself that
evening. His third book was a failure. The critics tore him limb
from limb, they knocked him down and stamped on him, and, to
quote one of Edward Driffield's favourite songs, then they lugged
him round the room and then they jumped upon his face: they
were quite naturally annoyed that they had mistaken a fluent
versifier for a deathless poet and were determined that he should
suffer for their error. Then Jasper Gibbons was arrested for being
drunk and disorderly in Piccadilly and Mr. Barton Trafford had
to go to Vine Street at midnight to bail him out.

Mrs. Barton Trafford at this juncture was perfect. She did not
repine. No harsh word escaped her lips. She might have been
excused if she had felt a certain bitterness because this man for
whom she had done so much had let her down. She remained
tender, gentle and sympathetic. She was the woman who understood. She dropped him, but not like a hot brick, or a hot potato.
She dropped him with infinite gentleness, as softly as the tear that
she doubtless shed when she made up her mind to do something
so repugnant to her nature; she dropped him with so much tact,
with such sensibility, that Jasper Gibbons perhaps hardly knew
he was dropped. But there was no doubt about it. She would say
nothing against him, indeed she would not discuss him at all, and
when mention was made of him she merely smiled, a little sadly,
and sighed. But her smile was the *coup de grâce*, and her sigh
buried him deep.

Mrs. Barton Trafford had a passion for literature too sincere to
allow a setback of this character long to discourage her; and however great her disappointment she was a woman of too disinterested
a nature to let the gifts of tact, sympathy and understanding with
which she was blessed by nature lie fallow. She continued to move
in literary circles, going to tea parties here and there, to soirées and
to At Homes, charming always and gentle, listening intelligently,
but watchful, critical, and determined (if I may put it crudely)
next time to back a winner. It was then that she met Edward
Driffield and formed a favourable opinion of his gifts. It is true

that he was not young, but then he was unlikely like Jasper Gibbons to go to pieces. She offered him her friendship. He could not
fail to be moved when, in the gentle way of hers, she told him that
it was a scandal that his exquisite work remained known only in
the narrow circle. He was pleased and flattered. It is always
pleasant to be assured ·that you are a genius. She told him that
Barton Trafford was reflecting on the possibility of writing an important article on him for the *Quarterly Review*. She asked him to
luncheon to meet people who might be useful to him. She wanted
him to know his intellectual equals. Sometimes she took him for
a walk on the Chelsea Embankment and they talked of poets
dead and gone and love and friendship, and had tea in an A.B.C.
shop. When Mrs. Barton Trafford came to Limpus Street on Saturday afternoon she had the air of the queen bee preparing herself
for the nuptial flight.

Her manner with Mrs. Driffield was perfect. It was affable, but
not condescending. She always thanked her very prettily for having
allowed her to come and see her and complimented her on her
appearance. If she praised Edward Driffield to her, telling her
with a little envy in her tone what a privilege it was to enjoy the
companionship of such a great man, it was certainly from pure
kindness, and not because she knew that there is nothing that
exasperates the wife of a literary man more than to have another
woman tell her flattering things about him. She talked to Mrs.
Driffield of the simple things her simple nature might be supposed
to be interested in, of cooking and servants and Edward's health
and how careful she must be with him. Mrs. Barton Trafford
treated her exactly as you would expect a woman of very good
Scotch family, which she was, to treat an ex-barmaid with whom
a distinguished man of letters had made an unfortunate marriage.
She was cordial, playful and gently determined to put her at her
ease.

It was strange that Rosie could not bear her; indeed, Mrs.
Barton Trafford was the only person that I ever knew her dislike.
In those days even barmaids did not habitually use the "bitches"
and "bloodys" that are part and parcel of the current vocabulary of
the best-brought-up young ladies, and I never heard Rosie use a
word that would have shocked my Aunt Sophie. When anyone
told a story that was a little near the knuckle she would blush to
the roots of her hair. But she referred to Mrs. Barton Trafford as

"that damned old cat". It needed the most urgent persuasions of her more intimate friends to induce her to be civil to her.

"Don't be a fool, Rosie," they said. They all called her Rosie and presently I, though very shyly, got in the habit of doing so too. "If she wants to she can make him. He must play up to her. She can work the trick if anyone can."

Though most of the Driffields' visitors were occasional, appearing every other Saturday, say, or every third, there was a little band that, like myself, came almost every week. We were the stand-bys; we arrived early and stayed late. Of these the most faithful were Quentin Forde, Harry Retford and Lionel Hillier.

Quentin Forde was a stocky little man with a fine head of the type that was afterward for a time much admired in the moving pictures, a straight nose and handsome eyes, neatly cropped grey hair and a black moustache; if he had been four or five inches taller he would have been the perfect type of the villain of melodrama. He was known to be very "well connected", and he was affluent; his only occupation was to cultivate the arts. He went to all the first nights and all the private views. He had the amateur's severity, and cherished for the productions of his contemporaries a polite but sweeping contempt. I discovered that he did not come to the Driffields' because Edward was a genius, but because Rosie was beautiful.

Now that I look back I cannot get over my surprise that I should have had to be told what was surely so obvious. When I first knew her it never occurred to me to ask myself whether she was pretty or plain, and when, seeing her again after five years, I noticed for the first time that she was very pretty, I was interested but did not trouble to think much about it. I took it as part of the natural order of things, just as I took the sun setting over the North Sea or the towers of Tercanbury Cathedral. I was quite startled when I heard people speak of Rosie's beauty, and when they complimented Edward on her looks and his eyes rested on her for a moment, mine followed his. Lionel Hillier was a painter and he asked her to sit for him. When he talked of the picture he wanted to paint and told me what he saw in her, I listened to him stupidly. I was puzzled and confused. Harry Retford knew one of the fashionable photographers of the period and, arranging special terms, he took Rosie to be photographed. A Saturday or two later the proofs were there and we all looked at them. I had never seen Rosie in evening dress. She was wearing a dress in white satin, with a long train and puffy sleeves, and it was cut low; her hair was more elaborately done than usual. She looked very different from the strapping young woman I had first met in Joy Lane in a boater and a starched shirt. But Lionel Hillier tossed the photographs aside impatiently.

"Rotten," he said. "What can a photograph give of Rosie? The thing about her is her colour." He turned to her. "Rosie, don't you know that your colour is *the* great miracle of the age?"

She looked at him without answering, but her full red lips broke into their childlike, mischievous smile.

"If I can only get a suggestion of it I'm made for life," he said. "All the rich stockbrokers' wives will come on their bended knees and beg me to paint them like you."

Presently I learned that Rosie was sitting to him, but when, never having been in a painter's studio and looking upon it as the gateway of romance, I asked if I might not come one day and see how the picture was getting on, Hillier said that he did not want anyone to see it yet. He was a man of five-and-thirty and of a flamboyant appearance. He looked like a portrait of Van Dyck in which the distinction had been replaced by good humour. He was slightly above the middle height, slim; and he had a fine mane of black hair and flowing moustaches and a pointed beard. He favoured broad-brimmed sombreros and Spanish capes. He had lived a long time in Paris and talked admiringly of painters, Monet, Sisley, Renoir, of whom we had never heard, and with contempt of Sir Frederick Leighton and Mr. Alma-Tadema and Mr. G. F. Watts, whom in our heart of hearts we very much admired. I have often wondered what became of him. He spent a few years in London trying to make his way, failed, I suppose, and then drifted to Florence. I was told that he had a drawing school there, but when, years later, chancing to be in that city, I asked about him, I could find no one who had ever heard of him. I think he must have had some talent, for I have even now a very vivid recollection of the portrait he painted of Rosie Driffield. I wonder what has happened to it. Has it been destroyed or is it hidden away, its face to the wall, in the attic of a junk shop in Chelsea? I should like to think that it has at least found a place on the walls of some provincial gallery.

When I was at last allowed to come and see it, I put my foot in it fine and proper. Hillier's studio was in the Fulham Road, one of a group at the back of a row of shops, and you went in through a dark and smelly passage. It was a Sunday afternoon in March, a fine blue day, and I walked from Vincent Square through deserted streets. Hillier lived in his studio; there was a large divan on which he slept, and a tiny little room at the back where he cooked his breakfast, washed his brushes and, I suppose, himself.

When I arrived Rosie still wore the dress in which she had been sitting and they were having a cup of tea. Hillier opened the door for me, and still holding my hand led me up to the large canvas.

"There she is," he said.

He had painted Rosie full length, just a little less than life-size, in an evening dress of white silk. It was not at all like the Academy portraits I was accustomed to. I did not know what to say, so I said the first thing that came into my head.

"When will it be finished?"

"It is finished," he answered.

I blushed furiously. I felt a perfect fool. I had not then acquired the technique that I flatter myself now enables me to deal competently with the works of modern artists. If this were the place I could write a very neat little guide to enable the amateur of pictures to deal to the satisfaction of their painters with the most diverse manifestations of the creative instinct. There is the intense "By God" that acknowledges the power of the ruthless realist, the "It's so awfully sincere" that covers your embarrassment when you are shown the coloured photograph of an alderman's widow, the low whistle that exhibits your admiration for the post-impressionist, the "Terribly amusing" that expresses what you feel about the cubist, the "Oh!" of one who is overcome, the "Ah!" of him whose breath is taken away.

"It's awfully like," was all that then I could lamely say.

"It's not chocolate-boxy enough for you," said Hillier.

"I think it's awfully good," I answered quickly, defending myself. "Are you going to send it to the Academy?"

"Good God, no! I might send it to the Grosvenor."

I looked from the painting to Rosie and from Rosie to the painting.

"Get into the pose, Rosie," said Hillier, "and let him see you."

She got up on to the model stand. I stared at her and I stared at the picture. I had such a funny little feeling in my heart. It was as though someone softly plunged a sharp knife into it, but it was not an unpleasant sensation at all, painful but strangely agreeable; and then suddenly I felt quite weak at the knees. But now I do not know if I remember Rosie in the flesh or in the picture. For when I think of her it is not in the shirt and boater that I first saw her in, nor in any of the other dresses I saw her in then or later, but in the white silk that Hillier painted, with a black velvet bow in her hair, and in the pose he had made her take.

I never exactly knew Rosie's age, but reckoning the years out as well as I can, I think she must have been then thirty-five. She did not look anything like it. Her face was quite unlined and her skin as smooth as a child's. I do not think she had very good features. They certainly had none of the aristocratic distinction of the great ladies whose photographs were at that time sold in all the shops; they were rather blunt. Her short nose was a little thick, her eyes were smallish, her mouth was large; but her eyes had the blue of cornflowers, and they smiled with her lips, very red and sensual, and her smile was the gayest, the most friendly, the sweetest thing I ever saw. She had by nature a heavy, sullen look, but when she smiled this sullenness became on a sudden infinitely attractive. She had no colour in her face; it was of a very pale brown except under the eyes, where it was faintly blue. Her hair was pale gold and it was done in the fashion of the day high on the head with an elaborate fringe.

"She's the very devil to paint," said Hillier, looking at her and at his picture. "You see, she's all gold, her face and her hair, and yet she doesn't give you a golden effect, she gives you a silvery effect."

I knew what he meant. She glowed, but palely, like the moon rather than the sun, or if it was like the sun it was like the sun in the white mist of dawn. Hillier had placed her in the middle of his canvas and she stood, with her arms by her sides, the palms of her hands toward you and her head a little thrown back, in an attitude that gave value to the pearly beauty of her neck and bosom. She stood like an actress taking a call, confused by un-expected applause, but there was something so virginal about her, so exquisitely spring-like, that the comparison was absurd. This

artless creature had never known grease-paint or footlights. She
stood like a maiden apt for love offering herself guilelessly, because she was fulfilling the purposes of Nature, to the embraces
of a lover. She belonged to a generation that did not fear a certain
opulence of line, she was slender, but her breasts were ample and
her hips well marked. When, later, Mrs. Barton Trafford saw the
picture she said it reminded her of a sacrificial heifer.

CHAPTER XV

Edward Driffield worked at night, and Rosie, having nothing
to do, was glad to go out with one or other of her friends. She
liked luxury and Quentin Forde was well-to-do. He would fetch
her in a cab and take her to dine at Kettner's or the Savoy, and
she would put on her grandest clothes for him; and Harry Retford,
though he never had a bob, behaved as if he had, and took her
about in hansoms too and gave her dinner at Romano's or in one
or other of the little restaurants that were becoming modish in
Soho. He was an actor and a clever one, but he was difficult to
suit and so was often out of work. He was about thirty, a man
with a pleasantly ugly face and a clipped way of speaking that
made what he said sound funny. Rosie liked his devil-may-care
attitude toward life, the swagger with which he wore clothes
made by the best tailor in London and unpaid for, the recklessness
with which he would put a fiver he hadn't got on a horse, and
the generosity with which he flung his money about when a
lucky win put him in funds. He was gay, charming, vain, boastful
and unscrupulous. Rosie told me that once he had pawned his
watch to take her out to dinner and then borrowed a couple
of pounds from the actor manager who had given them seats for
the play in order to take him out to supper with them afterward.
    But she was just as well pleased to go with Lionel Hillier to his
studio and eat a chop that he and she cooked between them and
spend the evening talking, and it was only very rarely that she
would dine with me at all. I used to fetch her after I had had my
dinner in Vincent Square and she hers with Driffield, and we
would get on a bus and go to a music-hall. We went here and
there, to the Pavilion or the Tivoli, sometimes to the Metropolitan

if there was a particular turn we wanted to see; but our favourite was the Canterbury. It was cheap and the show was good. We ordered a couple of beers and I smoked my pipe. Rosie looked round with delight at the great dark smoky house, crowded to the ceiling with the inhabitants of South London.

"I like the Canterbury," she said. "It's so homey."

I discovered that she was a great reader. She liked history, but only history of a certain kind, the lives of queens and of mistresses of royal personages; and she would tell me with a childlike wonder of the strange things she read. She had a wide acquaintance with the six consorts of King Henry VIII and there was little she did not know about Mrs. Fitzherbert and Lady Hamilton. Her appetite was prodigious and she ranged from Lucrezia Borgia to the wives of Philip of Spain; then there was the long list of the royal mistresses of France. She knew them all, and all about them, from Agnes Sorel down to Madame du Barry.

"I like to read about real things," she said. "I don't much care for novels."

She liked to gossip about Blackstable and I thought it was on account of my connection with it that she liked to come out with me. She seemed to know all that was going on there.

"I go down every other week or so to see my mother," she said. "Just for the night, you know."

"To Blackstable?"

I was surprised.

"No, not to Blackstable," Rosie smiled. "I don't know that I'd care to go there just yet. To Haversham. Mother comes over to meet me. I stay at the hotel where I used to work."

She was never a great talker. Often when, the night being fine, we decided to walk back from the music-hall at which we had been spending the evening, she never opened her mouth. But her silence was intimate and comfortable. It did not exclude you from thoughts that engaged her apart from you; it included you in a pervasive well-being.

I was talking about her once to Lionel Hillier and I said to him that I could not understand how she had turned from the fresh pleasant-looking young woman I had first known at Blackstable into the lovely creature whose beauty now practically everyone acknowledged. (There were people who made reservations. "Of course she has a very good figure," they said, "but it's not the sort of face I very much admire personally." And others said: "Oh, yes, a very pretty woman; but it's a pity she hasn't a little more distinction.")

"I can explain that to you in half a jiffy," said Lionel Hillier. "She was only a fresh, buxom wench when you first met her. *I* made her beauty."

I forget what my answer was, but I know it was ribald.

"All right. That just shows you don't know anything about beauty. No one ever thought very much of Rosie till I saw her like the sun shining silver. It wasn't till I painted it that anyone knew that her hair was the most lovely thing in the world."

"Did you make her neck and her breasts and her carriage and her bones?" I asked.

"Yes, damn you, that's just what I did do."

When Hillier talked of Rosie in front of her she listened to him with a smiling gravity. A little flush came into her pale cheeks. I think that at first when he spoke to her of her beauty she believed he was just making game of her; but when she found out that he wasn't, when he painted her silvery gold, it had no particular effect on her. She was a trifle amused, pleased of course, and a little surprised, but it did not turn her head. She thought him a little mad. I often wondered whether there was anything between them. I could not forget all I had heard of Rosie at Blackstable and what I had seen in the vicarage garden; I wondered about Quentin Forde, too, and Harry Retford. I used to watch them with her. She was not exactly familiar with them, comradely rather; she used to make her appointments with them quite openly in anybody's hearing; and when she looked at them it was with that mischievous, childlike smile which I had now discovered held such a mysterious beauty. Sometimes when we were sitting side by side in a music-hall I looked at her face; I do not think I was in love with her, I merely enjoyed the sensation of sitting quietly beside her and looking at the pale gold of her hair and the pale gold of her skin. Of course Lionel Hillier was right; the strange thing was that this gold did give one a strange moonlight feeling. She had the serenity of a summer evening when the light fades slowly from the unclouded sky. There was nothing dull in her immense placidity; it was as living as the sea when under the August sun it lay calm and shining along the Kentish coast. She reminded me of a sonatina by an old Italian composer with its wistfulness in which there is yet an urbane flippancy and its light rippling gaiety in which echoes still the trembling of a sigh. Sometimes, feeling my eyes on her, she would turn round and for a moment or two look me full in the face. She did not speak. I did not know of what she was thinking.

Once, I remember, I fetched her at Limpus Road, and the maid, telling me she was not ready, asked me to wait in the parlour. She came in. She was in black velvet, with a picture hat covered with ostrich feathers (we were going to the Pavilion and she had dressed up for it) and she looked so lovely that it took my breath away. I was staggered. The clothes of that day gave a woman dignity and there was something amazingly attractive in the way her virginal beauty (sometimes she looked like the exquisite statue of Psyche in the museum at Naples) contrasted with the stateliness of her gown. She had a trait that I think must be very rare: the skin under her eyes, faintly blue, was all dewy. Sometimes I could not persuade myself that it was natural, and once I asked her if she had rubbed vaseline under her eyes. That was just the effect it gave. She smiled, took a handkerchief and handed it to me.

"Rub them and see," she said.

Then one night when we had walked home from the Canterbury, and I was leaving her at her door, when I held out my hand she laughed a little, a low chuckle it was, and leaned forward.

"You old silly," she said.

She kissed me on the mouth. It was not a hurried peck, nor was it a kiss of passion. Her lips, those very full red lips of hers, rested on mine long enough for me to be conscious of their shape and their warmth and their softness. Then she withdrew them, but without hurry, in silence pushed open the door, slipped inside and left me. I was so startled that I had not been able to say anything. I accepted her kiss stupidly. I remained inert. I turned away and walked back to my lodgings. I seemed to hear still in my ears Rosie's laughter. It was not contemptuous or wounding, but frank and affectionate, it was as though she laughed because she was fond of me.

CHAPTER XVI

I did not go out with Rosie again for more than a week. She was
going down to Haversham to spend a night with her mother. She
had various engagements in London. Then she asked me if I
would go to the Haymarket Theatre with her. The play was a
success and free seats were not to be had, so we made up our
minds to go in the pit. We had a steak and a glass of beer at
the Café Monico and then stood with the crowd. In those days
there was no orderly queue and when the doors were opened
there was a mad rush and scramble to get in. We were hot and
breathless and somewhat battered when at last we pushed our
way into our seats.

We walked back through St. James's Park. The night was so
lovely that we sat down on a bench. In the starlight Rosie's face
and her fair hair glowed softly. She was suffused, as it were (I
express it awkwardly, but I do not know how to describe the
emotion she gave me) with a friendliness at once candid and
tender. She was like a silvery flower of the night that only gave
its perfume to the moonbeams. I slipped my arm round her waist
and she turned her face to mine. This time it was I who kissed.
She did not move; her soft red lips submitted to the pressure of
mine with a calm, intense passivity as the water of a lake accepts
the light of the moon. I don't know how long we stayed there.

"I'm awfully hungry," she said suddenly.

"So am I," I laughed.

"Couldn't we go and have some fish and chips somewhere?"

"Rather."

In those days I knew my way very well about Westminster, not
yet a fashionable quarter for parliamentary and otherwise cultured persons, but slummy and down-at-heel; and after we had
come out of the park, crossing Victoria Street, I led Rosie to a
fried fish shop in Horseferry Row. It was late and the only other
person there was the driver of a four-wheeler waiting outside. We
ordered our fish and chips and a bottle of beer. A poor woman
came in and bought two penn'orth of mixed and took it away with
her in a piece of paper. We ate with appetite.

Our way back to Rosie's led through Vincent Square and as we passed my house I asked her:

"Won't you come in for a minute? You've never seen my rooms."

"What about your landlady? I don't want to get you into trouble."

"Oh, she sleeps like a rock."

"I'll come in for a little."

I slipped my key into the lock and because the passage was dark took Rosie's hand to lead her in. I lit the gas in my sitting-room. She took off her hat and vigorously scratched her head. Then she looked for a glass, but I was very artistic and had taken down the mirror that was over the chimney-piece and there was no means in the room for anyone to see what he looked like.

"Come into my bedroom," I said. "There's a glass there."

I opened the door and lit the candle. Rosie followed me in and I held it up so that she should be able to see herself. I looked at her in the glass as she arranged her hair. She took two or three pins out, which she put in her mouth, and, taking one of my brushes, brushed her hair up from the nape of her neck. She twisted it, patted it, and put back the pins, and as she was intent on this her eyes caught mine on the glass and she smiled at me. When she had replaced the last pin she turned and faced me; she did not say anything; she looked at me tranquilly, still with that little friendly smile in her blue eyes. I put down the candle. The room was very small and the dressing-table was by the bed. She raised her hand and softly stroked my cheek.

I wish now that I had not started to write this book in the first person singular. It is all very well when you can show yourself in an amiable or touching light, and nothing can be more effective than the modest heroic or pathetic humorous which in this mode is much cultivated; it is charming to write about yourself when you see on the readers' eyelash the glittering tear and on his lips the tender smile; but it is not so nice when you have to exhibit yourself as a plain damned fool.

A little while ago I read in the *Evening Standard* an article by Mr. Evelyn Waugh in the course of which he remarked that to write novels in the first person was a contemptible practice. I wish he had explained why, but he merely threw out the statement with just the same take-it-or-leave-it casualness as Euclid used when he made his celebrated observation about parallel straight lines. I was much concerned and forthwith asked Alroy Kear (who reads everything, even the books he writes prefaces for) to recommend to me some works on the art of fiction. On his advice I read *The Craft of Fiction* by Mr. Percy Lubbock, from which I learned that the only way to write novels was like Henry James; after that I read *Aspects of the Novel* by Mr. E. M. Forster, from which I learned that the only way to write novels was like Mr. E. M. Forster; then I read *The Structure of the Novel* by Mr. Edwin Muir, from which I learned nothing at all. In none of them could I discover anything to the point at issue. All the same I can find one reason why certain novelists, such as Defoe, Sterne, Thackeray, Dickens, Emily Brontë and Proust, well known in their day but now doubtless forgotten, have used the method that Mr. Evelyn Waugh reprehends. As we grow older we become more conscious of the complexity, incoherence and unreasonableness of human beings; this indeed is the only excuse that offers for the middle-aged or elderly writer, whose thoughts should more properly be turned to graver matters, occupying himself with the trivial concerns of imaginary people. For if the proper study of mankind is man it is evidently more sensible to occupy yourself with the coherent, substantial and significant creatures of fiction than with the irrational and shadowy figures of real life. Sometimes the novelist feels himself like God and is prepared to tell you everything about his characters; sometimes, however, he does not; and then he tells you not everything that is to be known about them but the little he knows himself; and since as we grow older we feel ourselves less and less like God I should not be surprised to learn that with advancing years the novelist grows less and less inclined to describe more than his own experience has given him. The first person singular is a very useful device for this limited purpose.

Rosie raised her hand and softly stroked my face. I do not know why I should have behaved as I then did; it was not at all how I had seen myself behaving on such an occasion. A sob broke from my tight throat. I do not know whether it was because I was shy and lonely (not lonely in the body, for I spent all day at the hospital with all kinds of people, but lonely in the spirit) or because my desire was so great, but I began to cry. I felt terribly ashamed of myself; I tried to control myself, I couldn't; the tears welled up in my eyes and poured down my cheeks. Rosie saw them and gave a little gasp.

"Oh, honey, what is it? What's the matter? Don't. Don't!"

She put her arms round my neck and began to cry too, and she kissed my lips and my eyes and my wet cheeks. She undid her bodice and lowered my head till it rested on her bosom. She stroked my smooth face. She rocked me back and forth as though I were a child in her arms. I kissed her breasts and I kissed the white column of her neck; and she slipped out of her bodice and out of her skirt and her petticoats and I held her for a moment by her corseted waist; then she undid it, holding her breath for an instant to enable her to do so, and stood before me in her shift. When I put my hands on her sides I could feel the ribbing of the skin from the pressure of the corsets.

"Blow out the candle," she whispered.

It was she who awoke me when the dawn peering through the curtains revealed the shape of the bed and of the wardrobe against the darkness of the lingering night. She woke me by kissing me on the mouth and her hair falling over my face tickled me.

"I must get up," she said. "I don't want your landlady to see me."

"There's plenty of time."

Her breasts when she leaned over me were heavy on my chest. In a little while she got out of bed. I lit the candle. She turned to the glass and tied up her hair and then she looked for a moment at her naked body. Her waist was naturally small; though so well developed she was very slender; her breasts were straight and firm and they stood out from the chest as though carved in marble. It was a body made for the act of love. In the light of the candle, struggling now with the increasing day, it was all silvery gold; and the only colour was the rosy pink of the hard nipples.

We dressed in silence. She did not put on her corsets again, but rolled them up and I wrapped them in a piece of newspaper. We tiptoed along the passage and when I opened the door and we stepped out into the street the dawn ran to meet us like a cat leaping up the steps. The square was empty; already the sun was shining on the eastern windows. I felt as young as the day. We walked arm-in-arm till we came to the corner of Limpus Road.

"Leave me here," said Rosie. "One never knows."

I kissed her and I watched her walk away. She walked rather

slowly, with the firm tread of the country woman who likes to feel
the good earth under her feet, and held herself erect. I could not
go back to bed. I strolled on till I came to the Embankment.
The river had the bright hues of the early morning. A brown barge
came down-stream and passed under Vauxhall Bridge. In a dinghy
two men were rowing close to the side. I was hungry.

CHAPTER XVII

After that for more than a year whenever Rosie came out with
me she used on the way home to drop into my rooms, sometimes
for an hour, sometimes till the breaking day warned us that the
slaveys would soon be scrubbing the doorsteps. I have a recollection of warm sunny mornings when the tired air of London had a
welcome freshness, and of our footfalls that seemed so noisy in
the empty streets, and then of scurrying along huddled under an
umbrella, silent but gay, when the winter brought cold and rain.
The policeman on point duty gave us a stare as we passed, sometimes of suspicion; but sometimes also there was a twinkle of
comprehension in his eyes. Now and then we would see a home-
less creature huddled up asleep in a portico and Rosie gave my
arm a friendly little pressure when (chiefly for show and because
I wanted to make a good impression on her, for my shillings were
scarce) I placed a piece of silver on a shapeless lap or in a skinny
fist. Rosie made me very happy. I had a great affection for her.
She was easy and comfortable. She had a placidity of temper that
communicated itself to the people she was with; you shared her
pleasure in the passing moment.

Before I became her lover I had often asked myself if she was
the mistress of the others, Forde, Harry Retford and Hillier, and
afterward I questioned her. She kissed me.

"Don't be so silly. I like them, you know that. I like to go out
with them, but that's all."

I wanted to ask her if she had been the mistress of George
Kemp, but I did not like to. Though I had never seen her in a
temper, I had a notion that she had one and I vaguely felt that
this was a question that might anger her. I did not want to give
her the opportunity of saying things so wounding that I could not
forgive her. I was young, only just over one-and-twenty, Quentin

Forde and the others seemed old to me; it did not seem unnatural to me that to Rosie they were only friends. It gave me a
little thrill of pride to think that I was her lover. When I used to
look at her chatting and laughing with all and sundry at tea on
Saturday afternoons, I glowed with self-satisfaction. I thought of
the nights we passed together and I was inclined to laugh at the
people who were so ignorant of my great secret. But sometimes I
thought that Lionel Hillier looked at me in a quizzical way, as if
he were enjoying a good joke at my expense, and I asked myself
uneasily if Rosie had told him that she was having an affair with
me. I wondered if there was anything in my manner that betrayed me. I told Rosie that I was afraid Hillier suspected something; she looked at me with those blue eyes of hers that always
seemed ready to smile.

"Don't bother about it," she said. "He's got a nasty mind."

I had never been intimate with Quentin Forde. He looked upon
me as a dull and insignificant young man (which of course I was)
and though he had always been civil he had never taken any
notice of me. I thought it could only be my fancy that now he
began to be a little more frigid with me than before. But one day
Harry Retford to my surprise asked me to dine with him and go to
the play. I told Rosie.

"Oh, of course you must go. He'll give you an awfully good
time. Good old Harry, he always makes me laugh."

So I dined with him. He made himself very pleasant and I
was impressed to hear him talk of actors and actresses. He had a
sarcastic humour and was very funny at the expense of Quentin
Forde, whom he did not like; I tried to get him to talk of Rosie,
but he had nothing to say of her. He seemed to be a gay dog.
With leers and laughing innuendoes he gave me to understand
that he was a devil with the girls. I could not but ask myself if he
was standing me this dinner because he knew I was Rosie's lover
and so felt friendly disposed toward me. But if he knew, of course
the others knew too. I hope I did not show it, but in my heart I
certainly felt somewhat patronising toward them.

Then in winter, toward the end of January, someone new appeared at Limpus Road. This was a Dutch Jew named Jack
Kuyper, a diamond merchant from Amsterdam, who was spending
a few weeks in London on business. I do not know how he had
come to know the Driffields and whether it was esteem for the

author that brought him to the house, but it was certainly not that which caused him to come again. He was a tall, stout, dark man with a bald head and a big hooked nose, a man of fifty, but of a powerful appearance, sensual, determined and jovial. He made no secret of his admiration for Rosie. He was rich apparently, for he sent her roses every day; she chid him for his extravagance, but was flattered. I could not bear him. He was blatant and loud. I hated his fluent conversation in perfect but foreign English; I hated the extravagant compliments he paid Rosie; I hated the heartiness with which he treated her friends. I found that Quentin Forde liked him as little as I; we almost became cordial with one another.

"Mercifully he's not staying long." Quentin Forde pursed his lips and raised his black eyebrows; with his white hair and long sallow face he looked incredibly gentlemanly. "Women are always the same; they adore a bounder."

"He's so frightfully vulgar," I complained.

"That is his charm," said Quentin Forde.

For the next two or three weeks I saw next to nothing of Rosie. Jack Kuyper took her out night after night, to this smart restaurant and that, to one play after another. I was vexed and hurt.

"He doesn't know anyone in London," said Rosie, trying to soothe my ruffled feelings. "He wants to see everything he can while he's here. It wouldn't be very nice for him to go alone all the time. He's only here for a fortnight more."

I did not see the object of this self-sacrifice on her part.

"But don't you think he's awful?" I said.

"No. I think he's fun. He makes me laugh."

"Don't you know that he's absolutely gone on you?"

"Well, it pleases him and it doesn't do me any harm."

"He's old and fat and horrible. It gives me the creeps to look at him."

"I don't think he's so bad," said Rosie.

"You couldn't have anything to do with him," I protested. "I mean, he's such an awful cad."

Rosie scratched her head. It was an unpleasant habit of hers.

"It's funny how different foreigners are from English people," she said.

I was thankful when Jack Kuyper went back to Amsterdam. Rosie had promised to dine with me the day after and as a treat we arranged to dine in Soho. She fetched me in a hansom and we drove on.

"Has your horrible old man gone?" I asked.

"Yes," she laughed.

I put my arm round her waist. (I have elsewhere remarked how much more convenient the hansom was for this pleasant and indeed almost essential act in human intercourse than the taxi of the present day, so unwillingly refrain from labouring the point.) I put my arm round her waist and kissed her. Her lips were like spring flowers. We arrived. I hung my hat and my coat (it was very long and tight at the waist, with a velvet collar and velvet cuffs; very smart) on a peg and asked Rosie to give me her cape.

"I'm going to keep it on," she said.

"You'll be awfully hot. You'll only catch cold when we go out."

"I don't care. It's the first time I've worn it. Don't you think it's lovely. And look: the muff matches."

I gave the cape a glance. It was of fur. I did not know it was sable.

"It looks awfully rich. How did you get that?"

"Jack Kuyper gave it to me. We went and bought it yesterday just before he went away." She stroked the smooth fur; she was as happy with it as a child with a toy. "How much d'you think it cost?"

"I haven't an idea."

"Two hundred and sixty pounds. Do you know I've never had anything that cost so much in my life? I told him it was far too much, but he wouldn't listen. He made me have it."

Rosie chuckled with glee and her eyes shone. But I felt my face go stiff and a shiver run down my spine.

"Won't Driffield think it's rather funny, Kuyper giving you a fur cape that costs all that?" said I, trying to make my voice sound natural.

Rosie's eyes danced mischievously.

"You know what Ted is, he never notices anything; if he says anything about it I shall tell him I gave twenty pounds for it in a pawnshop. He won't know any better." She rubbed her face against the collar. "It's so soft. And everyone can see it cost money."

I tried to eat and in order not to show the bitterness in my heart I did my best to keep the conversation going on one topic or another. Rosie did not much mind what I said. She could only think of her new cape and every other minute her eyes returned to the muff that she insisted on holding on her lap. She looked at it with an affection in which there was something lazy, sensual and self-complacent. I was angry with her. I thought her stupid and common.

"You look like a cat that's swallowed a canary," I could not help snapping.

She only giggled.

"That's what I feel like."

Two hundred and sixty pounds was an enormous sum to me. I did not know one *could* pay so much for a cape. I lived on fourteen pounds a month and not at all badly either; and in case any reader is not a ready reckoner I will add that this is one hundred and sixty-eight pounds a year. I could not believe that anyone would make as expensive a present as that from pure friendship; what did it mean but that Jack Kuyper had been sleeping with Rosie, night after night, all the time he was in London, and now when he went away was paying her? How could she accept it? Didn't she see how it degraded her? Didn't she see how frightfully vulgar it was of him to give her a thing that cost so much? Apparently not, for she said to me:

"It was nice of him, wasn't it? But then Jews are always generous."

"I suppose he could afford it," I said.

"Oh, yes, he's got lots of money. He said he wanted to give me something before he went away and asked me what I wanted. Well, I said, I could do with a cape and a muff to match, but I never thought he'd buy me anything like this. When we went into the shop I asked them to show me something in astrakhan, but he said: No, sable, and the best money can buy. And when we saw this he absolutely insisted on my having it."

I thought of her with her white body, her skin so milky, in the arms of that old fat gross man and his thick loose lips kissing hers. And then I knew that the suspicion that I had refused to believe was true; I knew that when she went out to dinner with Quentin Forde and Harry Retford and Lionel Hillier she went to bed with them just as she came to bed with me. I could not speak; I knew that if I did I should insult her. I do not think I was jealous so much as mortified. I felt that she had been making a damned fool of me. I used all my determination to prevent the bitter gibes from passing my lips.

We went on to the theatre. I could not listen to the play. I could only feel against my arm the smoothness of the sable cape; I could only see her fingers forever stroking the muff. I could have borne the thought of the others; it was Jack Kuyper who horrified me. How could she? It was abominable to be poor. I longed to have enough money to tell her that if she would send the fellow back his beastly furs I would give her better ones instead. At last she noticed that I did not speak.

"You're very silent to-night."

"Am I?"

"Aren't you well?"

"Perfectly."

She gave me a sidelong look. I did not meet her eyes, but I knew they were smiling with that smile at once mischievous and childlike that I knew so well. She said nothing more. At the end of the play, since it was raining, we took a hansom and I gave the driver her address in Limpus Road. She did not speak till we got to Victoria Street, then she said:

"Don't you want me to come home with you?"

"Just as you like."

She lifted up the trap and gave the driver my address. She took my hand and held it, but I remained inert. I looked straight out of the window with angry dignity. When we reached Vincent Square I handed her out of the cab and let her into the house without a word. I took off my hat and coat. She threw her cape and her muff on the sofa.

"Why are you so sulky?" she asked, coming up to me.

"I'm not sulky," I answered, looking away.

She took my face in her two hands.

"How can you be so silly? Why should you be angry because Jack Kuyper gives me a fur cape? You can't afford to give me one, can you?"

"Of course I can't."

"And Ted can't either. You can't expect me to refuse a fur cape that cost two hundred and sixty pounds. I've wanted a fur cape all my life. It means nothing to Jack."

"You don't expect me to believe that he gave it to you just out of friendship."

"He might have. Anyhow, he's gone back to Amsterdam, and who knows when he'll come back?"

"He isn't the only one, either."

I looked at Rosie now, with angry, hurt, resentful eyes; she smiled at me, and I wish I knew how to describe the sweet kindliness of her beautiful smile; her voice was exquisitely gentle.

"Oh, my dear, why d'you bother your head about any others? What harm does it do you? Don't I give you a good time? Aren't you happy when you're with me?"

"Awfully."

"Well, then. It's so silly to be fussy and jealous. Why not be happy with what you can get? Enjoy yourself while you have the chance, I say; we shall all be dead in a hundred years and what will anything matter then? Let's have a good time while we can."

She put her arms round my neck and pressed her lips against mine. I forgot my wrath. I only thought of her beauty and her enveloping kindness.

"You must take me as I am, you know," she whispered.

"All right," I said.

CHAPTER XVIII

During all this time I saw really very little of Driffield. His editorship occupied much of his day and in the evening he wrote. He was, of course, there every Saturday afternoon, amiable and ironically amusing; he appeared glad to see me and chatted with me for a little while pleasantly of indifferent things; but naturally most of his attention was given to guests older and more important than I. But I had a feeling that he was growing more aloof; he was no longer the jolly, rather vulgar companion that I had known at Blackstable. Perhaps it was only my increasing sensibility that discerned as it were an invisible barrier that existed between him and the people he chaffed and joked with. It was as though he lived a life of the imagination that made the life of every day a little shadowy. He was asked to speak now and then at public dinners. He joined a literary club. He began to know a good many people outside the narrow circle into which his writing had drawn him, and he was increasingly asked to luncheon and tea by the ladies who like to gather about them distinguished authors. Rosie was asked too, but seldom went; she said she didn't care for parties, and after all they didn't want her, they only wanted Ted. I think she was shy and felt out of it. It may be that hostesses had more than once let her see how tiresome they thought it that she must be included; and after inviting her because it was polite, ignored her because to be polite irked them.

It was just about then that Edward Driffield published *The Cup of Life*. It is not my business to criticise his works, and of late as much has been written about them as must satisfy the appetite of any ordinary reader; but I will permit myself to say that *The Cup of Life*, though certainly not the most celebrated of his books, nor the most popular, is to my mind the most interesting. It has a cold ruthlessness that in all the sentimentality of English fiction strikes an original note. It is refreshing and astringent. It tastes of tart apples. It sets your teeth on edge, but it has a subtle, bitter-sweet savour that is very agreeable to the palate. Of all Driffield's books it is the only one I should like to have written. The scene of the child's death, terrible and heartrending, but written without slop or sickliness, and the curious incident that follows it, cannot easily be forgotten by anyone who has read them.

It was this part of the book that caused the sudden storm that burst on the wretched Driffield's head. For a few days after publication it looked as though it would run its course like the rest of his novels, namely that it would have substantial reviews, laudatory on the whole but with reservations, and that the sales would be respectable, but modest. Rosie told me that he expected to make three hundred pounds out of it and was talking of renting a house on the river for the summer. The first two or three notices were noncommittal; then in one of the morning papers appeared a violent attack. There was a column of it. The book was described as gratuitously offensive, obscene, and the publishers were rated for putting it before the public. Harrowing pictures were drawn of the devastating effect it must have on the youth of England. It was described as an insult to womanhood. The reviewer protested against the possibility of such a work falling into the hands of young boys and innocent maidens. Other papers followed suit. The more foolish demanded that the book should be suppressed and some asked themselves gravely if this was not a case where the public prosecutor might with fitness intervene. Condemnation was universal; if here and there a courageous writer, accustomed to the more realistic tone of continental fiction, asserted that Edward Driffield had never written anything better, he was ignored. His honest opinion was ascribed to a base desire to play to the gallery. The libraries barred the book and the lessors of the railway bookstalls refused to stock it.

All this was naturally very unpleasant for Edward Driffield, but he bore it with philosophic calm. He shrugged his shoulders.

"They say it isn't true," he smiled. "They can go to hell. It is true."

He was supported in this trial by the fidelity of his friends. To admire *The Cup of Life* became a mark of æsthetic acumen: to be shocked by it was to confess yourself a philistine. Mrs. Barton Trafford had no hesitation in saying that it was a masterpiece, and though this wasn't quite the moment for Barton's article in the *Quarterly,* her faith in Edward Driffield's future remained unshaken. It is strange (and instructive) to read now, the book that created such a sensation; there is not a word that could bring a blush to the cheek of the most guileless, not an episode that could cause the novel reader of the present day to turn a hair.

CHAPTER XIX

About six months later, when the excitement over *The Cup of Life* had subsided and Driffield had already begun the novel which he published under the name of *By Their Fruits,* I, being then an inpatient dresser and in my fourth year, in the course of my duties went one day into the main hall of the hospital to await the surgeon whom I was accompanying on his round of the wards. I glanced at the rack in which letters were placed, for sometimes people, not knowing my address in Vincent Square, wrote to me at the hospital. I was surprised to find a telegram for me. It ran as follows:

PLEASE COME AND SEE ME AT FIVE O'CLOCK THIS AFTERNOON WITH-
OUT FAIL. IMPORTANT.   ISABEL TRAFFORD.

I wondered what she wanted me for. I had met her perhaps a dozen times during the last two years, but she had never taken any notice of me, and I had never been to her house. I knew that men were scarce at tea-time and a hostess, short of them at the last moment, might think that a young medical student was better than nothing; but the wording of the telegram hardly suggested a party.

The surgeon for whom I dressed was prosy and verbose. It was not till past five that I was free and then it took me a good twenty minutes to get down to Chelsea. Mrs. Barton Trafford lived in a block of flats on the Embankment. It was nearly six when I rang at her door and asked if she was at home. But when I was ushered into her drawing-room and began to explain why I was late she cut me short.

"We supposed you couldn't get away. It doesn't matter."

Her husband was there.

"I expect he'd like a cup of tea," he said.

"Oh, I think it's rather late for tea, isn't it?" She looked at me gently, her mild, rather fine eyes full of kindness. "You don't want any tea, do you?"

I was thirsty and hungry, for my lunch had consisted of a scone and butter and a cup of coffee, but I did not like to say so. I refused tea.

"Do you know Allgood Newton?" asked Mrs. Barton Trafford, with a gesture towards a man who had been sitting in a big armchair when I was shown in, and now got up. "I expect you've met him at Edward's."

I had. He did not come often, but his name was familiar to me and I remembered him. He made me very nervous and I do not think I had ever spoken to him. Though now completely forgotten, in those days he was the best-known critic in England. He was a large, fat, blond man, with a fleshy white face, pale blue eyes and greying fair hair. He generally wore a pale blue tie to bring out the colour of his eyes. He was very amiable to the authors he met at Driffield's and said charming and flattering things to them, but when they were gone he was very amusing at their expense. He spoke in a low, even voice, with an apt choice of words: no one could with more point tell a malicious story about a friend.

Allgood Newton shook hands with me and Mrs. Barton Trafford, with her ready sympathy, anxious to put me at my ease, took me by the hand and made me sit on the sofa beside her. The tea was still on the table and she took a jam sandwich and delicately nibbled it.

"Have you seen the Driffields lately?" she asked me as though making conversation.

"I was there last Saturday."

"You haven't seen either of them since?"

"No."

Mrs. Barton Trafford looked from Allgood Newton to her husband and back again as though mutely demanding their help.

"Nothing will be gained by circumlocution, Isabel," said Newton, a faintly malicious twinkle in his eye, in his fat precise way.

Mrs. Barton Trafford turned to me.

"Then you don't know that Mrs. Driffield has run away from her husband."

"What!"

I was flabbergasted. I could not believe my ears.

"Perhaps it would be better if you told him the facts, Allgood," said Mrs. Trafford.

The critic leaned back in his chair and placed the tips of the fingers of one hand against the tips of the fingers of the other. He spoke with unction.

"I had to see Edward Driffield last night about a literary article that I am doing for him and after dinner, since the night was fine, I thought I would walk round to his house. He was expecting me; and I knew besides that he never went out at night except for some function as important as the Lord Mayor's banquet or the Academy dinner. Imagine my surprise then, nay, my utter and complete bewilderment, when as I approached I saw the door of his house open and Edward in person emerge. You know of course that Immanuel Kant was in the habit of taking his daily walk at a certain hour with such punctuality that the inhabitants of Königsberg were accustomed to set their watches by the event and when once he came out of his house an hour earlier than usual they turned pale, for they knew that this could only mean that some terrible thing had happened. They were right; Immanuel Kant had just received intelligence of the fall of the Bastille."

Allgood Newton paused for a moment to mark the effect of his anecdote. Mrs. Barton Trafford gave him her understanding smile.

"I did not envisage so world-shaking a catastrophe as this when I saw Edward hurrying towards me, but it immediately occurred to me that something untoward was afoot. He carried neither cane nor gloves. He wore his working coat, a venerable garment in black alpaca, and a wide-awake hat. There was something wild in his mien and distraught in his bearing. I asked myself, knowing the vicissitudes of the conjugal state, whether a matrimonial difference had driven him headlong from the house or whether he was hastening to a letter-box in order to post a letter. He sped like Hector flying the noblest of the Greeks. He did not seem to see me and the suspicion flashed across my mind that he did not want to. I stopped him. 'Edward,' I said. He looked startled. For a moment I could have sworn he did not know who I was. 'What avenging furies urge you with such hot haste through the rakish purlieus of Pimlico?' I asked. 'Oh, it's you,' he said. 'Where are you going?' I asked. 'Nowhere,' he replied."

At this rate I thought Allgood Newton would never finish his story and Mrs. Hudson would be vexed with me for turning up to dinner half an hour late.

"I told him on what errand I had come, and proposed that we should return to his house where we could more conveniently discuss the question that perturbed me. 'I'm too restless to go home,' he said; 'let's walk. You can talk to me as we go along.' Assenting, I turned round and we began to walk; but his pace was so rapid that I had to beg him to moderate it. Even Dr. Johnson could not have carried on a conversation when he was walking down Fleet Street at the speed of an express train. Edward's appearance was so peculiar and his manner so agitated that I thought it wise to lead him through the less frequented streets. I talked to him of my article. The subject that occupied me was more copious than had at first sight appeared, and I was doubtful whether after all I could do justice to it in the columns of a weekly journal. I put the matter before him fully and fairly and asked him his opinion. 'Rosie has left me,' he answered. For a moment I did not know what he was talking about, but in a trice it occurred to me that he was speaking of the buxom and not unprepossessing female from whose hands I had on occasion accepted a cup of tea. From his tone I divined that he expected condolence from me rather than felicitation."

Allgood Newton paused again and his blue eyes twinkled.

"You're wonderful, Allgood," said Mrs. Barton Trafford.

"Priceless," said her husband.

"Realising that the occasion demanded sympathy, I said: 'My dear fellow.' He interrupted me. 'I had a letter by the last post,' he said. 'She's run away with Lord George Kemp.'"

I gasped, but said nothing. Mrs. Trafford gave me a quick look. "'Who is Lord George Kemp?' 'He's a Blackstable man,' he replied. I had little time to think. I determined to be frank. 'You're well rid of her,' I said. 'Allgood!' he cried. I stopped and put my hand on his arm. 'You must know that she was deceiving you with all your friends. Her behaviour was a public scandal. My dear Edward, let us face the fact: your wife was nothing but a common strumpet.' He snatched his arm away from me and gave a sort of low roar, like an orang-utan in the forests of Borneo forcibly deprived of a coconut, and before I could stop him he broke away and fled. I was so startled that I could do nothing but listen to his cries and his hurrying footsteps."

"You shouldn't have let him go," said Mrs. Barton Trafford. "In the state he was he might have thrown himself in the Thames."

"The thought occurred to me, but I noticed that he did not run in the direction of the river, but plunged into the meaner streets of the neighbourhood in which we had been walking. And I reflected also that there is no example in literary history of an author committing suicide while engaged on the composition of a literary work. Whatever his tribulations, he is unwilling to leave to posterity an uncompleted opus."

I was astounded at what I heard and shocked and dismayed; but I was worried too because I could not make out why Mrs. Trafford had sent for me. She knew me much too little to think that the story could be of any particular interest to me; nor would she have troubled to let me hear it as a piece of news.

"Poor Edward," she said. "Of course no one can deny that it is a blessing in disguise, but I'm afraid he'll take it very much to heart. Fortunately he's done nothing rash." She turned to me. "As soon as Mr. Newton told us about it I went round to Limpus Road. Edward was out, but the maid said he'd only just left; that means that he must have gone home between the time he ran away from Allgood and this morning. You'll wonder why I asked you to come and see me."

I did not answer. I waited for her to go on.

"It was at Blackstable you first knew the Driffields, wasn't it?

You can tell us who is this Lord George Kemp. Edward said he was a Blackstable man."

"He's middle-aged. He's got a wife and two sons. They're as old as I am."

"But I don't understand who he can be. I can't find him in Debrett."

I almost laughed.

"Oh, he's not really a lord. He's the local coal merchant. They call him Lord George at Blackstable because he's so grand. It's just a joke."

"The quiddity of bucolic humour is often a trifle obscure to the uninitiated," said Allgood Newton.

"We must all help dear Edward in every way we can," said Mrs. Barton Trafford. Her eyes rested on me thoughtfully. "If Kemp has run away with Rosie Driffield he must have left his wife."

"I suppose so," I replied.

"Will you do something very kind?"

"If I can."

"Will you go down to Blackstable and find out exactly what has happened? I think we ought to get in touch with the wife."

I have never been very fond of interfering in other people's affairs.

"I don't know how I could do that," I answered.

"Couldn't you see her?"

"No, I couldn't."

If Mrs. Barton Trafford thought my reply blunt she did not show it. She smiled a little.

"At all events that can be left over. The urgent thing is to go down and find out about Kemp. I shall try to see Edward this evening. I can't bear the thought of his staying on in that odious house by himself. Barton and I have made up our minds to bring him here. We have a spare room and I'll arrange it so that he can work there. Don't you agree that that would be the best thing for him, Allgood?"

"Absolutely."

"There's no reason why he shouldn't stay here indefinitely, at all events for a few weeks, and then he can come away with us in the summer. We're going to Brittany. I'm sure he'd like that. It would be a thorough change for him."

"The immediate question," said Barton Trafford, fixing on me an eye nearly as kindly as his wife's, "is whether this young sawbones will go to Blackstable and find out what he can. We must know where we are. That is essential."

Barton Trafford excused his interest in archæology by a hearty manner and a jocose, even slangy way of speech.

"He couldn't refuse," said his wife, giving me a soft, appealing glance. "You won't refuse, will you? It's so important and you're the only person who can help us."

Of course she did not know that I was as anxious to find out what had happened as she; she could not tell what a bitter jealous pain stabbed my heart.

"I couldn't possibly get away from the hospital before Saturday," I said.

"That'll do. It's very good of you. All Edward's friends will be grateful to you. When shall you return?"

"I have to be back in London early on Monday morning."

"Then come and have tea with me in the afternoon. I shall await you with impatience. Thank God, that's settled. Now I must try and get hold of Edward."

I understood that I was dismissed. Allgood Newton took his leave and came downstairs with me.

"Our Isabel has *un petit air* of Catherine of Aragon to-day that I find vastly becoming," he murmured when the door was closed behind us. "This is a golden opportunity and I think we may safely trust our friend not to miss it. A charming woman with a heart of gold. *Vénus toute entière à sa proie attachée.*"

I did not understand what he meant, for what I have already told the reader about Mrs. Barton Trafford I only learned much later, but I realised that he was saying something vaguely malicious about her, and probably amusing, so I sniggered.

"I suppose your youth inclines you to what my good Dizzy named in an unlucky moment the gondola of London."

"I'm going to take a bus," I answered.

"Oh? Had you proposed to go by hansom I was going to ask you to be good enough to drop me on your way, but if you are going to use the homely conveyance which I in my old-fashioned manner still prefer to call an omnibus, I shall hoist my unwieldy carcase into a four-wheeler."

He signalled to one and gave me two flabby fingers to shake.

"I shall come on Monday to hear the result of what dear Henry would call your so exquisitely delicate mission."

CHAPTER XX

But it was years before I saw Allgood Newton again, for when I got to Blackstable I found a letter from Mrs. Barton Trafford (who had taken the precaution to note my address) asking me, for reasons that she would explain when she saw me, not to come to her flat but to meet her at six o'clock in the first-class waiting-room at Victoria Station. As soon then as I could get away from the hospital on Monday I made my way there, and after waiting for a while saw her come in. She came towards me with little tripping steps.

"Well, have you anything to tell me? Let us find a quiet corner and sit down."

We sought a place and found it.

"I must explain why I asked you to come here," she said. "Edward is staying with me. At first he did not want to come, but I persuaded him. But he's nervous and ill and irritable. I did not want to run the risk of his seeing you."

I told Mrs. Trafford the bare facts of my story and she listened attentively. Now and then she nodded her head. But I could not hope to make her understand the commotion I had found at Blackstable. The town was beside itself with excitement. Nothing so thrilling had happened there for years and no one could talk of anything else. Humpty-dumpty had had a great fall. Lord George Kemp had absconded. About a week before he had announced that he had to go up to London on business, and two days later a petition in bankruptcy was filed against him. It appeared that his building operations had not been successful, his attempt to make Blackstable into a frequented seaside resort meeting with no response, and he had been forced to raise money in every way he could. All kinds of rumours ran through the little town. Quite a number of small people who had entrusted their savings to him were faced with the loss of all they had. The details were vague, for neither my uncle nor my aunt knew anything of business matters, nor had I the knowledge to make what they told me comprehensible. But there was a mortgage on George Kemp's house and a bill of sale on his furniture. His wife was left without a penny. His two sons, lads of twenty and twenty-one, were in the coal business, but that too was involved in the general ruin. George Kemp had gone off with all the cash he could lay hands on, something like fifteen hundred pounds, they said, though how they knew I cannot imagine; and it was reported that a warrant had been issued for his arrest. It was supposed that he had left the country; some said he had gone to Australia and some to Canada.

"I hope they catch him," said my uncle. "He ought to get penal servitude for life."

The indignation was universal. They could not forgive him because he had always been so noisy and boisterous, because he had chaffed them and stood them drinks and given them garden parties, because he had driven such a smart trap and worn his brown billycock hat at such a rakish angle. But it was on Sunday night after church in the vestry that the churchwarden told my uncle the worst. For the last two years he had been meeting Rosie Driffield at Haversham almost every week and they had been spending the night together at a public-house. The licensee of this had put money into one of Lord George's wildcat schemes, and on discovering that he had lost it blurted out the whole story. He could have borne it if Lord George had defrauded others, but that he should defraud him who had done him a good turn and whom he looked upon as a chum, that was the limit.

"I expect they've run away together," said my uncle.

"I shouldn't be surprised," said the churchwarden.

After supper, while the housemaid was clearing away, I went into the kitchen to talk to Mary-Ann. She had been at church and had heard the story too. I cannot believe that the congregation had listened very attentively to my uncle's sermon.

"The vicar says they've run away together," I said. I had not breathed a word of what I knew.

"Why, of course they 'ave," said Mary-Ann. "He was the only man she ever really fancied. He only 'ad to lift 'is little finger and she'd leave anyone no matter who it was."

I lowered my eyes. I was suffering from bitter mortification; and I was angry with Rosie; I thought she had behaved very badly to me.

"I suppose we shall never see her again," I said.

It gave me a pang to utter the words.

"I don't suppose we shall," said Mary-Ann cheerfully.

When I had told Mrs. Barton Trafford as much of this story as

I thought she need know, she sighed, but whether from satisfaction or distress I had no notion.

"Well, that's the end of Rosie at all events," she said. She got up and held out her hand. "Why will these literary men make these unfortunate marriages? It's all very sad, very sad. Thank you so much for what you've done. We know where we are now. The great thing is that it shouldn't interfere with Edward's work."

Her remarks seemed a trifle disconnected to me. The fact was, I have no doubt, that she was giving me not the smallest thought. I led her out of Victoria Station and put her into a bus that went down the King's Road, Chelsea; then I walked back to my lodgings.

CHAPTER XXI

I lost touch with Driffield. I was too shy to seek him out; I was busy with my examinations, and when I had passed them I went abroad. I remember vaguely to have seen in the paper that he had divorced Rosie. Nothing more was heard of her. Small sums reached her mother occasionally, ten or twenty pounds, and they came in a registered letter with a New York postmark; but no address was given, no message enclosed, and they were presumed to come from Rosie only because no one else could possibly send Mrs. Gann money. Then in the fullness of years Rosie's mother died, and it may be supposed that in some way the news reached her, for the letters ceased to come.

CHAPTER XXII

Alroy Kear and I, as arranged, met on Friday at Victoria Station to catch the five-ten to Blackstable. We made ourselves comfortable in opposite corners of a smoking compartment. From him I now learned roughly what had happened to Driffield after his wife ran away from him. Roy had in due course become very intimate with Mrs. Barton Trafford. Knowing him and remembering her, I realised that this was inevitable. I was not surprised to hear that he had travelled with her and Barton on the continent, sharing

with them to the full their passion for Wagner, post-impressionist
painting and baroque architecture. He had lunched assiduously at
the flat in Chelsea and when advancing years and failing health
had imprisoned Mrs. Trafford to her drawing-room, notwithstanding the many claims on his time he had gone regularly once a
week to sit with her. He had a good heart. After her death he
wrote an article about her in which with admirable emotion he
did justice to her great gifts of sympathy and discrimination.

It pleased me to think that his kindliness should receive its due
and unexpected reward, for Mrs. Barton Trafford had told him
much about Edward Driffield that could not fail to be of service
to him in the work of love on which he was now engaged. Mrs.
Barton Trafford, exercising a gentle violence, not only took Edward Driffield into her house when the flight of his faithless wife
left him what Roy could only describe by the French word
désemparé, but persuaded him to stay for nearly a year. She gave
him the loving care, the unfailing kindness and the intelligent understanding of a woman who combined feminine tact with masculine vigour, a heart of gold with an unerring eye for the main
chance. It was in her flat that he finished *By Their Fruits*. She
was justified in looking upon it as her book and the dedication to
her is a proof that Driffield was not unmindful of his debt. She
took him to Italy (with Barton of course, for Mrs. Trafford knew
too well how malicious people were, to give occasion for scandal)
and with a volume of Ruskin in her hand revealed to Edward
Driffield the immortal beauties of that country. Then she found
him rooms in the Temple and arranged little luncheons there, she
acting very prettily the part of hostess, where he could receive
the persons whom his increasing reputation attracted.

It must be admitted that this increasing reputation was very
largely due to her. His great celebrity came only during his last
years when he had long ceased to write, but the foundations of it
were undoubtedly laid by Mrs. Trafford's untiring efforts. Not only
did she inspire (and perhaps write not a little, for she had a dex-
terous pen) the article that Barton at last contributed to the
Quarterly in which the claim was first made that Driffield must
be ranked with the masters of British fiction, but as each book
came out she organised its reception. She went here and there,
seeing editors and, more important still, proprietors of influential
organs; she gave soirées to which everyone was invited who could

be of use. She persuaded Edward Driffield to give readings at the houses of the very great for charitable purposes; she saw to it that his photographs should appear in the illustrated weeklies; she revised personally any interview he gave. For ten years she was an indefatigable Press agent. She kept him steadily before the public.

Mrs. Barton Trafford had a grand time, but she did not get above herself. It was useless indeed to ask him to a party without her; he refused. And when she and Barton and Driffield were invited anywhere to dinner they came together and went together. She never let him out of her sight. Hostesses might rave; they could take it or leave it. As a rule they took it. If Mrs. Barton Trafford happened to be a little out of temper it was through him she showed it, for while she remained charming, Edward Driffield would be uncommonly gruff. But she knew exactly how to draw him out and when the company was distinguished could make him brilliant. She was perfect with him. She never concealed from him her conviction that he was the greatest writer of his day; she not only referred to him invariably as the master, but, perhaps a little playfully and yet how flatteringly, addressed him always as such. To the end she retained something kittenish.

Then a terrible thing happened. Driffield caught pneumonia and was extremely ill; for some time his life was despaired of. Mrs. Barton Trafford did everything that such a woman could do, and would willingly have nursed him herself, but she was frail, she was indeed over sixty, and he had to have professional nurses. When at last he pulled through, the doctors said that he must go into the country, and since he was still extremely weak insisted that a nurse should go with him. Mrs. Trafford wanted him to go to Bournemouth so that she could run down for week-ends and see that everything was well with him, but Driffield had a fancy for Cornwall, and the doctors agreed that the mild airs of Penzance would suit him. One would have thought that a woman of Isabel Trafford's delicate intuition would have had some foreboding of ill. No. She let him go. She impressed on the nurse that she entrusted her with a grave responsibility; she placed in her hands, if not the future of English literature, at least the life and welfare of its most distinguished living representative. It was a priceless charge.

Three weeks later Edward Driffield wrote and told her that he had married his nurse by special licence.

I imagine that never did Mrs. Barton Trafford exhibit more pre-eminently her greatness of soul than in the manner in which she met this situation. Did she cry, Judas, Judas? Did she tear her hair and fall on the floor and kick her heels in an attack of hysterics? Did she turn on the mild and learned Barton and call him a blithering old fool? Did she inveigh against the faithlessness of men and the wantonness of women or did she relieve her wounded feelings by shouting at the top of her voice a string of those obscenities with which the alienists tell us the chastest females are surprisingly acquainted? Not at all. She wrote a charming letter of congratulation to Driffield and she wrote to his bride telling her that she was glad to think that now she would have two loving friends instead of one. She begged them both to come and stay with her on their return to London. She told everyone she met that the marriage had made her very, very happy, for Edward Driffield would soon be an old man and must have someone to take care of him; who could do this better than a hospital nurse? She never had anything but praise for the new Mrs. Driffield; she was not exactly pretty, she said, but she had a very nice face; of course she wasn't quite, quite a lady, but Edward would only have been uncomfortable with anyone too grand. She was just the sort of wife for him. I think it may be not unjustly said that Mrs. Barton Trafford fairly ran over with the milk of human kindness, but all the same I have an inkling that if ever the milk of human kindness was charged with vitriol, here was a case in point.

CHAPTER XXIII

When we arrived at Blackstable, Roy and I, a car, neither ostentatiously grand nor obviously cheap, was waiting for him and the chauffeur had a note for me asking me to lunch with Mrs. Driffield next day. I got into a taxi and went to the "Bear and Key". I had learned from Roy that there was a new Marine Hotel on the front, but I did not propose for the luxuries of civilisation to abandon a resort of my youth. Change met me at the railway station, which was not in its old place, but up a new road, and of course it was strange to be driven down the High Street in a car. But the "Bear and Key" was unaltered. It received me with its old churlish in-difference: there was no one at the entrance, the driver put my bag down and drove away; I called, no one answered; I went into the bar and found a young lady with shingled hair reading a book by Mr. Compton Mackenzie. I asked her if I could have a room. She gave me a slightly offended look and said she thought so, but as that seemed to exhaust her interest in the matter I asked po-litely whether there was anyone who could show it to me. She got up and, opening a door, in a shrill voice called: "Katie."

"What is it?" I heard.

"There's a gent wants a room."

In a little while appeared an ancient and haggard female in a very dirty print dress, with an untidy mop of grey hair, and showed me, two flights up, a very small grubby room.

"Can't you do something better than that for me?" I asked.

"It's the room commercials generally 'ave," she answered with a sniff.

"Haven't you got any others?"

"Not single."

"Then give me a double room."

"I'll go and ask Mrs. Brentford."

I accompanied her down to the first floor and she knocked at a door. She was told to come in, and when she opened it I caught sight of a stout woman with grey hair elaborately marcelled. She was reading a book. Apparently everyone at the "Bear and Key" was interested in literature. She gave me an indifferent look when Katie said I wasn't satisfied with number seven.

"Show him number five," she said.

I began to feel that I had been a trifle rash in declining so haughtily Mrs. Driffield's invitation to stay with her and then put-ting aside in my sentimental way Roy's wise suggestion that I should stay at the Marine Hotel. Katie took me upstairs again and ushered me into a largish room looking on the High Street. Most of its space was occupied by a double bed. The windows had certainly not been opened for a month.

I said that would do and asked about dinner.

"You can 'ave what you like," said Katie. "We 'aven't got noth-ing in, but I'll run round and get it."

Knowing English inns, I ordered a fried sole and a grilled chop. Then I went for a stroll. I walked down to the beach and found

that they had built an esplanade and there was a row of bungalows
and villas where I remembered only windswept fields. But they
were seedy and bedraggled and I guessed that even after all these
years Lord George's dream of turning Blackstable into a popular
seaside resort had not come true. A retired military man, a pair of
elderly ladies walked along the crumbling asphalt. It was incredibly dreary. A chill wind was blowing and a light drizzle swept
over from the sea.

I went back into the town and here, in the space between the
"Bear and Key" and the "Duke of Kent", were little knots of men
standing about notwithstanding the inclement weather; and their
eyes had the same pale blue, their high cheek-bones the same
ruddy colour as that of their fathers before them. It was strange to
see that some of the sailors in blue jerseys still wore little gold
rings in their ears; and not only old ones but boys scarcely out of
their teens. I sauntered down the street and there was the bank
refronted, but the stationery shop where I had bought paper and
wax to make rubbings with an obscure writer whom I had met
by chance was unchanged; there were two or three cinemas and
their garish posters suddenly gave the prim street a dissipated air
so that it looked like a respectable elderly woman who had taken
a drop too much.

It was cold and cheerless in the commercial room where I ate
my dinner alone at a large table laid for six. I was served by the
slatternly Katie. I asked if I could have a fire.

"Not in June," she said. "We don't 'ave fires after April."

"I'll pay for it," I protested.

"Not in June. In October, yes, but not in June."

When I had finished I went into the bar to have a glass of port.

"Very quiet," I said to the shingled barmaid.

"Yes, it is quiet," she answered.

"I should have thought on a Friday night you'd have quite a
lot of people in here."

"Well, one would think that, wouldn't one?"

Then a stout red-faced man with a close-cropped head of grey
hair came in from the back and I guessed that this was my host.

"Are you Mr. Brentford?" I asked him.

"Yes, that's me."

"I knew your father. Will you have a glass of port?"

I told him my name, in the days of his boyhood better known

than any other at Blackstable, but somewhat to my mortification
I saw that it aroused no echo in his memory. He consented, however, to let me stand him a glass of port.

"Down here on business?" he asked me. "We get quite a few
commercial gents at one time and another. We always like to do
what we can for them."

I told him that I had come down to see Mrs. Driffield and left
him to guess on what errand.

"I used to see a lot of the old man," said Mr. Brentford. "He
used to be very partial to dropping in here and having his glass
of bitter. Mind you, I don't say he ever got tiddly, but he used to
like to sit in the bar and talk. My word, he'd talk by the hour and
he never cared who he talked to. Mrs. Driffield didn't half like
his coming here. He'd slip away, out of the house, without saying
a word to anybody, and come toddling down. You know it's a bit
of a walk for a man of that age. Of course when they missed him
Mrs. Driffield knew where he was, and she used to telephone and
ask if he was here. Then she'd drive over in the car and go in and
see my wife. 'You go in and fetch him, Mrs. Brentford,' she'd say;
'I don't like to go in the bar meself, not with all those men hanging about'; so Mrs. Brentford would come in and she'd say: 'Now
Mr. Driffield, Mrs. Driffield's come for you in the car, so you'd
better finish your beer and let her take you home.' He used to
ask Mrs. Brentford not to say he was here when Mrs. Driffield
rang up, but of course we couldn't do that. He was an old man
and all that and we didn't want to take the responsibility. He was
born in this parish, you know, and his first wife, she was a Blackstable girl. She's been dead these many years. I never knew her.
He was a funny old fellow. No side, you know; they tell me they
thought a rare lot of him in London and when he died the papers
were full of him, but you'd never have known it to talk to him. He
might have been just nobody, like you and me. Of course we always tried to make him comfortable; we tried to get him to sit in
one of them easy chairs, but no, he must sit up at the bar; he said
he liked to feel his feet on a rail. My belief is he was happier
here than anywhere. He always said he liked a bar. He said you
saw life there and he said he'd always loved life. Quite a character
he was. Reminded me of my father, except that my old governor
never read a book in his life and he drank a bottle of French
brandy a day and he was seventy-eight when he died and his last

illness was his first. I quite missed old Driffield when he popped off. I was only saying to Mrs. Brentford the other day, I'd like to read one of his books some time. They tell me he wrote several about these parts."

CHAPTER XXIV

Next morning it was cold and raw, but it was not raining, and I walked down the High Street towards the vicarage. I recognised the names over the shops, the Kentish names that have been borne for centuries—the Ganns, the Kemps, the Cobbs, the Igguldens— but I saw no one that I knew. I felt like a ghost walking down that street where I had once known nearly everyone, if not to speak to, at least by sight. Suddenly a very shabby little car passed me, stopped and backed, and I saw someone looking at me curiously. A tall, heavy, elderly man got out and came towards me.

"Aren't you Willie Ashenden?" he asked.

Then I recognised him. He was the doctor's son, and I had been at school with him; we had passed from form to form together, and I knew that he had succeeded his father in his practice.

"Hullo, how are you?" he asked. "I've just been along to the vicarage to see my grandson. It's a preparatory school now, you know, and I put him there at the beginning of this term."

He was shabbily dressed and unkempt, but he had a fine head and I saw that in youth he must have had unusual beauty. It was funny that I had never noticed it.

"Are you a grandfather?" I asked.

"Three times over," he laughed.

It gave me a shock. He had drawn breath, walked the earth and presently grown to man's estate, married, had children and they in turn had had children; I judged from the look of him that he had lived, with incessant toil, in penury. He had the peculiar manner of the country doctor, bluff, hearty and unctuous. His life was over. I had plans in my head for books and plays, I was full of schemes for the future; I felt that a long stretch of activity and fun still lay before me; and yet, I supposed, to others I must seem the elderly man that he seemed to me. I was so shaken that I had not the presence of mind to ask about his brothers whom as a child I had played with, or about the old friends who had been my companions; after a few foolish remarks I left him. I walked on to the vicarage, a roomy, rambling house too far out of the way for the modern incumbent who took his duties more seriously than did my uncle and too large for the present cost of living. It stood in a big garden and was surrounded by green fields. There was a great square notice-board that announced that it was a preparatory school for the sons of gentlemen and gave the name and the degrees of the headmaster. I looked over the paling; the garden was squalid and untidy and the pond in which I used to fish for roach was choked up. The glebe fields had been cut up into building lots. There were rows of little brick houses with bumpy ill-made roads. I walked along Joy Lane and there were houses here too, bungalows facing the sea; and the old turnpike house was a trim tea shop.

I wandered about here and there. There seemed innumerable streets of little houses of yellow brick, but I do not know who lived in them for I saw no one about. I went down to the harbour. It was deserted. There was but one tramp lying a little way out from the pier. Two or three sailormen were sitting outside a warehouse and they stared at me as I passed. The bottom had fallen out of the coal trade and colliers came to Blackstable no longer.

Then it was time for me to go to Ferne Court and I went back to the "Bear and Key". The landlord had told me that he had a Daimler for hire and I had arranged that it should take me to my luncheon. It stood at the door when I came up, a brougham, but the oldest, most dilapidated car of its make that I had ever seen; it panted along with squeaks and thumps and rattlings, with sudden angry jerks, so that I wondered if I should ever reach my destination. But the extraordinary, the amazing thing about it was that it smelled exactly like the old landau which my uncle used to hire every Sunday morning to go to church in. This was a rank odour of stables and of stale straw that lay at the bottom of the carriage; and I wondered in vain why, after all these years, the motor-car should have it too. But nothing can bring back the past like a perfume or a stench, and, oblivious to the country I was trundling through, I saw myself once more a little boy on the front seat with the communion plate beside me and, facing me, my aunt, smelling slightly of clean linen and eau-de-Cologne, in

her black silk cloak and her little bonnet with a feather, and my
uncle in his cassock, a broad band of ribbed silk round his ample
waist and a gold cross hanging over his stomach from the gold
chain round his neck.

"Now, Willie, mind you behave nicely to-day. You're not to
turn round, and sit up properly in your seat. The Lord's House
isn't the place to loll in and you must remember that you should
set an example to other little boys who haven't had your advantages."

When I arrived at Ferne Court, Mrs. Driffield and Roy were
walking round the garden and they came up to me as I got out of
the car.

"I was showing Roy my flowers," said Mrs. Driffield, as she
shook hands with me. And then with a sigh: "They're all I have
now."

She looked no older than when last I saw her six years before.
She wore her weeds with quiet distinction. At her neck was a
collar of white crêpe and at her wrists cuffs of the same. Roy, I
noticed, wore with his neat blue suit a black tie; I supposed it was
a sign of respect for the illustrious dead.

"I'll just show you my herbaceous borders," said Mrs. Driffield,
"and then we'll go in to lunch."

We walked round and Roy was very knowledgeable. He knew
what all the flowers were called, and the Latin names tripped off
his tongue like cigarettes out of a cigarette-making machine. He
told Mrs. Driffield where she ought to get certain varieties that
she absolutely must have and how perfectly lovely were certain
others.

"Shall we go in through Edward's study?" suggested Mrs. Driffield. "I keep it exactly as it was when he was here. I haven't
changed a thing. You'd be surprised how many people come over
to see the house, and of course above all they want to see the
room he worked in."

We went in through an open window. There was a bowl of
roses on the desk and on a little round table by the side of the
arm-chair a copy of the *Spectator*. In the ash-trays were the master's pipes and there was ink in the inkstand. The scene was
perfectly set. I do not know why the room seemed so strangely
dead; it had already the mustiness of a museum. Mrs. Driffield
went to the bookshelves and with a little smile, half playful, half

sad, passed a rapid hand across the back of half a dozen volumes bound in blue.

"You know that Edward admired your work so much," said Mrs. Driffield. "He re-read your books quite often."

"I'm very glad to think that," I said politely.

I knew very well that they had not been there on my last visit and in a casual way I took one of them out and ran my fingers along the top to see whether there was dust on it. There was not. Then I took another book down, one of Charlotte Brontë's, and making a little plausible conversation tried the same experiment. No, there was no dust there either. All I learned was that Mrs. Driffield was an excellent housekeeper and had a conscientious maid.

We went in to luncheon, a hearty British meal of roast beef and Yorkshire pudding, and we talked of the work on which Roy was engaged.

"I want to spare dear Roy all the labour I can," said Mrs. Driffield, "and I've been gathering together as much of the material as I could myself. Of course it's been rather painful, but it's been very interesting, too. I came across a lot of old photographs that I must show you."

After luncheon we went into the drawing-room and I noticed again with what perfect tact Mrs. Driffield had arranged it. It suited the widow of a distinguished man of letters almost more than it had suited the wife. Those chintzes, those bowls of pot-pourri, those Dresden China figures—there was about them a faint air of regret; they seemed to reflect pensively upon a past of distinction. I could have wished on this chilly day that there were a fire in the grate, but the English are a hardy as well as a conservative race; and it is not difficult for them to maintain their principles at the cost of the discomfort of others. I doubted whether Mrs. Driffield would have conceived the possibility of lighting a fire before the first of October. She asked me whether I had lately seen the lady who had brought me to lunch with the Driffields, and I surmised from her faint acerbity that since the death of her eminent husband the great and fashionable had shown a distinct tendency to take no further notice of her. We were just settling down to talk about the defunct; Roy and Mrs. Driffield were putting artful questions to incite me to disclose my recollec-tions and I was gathering my wits about me so that I should not in an unguarded moment let slip anything that I had made up my mind to keep to myself; when suddenly the trim parlour-maid brought in two cards on a small salver.

"Two gentlemen in a car, mum, and they say, could they look at the house and garden?"

"What a bore!" cried Mrs. Driffield, but with astonishing alacrity. "Isn't it funny I should have been speaking just now about the people who want to see the house? I never have a moment's peace."

"Well, why don't you say you're sorry you can't see them?" said Roy, with what I thought a certain cattiness.

"Oh, I couldn't do that. Edward wouldn't have liked me to." She looked at the cards. "I haven't got my glasses on me."

She handed them to me, and on one I read "Henry Beard MacDougal, University of Virginia"; and in pencil was written: "Assistant professor in English Literature". The other was "Jean-Paul Underhill", and there was at the bottom an address in New York.

"Americans," said Mrs. Driffield. "Say I shall be very pleased if they'll come in."

Presently the maid ushered the strangers in. They were both tall young men and broad-shouldered, with heavy, clean-shaven, swarthy faces and handsome eyes; they both wore horn-rimmed spectacles and they both had thick black hair combed straight back from their foreheads. They both wore English suits that were evidently brand-new; they were both slightly embarrassed, but verbose and extremely civil. They explained that they were making a literary tour of England and, being admirers of Edward Driffield, had taken the liberty of stopping off on their way to Rye to visit Henry James's house in the hope that they would be permitted to see a spot sanctified by so many associations. The reference to Rye did not go down very well with Mrs. Driffield.

"I believe they have some very good links there," she said.

She introduced the Americans to Roy and me. I was filled with admiration for the way in which Roy rose to the occasion. It appeared that he had lectured before the University of Virginia and had stayed with a distinguished member of the faculty. It had been an unforgettable experience. He did not know whether he had been more impressed by the lavish hospitality with which those charming Virginians had entertained him or by their intelligent interest in art and literature. He asked how So-and-So was, and So-and-So; he had made lifelong friends there, and it looked as though everyone he had met was good and kind and clever. Soon the young professor was telling Roy how much he liked his books, and Roy was modestly telling him what in this one and the other his aim had been and how conscious he was that he had come far short of achieving it. Mrs. Driffield listened with smiling sympathy, but I had a feeling that her smile was growing a trifle strained. It may be that Roy had too, for he suddenly broke off.

"But you don't want me to bore you with my stuff," he said in his loud hearty way. "I'm only here because Mrs. Driffield has entrusted to me the great honour of writing Edward Driffield's Life."

This of course interested the visitors very much.

"It's some job, believe me," said Roy, playfully American. "Fortunately I have the assistance of Mrs. Driffield, who was not only a perfect wife, but an admirable amanuensis and secretary; the materials she has placed at my disposal are so amazingly full that really little remains for me to do but take advantage of her industry and her—her affectionate zeal."

Mrs. Driffield looked down demurely at the carpet and the two young Americans turned on her their large dark eyes in which you could read their sympathy, their interest and their respect. After a little more conversation—partly literary but also about golf, for the visitors admitted that they hoped to get a round or two at Rye, and here again Roy was on the spot, for he told them to look out for such and such a bunker and when they came to London hoped they would play with him at Sunningdale—after this, I say, Mrs. Driffield got up and offered to show them Edward's study and bedroom, and of course the garden. Roy rose to his feet, evidently bent on accompanying them, but Mrs. Driffield gave him a little smile; it was pleasant but firm.

"Don't you bother to come, Roy," she said. "I'll take them round. You stay here and talk to Mr. Ashenden."

"Oh, all right. Of course."

The strangers bade us farewell and Roy and I settled down again in the chintz arm-chairs.

"Jolly room this is," said Roy.

"Very."

"Amy had to work hard to get it. You know the old man bought this house two or three years before they were married. She tried to make him sell it, but he wouldn't. He was very obstinate in some ways. You see, it belonged to a certain Miss Wolfe, whose bailiff his father was, and he said that when he was a little boy his one idea was to own it himself and now he'd got it he was going to keep it. One would have thought the last thing he'd want to do was to live in a place where everyone knew all about his origins and everything. Once poor Amy very nearly engaged a housemaid before she discovered she was Edward's great-niece. When Amy came here the house was furnished from attic to cellar in the best Tottenham Court Road manner; you know the sort of thing, Turkey carpets and mahogany sideboards, and a plush-covered suite in the drawing-room, and modern marquetry. It was his idea of how a gentleman's house should be furnished. Amy says it was simply awful. He wouldn't let her change a thing and she had to go to work with the greatest care; she says she simply couldn't have lived in it and she was determined to have things right, so she had to change things one by one so that he didn't pay any attention. She told me the hardest job she had was with his writing-desk. I don't know whether you've noticed the one there is in his study now. It's a very good period piece; I wouldn't mind having it myself. Well, he had a horrible American roll-top desk. He'd had it for years and he'd written a dozen books on it and he simply wouldn't part with it, he had no feeling for things like that; he just happened to be attached to it because he'd had it so long. You must get Amy to tell you the story how she managed to get rid of it in the end. It's really priceless. She's a remarkable woman, you know; she generally gets her own way."

"I've noticed it," I said.

It had not taken her long to dispose of Roy when he showed signs of wishing to go over the house with the visitors. He gave me a quick look and laughed. Roy was not stupid.

"You don't know America as well as I do," he said. "They always prefer a live mouse to a dead lion. That's one of the reasons why I like America."

CHAPTER XXV

When Mrs. Driffield, having sent the pilgrims on their way, came back she bore under her arm a portfolio.

"What very nice young men!" she said. "I wish young men in England took such a keen interest in literature. I gave them that photo of Edward when he was dead and they asked me for one of mine, and I signed it for them." Then very graciously: "You made a great impression on them, Roy. They said it was a real privilege to meet you."

"I've lectured in America so much," said Roy, with modesty.

"Oh, but they've read your books. They say that what they like about them is that they're so virile."

The portfolio contained a number of old photographs, groups of schoolboys among whom I recognised an urchin with untidy hair as Driffield only because his widow pointed him out, Rugby fifteens with Driffield a little older, and then one of a young sailor in a jersey and a reefer jacket, Driffield when he ran away to sea.

"Here's one taken when he was first married," said Mrs. Driffield.

He wore a beard and black-and-white check trousers; in his buttonhole was a large white rose backed by maidenhair and on the table beside him a chimney-pot hat.

"And here is the bride," said Mrs. Driffield, trying not to smile.

Poor Rosie, seen by a country photographer over forty years ago, was grotesque. She was standing very stiffly against a background of baronial hall, holding a large bouquet; her dress was elaborately draped, pinched at the waist, and she wore a bustle. Her fringe came down to her eyes. On her head was a wreath of orange blossoms, perched high on a mass of hair, and from it was thrown back a long veil. Only I knew how lovely she must have looked.

"She looks fearfully common," said Roy.

"She was," murmured Mrs. Driffield.

We looked at more photographs of Edward, photographs that had been taken of him when he began to be known, photographs when he wore only a moustache and others, all the later ones, when he was clean-shaven. You saw his face grown thinner and more lined. The stubborn commonplace of the early portraits melted gradually into a weary refinement. You saw the change in him wrought by experience, thought and achieved ambition. I looked again at the photograph of the young sailorman and fancied that I saw in it already a trace of that aloofness that seemed to me so marked in the older ones and that I had had years before the vague sensation of in the man himself. The face you saw was a mask and the actions he performed were without significance. I had an impression that the real man, to his death unknown and lonely, was a wraith that went a silent way unseen between the writer of his books and the man who led his life, and smiled with ironical detachment at the two puppets that the world took for Edward Driffield. I am conscious that in what I have written of him I have not presented a living man, standing on his feet, rounded, with comprehensible motives and logical activities; I have not tried to: I am glad to leave that to the abler pen of Alroy Kear.

I came across the photographs that Harry Retford, the actor, had had taken of Rosie, and then a photograph of the picture that Lionel Hillier had painted of her. It gave me a pang. That was how I best remembered her. Notwithstanding the old-fashioned gown, she was alive there and tremulous with the passion that filled her. She seemed to offer herself to the assault of love.

"She gives you the impression of a hefty wench," said Roy.

"If you like the milkmaid type," answered Mrs. Driffield. "I've always thought she looked rather like a white nigger."

That was what Mrs. Barton Trafford had been fond of calling her, and with Rosie's thick lips and broad nose there was indeed a hateful truth in the description. But they did not know how silvery golden her hair was, nor how golden silver her skin; they did not know her enchanting smile.

"She wasn't a bit like a white nigger," I said. "She was virginal like the dawn. She was like Hebe. She was like a tea rose."

Mrs. Driffield smiled and exchanged a meaning glance with Roy.

"Mrs. Barton Trafford told me a great deal about her. I don't wish to seem spiteful, but I'm afraid I don't think that she can have been a very nice woman."

"That's where you make a mistake," I replied. "She was a very nice woman. I never saw her in a bad temper. You only had to say you wanted something for her to give it to you. I never heard her say a disagreeable thing about anyone. She had a heart of gold."

"She was a terrible slattern. Her house was always in a mess; you didn't like to sit down in a chair because it was so dusty and you dared not look in the corners. And it was the same with her person. She could never put a skirt on straight and you'd see about two inches of petticoat hanging down on one side."

"She didn't bother about things like that. They didn't make her any the less beautiful. And she was as good as she was beautiful."

Roy burst out laughing and Mrs. Driffield put her hand up to her mouth to hide her smile.

"Oh, come, Mr. Ashenden, that's really going too far. After all, let's face it, she was a nymphomaniac."

"I think that's a very silly word," I said.

"Well, then, let me say that she can hardly have been a very good woman to treat poor Edward as she did. Of course it was a blessing in disguise. If she hadn't run away from him he might have had to bear that burden for the rest of his life, and with such a handicap he could never have reached the position he did. But the fact remains that she was notoriously unfaithful to him. From what I hear she was absolutely promiscuous."

"You don't understand," I said. "She was a very simple woman. Her instincts were healthy and ingenuous. She loved to make people happy. She loved love."

"Do you call that love?"

"Well, then, the act of love. She was naturally affectionate. When she liked anyone it was quite natural for her to go to bed with him. She never thought twice about it. It was not vice; it wasn't lasciviousness; it was her nature. She gave herself as naturally as the sun gives heat or the flowers their perfume. It was a pleasure to her and she liked to give pleasure to others. It had no effect on her character; she remained sincere, unspoiled and artless."

Mrs. Driffield looked as though she had taken a dose of castor oil and had just been trying to get the taste of it out of her mouth by sucking a lemon.

"I don't understand," she said. "But then I'm bound to admit that I never understood what Edward saw in her."

"Did he know that she was carrying on with all sorts of people?" asked Roy.

"I'm sure he didn't," she replied quickly.

"You think him a bigger fool than I do, Mrs. Driffield," I said.

"Then why did he put up with it?"

"I think I can tell you. You see, she wasn't a woman who ever inspired love. Only affection. It was absurd to be jealous over her. She was like a clear deep pool in a forest glade into which it's heavenly to plunge, but it is neither less cool nor less crystalline because a tramp and a gipsy and a gamekeeper have plunged into it before you."

Roy laughed again and this time Mrs. Driffield without concealment smiled thinly.

"It's comic to hear you so lyrical," said Roy.

I stifled a sigh. I have noticed that when I am most serious people are apt to laugh at me, and indeed when after a lapse of time I have read passages that I wrote from the fullness of my heart I have been tempted to laugh at myself. It must be that there is something naturally absurd in a sincere emotion, though why there should be I cannot imagine, unless it is that man, the ephemeral inhabitant of an insignificant planet, with all his pain and all his striving is but a jest in an eternal mind.

I saw that Mrs. Driffield wished to ask me something. It caused her a certain embarrassment.

"Do you think he'd have taken her back if she'd been willing to come?"

"You knew him better than I. I should say no. I think that when he had exhausted an emotion he took no further interest in the person who had aroused it. I should say that he had a peculiar combination of strong feeling and extreme callousness."

"I don't know how you can say that," cried Roy. "He was the kindest man I ever met."

Mrs. Driffield looked at me steadily and then dropped her eyes.

"I wonder what happened to her when she went to America," he asked.

"I believe she married Kemp," said Mrs. Driffield. "I heard they had taken another name. Of course they couldn't show their faces over here again."

"When did she die?"

"Oh, about ten years ago."

"How did you hear?" I asked.

"From Harold Kemp, the son; he's in some sort of business at Maidstone. I never told Edward. She'd been dead to him for many years and I saw no reason to remind him of the past. It always helps you if you put yourself in other people's shoes and I said to myself that if I were he I shouldn't want to be reminded of an unfortunate episode of my youth. Don't you think I was right?"

CHAPTER XXVI

Mrs. Driffield very kindly offered to send me back to Blackstable in her car, but I preferred to walk. I promised to dine at Ferne Court next day and meanwhile to write down what I could remember of the two periods during which I had been in the habit of seeing Edward Driffield. As I walked along the winding road, meeting no one by the way, I mused upon what I should say. Do they not tell us that style is the art of omission? If that is so I should certainly write a very pretty piece, and it seemed almost a pity that Roy should use it only as material. I chuckled when I reflected what a bombshell I could throw if I chose. There was one person who could tell them all they wanted to know about Edward Driffield and his first marriage; but this fact I proposed to keep to myself. They thought Rosie was dead; they erred; Rosie was very much alive.

Being in New York for the production of a play and my arrival having been advertised to all and sundry by my manager's energetic Press representative, I received one day a letter addressed in a handwriting I knew but could not place. It was large and round, firm but uneducated. It was so familiar to me that I was exasperated not to remember whose it was. It would have been more sensible to open the letter at once, but instead I looked at the envelope and racked my brain. There are handwritings I cannot see without a little shiver of dismay and some letters that look so tiresome that I cannot bring myself to open them for a week. When at last I tore open the envelope what I read gave me a strange feeling. It began abruptly:

I have just seen that you are in New York and would like to see you again. I am not living in New York any more, but Yonkers is

quite close and if you have a car you can easily do it in half an
hour. I expect you are very busy so leave it to you to make a date.
Although it is many years since we last met I hope you have not
forgotten your old friend

ROSE IGGULDEN (*formerly Driffield*)

I looked at the address; it was the Albemarle, evidently a hotel
or an apartment house, then there was the name of a street, and
Yonkers. A shiver passed through me as though someone had
walked over my grave. During the years that had passed I had
sometimes thought of Rosie, but of late I had said to myself that
she must surely be dead. I was puzzled for a moment by the name.
Why Iggulden and not Kemp? Then it occurred to me that they
had taken this name, a Kentish one too, when they fled from
England. My first impulse was to make an excuse not to see her;
I am always shy of seeing again people I have not seen for a long
time; but then I was seized with curiosity. I wanted to see what
she was like and to hear what had happened to her. I was going
down to Dobb's Ferry for the week-end, to reach which I had to
pass through Yonkers, and so answered that I would come at
about four on the following Saturday.

The Albemarle was a huge block of apartments, comparatively
new, and it looked as though it were inhabited by persons in easy
circumstances. My name was telephoned up by a negro porter in
uniform and I was taken up in the elevator by another. I felt
uncommonly nervous. The door was opened for me by a coloured
maid.

"Come right in," she said. "Mrs. Iggulden's expecting you."

I was ushered into a living-room that served also as dining-
room, for at one end of it was a square table of heavily carved
oak, a dresser and four chairs of the kind that the manufacturers
in Grand Rapids would certainly describe as Jacobean. But the
other end was furnished with a Louis XV suite, gilt and upholstered
in pale blue damask; there were a great many small tables, richly
carved and gilt, on which stood Sèvres vases with ormolu decora-
tions and nude bronze ladies with draperies flowing as though in
a howling gale that artfully concealed those parts of their bodies
that decency required; and each one held at the end of a playfully
outstretched arm an electric lamp. The gramophone was the grandest thing I had ever seen out of a shop window, all gilt and

shaped like a sedan chair and painted with Watteau courtiers and their ladies.

After I had waited for about five minutes a door was opened and Rosie came briskly in. She gave me both her hands.

"Well, this is a surprise," she said. "I hate to think how many years it is since we met. Excuse me one moment." She went to the door and called: "Jessie, you can bring the tea in. Mind the water's boiling properly." Then, coming back: "The trouble I've had to teach that girl to make tea properly, you'd never believe."

Rosie was at least seventy. She was wearing a very smart sleeveless frock of green chiffon, heavily *diamanté*, cut square at the neck and very short; it fitted like a bursting glove. By her shape I gathered that she wore rubber corsets. Her nails were blood-coloured and her eyebrows plucked. She was stout, and she had a double chin; the skin of her bosom, although she had powdered it freely, was red, and her face was red too. But she looked well and healthy and full of beans. Her hair was still abundant, but it was quite white, shingled and permanently waved. As a young woman she had had soft, naturally waving hair and these stiff undulations, as though she had just come out of a hairdresser's, seemed more than anything else to change her. The only thing that remained was her smile, which had still its old childlike and mischievous sweetness. Her teeth had never been very good, irregular and of bad shape; but these now were replaced by a set of perfect evenness and snowy brilliance; they were obviously the best money could buy.

The coloured maid brought in an elaborate tea with *pâté* sandwiches and cookies and candy and little knives and forks and tiny napkins. It was all very neat and smart.

"That's one thing I've never been able to do without—my tea," said Rosie, helping herself to a hot buttered scone. "It's my best meal, really, though I know I shouldn't eat it. My doctor keeps on saying to me: 'Mrs. Igghulden, you can't expect to get your weight down if you will eat half a dozen cookies at tea.'" She gave me a smile, and I had a sudden inkling that, notwithstanding the marcelled hair and the powder and the fat, Rosie was the same as ever. "But what I say is: A little of what you fancy does you good."

I had always found her easy to talk to. Soon we were chatting away as though it were only a few weeks since we had last seen one another.

"Were you surprised to get my letter? I put Driffield so as you should know who it was from. We took the name of Iggulden when we came to America. George had a little unpleasantness when he left Blackstable, perhaps you heard about it, and he thought in a new country he'd better start with a new name, if you understand what I mean."

I nodded vaguely.

"Poor George, he died ten years ago, you know."

"I'm sorry to hear that."

"Oh, well, he was getting on in years. He was past seventy, though you'd never have guessed it to look at him. It was a great blow to me. No woman could want a better husband than what he made me. Never a cross word from the day we married till the day he died. And I'm pleased to say he left me very well provided for."

"I'm glad to know that."

"Yes, he did very well over here. He went into the building trade, he always had a fancy for it, and he got in with Tammany. He always said the greatest mistake he ever made was not coming here over twenty years before. He liked the country from the first day he set foot in it. He had plenty of go and that's what you want here. He was just the sort to get on."

"Have you never been back to England?"

"No, I've never wanted to. George used to talk about it sometimes, just for a trip, you know, but we never got down to it, and now he's gone I haven't got the inclination. I expect London would seem very dead and alive to me after New York. We used to live in New York, you know. I only came here after his death."

"What made you choose Yonkers?"

"Well, I always fancied it. I used to say to George, when we retire we'll go and live at Yonkers. It's like a little bit of England to me, you know. Maidstone or Guildford or some place like that."

I smiled, but I understood what she meant. Notwithstanding its trams and its tootling cars, its cinemas and electric signs, Yonkers, with its winding main street, has a faint air of an English market town gone jazz.

"Of course I sometimes wonder what's happened to all the folks at Blackstable. I suppose they're most of them dead by now and I expect they think I am too."

"I haven't been there for thirty years."

I did not know then that the rumour of Rosie's death had reached Blackstable. I dare say that someone had brought back the news that George Kemp was dead and thus a mistake had arisen.

"I suppose nobody knows here that you were Edward Driffield's first wife?"

"Oh, no; why, if they had I should have had the reporters buzzing around my apartment like a swarm of bees. You know sometimes I've hardly been able to help laughing when I've been out somewhere playing bridge and they've started talking about Ted's books. They like them no end in America. I never thought so much of them myself."

"You never were a great novel reader, were you?"

"I used to like history better, but I don't seem to have much time for reading now. Sunday's my great day. I think the Sunday papers over here are lovely. You don't have anything like them in England. Then of course I play a lot of bridge; I'm crazy about contract."

I remembered that when as a young boy I had first met Rosie her uncanny skill at whist had impressed me. I felt that I knew the sort of bridge player she was, quick, bold and accurate: a good partner and a dangerous opponent.

"You'd have been surprised at the fuss they made over here when Ted died. I knew they thought a lot of him, but I never knew he was such a big bug as all that. The papers were full of him, and they had pictures of him and Ferne Court; he always said he meant to live in that house some day. Whatever made him marry that hospital nurse? I always thought he'd marry Mrs. Barton Trafford. They never had any children, did they?"

"No."

"Ted would have liked to have some. It was a great blow to him that I couldn't have any more after the first."

"I didn't know you'd ever had a child," I said with surprise.

"Oh, yes. That's why Ted married me. But I had a very bad time when it came and the doctors said I couldn't have another. If she'd lived, poor little thing, I don't suppose I'd ever have run

away with George. She was six when she died. A dear little thing
she was and as pretty as a picture."

"You never mentioned her."

"No, I couldn't bear to speak about her. She got meningitis and
we took her to the hospital. They put her in a private room and
they let us stay with her. I shall never forget what she went
through, screaming, screaming all the time, and nobody able to do
anything."

Rosie's voice broke.

"Was it that death Driffield described in *The Cup of Life?*"

"Yes, that's it. I always thought it so funny of Ted. He couldn't
bear to speak of it, any more than I could, but he wrote it all
down; he didn't leave out a thing; even little things I hadn't
noticed at the time he put in and then I remembered them. You'd
think he was just heartless, but he wasn't, he was upset just as
much as I was. When we used to go home at night he'd cry like
a child. Funny chap, wasn't he?"

It was *The Cup of Life* that had raised such a storm of protest;
and it was the child's death and the episode that followed it that
had especially brought down on Driffield's head such virulent
abuse. I remembered the description very well. It was harrowing.
There was nothing sentimental in it; it did not excite the reader's
tears, but his anger rather that such cruel suffering should be
inflicted on a little child. You felt that God at the Judgment Day
would have to account for such things as this. It was a very
powerful piece of writing. But if this incident was taken from
life, was the one that followed it also? It was this that had shocked
the public of the 'nineties and this that the critics had condemned
as not only indecent but incredible. In *The Cup of Life* the husband
and wife (I forget their names now) had come back from the
hospital after the child's death—they were poor people and they
lived from hand to mouth in lodgings—and had their tea. It was
latish: about seven o'clock. They were exhausted by the strain of
a week's ceaseless anxiety and shattered by their grief. They had
nothing to say to one another. They sat in a miserable silence.
The hours passed. Then on a sudden the wife got up and going
into their bedroom put on her hat.

"I'm going out," she said.

"All right."

They lived near Victoria Station. She walked along the Buckingham Palace Road and through the park. She came into Piccadilly and went slowly towards the Circus. A man caught her eye, paused and turned round.

"Good-evening," he said.

"Good-evening."

She stopped and smiled.

"Will you come and have a drink?" he asked.

"I don't mind if I do."

They went into a tavern in one of the side-streets of Piccadilly, where harlots congregated and men came to pick them up, and they drank a glass of beer. She chatted with the stranger and laughed with him. She told him a cock-and-bull story about herself. Presently he asked if he could go home with her; no, she said, he couldn't do that, but they could go to a hotel. They got into a cab and drove to Bloomsbury and there they took a room for the night. And next morning she took a bus to Trafalgar Square and walked through the park; when she got home her husband was just sitting down to breakfast. After breakfast they went back to the hospital to see about the child's funeral.

"Will you tell me something, Rosie?" I asked. "What happened in the book after the child's death—did that happen too?"

She looked at me for a moment doubtfully; then her lips broke into her still beautiful smile.

"Well, it's all so many years ago, what odds does it make? I don't mind telling you. He didn't get it quite right. You see, it was only guesswork on his part. I was surprised that he knew as much as he did; I never told him anything."

Rosie took a cigarette and pensively tapped its end on the table, but she did not light it.

"We came back from the hospital just like he said. We walked back; I felt I couldn't sit still in a cab, and I felt all dead inside me. I'd cried so much I couldn't cry any more, and I was tired. Ted tried to comfort me, but I said: 'For God's sake shut up.' After that he didn't say any more. We had rooms in the Vauxhall Bridge Road then, on the second floor, just a sitting-room and a bedroom, that's why we'd had to take the poor little thing to the hospital; we couldn't nurse her in lodgings; besides, the landlady said she wouldn't have it, and Ted said she'd be looked after better at the hospital. She wasn't a bad sort, the landlady; she'd

I

been a tart and Ted used to talk to her by the hour together. She came up when she heard us come in.

"'How's the little girl to-night?' she said.

"'She's dead,' said Ted.

"I couldn't say anything. Then she brought up the tea. I didn't want anything, but Ted made me eat some ham. Then I sat at the window. I didn't look round when the landlady came up to clear away, I didn't want anyone to speak to me. Ted was reading a book; at least he was pretending to, but he didn't turn the pages, and I saw the tears dropping on it. I kept on looking out of the window. It was the end of June, the twenty-eighth, and the days were long. It was just near the corner where we lived and I looked at the people going in and out of the public-house and the trams going up and down. I thought the day would never come to an end; then all of a sudden I noticed that it was night. All the lamps were lit. There was an awful lot of people in the street. I felt so tired. My legs were like lead.

"'Why don't you light the gas?' I said to Ted.

"'Do you want it?' he said.

"'It's no good sitting in the dark,' I said.

"He lit the gas. He began smoking his pipe. I knew that would do him good. But I just sat and looked at the street. I don't know what came over me. I felt that if I went on sitting in that room I'd go mad. I wanted to go somewhere where there were lights and people. I wanted to get away from Ted; no, not so much that, I wanted to get away from all that Ted was thinking and feeling. We only had two rooms. I went into the bedroom; the child's cot was still there, but I wouldn't look at it. I put on my hat and a veil and I changed my dress and then I went back to Ted.

"'I'm going out,' I said.

"Ted looked at me. I dare say he noticed I'd got my new dress on and perhaps something in the way I spoke made him see I didn't want him.

"'All right,' he said.

"In the book he made me walk through the park, but I didn't do that really. I went down to Victoria and I took a hansom to Charing Cross. It was only a shilling fare. Then I walked up the Strand. I'd made up my mind what I wanted to do before I came out. Do you remember Harry Retford? Well, he was acting at the

Adelphi then, he had the second comedy part. Well, I went to the stage door, and sent up my name. I always liked Harry Retford. I expect he was a bit unscrupulous and he was rather funny over money matters, but he could make you laugh and with all his faults he was a rare good sort. You know he was killed in the Boer War, don't you?"

"I didn't. I only knew he'd disappeared and one never saw his name on playbills; I thought perhaps he'd gone into business or something."

"No, he went out at once. He was killed at Ladysmith. After I'd been waiting a bit he came down and I said: 'Harry, let's go on the razzle to-night. What about a bit of supper at Romano's?' 'Not 'alf,' he said. 'You wait here and the minute the show's over and I've got my make-up off I'll come down.' It made me feel better just to see him; he was playing a racing tout and it made me laugh just to look at him in his check suit and his billycock hat and his red nose. Well, I waited till the end of the show and then he came down and we walked along to Romano's.

"'Are you hungry?' he said to me.

"'Starving,' I said; and I was.

"'Let's have the best,' he said, 'and blow the expense. I told Bill Terris I was taking my best girl out to supper and I touched him for a couple of quid.'

"'Let's have champagne,' I said.

"'Three cheers for the widow!' he said.

"I don't know if you ever went to Romano's in the old days. It was fine. You used to see all the theatrical people and the racing men, and the girls from the Gaiety used to go there. It was *the* place. And the Roman. Harry knew him and he came up to our table; he used to talk in funny broken English; I believe he put it on because he knew it made people laugh. And if someone he knew was down and out he'd always lend him a fiver.

"'How's the kid?' said Harry.

"'Better,' I said.

"I didn't want to tell him the truth. You know how funny men are; they don't understand some things. I knew Harry would think it dreadful of me to come out to supper when the poor child was lying dead in the hospital. He'd be awfully sorry and all that, but that's not what I wanted; I wanted to laugh."

Rosie lit the cigarette that she had been playing with.

"You know how when a woman is having a baby, sometimes the husband can't stand it any more and he goes out and has another woman. And then when she finds out, and it's funny how often she does, she kicks up no end of a fuss; she says, that the man should go and do it just then, when she's going through hell, well, it's the limit. I always tell her not to be silly. It doesn't mean he doesn't love her, and isn't terribly upset, it doesn't mean anything, it's just nerves; if he wasn't so upset he wouldn't think of it. I know, because that's how I felt then.

"When we'd finished our supper Harry said: 'Well, what about it?'

" 'What about what?' I said.

"There wasn't any dancing in those days and there was nowhere to go.

" 'What about coming round to my flat and having a look at my photograph album?' said Harry.

" 'I don't mind if I do,' I said.

"He had a little bit of a flat in the Charing Cross Road, just two rooms and a bath and a kitchenette, and we drove round there, and I stayed the night.

"When I got back next morning the breakfast was already on the table and Ted had just started. I'd made up my mind that if he said anything I was going to fly out at him. I didn't care what happened. I'd earned my living before, and I was ready to earn it again. For two pins I'd have packed my box and left him there and then. But he just looked up as I came in.

" 'You've just come in time,' he said. 'I was going to eat your sausage.'

"I sat down and poured him out his tea. And he went on reading the paper. After we'd finished breakfast we went to the hospital. He never asked me where I'd been. I didn't know what he thought. He was terribly kind to me all that time. I was miserable, you know. Somehow I felt that I just couldn't get over it, and there was nothing he didn't do to make it easier for me."

"What did you think when you read the book?" I asked.

"Well, it did give me a turn to see that he did know pretty well what had happened that night. What beat me was his writing it at all. You'd have thought it was the last thing he'd put in a book. You're queer fish, you writers."

At that moment the telephone bell rang. Rosie took up the receiver and listened.

"Why, Mr. Vanuzzi, how very nice of you to call me up! Oh, I'm pretty well, thank you. Well, pretty and well, if you like. When you're my age you take all the compliments you can get."

She embarked upon a conversation which, I gathered from her tone, was of a facetious and even flirtatious character. I did not pay much attention, and since it seemed to prolong itself I began to meditate upon the writer's life. It is full of tribulation. First he must endure poverty and the world's indifference; then, having achieved a measure of success, he must submit with a good grace to its hazards. He depends upon a fickle public. He is at the mercy of journalists who want to interview him and photographers who want to take his picture, of editors who harry him for copy and tax gatherers who harry him for income tax, of persons of quality who ask him to lunch and secretaries of institutes who ask him to lecture, of women who want to marry him and women who want to divorce him, of youths who want his autograph, actors who want parts and strangers who want a loan, of gushing ladies who want advice on their matrimonial affairs and earnest young men who want advice on their compositions, of agents, publishers, managers, bores, admirers, critics, and his own conscience. But he has one compensation. Whenever he has anything on his mind, whether it be a harassing reflection, grief at the death of a friend, unrequited love, wounded pride, anger at the treachery of someone to whom he has shown kindness, in short any emotion or any perplexing thought, he has only to put it down in black and white, using it as a theme of a story or the decoration of an essay, to forget all about it. He is the only free man.

Rosie put back the receiver and turned to me.

"That was one of my beaux. I'm going to play bridge to-night and he rang up to say he'd call round for me in his car. Of course he's a Wop, but he's real nice. He used to run a big grocery store down-town, in New York, but he's retired now."

"Have you never thought of marrying again, Rosie?"

"No." She smiled. "Not that I haven't had offers. I'm quite happy as I am. The way I look on it is this: I don't want to marry an old man, and it would be silly at my age to marry a young one. I've had my time and I'm ready to call it a day."

"What made you run away with George Kemp?"

"Well, I'd always liked him. I knew him long before I knew Ted, you know. Of course, I never thought there was any chance of marrying him. For one thing, he was married already, and then he had his position to think of. And then when he came to me one day and said that everything had gone wrong and he was bust and there'd be a warrant out for his arrest in a few days and he was going to America and would I go with him, well, what could I do? I couldn't let him go all that way by himself, with no money perhaps, and him having been always so grand and living in his own house and driving his own trap. It wasn't as if I was afraid of work."

"I sometimes think he was the only man you ever cared for," I suggested.

"I dare say there's some truth in that."

"I wonder what it was you saw in him."

Rosie's eyes travelled to a picture on the wall that for some reason had escaped my notice. It was an enlarged photograph of Lord George in a carved gilt frame. It looked as if it might have been taken soon after his arrival in America; perhaps at the time of their marriage. It was a three-quarter length. It showed him in a long frock-coat, tightly buttoned, and a tall silk hat cocked rakishly on one side of his head; there was a large rose in his buttonhole; under one arm he carried a silver-headed cane and smoke curled from a big cigar that he held in his right hand. He had a heavy moustache, waxed at the ends, a saucy look in his eye, and in his bearing an arrogant swagger. In his tie was a horse-shoe in diamonds. He looked like a publican dressed up in his best to go to the Derby.

"I'll tell you," said Rosie. "He was always such a perfect gentle-man."